THE MARSCO DISSIDENT

A Futuristic Novel

BOOK ONE OF

THE MARSCO SAGA

BY JAMES A. ZARZANA

Dedicated to Marianne and Elaine

ISBN: 1495925838
ISBN 13: 9781495925832
Library of Congress Control Number: 2014903178
CreateSpace Independent Publishing Platform
North Charleston, South Carolina

ACKNOWLEDGEMENTS AND THANKS

Thanks to Marianne for all her careful reading and editing. Additionally, to Elaine, who supported this effort from start to finish. And to Barbara Booth whose early look gave me such encouragement. Thanks also go to Cheryl Seehorn for her knowledge of roses. Acknowledgement must go to the late Professor Eric Markuson for his information on genocide and "grassfire wars." His visuals helped in countless ways. Lorien Downing read this manuscript carefully and pointed out many ways to improve my prose.

I am absolutely indebted to Cathy Bernardy Jones for the final proofing, editing, and formatting of this text. The completion of this project would not be possible without her efforts.

I also wish to thank Dana Yost and Marcy Olson for their editorial and artistic help with this work in its final stages.

Lorien, Cathy, Dana, and Marcy: Southwest Minnesota State University prepared you all so very well.

Finally, thanks to all those others whose encouragement and faith gave me strength to continue.

AUTHOR'S NOTE

This work is entirely a piece of fiction. "Marsco" is a completely invented entity, created solely for the purposes of this fictional work. It is not to be mistaken for any past or currently existing corporation or business. Any similarity of name or of characteristics to existing corporations or businesses in the use of the name "Marsco" is purely coincidental. Similarly, all characters in this work, except known historical figures, are fictional and created solely by the author.

A glossary of specialized Marsco terms and slang is located at the end of the novel.

The Marsco Dissident

"The times scientific, as evil as ever."
"Toward Lillers"
1933
Ivor Gurney

"It had all the unknownness of
something of immense realness."
In Parenthesis
1937
David Jones

"Everything off the Earth goes Marsco."
Marsco Lunar Fleet Motto
2034

ONE

THE DISSIDENT'S DAUGHTER

(The Sac City Subsidiary, formerly Sacramento, California, 2092)

It's a Marsco world, thought Lieutenant Tessa Miller as she left the battered light rail, ravaged by age, gloomy with rust and neglect.

Her long day of travel almost over, she hustled along the dingy platform through a crowd of Sac City subsidiary residents. Stepping over a sleeping PRIM just beyond the broken escalator, she noticed he smelled of urine. The subcutaneous disk at the back of his left hand flashed amber, alerting the officer it was faulty.

Let an Auxxie deal, Tessa rationalized.

At street level, she surveyed the once-prosperous neighborhood still well within the rambling Sac City Sid. Twenty-two years after the Armistice, the area looked vastly different than from before the C-Wars. A seven-story building down the block was salvageable, yet no robotic cranes stood beside it. Instead, a scaffold surrounded the gutted structure on which sid-overseers supervised dozens of PRIMS brought in from the outlying unincorporated zone. These gangs scurried up and down the skeletal scaffolding, chipping off bricks and useable metal; a frenzy of PRIM-labor rather than cyber driven machines picking the bones of this sid for Marsco.

Once, seeing such gangs with her father, she heard him mutter about them being like coolies from a past era, but she didn't know what he meant and later couldn't find out on the Marsco-Wiki. Today near the light rail platform, she shook her head and looked the other way.

It was the lack of LR service that most occupied her mind. Without a continuing line, she had few choices left to reach her father's isolated grange twenty-five clicks in the distance. Rather than returning to Seattle—Tessa was on the verge of that—or going back to the secure Marsco cantonment and grabbing a hover flight craft, she decided to proceed.

Before leaving her flat she had checked the Marsco Net, which indicated that the commuter line continued for several more stops to the edge of the subsidiary, terminating closer to where these outlaying districts gave way to the greenbelt. Why Marsco's own Net was inaccurate, Tessa didn't know. Unflustered by this inconvenience, she shouldered her small backpack, slipped on her wraparound dark glasses and walked to the curb amid the dispersing crowd of PRIMS and sids just below the elevated platform.

To ensure her safe transit but mostly to avoid delays at any checkpoints (although her palm unit marked none along her route), Tessa wore her Marsco uniform, medium gray with red piping and prominent officer bars. Her shoulder patch designated her professor status at the Marsco Academy, the flagship campus within easy distance of the Seattle HQ itself.

Beyond those quads, her uniform carried little weight. Within greater Marsco, she wasn't a member of its elite Asteroid Shuttle Fleet or even a member of its celebrated Lander Fleet making routine jaunts to and from the lunar colonies. And she wasn't Security and Hygiene, even though her uniform prompted deference as she approached. To anyone non-Marsco, she *was* Marsco; that was enough to keep her from seeming fully integrated anywhere she traveled.

As a matter of course, she strapped an Enfield in a leather holster on her hip and wore cotton gloves to cover her eight finger disks embedded in the tips and on the phalanges of her right hand.

Earlier that morning, Tessa had been encased in secured chrome and stainless steel, speeding along on a MAG LEV train at 300 kilometers per hour. The 1200-click trip, with its one stop at the Portland Sector, took her just over five relaxing hours. She ate a lunch of fresh poached salmon, dozed in the plush comfort of the first-class compartment, associates only. Behind glass tinted with asteroid gold to filter the sun's glare, she accelerated from the gleaming Seattle Sector to the Sac City Cantonment as if in a pneumatic tube detached from the remainder of the world. Since the Armistice, Seattle shone as Marsco rebuilt its HQ. Subsidiaries, such as the former capital city of Sacramento, were also thriving via their connection to Marsco, or so Marsco reported to its associates like Tessa. The traveler looked for evidence of this flourishing, but found none.

As often happened on the magnetically levitated bullet, a few older associates had recognized her as Walter Miller's daughter, a point that she never openly acknowledged even though curiosity about him was frequently on fellow associates' minds, in their eyes.

Whether seeing her in transit or during the course of her weekly duties, some longstanding associates who knew both her parents periodically took note of her similarity to Bethany Palmer, her mother. Tessa's auburn hair, shaped stylishly, a brush of freckles that made her seem younger than she was, her keen determination—these maternal traits gave her away, caused some associates to take a lingering look.

She had much of her father as well: his lively, ready smile and his eyes.

From both: a slender, athletic build and an unrelenting stubbornness.

From Marsco: a withering stare that never seemed to fit her even though an absolute necessity for survival in its world.

The inquisitive gazes above digital projection screens from several passengers on the bullet train, those raised eyebrows, prompted Tessa to initiate a "Question and Answer" game with herself somewhere below the Portland Sid.

Q: *Your folks were such illustrious associates. But did you make it in Marsco based on your own skills?*

A: *Affirmative with a cap "A". An aerospace engineering prof by my own dogged work.*

Q: *Impressive! So, a propulsion wonk like your father?*

A: *Not exactly. He's more theoretical. I'm more applied.*

Q: *Has it hindered you being the only child of Marsco's most famous dissident?*

A: *No comment.*

Q: *How do you explain this inherent contradiction in your life and his?*

A: *It's a Marsco world.*

Q: *Is that your answer?*

A: *Affirmative.*

Q: *Can you elaborate?*

A: *Unnecessary. The nature of the world has become (or remains?) a contradiction.*

Q: *Is that your final answer?*

A: *Pass.*

Q: *Do you wish to add any other pertinent information to this conundrum?*

A: *Unnecessary.*

Q: *And what of Zot?*

A: *Do you mean Ensign Anthony Grizotti?*

Q: *Who else? Besides, logically, you can't answer a question with another question. Do you still love him?*

A: *Why even ask?*

Q: *Why not?*

A: *Pass.*

Q: *A strange reply. Do you wish to add anything else?*

A: *As I said, it's a Marsco world.*

Q: *And what is Marsco after all?*

A: *A hyper-country. A meta-nation. It exists beyond conventional post-statehood. For twenty-plus years, it has brought stability and prosperity to the world. Since the end of the Continental Wars, it has insured peace from here to the asteroid belt. But why can't I answer my own question with my own question? After all, I* am *an associate, am I not?*

Q: *Is that your question or your answer?*

Napping or watching the subsidiaries and cantonments rush by, Tessa had glided steadily south to the main Sac City terminal. Once there, it was only a few steps from the posh, spotless bullet to the run-down local service lines. After a delay, the associate left behind the cantonment at city center. It was from its guarded cantonments that Marsco assisted subsidiaries in keeping good order and tranquility. From them, Security often lent a hand in patrolling the contiguous PRIM unincorporated zones.

Like most pockets of Marsco power, the Sac City cantonment boasted almost all the comforts of Marsco with its gleaming metal and glass towers. Above and amid that part of Sac City's skyline, a handful of HFCs skimmed, settled at street level or alighted on a rooftop. By midcentury, the hover flight craft had moved much mechanized traffic off ground. Taking a four-seater down to their final destination was generally the automatic choice for most associates (*why go ground when you can skim?*), but today Tessa wanted to make her way without avoiding indigenous contact, without avoiding the PRIMS and sids who populated Sac City.

Leaving the guarded cantonment at the center of the subsidiary, the solitary associate rattled along on a deteriorating local for more than an hour, still ever southward.

Once at the broken curb below the LR platform, Tessa quickly hailed an idle jitney with an old driver and his teenage son. They surely bought their banged-up prewar rover at auction, the woman concluded. Its faded navy blue paint showed the urban-gray color scheme of Security underneath.

“Sure, mizzy, sure?” the eager driver inquired. A thin, stooped PRIM, he counted it a blessing to have an associate grace his threadbare back seat. His tawny face was smooth except for a permanently wrinkled forehead common among PRIMS. “Sure y’wish, go *there?*” His brown eyes conveyed reluctance.

Such a noteworthy passenger, such a tenuous trajectory! The associate read his thoughts in the worry lines along his face, although she knew he could never have used such words. Father and son didn’t have language disks, Tessa noticed, so command of English was not expected. They were from off-continent, as so many PRIMS often were, an aspect of the prewar world that still existed.

“The way’s direct, even if far. And if it’s off your route, I’ll pay whatever’s fair.” Tessa was insistent; she had little choice. Only six vehicles, all in the same condition as this jitney, crept along the wide street they shared with scores of pedestrians and dozens of bikes. “I have the coordinates.”

The old PRIM knuckled under and offered Tessa a seat patched with duct tape. The boy lit two joss sticks poking out from the dash to mask any odor. In a trail of blue smoke, they were off, the driver and his son jabbering in a language Tessa didn’t recognize.

The glowing green of PRIM-disks at the back of their left hands reassured her.

Each click brought Tessa deeper into the surrounding subsidiary. Viewing her palm unit, she followed the progress of her journey down to the exact GPS coordinates.

Marsco precision.

Eventually, looking up from the unit’s screen, she watched the now-crowded street. A chaotic mesh of scooters and bicycles and a handful of other jitneys jammed the avenue. Several overloaded flat-beds moved through the jumble. They passed a pair of alcohol-fueled buses crawling along, both with riders precariously hanging on the outside. And always, ubiquitous rovers filled with Auxilliary personnel, Auxxies, patrolled.

The late afternoon was hot for mid-May, almost like full summer. The A/C wasn't working, so the rover's windows were open, one only partially, because it was cracked. When the jitney slowed amid a swell of humanity along the road, smells wafted into the interior: curry and sweet, pungent incense.

Old neighborhoods, inhabited once more, showed signs of revitalization, even if some dwellings needed fresh paint and window glass. Passing through this non-associate world, light years from the sparkling marble, glass, and chrome world she inhabited, Tessa felt a mix of power and exposure.

Estimating that her last leg would take about forty-five minutes, Tessa continuously checked her progress. As close to "on course, on time" as a Masco shuttle, she mused, given this antiquated equipment.

A twitch of her finger disk on her mobile palm unit opened her personal files. Three emails waited, all with disappointing news. Five more cadets, newly commissioned lieutenants, had been transferred to Security and Hygiene, their appointments to Flight School canceled. Marsco had a greater need, a pressing need, for patrol officers rather than shuttle pilots. She had access to no accurate numbers, but extrapolating from her own students, it seemed like 33% of this year's graduating class had been sucked into the S and H. Last year's total was a higher-than-normal 25%. Tessa had no firm verification of her numbers, only chilling rumors backed by her unofficial but conclusive stats.

Pulling her eyes up from the disappointing screen, she watched her driver's head move as like an early century bobble-head on a dash. His son, an undersized teen, now sat silently. They were PRIMS, to be sure, ones working too hard to stay on the bottom, she noted, then grew ashamed of such standard-issue thoughts.

She knew her father would offer an alternative theory—with sufficient evidence to appear totally logical—to counter her own Marsco-endorsed hypothesis.

It was easy, Tessa cautiously reassured herself, that as a Marsco associate she had put herself in the hands of PRIMS. Associates lived and worked in Marsco safe havens (sectors and cantonments); their finger disks gave them total access to the Marsco Net thus unlimited access to every comfort and security imaginable. All of this, far from PRIMS. Sids, residents of subsidiaries, (those locales coupled with Marsco in the main), benefited from Marsco largess, but more than likely these sids were without finger disks and always without the elevated standards of a typical associate's life.

And sids were a constant buffer for Marsco against PRIMS, both the residents themselves—who worked directly with PRIMS so an associate never had to—and the vast locations of their subsidiaries—these more than likely surrounded Marsco sectors. And these subsidiaries in turn shared tenuous borders with unincorporated zones, the lands of PRIMS. Unless an associate wanted to, actually went out of her way to, as Tessa had done today, an associate might live in a totally PRIM-free world.

The jitney traversed an area below the cantonment but one still well within regularly patrolled stoplines. Tessa's palm screen gave her proof of that. Yet as she moved farther south, the sights changed radically. It did strike her though that this subsidiary had more than its share of PRIMS, and it showed signs of being more like an unincorporated zone than a true, thriving sid on a path to emulate Marsco success. A patina of dust covered everything, a layer of abandonment and despair. The air reeked of a teeming PRIM population, of feces, decay, and death.

Without warning, her palm lost all contact. Even com-link connections went dead. Tessa looked up in disbelief. "Stop, stop," she shouted. "Pull over! You must've taken a wrong turn."

The driver obeyed, but at the curb began to argue in that wheedling PRIM way when one of them is caught doing something underhanded. "Mizzy, sometin' wrong? I know way, yes-yes."

"You can't be right!" She held up her palm unit to show him its display as though he would have no trouble following the downloaded map's exact route. "We're in a sid! Never to leave it! But look!"

The old PRIM knew to look around on an associate's order.

This subsidiary sure seems mogged, the lieutenant thought. Dating from the late-twentieth century, *mogged* (coined by international troops patrolling Mogadishu) described scenes of the internal destruction of a society as legitimate governments and the rule of law failed. What had become an open wound and stark reality on the Horn of Africa a century back then became the wretched, dismal template for the prewar world, a world Marsco now ruled and vowed to restore.

Along the boulevards once known for their luxury, streetlights and traffic signals had long since been scavenged for metal. Here, late-twentieth century elegance and prosperity had been systematically dismantled by PRIM brick-gangs, the materials of the houses and shops used for makeshift dwellings that jammed the edge of the wide road. *Barely functional habs.* Tessa shuddered. Although she was moving through a location still designated by Marsco as a subsidiary area, it had all the unmistakable markings of an unincorporated zone.

"None of this makes sense," she grumbled, half-blaming the driver.

She wasn't positive, but she swore the son muttered to the back of his left hand, as though his PRIM-disk wasn't a RFID transponder for tracking his movements but a mic, "It's a Marsco world!"

No, he couldn't have said that! She looked directly at the gaunt boy. *Wouldn't have dared to utter that.*

"Bad-bad here," the driver insisted nervously. "No understan' y'that, mizzy," he motioned to her palm unit. "But this—" he swung a roundhouse motion "—it's been like ever-ever."

"He is meaning, my father, beens this years and years," the son added in feeble defense.

"Yes, year an'year," echoed the old man.

Tessa shrugged, not defeated but confused. She knew that over the passing decades, with their series of asymmetrical urban wars, pandemic plagues, and dwindling populations, the late twenty-first century had given way to *this* aspect of the Marsco world. *What associate didn't know that?*

"You wan' go back, mizzy? Go back, Mar'co! All this no-no." His brown eyes pleaded. His bronze brow wrinkled.

"No, carry on." Sitting back in her seat, Tessa laid a reassuring hand on her Enfield.

The associate's route grew increasingly crowded with small living spaces and scattered shops. Some were made of cannibalized building materials, tarps and plastic sheeting, corrugated metal, and planks. Here and there, high stone walls and steel gates stood at the entrance of larger, more permanent structures. *Local warlords and thugs who ruled a few run-down city blocks*, Tessa assumed. *A bribe, a promise of compliance to Security, probably all it takes for an urban fiefdom.* The streets throbbed with people and traffic, bicycles and mopeds, the crowd a mixed batch, an amalgam of sids and PRIMS.

The noise and snarled movement suddenly stopped as a Security Brad turned the wide corner. Tessa's PRIM pulled to the side and waited. The associate, accustomed to taking matters into her own finger disks, got out and stood quietly beside the jitney as the armored personnel carrier approached.

Moving down the subdued street, the squat APC swung its nonlethal snout right and left, eyeing the crowd. Typical of Security, always watching. Although only meant to immobilize, its stunner and oozer nozzle looked sinister. The black Brad, four-times the size of the jitney, seemed to single out Tessa for scrutiny. A cam focused, lingered. After a pause, the patrol vehicle moved on, concluding that a uniformed associate must know her own business even down here.

"Do they come around often?" Tessa shouted above the returning street noise before her driver restarted his engine.

"Yes-yes, mizzy. Many patrols here. Keeps all saved here, it does."

"All very goods here, safe yes-yes, and very, very goods," added the boy, shouting to be heard. "Sid and PRIM here, goods all here."

"Yes, no trouble Mar'co heres," the father joined in, shaking his head eagerly, making up for his earlier complaints.

It's all as incongruous as my crashed palm, Tessa thought. *Yet, if this driver's from around here, it's no wonder he's working so hard. He wants out, that's for sure, and he has the initiative and self-determination to move up and away.*

As their journey continued, the associate noted that a CCTV unit stood inconspicuously every few hundred meters, each a slender stanchion resembling a tall lamppost with a surveillance housing where the light dome should be. They were sacrosanct and never touched by sids or PRIMS. Throughout the Marsco world, CCTV devices, or I-ON-Us as they came to be called, were so omnipresent no one gave them any attention.

They, on the other hand, paid meticulous attention to everything.

Three clicks down the once-thriving boulevard, the broken macadam rose gradually up an incline, where a layer of dust seemed to thicken. In times past, at the crest of the rise the south road curved to join a larger transit system coming from the east. But today, Tessa was confronted by the sure signs that during the C-Wars this shallow valley had taken a direct V-hit.

The jitney slowed to a crawl, giving her a view of the stretching remains of this quarter of the city. Never a megalopolis like those lining the coast, at midcentury this was a sprawling metro area, influential in its own right, vital to the Continental Powers at their end. And always a significant military target.

But this suburb? What was here to merit a V-strike? She looked around a moment at the destruction. *Explains the malfunct light rail,* she noted without emotion.

The pavement ended where it had once joined the major thoroughfare. Up along the hillside, the cliffs had given way. Tessa was unable to judge if this was due to the initial Vanovara blast or the twenty-five years of disrepair since. Her jitney cautiously edged along where over the years tenuous traffic had made a compacted dirt road out of the remaining debris and hillside. Finally, after a forty-meter stretch, the unpaved route reached the remaining cement ribbon in a cleft through the west ridge.

Tessa turned in her seat to look back into the charred valley. Stanchions and supports for the old freeway stood stripped of suspended sections, lonely sentinels rising above the ruins they guarded. The Vanovara had exploded as an airburst above the crammed basin, flattening everything beneath its fireball. A comet nucleus composed of frozen methane blasted with dozens of kilotons of blinding force. Cracked pieces of the once-elevated pavement rested on the ground. The demolished buildings and rubble-strewn streets attested to the tremendous shockwave of that detonation.

The associate remembered her own early Academy lectures. *V-1 type, comet head, methane, explosive. V-2 type, iron asteroid honed to a guidable shape, much smaller and used for precision hits.*

"The ensuing fireball from a V-1 creates one of two situations," her animated professor lectured a dozen years ago. "A *firestorm* or a *conflagration*—know the difference for Tuesday."

In the Sac City Sid, Tessa clearly saw the evidence of a conflagration; the reaches of its all-consuming flames had scorched the hillside and continued in every direction.

"No matter which inferno, you want to avoid both," whispered an older-looking cadet next to Tessa. His grin showed new braces, a post-sid luxury made possible by joining Marsco. "Grew up in the Chicago Sid," he hastily explained under his breath.

"Took several hits, didn't it?" another cadet asked, trying to occupy the dark-eyed young man all by herself.

"Closer to thirty-five, forty."

The cadet with braces was Anthony Grizotti, born of sids, now a fledging associate.

"And so, Cadet Miller," their prof stood over the three whispering plebes—hers was the only name he knew—"either way, you plebes are here at the Academy to make sure that this never, never happens again."

In another twenty minutes, Tessa's ride took her near an open-air market, close to a stopline and PRIM-accessible.

Inexplicably, she motioned for her driver to pull over. Even as he cautioned, "No-no, mizzy, no. Y'no stop here," Tessa was out among the sids, PRIMS, and vendors. Scores of bartering booths covered a lot next to a deserted mall. If Tessa wanted lavish shopping, Seattle offered her everything. Here were rows of tables with last-century's hand tools, clothes, farm produce, and MREs past code date but still edible.

Someone has an insider in Security, she realized, *willing to fence.*

Nothing appealed to her at first, and yet as she moved from kiosk to kiosk, the associate relished the freedom of a world so different from Marsco's.

Leaving his son to guard the jitney, the driver hovered protectively behind Tessa at a respectful distance, his own quick PRIM eyes distrustful of so many other PRIMS around *his* missy.

They created an odd sight: a sole associate among a swarm of indigenous skinnies going about their frenetic bartering, and her PRIM trying to keep this unpredictable woman out of harm's way. He knew if anything *did* happen to her, he would be blamed by Security. Thinking of that Brad, his mind raced, trying to avert any possible disaster.

Tessa stopped at a clothing stand; most of its pieces were PRIM-made and slightly flawed. The asking price jumped advantageously as the seller realized an associate had miraculously appeared with ready MMUs. Tessa's eye fell on a gray cotton T-shirt with red block letters simply stating MARSCO, a standard-issue part of a plebe's training uniform, unadorned with any patches or insignias. The one she chose had sleeves of slightly different lengths, unnoticeable without careful inspection.

Marsco had noticed.

Without haggling over the price, Tessa handed over a single Marsco Monetary Unit.

"Too-too, mizzy, too high," her driver whispered hoarsely behind her. "PRIM hem douwn, mizzy! PRIM hem douwn!"

When she ignored him, he circled around her, acting as her mediator, waving his arms and grimacing.

Even as she moved to the next booth selling palm units three or four generations older than hers, and then the next with local jams and preserves, the driver's appeals on her behalf continued. "Mizzy shouldda getta two deese," he urged through broken teeth, grabbing up a shirt from a separate pile. The vendor, with judicious sidelong glances, cautioned against such a selection. She displayed the reverse side which verbally modified the front proclamation of "MARSCO," stating simply, "SUCKS!"

Through her driver's intercessions, Tessa received an additional single-worded, gray tee. Her protective old PRIM wouldn't let her be cheated.

Her driver caught up to her amid other stalls selling individual items, barter items: bars of soap, bottles of shampoo, canned food, new and cleaned-up pots and pans, refurbished computers that couldn't get anyone onto the Marsco Net but did minimumly function. Many products superior to these any associate in a sector or cantonment might order by the gross off the Marsco Net.

Tessa was sure, just beyond her vision, a black market offered more besides. Weapons and drugs and human flesh, undoubtedly: anything and everything to satisfy any vice.

As much as Marsco cracked down on such illicit sales, they flourished, festered. *Although clearly designated as a sid,* she thought back to her blank palm screen, *it's one not yet totally regulated.* The noise of a mélange of languages hawked out in fits and starts, the shouts of merchants and buyers alike at grubby stalls, the knots and crowds of idle PRIMS both fascinated and depressed her. It could have been a scene from another century, not the end of the twenty-first.

Marsco has much housekeeping still to do, she thought.

With eager help from her driver, Tessa climbed back into the dented-up rover and was off.

The PRIM found his way instinctively. He kept to wider streets, slowing for the crowds that clogged them but running parallel to the main stopline on his left. He knew enough to cross only at a checkpoint and not to attempt any other way beyond.

Eventually, they slowed to approach a CP at an internal stopline. *Another incongruity,* the associate noted. Her download hadn't designated either the in-sid line or its CP.

The fuel cell engine sputtered, not one of the finest the twenty-first century ever produced. Two S & H troopers suspiciously eyed the bent PRIM and his son. A barrier closed the stretching road to traffic, and beyond the gate Tessa saw few signs of habitation or postwar restoration.

Such a drastic change here within a subsidiary made no sense; by all Net accounts, she had never actually gone *outside* the sid. The look of this locale told her otherwise.

If anything, before her was a separation point between a subsidiary area and an unincorporated zone. If so, Marsco wasn't web-reporting accurately. It made no sense to her that *it* was wrong. Making allowances, she rationalized that perhaps she simply misunderstood these sights before her.

To her left in the shade of a tall tree, a Brad sat with its menacing 20 mm weapon, not the usual McGrath stunner and

Evans immobilizer ooze-nozzle like she had seen earlier. Leths had replaced nonleths. These Security troopers, clad in mottled cement-gray uniforms, all had shoulder-fired Enfields in addition to handhelds like hers. Besides being heavily armed, they were doing a job usually performed by Auxilliary units, Auxxies, who were recuited and trained by Marsco to keep the peace in subsidiaries. *Someone's expecting trouble, serious trouble.*

Two rovers were parked near the armored vehicle, one having brought a meal out to the troopers. Half a dozen ate and relaxed to the side; another six eyed Tessa up and down. The contingent didn't seem members of Marsco's finest, the kind stationed in Seattle near Marsco HQ. These troopers had skinned their knuckles—and more—plying their trade here. Rotors in an I-ON-U housing whirred; a cam angle changed, focused.

Without hesitation, one hardened trooper was in the old driver's face and retina-blinked him. He then had the gall to in-face Tessa as well, infuriating the officer.

Instantly, the trooper's reader gave a green report on the driver. Tessa's file acknowledged clearance notification and classified status, as expected for an associate and officer.

Her irritation changed slightly when she realized the retina system was up and running again. Only a few days before, Luddite hackers had phreaked the system, an all too common occurrence. Her own palm unit once more flickered to life, still reporting her inside Sac City and nowhere near a checkpoint.

The warrant officer in charge, realizing the jitney passenger intended to cross his stopline, barked at her, "Here on out, mizzy, s'nothing but RPA."

The wide avenue beyond the checkpoint had become an unpaved road used mostly by PRIMS on scooters or bicycles. "Where y'up to anyway, wallah?" the haggard trooper drilled her without the expected Security courtesy. This wasn't the heart of a Marsco sector; he needn't bother with such niceties here.

"Is that how you address a superior officer, mister?" Tessa shot back. She leaned forward from the back seat so he could see her uniform better. The red piping and bars made it clear what he was dealing with. Had she been quicker to move forward, the retina scan would have been uncalled for.

The warrant officer remained unimpressed. *He* had his orders, and at *his* stopline, no one and nothing moved into this Random Patrol Area without his approval.

Tessa knew the routine, knew the way to circumvent this annoyance. She removed the cotton glove from her right hand. When that imposing array of finger disks failed to impress the warrant officer (*a stubborn bastard to be sure,* Tessa noted) she made a display of starting to remove the left-hand glove. She needn't go *that* far. The warrant officer, a mere two-disk centurion with a three-centimeter PRIM-disk removal scar at the back of his left hand, relented. The former PRIM balked at crossing someone of Tessa's status. With a resigned gesture, he signaled his troopers, who had finished eating, to raise the barrier. He knew when he was beaten.

But in one last act of defiance, the warrant officer stopped Tessa's PRIMS, father and son, from moving on. "Him and him don't have no clearance. Y'll have to walk." His smirk stated, *Permission to enter granted, but upon more thoughtful-wise consideration, y'won't go no further at all. Top that, wallah.*

The Security warrant helped her out of the rover's back seat, his Marsco courtesy suddenly oozing forth. It gave him an opportunity to admire her close up; his forced gallantry was worth the price to pay for that view. She was nothing like the PRIM skanks he poked, well out of his sphere. *Fine T and A even in uniform,* he futilely schemed, *and as a bonus—no trace of the clap or crabs near her.*

Tessa paid her driver and his son five MMUs, double what PRIMS might have expected from an associate, even a generous one. She gave the boy her second T-shirt. "Careful wi' *that* un, mizzy wallah," the old man whispered earnestly but politely. "Y'know troopars," he went on carefully through his broken-tooth grin. "If y'cross'em, they tak't ou' uv y'un way o' another."

As she turned to enter the RPA, the warrant cautioned her one last time. "Only thing out *there,*" he motioned emphatically, "is Indie sids, renegade PRIMS, and ol' Doc Miller's grange—you know, that gnarly crackpot." He gave a smarmy grin. *Don't git your prime-osity of an ass in a bind, wallah; I haven't the troopers nor inclination for any Air Cav nick-of-time rescues.*

Tessa glared, replacing her right-hand glove and shouldering her pack.

Looking up at one of the troopers, she instantly saw her chance. Jumping to an aggressive, in-your-face stance, she eyed a young woman who stood slightly shorter but thicker set than her superior. Without taking her eyes off her victim, the officer shouted at the warrant, "Why's this trooper out of uniform?"

The Security trooper—clearly of PRIM stock, her left-hand scar proved that—had a ring through one eyebrow.

Tessa didn't let up. "She has a fishing lure over her damn right eye! Is that standard issue?" She pointed her glove hardly five centimeters away from the objectionable eyebrow. The grinning abruptly stopped as broken nails fumbled to remove the offensive facial ornament.

The commanding officer was speechless; the suddenness of this counterattack caught him flatfooted. "No, ma'am!" He eventually got out, "She's new to my squad, ma'am!"

"No excuse, mister!"

The victim kept a vacant stare, knowing if she caught the officer's eye, more hell would thunder down on her. Yet Tessa's green eyes never left the woman's, whose own were green as well. Like the officer's, the trooper's nose was bridged with freckles, more so since her duties brought her into the elements. The other woman could have been Tessa's doppelganger. Had things been different, *she* might have been standing there, sweating under the glare of a fierce officer. It was that easy, Tessa knew, to be on the other side—*the wrong side*—of any stopline.

"Roger," the warrant officer shouted into his com-link, "got yur back!" Ignoring Tessa's glare-down, the detachment commander gathered his troopers, including the officer's double. "There's twenty-some PRIMS refusing to move back out! They've crossed the stopline six blocks to our east. Auxxies can't get no co-op from 'em."

The warrant glared at Tessa; it was his time to be in total control. "Take these four," he ordered his second-in-command, "give Teri-Shay here," he motioned at the eyebrow woman, "the SAW." Tessa's trooper ended up lugging the heavier squad automatic weapon, punishment of sorts for her unauthorized embellishment of the uniform. "Back up the Auxxies—but git them PRIMS out if they're in here without authorization."

Troopers hastily gathered gear, walking around Tessa as though she were no longer standing there.

"Auxxies visualled twenty," the warrant explained to his second, "but disk-RFID has only a dozen." A PRIM without a correctly working disk was in considerable trouble; PRIMS knew to report themselves to Security if their disk went from green to amber. Tampering with a PRIM disk was met with severe punishment, often expulsion from the PRIM's home to some other dismal unincorporated zone half a world away.

"P-W/O-Ds!"

Tessa knew the seriousness of PRIMS without disks crossing a stopline and the capability of Security troopers backing up an Auxiliary patrol.

As troopers scrambled about, Tessa began walking away. When she stepped into the RPA beyond the gate, she heard a trooper yell at her jitney driver. "Git this kludgosity outta here!" The trooper's voice was one of envy; he sensed that father and son would be leaving PRIM status by dint of their hard work together. The trooper's father had lied about his son's age and gave his own boy over to become an Auxxie at fourteen. Clearly this PRIMS'son was moving toward sid-level soon. Not by becoming a Security legionnaire after being forced into the Auxillary, either.

Tessa didn't hear a trooper whisper to his warrant officer a caution, "Better watch how ya treat dem brass wallahs, dey get back a' ya eve'time."

Before she had gone far, a Security & Hygiene HFC skimmed slowly down the stopline. The hover flight craft glided thirty-five meters in the air, heavily armed, more so than usual. The HFC examined everything to its port and starboard, watching the barrier that kept things separate, categorically discrete. Only the two PRIMS bothered to watch it move down the stopline.

Thirty meters into the RPA, Tessa gave the bulge on her hip a reassuring tap. She was strapped and ready. As she walked farther beyond the checkpoint, she sensed the I-ON-U still focused on her.

As the associate paced herself for her final walk toward her father's, her first visit in three years was steadily growing to be more trouble than it was worth.

In the past, she had come by lander from Seattle to the cantonment. Ordinarily, this last leg from city center to the grange was a quick HFC skim. Those had been uneventful jaunts she made regularly every few months over the past several years until her visits abruptly ended when she took a faculty position at the Academy. By skimming over subsidiary checkpoints, she kept herself from witnessing what she had seen this trip. Today's more lengthy and tactile travels showed her that an abrupt change was going down, a change with Marsco's veiled iron fist behind it. It was a realization that most associates, zipping sector to sector, kept at bay.

The troopers at the checkpoint carried Enfields. Any random Auxiliary patrols she had previously encountered in the sid green zone were armed only with nonleths, show-of-force deterrents more than anything else. Troopers stayed in the distance. Today was atypical, as the heavily armed contingent at the CP showed.

A palpable change, Tessa noted.

Preparing to meet her father, she let the troopers at the stopline fade from her mind.

As she continued on, she passed next to thick, guarding hedgerows and jagged walls of scavenged stone that surrounded several isolated granges. Out here, hardscrabble farmers needed each other, but they still relished the notion of independence from everything, especially Marsco.

Before the twenty-first century plagues had decimated the population, these remote residences stood on several-acre plots. From the first, their owners relished seclusion and grand architectural statements. These trophy estates had HFC landing pads and hangers, artificial lakes with faux waterfalls and gaudy fountains, and even small replicas of Greco-Roman or Oriental temples in their rambling gardens. European manors transplanted to a different continent and era, each far removed from the polluted, congested city to the north.

Eventually, Independents claimed the abandoned lands to make a stab at primitive farming.

Until the C-Wars disabled the interconnected tech-world, which Marsco was working to restore, earthmovers and heavy tractors had re-contoured the land. After the Wars, PRIM gangs worked the decorative landscape into something useful, salvaging what they could by hand. Each grange reclaimed an expansive house and possibly a garage or two for adaptive barns. In these hedge-surrounded farms, showcase lawns and gardens were slowly transformed into cultivated fields and pastures. Swimming pools were chipped into pieces then filled in or were used as cisterns, the great irrigation system of the last century having been destroyed in the C-Wars.

Another click on past the first grange, the solitary associate walked through a desolate area that still showed signs of the neglected midcentury community it once had been. She stepped over a stretch of a crumbling bike path and around an open storm drain sprouting tufts of thistle. This was not, she realized, the prime farmland of the Food Consortium.

"He'p a fella', missy wallah," a PRIM voice burst forth at her from under a thorn bush next to the path. The spiny hedge enclosed a grange close to her father's.

Tessa's first reaction was disbelief—that a PRIM might bother a uniformed associate. Her second thought, simultaneous with the first, was to shift her hand to the Enfield's grip, taking no chances. The weapon hissed its distinctive recharge venting; its targeting laser blinking red on the PRIM's chest. She was alone, without backup, out here many clicks from anyone or anything Marsco. A soft target. She also carried items easily disposed of on the black market—her palm unit, her backpack, the Enfield.

The lone associate assessed the situation. The old PRIM probably picked up day labor locally, but with most spring planting done on the larger granges, little extra help was needed. He held his palms up, showing he wasn't armed, a submissive gesture. His PRIM-disk glowed green although the scars at the fingertips of his right hand indicated he once had implanted disks, just like Tessa and everyone else fully functional in the Marsco world.

Clearly, she realized, *he's had DRP.* Disk Removal Procedure, the stripping of disks, was common practice after the Continental Wars, during the purges of the Troubled Times immediately after the Armistice. Quite painful if forced and especially painful because of its lifetime repercussions, even if voluntary.

While a PRIM without finger disks was axiomatic—only one type of implant awaited PRIMS—his assertiveness wasn't.

This one was Tessa's father's age but beaten down by hardship and privation. According to Marsco, all subsidiary areas worldwide were thriving once more. But even so, she realized that PRIM life was relentlessly grinding.

It's especially arduous for someone stripped of FDs, for someone deleted from the Marsco world or its subsidiaries—but that's just the way things are, Tessa thought, forcing herself to be numb to that conclusion.

Then, her associate's training gave way to her parents' attitude toward PRIMS. She offered a five-unit token, not a credit strip, which he could hardly be expected to spend.

As quickly as the PRIM had appeared, he vanished into his bush, leaving the path ahead clear. *That would never happen near a sector or in a cantonment,* she knew, thinking once more as an associate.

The begging didn't bother her; the five MMUs were hardly a widow's mite. What bothered her was the interruption itself. Approaching her father's home always took a certain degree of steeling herself, psyching herself to enter his world. Part of that preparation was why she chose the bullet instead of the expeditious lander. Returning had never been easy; her extended absence only made it worse.

She stopped 200 meters from the grange. First as an undergraduate at the Academy, and then as a graduate student at the Marsco Institute of Technology, she had regularly made this trip. Today, she was making her visit out of duty to her father and respect for her parents, although her mother had been dead nine years.

Nonetheless, as her uniform attested, she was crossing into his world not only as a daughter but also as a symbol of all that he had rejected.

Tessa knew the Marsco world was filled with incongruities. But the greatest symbol of that world wasn't her uniform, it was her finger disks, and her father—a lefter still—sported all his. Yet another incongruity among innumerable others.

Uncharacteristically for anyone who constantly used disks without paying the slightest attention to them, Tessa stood a moment to think about hers. Removing her right cotton glove, she turned her palm upward to examine the blue-green disks implanted under her epidermis. That hand had eight disks at the fingertips and on the phalanges, an impressive array. Her index finger disk, always the prime, held her identity in Marsco and opened the world to her as nothing else on- or off-planet did. Her disks had a functionality completely opposite that of a PRIM-disk; hers expanded, not closed off, everything.

Months before, her father had sent her a portion of a history of Marsco that he was writing. One file, "The Development of Finger Mouse and Finger Disk Technologies," sat in a folder, essentially unread. She had dutifully clicked through it once, a cursory glance. But she excused herself from delving into the piece by noting how busy teaching and her unfinished dissertation kept her.

Miller dwelt on history, his daughter conceded, while she dwelt with the here and now—this was the Marsco world she had inherited, that was all.

But Tessa accepted one part of her father's historical theory, his assertion that finger disks and Marsco were inexorably linked. Granted, some high-ranking sids might utilize midcentury finger mouse technology if they didn't sport a few right-only disks, but for the most part, computer access came *with* an implant and, more likely than not, *only* with an implant. This was the central reality every associate accepted as part of the world.

A world her father, after a stunning thirty-year career, had rejected.

Doctor Walter C. Miller chose instead to live outside Sac City, well beyond its thriving cantonment at the subsidiary's core, and to settle in an oddly defined gray area almost inside a conjoined unincorporated zone itself. He stayed amid autonomous neighbors who made a sort-of life for themselves, not as associates or sids or PRIMS.

Taking in a deep breath, Tessa slowly walked along a dirt road that once had been a winding, shady avenue. As she approached her father's residence, an incongruous, fully functional I-ON-U rose above the height of the grange. Of early-century design, this stanchion initially had been placed on a bridge or in a city center for illumination. It had all the tech pieces to serve that function, including a solar panel generating enough power for continuous service, but here it lit up no passing traffic. Near its top, a surveillance cam in an onion-shaped housing focused down into Miller's grange.

Why can't it just leave him alone?

Tessa already knew the answer.

TWO

THE DISSIDENT'S GRANGE

(Miller's near the Sac City Sid, 2092)

"D'ya miss me? Did ya?" Tessa went on like a PRIM in the hopes that the pair would understand her better. "Oh, I've missed you!" She singled one out, "And *you've* grown so much!"

Io and Deimos circled about Tessa's feet yelping and pawing at her as she neared the entrance to her father's grange. Io was oddly shaped with all the characteristics of a black Lab except height. Her squat legs kept her close to the ground, but this didn't deter her wild jumping. She even bayed like a hound at times. Deimos stood taller, with a long, auburn coat nearly the color of Tessa's hair. While Deimos was assertive, Io was lovingly enthusiastic.

Standing in the trellis break of his hedge, Miller watched the scene unfold. Tessa seemed almost girl-like with his dogs. She petted them, shook them playfully by their scruffs, and ended up in a crouch with each under an arm, letting them lick her face excitedly.

Noting Deimos' ruddy coloring, Miller remarked, "With you two having the same hair, it's hard to tell he's adopted." Tessa looked up at her father and smiled. His wry humor was a better way to begin than the expected argument.

"How'd you know it was me?"

"*They* knew. I can tell by their commotion. My low-tech early warning system."

"So that's why you came to the gate without that Enfield I left you." Tessa walked around a sore spot between them.

"I always come to my gate 'without the Enfield you left me.'" His voice was a whining, nagging mimicry of hers. It next took on a flat take-it-or-leave-it tone, "And I leave my gate unlocked. Anyone may enter here."

Weren't we, not our parents, supposed to rebel against authority? Tessa thought wistfully. The bantering humor of their conversation dissipated. Still, she was glad to be at the grange at last, even with her guard up.

An hour later, Tessa sat comfortably in a shady garden behind the house. She had applied a trace of makeup imported exclusively for associates from a thriving Swiss subsidiary. And because she was off duty and out of uniform, she allowed two pieces of jewelry. Her earrings were matching Martian emeralds set in asteroid-derived platinum, originally a gift from her father to her mother years ago. The gems played off her green eyes. A simple platinum herringbone chain graced her neck, a gift from Zot in better times.

The pair remained mostly in silence looking over spreading rosebushes just beginning to bloom. On Mars at Dr. Herriff's VBC, even with cramped garden space and limited water, Bethany had insisted on roses. "Everyone must see something beautiful," was her rationale to Herriff, as she nurtured bushes that climbed up the exposed interior framework of the Von Braun Center.

Beyond Miller's roses, a dozen apple trees showed their first green fruit. A stack of his neighbor's white beehives sat on a carpet of clover amid the rows of trees. The flourishing, well-tended orchard would produce a bumper crop later that autumn.

As the evening deepened, both Tessa and her father were in better spirits, the initial tension diffused. Sipping iced tea, she asked how such refreshment was possible. "I've gotten hold of some deep-space solar panels and fridge units," Miller replied. Without a sense of arrogance or inconsistency, he often alluded to his many connections within Marsco.

"Plus your skill to cannibalize any castoff and obsolete equipment, I'm sure," added Tessa.

"Certainly," he explained. "I couldn't make it without water recovery." He drew a thoughtful, reminiscing breath. "Water never used to be an issue here. Wasn't like this when I was a boy."

Around them, his gardens flourished. Computer analysis of moisture content kept his drip irrigation system at optimum. Not a liter was wasted. His high-tech system allowed him to do so well while the neighbors struggled.

To this tranquil scene, she thought, add a pressurized, Plexiglas dome and, beyond its clear panels, a wind-driven dusty sky—then take away the sleeping dogs at her feet—and father and daughter might be back at her girlhood home on the Red Planet. "It does have a colony feel about it, your gardens. Mars colony, I mean."

"I know," Miller continued, taking their conversation in another direction, "but, I think that your childhood, your teen years on Mars, gave you such a distorted view."

"Well, I was the only child at Von Braun for years. A bit of everyone's niece, everyone's princess."

"Well, yes, that, but I meant about Marsco itself."

Tessa was reluctant to add much to his assertion. Born on Earth several years before the C-Wars, she had been whisked away as a child on one of the last shuttle flights before fighting erupted. She spent the rest of her girlhood at the Von Braun Center, Marsco's flagship for propulsion and space research, where her father was the chief engine designer under Dr. Herriff. Her mother was the colony's hydrologist. Under her auspices, indigenous frozen water was found, analyzed, melted, and purified. Only Tessa's entrance to the Marsco Academy brought her back to Earth, more or less for good.

Wanting to say something, she admitted, "My memories of those early days are of the victorious Marsco. When I left Earth that first time, Marsco was a computer conglomerate. A multinational corporation universally praised for its research, its diversity, and its philanthropy. When I returned, it'd become the sole world power."

"Yes," her father admitted with no enthusiasm.

"*Something* had to step in!" Tessa reacted sharply. "My God, you knew the chaos facing the world back then! Knew it better than I do! Some power needed to stabilize things."

"Of course, of course," her father noted with a touch of associate's pride he displayed as a younger man. "Everyone believed in Marsco's promises before the Continental Wars. Bethany did. I did. When the conflagration erupted, it had to, as you say, step in and stabilize all the chaos."

"And its measures are only temporary, surely," insisted the daughter.

"As a point of hypothetical argument, I'd say, its measures currently have become more or less permanent."

"Twenty-some years is hardly permanent," the younger associate smirked.

"I'm not so sure its time horizon is much shorter than permanent."

Much to the benefit of humankind, Tessa noted in some curious combination of smug satisfaction and ambivalence toward Marsco. Yet, she insisted, "Once an acceptable degree of political stability's assured worldwide, it'll step back."

"That's not what its actions suggest. It seems determined to keep control indefinitely."

"Well, I'm not sure that's so reprehensible. For instance, look at the record of the Continental Powers, Walter, just look."

"I don't have to look. I was there. I grew up with them." He paused to gather his thoughts. "There's plenty of blame on the Powers' part to justify *anything,* if that's what you want me to admit." He paused once more, trying to say everything in an inoffensive a manner; fighting with his daughter was not his intention. "However, I suppose you mean something like the poet's line: 'Better a present like this than a past like that.' But, you're thinking too much like an associate—"

"I *am* an associate! And so are you!"

"You know what I mean. That binary reasoning: either you're *for* or *against* the Continental Powers. And if *against,* therefore you're *pro* Marsco. Quite Boolean. Can't there be a third way?"

Tessa had had enough, so she tried a neutral topic. "The gardens and orchards look fantastic."

"Thanks." Her father allowed this segue.

"Mom would be proud."

"Yes, she would."

"And you should be, too." A reluctant admission of tolerance.

"I am. It's not been easy, but I seem to have made it work." Kludgy but working water condensers, up- and down-links, an antenna array, his drip irrigation systems like those Bethany had originally designed for the Martian gardens. He was well supplied, better than any other nearby Indie grange.

As she felt the tension ease slightly, Tessa ventured onto a potentially touchy topic. "I had to cross a checkpoint that seemed under heavy guard this afternoon. Security troopers there, not Auxxies. Anything up?"

"You mean aside from living so near the stopline of a subsidiary and a sprawling UZ? No, nothing I know of." His sarcasm lingered until he reflected further. "This is an odd place." He swept his right hand around to signal his grange and the others like it beyond the hedge. "Marsco likes its world binary—yet this location's neither sid nor zone—and certainly not a Marsco sector or cantonment."

"A gray area?"

"In the Marsco world, almost an impossibility."

She let the subject drop to sip her tea. She wanted her feelings to be as happy as they were on Mars so many, many years ago.

In her silence, Tessa studied her father. He stood 1.85 meters tall, exactly six feet using last century's measurements. His green eyes still glanced at everything brightly with good humor. His once-blond hair, which he kept short, was going silver. When he stood, he went straight up, with a vaguely military air, a Marsco mien.

He hid his age well, because he was over sixty but hardly looked mid-forties. Repeated hibernation flights from Mars kept him from aging naturally even though he hadn't been in space, much less hiber, for a good ten years. Fearing he would age more slowly than Bethany, during Tessa's childhood, her parents made several trips to Earth together, leaving her well-tended on Mars. It was a solitary childhood, a Marsco childhood.

Only later, when she returned to Earth to matriculate at the Academy did she realize why she had been kept on Mars for so long. The whole world had suffered incredibly from the recurring AIDS-spawned scourges throughout the twenty-first century, dating from long before the C-Wars. And when those hostilities had finished devastating the planet, another round of virulent pandemics re-emerged with a vengeance.

In the following desperate years after the war, "the Troubled Times" as they euphemistically came to be known, the world suffered its forlorn Marsco Winter. Three years of often frigid and nearly sunless existence. Another persistent, decimating pandemic brought death to countless millions. As a first-year Academy student, Tessa saw from that insulated campus what the Earth had suffered. Even today, twenty years on, the winters continued to be colder, the summers hotter, as the planet struggled to stabilize after the carnage. According to Marsco (the only authority on such matters) the Earth was beginning to recover worldwide. And yet disease outbreaks still terrorized every non-associate.

The Martian colonies, on the other hand, had remained unscathed. As harsh and limiting as the Red Planet was, colonists fared far better there than their Earth-side counterparts did.

Still tense after her three-year hiatus, Tessa was reluctant to continue with any flashpoint topics. Even so, she quickly noted that during the evening's lazy chat, her father routinely and pointedly referred to the *C-Wars* as the *Continental Wars*. There was no mistaking his intentions. "Calling those times the 'C-Wars,'" he explained, "makes people think the abbreviation is for the 'Cyber Wars.'"

"Well, wasn't that part of it? All those cyber attacks on systems and whatnot?"

"It's the vagueness of the 'whatnot' that bothers me. Of course, both sides launched third-wave weapons, cyber strikes that disrupted computer networks worldwide. We continue to suffer the ravages of what those digital attacks and magnetic mines (that 'whatnot') left behind in practically every OS."

Marsco still struggled to rid its own operating systems and integrated networks of all those lingering viruses planted two decades ago. Everything was infected, corrupted. Most of the longed-for advancements in the sciences and in medicine were arrested, or even destroyed, in those e-strikes and counterstrikes. No data was immune; no OS existed at that time without some corrupting exec commands. Finger disks existed before the Wars; since then, they were an insurance against anyone trifling with Marsco's rebooted systems.

"Well, then, 'Cyber Wars' nails it, doesn't it?" Tessa returned to her rational point.

"But it was so much more. Hundreds of millions of people died! More than that, I'm convinced. Perhaps two to three billion! This wasn't a role-playing software package. After that many casualties—hardly a mere cyber war, like it was some planetwide, each-player-gets-a-turn computer game."

"Well, the Continental Powers were the ones who ended democracy. They started Divestiture and the Wars," Tessa responded, hedging without enthusiasm in the standard Marsco explanation.

Chiding, Miller laughed. "Is that all you can say?"

Knowing she had no real defense, she let his retort drop.

The next morning they spent in the garden before it grew too hot. Both wore baggy cotton clothes and wide PRIM-made straw hats.

Tessa felt she was going through PRIM-ification but oddly enjoyed this simplicity.

On the far side of his orchard, Miller had his main vegetable garden. "Nearly a hundred meters a side," he proudly explained. The checkerboard field was fully tilled but only partially planted. Already some rows of crops had sprouted. Hundreds of hothouse seedlings waited transplanting.

"It's humongous. And you take care of all this?"

He laughed at himself lightly. "Lord of the Manor!" His eyes rolled skyward.

His daughter arched an eyebrow.

"I employ a dozen PRIMS, supervised PRIMS."

Tessa looked surprised at first then laughed with him. "Yes, Lord of the Manor, indeed."

"But the garden's more than enough for me."

"Must have doubled since my last visit."

"Right. I've plenty to sustain myself, plus ample for paying the PRIMS. And I do pay them well. With any surplus I barter for flour and honey, milk and meat, since I keep no animals except the dogs." He did admit that coffee was difficult to secure, so Tessa made it a point to bring some of Seattle's finest this visit.

"But with this subsidiary thriving once more," she reassured him, "you'll find quality coffee there."

Miller shrugged her off. "Since you last visited, I've also added something else."

Just south of his hedge-surrounded garden and orchard, the granger explained, "Last summer, I took control of a large pasture, nearly seven acres, formerly a school playground and part of a country club." They walked down to the enclosure, something akin to a medieval field surrounded by a low wall of PRIM-scavenged stones. "I allow a dairy herder, about two clicks away, to graze his twelve cows here. His grazing rights procure me butter and cheese."

"And your harvest?"

"Most of my own fruit I dehydrate or preserve when I can get sugar. But I tinker with my neighbors' tech equipment, repairing condensers or computers, any odd assortment they might use. An hour's work might bring six eggs or a half-kilo of meat."

"Is that it for income?"

"I still draw my salary at the reduced sabbatical rate, but I have to manage it as efficiently as possible."

More than likely, Tessa assumed, he gave away plenty of that ready supply of MMUs. But, she knew, such while-on-leave pay wouldn't go on forever.

Caught between her own pride and envy of his freedom, Tessa noted that he made do. He lived in his eclectic non-Marsco way. He was happy and contented. Relaxed. He survived mostly by sid service, and at times PRIM labor, but it suited him.

During these mornings of planting, conversations came and went. Some of their talk was reminiscences: how Bethany loved her garden domes on Mars, her life at Von Braun, especially early on when Tessa was a child there. They touched gingerly on Miller's decision to come back here to his boyhood home and live outside of the direct auspices of Marsco—that was just after her mother's death nine years ago. Bethany had never lived at the grange, but her presence was constantly felt, her ashes mixed into the parched, reluctant soil.

When they stopped working for a noon meal, the son of a neighbor appeared, in a panic.

"Doc," the gap-toothed young man explained between gulps of breath, "water condenser ain't *nominal.* We're not getting nothin' fur the herd." To Tessa, the son of the dairy herder looked to be out of a Twain novel rather than the Marsco world—barefoot, his grain-blond hair covered with a PRIM-woven straw hat. Tessa wouldn't have been shocked if he smoked corn silk from a cob pipe.

"What's the rating?"

"Ain't more than 40%, well, 38.0727%."

"Fragmentary information—don't want to draw a conclusion right away. A loss like this might just be a clogged line. Simple to locate and repair. Double-check your hoses and couplings, and if that's not it, we'll have a look."

Typical, thought Tessa, *we'll* have a look. Not *I'll* have a look. That was her father, incapable of seeing (or admitting) that those around him often differed with his opinions.

When Huck left (Tessa didn't bother to remember his name; after all, he was clearly a sid) Miller explained, "I've been barter-tutoring the boy in calculus to enhance his chances on the entrance exam. Scientific accuracy's a must for matriculation; his grammar'll come later."

"Yes, he might need a language disk."

"Only temporary, I'm sure. Smart, that one. And wait 'til you see his younger brother—both will do very well indeed."

"In Marsco, you mean."

"The older one, yes. He's interested in the Academy."

Walter helping an Indie's son enter Marsco? The incongruities of her father's world grew.

Tessa asked, "Why all this reliance on water condensers? This area always had ample water."

"Yes, but all via massive irrigation and reservoir systems, dating from, oh, well over one-hundred seventy years ago."

"So now?"

"The whole system took e-strikes on their management computers. Every dam and most irrigation canals also took Vanovara hits during the Wars."

"But that was years ago. Marsco's repairing the war damage steadily, worldwide."

"My dear," the father said without parental condescension, "it isn't repairing this subsidiary area. Most of the devastation here hasn't been rebuilt. And what's still serviceable's been removed, relocated for use elsewhere." After a pause, he added, "The cyber damage's probably beyond repair. But y'know that." Every associate did.

Tessa thought back on the evidence of V-strikes she'd seen from the jitney. *Throughout this sid,* she realized, *so much infrastructure's non-recoverable. So much of the computer network that this area extensively relied upon must be beyond restorability.* Contrary to Marsco claims, nothing seemed to have been replaced.

This struck Tessa as odd. Marsco proclaimed that all subsidiaries globally were improving. It needed them to thrive for it to thrive.

"Regardless of its pronouncements," her father added as an afterthought, "this subsidiary languishes in acute decline. The wrecked irrigation system—oh, it's been repaired enough to assist the Food Consortium, which leases much of the prime farmland throughout the Central Valley. Little's left for anyone else not closely connected to Marsco. You can see why: it prefers everyone dependent on it."

Miller's statement was the only one that approached a direct complaint or affront to Marsco.

"And, of course," he continued, "since the Continental Wars, the weather patterns have changed. First it was three years of unprecedented cold, 'the Marsco Winter,' while Vanovara dust settled out of the atmosphere. They created a hell of a mushroom cloud!" A trio of frigid winters, wet and cold springs, and cool, weak-sunned summers followed the Wars, but Miller needn't explain something his daughter already knew.

It didn't take much raking the garden dirt with his covered fingers for the granger to find pea-sized remnants of the asteroid weapons. "More than dust," he concluded, taking off his gloves. The nickel and iron pebbles sat in his palm, black against his calloused skin and blue-green finger disks.

"Since then, weather's gone to extremes. No area in the world's received normal weather in the past two decades. This whole area is suffering from a lingering drought for five years running. Even Marsco boffins can't fix that."

"Still, it surprises me Marsco isn't doing more here," the associate replied in a tone too defensive to go unnoticed.

"Have you seen the UZ just south of here? PRIMS take dilapidated light rails into city center to their work sites. They don't have more than three or four dozen water stations for the whole unincorporated zone. Marsco's sending an expedition to orbit Jupiter, but it can't fix that?"

"Clearly it should do more." And then, relying on last century's cliché, she added, "'Rising water raises all boats.'"

Giving her no response, he tossed the asteroid weapon shards aside.

After their long day in the garden, broken by a siesta during the searing afternoon heat, they walked along the thick hedges and trees of the nearby granges. Io and Deimos tagged along, trotting over the still-hot ground, some of it showing signs of former pavement and curbing.

Tessa insisted on carrying her Enfield whenever leaving the grange.

As they walked amid lengthening shadows, the younger associate confided, "Martin's asked me to join his VBC research team once I've finished my dissertation."

"Not surprising, you're a wonderful researcher! And Mars'll be an excellent opportunity for you. You'll do well as part of Herriff's Center."

"Thanks," she replied with sincerity. "He thinks I'll be happier pursuing pure research. He's seen a sampling of the preliminary test results I've compiled."

"Dare I ask someone in the midst of finishing a dissertation that eternal nagging question?"

Tessa looked stern then smiled. The code of friends and family of those slogging through an interminable thesis—*Don't ask.* "No, I forbid it," she pronounced with a queenly air, "but I don't mind telling you. I've finally collected all my data. My test results compute exactly as I predicted. Perfect sine curve with minimal derivation. It's a matter of finishing the written explanation."

"Ah, yes," her father interjected. "'There's no end to the writing of books; that much work wearies the soul.'"

"Precisely, but I'm not offering any classes this summer and I'm on reduced teaching load next year. I'll get it done."

He rested his hand reassuringly on her shoulder. "Take some advice: 'Better done than done better.' You're not reinventing the rocket engine—just explain your data and be done with it."

"I know. And my thesis director also wants me at MIT when I'm done—like Herriff, she wants me doing pure research."

"If a father might offer some advice?"

"Yes, you may."

"I'd go to Mars. Herriff'll give you more room to work, professional room."

"But will I go there in your shadow? You were never at the Marsco Institute of Technology. I'll be able to grow there without your stature becoming my measuring stick. At the VBC, your shadow's still lengthening."

"Are you in my shadow now? You've made your own way." He added as humorously as possible, "Besides, is being connected to me currently helping you?" She didn't answer at first. Yet, after looking at each other, they burst out laughing like siblings sharing a comical secret.

"Sometimes that's the only way to respond," Tessa concluded with a bemused sigh.

They crossed a winding dirt path that had been a tree-lined avenue of luxurious home sites, all gone now. Miller threw a stick for his excited dogs until it bounced down an old storm drain. They leaned against a brick foundation of a collapsed house next to a thick-branched oak void of any greenery.

Finally, after a silence, Miller offhandedly remarked, "Herriff asks me to rejoin him every year on Bethany's anniversary."

"Anniversary of mom's death?"

"Yes."

"Is there a connection here?"

"I didn't notice one; coincidence I guess."

"Or something else?"

"Yes, I suppose it could be guilt."

"I thought he was your friend. You don't see eye-to-eye with him anymore."

"Martin Herriff was my collaborator and my best friend, aside from your mother." He paused. "It isn't that we don't see eye to eye. *I* see. *He* doesn't." Miller's words hung in the air as he left the abandoned house and headed home.

"'Marsco ambivalence'—that's Father Cavanaugh's term for it," Miller explained. He and Tessa enjoyed the springtime smell of renewed life coming off the grange's irrigated fields that filled the cool evening air. "Marsco gives so much, say periodically to an individual PRIM, while on the whole it holds them back as a group."

Unseen in the darkness, Tessa suppressed a yawn. *No,* she thought, mentally correcting her father, *that's not it exactly.* In all her years of being an associate, especially one of such a famous parent, she learned to ignore his hyperbolic polemics. Marsco had given her much. And yet, in so many ways, it had taken her father from her. And others she once loved so passionately. She forced Zot out of her mind.

Marsco ambivalence.

A dream of Zot woke Tessa early the next morning. He was on her, in her. She embraced him, welcomed him. Her breath shortened; her body ached for him. Awake, she lingered in bed, first savoring then fearing the fragmented images of her loss.

Moving aside her mosquito nets, Tessa stood up. Through the window, the moon cast a gray light into her room. Deimos woke as well and stretched his legs while still lying on his side.

Zot, Ensign Anthony Grizotti, often came to Tessa in dreams, in daydreams, in frustrated conversations with herself. She always tried to suppress these episodes. Shivering, she lay back down on the bed but let the memories overwhelm her. She didn't want to admit she still loved him, yet that thought was not far below the surface of her conscious mind. "Oh, well," she whispered to the dog and shrugged, "there're lots of associates in the Marsco world."

They often spoke, when they first met as plebes at the Academy years before, of their mutual desire to improve Marsco. Only a fool didn't notice its excesses, its delays in worldwide housekeeping to improve the life of so many, the PRIMS especially. "New associates for the new Marsco," they boasted of themselves while pledging their idealistic commitment to upgrade Marsco's methods.

"We will build that better world it has promised."

Their shared dream. Their shared passion. Their deep love.

Then his bewildering and unexpected shift. His matriculation not in Flight School but in Hibernation Specialization Training. His sudden reticence. He might as well have joined a mercurial and treacherous Luddite cell like the Nexus for the way he suddenly acted. It was all too much for Tessa.

Outside, the wind stirred a bit. She noticed tree branches swaying in the strong gray light of the Marsco Moon. The Earth-side wind had no effect on the illuminated dust clouds stringing out from the lunar sphere.

Forcing herself not to think again of Zot, Tessa willed herself to sleep by listening to the rhythms of Deimos' breathing.

They wore gardening gloves to protect their finger disks and planted bedding tomatoes and basil the next morning before it grew sweltering. Against her wishes, the seedlings brought Zot to mind. Tessa asked in an absent-minded way, "Do you still make pesto with Zot's recipe from Nona Grizotti?"

"Of course. I freeze enough for all year."

"Damn, Zot, that bullshitter," Tessa sighed off-handed. Miller heard, but said nothing as they continued digging. She added, "He loves fresh tomatoes."

"Yes, he ate his way through nearly two dozen last August."

"Zot—Ensign Grizotti—*here*?"

"He's been promoted."

"Very well, *Lieutenant* Grizotti, here?"

"Not as formal as that, but yes, here last summer." Catching her eye, his tone held the slight reprimand of a parent disappointed that a child wasn't listening. "I told you all about it. Well, tried to. I had to leave you a voice mail last Christmas."

Tessa knew she had to respond with something. "End of semester. Grading and prepping. Squeezing in my dissertation research. It must have slipped my mind." They both knew a feeble excuse when they heard it.

Her father wondered, *how does a man like Zot slip your mind?* As eager as he was to find out what, if anything, was on between them, Miller tended his garden, saying nothing more. He continued planting, removing bits of Vanovara metal as he worked.

Three bedding plants later, Tessa asked, "Do you know where he is?"

"He who?"

Daughter and father crossed glances. *As if…*

Under Tessa's withering gaze—so like her mother's—Miller replied, "Let me explain completely as I'm sure I did in December. He was here with a shuttlemate in the middle of last August. He'd been promoted. I'm sure I told you all that. He was to leave the next month for deep space. He's chief hiberman on the *Yuri Gagarin*. I'm sure you know of that. Marsco's certainly touting that run."

"Of course, the Jupiter expedition."

"Yes, the first manned trip beyond the asteroid belt."

"But I don't know the crew manifest," she lied.

"Well, he's nowhere else. Is there any getting off a shuttle on a four-year mission into the never-never?" Miller asked calmly.

Returning to her planting, Tessa tried to appear disinterested. Eventually, however, she asked, "Who's this shuttlemate?"

"Jamie Maissey."

"Oh." The woman seemed to shrink with the news.

"That's *his* name. He's been assigned a routine Mars-to-belt mission—as if that duty could in any way be routine," Miller emphasized.

"Leave it to Zot to volunteer for the most dangerous expedition in the world. In the solar system. I swear, the man has a death wish."

"Well, hardly that. He's young. Restless. Running from something. Or someone, I'd imagine." Miller touched a nerve. He then added almost as an aside, "Why would you think, that if Zot *were* in love with someone else, he'd bring her here?"

Tessa bit her tongue, although she wanted to ask if he definitely knew if Zot loved someone else.

"Besides," Miller remarked a row of basil plants later, "you broke his heart."

Tessa shot back, "He said that?"

"He didn't say anything. I read it in his looks. I see it in yours."

Planting more seedlings, Tessa brushed off her father's comment but asked, "So why did he come here?"

"I think he thought you'd come down from Seattle." Without offering this as a defense, Miller added a longer explanation, "Besides, many people come here. Stephen Cavanaugh visited recently. Also the heir-apparent Dalai Lama. Several Auxxies who've built the Colony drop by on occasion."

A motion of Miller's head signified where the Colony was in reference to his grange, about fifteen clicks due east. It was home for much of the Auxiliary and their families, those who helped Security patrol the Sac City Sid and its UZ. "When they do visit, they always bring me black and oolong teas. My chief suppliers."

Tessa knew that the leader of a nonviolent Luddite commune visited occasionally. She'd heard of, but never met, Allison. This Ludd had once been disked although she was formerly a sid, never an associate. And never a lefter. To become a Ludd, she had all her finger disks surgically removed. Not a forced DRP, but a voluntary disk removal procedure. *Totally insane maneuver,* the associate concluded, *dot.*

Tessa also knew that Miller attracted an endless stream of guests—active supporters of Marsco, active dissenters. Sometimes, associates and avid detractors sat opposite one another, seemingly at ease with the contradictory juxtaposition. All greeted by Miller without ceremony or rancor.

"I've even had the head of the sid's Security and Hygiene detail drop by for tea. 'A courtesy visit.'"

"To spy undoubtedly."

"Possibly."

"And while you had a house full of Ludds, I'm sure."

"And itinerant PRIMS camped out in the garden."

This was Miller's world. Associates, sids, PRIMS, Luddites. A disparate amalgam of visitors and guests. Some invited. Others random travelers who happened to wander in. And still others with ulterior motives. All welcomed with the same warmth and generally the same simple meal. No wonder an I-ON-U focused down on his isolated grange. Tessa wondered what bugs Security had planted around the garden.

"You'll meet with anyone, won't you?" Her voice had more concern than annoyance, although as a Marsco officer, it should have had the latter.

"Stephen Cavanaugh was Bethany's closest friend from childhood. I've known him, or of him, since I first met your mother years and years ago on Mars. Allison and all those others who visit, oh I don't know, they just want to come here. To talk. To garden. There's no law against me having visitors. I *am* an associate, still in good standing by any measurable meaning of the term. That gives me some rights, I assume." He defiantly held up his left hand covered by a soiled work glove, the gesture reiterating his lefter status.

After a pause, he clarified, "But I won't let just anyone come to the grange. The head of the Nexus wanted to meet here, but I wouldn't allow it, not here."

"Well, that shows some sense." His daughter sharply reacted in the same tone Miller himself often used when annoyed. She knew of this Luddite and his infamous reputation. Prominent for all the wrong reasons, advanced by his grandiose attitude of his own particular importance. Among his many self-designated sobriquets, "The Scourge of God" proved her point. But mostly, he was known plainly as just "Leader." His Nexus followers were the most violently opposed to Marsco's current rule of law.

Tessa drew a breath. *At the grange? Here? Had they actually met elsewhere?* She didn't know but feared to probe.

The Millers worked another few minutes planting basil. In front of three rows of rosebushes, irises grew. "I need to thin those or they'll take over," the granger noted in passing. Offhandedly, Miller remarked, "He seems friendless, and Zot's taken him under his wing."

"What? That Luddite? Who're you talking about?"

Miller caught his daughter's attention. He too had a withering professorial stare when needed. "*Maissey,* Zot's friend, the other iceman with him last summer. I thought we were talking of Grizotti's visit."

"Were we?" Tessa's retort ended the conversation. As the heat rose, they planted in silence until stopping for lunch.

Their work done that evening, Tessa ventured a question, "What was it like? Before the C-Wars?"

Miller hesitated at such an odd query from an associate. "I'm writing about that world, you know. I've sent you pieces of it. Herriff as well."

Tessa looked down, that undergraduate lowering of eyes, always a signal when a student hadn't read an assignment carefully or at all.

Miller himself looked over Tessa's shoulder as if into another world. *How do I describe Caesar's Rome? Napoleon's Paris? And all those other lost empires?* He didn't notice his daughter watching him with concern. *Midcentury, the cities emptying due to fear of disease and the techno-ability of so many to live and telecommute outside of and away from urban centers.* He surveyed his gardens, his grange an example of such an escapist's home. *That prewar cyber world altered, destroyed, distorted everything.*

"I don't know how to explain it, Tess, except that the tech-world that evolved, that world seemed to make *this* unnecessary." He placed his bare hand gently on her forearm. His implanted FDs gave her skin a slight electrical tingle. "Human touch became unnecessary to some—to enough. Cyberspace became authenticity for far too many. V-logs replaced community. Web-reality replaced actual contact." He drew a sad breath, "But we *are* human. We need this touch. In the long run, it cost us, that loss of human connection."

He grew contemplative once more. *How do I explain the decay of life? The eroding of societal and social bonds? How to explain that some citizens no longer felt any need to be part of any society but a blogged one?*

Still others felt that destroying—or at least striking out against—the last vestiges of that civilization was their only response. The natural response. Violence. Luddites spawning more violence.

"It seems a thing I ought to be able to voice," Miller eventually went on, "but I find speaking of it somehow silencing."

His thoughts, however, ran on. *Still others played off this furious cadre and asked, "Why have schools for someone else's deadhead kids?" Or they asked, "Why support hospitals for those sick and dying of HH GAS? Herpes. Hepatitis. Gonorrhea. AIDS. Syphilis. These diseases might as well take 'em all." Or they declared, "If they want to go their own way—that rabble and their malcontent ilk, those Ludds who reject everything, hate everything, destroy everything—dammit, then let them. But on their side of a stopline." And thus, one type of PRIMS came into existence, the low-end castoffs, the self-castaway citizens of so many countries, living or existing in sealed neighborhoods, even inside the longstanding borders of their countries of origin.*

Seeing his anguish, Tessa wished she hadn't asked the question.

Rebelling Luddites making civilian rule impossible. AIDS and TB and other virulent diseases destabilizing so many countries. The end of democracy. The rise of the Divestiture Movement. The Policy of Abandonment.

How do I explain all that?

And a second type of PRIMS (off-continent mainly) forced into relocation camps by near-continuous civil wars, the ceaseless politics of terror, never-ending droughts, and recurring deadly plagues. Unaided until Marsco stepped in to care for them. "Marsco Philanthropy." How do I explain it all? Pandemics decimating the world's population time and again, dividing the digital from the non-digital all the more?

As though his daughter was privy to his tormenting thoughts, Miller stated, "There came to be armed militias and Auxiliaries patrolling the cities."

The Continental Powers arising by cutting themselves to pieces, the Divestiture Movement, divesting themselves of their own unwanted citizens. Creating new "countries" where none had previously existed. Taking the lion's share of educated citizenry and wealth and technology and then excluding the rest. Democracy becoming kleptocracy.

All this created in part by the digital divide between peoples. Creating it or upgrading it. Certainly making it all possible.

And then the Continental Wars when the Powers tried to rein in Marsco.

"I'm not sure I can explain that prewar world, Tessa. I'm putting together a manuscript on it. A type of *samizdat*."

Pensive, Tessa shuddered at the implications of his provocative writings.

"Maybe that'll explain some of the beginnings." He paused thoughtfully. "Although in all fairness, there's blame enough to go around—on the Continental Powers, on scores of spiteful Luddite factions, on the Divestiture Movement, on Marsco, on nature unleashing waves of disease. On *us*—" he wiggled his fingers laden with disks "—we who helped Marsco, fostered it over all those years."

Melancholy grabbed Miller as he grappled with all the lingering demons he carried. He was paying the price for misplaced loyalty. Glancing at her, he added softly, "I know you and Zot have plans to improve and change it—"

"Yes, from within." An ardent response.

Miller said nothing more.

Tessa was saddened that her father still struggled to understand, to overcome this world. She knew he was out of touch about Marsco. *This is the world—my world—deal with it. Make the most of it. Especially since you bequeathed it to us. But what a world, what a world, one filled with e-viruses and real viruses.*

His words gave her pause, but the associate felt she must say something in defense of Marsco. She asked pointedly, "Marsco didn't destroy democracy, did it?"

"Oh, no, elections were gone long ago—thanks in large part to the Luddites, the ferocious kinds. Hard to hold them amid all that continuing upheaval. No elections, thus martial law became common, accepted. A natural progression."

Taking it all in, Tessa continued her syllogism. "And did Marsco create unincorporated zones originally?"

"No, clearly, they're of C-Powers origin."

"But didn't Marsco step in to help PRIMS in those zones that so many Powers created?"

"Yes, certainly. 'Marsco Philanthropy,' no doubt."

"It has a history then, a long history, of helping PRIMS, wouldn't you say? From even before the Wars?"

"I can't argue with your facts. But what's your point?"

"Only that Marsco's a damn sight better than the Powers it replaced."

"It didn't replace the Powers. It's replicated them!" Miller thundered, slamming his daughter's logical step harder than either expected.

At his outburst, Tessa rose and walked back into the house.

Miller sat silently in his garden for twenty minutes, then finished putting away some tools and refilling his dogs' outdoor water bowls. He texted instructions to his sid overseer about tomorrow's tilling for a few acres of winter wheat.

Tessa showered and returned for iced tea in her off-duty uniform. Except for a periodic associate stopping by for one reason or another, that uniform was rarely seen here. And yet Tessa was proud of her red-trimmed grays, and why not? Marsco had brought stability to the world. "If you want peace, work for Marsco" wasn't just some adage. It meant something. Since the C-Wars, the world had witnessed no major wars. No nationalism. No arms race. After a fashion, no crime or urban problems. Those were negative facets of the past.

Once finished with a silent evening meal, Miller gently offered some paternal advice, "Tess, don't surrender your ideals." He paused. "I should've said that to you earlier. And I sincerely mean it—don't surrender your laudable goals for Marsco."

THREE

THE DISSIDENT'S SCHEME

(Miller's Grange, 2092)

"Boys with toys!" Tessa teased.

"Perhaps a bit," Miller replied two nights later as he brought her to a renovated garage beyond the greenhouse at the farthest edge of his hedge-surrounded grange.

They walked in brighter-than-full moonlight. A rising Marsco Moon, its dust clouds extending into deep space, illuminated the gardens in a soft blue. Even Io and Deimos cast long shadows in the abnormal glow.

The outbuilding, used for storage and workspace, had once stood next to what would have been the third house down from his along the winding avenue. The granger had all the abandoned structures removed by PRIM work gangs to create an open space for cultivation. Other than his home and greenhouse, only two swimming pools turned into cisterns and two garages (this one and another closer to the gardens) remained of the ostentatious, widely spaced houses that once stood here. *Starter castles,* as he facetiously referred to them.

Miller used his left disks to unlock the door. Inside, in a rectangular workspace a dozen meters at its longest, the engineer showed his daughter the first of his two projects. "There she is." He pointed to a horizontal/vertical hover flight craft that sat on its landing struts. "I've nearly restored her to skim-worthy status." Before them stood an H/V HFC of early design. Once completely refurbished, it would be capable of vertical climbs and horizontal skims as well as hovering by means of its vector jets.

Tessa's eyes grew large, so similar to those her father knew when she was a child.

Reluctant to break the spell, Miller finally noted, "It's one of the first models that Herriff developed while still Earth-side."

"My God," Tessa burst out, "that old? What do you do for spares? This model's so obsolete."

"For parts, I cannibalized a pair of outmoded HFCs I keep stored under that blue plastic sheeting alongside the garage." He paused as if remembering, "Oh, and *this*."

As he pulled back a grease-stained canvas tarp, Tessa jumped away horrified. In a dark corner of his storage space stood an archaic bot warrior acting as a lonely, watchful sentinel.

"I've only read about such things!" the shocked younger associate murmured, moving slightly behind her father and farther from the terrifying metallic specter. "Watched them in virt-history programs. Never actually saw one."

"There it silently waits," Miller stated grimly with no hint of sarcasm, "mute testimony to the thankfully short era of independent robotic warfare."

The humanoid stood almost half a meter taller than its owner. Its burnished metal skin had lost its luster. Miller had taken off an arm and a breastplate to reach its circuitry innards. The bot's face mimicked a man's but with mismatched eyes, one an infrared cam, the other an optic lens for streaming real-time data.

"Although their ilk supposedly ran fully functional AI," Miller explained, "they proved useless." He smirked with acerbity. "*Artificial intelligence*—their inventors needed their own intelligence instead of the hubris to create such a savage weapon."

As though understanding, the metallic face seemed to grimace in shameful pain. "One of the midcentury's finest inventions," he scoffed, poking its ribs, "utter junk."

"But, the *finest?*" Tessa asked, being contradictory but just as cynical. "I'd say there were plenty of other blunders."

"Certainly—voice activation and face recognition, to begin with."

"Which were so easily cracked."

"Don't dignify breaking into their moatless OS with the verb *crack.* Anyone with a wire-attached mouse—from zitty tweeners and scheming Ludds—phreaked those systems; they were that porous."

"Yes, I know."

"Until these." Miller held up his right hand to signify his impressive finger disk array. "Today, twitching in's about the only way to enssure access." He left it unstated that only with Marsco's permission did anyone have FD implants. "But I guess I explained all that thoroughly enough in that chapter of my history, on the development, first, of the finger mouse, then the finger disk."

He saw that Tessa avoided his gaze. To ease things, he went back to his disabled robot. "Well, I guess my Tin Man here isn't totally useless."

"How do you mean?"

"Metal's hard to come by in this sid, so my Man here provides me with titanium, stainless steel. And, of course, tubing, couplers, other hardware."

"Weapons?"

Miller momentarily thought, *She's analyzing this like a true associate.* "No, it'd been stripped of those before I got it."

"And where was that? Black market?" Tessa shivered fearing that was the truth.

"No, an Indie auction, quite above boards even to Marsco. I actually obtained a scavenger's license from Security before I bid on them. This one's the second of the pair; I've already totally scrapped the first."

"For its chips?"

"Hardly! All processing hardware's hopelessly out of date. It's decades-old technology, after all."

"So, everything inside that's e-corrupted?"

"Truly. Although goths loved bot-tipping—any bot, not just armed ones—in the end it was cyber attacks that ultimately curtailed their use. That generation was almost a precursor, a foreboding specter of events to come during the Continental Wars. These were rendered obsolete long before the fighting. That conflict had its own drone warfare systems that went amuck."

"We're still dealing with that cyber debris."

"Yes, as you know, quite a serious lingering problem."

Covering up the distorted mechanical face, Miller mused philosophically. "Well, at least those disrupting cyber attacks against drones did one good thing, such as it was. E-strikes made war *war* again." He paused, tying off the tarp around the open torso of the robotic warrior. "Not that I'm in favor of war. But the Continental Wars almost immediately degenerated into savage PRIM versus trooper fighting." He looked away into the shadows of his storage area as though seeing scenes of the carnage there.

"Almost early twentieth-century warfare with trenches and mud and muck. And slaughter. None of this GPS-guided and bot-waging telescopic carnage that made war seem like a virtual game, a distant cyber contest. Something witnessed on a screen with no consequences as though war could really be bloodless, without victims, with no casualties. It's easier to hate the real thing when it *is* the real thing, not some virtual copy, not some pixel display. To know that the real thing's horrific beyond reckoning—well, Marsco gave us that at least."

Tessa's mind ran along other lines. Since Marsco's victory, there were no longer global conflicts. Associates took pride in that; Tessa took pride in that.

The engineer opened the pilot's hatch of the restored HFC. The hinges on the bulkhead swung the hatch upward, making the small craft look like a captured bird with one wing uplifted awkwardly. While in skim mode, the runabout used its body for lift, thus avoiding many flight characteristics of a fixed-wing aircraft. Vectoring exhausts maintained the hover capability and provided horizontal/vertical thrust.

"I've upgraded the avionics," the engineer explained proudly.

Tessa looked at the control console of the four-seater. "Fuel systems?"

"Herriff's original converter. Reactor needed better shielding. I've doubled the preflight storage tanks so in-flight conversion needn't be at max to extend the range."

"Sound retro-maintenance."

"I also finessed the onboard reactor for better water vapor efficiency. Retrofitted miniature engine jets for peak efficiency of the hydro/ox reutilization. Herriff was brilliant—is brilliant—but you can see where he wasn't thinking of designing this initial project for ease of mass production. He wasn't yet messing with any refinements."

Miller had remained busy during her self-imposed hiatus, Tessa realized.

The daughter felt a surge of pride admiring her father's handiwork. He was a theorist, as brilliant as Herriff in his own way but also a tinkerer at heart. His tweaking paid off. The HFC was beautiful. His restoration confirmed the Marsco adage, "All good engineering begins with finger disks."

As the woman sat in the command seat, she ran her hand along the flight instruments.

"Soon I'll have everything but nav systems working," he explained. "No GPS coordinates are currently transmitted around here anyway. Marsco blocks all reception to this area for some reason."

"I noticed faulty info and lack of signal on my mobile when I came down."

"Perhaps not so accidental," her father hypothesized with a pointed tone.

"I can't imagine Marsco," Tessa replied defensively, "being imprecise and uninformative on its own Net."

"There's no Herriff-Grid rebooted and refunctionalized as yet, anyway," Miller went on trying to ease the situation, "so why worry about those downlinks?" Over areas crowded with HFC traffic, the

Grid kept patterns smoothly flowing and collision-free. The sparse traffic over Sac City negated its need.

Her quiet admiration for the restoration was followed by a surprised outburst, "This flight console doesn't need finger disks!"

"Herriff was a firm believer in avoiding them whenever possible. Her joystick and dedicated systems take—oddly—fingers, not even a finger mouse. Quite intransigent of Herriff, considering the times. Anyone might have skimmed her back then; anyone can now."

Although not yet fully hover-worthy, the runabout showed her lines proudly. From the command seat to its conical nose, anti-glare green gave it a military aircraft look. The rest of the fuselage was clearly of twenty-first century design with stubby canards and a single-piece empennage. The polymer composite body gleamed from countless hours of polishing. When it skimmed in the near future, it would rise off the ground majestically, as glittering as the day it first hovered before initiating level flight.

Tessa imagined her father working there, using the monotonous polishing almost as a meditation. *Thinking of what? Of whom? Pondering what? Remembering Bethany? Imagining things that might have been? Thinking of me, his only child and my own career choices?*

This reverie was broken by her father's comment about the computers. "Instead of trying to purge them of any latent, dormant viruses, I didn't even bother with the existing onboards. I wired in a separate M-1 Lander system."

"That's ten times more functionality than you need."

"More like twenty-five times. But rather over than under."

"Have you flown it?"

"Just up toward the rafters to make sure all the vector jets worked. I raised her a meter or so to swing her about one-eighty three weeks ago."

"All within this confined space? And she's how long? Five meters?"

"Just over."

Impressed, Tessa added under her breath, "Incredible disking skills."

Miller lifted a canvas cover from the aft portion of his restoration. Along the now-exposed fuselage, a hand-painted emblem greeted Tessa. It showed a stylized Earth and Moon linked by a sideways figure eight that suggested a spacecraft egressing orbit around the planet, reaching the lunar sphere, and returning to its Earth-based home.

In navy blue letters above the emblem ran the heading: *Sac City Aerospace Associates*. Below ran the bold statement: *Independent Conglomerate of Lander Manufacturers and Operators.* The emblem and slogan suggested a smartly done advertisement campaign from the last century.

Tessa's face posed the question.

"Oh, this?" He answered.

"*Conglomerate?*"

"Bit pretentious, I know." He unassumingly patted the enigmatic lettering before explaining. "I've cobbled together a research team and a few abandoned assembly plants. We're getting started, making do. Sac City has a fine history of making rocket engines. Seattle, where our fuselages are built, had a thriving aerospace industry once, pre-Marsco."

"So your SCAA's still in its infancy, its grandiose infancy."

"*Marsco* started with *Mars* in its name way back in 1999 because it was aiming heavenward. Three geeks, a rented office, a name. Not much more. Now look!"

Tessa had no rejoinder for her father except the knowledge that he was always a dreamer. She shrugged then mentally added, *Fortune favors the bold!*

"Now for my second surprise," Miller finally stated.

In a smaller workroom off the larger one, Miller stowed a gray, plastic mock-up of a sublunar lander, just over a meter in length, sitting on a studio table. A full-size lander of this design would be capable of easily making the Earth-to-Moon journey suggested by the runabout's emblem.

"It's a standard Herriff design, more or less. I've worked on the engines mostly. They'll be much more efficient than anything going today."

"Propellant?"

"Standard Marsco-approved hypergolics." Miller explained the components of such a fuel needlessly to the other aerospace engineer. The hydrazine and dimethylhydrazine mixture, when in contact with nitrogen tetroxide in a ship's combustion chamber, instantaneously ignite with an explosive reaction. In space, it had been the standard chemical fuel for well over 125 years.

"Walter," she reminded him patiently, "this is first-semester lecture material. I explain this to my plebes all the time."

"Yes, but shouldn't we be beyond that by now?" the senior engineer asked rhetorically. "Chem fuels, for heaven's sake. Obsolete in the first decade of this century."

"Well, come up with a viable alternative."

"Don't think I haven't tried."

"At the VBC, you'd have plenty of opportunity to try. More than *try*."

He responded more sharply than intended, lashing out when he knew he shouldn't, "Is this why you're here? To talk me back into Marsco for Herriff?"

"No!" she shot just as sharply. "Yesterday what did you call yourself? 'An associate who was still in good standing'? Today you deny you're even in Marsco."

"Rather a moot point, don't you think? I'm certainly not an associate in the sense that you want me to be."

As their discussion simmered, Tessa sensed it was ranging out beyond her control. Before he moved into that territory (a précis of "What might have been in this century"), she reached for a safe question. "Have you flown this one yet?"

"Flown it? I don't even have a full-sized mockup. I haven't even tested the engines yet, but I'm working on them. I'm quite close to that actually."

"Finishing the engines?"

"Yes."

"Here?"

"Out at the old aerospace test site thirty-five clicks to the east. But I'll have to test them horizontally on Earth, not in orbit as we did back at Herriff's center." Slipping into a description of his dream, he continued. "Their lifting capacity is, via computer simulation, 55.0762% higher than anything Marsco currently operates. I think with a few refinements, we'll top 60% higher."

"What's the scale?" Tessa asked, fingering the intricate workings of the plastic model on the table and wishing to avoid any more flashpoints.

"One to seventy-five."

"She's a massive brute, isn't she?"

"Yes, that's for sure," Miller replied with a hint of justified pride.

"When do you build your dog ship?"

"Our prototype's a ways off. In the works, of course, but only a long-range plan. We'll build the engines here and the fuselage in Seattle."

"This craft'll be bigger than any standard sublunar orbiter."

"That's the whole point—larger, more capacity. A buff, as an old airman might say. But more efficient. Meaning: she won't need to refuel in space for a return trip to Earth." Miller let that remark hang in the air without further comment. He watched his daughter think over the implications of that fact.

"I don't see the need," the Marsco officer eventually responded, not readily wishing to admit the ramifications of a craft with such muscled-up specs. "Marsco already has an extensive, expanding, and dedicated lander fleet, plus ample docking ports on its orbiting lunar stations."

"Now who's lecturing? But I'm thinking of working with Independent concerns."

"But even Indies utilize Marsco ports."

The engineer's eyes gleamed with boyish excitement. "I'm thinking of bypassing Marsco."

"Bypassing Marsco in space? How? By getting around its Twelve Thrusters Policy? Is that your implication? I don't see how that's possible."

"She won't need servicing in space, that's how. Twelve Thrusters keeps every Independent tied to Marsco. Those regs have kept Marsco the sole operator in space for nearly seventy years."

"What's wrong with that?" The associate sought to keep her employer's reputation intact. "Every craft is serviced. No exceptions! They're no systems allowed in orbit that *can't* be maintained out there all the way to the asteroid belt. All's standardized."

"Yes, my point exactly. Twelve Thrusters gives Marsco a crushing monopoly on space travel. They have had it, maintained it, for the past seven decades."

"But there are Independents!" Now Tessa's eyes flashed. "Marsco allows them to operate."

"But always through *its* ports, using only *its* registered and regulated thrusters, and buying only *its* fuels."

"Exactly!" Tessa stated firmly, reiterating the right of eminent domain. "'Everything off the Earth goes Marsco.'"

"So with her," he motioned to his detailed model reverently, "we avoid Marsco."

Tessa's mind worked to find all the hidden pitfalls in such a quixotic program. But she was also multitasking and working to find the value in such labor spent on a seemingly futile project. "Why would you want to avoid Marsco?"

Dead silence surrounded father and daughter for a moment.

Finally, he broke the tension. "Just to manufacture something legal and positive that its HQ doesn't totally control. Just to show it that it isn't the only game in space anymore. Maybe to give this subsidiary a reason to exist when we make half a dozen landers to compete with Marsco's hundreds."

As her father twitch-locked the work areas, Tessa stood silently in the pale blue-gray of the Marsco Moon beside him outside the secret-filled garage. *Lofty dreams,* she thought. *Always been a dreamer, aiming for the stars. Well, his engines are on their way to Jupiter as we speak; some dreams do come true.*

Faint mechanical clicking and whirring noises from behind them caught Tessa's attention. The dogs at her heels whimpered and futilely tried hiding themselves in the shadows. The associate reacted as any trained officer would to an unknown threat. A hissing sound filled the air. Her taut arm leveled an Enfield.

A surveillance drone hovered ten meters from the Millers. The saucer-shaped craft, less than a meter in diameter, trained its IR scanner on the pair and aimed a small dish antenna toward its central coordinating unit somewhere off in the distance beyond the hedges.

"Predictable, isn't it?" commented Miller, his hand lowering Tessa's Enfield. "God only knows what insect-sized snoopers it sends."

"You expected this drone, didn't you? Who sent it?"

"Oh, my dear friends with that I-ON-U by my gate send it to take a closer look every time I tinker in my barn. It floats over my hedge with ease. Comes so quietly, the dogs're too frightened to bark. They duck for cover rather than make any fuss."

"Why's it here?"

"In a few weeks when I test fly that HFC, it'll get a real treat."

"That doesn't answer my question."

"You're Marsco. Figure it out—why scrutinize a has-been associate and terrorize my dogs?" Down on a knee, he called to comfort the quaking pair. Their tails between their legs, they shook noticeably, reluctant to even step toward their consoling master. Looking up, he asked, "What sort of threat do I pose?"

"You're not making any sense."

"It's a Marsco world."

Tessa tossed without sleep. She adjusted the mosquito net, counted asteroids. But sleep eluded her.

At the grange, Miller set aside a suite of rooms solely for her. She kept some off-duty clothes in a closet to make it easier to travel here on her increasingly rare visits. She also kept a few mementos from Mars. Restless, she fingered them. A Martian turquoise stone and a nickel meteorite found near the VBC, both fist-sized, gathered dust. In a gesture similar to her father polishing his restored HFC, Tessa dusted them mindlessly.

Next to the girlhood keepsakes sat a picture frame on an oak chest of drawers. The frame had a dozen embedded images that, every two minutes, whether anyone was there to watch or not, changed to the next in a random, continuous sequence.

The first digital was of her mother, one posed at an actual studio. Bethany wore a pearl necklace and a formal black dress, flattering but already out of fashion at the time of the sitting. Nonetheless, she looked young, vibrant, attractive, aspects difficult for Tessa to remember. It was easy enough to reproduce the shot so she might have a copy for her Seattle flat, but she hadn't bothered.

Bethany's portrait faded to Walter holding Tessa as a baby. Next, the image of her parents with their infant came into focus. Both were taken on Earth before the three moved to Mars.

These digitals did little to settle Tessa's restlessness.

The next display sent a shudder through her. The frame refocused to a casual snap of Zot arm-in-arm with her at their Academy graduation. They both beamed with pride and love that their formal uniforms did not hide, could not hide. Zot's strong Mediterranean features held her attention until it segued. He looked handsome, she strikingly pretty. Physically and mentally, she realized, they made a wonderful couple.

These were old-fashioned words, but they fit him and their relationship. He had many traditional aspects, most of them rock-solid. Even several years later, that image and her flooding memories of those times still made her shiver.

Of all the digitals in the frame, Tessa had only this one in Seattle where she periodically and reluctantly studied it as she did right then.

The frame changed. Tessa felt better seeing Io as a puppy climbing on the larger and older Deimos. In the background stood sids or Ludds that Tessa didn't recognize.

That collection of strangers reminded her of the constant stream of visitors at the grange, some she approved of, some she didn't. Miller, however, always seemed to have a vacant house whenever she visited.

Restless, Tessa wandered around room to room in silent darkness. Much had changed in the past few years.

The massive house was initially conspicuously ornate and ostentatiously lavish even by the midcentury standards of its construction. The original dwelling was in a palazzo villa-style. It consisted of eight bedroom suites laid out around two vestigial courtyards. Miller had retained the same floor plan with several key modifications, mostly changes that stripped the garish style and kept the practical aspects of the house, its size and privacy.

Nine years earlier, hiring a PRIM brick-gang, Miller had worked side by side with them to enhance the place. Wearing work gloves and doing as much physical labor as possible without damaging his extensive finger disk array, he transformed his home into a self-sufficient dwelling. He thickened the existing walls with used bricks to create maximum insulation. The mismatched masonry kept out the penetrating winter damp and the searing summer heat.

Going aimlessly from one room to the next, Tessa assured herself she wasn't spying.

She entered the largest room, which had a fireside commanding one end. In the chic fashion of the previous era, fireplaces were essentially wasteful, nonfunctional decorations, their appearance only a suggestion of their real purpose. Tessa saw that her father had retrofitted his to be a hearth capable of efficiently throwing heat into the surrounding room. It stood empty of flames in the warm spring. In the autumn, the granger hired PRIMS to split and stack firewood for the winter months. Before this grate a cluster of leather couches and chairs stood where Miller discussed everything and anything with his visitors. The spot seemed used for nothing else.

When Tessa visited, she and her father rarely sat here.

Off to the left was a large suite the granger transformed into his library and study.

The windows once had overlooked a courtyard. Miller had bricked them up entirely so that the room was totally enclosed. A solar-powered ECS with a wind-charged battery backup system kept the extensive library and sophisticated Marsco equipment safe in controlled humidity and temperature. The room might have been located in a sector or on a MAS shuttle, not in this no-man's-land.

A single well-worn Morris chair and standing lamp fit snugly into one corner bordered by built-in shelves. The two walls meeting here were lined with an extensive book collection.

Sitting on the arm of the chair, Tessa fingered the bindings of the books. Art, literature, tech manuals. Old atlases and photo-travel guides. Tomes on the history of technology and spaceflight. Collections on philosophy, theology, biography. Novels. Poetry.

She recognized few of the titles or authors. Shakespeare was among those she did know. Alan Paton and Erich Marie Remarque were names that meant nothing to her; lab manuals and research occupied her time. The granger had works by Laurie Garrett on resurgent plagues and by Margaret Drabble about rampant genocide in the late twentieth century, odd topics for a theoretical aero-engineer, she concluded. Some of the volumes were original published editions dating from the last century. Others were computer printouts, individually bound in PRIM-made leather covers.

A peculiar and an extraordinary mix of works as eclectic as her father.

Small, handmade signs hung above the shelves, printed in a calligraphy that needed more sustained practice. She assumed they were her father's attempts. Why he had meticulously shaped characters with the age-old pen-and-ink system instead of using a common Marsco printer, she didn't know. His obstinacy, the obvious reason. The neat signs caught her attention because they were not there last time she visited.

Their contradictory nature was startling even to the associate.

One in stark, red lettering declared, "'Understand the great secret: Cruelty is the cutting edge of history. The deciding factor is always the greatest degree of cruelty most intelligently applied.' —Stalin." Next to it, a second in black stated, "'We should not minimize our sacred endeavors in this world, where, like faint glimmers in the dark, we have emerged.' —A. Sakharov."

Reading both several times, Tessa forced herself to respond to neither.

Besides these, also in Miller's hand, were two additional signs, mere fragments: "Exterminate the brutes" in red and "a government of the people, by the people, and for the people" in blue.

"You're losing it, Walter," Tessa mumbled after scanning his obscure quotes.

On a long table were several neat stacks of materials. Among them she encountered an unauthorized printout of the *Gagarin's* performance data, providing engine utilization logs. Herriff-Millers powered the experimental ship. It was understandable that an engineer and co-designer of those units was following the progress of that deep-space Jovan trek, even if he had to crack Marsco encryption to get this material. And yet for nearly ten years, most of them at this grange, he purposely remained sequestered outside the Marsco mainstream. He wished to live here, in self-imposed exile cut off from the only thriving entity left in the entire world.

A file disk from a finger mouse PC was neatly labeled in a woman's handwriting: "Report of cholera outbreak, Sac City UZ, 2091." Clearly not his field of expertise. Another disk had the ambiguous title in Miller's own hand, "Engine test specifications, S.C.A.A., April '92."

Tessa also found a hard copy of a letter, sitting by itself, dated 2/15/92 addressed to her, one she'd never received. It began, "Tessa, I've much to show you should you visit again..."

Why would he think that I might not? She preferred not to read any further.

Above an alcove that originally boasted an ornate faux fireplace, an elegant mantel still stood. Tucked beneath it, a small desk created a workbay where her secretive father kept some obsolete but still functioning computer equipment. He had a pre-Marsco external storage tower, with limited terabytes of space, hooked up to a still bootable wire-attached mouse system. Several old-style storage collections showed that he had been compiling a comprehensive document and ripping copies onto standard memory units. Whatever humongous multimedia work he was assembling, he was keeping it secret and secure.

The woman quickly registered in her associate mind that the electronic unit in the alcove was standalone. It was too kludgy for connection to anything Marsco made these days, although it seemed that Miller had it booted and functioning flawlessly. The granger was making sure, the associate observed, that no one hacked into this muscled puppy. His system was intruder-secure and snooper-protected unless someone was sitting in front of the obsolete monstrosity.

A printout title page of a document ran: *The Ascendancy of Marsco: An Unauthorized History. By Walter C. Miller, Ph.D., an associate in good standing.* It rested on top of a stack of perhaps 600 pages of PO on traditional business stationery. The first page had an epigraph. "'Oh happy posterity who will not experience such abysmal woe and will look back upon our testimony as a fable.' —Petrarch."

Tessa read the title page and quote again, but no more.

The associate found the room's contents disturbing. *What's the meaning of all this e-storage?* Miller even possessed a finger mouse PC of relatively contemporary design; a similar unit was routinely issued to an associate, usually from Security, in utmost need of top secret status.

As a commissioned officer, she felt compelled to look around the library, to ask penetrating questions. As the child of two associates of considerable consequence, she grew up surrounded by such equipment, so why take notice? Wasn't this a typical Marsco child's experience?

For the sake of all they had given her, she ignored any misgivings.

She smirked, musing, *I thought nerdy geeks, thinking of firewalls as challenges, became crackers. Who'd ever suspect their parents?* She concluded it best to remember nothing she saw here although she was quite sure that somehow Internal Security knew the contents of this room. If they seemed satisfied to merely watch the dissident granger, she wouldn't interfere with him.

Tessa walked in the early light before the rising sun. After surveying the library, she slept only an hour more when she woke from another passionate dream. Zot stood before her, Med features, eyes. A face etched with worldly knowledge yet tenderness. He readily opened his arms to her, but she froze, unable to accept his advance—then she sat up. After such blunted desire, a quiet morning walk made more sense than continued broken sleep.

She was anxious, on edge, but not so confused that she neglected strapping on her Enfield.

Soon after sunup, not far from her father's, she met the two older sons of the neighbor dairyman. "Huck," the senior, she had seen recently at the grange. At first she mentally thought of the younger boy as "Tom." It made sense to Tessa, their tattered clothes, their spunk and playfulness, their friendly shyness when confronted by an older and polished woman, an associate.

The brothers had finished their laborious morning milking and were carrying their two-handled cans to a buried cooling chamber.

Tessa's reluctant "good day" initiated a conversation. The brothers were old enough to be enchanted by her, young enough to bumble and stammer innocently. Stopping to talk with them, she learned that their real names were Aaron and Jeremy Truman.

Unintentionally, the associate crossed an invisible stopline and put a name onto the face of an anonymous sid. She walked along chatting with them until they reached the earth-cooled storage chamber where all three took turns hand-cranking the milk separator.

"This must make excellent ice cream," the woman commented absently.

"No way!" responded Aaron. "You've had *ice cream?*"

Jeremy stammered, "We ain't got no way to 'frigerate nothing or make no ice."

The older boy hastily explained that they didn't have a solar-powered refrigeration system like Miller's. Without such a device, they needed to use the buried chamber for storage.

Tessa invited the young men down to her father's later that afternoon. "Bring six liters of your best cream," she instructed. Accustomed to bartering with her father, the brothers came dutifully as required after chores with a partially filled milk can between them.

Tessa had spent the rest of the day preparing slabs of ice at the grange, using units that once equipped an asteroid shuttle. The brothers broke the ice with a wooden mallet and, under her guidance, arranged the pieces around an ice cream churn, a cherished Miller family heirloom. "Start cranking," she ordered with older-sister authority.

Two sweaty foreheads later, when the cream finally solidified, she had her young men put the tub into one of Miller's freezers, another salvaged shuttle component. They were impressed with their neighbor's collection—refrigerators, generators, and solar panels.

"Here's a second treat," Tessa explained, "an old-fashioned meal before dessert." Her father's kitchen ran on passive energy but was equipped as though a midcentury home. Earlier in the day Miller purchased some beef from another neighbor for which Tessa supplied the MMUs. (They had eaten little meat during her time there.) With rooftop panels supplying ample voltage, she ground the fresh meat. She next made patties and fried up traditional backyard summer fare. The potatoes she cut in long strips, the meat she even topped with cheese.

Miller enjoyed their throwback dinner as much as the boys did. It crossed Tessa's mind that this tableau might have been a real family: grandparent, his daughter, her sons. She was almost old enough, discarding hiber-retarding, to be their mother. Playing their part, the boys treated her respectfully, as if a distant, older sister or an unmarried aunt.

Conversation continued with ice cream served in the garden. Miller explained to the associate, "Aaron wants to enter Marsco. I tutor him in preparation for his service exam, but he only has access to finger mouse units." Miller wriggled his FDs. "The likelihood of him getting implants pre-Marsco is remote."

"When you matriculate," Tessa added spiritedly, "you'll then be disked." With encouraging earnestness, she explained, "Plenty of plebes at the Academy come from sid-status."

"Or enlist for other branches," Miller added.

Only Tessa understood the allusion about jumping at anything to enter Marsco, including upping to Security.

But the granger knew that if Aaron hosed his entrance exam, the boy would never rashly enlist in Security and become just another legionnaire at some stopline checkpoint. He had higher goals and aspirations.

"And the younger scholar here, Jeremy, wants to study veterinary medicine," Miller commented.

The boy grinned in pleased acknowledgment.

"How's that?" asked Tessa.

"Via a sid apprentice system, the time-honored method of hands-on instruction," her father explained.

"I'm most inner'sted in surg'ar'rey," the boy added as he blushed, staring at his feet for fear of looking at the fascinating associate too deeply.

Miller filled in for the shy boy. "He'll primarily learn methods of surgery. He's already helped an itinerant vet spay Io."

Through his blushing, the boy confided. "I like hep'ping with the birthin' and cast'ratin'."

Tessa smiled. "Surgery in its broadest sense."

"He'll also learn to make his own rudimentary medicines."

Tessa gave a quizzical look.

"Even though some vaccines for rabies and distemper are still viable and available in the sid open markets, other resurgent animal diseases are antibiotic-resistant—like most human ones. Microbes take their toll on all mammals."

"Doc here's hep'ping work on syn'sizing new ant'biotics." He was nearly beet-red from the few words he spoke.

Without false modesty, Miller explained, "I've put him in touch with friends who're trying their hands at it. Jeremy's been doing some field testing for them."

Still blushing, the boy sneaked another glance at the younger associate. Her auburn hair glistened. Her skin was radiant. She had no pox marks, no wheezing cough from untreatable Neo-Con, one of the world's many resurgent, rampant diseases. She seemed a goddess to the young granger, a vision from another world.

Tessa had dressed herself with special care that afternoon, not in the baggy grey T-shirt she had gotten last week, but a finely knit lilac sweater that fit her perfectly. Zot's platinum chain graced her neck. It was as though she was preparing to dine with an associate. Her accidental mixed-message, this inadvertent posture of a siren before the brothers, was unintentional. She hadn't realized how much she longed for companionship.

Tessa gazed a long time at the siblings and then her father. Her mind was brimming with analogies. *An associate neophyte. A sid vet. Two brothers. Two pathways. One Marsco, one non.* She reflected further. *Father and daughter. One Marsco, one non. Or more accurately, one no longer.* A jarring contradictory tableau.

FOUR

ZOT

(Miller's, 2092)

I'm so not up for this, Tessa admitted to herself.

The day after the ice cream was her last full day at the grange. As the Millers prepared their final dinner, Allison from the Luddite commune joined them. It was a simple meal: lentils and rice, fresh green salad, fruit from the orchard.

Tessa had the sense that Allison, whom she'd heard of intermittently over the years but never met, was here on approval. A nagging sense came to her that she and her father had reversed roles one more time. *Shouldn't I be bringing associates for his approval?* That question running through her mind came and went part humorously, part seriously. In the end, she kept reassuring herself with the knowledge that Walter liked and admired Zot, no question, for all the good it did her.

Allison arrived quietly through the opening in the hedge. Io and Deimos greeted her with wagging tails and excited barks. They begged to play, offering frolicking yelps instead of menacing snarls. *She's been here many times,* Tessa noted. The associate also observed that it was indeed true; as a Luddite, Allison had undergone voluntary DRP—disk removal procedure.

Icily, Tessa wondered why.

The visitor was dressed austerely in gray cotton. She was, like Miller, wiry and strong from working long, hard hours in the sun, but her skin was more leathered. Her gray hair showed traces of its original honey-blond color. Had she styled it better, Tessa thought, she might look more graceful.

Although Allison was about her host's age, he looked twenty years younger. She hadn't been fortunate enough to ever hibernate. To Tessa, it showed. Bethany had died well before reaching this age but wouldn't have looked it if she had. But Bethany wasn't here, Allison was. That thought pained Tessa.

All things considered, the younger associate reluctantly acknowledged that the guest's face was striking, her blue eyes still intense. Her countenance had a hint of familiarity, like a distant childhood memory.

As soon as the Ludd arrived, she greeted Walter warmly and spoke pleasantly to Tessa. Witnessing these straightforward gestures, the worrying daughter knew her stinging apprehension was misplaced. The old friends' conversation betrayed nothing more than the fact that both had been young long before the Continental Wars. They once knew the same world: an irretrievable era that each had had a hand, however small, in shaping.

After their opening talk over iced tea in the rose garden, Miller served their meal outside. The evening grew dark before they finished. A late rising Marsco Moon re-illuminated the orchards in blue-gray hues as they lingered tableside.

The salient discussion was *cyber truth.* Both Allison and Miller knew well the days before the Wars. What they spoke about was hardly a reminiscence of better times. "Those days saw the end of *truth, objective truth* one ought to easily recognize even today." Allison quietly spoke, like Miller, without rancor or accusation.

Throughout, Tessa noted how reserved the Ludd was, due not only to her memories of those turbulent days, but also to a sense of remorse she was trying to suppress.

What a trio we make, thought Tessa bitterly, *all three of us holding down our churning emotions.*

Someone who seemed never to hold back, Tessa remembered, was Bethany. Her animation lit up a conversation. She captivated her audience from the start, not necessarily by exceptional looks alone but by her radiating personality. Nothing at all like Allison that evening. *In her younger days perhaps she was the center of attention but not now.*

Tessa felt more and more reassured as the night passed; she no longer perceived Allison as a threat to her mother's memory. Bethany was irreplaceable.

Some deep and lingering pains masked that intrinsic spark Allison had once possessed. Ghosts slow to cease their haunting. Indirectly, the associate guessed, this Luddite was trying to say so much more than she was willing to admit.

"The Web and all the instantaneous media," Allison softly explained to Tessa, "made for shrill, confused shouting."

Miller agreed with her insights, nodding as she spoke.

The Luddite woman's harsh perception was in sharp contrast to her quiet way of talking. "When one view of *the truth* was presented, other views came in fast and furious, often without any credence. But few observers or bloggers had the ability to discern what really happened."

"Yes," Miller added. "With so many so-called 'news' outlets 24/7, even accepted truth was waylaid. Some programs even assured viewers that the Earth was flat, that Armstrong never walked on the moon, that evolution didn't happen."

"Worse yet, that Hitler hadn't exterminated millions."

"That hundreds of millions weren't struck down by AIDS."

"That sea levels hadn't risen."

"*Truthiness* became accepted as truth."

Tessa raised an eyebrow at her father's word. Allison smiled then explained. "'That which has all the appearance of truth until confronted with irrefutable facts.'"

Miller nodded then went on about the effects to the society he knew as a boy. "Most citizens hadn't the inclination or sophistication to understand what was going on around them politically."

The engineer paused. "For as scientific and technical as the times were, imagine schools closing, then children going uneducated by design." He paused once more, searching for the precise words. "I think that made Divestiture possible, in part—that lack of education. It got underway, in its beginnings, for example, with far too many citizens not comprehending the far-reaching aspects of it. The catastrophic ramifications if you found yourself on the *wrong* side of a stopline, the *wrong* part of PRIM-ification."

"And for far too many others," Allison clarified, "if they weren't affected, if they *were* on the right side, they were content to let life flow on. The ultimate laissez-faire attitude."

"Yes, the pandemics created a cocky attitude in some survivors: 'Since it wasn't me, why should I care?'"

Tessa knew parts of this history already. And most associates, those honest with themselves, admitted to some of this guilt about being in Marsco.

"In the past," Miller continued, "the distant past, governments often censored or controlled the press and other media. Ironically, in the halcyon time well before the Continental Wars, governments thrived for the opposite reason, because there was too *little* information—not too much. Then midcentury, it was all there to Google, yet few citizens cared to—or had the ability to—discern the truth, glean the truth."

"'Devoured not by a roaring lion but 100 rats,'" Allison concluded.

"Well," Miller played off Allison's ideas, "it happens even today." The granger laughed his way through tales of contemporary cyber misinformation not much different from the disseminated political lies of old. His obituary had been recently posted; no one bothered to check whether he was alive or dead first. "As Twain said, 'Reports of my death have been greatly exaggerated.'"

Besides these false rumors, countless blogs claimed he had joined a Luddite splinter, a violent faction, hinting it was The Nexus. Other absurd proclamations were posted with his name attached. Some declared sanctimoniously the Second Coming of the Messiah was near with Marsco as the Dragon-Satan. Another self-righteous posting, allegedly by Miller, asserted Marsco was totally right and just in all its actions.

The granger and his guest could only speculate at how many other such notices out there in cyber never-never were actually Marsco postings. "To create whipping boys," they concurred.

One circulating Net rumor that repeatedly ended up on various clandestine sites stated assuredly and factually that Bethany Palmer's hydroponics gardens on Mars initiated the plagues on Earth. Martian microbes infecting human immune systems. "As if bio-terrorists hadn't had a hand in all that," Tessa stated defensively, knowing how deeply these postings hurt her father as well as herself.

"Some blogs are reminiscent of the prewar info-anarchists at work," Allison commented, "destroying the credibility of the whole Net. The bigger the lie, the more often it's repeated. The more repeated, the more believed."

Miller half-heartedly tried to laugh it off. "Net *chaosity*. The inability to garner *anything* from too much of *everything*. Much of it unreliable."

Father and daughter, mumbled in unintentional unison, "It's a Marsco world." Their heads whipped around; their green eyes met.

The three talked until nearly midnight. Finally, Allison rose. Turning to Tessa, she took the associate's right hand in both of hers. "Find your peace," she whispered. "Be your peace." To her host she stated softly, "Walter, I've considered your offer, but no, I can't narrate your *Ascendancy*—much as it needs a strong voice."

"For obvious reasons," Miller argued, "you'd be perfect. The logical choice."

Allison raised her hand slightly to cease his entreaties. Tessa saw that he was once more frustrated, his attempts at persuasion muted. "I played my part then," the Ludd explained, "but it's best to distance myself now. Call it a personal space issue. I'll give you whatever statements you wish, access to some journals and documents I've saved—you'll be pleased with them—but I can't be a greater part of the whole."

As prearranged, two young men waited outside the hedge to escort Allison back to the commune. As silently as she had entered, she was gone. As jealous as Tessa was at first, she grew calmer after witnessing old friends merely reminiscing together.

After their late evening, Miller took Tessa back to a locked room next to his library.

Along the far wall, a working Marsco computer dedicated to deep-space communications and two other high-end units linked to the Marsco Net sat in a row on top of an oak door used as a tabletop. Yet another fully functional unit stood to the side. "This," he explained, "acts as a proxy server creator and filters all my computer use."

Why's he admitting all this?

"Whenever I use the Net, I do so with total anonymity. These firewall systems keep me free from any E.T. programs snooping me." He announced proudly, "No cookie's phoning home on me."

Tessa saw at a glance that this vast layout masked all his outbound communications and thwarted all (Marsco's and anyone's) incursions into his privacy. "You're certainly risking *MR SoD,* that's for sure," Tessa remarked, pronouncing the term *Mr. Sod.*

Miller, busy with his booting, respond off-handedly. "'Marsco's Red Screen of Death'? Hardly!" At the console of the largest unit, he silently removed his gloves and, twitching his lefter disks, called up a series of windows.

Tessa watched the brightening screen in amazement. The use of his left hand wasn't so surprising; she worked around lefters every day. She had become one herself, after all, although with only a recent second disk. It had been years, however, since she actually saw her father twitch any lefts over an access pad.

The startup came to rest on a cerulean screen, not a Marsco red screen. Several GUIs glowed against the sky-blue background. As an associate, Tessa grew even more amazed, even a bit worried.

"You're standing before unauthorized digital territory, *cyber incognita.* Sites Marsco officially denies actually exist even while IOSS secretly tries to snuff them out and crash them permanently." Her father had opened a non-Marsco hotbox mail server of midcentury design that Internal Operating Systems Security was unable to police. He explained that an e-sophisticated Luddite faction maintained and linked this underground page to the Marsco Net.

Although no security expert, it was clear to Tessa that his software bypassed or frustrated any security moat or return trail surveillance. *Why does he need—or want—to stay this tied to Marsco's central communications? Who's he communicating with? Why such a veil of secrecy about all this?* A parental enigma, as deep as Marsco's.

"Two things," Miller explained further. "This GUI is a file from Zot."

"Who? What?" Tessa yelped. "To you?"

"Yes, *me,* not *you.*" Miller let that information sink in. "Sent recently for reasons you'll quickly understand should you wish to activate it."

Getting no response, he continued.

"It's fragmentary. Not sure if it was jammed at his end or warped by cosmic wind. But if you want to hear what he had to say, it's available to you." He paused a moment before continuing. "With this second link, you access a freenet portal through which you can contact anyone, associate or not. Your message will be laundered through a series of linked sites—anything you send will come through clean and not be traced."

"Anyone? Someone non-Marsco?"

"Even someone without disks, someone still on an old finger mouse unit."

"Aren't you chancing MR SoD doing all this? IOSS wouldn't be happy to see your network setup here." Tessa spoke with a daughter's concern only, not an associate's.

"I don't fear Internal. My system's failsafe."

Tessa's confusion with her father grew. Why had he kept Zot's message from her until now? And why give her an open invitation to contact anyone? Even someone on a Marsco shuttle beyond the asteroid belt on his way to Jupiter? *How'd he known? What does he know? Or suspect? To initiate all this because I might want to contact some other associate? He's guessing.*

But he guessed correctly.

Miller provided answers to her unasked questions. "This is a Luddite cobweb site. Taken from a Eudora that predates even Marsco. Graphics and GUIs are primitive, but it still works."

"Luddites? Doing this?"

"You believe too much of what Marsco transmits about Ludds. Many are against FDs only, their implantation. A finger mouse achieves the same results if the QCA chips have been programmed for parallel compatibility. Basically, many Ludds believe in technology when used properly and within reason." Her father's unspoken message was that no Luddite believes in Marsco. "Most I know are nonviolent, like Allison, but unfortunately, those types are disappearing fast."

Tessa only nodded.

"If you thought a plethora of voices were rising up to block or distort *truth,* imagine the extremes some voices'll go to, to shout down, to bring down Marsco. And, you can imagine how it responds to any perceived threat."

Tessa didn't need to imagine. As an associate, she knew: more than voices, more than shouting.

"Well, I'll leave you to it," Miller finally said. "Everything right-disked from here. I've rewritten the protocols to take standard commands; all the pathway-cloaking proprieties are imbedded."

Initially, Tessa was intrigued by the two links and secretly desired to open the first. Then she thought, *How veiled am I being if he knew, if he suspected, that I wanted to twitch this system?* She sighed at the uncanny abilities of parents toward their children no matter their age. *But what an opportunity—to send Lieutenant Grizotti an unencumbered message.*

As he was leaving, Miller gave her a parting shot, although he failed to disguise the concern in his voice, "I'll leave you the dogs; you look lonely."

Tessa exploded at her father, "You seem intent on having me talk to Zot!" The daughter saw the sudden pain in his eyes.

"I only make the offer. As always, it's your decision."

For a long time, Tessa did nothing. Deep into the night, while her father slept alone at the back of the rambling house, Tessa sat in front of the glowing screen, the only light in the room. Finally, she started some mindless tasks, viewing last semester's roster to double-check her posted grades. She found them all correct. She tapped into her messages, deleting most and skimming only a few. She texted to her laundry and contacted her flat super about the A/C filter needing cleaning.

Only after much busywork did she twitch her right-hand finger disks and open Zot's message to her father. Without warning, three projection units behind her booted; in a nano, a life-size virtual Zot stood next to her. Startled then pleased by this unexpected holograph, Tessa listened transfixed even though the beginning of the projection was tedious techno-blah-blah. But it wasn't the meticulous scientific summary that held her attention even if she was a specs-wonk herself.

The virtual of Zot, *that* she scrutinized. As he stood before the VIOS, one of Marsco's finest, the system hid nothing. The virtual intake optical scanners even digitized his backside, so that before her was projected a corporeal composite of Zot, lifelike, breathing, almost tactile.

Even though a holograph she reached for his hand instinctively but clutched only air. She froze his image. His dark hair and beard (a perk of the Hibernation Service) were tinged with recent gray. He was leaner, more sinewy than she remembered. His face looked strong though stern. She knew more sides of him than just his Asteroid Fleet side.

With a twitch, his message continued with a system's analysis of Miller's engines; more specifics were downloadable through a left click. (*Pretty techie bumf for an iceman to handle,* Tessa scoffed mentally at the image. Marsco attitudes toward hiber specialists closed down hard.) Zot explained the swing-by of the asteroid Orion Rex during the past week, a maneuver that propelled the *Gagarin* even deeper into unexplored space. Tessa focused, wishing over and over that she had kept this file closed. It had churned up so much more than she anticipated.

She was about to shut down the whole virtual when a remark piqued her curiosity. "All systems continue after shattering the six-month hiber-cycle barrier. I've engaged several prewar specs and safety paradigms from Powers experiments on extended cryogenic stasis, and now believe that *years* of, perhaps a *dozen* years of, hiber in CS-mode, is indeed possible."

With that, the virt suddenly froze, leaving its projection like an ethereal statue before her. Tessa spoke bluntly to this motionless specter. "Iceman, what the hell are you doing accessing Continental Powers databanks? That's a high security–clearance area, lefters only." She held up her dual-disk left hand for emphasis to the arrested right-only Zot. "For secure and cleared lefters *only,* not hibermen who are usually chasing iced ass. C-Powers' sites are *not, not* something for a lowly iceman to deke about in."

Then she grew angry with her father for receiving classified intel from this experimental mission. *Was Zot aiding Miller's espionage?* Her mind raced through all the possibilities, none particularly inviting, none comforting. *A mole in this operation?* She tried rationalizing. *Perhaps curiosity by my father. After all, it was his initial engine design on the Jovan craft.* She tried holding that hypothesis but had to drop it for lack of any credence. *I ought to report this,* she thought. Aloud she muttered, "I *have* to report this!"

The virtual flickered to life unexpectedly. At first garbled, the iceman's voice soon continued clearly. "—so I thought I should tell someone. I guess you're it." More flickering caused Zot's head to list sixty degrees to starboard. "—using prewar, we've cracked the six-month hiber-barrier months ago. We're still running on, as I said. Walter, are you getting all this?" (Reaching to adjust something below the optical scanner, Zot faded out. The projection blurred and then refocused.) "The Powers might've gone beyond experimental to actual implementation well before the Wars. Not really hiber as we know it, rather a *cryogenic stasis* based on—"

The virtual froze once more, losing its intensity. Zot's skin paled and grew tinged with yellow. He looked pallid, death-like, worse than a victim of hiber-sickness. In a blink his virtual flickered off altogether. Several of Tessa's twitches revealed that three seconds of broadcast remained.

A moment later, he reappeared unexpectedly. The virtual startled Tessa since she was bent forward looking closely at the monitor, trying to restore the projection. "—still love her—" he announced bluntly, the virtual fading, then disappearing completely. Whirring sounds of the projectors automatically storing themselves confirmed that Zot was no more.

The iceman running tests on extended hiber, clearly connected to the VBC. Worse yet, vaguely connected to the C-Powers! And super secret.

From Seattle, she had checked on this mission. Even using lefter clearance, she found nothing in the daily status reports to suggest anything more than an expedition beyond the asteroid belt to Jupiter and its ice moon Europa. A system recce, nothing more. As if such an extraordinary feat needed any additional bells and whistles—it was a technical triumph in itself.

But this? Wasn't this mission only engine and system endurance tests? That's all his mission was to be—not one to test some buffed-up hiber bay, what did he call it, "a cryogenic stasis system"? Zot was there to cover crew icing, not engage in experiments! And covert experiments at that! Tessa ran her hands through her auburn hair before letting another thought cross her mind. *And how's all this connected to Walter?*

Still sitting at the secure communications console, she pondered all these enigmas well into the night. When the saver came on, she hardly noticed its antiquated graphics. Pixels of white stars on a black screen came at her. She sped through digital space just as Zot was doing in real space.

After an hour, she went so far as to open the second GUI. A while later, tapping a finger disk to initiate a message template, Tessa looked at the white screen trying to think of what to say and how to say it. So much was coursing through her mind.

Io and Deimos nudged each other at her feet. Her father had been right; she appreciated the nestling dogs. Deimos rose to stretch. Io put her muzzle on Tessa's knee.

What can I say after so long? she wondered. The engineer considered at first, "Zot, Walter tells me you're on the Jupiter run." What a bogus beginning. Anywhere in the solar system, Tessa had access to daily mission reports. Although now she realized that Marsco was indisputably cloaking Zot's real mission; much of what the iceman was actually doing was black.

And she had to be truthful with herself. She had periodically checked on this flight to scrutinize practically his every move. And not for scientific or technical reasons either. Yes, she admitted that.

She failed to grasp that she wasn't all that different from Miller. While her father monitored (cracked?) scrambled information about his propulsion units and received covert transmissions from Zot, she read his actual hiber reports. But what of those reports? Clearly nothing was available to her on the cryogenic protocol experiment he obviously was engaged in.

Regardless, she had known (or thought she had known) which crewmembers were iced. She had known (or thought she had known) which crewmembers were dehibered as the shuttlemates worked in relays across the ponderous black emptiness between the Belt and Jupiter. She was especially relieved when all the women on the crew were iced and no longer awake.

Since seeing the virt, Tessa instantly realized that not all the Marsco reports she read were accurate. Had Zot really remained all alone on his lengthening mission? A hookup on a shuttle wasn't inconceivable. It was more conceivable than an Earth-side one for her in her self-imposed, sterile hermitage at the Academy.

Letting her guard down, other memories flooded through the associate's distracted mind. Back in Seattle, two of Tessa's closest friends, Tiffany Zwack and Darin Lyons, knew her well. Best of friends, the couple didn't hold back when Tessa was sabotaging herself with her denial of reality.

Like Tessa, they were children of associates. In the Marsco world, few paid much attention to ancestral origin, since the concept of nations had so shifted. Clearly, however, both Tiff and Darin were mixed, with distant African extraction mingled with Euro. Darin was a lander pilot whose duties took him to the lunar docking ports for extended monthlong tours. Tiffany, like Tessa, taught at the Academy. Her specialty was space psychology, but the engineering colleague found in her a kindred spirit. Tiff had taken a year's leave to have Emma, their first child.

At her father's when Tessa was frozen with indecision Tiff's words came back. "You two never really ended—*that's* the issue. You don't have a sense of closure."

"So, how do I get this closure—ask him to finally point an Enfield at my head? Like a race horse with a broken leg?"

"In a sense, yes, although your metaphor sucks; especially since he isn't at all violent. But you need to ask him for a full explanation, that's all. An honest clarification—what happened? 'Why did this happen *to us*?' Ask as neutrally as possible."

Tessa had been holding Emma, her goddaughter, in her friends' apartment overlooking the whole of Seattle, its skyline illuminated as only a thriving Marsco sector could be. Tessa felt a sharp pain, part envy, part realization that she might never hold her own child.

"The fact that you don't see others—"

"How quaint an expression."

"I studied under old-fashioned shrinks." The women shared a gentle smirk. They knew each other well and confided deeply, especially when Darin was posted away for a thirty-day rotation. That particular night, Tessa's classes for the week finished, was one of those times.

"Look, I'm not prying. It's hard picking up after a crash—any crash, any loss. But the way you two just parted—you see, don't you? You don't know for sure if there's been a breakup."

God, Tessa thought back then in Seattle, and again at her father's, *if I hurt this much with "no breakup," then imagine the real thing!* Her guts told her it was real; they told her repeatedly in undeniable pain. She felt it then; she felt it now. She shut down then; she shut down now.

That night with Tiffany and Emma, Darin com-linked in from his lunar colony quarters. In his projection—as lifelike as Zot's virt to Miller—the pilot looked tired but beamed when he saw his wife and daughter. He greeted Tessa with the same cordial smile.

Tessa moved Em's arm with canned wave-to-daddy cooing. When the child lost interest, the engineer slipped in a trial balloon. "Have you seen any shuttle pilots preparing for a Mars run?"

"Lots. Any in particular?"

Both Darin and Tiffany picked up at the pilot's name, a shuttle jockey Tessa had allowed herself to seem remotely interested in. Tessa caught it—*they know something, suspect something.*

"You're crossing into classified information," Darin alluded. A virtual link like this was open to any Security snooping. In the Marsco world, associates protected themselves in every possible way. "But," he went on guarded, "look for him Earth-side. I think, but can't confirm or deny, he's been transferred to some S & H posting."

"Security? He might as well go to Hiber—" Tessa stopped herself.

After the holograph closed, and Em was finally down, Tiffany announced pointedly, "There's something you want to bring up."

"You asking me?"

"No, I can tell—you have something on your mind."

"I'm not sure what you're getting at."

"Look," Tiff stated, her blue eyes penetrating Tessa's green. "Darin's away for a monthlong rotation, lunar duty. But I lander up to his colony base for at least one weekend while he's away. Then, after his extended tour, he's here working out of Seattle for another month, sometimes two."

"Where's this going?"

"We *have* a life, that's where. An iceman? A shuttle pilot? And you clearly based here. Prof at the Academy—completing your doctorate. Why these long-distance—and seemingly self-destructive—relationships? The men are gone."

"Are you suggesting?" Tessa stopped short.

"No, not *that.* But even so, I'd be concerned about your partner only if you kept repeating the same zero-success pattern."

"But it's more than all this, isn't it? You two, your looks, you know something!"

"Only suspect, Tes, only suspect. You'll have to sort it out."

Finally, Tessa confided, "When he told me he was *not* leaving soon on a belt run, I did grow suspicious." Both Earth-side associates knew that crews in the Asteroid Fleet aren't just reassigned at whim. Mission training was months long. Marsco spent too much time and resources prepping such crewmembers. "We'd had dinner—just dinner, Tiff. Don't go there. I didn't. I thought, 'Certainly he'll be egressing on a lander to a lunar docking platform soon and then outbound on a shuttle. That'll end it!' So, Tiff, I actually knew by then, that this is it, it's all over, he's nothing to me. But he told me, 'No, I'm staying put.'" Tessa concluded with a conceding shrug.

"So, y'knew before you asked Darin."

"*Knew, suspected?* What's the diff?"

"Or *denied?*"

"Yes." Another despondent shrug.

"Doesn't that suggest something—about *him* and *you?*"

"In what way?"

"All the permutations you want. About him. About you. About any possibility of you two making a real couple, not just being fuck buddies."

"Shit, please don't even—"

"Nonetheless, it sucks, his lack of honesty."

"Worse yet, he told me he was being transferred into lunar-run landers, a horrific career crash—"

"And a lie!" The psych prof then arched an eyebrow playfully. "Oh, so now you're implying that a shuttle commander's better than a lander jockey! Look, Darin passed up shuttle duty so we could—"

"That's not it, and you know it. Look, I was in love with an ice-man—do I care about these artificial Marsco distinctions?"

Tiffany caught the word *love*—one of the few times in months that a reference to Zot came up even vaguely.

"But my new pilot: it makes no sense, this transfer."

"Especially to Security. Patrolling zones. Busting up PRIMS in food riots." From the apartment, all Tiff needed to do was look over her shoulder. Out the picture window in the nighttime sky-line, Security HFCs were visible in the distance, their searchlights probing the nearest PRIM res area. "That's really a career crash."

On that night with Tiffany four months before, Tessa wanted to confide totally, as she wanted to do with her father, but she sealed herself up—her characteristic response. The flyboy had been moving on her too fast—in the Marsco world, always worrisome. It wasn't that sort of world anymore. Everyone knew it.

Tessa wasn't that lonely.

A few weeks later, just after Tessa received her first left disk implant, she had access to much more than an ordinary associate would ever see. With almost her first left twitches, she sniffed out his background. Cyber locks and security moats clicked open for her without question. She was a lefter, had full authorization to those sites.

In the era of rampant diseases, the *Hygiene* segment of Security and Hygiene kept busy. Not just with outbreaks of neo-consumption or Ebola in some out-of-the-way unincorporated zones, not just with controlling extremist-initiated bio-attacks. The last thing the MAS Fleet wanted was some outbreak in space. Preventing another *Plague Ship* episode was foremost on Hygiene's mind, on Marsco's agenda.

Moreover, personally, associates protected themselves in this world. It was no wonder that in so many times and places when an associate had to deal with PRIMS, Marsco had a sid act as the intermediary. The world of PRIMS remained the most disease-ridden.

And so, to keep safe, to be within Marsco, a certain degree of privacy was sacrificed. It was a Marsco world, one riddled with rampant PRIM-related diseases and HH GAS. Population depletion had run its inevitable horrific course. *Herpes, hepatitis, gonorrhea, AIDS, syphilis. "Ha Ha gas"* as it was termed.

Any signs of "behavior detrimental to the good order and health of Marsco" and an associate might suddenly be without a commission, in some cases without disks. Demotion out of the Asteroid Fleet was not uncommon. In rare cases, deportation to a UZ was dictated.

Not that there wasn't a wild, licentious side to Marsco—there was. It happens any time you gather young and fit people, or old and unfit. But, to stay an associate you tempered some things and routinely checked your partners.

Twitching her then-solitary left disk, Tessa first scanned her pilot's Hygiene records. When it put its mind to the task, there was little that Internal Security and Hygiene didn't find about an associate. Within its ranks, "Hygiene" reports were common. The rogue pilot's file was bytes and bytes long. More than 4.3067 MB. Quite a list but in dry bureaucratic observations.

That particular left-twitch night back in Seattle turned out to be like this one at her father's grange. On both nights, Tessa sat frozen by indecision before a monitor. On this night, while her father slept, Tessa linked with no one. On that Seattle night, she c-phoned Tiffany.

"Did I wake you?"

"No, the ringtone of my mobile did."

Tessa, too excited to react, missed the sarcasm. Without an apology, she jumped in. "You near a monitor?"

"No, near my husband actually."

Still missing the pointed remarks, Tessa ordered, "Get to a monitor and look at what I'm sending you." Tessa uploaded the file and left-twitched a copy to her friend's screen.

The agitated associate heard Tiffany talk briefly with Darin. "Give Em a bottle of expressed milk from the freezer."

It suddenly dawned that Tessa was overhearing a couple's exchange about domestic chores, something unchanged even by Marsco. "Oh, I'm so sorry. Look, I'll call back later."

"Bloody hell! You've woken me at 0311 for a reason—give it to me."

"But—"

"This is what friends are for."

In a file that both women soon examined at their separate monitors, the history of Tessa's pilot was spread before them. His cyberfile was the link-tree of his sexual genealogy. Both women scanned the data. Tiffany jumped on the part that sickened her most, "Look at all his trips to zones."

Neither commented on the fact that in most UZs, PRIM skanks or unspoiled girls—or boys, for that matter—were only a few MMUs away. The single token that Tessa had willingly given to that begging PRIM bought human flesh for any purpose, no questions.

In amazement, both women found connecting lines coming and going from partner to partner, listing possible transmissions and highlighting known infections. Like any warning glyph, these were color-coded. *Yellow caution. Orange suspected. Red known.*

Most of his were yellow. H^1 for herpes, H^2 for hepatitis strains. But at least eight blinked orange. Tiffany had counted.

"And two *red,*" Tessa commented in a depressed voice. The cautioning blips screamed his total disregard for any personal safety protocols.

"Look!" Tessa blurted.

"He grows sleazier and sleazier." Links showed the pilot's proclivity for cam recording and posting his exploits. "Christ, what a vlog!"

"Vlog, hell. What an exhibitionist! If careful and with consent, who gives a fricking rip? Even Hygiene doesn't. But Netcasting his shit?"

"I know."

"About the only thing missing from his triumphs is any note of *SWR.*" *Sex with resistance:* the bureaucratic euphemism for dealings with a sid or PRIM who clearly lacked the power to resist.

"Small consolation. He'd have digitally recorded it if he had."

"Well, Tes, he's a charmer, but—"

"I know. Sending me flowers and a damn talking digital image frame that plays music with his love message as a voiceover."

"This is more serious than I thought! The sick shit!"

"Y'know, frankly, when he sent that gift, I thought he might be producing these by the dozen."

"Then why ever go there?"

"I don't know—to piss off Zot, I guess."

"Your anger's a sign of how much you love him."

"Him who?"

"Don't play the dumb brunette. Zot!"

"*Loved* him," Tessa insisted. "Past tense."

"Whatever!"

Four months later at her father's grange, the memory of that night in Seattle still pained her. In that nano, she saw the truth—was forced to accept the truth—of her pilot in blinking red and orange blips. She had suspected all this but hadn't paid attention to her own misgivings. After closing her palm link to Tiffany, Tessa smashed the talking frame. His voice, as relentless as his come-ons, came through the still-speaking bits. A pathetic high-pitched appeal, committing himself to her with unceasing devotion.

"And incurable diseases!" Tessa shouted to the shattered pieces.

When she picked up the fragments, she discovered not only a voice unit to repeat his devotion but a cam to record her movements around her flat.

On that infamous night of checking and smashing, she had next accessed her own file. She called Tiffany back. "You said call any time."

"Don't you take such polite comments with a grain of salt?"

"What time is it now?"

"Only 0505."

"Well, look at *my* records." A few twitches sent the data. "Where's Zot in my file? Don't tell me Hygiene's not doing its job?"

"Since he's above board, he's not even listed." On a mostly blank page, there was a single orange glyph: *One suspected infected partner.*

Tessa reflected a moment on what might have happened. The hunk pilot *had* brought to her (according to the inaccurate Hygiene report) or *might have* brought to her (according to her full knowledge of things) everything: H^1, H^2, *GAS*.

"Reluctance has its virtues," Tiffany commented.

"And its safety parameters."

That first lefter night in Seattle, Tessa also checked on Grizotti. "I want to assure myself," she snickered to Tiff who loyally and patiently listened, "that all men are such diseased assholes they aren't worth it."

"Anger's a natural response."

In a moment, Tessa cursed then replied, "His file's blank." She drew a breath and pointed at the monitor as if Tiffany could see her gestures. "Look! No tree of partners. No genealogy of possible transmissions. Although he's currently in space, there's been plenty of time for another associate. He must've had better luck than I've had." Tessa couldn't believe it. "The guy's had time for a furlough fling that might have meant something, or even time for a quickie in a zone."

Without judgment, Tiff concluded, "He's being careful, that's all. 'Consenting and safe!' Hygiene doesn't care, doesn't snoop." A cruel way to imply it, the counselor knew, but necessary. Shock and awe therapy. *Get over him, Tes, or admit that you really do still love him.*

"That's why his file's empty," the psychologist went on. "And from your pilot's file, we can conclude he's a boinger, a score-keeper with a long line of previous successes and no history of commitment."

"Just imagine my students seeing me on the Net! Stepping out of the shower? That cam in the frame caught me for sure," she fumed out of injured pride. "Shit, just the sort of self-absorbed asshole I'd never spend a moment with!"

"With your mind on Zot, you're susceptible to taking this charmer's bait."

"That doesn't help."

"The truth hurts."

That initial use of her first left disk cost Tessa much. It brought her continued loneliness mostly. She was a private person to begin with. First, her career demanded much of her attention, plus her personal history necessitated some degree of anonymity. (A rare commodity in Marsco.) "Besides," Tessa told Tiffany a few weeks later, Darin gone back to lunar rotation, "I'm not in need of some *man* to give my life meaning. What I ever saw in that jockey—aside from the fact that he was so totally different from Grizotti—I'll never know."

Ever the shrink, Tiffany stated, "Loneliness and denial and depression will lead you into many foolish mistakes, some deadly mistakes."

"You know, besides his proclivity for amassing a higher and higher victory tally—"

"Which he cam-shared—"

"—that player lacked something *vital,* something *essential.*"

Tiffany nodded.

"My mother and father had this, this passion for something beyond, something transcendent." Tessa believed she had it—as difficult as it was to possess this kind of passion in the world they inhabited. "It's not in machines, not in Marsco." It had been driven out of a world where so many scramble to eke out a day-to-day, moment-to-moment existence. An essential *something* lacking in the lives of most associates, to say nothing of the lives of sids and PRIMS.

At the grange, Tessa let these past conversations with Tiffany surge through her memory. She still smarted with the realizations. She re-crossed her legs, waking the dogs at her feet. Much to her annoyance, Tessa felt that Zot still burned with this indescribable passion in his heart, to his core.

She hated and loved him for that.

From her father's networked portal, Tessa wanted to send Zot a visual message. She knew she'd look hot even as a digital projection. She wanted to let him see what he was missing. Her auburn hair. Her green eyes. A flattering sweater. But with little self-arguing, she declined. *No more mind games with the man. Strictly a written, eyes-only message.*

Tessa twitched out an opening sentence, "*WELL, GRIZOTTI,*" she screamed across the screen, "*YOU MIGHT'VE TALKED WITH ME BEFORE YOU EGRESSED!*" An absurd remark and she knew it.

He had tried to see her several times before Jupiter, but she blew him off. She even alluded to her new shuttle pilot to burn her iceman.

Tiffany had chided her severely. "Suck-tactics, playing the fly-boy off Zot."

Embarrassed, Tessa admitted to herself, *I was childish! My actions bogus crap! At least I might've given him common courtesy. He deserves that.*

Finally toward dawn, Tessa deleted her screaming-caps statement, closed her eyes, and began tapping out another message. Her finger disks glowed blue-green as they worked over the pad.

Rather than read her note, she petted Deimos on the head. This woke Io, and the reluctant writer needed to pet her as well.

Eventually, Tessa looked back at the screen. She had hastily tapped the first thoughts that came to mind to express what she felt for the distant iceman. *Instantaneous reactions are usually the truest,* Tiffany repeatedly told her. *What comes first is often the deepest, unfiltered by personal defense. A Rorschach test.*

She read, "Zot, I love you." It was a prelude of the freefall of bottled-up emotions she still harbored for him. But instead of disclosing any more, she froze as tight as a crashed hard drive. Shutting down was her emotional default option.

Tessa scratched the dogs' heads until finally frustrated and exhausted, she hit "delete," clearing the screen of her message.

FIVE

THE BOY, RAM

(On the asteroid Vesta, 2094)

"She's awesome," mouthed Ram Chaudhuri, convincing himself he was praising the MAS *Piazzi,* a shuttle that hung white against the black backdrop of space just beyond the viewport.

The Marsco Asteroid Shuttle was fully reconfigured from several interchangeable components—command and crew modules, two passenger and four cargo mods—all arranged around a massive pair of Herriff-Millers. Those dual propulsion units measured all of 100 meters but seemed smaller, with only a gantry stretching up from a distant colony dome for comparison. Also confounding a sense of the *Piazzi's* size was how quickly she was bathed in dim sunlight then plunged into near-total blackness, an effect caused by the rapid rotation of the asteroid Vesta itself.

But Ram paid little heed to all this. In the Plexi-panel, he scrutinized the reflection of two crewmembers from that very shuttle. The woman had him transfixed. The boy was at that between-age, made worse by his natural aging being retarded by periods of extended hibernation. His slender build and pre-pubescent awkwardness made him look eleven or twelve. His mind, however, was fully sixteen. Such a hiber-gap in adults was a perk of the MAS service. In the growing boy, it only made touchy tweener matters worse. He looked like a clumsy preteen; he thought like a self-conscious adolescent. Ram's world was a hefty slice of both, creating constant physical and mental torment.

Gazing through the panel and then letting his eyes readjust to the reflection, he watched her animated conversation with another officer.

Captain Mei-Ling Chen and Lieutenant Julio Fuentes sat alone in a crew mess tucked to the side of one of the colony's smaller domes. Both officers wore cerulean flight suits with a Marsco Asteroid Shuttle patch. The square emblem had a midnight-blue background. In the center was the Earth with a monogrammed "M" superimposed over it. In the four corners were stylized depictions of the Earth's colonized Moon and red Mars, plus storm-spotted Jupiter. Three ashen asteroids in the lower right corner finished the representation of Marsco's dominance over the solar system.

"At least," the captain sighed, more mentally spent than physically, "shuttle refueling's automated enough for the station crew to handle." She let her bars slip out of keen interest in the junior officer.

"Yes," Julio replied, his liquid brown eyes caught in hers.

For the past week, they had both donned EVA suits to float around the shuttle's mods to complete refabrication. Grueling and fatiguing work, levitating amid the giant pieces of their next shuttle assignment. *Besides,* he smiled mentally, *a bulky EVAs hides too much of her.*

Like the modular components of the shuttles themselves, flight crews were often configured differently each trip. Neither Fuentes nor Chen had met their commander, Lieutenant Colonel Arnold Wilkes, before pre-separation briefings began two weeks prior at the Vesta spaceport. However, Fuentes had known Chen slightly from the Academy in Seattle. "My plebe year," she noted, a point she had made before, "overlapped with your fourth. It seems so recent."

"Even if, what, eighteen years ago?"

"Icing speeds time along." For Mei-Ling, hibernation also kept her looking in her twenties, even though she was a dozen years older. Her porcelain skin, her shapely stature, kept her deceptively young. But her intense eyes and demeanor, brought on in part by her officer status, alerted everyone she was a force to be reckoned with.

Born of associates in the Shanghai Sector more than a decade before the C-Wars, she grew up next to one of Asia's largest Continental Powers. Hong-Shang had been cobbled together from the best pieces of coastal China in the '30s. This Asian Power was one of the world's first to rise from the political and economic chaos of the century's second decade. Living so close to a ruthless regime, Mei-Ling knew Marsco as the sole guardian and protector of world peace.

"That was about the time—" Julio began tentatively.

Mei-Ling looked quizzically but remained silent.

"Eighteen years ago. When I was unexpectedly posted to Security after graduation." He sipped coffee to dodge questions, angry that he had let this slip out.

Fuentes had learned from bitter experience that knowledge of his off-kilter "posting history" didn't foster warm collegiality from most of Marsco. A five-year tour in the S & H such as his derailed many an officer's career.

Called from the Academy, he had served as ordered. Prior to that, his had been a normal Marsco upbringing. Born near Pensacola in what had once been Florida, he was raised amid Marsco sectors and cantonments in several Euro and SoAm Powers—governing entities like Hong-Shang, jerry-rigged from the best pieces of early-century countries then in tatters. As was the case with Mei-Ling, being from associates, his trajectory was set early: he was Marsco-bound. From youth, he aimed for the stars or at least the asteroids. Standing 1.75 meters, and with his innate Marsco mien, he was a natural for the MAS, as delayed as his space service had actually been.

"It's a common enough experience," Chen reminded him, "coming in later than planned. Marsco has needs in many arenas."

He nodded. When he did rejoin fleet training, he entered a year behind her at flight school. "An odd switch, from your superior to your junior."

Chen's eyes sparkled.

"I took a two-step reduction in rank. But a Security promotion's not really a—" he shrugged, thinking it best not to finish his comment.

Intent on being supportive, she held his gaze.

Since their initial briefing, those eyes had flashed more each time they were off-duty and relaxing. Neither had a history with the other. And both were HH GAS-free; separately they had each made the obligatory background check.

"Yes," Julio continued, enjoying their lingering coffee, "I'd been your senior until I finally matriculated to Flight."

"By then, I was in my second year of training."

Fuentes shifted his eyes as he remembered his Security tour. He appeared to look at the dozen mining asteroids and scattered components of shuttles waiting reconfiguration, dimly visible through the Plexiglas, orbit-parked near the large Vesta asteroid. Chen knew him well enough already to know his thoughts were millions of clicks away.

The unexpected duty of patrolling mogged zones for five years, the former S & H officer thought with acrimony about his whole Earthside hitch. "When finished with that assignment," he confided slowly, "I was fortunate to be allowed into Flight at all. Security duty scuttles many a career."

"At least it wasn't hiber-tech."

"Granted." They both shared a laugh, breaking the hold of the resentment Fuentes harbored.

"What was it like?" She reached for his hand across the mess table, taking his right with both hers. Her finger disks gave his skin a slight tingle. "On those patrols?"

"Let's talk of this on the *Piazzi.*" He glanced side to side, already thinking of the shuttle as a haven. "Where it's private."

Her hands gradually withdrew. It was too soon for her to totally cast aside her second-in-command role.

Even so, after a sip of coffee, Fuentes felt free to muse about their commander. Crew chatter, crew stewing. "I've tried getting a fix on Wilkes. At first, I sensed that he just might be a C-Wars vet."

"If so, he's ancient," Chen continued, "much older than he looks."

"You're right, plus I don't think he's a C-Power fossil. He seems too gung-ho, zealously obeying orders."

The woman acknowledged his line of reasoning. Immediately after the Wars, Marsco granted amnesty to hundreds of shuttle jockeys—not Lightning pilots—who had served the Continental Powers. "Those wuss-warriors love being in space but won't do anything to call attention to themselves. They don't want anyone scrutinizing their records."

The pair struggled with the continual problem facing shuttle crews: calculating the age of someone who has two ages, chronological and physical.

Fuentes wondered—but didn't state—if Wilkes had endured a veering-off career like his own. Many Marsco officers spent *some* time in Security. Refusing to share this last thought was defensive nature: he might not yet have the full trust of Mei-Ling. She was still holding back, as was he.

"So then," Chen stated casually, knowing she didn't look authoritative enough for her rank at present, "our course is all laid in."

Fuentes shot back, ignoring rank, "Don't you hate this recent directive?"

"Yes," Mei-Ling responded, more to dissipate her frustration than explain what they both knew. A quick, safe egress trajectory had been the SOP for nearly fifty years—as long as Marsco had mined the belt. Standard protocol instructed shuttles to maneuver within designated flight paths with nav beacons and instrumentation assisting every move and head for open space, stat.

Wry smiles crossed their faces as the pair mimicked a professor from their Academy days, "'For this reason, most Marsco colonies and docking ports are on large spherical asteroids at the edge of the belt, even though their positions shift continuously.'"

"Now," Fuentes shrugged, "a shuttle wanders through the belt. Our egression'll be several harrowing hours. Last time on the *Chawla,* we were out in less than an hour-thirty, out to the relative safety of deep space. We accelerated perpendicular to the belt's orbit and looped around the last fat asteroid—that was it."

"And once out, final burn from the twin Herriff-Millers."

"Roger that."

Both fliers shuddered. In a week, their trajectory would wind through a series of unexplored belt sectors, through teaming families of not-yet-mined asteroids. Fuentes knew that it would take a cool head and quick twitches to pilot amid those ever-dangerous objects. And it wouldn't be his finger disks. "Marsco's been navigating the belt for five decades and building supercomputers for nearly 100, but even so, computers still haven't replaced that human finger-disk-touch at the controls."

The senior officer's smile conveyed understanding and amused tolerance. She almost let her real concerns about her crew slip out when someone approached their table.

"Are you the crew of the *Piazzi?*" a young boy interrupted them.

Fuentes slapped his hip where an Enfield holster would be on Earth. "Who let you in here? This area's restricted!" To the former Security officer, the boy looked PRIM, even though he had to be at least a sid to be in space.

"My father's a mining engineer," he replied defensively. "I have a pass."

The captain eased the sudden tension. "Nearly everyone does on this colony; it's easy for us to forget that. We transit through so many docking locales."

"Yes," the boy stated confidently, looking directly at the woman, "nearly 1,000 associates live here, and all have clearance, assuredly." Extending his hand to shake Chen's, he hastily introduced himself before the conversation ended abruptly, "I'm Ram Chaudhuri."

Chen greeted him politely, giving their names. "Well, to answer your question, Ram, yes, we're the crew of the shuttle *Piazzi*."

"Is *he* ship's commander?" The boy looked at Chen the whole time, motioning only to Fuentes with a tilted head.

"No, Colonel Wilkes's still on board. I'm copilot."

"He's not an iceman?"

"No, second officer," Fuentes snapped. *I've handled allegedly innocent intruders like you, sneaking up, begging for burger vouchers but really—.* He gulped a calming breath. *No, not here. Not at a space colony.* The lieutenant forced himself to say civilly, "Anything we can do for you?"

Still facing Chen, the boy explained that he and his family were leaving on their shuttle. His hints for a flight deck tour were answered with a promise from Chen "only if time permits before you hibernate."

"Ah, yes, that all-important tech advancement," Ram launched himself into an explanation. "Quite a feat. And quite necessary." As Chen listened calmly to the intelligent child, Fuentes grew increasingly impatient.

Ignoring the junior officer, the boy went on, trying to impress the senior. "Because of the current close location of Vesta relative to Mars orbit, we're able to fling around that planet to continue toward our lunar rendezvous. Our trip's a short six-month jaunt," he commented with authority. "Half a year's still the max hiber duration."

"You know much about travel from the asteroid belt," Chen encouraged.

Ram beamed. "Yes, I know that our proposed trajectory takes four months to Mars, then two to the Earth's Moon. But nonetheless, it's one of Marsco's quickest flights. The planets are aligned exactly right. Mars has left its conjunction with Earth and is setting up perfectly for a flyby."

Fuentes pushed into their private conversation. "Are you planning on entering the Fleet?"

"Possibly," Ram answered, "but regardless, ours is short compared to the first ones fifty years ago. Back then," he continued, straining to impress the pair of officers, "just the Earth-Mars link took six months and only on flights initiated when the launch window was opportune—every twenty-six months. At best speed, the Mars-to-Belt leg was at least another year. So, six months is nothing. A nano." The boy added, "Vaunted Marsco efficiency."

Chen asked him a leading question. "How does hiber play into all this?"

"It's better to sleep through such a long trip. Furthermore," Ram explained excitedly, "it's not practical or possible to carry enough supplies—food, water, and oxygen—to sustain a crew complement and twenty-three passengers for that duration. The number I use is the current manifest for the *Piazzi.* With most of the passengers and crew iced, necessary supply requirement are reduced by 94.0506%."

"My, my," Chen replied sincerely, placing her hand on Ram's shoulder, "you do know your stuff."

Fuentes kept himself from asking if this kid knew anything of more practical value, like how to patrol a tense zone with a pack of half-trained Auxxies in tow.

Ram changed the direction of the comments. "I don't particularly like being iced," he announced. "But, I'll get a second disk." He held up his right hand. Under the skin of his index finger, a single blue-green disk was visible.

Chen took his hand delicately. Ram felt his face heat up. "So, this is your first adult implant," she remarked with that particular voice grownups use to praise a child.

"Yes, and I know lots of other things," Ram answered, teetering between a child's and a man's response.

Beside himself with frustration, Fuentes played along, hoping to hasten the interloper's departure. "Like what else? You've covered the basics of interplanetary spaceflight and hiber tech."

Chen shot him a look that commanded *be kind to the offspring of associates.* "Well, what else do you know?" she asked.

He doesn't need to be egged on, Fuentes thought with irritation.

The boy launched into a science lecture for the shuttle officers, one polite, one annoyed. This suited the student. It gave him tacit permission to stare at the enchanting Chen. "Most people—Earthside—they think the belt constantly thrashes about."

"Is that so?" Fuentes probed. "And *you* know?"

"I've lived on-colony for two tours; I ought to know something." He drew an excited breath. "Asteroids don't zip around like in some virtual game." He motioned through the dome at a completely black view punctuated by motionless shapes blocking out stars.

Chen reassured him, "Affirmative! They drift along slowly."

"Yes, collisions happen periodically, but those on impact courses near colonies are diverted to keep docking lanes open, debris-free." He had seen a video of a purposeful collision, initiated by a mining crew like his father's, to break up a gigantic slab-shaped asteroid into manageable pieces before sending them on their trajectory across space. "I've only seen a few real collisions in my whole awake life!"

"Oh, and I suppose," Fuentes jumped in, "you're waiting for one to whack a shuttle!"

Chen touched her subordinate's hand and encouraged Ram to proceed.

"The asteroid belt's essentially Marsco's asteroid belt," the boy stated confidently. He sounded like he had been practicing every word. "It's an orbiting ring of minor planets of various shapes and sizes, each one representing potential riches—and potential collisions." The boy's right eyebrow arched as he leaned toward Chen for emphasis.

He memorized this, Fuentes conjectured, *for some school project.*

"Just those planetoids with a diameter of 100 kilometers number 50,000 or more." His voice slowed for emphasis. "Millions of others a mere fraction of that size orbit around the sun between the major planets of Mars and Jupiter. The asteroid belt's no place for an inexperienced pilot," the boy whipped an accusatory glance at Fuentes.

"My, Ram, you do know a great deal," Chen remarked, charmed by the ingratiating child-teen scholar.

"Wait, wait. It goes like this: In eternal, relentless orbit, nothing ever seems to change in the belt. The gravitational capturing by one of the Big Four—the quartet of the largest and first-known asteroids, Ceres, Pallas, Juno, and Vesta—or by Jupiter passing even at its astronomical distance may shift the natural orbit of a smaller asteroid from time to time."

Fuentes suppressed a yawn. *Aren't school speeches timed?*

"Caught in an orbital perturbation," the boy emphasized again with an eyebrow arching at Chen, "an erratic asteroid may be transferred to Jupiter or may drift randomly for a time until transferred to a close-approach orbit around the Earth. Or it may collide violently with a neighboring body." He drove his fist into his palm.

"Don't pop your disk," Fuentes muttered snidely. Chen's eyes silenced him.

"Marsco's recorded many of these asteroid-to-asteroid collisions—and other asteroid-to-passing-object collisions." (The boy heaved a telling look at Fuentes as if to suggest, *Probably on your watch!*) "It scrupulously updates its accurate celestial database of the belt. But for the most part, asteroids drift with little noticeable alteration."

While the boy paused again, Fuentes fidgeted nervously. Chen glared at the officer until he grew still.

Ram sensed this. "Wait, wait, almost done." Swallowing hard, he stressed dramatically, "*Until Marsco!*"

He smiled, making a slight bow. "How'd you like it? I learned that for my science project. Was best in my class, second among all asteroid entrants. I was virtually linked to the finals, but I ended up only twelfth."

"Out of how many?" Fuentes demanded.

"Seven-fifty Earth contestants. Two-fifty from colonies—lunar, Martian, and—" He swept his hand to show the asteroids.

"That many? Bravo!" Chen applauded. She reached down to shake his hand, her finger disks giving him a slight electric tingle. The boy was beside himself. While he beamed, Mei-Ling glanced at Julio. *You'll get yours later,* her brown eyes reassured him. "Now, Ram, my crew and I must finish up some duties, so you'd best be running along." It was the first time she responded to his boyish aspect and not his adult-like mind.

"Quite, but I'll get a tour of the flight deck, right-o?"

"Roger, if practicable."

The two members of his crew knew that Lieutenant Colonel Wilkes was a skilled pilot as he twitched the controls, guiding the Marsco Asteroid Shuttle *Guiseppe Piazzi* on its weaving course.

As copilot, Captain Chen sat next to the commander, keeping all systems on task. Lieutenant Fuentes, to the right and slightly behind his superiors, hunched over an IR scope, searching for trouble.

"Check my six again," Wilkes barked.

"Yes, sir," the junior officer replied smartly. He went to work, looking for what the computers may have missed.

Sensors ringing the shuttle fore and aft provided him with a 360-degree vista of scrutiny, although the craft's 10 percent thrusters made rearward IR readings virtually useless because of heat distortions. Even so, it was SOP that Fuentes complete continuous searches.

With a routine sweep negative and with no computer finds to double-check, the officer glanced up toward the flight deck with envy at the way his pilot was handling the *Piazzi.* Impatient for command, Julio groused inwardly, *Without a Security detour, I'd be sitting up front.*

The commander's calm hands moved the joystick gracefully, navigating the slow-stick vessel through the drifting flotsam. His twitching implants glowed blue-green as another command to steering nozzles changed the ship's bearing.

Shuttles are not delta-winged attack fighters, Fuentes knew. They were nothing like the infamous and lethal Lightnings of the Continental Forces. Whether manned or drone, those fighters were designed for speed and maneuverability. But shuttles hauled cargo and passengers for Marsco. *Even if they're unceremonious drudges,* Fuentes noted with confidence, *I want my own!*

Between sweeps, Julio glanced at Mei-Ling's silhouette. He made it a point to study the arresting copilot whenever possible.

"Lieutenant, what's below?" came a harsh request from Chen, breaking his reverie. When she needed it, she had as stern a Marsco voice as anyone.

"Checking, sir." He buried his face in the hood of his scope.

Two hours more and still in the belt. Fuentes's agony increased as his pilot adroitly maneuvered the *Piazzi* uncomfortably close to several binary asteroids. The lieutenant had that urge of many officers to be in complete control whenever possible. In the belt, however, guiding the shuttle was a single-set job; everyone else kept their intruding disks out. Restless, the officer dutifully re-engaged his scope, swept starboard, and waited.

In egression, the second officer had one primary duty, and it had little to do with actually piloting the craft. Pressing his face to the pads on the scope's hood, he scoured the darkness for the smallest solid celestial bodies that escaped detection on other sensor instruments.

Through this thermal scope, Fuentes saw the fuzzy images of several passing asteroids. The closest was potato-shaped with several craters, each from a violent collision. Another bogey was a jellyfish on its side with a trailing school of fish. The larger asteroid had captured several icy, miniscule ones in its infinitesimal gravitational tug. But even these inconsequential strays could severely damage a shuttle in an impact.

In a neutral voice, Fuentes dutifully informed his pilot, "Avoid large asteroid family to starboard."

If his subcutaneous disks were at the controls, his wouldn't be distracted by the unplanned trajectory, one that plotted their craft so close to obvious danger. Instead, he twitched from Port/ Starboard to FLIR and scanned ahead.

Sitting beside the commander at the flight deck, Chen worked her SDC, providing crucial information to the pilot's HUD by filtering out unnecessary data from the sophisticated sensors.

Scanning plots on the situation display computer meant rechecking multiple sources of information: intersecting trajectories of known mining asteroids and of larger marked and unmarked asteroids. The plots of recent debris fields. Asteroids on known collision courses with other asteroids. An occasional mining ferry unexpectedly entering their safety envelope. The list was exponential.

Objects creating potential trouble Chen sent "forward" as glyphs to be plotted on the pilot's heads-up display. Green for benign but ones he should be aware of. Yellow for caution. Red for impending danger.

Although his officers didn't actually fly the craft, the commander relied on their close cooperation. Caught up in piloting the wandering shuttle, Wilkes might not see trouble. Smaller asteroids were not easily picked up on visual, no matter how sharp the pilot's eyes. And anything approaching from his "six" or below the ship was unseen by the pilot.

Amid countless asteroids anything unseen was menacing, but no one accused Commander Wilkes of being out of his league at the controls.

"What's this?" the pilot abruptly demanded.

Jerking his head out of the scope, Fuentes saw that in zero-g his flight instruction packet had drifted into the pilot's field of vision.

"Sorry, sir," he apologized, retrieving his materials.

"Anything forward to report?"

"No, sir. All the usual."

"That's what I worry about; the *usual's* often the most dangerous. I don't want any surprises creeping up my arse," the colonel retorted. His gray eyes bore down on the lieutenant as though he were still a plebe.

The copilot shot the junior officer her own commands. "Double-check steering nitrogen reserves and burn-ready status of main engines."

Crisply, Fuentes turned to examine propulsion analog readouts. *All my training to watch a screen,* he fumed.

That task done, he went back to the scope. At this distance from the sun, the magnitude of an asteroid's reflected light gave little to read, but he kept looking for prospective trouble inconceivably missed by computer-controlled sensors. He began another tedious sweep around the *Piazzi.*

And yet Fuentes questioned more than searched. The crew's task was to avoid such a hazardous path, not take their shuttle deeper onto one. Precautionary sweeps weren't for piloting off a programmed trajectory. For all his prudence, the commander was slipping more and more from the *Piazzi's* designated preflight course—one filled with enough of its own risks. *This uncharted sector is for a zipping mining ferry,* thought Fuentes, *not a lumbering deep-space shuttle.*

Satisfied nothing dangerous was approaching, with a few disk-flicks, the lieutenant dashed off a message to the copilot's console, "Remember what we learned at Flight? 'There are *old* pilots and there are *bold* pilots, but....' Where's Old 'n Bold going? What's he doing?"

Chen at first ignored the message. Like the commander, she was extremely preoccupied. Exiting was difficult enough when it was through prearranged flight paths. *But this uncharted route?* the copilot questioned. They were off as though on a whim—without any meticulous planning—off on their own into an unplotted netherworld teaming with clusters of threats.

Neither she nor Fuentes appreciated this tangent into *spatium incognita.* This was dangerous stuff, pure and simple, not something engaged in by a generally watchful breed of pilots like Wilkes.

The copilot continued to hide her concern even with all the danger out there. Besides the possibility of random asteroids, there skulked massive mining asteroids, honed shipments measuring nearly a click in length, powered by steering rocket pods that were regularly shipped out of the belt. Here these mining asteroids were out of harm's way. But because Wilkes was no longer heading where the *Piazzi* had planned to, the steadfast subordinate wondered if she was getting accurate information from Vesta about surrounding traffic.

And what about space debris reports? She tried not to think of those rare shuttle entanglements with an asteroid. Because they were crossing a sector typically unused by shuttles, did she have any data about known—or suspected—debris fields? And nimble, five-seat ferries transporting engineers to the mining asteroids? Were their crews paying attention, looking for an unanticipated shuttle plowing through crowded space where she didn't belong?

A constant complaint among flight crews was that some cheeky space-based geologist purposely aimed mining asteroids at passing shuttles out of boredom—as if spaceflight wasn't thrilling enough. These same engineers even buzzed gigantic shuttles—a reckless and potentially lethal game—or so shuttle crew grumbling went. For plenty of reasons, guiding a shuttle out of the belt was a daunting task, even before the recent directive came down ordering shuttles to loiter inside the belt, almost like a recce drone over a hot arena.

After a dozen harrowing minutes, Mei-Ling found a safe moment to return to Julio's message. In a few twitches, she tapped out, "'...but there are no *old, bold* pilots.'" Then she defended her superior. "Still, he's w/in safety envelope—new MAS SOP. Remember?"

While Chen answered, Fuentes made another complete sweep. Her reply gave him a distracting rush. The impatient flier tried to catch a glimpse of her full face but couldn't.

Unless tucked under her soft flight cap and headset as it was now in the weightless environment of space, her black hair framed her delicate distinct features. Her brown eyes smiled naturally when they were alone, even if she looked every centimeter an associate when she needed to.

She was right, however, about the new orders. Regardless, Wilkes didn't have to wallow through the belt forever.

Joy ride in deep space, Fuentes willed his commander, *not in the belt.*

As Wilkes sidled perilously close to an unnamed planetoid, the twenty-four weightless passengers sensed the same discomfort as his officers.

The nineteen strapped in Passenger One were all Marsco mining engineers and astrogeologists who operated from dozens of bustling colonies. From experience, they knew what a collision with a mining asteroid was like. Some thought pilots still routinely moved into deep space immediately, taking their shuttles to vacuous safety with Marsco dispatch. No one argued against that conventional wisdom.

In Pass Two, five passengers were strapped in. Before separation, the ship's hiberman, Jamie Maissey, had made two suites in the nearly empty module. Up front he placed a family of four. At the rear he configured a private area for a solitary mining consultant, a late addition to the manifest obviously traveling alone and wishing to remain so.

The hiberman had arranged these with collapsible partitions, although he kept all hatchways open in case they needed emergency evac pods. The partitions didn't touch the conduits lining the upper bulkheads, so the family at times heard the associate cough and twitch his FDs over a pad, although they didn't see him. The father made sure, by silent gestures, that his children did not bother this lefter.

Hari and Jyoti Chaudhuri and their two children were returning to Earth after his second four-year belt tour. For Hari, shuttle separation from an asteroid was routine. He settled back for a quiet and short (or so he thought) departure from the belt. A small, scholarly-looking man, he sat between his daughter and his wife.

Indera, their eleven-year-old—who looked eight—sat at the starboard viewport watching Vesta, with its colony domes and ancient collision-pocked surface, fade into the surrounding blackness. Her palm viewer and drink pack drifted aimlessly around her head.

"Are you all right, Mother?" she asked.

"Just a bit muzzy," Jyoti answered in singsong nervousness. She had made these trips before, but she was a preschool teacher, not someone ordinarily engaged in space travel. Both the woman and the girl held the man's steady hands for comfort.

"You'll be fine out of the belt," he reassured. As an astrogeologist, he had much experience in space. He had traveled several times to Mars before bringing his family here. In the course of duties, he routinely moved about in an agile ferry, the safest craft amid this swath of gigantic rocks.

On the opposite side of the passenger mod, Ram sat apart from his family. Just like a fully-disked adult with his single hypodermal disk, he activated an info presentation. The option was interactive, designed for someone his sister's age. He didn't call her over, something he might have done just a few months ago; instead he demonstrated more independence and maturity.

Ram twitched the crew bios. Colonel Wilkes's digital showed a younger version of the pilot, making it difficult to guess his real age. He was born in Brisbane, date not listed. *Probably well before the C-Wars,* Ram assumed. The flier had gray eyes and a faded scar running along his lower jaw. *He's hibered a lot,* the boy concluded.

Ram skipped through the file devoted to Lieutenant Fuentes. Even though he had a magnetic flair—dark eyes and hair, thick eyebrows—to the boy he was just another nondescript officer, a common sort often seen on Vesta.

Twitching Chen's file, Ram studied the mesmerizing officer, her soft features and arousing looks. In the graphic, her long hair was woven in a braid tucked up in back, not hanging down like his sister's. The officer now wore hers shorter to frame her face. Even the dated image made her alluring to the dual-aged eleven- and sixteen-year-old boy.

As Ram studied his screen, the rest of his family looked out the starboard viewport. A brain-shaped asteroid slipped past.

In zero-g Indera's own black braid floated at will, gently tickling her right ear. It amused her mother, who was feeling better.

"We're passing through a remote sector," Hari elaborated in a professorial tone. "Only four months ago, I led the first recce here."

Indera's eyes grew large. She had heard all this before, but to actually see it was all the more exciting.

Her father pointed out two newly assayed asteroids. "Davida and Maya, each only one-fiftieth the size of the largest, Ceres." In the near-sunless view, they were so close that the irregular shapes blotted out everything.

"Are those flashes stars?" Indera asked.

"No, satellites." Three brilliant warning lights orbited around the newly explored asteroids.

"But they're the only lights visible," the girl noted.

"That'll change as our alignment changes. Keep watching; you'll soon see more stars than from Vesta."

She tried counting the first ones that came into view above the jagged rim of the irregular shapes, but soon there were far too many.

This is becoming so close, too close, the father worried. *A craft like this shouldn't be approaching such asteroids.*

Removing his right hand from his daughter's grip, he activated a view screen. He selected the telemetry option, a presentation that ran the preprogrammed flight path in red with the actual route overlaid in blue.

Hari was alarmed that the two no longer matched exactly. The past thirty minutes showed a widening divergence. He kept his concern about this discrepancy to himself. It was so unlike a Marsco pilot to deviate from a proscribed flight path. *This sector's no place for a shuttle,* he thought once more.

"I don't see any colony," Jyoti remarked, expecting to see a multi-domed outpost with its raised docking tether.

"They're only recently explored," the geologist patiently explained. "They've none yet—just emergency ports in case of ferry difficulty."

Chaudhuri knew this from direct experience. Three months prior, he and his crew had spent forty nerve-racking hours in a safety port awaiting rescue, but neither child knew; he was routinely away for weeks at a time.

The parents looked at each other, reconfirming their commitment to silence.

"Is it always this long amid all these rocks?" Jyoti stated fitfully, not hiding her anxious tone. She tightened her grip on Hari's arm. Her action made Indera take back her father's other hand.

Ram pretended to be watching his screen but was listening as well.

"This is becoming extremely unusual," Hari answered with authority and deep concern. "We should have been making for deep space immediately."

Ram and his family settled back into a tense silence for another hour.

Finally, Indera drank an aseptic juice pack, but Jyoti wouldn't let her son have one until the ship was at cruising G. Indera smirked at her brother and squirted several droplets. Her parents snapped the weightless balls into their mouths before they traveled too far. They scolded but in a perfunctory way that indicated indulgence more than admonishment.

Ram, meanwhile, twitched every link on his screen, seeing what he might crack. Before he knew how, a message scrolled, "VR ready." Fumbling around in his backpack, he slipped on a visor. Suddenly the virt screen showed a throbbing, dark rave scene—eerily silent as though he hadn't clicked in correctly.

In staccato strobe lights, a solitary dancer beckoned him on.

Without a thought, the boy released his safety harness to float free. Airy, like a demigoddess floating above, a woman's shape urged him to follow. Virtual or not, the graphics were stunning. As he felt himself swim upward, the shape took form. She was Chen, like a siren, a temptress moving gracefully just out of reach, exhorting him on. She never faltered or showed any reaction to her dance partner. Her lips were pink, slightly moist with an inviting shine.

The older part of the boy was beside himself with longing and desire; the younger confused, reluctant.

Moving away from his seat, Ram gyrated toward the free-floating woman who filled his VR visor. Bouncing off the conduit-lined bulkhead, he ignored everything but the swaying virt. Chen wore a tight short skirt and a halter. He focused on her alone, dancing to notes unheard. It was like swimming deep with her under water.

Obviously someone had hacked up this computer program and had forgotten to set any safeguards, or the boy would never have gotten in by twitching aimlessly. But such thoughts were too rational for the eleven/sixteen-year-old boy who danced in unison with the limber VR Chen.

In this rave mode, the virtual woman continued to move out of reach. She seemed absolutely real, although two massive breasts distorted her otherwise slim body. They were held in place by a violet day-glo halter just covering her erect nipples.

Someone's definitely customized this protocol, the transfixed boy realized. He thought he should close down the virt program, but he fought off that temptation.

He continued on, dancing in the flashing light to the silent rhythm of the deep-cleaved halter glowing in black light. He had it all: their floating, Chen's dance, her delicious breasts swaying just beyond his outstretched arms.

Then the whole psychedelic dance stopped in a nano. His imaginary, erotic, untethered world ended with a gray screen. He still drifted about weightlessly but in an ashen void. Confronted with a blank VR visor and thick silence, Ram felt his parents glaring at him.

His suddenly vacant visor flickered back to life and a message commanded in screaming print: "RETURN TO YOUR SEAT!!!!"

Shit! There they go! thought the boy, taking the virtual tech from his eyes.

"Ram!" Hari's voice came without warning or characteristic gentleness. "What are you doing?" The simmering edge to his voice made Ram realize that the wallah had sent his father a message after he had drifted over the partition and floated rearward into the private compartment. *That* annoyed associate had shut down the virt dancing and sent the ripping message across the visor, not his parents.

"It's good he disturbs only one other," Jyoti whispered in an irritated tone.

"But he's annoying such a passenger," the scowling father answered under his breath. Her son had made a scene, disturbing that lefter.

Indera smirked. She wasn't causing any trouble.

SIX

THE HIGH WALLAH

(The Belt, 2094)

"That settles that!" muttered Martin Poindexter, the Marsco mining consultant at the rear of Pass Two.

As soon as he shut down that floating nuisance of a boy, he turned his attention to the *Piazzi*. He twitched a view screen that showed that the preflight trajectory and actual exit path through the belt were no longer the same. Not content with the mealy pap provided to ordinary passengers, the high wallah set about rectifying the situation. Removing his black gloves (each with a red monogrammed *M*), he engaged his subcutaneous disks—first his left set, then his right—to access Chen's SDC. In a blink, he was reading the copilot's display.

"Well off our course!" he grumbled with as much venom as he had spit at that boy. "Deliberate and without prior authorization," he mouthed.

But his scrutiny of this course discrepancy didn't hold his attention for long.

Outside the starboard viewport, the shuttle approached an extraordinary trinary planetoid, three distinct lumps of rock coalesced into a single gigantic phenomenon. As the wallah watched, the shuttle moved so close to the pocked surface that the asteroid blocked out the Milky Way. The passenger realized how dangerously close to the triple-contoured asteroid the shuttle now was.

"But look at that mother's unusual g-flux!" He whispered in excitement after reading Fuentes's screen. "This might be it!" He nodded before adding silently, *Yes, this might be it!*

Its gravity and uncharacteristic size, plus its circling family, made for a tense maneuver. And yet, risks and all, Lieutenant Colonel Wilkes slid his shuttle toward the asteroid as if the *Piazzi* belonged there.

Transfixed, the consultant still worried about the shrinking distance between the craft and the surface. And yet he couldn't help but calculate the value of all that iron, nickel, and precious metal awaiting harvest. Even a few frozen methane comet nuclei gathered in this extraordinary family. "Yes, this might be it!" he concluded once more.

The opportunistic associate had to admit finally that this three-lobed discovery, along with its rich pickings, was a valuable find, albeit a precarious one to explore in a slow-stick shuttle.

Activating the crew com-link, the wallah abruptly demanded, "Commander, shouldn't we be leaving the belt soon? We left Vesta colony several hours ago."

Wilkes froze mid-twitch, hardly controlling his anger. His grey eyes and jaw locked into an inflexible expression. The brazen passenger had overridden a com lockout, always engaged during separation from docking before fling. He had accessed Chen's console with ease, as though he were a senior member of the flight crew. The pilot had long suspected that this passenger was no ordinary associate. With such power in the wallah's left hand, the commander's suspicions were confirmed. The flier's forehead grew deep furrows.

The seething senior officer gave a "you-handle-the-VIP" nod to his subordinate. Chen activated the com-link, but even with her extensive FD array, she didn't have the disk power to override a command lockout. *He's one well-disked associate,* she realized.

Before speaking, she watched Poindexter as he carefully replaced his cotton gloves. His light-colored palms clearly showed several blue-green disks implanted under the skin, plus an ominous red command-and-control disk on his right index finger identical to Colonel Wilkes's. Also like the commander, Poindexter seemed ageless. His position undoubtedly took him into deep space regularly, thus into hiber. His round face was wrinkle-free. His curly hair was cropped short in military style, rather like the colonel's. It was black with a few twisted strands of gray. His ebony complexion was common enough in Marsco; he didn't stand out as unusual in his cerulean flight suit.

Gruffly, the wallah demanded of Chen, "Are you going to explain this trajectory, or do I have to speak directly with the commander again?"

With a soothing voice, the captain explained, "We're following recently upgraded Marsco procedures, Mr. Poindexter. Our protocol calls for us to check unmarked planetoids for signs of intruding vessels in unmined or unexplored sectors before we fling." With the poise of a sophisticated beauty firmly rejecting an iceman on the make, she added, "We don't want any unwelcome competitors mining our ores, do we?"

"No, course not," Poindexter snapped. "Mining's my business and still one of Marsco's most profitable operations."

The copilot and the consultant eyed each other guardedly over the visual link.

Rumors had circulated throughout Vesta that this lefter's mining visits consisted entirely of inspecting the adjacent quadrants for unauthorized harvesting.

With only a set of steering rocket pods and not much else to create notice, unlicensed scavengers working off any number of Indie shuttles often sent scores, perhaps hundreds, of unsurveyed rich asteroids speeding toward any number of waiting customers. Periodically, even licensed non-Marsco operators over-harvested their strict allotments. Either way, this was a ruinous business practice, letting renegades snatch valuable assets from right under Marsco's nose.

To protect the vast conglomerate he served, Poindexter was bound to stop them. In fact, the *Piazzi's* erratic egress tactic was one of his primary directives. "Entering and exiting shuttles must survey the belt before they dock or fling homebound. Periodic and random surveillance in unexplored sectors by shuttles is absolutely imperative," he had previously suggested in a series of ultra-secret memos to Marsco HQ. "These unpredictable pathways will ward off even the most adventurous scavengers and examine quadrants that have a high probability of activities counter to the best interests of existing mining ops."

The irony of his situation was not lost on Poindexter. He realized that staring down a potential collision definitely made atheists pray and wallahs question their own wisdom.

The passenger tried to relax. Although a former fleet pilot (he had distinguished himself during the Continental Wars and in the following unrest, the so-called Troubled Times), he never flew as well as this Wilkes. That thought brought some comfort and much envy.

"Pallas's coming up in thirty minutes, Mr. Poindexter. ETA in exactly 28 and 32.5." Her Marsco exactness suggested that all was in skillful and experienced finger disks. Then the copilot reminded him, "Our commander'll use the gravity of that minor planet to help fling the shuttle into space beyond the belt, as planned in our preflight trajectory schematics."

"Of course," the wallah noted, "however, your commander's transitioned from Point A to Point B by winding needlessly through Points C, D, and E."

"Excellent celestial navigation, sir." The smarmy remark actually soothed the cantankerous VIP. "And, sir," the officer concluded with an outpouring of charm, "do be careful moving about the pass mod until our highly trained and competent hiberman's ready for you."

"Highly trained and competent?" the wallah thought. *An iceman? They're the laziest rat bastards on the crew. Hell, throughout all Marsco.*

Chen closed and then locked down the com system. *Try cracking that security measure,* she challenged.

Poindexter didn't bother with the com-link immediately. Instead, he utilized his FDs to activate the terminal in front of him. Chen's calm demeanor and fascinating face intrigued him; he was not the only one to come under her beguiling sway.

With a few swift twitches, he began checking up on her. By asking for the bios of the current crew, with an additional lefter twitch, he was soon crosschecking additional intelligence. A few more left clicks and he had access to the genealogy records of every associate and was viewing Chen's family history.

As he suspected, the flier was second-generation Marsco. Although her maternal grandparents were a mixture of European ancestry tightly tied to Marsco, her paternal grandparents were from Shanghai in the former nation of China. The megalopolis still existed, but the prime part was in the East Central Chinese Subsidiary that operated independently, yet under Marsco's characteristic benevolent guidance. The largest remaining section—holding the dregs and dross, the diseased remnants of its PRIM population—was a temporary, sprawling unincorporated zone. But these locales were unknown to the likes of Chen. Her parents were both associates when they married. Even with her predominate Asian features, Chen was a blend of both backgrounds.

A merger like myself and so unlike someone from the C-Powers. His own distant African ancestry fit proudly into Marsco. Although born on the NoAm continent in an Atlantic & Pacific League Power, both his parents were associates. Poindexter himself had lived most of his Earth-side life in Africa, the Johannesburg Sector. Since then, he remained active in the space-based arm of Marsco.

She's an excellent Marsco amalgamation, the wallah thought. And such cultural combinations were one of the keys to its phenomenal and continuous success.

When finished with her lockout, Chen had a few moments to herself. In an uncharacteristic gesture, she examined her finger disks, so often used, so infrequently contemplated.

She turned her right hand palm-side up. She had five implanted blue-green disks, one at each fingertip and a fifth on the middle phalange of her index finger. This last one, her security disk, commanded the entire lockout system. Indeed, the officer had authorization to open, access, or shut down any number of Marsco windows, programs, and systems throughout its shuttle fleet and its Earth-side Nets.

With her thumbnail, Chen picked at the skin covering her index finger disk, her first, her main disk, her identity within Marsco. *Sometimes it's the smallest change that has the most significant effect in the long run,* she thought, scrutinizing this disk. It was small and thin layer of polymer, one centimeter in diameter but only hundreds of molecules thick. *How these blue-green implants—and in rare cases, red ones—have so changed the world. "It's a Marsco world" isn't merely a passing remark; it's a stark reality.*

The copilot's conversation with the meddlesome VIP and her musings had kept her mind off the *Piazzi's* critical situation.

Fuentes masked his concern by offering cautionary information to their commander. "The main asteroid's mammoth by any standards, certainly larger than the two we passed last hour. Can easily hold not only a permanent colony."

When that didn't seem to register with Wilkes, the second officer added, "It's got quite a g-flux kick as well."

Through the Plexiglas panels in front and to the sides of the flight deck, all three crewmembers watched the passing celestial show, two of them trying to warn the third of the obvious danger.

Orbiting and surrounding the three-lobed monstrosity were at least eighteen smaller asteroids. These moved at different rates and at varying rotations and distances around the main body.

Wilkes let his crew ramble on while nitrogen jets angled the *Piazzi* lengthwise down the huge asteroid, one lobe at a time. It was a slow, harrowing pass, well inside and amid the orbiting family.

"They're all just waiting to be sent out of orbit," Chen stated, her dry facts acting as a warning about the attendant family of asteroids the shuttle was cautiously moving through.

"Yes," Fuentes picked up on her prudence, "several are already the perfect size and shape of a mining asteroid."

The family around the main asteroid created another oddity. Drifting together was a mix of rich S-class iron-based asteroids and several C-class carbon-based ones. Both types blended together even though they were inner- and outer-ring asteroids from different parts of the belt. Even three comet nuclei drifted in the swath.

"Metals, carbon, water ice under the surface of a few—all that's needed to sustain a thriving colony," Fuentes noted after an instrument scan.

"Methane, too, I'm sure—in those comets," the copilot theorized. "Plenty of potential fuel."

"Damn odd collection for this part of the belt," Fuentes stated, bent over his scope. "It's almost like a shunting point. Unlicensed freelancers may be working this sector."

"Okay, people," Wilkes admonished as if coming out of a trance, "we've a fling to set up."

After single-mindedly bringing their shuttle out of the way to what appeared to his crew to be this one particular asteroid, their commander was unexpectedly all dispatch and anxious to move on.

Fuentes readily agreed. *We've stomped around here unscathed long enough. Let's not press our luck. Let's fling before one of those rogues kisses us.*

The second officer returned to his IR scope, the copilot to her SDC.

For some unknown reason, the lieutenant's systems suddenly gave a fluctuating reading. Fuentes rechecked his instrument but thought nothing further of the situation. The dangers were clearly visible. Pursuing a reading spike was not essential or obligatory.

"Surprised no one's done a complete recce of this sector," the commander finally commented, more to himself than to his officers. He caught the two others off guard; the colonel was taciturn for the most part.

Assuming the senior officer's off-handed remark was actually a request for precise information, Fuentes twitched up a data file. "Last navigation beacon we passed was placed in 2056, just fifteen years into hiber treks." After a few more twitches, he added, "It wasn't even ours."

"We're probably crossing a sector even the MAS hasn't seen," the CO commented in a distracted manner.

"Hard to believe that anyone beat Marsco to any part of the belt," answered Chen while thinking, *What's this brick doing acting like an exploration vessel?*

"Records indicate that beacon was licensed to a consortium representing the Continental Powers," Fuentes stated dryly. Then he added sarcastically, "Guess they won't be cashing in up here after all. Their party's over!"

"Asteroid ephemeris already lists this minor planet," Chen expained after checking her own data file. "Although large enough to be named, it's only numbered: S2863-56JH. Discovered 2056 by Jarrod Hawkins, whoever that was, in a Powers craft. Only recorded survey of this sector was by the Hawkins vessel from well before the Wars."

With a twitch of her implants, the screen displayed a visual of S2863 plus the six largest of its accompanying family of asteroids. "Wait, what's this?" Her voice trailed off. She studied her view screen and added, "Let me confirm this anomaly by virtual."

Well-trained movements of her disks produced an enlarged projection of the planetoid within a 2.5 meter square in the VR bay behind the flight deck. The crew examined the projected planetoid carefully.

Three of its captured asteroids were enlarged as well. The glowing holograph was accurate down to the pocked impact hits on their surfaces. Where the scanners couldn't observe, a smooth gray scheme filled in. The trinary body and its three family members (potato-shaped, peanut-shaped, lizard-headed) seemed to float in the rear cabin, illuminated with an eerie light produced by the VR projectors.

"Look at that!" Chen aimed a laser cursor at one of the trailing asteroids; its virtual suddenly filled the whole VR bay, growing to a meter and a half in length. The details from the shuttle's scanners were remarkably accurate. This single actual asteroid virtually represented in the bay was nearly ten times the length of the *Piazzi.*

Chen pointed out what she thought was so odd: the asteroid had bumps along it while conventional astrogeology suggested its surface would be pockmarked with impact craters, much like the Earth's moon. Even comparatively minor impacts left their unmistakable spherical indentations. "How do indiscriminate natural actions produce *bumps* where *craters* should exist?" Chen wondered.

Even more peculiar, the mounds seemed regularly and evenly spaced, not randomly scattered. "Eighteen bumps are visible," she noted, "but where the scanners don't project, there's room for another six." With her laser pointer, she traced the lumps. "Their arrangement does suggest a discernable pattern, intelligently contrived, not naturally occurring."

"Ominous number, twenty-four," added Fuentes, trying not to let his imagination run away with the anomaly.

"Space holds many mysteries," Wilkes insisted, "perhaps this phenomenon is just another."

Chen beat the misgiving Fuentes to any conclusions, "*Twenty-four!* The number of Lightning fighters in two squadrons; the contingent on an attack carrier—one of the largest."

"Quite an intuitive leap," the commander remarked hotly.

"If we can loiter, the natural rotation of the asteroid *will* confirm my hypothesis," she insisted. "We will see all twenty-four!"

"Or little green men?" the senior officer retorted. "Aliens and predators or those unfortunates once abducted from Earth? Is that what you had in mind? No, we're off." The previously dilatory pilot was suddenly in a hurry.

As Chen and Fuentes prepared the *Piazzi* to leave the area, they worked together on their secret project to solve the mystery of this tri-part asteroid.

The belt *did* hold mysteries. And one it might still be concealing had Continental ties. The two officers had been born before the devastating Wars that still affected their world. As children, they had witnessed the horrors unleashed by the Powers. As adults, they had never seen any forces opposed to Marsco, except the pernicious rebellious Ludd fanatics Fuentes knew firsthand. As officers they had never experienced anything as well-organized, as well-trained, as well-equipped as the coalition of nations, the Continental Powers, bent on destroying Marsco.

Fervently believing in Marsco's peace, both officers would do anything to protect their world from another determined onslaught by C-Powers forces, hence the pair's obsession with the remarkable asteroid and its coincidental shape and intriguing family. Chen called up *Jane's Encyclopedia* a virtual representation of the C-Powers's last commissioned deep-space attack carrier. The JPEG showed it with its full complement of two squadrons, twenty-four Lightning fighters. "This entry is for the *Akagi*, the C-Powers's largest spacecraft."

"A craft, incidentally," the onetime Security officer noted, "not accounted for at the Armistice."

Twitches by Chen put the two—her bumpy asteroid's virtual representation and *Akagi's* schematics—into the same ratio of dimension. The virtual silhouette of the attack carrier fit exactly on top of the asteroid holograph; aligned correctly, each bump lined up in the precise location of an armed, ready-to-launch Lightning fighter poised on the carrier's hull.

The pair watched the overlaid virtual in rapt silence. *What have we found?*

"And those bumps're distinctively shaped, aren't they?" she remarked, "almost delta-winged."

"Each does have the profile of a Lightning, if someone wanted to mothball it for deep space. The craft might have been covered to shelter it during transit, but that protective covering still creates an outline indicative of a fighter."

"If only that asteroid would rotate faster, we'd see its other side before we leave."

Even without total observation, the evidence was overwhelming. This was more than an intuitive leap. The two were convinced; this was fact.

Except the commander.

He barked, "We're preparing for fling, and you two are playing 'Guess the Shape'!"

Fuentes stuck his head in his scope's hood but downloaded Chen's virts for later scrutiny.

The *Piazzi* distanced itself from the asteroid family. And yet minutes later with fewer dangers to concern them, Chen and Fuentes surreptitiously went back to examining their discovery like pupils believing they would never be caught by their teacher.

After closer inspection of her display, Chen found steering rocket pods completely visible at the near end of a different arrow-shaped S-class asteroid in the family. "But where's the command pod?" she tapped to Fuentes's screen. Steering rockets without a pod suggested that a freelance scavenger had diverted the asteroid.

Without a command pod, the asteroid might be sent out of the belt, but once out, it would have no internal control over its flight path. A randomly drifting asteroid was a common enough event. Once outside the belt, drifting on its own, it was "salvageable" under space law; anyone might freely claim it. Chen twitched,

"I'm absolutely convinced I've discovered the duplicitous means Independents employ to cover their astro-piracy."

Fuentes turned in his seat and shrugged.

"Look," Chen whispered under her breath. "Rockets without a pod—that points to the fact that this asteroid was clearly stolen from Marsco—yet its systems somehow failed before it managed to leave the belt."

"Maybe there *is* a com-pod, Mei-Ling. Might be situated beyond liberation," Fuentes conjectured.

Chen snapped, her whisper growing louder, "No, the pods're always adjacent to the rockets."

"Somewhere our scanners can't reach?" The lieutenant tapped out to her even while knowing his question was one a lowly plebe was capable of answering. "Only twenty-two minutes before rotation exposes the other side. Be long gone by then."

She rotated the virtual to double-check that no command pod sat behind, although without a total scan she was unable to project the far side of the asteroid. Convinced on fragmentary evidence, she concluded, "Looks like a toasted scavenger's job to me."

Wilkes suddenly interjected, "Affirmative! Some bugger bungled that job."

Busted, Fuentes realized.

Chen, however, was more struck by the words *bugger* and *bungled,* which she thought oddly archaic. Wilkes was showing his hiber-elongated age. Additionally, when excited, his Australian accent thickened, his voice losing its Marsco standardization.

Speaking normally for the first time, Fuentes asked, "Should we try to retrieve it, commander?" In deep space, that would be Marsco SOP. "A speeding and unmarked mining asteroid running wild outside the belt might become a navigation hazard."

Wilkes responded bluntly, "But this one's harmlessly adrift. It's stuck in the gravitational sway of that massive brute, tucked well into the belt itself, one of ten thousand others like it."

"But, sir, regs *are* clear—"

"In this case, regs don't apply. Here's a single lost mining asteroid accidentally propelled to a new location in a random orbit around the unsurveyed S2863. One of hundreds of potential mining asteroids in the immediate area."

"But shouldn't we retrieve it, sir?" Purposely, Fuentes asked formally. "The pods're worth salvaging, if nothing else."

Mr. Poindexter's voice unexpectedly broke into the com-link; he had effortlessly intruded through Chen's last attempt to lock him out. "That's an excellent question for our commander," the passenger speciously stated, seeming pleasant while demanding action. He was showing as much interest in the planetoid as the copilot and second officer had but with more authority behind his words.

That bloody bastard! thought Wilkes. *Been listening this whole time. He's powerful, he is.*

Temper flared in the colonel's gray eyes. Chen and Fuentes both thought that Wilkes, accustomed to getting his own way, was preparing to eject the passenger. Chen shot her superior a *jettisoning-of-passengers-is-not-standard-practice* glance.

Wilkes constrained himself (not because of Chen's looks—he was immune to them) and answered the lefter himself. "Mr. Poindexter, take a look around. We're moving through a target-rich environment, passing hundreds of mining asteroids. And I've got my finger disks full as it is. One mining asteroid with malfunctioning steering pods is bloody valueless. Retrieving it would cost more than grabbing another closer, safer one. Besides, this shuttle's totally modularized and not extremely maneuverable. I can't jink around trying to retrieve some lost chuck of ore. Let some bloody mining snapper re-procure it."

His copilot and lieutenant understood the logic of this argument. To silence any Marsco wallah, remind them of potential cost overruns and equipment degradation implications. Smashing an MAS shuttle into an asteroid was an unsound business policy.

The navigational computer beeped a soft reminder. The near-spherical Pallas was coming into visual range; it was time to initiate acceleration around it to fling out of the belt. Time to head for home.

"Should I mark this family with a nav beacon?" Chen asked. The different orbiting speeds of Pallas and the anomaly caused the two to be in the same proximity only temporarily. They would eventually drift apart. The triad-shaped asteroid had a unique and decidedly faster orbit than the other bodies in this sector. It wouldn't take long for it to be lost again in the endless asteroid-populated swath.

"Don't waste your effort. I'm reluctant to interfere with an astrogeologist on this," the colonel explained.

The flight deck officers distinctly heard Poindexter draw a sharp, disapproving breath. He continued listening, watching everything regardless of Chen's security precautions.

The copilot muted the com-link and whispered to the commander, "Maissey'll have him iced and out of our hair soon." Well-disked or no, she locked him out once more.

"That's about all the iceman's good for," the colonel smirked.

"Should we fling around it?" Fuentes asked. "Give us a chance to scan it more closely, have better measurements."

"No. Stay on present course. Now that we're past, let's not reenter its g-sway. I don't want to get mired in its family. Continue to Pallas. Its family's been mined for years."

Fuentes understood. Few could predict how difficult it would be to extricate a shuttle from an unknown g-flux amid the dangers of those smaller, orbiting asteroids. *Why press our luck a second time?*

In the vicinity of the mined-out Pallas, no other asteroids floated. Marsco mining-boffins had removed all those asteroids years before. Pallas, a lumpy ball of basalt, was one of the first that Marsco engineers had excavated. Even its colony was abandoned, maintained as an isolated emergency port. A ghost town in space, Pallas had drifted away from a once-thriving mining sector and into this unexplored area. The asteroid remained useful to a shuttle only as a huge barren rock, a gravitational pull to initiate fling.

—•—

As automated controls took over, Chen analyzed the readout from her console and examined the virtual of the enigma. "Many of the smaller asteroids haven't been here long. The core of the largest one must be denser than it looks, capable of capturing a number of random drifters."

"A discovery that's generated this much discussion at least deserves the distinction of a name," Mr. Poindexter commented from Pass Two.

He's at it again, Chen realized, *left-overriding my lockout.*

Although the consultant didn't come right out and say it, he wanted the baffling mystery marked for a later survey team. He was certainly snooping—for new rich mining deposits, for illegal free-lancers. No doubt about it, the flight crew concluded with knowing glances to one another.

With her superior's approval, Chen called up a list of pre-determined but unassigned names from the Marsco Institute of the Minor Planets. Housed in the Moscow Cantonment, where a Minor Planet Center had stood since the last century, this institute recorded all asteroid registrations. *Siberius* was top on the list. *Apt name,* thought Chen.

"Thank you all," commented Poindexter over the link, a perfunctory remark. "We'll have to survey this sector again soon."

Bloody well won't be your buggering bum in the command seat, Wilkes assured himself.

Computer controls guided the *Piazzi* in its final fling around Pallas and set her spiraling trajectory across vacuous space, Marsward. The shuttle's two main thrusters came to life at fifteen percent, a small taste of the main burn that would take place in several more days. The slight gravitational tug of their partial, elliptical orbit around Pallas nosed the egressing shuttle toward a point in space where she would initiate full throttle up and start her planetary rendezvous.

As soon as the shuttle broke into the unencumbered emptiness beyond the main swath of belt asteroids, Chen activated artificial gravity. Soon the essential crew and pass mods were at a comfortable 75 percent of Earth-g.

Sitting near the VR bay, Wilkes called up the virts, first of Siberius and then two additional asteroids, the one with its bumps at regular intervals and the other with its steering rockets.

The commanding officer grew as absorbed in the holographs as his crew had been, raising his eyes only when Chen reported more alarming info.

Her readings indicated that many of the asteroids near Siberius were recent arrivals. "Disregard outright the one gone astray because of rocket malfunction," she stipulated, "since that one had to have come into orbit within the past forty years. But the others seem to have been caught relatively recently. Readings suggest they all arrived in the past *twenty years.*" For asteroids ceaselessly orbiting the sun, twenty years was a nanosecond, the woman insisted. "And for any asteroid, even of this one's surprising density, to pull in so many—I've counted at least fifteen—is an anomaly of immense proportions."

When she brought this to the commander's attention, he remarked blandly, "Yes, but there are millions of mysteries in space."

"But, sir," she continued eagerly, "my sensors also record an ECM pulse emanating from Siberius."

"Impossible!" barked Wilkes. "*Electronic countermeasures?* From a solid, lifeless mass? A rock? Bloody impossible!"

Even Fuentes seemed incredulous but tried to hide his skepticism by asking, "Passive or active?" *After all,* he reasoned, *this might explain my sudden spike in sensor readings.*

"Active. Definite wave modulation comparisons," the copilot insisted.

"There must be a *hidden* colony on the far side—beyond sensor liberation," Fuentes remarked. "We should of waited for it to fully rotate."

"*Hidden?*" the commander repeated.

"Yes, hidden on purpose or because of the size, *hidden* from our view." Fuentes spoke fast in his excitement. "But I think it's a secret base—something someone wants to keep hidden."

"Yes, maybe it's the base of the Lost Squadron!" Chen was sure of herself; sensor readings were too strong to be anything else but an ECM umbrella emanating from the mysterious asteroid.

"You mean *Lost Fleet,* captain."

"Sir?"

"Rumors of the Lost Fleet abound throughout Marsco; they circulate as regularly as the stories about the *Plague Ship,*" scoffed Wilkes. "These myths grow more fantastic with each retelling. Even postings on e-boards spread various histories of these apparitions. No rendition's ever the same."

Chen and Fuentes eyed each other. She wanted him to know what she was thinking, but that was impossible in front of their commander. She knew the rarity of the triad asteroid fascinated their CO. This was all the more plausible since he had seemed to be searching for something definite coming all this way off their flight path. She had no proof for her hypothesis; instead she willed Fuentes to understand her thoughts, the telepathy of incipient love.

"All this talk's someone's leftover breakfast," continued Wilkes. "Chatter and rumors, all inventing three attack carriers out of the vacuum of space, each craft humping a Lightning fighter squadron, or four, or a dozen. All in preparation for a sneak attack against Marsco by the defunct C-Powers. The alleged fleet left Earth orbit early in the Wars heading for the belt, never to return even after hostilities subsided. Supposed to come back to Earth—or at least lunar orbit—after the Armistice but failed to arrive. Marsco presumed it lost, perhaps in order to hide the failure of its Security Forces to find that damned mysterious fleet."

The commander looked at his junior officers, who expected him to be finished. But abruptly he added, "The *Akagi,* the largest carrier ever. Humps two squadrons, as you've conjectured earlier.

Two other attack carriers, the *Hiryu* and *Soryu.* Smaller sister ships, one squadron each. At least forty-eight Lightnings in all, or so the rumors go. An enemy fleet waiting in a hidden, remote redoubt, waiting to reemerge and strike at Marsco! Those rumors?"

For someone denying rumors, he's got all the details down cold, Fuentes thought.

"Are you suggesting, Captain Chen, that you found a covert base of the C-Powers? That's an old bogyman's tale hibermen tell children. Lost Lightning squadrons! Preposterous!" With each emphatic statement, his creased forehead suggested, *What sort of a crew do I have?*

"Secret bases!" More wrinkles, more insinuations that the pair lacked analytical minds. "Hibernating fighter crews!"

Chen reluctantly countered, "I hadn't suggested anything of the kind, sir, at least not based on this partial and fragmentary analysis. I state nothing conclusive about my readings *as yet.* I only report that I have *definite* humanly produced ECM readings."

Fuentes joined in support of the copilot. "Maybe an old crashed fighter craft with its stealth array still operating."

"Impossible. How would a fighter get all the way out here," asked Wilkes, "350 million kilometers from Earth, give or take 10 million clicks? And once here, still have a functioning transmitter after all the years since the Continental Wars? Your conclusion's utter and total rubbish. Get a hold of your fanciful imaginations, you two! Don't go space happy on me *before* our crossing even starts."

His intense eyes bore down on Chen. "Put it down to false readings. 'Faulty computer comparison program.' Background radiation from a galaxy light years from here bollixing up your computer's analysis. 'Readout states categorically that an unknown natural anomaly is inaccurately being read as a known ECM emission!' You should override your computer reasoning with ordinary *human* sense, something I believe a highly trained officer's expected to display at all times."

"But, sir," the copilot countered, "there seems to be an electronic umbrella over part of that asteroid. *If* these are emissions from an exact source *and if* they can be traced *and* calibrated but *not* modulated for comparison to—"

"Don't go Boolean on me either, Mei-Ling." The captain's remark ended the discussion. Wilkes rarely called the woman by her first name and when doing so, always without softness or concern; he was totally devoid of those qualities.

Chen understood completely. She had too many other pressing duties in preparation for final burn to pursue her observations. While setting their course toward Mars and checking engine status, she never again looked at the virtual of Siberius.

Wilkes, however, continued studying the projections. He examined several of the recent arrivals as well. *Yes, enough ice and carbon and methane floating nearby to service quite a colony for years.*

The display began blinking, and a script notice streamed across the bottom of the virtual bay as though the letters were floating amid the asteroids. An info-blurb drifted along: "Degradation of virtual imminent. Scanners losing visual contact. Save to existing datum file or disengage."

The colonel found that Fuentes had created such a file. Using his left-hand disks, he twitch-deleted it. The virtual anomalies flickered and disappeared forever.

Once satisfied with the progress of his subordinates, the senior officer left the command mod.

SEVEN

ICEMEN CONCERNS

(On the *Piazzi*, 2094)

"Is it true?" an excited voice asked.

The unexpected question caught the iceman totally off guard. He hoped he hadn't sent the wrong command to his program. Petty Officer Jamie Maissey, Hibernation Specialist, paused to rethink his last twitches.

While most shuttle crewmembers were fit and trim, Maissey thickened more than most around the middle. His extra seven kilos gave him a chubby, boyish look, making it difficult to judge his age. He might have been thirty; he might have been only several years older than the impetuous boy pestering him.

Standing in the hatchway of the hiber station, Ram didn't lighten up. "Well, is it?"

"How'd you get in here?" the iceman stammered, thunderstruck at the presence of the boy, *here,* in crew territory.

"That Mr. Poindexter, he can be *so* nice when he wants. He said he was busy, so why don't I just go talk with the crew."

"But, the hatch's locked down. I know that Mei-Ling—Captain Chen—did so herself."

"Yes, I know." The boy oozed precocious charm, "but with all those left disks, a few—" He air-twitched his left fingers. "Mr. Poindexter's array's rad. I bet he can *crack,* I mean, *access* anything. But, anyway," he went on, trying to sound older, "I'm here to ferret out reliable intel—is it true?"

Maissey did a double-take. *How old is this boy?* "About what?" he managed to get out.

"Mars swing-by. Will we, my sister and I, be awakened?"

Self-importantly, the iceman studied the passenger requests on several screens before replying. "Yes, here it is. Your parents want you two hibered first but then awakened during flyby, four months away."

"Right-o!" the boy beamed, then caught his runaway, keyed-up younger self. "I mean," he went on in a controlled voice, "the *Piazzi's* fortunate to be making her journey during this period of trek-enhancing planetary alignment."

"Yes, indeed." Maissey eyed the child, marveling at his vocabulary and knowledge. *And only eleven or sixteen.* "It's not an unreasonable request. Kids safely come out of icing fifty percent faster than adults. Returning you to hiber three days later for the lunar leg will be routine. Cake."

Mr. Chaudhuri not only asked that his children be iced as soon as possible but that he and his reserved wife be left until last for a few peaceful days to themselves. He had requested this discreetly, and the specialist disclosed none of this to his son. These were all requests icemen handled with tact, although passengers usually welcomed hiber, for once out of the belt, the view was changeless, ceaseless, and mostly black.

Waiting around for the complete attention from the crewman, the boy commented, "Seeing the Red Planet from space is a spectacular sight not to be missed, so I'm told." He spoke as though the iceman had never even been in space. "Most passengers, like Mr. Poindexter and those in Pass One, prefer to hiber during the maneuver. Fascinating to children but to adults, quite mundane."

The iceman mumbled, "Yeah, kids're a different story."

"Oh, yes, yes, I see," Ram replied, as though he were not in that general category of "children." "To most youngsters, it's all so exhilarating—the long months of spaceflight, the hiber bays, the sleep-packs." The inquisitive boy looked at the primary hibernation screen with all its readouts and GUIs. "Will anyone be awake the whole time?"

"I will."

"SOP?"

"In a way, yes. The systems're fully automated, however. I could, if I chose, self-ice and go down with the rest. Our on-boards—"

"Marsco computers!"

"Affirmative. On-board computers will handle everything perfectly. But, I like to monitor everyone myself. It's my choice, that's all."

The boy's arched eyebrows asked the question *Why?* But Maissey didn't go into it. Like a typical hiberman, the petty officer never underwent icing himself and religiously avoided any duty that necessitated it.

"How does that work? Shuttle navigating and all? Do *you* steer the ship?"

"Oh, no. Hibermen stay off the flight deck. Pilots are *very* territorial. Lieutenant Fuentes will enter hibernation about seven days after Captain Chen. The copilot is right now laying in the course for Mars. But it falls to her subordinate, Fuentes, to monitor the auto-systems at the outset, until we're well passed the PNR."

"That's the *point of no return,*" the boy said, then quoted, "'a navigational distinction more than any discernible landmark.'" He drew a confident breath. "Comes after our final hour-long burn, but beyond that it's a monotonous journey across the eternal blackness."

I have to impress this wunderkind somehow, the hiberman thought. "Once past PNR, it's impossible—I'm sure you know—for a shuttle to return to the belt."

"That has to do with chemical rockets for propulsion and the amount of fuel every shuttle carries," Ram stated, completely cognizant of the decades-old system.

The iceman, on the other hand, didn't fully comprehend why Marsco was so negligent in developing better propulsion systems. He knew from his single meeting with Walter Miller that real advancements in space travel were stalled, mostly by Marsco's design.

The boy continued. "Since there isn't a significant, astrological body out beyond the belt whose gravitational pull might redirect the shuttle—a moon or large asteroid—the point of no return's actually not that far ahead." The boy arched an eyebrow, seeking acknowledgement. Receiving none, he continued anyway, "After our final burn, there won't be enough fuel for a return even if we needed to turn around. Rather, we'll be forced to continue toward Mars—letting planetary gravity steadily accelerate us throughout our spiraling elliptical orbit."

"That's right," Maissey reluctantly agreed, impressed by Ram's celestial comprehension to the state of exhaustion. "But nothing is going to happen."

"Nonetheless, *if*—hypothetically of course—*if* an emergency *did* develop, no spaceship exits that has the capacity to start out from the belt behind us and then have enough acceleration to rescue us."

"Affirmative. Help'd have to come from Mars, if we're close enough. More or less, each shuttle's at the mercy of safety protocols—and her well-trained crew."

"Oh, I believe that," said the boy. "I've met the copilot."

The boy and man exchanged knowing glances.

"Oh, and luck," Ram added, "during the seemingly endless inbound trip."

"Affirm that, our crew skills first though."

"Yes, it's 1.2 AUs from here to Mars with another .6 AU from Mars to the lunar docking ports. Close to 270 million clicks across an unforgiving void." Ram tossed around the scientific terms breezily, discussing astronomical units—the distance from the Earth to the Sun—as though in an Academy lecture hall with conversant peers.

Maissey's eyes glazed over while the boy continued his detailed précis of outer space. All this talk made the iceman think of Zot.

Anthony Grizotti and Maissey had endured two years of hiber training together, a time that went much smoother because of Zot's mentoring. *He was, after all,* Jamie recalled, *a sort of big brother.* Around him, there were fewer putdowns and snide remarks from others. Jamie remembered all too vividly how he often suffered the butt of many pranks. Not so under Grizotti's wing. Zot's Academy-grad status and his officer's rank cast a protective aura over Maissey during those months. They remained close friends since.

The hiberman muttered to the ceiling conduits, "I've a friend on the expedition ship *Gagarin.* Think of the inconceivable distance from here to Jupiter. It's two AUs."

"Closer to 2.4—360 million clicks." The iceman whipped his head to glare at the boy. But Ram only stated excitedly, "That must be awesome! But the belt to Jupiter's more than twice the distance of abysmal nothingness than from the Earth to the Sun."

"And the last leg of his journey started from a band of rocks floating in space," Jamie noted, "from nowhere through empty oblivion back to nowhere."

For once, the boy listened, transfixed.

"We've plenty of night inside the belt going to Mars," Maissey mumbled.

A chime from Ram's wrist chronometer ended their conversation. "Look, 1430 already!" With that, he was gone.

"—so it makes some sense to me at any rate," Mei-Ling explained.

She and Julio sat at the flight deck, preparing the shuttle for her four-month Mars crossing.

"To recce an unexplored sector," the copilot elaborated, rationalizing the commander's actions, "takes that much longer. New regs, remember?"

"I guess so," Julio groused. "But first HQ sends that asinine directive to wander off established flight paths. Then Wilkes dutifully takes up the call and sets our post-dock route through a dense collection of moving crapola. Mostly through uncharted rocks. Sets it all preflight—with us right there. A clear, safe path outward yet within this directive to snoop around. But then, he unexpectedly changes the path yet *again*—this time mid-flight. Takes us into an even denser collection—" He broke off his words in disgust.

"How dense?" Chen asked.

"The densest known to Marsco!"

"Says it all," she playfully mocked.

"Each one of them capable of—!" Fuentes let her draw the conclusion. "And there's Wilkes, finger-disking it rather than letting auto-controls run the show. He nearly skimmed the surface of that fat mother as though jockeying a hovercraft on Earth." He stopped short then drilled her like a plebe, "Think of that! No confirmed perigee since we were on a partial orbit. No way to be sure of our Hohmann transfers."

"Doesn't matter now. We're out, approaching final and PNR."

"Still," Fuentes insisted, "he should've informed us before changing his—*our*—flight plan. I mean, we are his crew." His last remark brought them face-to-face; two sets of brown eyes met. She reached over to squeeze his neck; his tense shoulders relaxed. He smelled her lingering jasmine fragrance.

Then, back to duty. Twitching, the officers worked on Mars rendezvous. Migration of commands, sequencing of emergency computer procedures and safety protocols took up their time with hardly a moment for other comments.

Their inputting finished, the junior officer began establishing the reliability of the inertial guidance platform, essential for any movement through space. Eventually, he announced, "I'll check the gyros myself."

Chen laughed, "Don't trust Marsco computers to run that diagnostic?"

"Just cautious—three gyros, three quick checks." Without the trio of perfectly functioning gyroscopes, especially without a planet beneath them to provide a horizon for direction, any breakdown in the inertial guidance would be catastrophic with the command crew iced. Unlike an HFC or lander in Earth orbit, spaceflight navigation was exponentially more intricate. Accurate gyros created a consistent geometrical axis to substitute for the planet's horizon. The ethereal void was without landmarks, so spacecraft needed to provide their own.

Chen laughed at his vigilance. And yet, as a well-trained officer and his superior, she double-checked his work when he was finished.

After four hours without any let-up, Chen glanced over her shoulder, looked into a cold opt-scanner, and whispered, "Icing isn't my favorite."

Mimicking Ram, Fuentes responded, "But it saves 90.9078% of our onboard supplies."

"Your stats are wrong, but your parody's accurate—cruel of you to pick on that defenseless boy!"

"He's a walking encyclopedia link!"

She jabbed his ribs, using her knuckle so as not to hurt her fingertips. The joshing motion brought her face closer to his, but with a serious expression. "I have a *feeling*," she shuddered; there was some doubt as to its meaning for Fuentes.

"Feeling?"

"About *him*, Maissey, and his attitude toward me. I'm probably just guessing. We did a rotation together a few years back. Outbound to Mars—the long trek—three months. So, I feel mine are legitimate concerns, not just negatory feelings of our iceman."

"Yes," Fuentes replied, missing the exact reason for her anxiousness, "They're mostly sandbaggers and shirkers. Ever see one volunteer for anything beyond the ordinary?"

"But even the ordinary's risky out here," rejoined Chen, now sounding like she was defending her shuttlemate. "Especially since 'there're millions of mysteries in space,'" she added, her slam of the colonel cooling any notion of support for Maissey.

"I'm sure he likes the ice service," Fuentes commented, "especially the pay-cycle."

He drew a breath while they both marveled at the vagaries of pay that allow hibermen to earn MMUs at a phenomenal rate. Owing to complicated historical reasons having to do with early century unions and tangled guidelines long forgotten, icemen were essentially paid per diem. Moreover, their daily rate changed while the shuttle commander and crew were under, when technically the iceman was acting commander. The bonus for that temporary status made the dullness of space economically worthwhile. "Pay alone almost makes it attractive to be an iceman."

"*Almost!*" Chen insisted then added, "Glad you're not." She leaned into Fuentes and kissed him gently, her tongue just wetting his lips.

"Regs forbid PDA on the flight deck."

"You're right, of course, it's verboten. But we'll have time soon."

The silence after the boy left depressed Maissey. He felt mentally incompetent, physically drained. *Maybe I should read something while the others are iced,* he thought. He would do anything to impress that dual-aged kid-genius—and Mei-Ling.

As it was, the hiberman planned to spend his wake-time floating—and more—with his rave scenario. Digital or no, *that* thought sent a sensation throughout his body.

But Chen and his lucrative watch both had to wait. He had preps to complete as the *Piazzi* left the relative safety of the belt further behind. The petty officer would soon be on duty alone: monitoring, checking, making sure everyone hibered safely. Raving with his virt Chen in deactivated artificial gravity and watching all those monetary units cha-ching up and up.

A dozen years or so, he mused, *and I'll retire to some tropical island, team up with a bodacious HH GAS-free babe (or several) and my life'll be sweaty-luscious.* Wistful, he wondered, *Will Mei-Ling come with?*

Daydreaming finished, Maissey's protocols called him back to sustained work for an hour.

While the hiberman prioritized, Wilkes interrupted him over the com-link. "How y'coming?" The iceman looked up, but he didn't see anyone on his blank monitor. He was receiving only audio. The pilot saw him clearly and added, "Come to my quarters once finished with your schedule."

Thirty minutes later Maissey strained to remain standing upright. One step inside the colonel's meager quarters and he realized that the AG was set at 1.5—double that right outside the bulkhead.

Wilkes squatted on the deck by his bunk, having completed a regimen of strenuous calisthenics. The increased gravity provided more resistance. Sweat ran off him at an accelerated rate. *No excess fat on that frame,* the petty officer noted with envy.

It struck Maissey that the commander had a military mien about him. He insisted on the crew adhering to Marsco chicken shit that most COs eased in deep space: hair length, clean shaving, that sort of nuisance. Hibermen, especially when alone, didn't follow such atavistic routines. The officer also had other vestigial martial characteristics. Athletic build. Cropped hair. Healed scar from a deep wound along his jaw. A battle wound, Maissey guessed.

And an ominous command-and-control implant at the tip of his trigger finger. The red disk stood out since the rest of his well-disked fingers on both hands were the typical blue-green. *He'd been in the service all right.* Maissey knew it. *And yet he doesn't seem old enough to have been in the C-Wars.*

Wilkes motioned Maissey to a chair that the iceman fell into with a 1.5-g-thud. He immediately realized why he hadn't seen Wilkes on visual. The cabin's com lens was duct-taped over.

"Luddite trick to frustrate technology," the commander remarked casually. "Don't want that bloody arse Poindexter snooping on me."

The expression *bloody arse* struck Maissey as old-fashioned and seldom used.

"He's a god-almighty wallah," Wilkes continued after another set of g-enhanced push-ups, "who overrides any lockout at will. He must have bloody implants up to both frigging elbows."

"Yes, sir, I noticed." Then the petty officer thought, *Look who's talking about disks to the elbows!*

The duct tape struck Maissey as evidence of another time-honored military tradition. Ignore regs when they didn't suit an officer, and enforce them when they did. But whose regs, Maissey wondered. Since the defeat of the C-Powers, there hadn't been any military forces per se. Marsco had its Security and Hygiene battalions and special ops units honed to precision. Plus the S & H trained numerous Auxiliary contingents, mostly for urban patrols of PRIM-infested zones, but Auxxies were hardly armed forces in any conventional sense.

The iceman made a mental note to check Wilkes's age later when everyone was completely iced. Wilkes looked in his forties, but if he had been under ice routinely, his actual age would be—must be—much older. Doesn't take long to have a high actual year count but remain relatively young looking if two-thirds or three-quarters of your years are spent in near suspended animation. Even the boy, Ram, manifested this discrepancy.

The petty officer briefed the commander, who listened with his back on the cabin deck but his legs held up twenty centimeters in the air against the 1.5-g resistance.

Settling everyone into the hiber bays would take Maissey four days. Chen would hiber first among the crew, which was a shame. The hiberman was looking forward to spending some actual time with her, even though she was an officer. *It sucks,* Maissey thought, *that I can only look.* Marsco frowned on fraternization between commissioned associates and non.

"And you, sir, have requested being under for only three months of the belt-to-Mars trip, a typical senior officer request."

"Yes, I want to be awake during flyby to monitor what Chen's preset in the nav-computer."

"Even so, during the longest segment of the flight, all passengers and crew will be under."

"All except you," Wilkes shot.

In too breezy a tone, Maissey replied, "Yes, well, like so many comrades in my fraternity, I like to stay upright."

"And you've a way of making sure you look damn busy when everyone's awake."

"Sir?"

"Nothing."

But once iced, Maissey replied with mental insubordination, *you can't very well check up on me, can you?*

"Let me understand," the commander went on between sit-ups and push-ups, "the children and their parents, those *wogs,* plus Poindexter, the *nig*—well—that black wallah, they'll be the only ones in Pass Two hiber bay."

Wogs? Nigs? Maissey thought, *he gets murkier and murkier!* "Yes, sir, that's correct."

"Very well," the commander said. After a pause, he shifted subjects. "Did anyone notice vibrations, *unusual* vibrations during docking separation?"

"I didn't, sir."

"Feel anything at all out of the ordinary?"

"Like what exactly, sir?"

"Like *anything.*" Wilkes gave the look: *I'm not accustomed to having my suggestions questioned.*

"No, sir."

"Anyone say anything, although I suspect that bloody arse Poindexter was spitting the dummy—" Maissey looked confused, so Wilkes added, "*complaining up the bloody bum* if something did seem amiss."

The iceman chuckled, "Yes, he's an exec file all to himself."

"But no one said anything?"

"No, sir."

"Of course, the wogs wouldn't have, too timid."

After a pause, the hiberman inquired, "May I ask why, sir?" Maissey knew instantly he should have said, "Not my area of concern, sir." He should have followed the maxim, "Flight crews stay out of hiber territory, icemen out of command mods."

"Chen was duty officer when the ship was reconfigured two weeks before departure. I hadn't arrived yet, that's all."

"Yes, sir, refabrication's standard copilot duty, even when the senior officer is present."

"I hope all mods're sequenced correctly within safety protocol."

With great animation, Maissey defended Chen, letting slip more than he intended. "She is experienced! Why, she's made the Mars relay several times—I've been with her once. Our current run's her third belt trip as copilot." Wilkes didn't seem to pay attention or care. Maissey plowed on, his superior's displeasure notwithstanding. "Plus, she's fully certified to take command of this ship. Her promotion rating's the highest."

Even though he didn't let on, it amazed Wilkes just how much Maissey *did* know about his crew, especially Chen. *Perhaps this iceman knows more than he should,* the commander thought, with a long-honored distrust for hibermen in general and this one in particular. "Enter that in your log, nevertheless," the commander eventually stated. His glare said, "Do it now, mister! That's an order!"

"Sir? I don't quite understand, enter *what*?"

"'Vibrations noted in Pass Two possibly emanating from Cargo One.'"

"'Vibes in Pass Two,'" he repeated. "Very well, sir."

Were there any? the iceman wondered as he left the high-g quarters. An experienced space traveler, he had felt nothing out of the ordinary.

Misgivings aside, he duly noted in his log, "Colonel Wilkes notes vibes in Pass Two and Cargo One during dock-sep before fling. Captain Chen, copilot, duty officer at reconfigure."

While his log file shut down, he thought, *wogs? Didn't the term predate the C-Wars?*

Maissey prepared Ram and Indera for hiber in Pass Two. They were dressed in self-sterilizing sleep-suits, the white gauzy material keeping their bodies decontaminated throughout the long passage. The Chaudhuris had already wished their children goodnight as if just another evening on Vesta. Both kids chattered away, their comments and questions interspersed with Maissey's explanations of his procedures.

The petty officer had discovered that continuous explanations made his prep much easier on children. Icing did have a frightening clinical aura about it with heart monitors, sterile drips, and sleep-suits reminiscent of hospital gowns. Five-year-olds, Maissey had learned the hard way, were the worst to hibernate, but these two were at the optimum ages.

As the iceman made sure that their left wrist shunts were in place and that each drip was correctly adjusted, Ram asked, "Do you think Colonel Wilkes *was* in the Continental Wars?"

Maissey gave no reply.

"Father explained," the boy stated, "that Marsco graciously offered amnesty to many enemy pilots—only crews on shuttles, not Lightnings. Hundreds of older ones today, says father, began flying for Marsco only after Armistice."

Indera wanted her share of the conversation, so she burst in, "Oh, that was twenty-five years ago. He looks too young." She had no way to judge his age and was only repeating what her mother said.

"Strictly speaking, it is possible," the hiberman remarked off-handedly.

"You don't age in hiber," the girl declared with total assurance, trying to show that she knew as much about space travel as Ram.

"*Wrong!*" her brother interjected, delighted to catch his sister on a technical point. "You do age but extremely slowly. Isn't that right, Officer Maissey?"

"You are both right in a sense," the iceman responded, trying to keep control.

Feeling vindicated, Indera smirked at her brother.

"Your physical age is slowed," Maissey explained his dry tech knowledge in terms they could understand. "You age thousands of times slower than when awake—or sleeping normally, for that matter." They listened intently. "In hibernation, your body enters a state something like, well, *hibernation,* since it is like that—*hibernation.*"

Ram stared at the man, not sure he wanted this dolt putting him on ice.

"Like a screensaver," Indera declared.

"Well, yes, something like that. But, while your body's slowing down, your chronological age, your real actual age—" he thought for a second, "that keeps increasing at the same yearly rate. So you see, after you've been hibering, you start having two ages, your *physical age*—the age of your body's wear and tear—and your *chronological age,* the actual time span of your life."

"Huh?" blurted Indera. She still didn't understand the concept that her brother had been trying to explain to her for several months.

"Let me see," returned the hiberman. "In the late twentieth century, a boy of sixteen and a girl of eleven—"

"Eleven and a half—"

"—a girl of *eleven and a half* would have only counted their chronological age, because their actual age and physical age were the same."

"Because hiber wasn't yet invented," Ram jumped in.

"Shh, let him explain."

"You're right, Ram. Do you know when it was?"

"Of course, 2041."

"That's right. Now, back before hiber, no one ever thought of counting age two ways. When they said someone was 40, that was their age although they might say, 'She's a young 40' or something like that." Maissey saw that his example confused the issue.

"Don't worry about that at this point. As for the late twenty-first, during a year, a shuttle member might age one year on the chronological scale but may physically age only a few months, that being the wake time between their six-month hiber periods."

"And so," commented Ram, "some associates have two ages. Chrono age is consistent, like a baseline, but physical age is slowed down by hiber, slowed way down. And physical age is a *variable,* not a *constant.* It's different for different people depending on how much they've hibered."

Maissey marveled at the boy's explanation of scientific concepts he once painstakingly struggled to comprehend. "That's why you both have two ages already," he began haltingly. "You're sixteen and eleven *and a half* chronologically, but on your flight out to the belt originally, you hibernated for six months total and aged only a few days."

"It's especially noticeable in Ram," Indera stated pointedly. Then retreating, she added, "Like father. He was 42-chrono on his last birthday, but he says he's still thirty."

"Or like Commander Wilkes," Ram chimed in. "Father thinks he's much older chrono-wise than his physical age suggests. He looks, says father, in his mid-forties, but he must be an old man."

"He would have to be if he'd fought in the C-Wars," added Maissey without thinking. He mentally kicked himself for letting his guard down.

The hiberman continued to work. The children leaned back on the sterile mattresses of their bunks and watched. He started one procedure on the boy, who was on the top bunk of one pair of hiber-units, and then repeated the same on his sister, who was on the top of the opposite set.

Maissey examined their upper left arms to evaluate the children's Neo-Consumption test blotch. A nurse on Vesta had administered these mandatory tests and verified that all passengers were totally healthy. No one entered a shuttle unless they were "Marsco pink." If not totally disease-free, Neo-Con would lay waste to the victim's lungs during their prolonged sleep—a slow and torturous way to die, a certain way.

Maissey placed a color-bar test card next to each blotch to match it. The top color was vibrant blood red with pricks of sickly yellow pus. Anyone with this blotch, the iceman explained, "was beyond medical assistance and highly contagious. Plus nearly dead." Once more he wished he had been more guarded, but the iceman added, "Maybe a dying PRIM has such a blotch. I don't know. I've hardly ever seen a real PRIM, much less tested one for Neo-Con."

The next test color was orange, then pale yellow. Finally, a pink tone of a healthy, recent scar. The Chaudhuri children were both a robust Marsco pink, totally free of any trace of disease.

Ram stated confidently, "Only PRIMS get Neo-Con."

"Not necessarily," the iceman replied, glad he caught the boy in an error, the reason he went on with such bluntness. "Anyone just traveling through a zone can get it. Or a host of other opportunistic diseases. It's not just PRIMS who're at risk, although, of course, they spread things among themselves at an alarming rate. In some locales, Neo-Con's rampant."

His reckless statements had a sobering effect on the children, so he clarified, "As expected, you're like everyone else who's lived in space for four years—totally free of any disease." Finally, he added, "I've never seen an associate with any other reading but pink. And you two are in the pink all over: heart, lungs, blood pressure. Just raring to go to sleep."

Once finished with the tests, the iceman attached the boy's heart monitor. When he started to do the same for the girl, he found she was wearing a gold chain. Attached to it was a 100-rupee piece minted in the year 2000—millennial objects in fashion at the end of the twenty-first century.

The iceman gently reminded, "You can't wear anything except the sleep-suit; nothing else must touch your skin."

Without warning, tears rolled from the girl's large innocent eyes. She burst out, "Grandfather was a *PRIM*—"

Her brother tried to silence her but couldn't. His own brown eyes narrowed and flashed side to side nervously, displaying the same embarrassed expression of his mother earlier in the flight.

Even though Maissey had explained every step, Indera was overcome by all the humming and glowing apparatus surrounding her. Frightened, she began telling long-hidden family secrets. "Grandfather and grandmother, my father's parents, yes, PRIMS. Although, they never had Neo-Con. Father passed his Marsco exam. He was born a PRIM but isn't one now." She looked at her brother, "Neither are we, isn't that right, Ram?"

Maissey gently urged her back down onto her sterilizing mattress. "It's okay," he whispered several times.

To dispel his discomfort at her outburst, Ram explained, "Our grandparents now live in a thriving subsidiary near Calcutta. So that makes them sids." The boy chattered on, "And Father's quite a successful astrogeologist. His crew broke two records this rotation: largest single mining asteroid—3.5 million tons, 14.4% larger than the record—and highest monthly tonnage average."

The hiberman continued to work, hoping his repetitive movements would calm them for sleep. In their opposite bunks, offset from the bulkhead so that the iceman could move on either side of them, he checked their IVs for the last time. "This'll give you melatonin for sleep and this serotonin for dreams. And this," he arranged their headsets with its dozen electrodes, "will reproduce your exact brain wave pattern that you gathered."

"Remember, Ram, how you kept having nightmares?"

"Yes," he answered flatly.

"Ruined part of his sleep-pack, Officer Maissey," she informed him, trying to shift her embarrassment onto her brother, a longstanding sibling ploy.

Realizing Ram's self-consciousness, the hiberman explained, "It's okay if, while you're assembling all your patterns, you have a few terrible nights. Technicians edit them, gather months of normal sleep, then arrange everything into a seamless, continuous pattern of alpha, beta, and delta waves. The pack stimulates your brain to mimic your common nightly patterns; it keeps your brain in them continuously. In addition, while you're under, you'll get much more."

"School lessons!" Ram muttered with disappointment. "And I just want to dream."

"Once iced," Maissey explained, "through these electrodes, your waves are controlled by the rhythms of a sleep pattern, only decreased to their slowest possible algorithm. In addition, children and adults can be instructed."

Ram nodded. He was learning calculus and inorganic chemistry. Indera was only on algebra, but she would also be learning disk commands.

While under, Maissey would perform scheduled upgrades. Ram was getting his second adult disk, the new one at the tip of his right middle-finger.

Indera was having her child-sized oblong finger disk replaced by an adult one. The small size of children's fingers, girls in particular, often kept them from having a circular disk implanted when they turn seven, the optimum age for an initial implant. "This's why," the iceman explained to give this average youngster a defense against her high-end brother, "girls're often slower in the sciences and tech. Until their hands grow larger, they have to utilize a slower child's disk while still mastering overall twitch-coordination. Girls often get their first adult disk later."

The younger child smiled, understanding.

"When you awake," Maissey assured Indera, "you'll have a full-size disk."

Ram teased, "And be expected to twitch it with the same finesse as me."

"You'll have no probs." Maissey smiled at her. "You're bright, and with Marsco parents, nothing'll be spared for you to master the art of finger disks."

Another technique that the iceman had learned with children was to sit with them until they were fully asleep. And so, as both drifted silently toward natural sleep, he sat quietly between their bunks, looking over his protocol for the remaining passengers.

When Ram heard his sister's rhythmic breathing, he opened his eyes and remarked, "The whole shuttle doesn't have artificial gravity right now, correct?"

"That's right," the hiberman replied quietly. "Unless hauling sensitive equipment or using the cargo mods for a process requiring gravity—"

"—like hydroponics—"

"Yes, something like that. The mods are without AG to conserve power output." Maissey didn't encourage the boy to continue.

Even so, Ram went on. "The orbital retardation of Mars's less than the equivalent ratio of the thickness of a coat of paint to the overall length of the *Piazzi* itself. An insignificant and inconsequential fraction of overall orbital speed."

Nearly dumbstruck, Maissey admitted, "Yes, asteroids coming to Mars, shuttles flinging around the planet, they've slowed its orbit."

"And the Moon's."

"Yes," Maissey concurred. "If you knew lunar astronomy, you'd be able to tell from Earth just how much Marsco asteroids and shuttle launch flings have slowed the Moon down."

"Well," the boy replied, "I think it's max-cool that Marsco's able to alter so much in the solar system—planet orbit duration, the belt's asteroid population, the age of a person."

The iceman didn't respond, so the boy went on, "Doesn't that wondrous Chen act as sparks?"

Thinking he should be the adult here, Maissey shot a glance at the boy.

"She's boss, but I didn't get a tour of the flight deck."

The hiberman remained motionless to calm the boy down.

Finally, Ram began once more. "Marsco's extremely efficient in its use of this modular system, isn't it? And on shuttle flights, aren't humans transported first?"

"That's right."

"On Vesta, it seemed that shuttles heading to or departing from the belt mainly haul cargo."

"Correct again."

"From lunar ports or Mars they'd bring replacement personnel, supplies, and tech equipment."

"That's right."

"Food, water, and fuel are commonly produced on colonies but never in sufficient quantities to sustain them," the boy chattered, sounding like his father. "Links to Earth, directly via the Moon, or when movement allows via Mars, are essential for colony viability."

"You seem to understand the system." The iceman refrained from giving the boy any more encouragement.

After a pause, Ram spoke further. "I was playing around with the computer, just using my disk, clicking here and there, when, something weird happened—" he caught himself.

Maissey and Ram instantly froze. In the dim light, they looked suspiciously at one another. They each knew a secret which they refused to share. The moment passed as the boy lay back down on his bunk.

The pair remained still for several minutes, so much so that the hiberman thought the boy was asleep. Then, eyes wide, Ram asked neutrally, "We stayed in the belt a long time, didn't we?"

"Yes, it seemed a bit longer than usual."

"Mother was scared. And a bit spacesick, I think. She held father's hand until we'd flung around Pallas."

"That's something married people do."

"Something girls do as well. Indera held his other hand."

"Hmm," Maissey replied, trying to end their conversation.

Ram shifted topics again. "Mr. Poindexter claims he's a mining engineer, but Father has visited every mining site in our sector, and he never saw him once at any of them. Father says he spent his whole time in a surveillance shuttle with the colony's security chief." After a pause, during which Maissey was expected to add something, the boy continued, "He has a finger mouse notebook. Father thinks for secret files—no one can crack an NB."

"I wouldn't know anything about your speculation."

The boy realized the petty officer was not going to discuss Marsco policies with him the way that his parents privately did. He shifted topics, "Chen's bodaciously awesome, isn't she?"

"*Captain* Chen—" the petty officer corrected, no longer in his soft go-to-sleep voice.

"Anyway, she's a hottie, don't you think?"

Maissey didn't respond.

"Does she have anyone?"

The adult continued to ignore the child.

"What if she hibernates repeatedly, each time for a long duration, you see, and so her physical age slows down? And if I never hiber at all—after this time—and I keep growing older because I never slow down. If all that happened, I could marry her one day, couldn't I?"

It took Maissey a moment to see the adolescent logic of the boy's question. Finally he said, "Yes, that's true. If you lived on Earth normally, you'd age normally. If she traveled in space—"

"But hibernating, not just on a sublunar lander which has no icing—"

"Affirmative. If she hibernated in enough cycles, you might, at least conceivably, pass her age. Theoretically."

"Once back on Earth, first I want a segway and then a dog, and then a kickin' girlfriend."

With that pronouncement, Ram became motionless at last. Soon both children were entering a natural sleep cycle.

Each had suspended a toy on the bulkhead above their hiber bay. The boy placed an astro-engineer clad in a mobile EVA suit as though in the belt. His sister had a furry blue monkey. If she slept with it touching her, it would be grotesquely attached to her skin in four months. It wouldn't have gone unnoticed for that long, though. Maissey performed methodical inspections of the vitals twice daily during their hiber-cycle. He put the chain and rupee around the monkey's neck.

Next he double-checked their elimination tubes. Indera's mother had helped fit hers properly. The girl was at a sensitive age to have a stranger asking her about elimination. She wasn't old enough to menstruate, so the iceman expected her to have no complications. The boy had put on his own elimination tubes to impress the hiberman with how grown up he was.

Half an hour later, the iceman initiated all systems by disking a command pad. He sealed the hoods over the units and dimmed the lights as though putting children to bed on Earth.

EIGHT

POINT OF NO RETURN

(In deep space, 2094)

"Permission to remove my tunic, sir."

Initially, Fuentes didn't realize that Chen was mocking the skipper until she took off the top of her regulation cerulean shuttle suit with its badge of rank and MAS fleet patch.

Usually crewmembers wore issued tees underneath their uniforms. Yesterday, when Chen and Wilkes stood watch, she dutifully asked formal permission to uncover her upper arm because her Neo-Con test was itching. The senior officer had reluctantly granted the request. The copilot then worked the rest of her shift in a loose-fitting gray T-shirt.

Today, she uncovered a silk and lycra sleeveless top, a lustrous navy blue with a plunging V-neck that hugged her well-toned figure. Fuentes smiled his approval. Without her flight cap, her hair hung naturally in cruising-g. Shimmering black, it framed her face gracefully. A hint of jasmine lingered.

"Does your blotch hurt much?"

"No, it's a bit irritated, that's all."

He examined her upper arm. "Your reaction's normal," he declared.

Lowering her almond eyes, Chen whispered, "I'm hoping yours is too."

"I'm happy you're on board, that we have time together." He touched her hand and looked directly at her. She held his gaze.

Their work went smoothly with this informality between them. They knew each other well enough from before so that they didn't go through an initial awkward stage with someone of definite interest. Yet in many ways, they were just beginning to know each other beyond the superficial. Both had histories, all HH GAS–free. Each had checked the health status of the other. After the worldwide depopulating epidemics, associates became and remained cautious.

Eternal night was all before the *Piazzi.* Behind the shuttle, several belt colonies were still visible as brighter-than-stars spheres. Each hour they dimmed more. Amid the countless specks of light, Mars grew larger, brighter, an orange-red ball nearly four months away.

The silent ship seemed empty. Alone on the flight deck after passenger hiber but still before final burn and PNR, Chen and Fuentes worked to make certain all systems were ready for the last ignition of their Herriff-Miller units. For the next hour, they studied data readouts, verifying that all systems maintained their green lines when successfully transferred to auto-ops. Any equipment failure, even for those systems with a triple redundancy, called for emergency crew deicing. It was axiomatic: "No one wants to dehiber dead."

Another hour of inputting occupied the pair.

"Migration needs to run smoothly," Fuentes stated half-heartedly, knowing that his coworker knew her business. Chen accepted his low-key lecture; she liked his voice.

Seemingly out of nowhere, she brought up the inevitable. "You were going to tell me about your Security and Hygiene hitch."

His FDs froze, arrested mid-flick. “That’s an odd segue.”

“Well?” Her eyes met his, burning with understanding and concern.

“I served,” he replied with controlled emotion, “between the Academy and Flight—an assigned duty, not a request. Five years. You knew that.”

“What was that like?”

He took his time responding. When he did so, it was with an openness that masked the roiling tension these memories brought on. “At first, there was the exhilaration of commissioning and of being accepted into Flight. Then frustration, almost disillusionment at my new, changed orders just a few days later. ‘Security needed officers, stat!’ I had nine weeks at Basic. Running and calisthenics to whip us into real shape. Tough even though fresh from the Academy. The DIs took special delight in taunting officers; it was a drill instructor’s—warrant officers all—only chance to harass superiors.”

He paused, gazing at the blackness beyond the viewport. “I was then three months at an officers’ training center. Met many centurion-wannabes there.” Fuentes stopped to reiterate his point. “I was *never* in Security before the Academy. I got in straight away. Certainly, I’ve associate parents, which helps, but I aced my entrance scores. *I* didn’t get in over the bodies of—”

Breaking off, he went back to assessing readouts. Chen thought he might never return to the subject at all. Far from hurting their incipient relationship, she felt closer because of his frankness.

She shared her life story although she felt somewhat embarrassed by it. “Born of associates and grew up in the Shanghai Cantonment, went to a Marsco Prep. Sid instructors, of course, but as close to associates as possible. They were even given permission to live in the cantonment—a perk. Their children made the step into Marsco as easily as we did.”

Chen paused, pleased that their mutual honesty was deepening what feelings were already there. “Had three disks by sixteen,” she said with no sense of boasting. “Was skimming an HFC at seventeen.

My folks, though Earthbound, took holidays to lunar colonies so I'd be experienced with spaceflight before the Academy. As associates, they understood that the Fleet was the pathway." She thought of those two hibering children on board. Although they had spent years in deep space and as a girl she hadn't, their childhood and hers seemed quite similar.

In time, Fuentes returned to unburdening himself. "I had three months to train with my new unit, with legionnaires, both sids and PRIMS."

"When was this?"

"Autumn after the Academy." He paused. "My grunts were men and women, a few hardly more than children, who'd do anything to get into Marsco—*anything*." He paused once more. "Those were tumultuous times. A violent rebellion on three continents. Bio-outbreaks—all Ludd-induced. Dozens of urban zones rioting. The months, the years became a blur."

Yes, thought the copilot, *MAS saved many associates from all that. I was safe at the Academy or in Flight during all that chaotic time!*

After a natural silence, she asked, "Have you ever killed a man? Killed anyone at all?" Although blunt, her surprise question was neither harsh nor accusing.

"I was deployed worldwide for four and a half years," he whispered.

"That doesn't answer my question," she replied, gently placing her hand on his arm.

"I served a long deployment. I led countless patrols and recce sweeps. *Some* incident of *some* kind was bound to happen—let's just leave it at that," he answered. "Perhaps in the future, such events won't be necessary. Perhaps—who knows? Maybe the Marsco I constantly imagine as possible will eventually evolve, one with—" He stopped, not knowing the exact words to utter.

"With?" She didn't remove her hand or cease gazing into his dark eyes.

"With more of what it promises. I envision a different Marsco, an upgrade from the one we currently have."

"Who doesn't?"

"Perhaps Wilkes," Fuentes hypothesized.

"He certainly operates by his own exec commands."

"Ready for primary burn countdown, sir," Chen reported to her superior, who had not been on the flight deck for most of the day.

"Very well," Wilkes answered over the com-link, "have Fuentes stand by to commence."

Julio? Chen hoped her sharp reaction didn't betray her shock.

"Yes," replied the commander, comprehending the disbelief on her face. "That's an order! Have Fuentes fire the burn and control the ship."

The junior-most officer put a hand to his mouth so a cam could not pick up his lips. He whispered as softly as possible, "Is this a test?"

Seemingly not hearing, Chen went about her preps without a pause or a reaction. In ten minutes, however, a message went across his monitor, "Yes! Can't imagine why! :("

"Hibernation report?" Chen requested final verification from Maissey.

At first, the hiberman did a double-take. This status request ordinarily came from Fuentes. "We have a mutiny on the flight deck?" the iceman joked.

"No, commander's whim," Chen answered in a flat tone.

"All passengers under. Pass One and Two on lockdown. All's ready and prepped here for initial firing." The petty officer sat at the Pass One workstation with a jettison protocol called up to the screen before him. At the first sign of verifiable trouble, he was to disengage the two modules that would in turn act as gigantic life rafts.

Even over the com-link screen, the flier saw that the iceman was uncomfortable as burn approached. He had to know, as certainly every iced associate in his safekeeping knew, that should the Herriff-Miller pair malfunction, escape from the ensuing explosion was unlikely. Even if the mods got clear of the flames, their survival chances in the vagaries of space approached zero.

"On your mark, Captain Chen, if you please," requested Lieutenant Fuentes, the last command before the fleeting seconds prior to primary burn. As the copilot counted down, the juniormost officer sat poised in *her* command seat with *his* finger disks at the ready.

"Ten, nine—"

"Go for candle flaming."

"—eight, seven—"

"Fuel pressure at optimum."

"—six, five—"

"Nominal readings of isolated fuel component flow."

"—four, three—"

"Fuel mixturization imminent!"

"—two, one!"

"Ignition!"

From the enormous storage tanks fitted at the rear of the awakening Herriff-Miller engines, tons of hypergolic fuel ran through pipes leading to the combustion chambers immediately behind the engine bells. Fuel little different from what propelled Armstrong on the *Apollo 11* rushed toward detonation. Hydrazine-dimethylhydrazine met nitrogen tetroxide in a catalytically thunderous combination; the hypergolic compounds ignited spontaneously as they combined. An instantaneous reaction of fire and light vented from the initial chambers then out through the massive engine bells.

The century-old chemical propulsion system worked flawlessly. As the Herriff-Miller thrusters exploded from partial to full power, the *Piazzi* went from placidly gliding to steadily increasing from the enormous thrust out-throw. The initial acceleration began violently shaking the shuttle about.

"We have ignition confirmation!" Chen reported with excitement in her voice and no need to read any monitor. But read she did, searching for any flashing warnings that engine firing was in fact burn failure. If she found a sign, it meant only a second or two longer to imagine her fiery death. Escape protocols would never jettison the crew out of the ensuing fireball.

"All systems go!" she reported, sitting at Fuentes's monitor, away from the action.

In the shuttle's sudden gyrations, Fuentes at the command seat gripped the joystick to keep the craft straight and level. In space, without a planetary horizon, "straight and level" was an imaginary plane on the projected trajectory. His task was not that of a gravity-captured lander circling the Moon or the Earth, so lack of control here would be disastrous. His disk-finesse with the craft, however, was noticeable to Wilkes, although not by Chen, who had her back turned toward the command monitor and her own finger disks full of safety checks.

Unlike a ship blasting off from Earth in the early days of spaceflight when a burn lasted only a dozen minutes, this one stayed lit an hour as ton after ton of hypergolic fuel fed the twin Herriff-Millers. With no gravity or atmosphere to create resistance, the belching red-orange flames and dispersing condensation trails vaporized instantaneously. Even so, the continuous explosive reaction grew so bright that it was visible from several colonies in the Belt.

With each passing minute, Fuentes stayed on task, spelled only for a few moments by the commander himself. Chen remained relegated to junior-officer duties. Even as the *Piazzi's* speed increased, the enormous distance to Mars still meant a four-month trip. Ahead lay a long elliptical swoop toward a rendezvous with the planet. There, the shuttle wasn't stopping, only partially orbiting to reorient toward the Moon, her ultimate destination.

"Congratulations, Lieutenant Fuentes," the commander finally complimented after the hour-long burn had emptied the Herriff-Miller tanks down to flammable—and still explosive—vapors. "Was that your first at the helm?"

"Yes, sir." Looking a bit apologetic toward Chen, Fuentes added, "Thanks for the opportunity."

"To everything, there's a first time," the stern officer replied with no kindness or emotion.

In zero-g Mei-Ling and Julio floated together. His quarters were confined, but duct tape over the cam lens kept them private.

Music mingling with crashing ocean waves drifted in the air just as they did. Soft light lit their weightless bodies; their skin glowed in a reproduced full moon, a virtual of the historic one, not a cloudy Marsco Moon.

Julio believed in the pith of his being—a place no one else had ever touched—that through their love, they would change the Marsco world for the better. Transform it, reformat it into what it claimed to be already. Together they would remake their future Marsco into a humane set of disks guiding the world.

That first night together, they floated, bumped, giggled like children. Not for mere sensation; that was easy enough for every careful associate. Their confident candor made their initial love-making more than just a mechanical act. They both sensed a commitment, an opening up to another, an immediate depth, an unimaginable certitude. *This is real,* Mei-Ling reassured herself, *something deep and lasting even in its delirious suddenness.*

Pushing off a bulkhead like a swimmer, Julio came up behind her. Her body was silken. He wrapped her in his strong arms, where she belonged.

The newness, the renewal, Mei-Ling thought enraptured, *of us and of our Marsco.*

They floated apart but embraced a moment later, forming a weightless union.

"This won't work," she whispered.

"What," Julio asked, politely, "aren't you—"

"It's okay; I'm BC compliant. But I need some gravity." They couldn't keep from laughing.

He reached over and twitched the AG to normal. As the increasing pull of artificial-g brought them gently to his cot, she whispered eagerly, "That's not enough."

"You're right," he grinned, complying with a more satisfying 1.1225-g setting.

This isn't just about us, Mei-Ling insisted, *it's about re-creating Marsco, about giving it a new birth through us.* Neither had ever felt such boundless faith in another associate before.

Exhausted, Mei-Ling softly breathed in his ear, "You're what love's supposed to be."

Neither wanted to appear eager for more of the other, as though too much would suggest shallow feelings. Julio kissed her check gently. Their lips met lightly, then firmly. Passion rekindled until duty brought them back to the flight deck ninety minutes later.

After Chen's final pre-hiber watch, Wilkes hosted dinner for his crew, the only ones awake on the *Piazzi*. The festivities, a simple meal of space-packed Spam and camaraderie, celebrated the approaching PNR now that final burn was successful.

The commander unexpectedly turned their discussion to the Continental Wars. "Nearly thirty years ago now, as the Powers tried to rein Marsco in," he emphatically stated, "Seattle persuaded the PRIMS to form an alliance." His gray eyes swept the cramped table as a victorious general surveys the vanquished. "Their coalition made for an unprecedented war."

One that still leaves a lot of unanswered questions, thought Maissey, *even this long after the fighting.*

It wasn't easy. And yet at Walter Miller's suggestion, whom he'd met two years before at the dissident's grange, the iceman had managed to garner info about those times. He didn't share his knowledge immediately, but during his months of nocturnal Net searches, he found many old links made active by Ludds, he assumed. Other pages suddenly appeared as links only to be ruthlessly suppressed by IOSS; the cyber vigilance of Internal OS Security was relentless.

Maissey's furtive excursions found cyber docs that clearly Marsco hadn't vetted. One site was an assortment of fragmentary manuscripts, wiki-posts, blogs, each giving a personal history and description of the conflagration, the outbreaks of disease, the Vanovara-wrought winter, the planetary butchery during the late '60s.

He was certain that Miller had actually posted this collection.

As the iceman thought of his discoveries, the commander leapt into his topic. "The Continental Powers were suddenly fighting against what enemy?" he asked rhetorically. "Part of their very own tech and computer networks, the vast telecom infrastructure that every advanced society needs."

He paused only a moment; his glare didn't invite a collegial response.

"And how do you make this essential part of yourself your enemy?" he asked excitedly. "How do you rid a country of its cyber and technical self—its vibrant self—without destroying the advanced country you wish to liberate?"

His burning questions hung in the air.

"And how do you fight a modern war when the first attack's a cyber strike that renders your entire C-and-C network inoperable?" His face flashed with furious anger, as though his own red command and control disk was giving him excruciating pain. "Com goes down. Drone Lightnings fail to respond. Satellite surveillance grows blank."

Fuentes commented softly, with a veteran's shared experience: different war, same anguish. "You speak from firsthand knowledge."

"You three were all children then. I was there," the CO stated, tapping his red disk on the table. "How do you control weapons when Marsco wrestled away their command configurations before the first real shot was fired? Marsco knew what it was doing; it planned and waited, waited and planned. It had spies and moles. It wrote the basic language and hid links to its own HQ; it left Trojans, trapdoors, dormant command protocols. Its fingerdisks were in the offing just waiting to control our networks. Twenty-first century forces suddenly reduced to fighting as though in the early twentieth. A digitally brilliant opening sortie, a bold coup de main brought on by a few twitches."

Chen shifted nervously in her seat, not from squeamishness, but because associates didn't talk this way, anywhere, anytime.

"Of course, an opening strike invites retaliation. Marsco was caught off guard by the ferociousness of the Continental's return e-strikes. And so, in that interconnected, seamless e-world, the system destruction ran rampant. In a matter of minutes, most of the cyber world crashed. No firewall, no virus scan could stop *that.*"

"Even today," Maissey stated with rare self-assurance among ranking officers, "computers periodically stumble onto destructive programs."

"Yes, they've stayed dormant for years," Wilkes concurred, "waiting for the right conditions to replicate."

"Although," Fuentes cautioned, "there's a chance that a spreading virus *is* a recent phenomenon initiated by some violent Ludd faction; thus Security—"

A man speaking from experience, Chen thought, surprised he let such a point slip out.

"Additionally, on the real battlefields," the commander pronounced as though inebriated by this knowledge, "Marsco deployed hordes of PRIMS—abandoned human castoffs—but now well-armed and well-led. What then of the C-Powers that'd oppressed them for years?"

Wilkes continued on, aiming venom at the conduct of the combatants. "PRIMS inexplicably were in league with the most sophisticated cadre in the world. How did the most electronically advanced become the champions of such disenfranchised human waste?" The commander posed his idea rhetorically. "And how could the Powers conceivably subdue this enraged rabble?" The crew dared not answer his searing questions.

As though reading their collective minds, the commander answered bluntly. "Like all wars, these were a bollixed cock-up—a bloody shambles."

"God-awful debacle," remarked Chen, too pointedly for an associate, remembering her childhood near one of the worst theaters of war.

"And thus the resulting horror and destruction we inherited," Fuentes added.

Wilkes, paying no attention to them, launched another wave. "As soon as the serious belligerence ceased, the plagues reemerged." It was, the crew knew, the fourth time in the carnage-ridden century that epidemics swept the globe. Like the rise of Marsco itself, the outbreaks were defining elements of their century.

The only one of sid background, Maissey remembered this era of unprecedented mass death as virulent diseases ravaged a weakened world.

"Neo-Con," the commander went on, "wasn't the most contagious illness sweeping the world, even though it sickened PRIMS the most. Other pandemics, like Ebola and hantaviruses, brought agonizing death within a matter of hours. Penicillin-resistant strains of streptococcus and anthrax emerged."

Riveted by the commander's frank revelations, Chen nonetheless thought, *He shouldn't go on. He shouldn't go on.*

"Antibiotics," Wilkes noted firmly, "are still virtually useless."

He seems, Chen felt, *to be blaming Marsco.*

"Immediately after the C-Wars," the CO insisted, "PRIMS *refused* Marsco's aid."

"Even with all those diseases pillaging their zones," Maissey unwisely added. "Or, at least, that's Marsco's official history of the times."

"Quite so," returned Wilkes. "But PRIMS never fully understood Marsco from the start." Abruptly, he defended Marsco. "And so, resurgent plagues ran rampant everywhere PRIM masses assembled, in every corner of the world. Some diseases even reached its lunar and Martian colonies. How this occurred has never been understood fully, considering all its hygiene consciousness." He motioned to his left arm with its test blotch as evidence.

Brazenly, Maissey interjected. "Or was it the other way around? Persistent rumors still circulate that these outbreaks originated when human anatomy was exposed to Martian microbes, when crops grown in domes fed the burgeoning colonies on Mars."

Chen and Fuentes first looked at each other, then at the lowly iceman. "Utter nonsense," the former Security officer retorted.

Wilkes silenced him by placing a hand on the flier's forearm. His disks tingled on the flesh.

Taking a breath, Maissey continued. "Marsco—so the whispers go—brought the plagues to Earth years *before* the C-Wars. Many disgruntled Luddites place the blame on Walter Miller's wife, Bethany Palmer. Certainly Miller denies these allegations, but info-terrorists still targeted her reputation."

"And these rumor mongers—can't they actually be Ludd operatives?" Fuentes used Maissey's own argument against him.

The iceman shrugged. "I'm not sure. We are in a world where truth is dead."

"That's *not* Marsco's fault," Chen shot back. "Besides, it brought stability to the world when none existed! It deserves credit for *that!*"

The hiberman shrugged her off with a hint of insubordination, rolling back into his original argument. "I know this much for sure, that the conflict gave many opportunistic diseases a chance to spread rapidly, widely." He spoke with a degree of credibility. Icemen were highly trained in a quasi-medical field.

The petty officer knew he should hide his clandestine searches of unauthorized writings posted on the Net; nonetheless, he recklessly leapt into his topic with the same ferocity as Wilkes. "Who knows the real history of those times? Certainly not me, even with all I've gleaned." He knew he shouldn't confide so much, and yet he went on with abandon. "Especially since any postings may not be trustworthy."

"At any rate," the commander stated, trying to make his remarks the focus once more, "the C-Wars were only the half of the holocaust. We can establish that."

The other three around the table nodded assent, remembering the lingering Marsco Winter with its frigid darkness more clearly than the Wars. "By the time PRIMS accepted Marsco's help, their dead numbered beyond counting. The plagues easily took two billion, on top of the three-quarters killed in the fighting itself."

Maissey suspected, based on Miller's assessment, that the numbers were at least a billion-and-a-half light.

Chen sighed with earnest sympathy, "Mind-numbing numbers. Another reason why Marsco stepped in to restore order. It was the only organization left powerful enough to bring stability."

"Yes, yet Marsco perpetuates the unincorporated zones," Wilkes said. "It needs to, considering how ignorant PRIMS are. Their homelands carved up from former countries to keep disease-ridden PRIMS away from disease-free Marsco. All only temporary, of course, but hardly any different than what the Powers initiated. This time, though, truly transitory—or so Marsco insists. A fleeting necessity."

Alone with Mei-Ling their last time before her icing, Julio said, "Wilkes is as hard-assed on PRIMS as I suspected."

She agreed. "He sure arrogantly defends Marsco's excesses." Even if fed on the standard-issue line, they questioned official history. It was an irony lost on neither associate that, although PRIMS helped bring about this world, they were now nearly totally shut out from it.

"An old-timer's attitude we'll change," Julio vowed.

"Yes, all those prewar ideas must go."

"After all, didn't we join Marsco because it alone brought continuity and normalcy to a chaotic world? Peace at last."

"That's the part of Marsco we want to see succeed."

"An ideal more than an entity. A cyber nation. A meta-nationality."

Mei-Ling nodded her agreement. "All committed to a renewed world."

"Rid ourselves of flint-jaws like Wilkes, and Marsco's all the better for it."

"Well, let's not talk of him now." She kissed him deeply. "I'll miss you, Julio, but will dream of waking to find you."

Running his hand over her breasts and down her stomach, he promised to be there when she woke. "We'll talk more then," he assured her.

"Yes, our whole lives together afterward," she whispered. Nestling into his shoulder masked her deep concerns about going under icing.

"You have a secret admirer on board, captain," the hiberman smirked as he readied Chen for hibernation. The *Piazzi* was eighteen hours beyond PRN although months from swing-by around the Red Planet.

As the iceman recounted Ram's comments and questions, the copilot tried to end the conversation with a glib remark, "I don't think he's my type."

"What is your type, sir?" He feigned being ingratiating but failed.

The officer was annoyed with the hiberman's lack of tact. Not only did his question border on insubordination, it struck her that he intended it to be crude. It was unpleasant enough that he bluntly requested information about her pregnancy status, although a pre-hiber necessity and a routine inquiry of every woman. Pregnancy during icing was a potentially serious health threat. She knew that and had acted accordingly.

"Y'know, some called us 'morticians of the living.'"

"Never heard that one," Chen lied coldly.

"Throughout the fleet, we're generally considered disreputable, if not downright deceitful."

"Even though a flight crew, once iced, has to depend upon you totally," noted the flier, trying to gloss over any hard feelings.

"That's right, but as you know, there's been several open-secret scandals involving the hiber service." While prepping this officer, as he had the children, he continued rambling. "The most notorious happened probably fifteen years ago, before Herriff-Millers increased crossing speed."

As his tale unraveled, Maissey savored each insidious detail.

"Hate to speak ill of anyone in our guild, but one particularly depraved iceman substituted an innocent ensign's sleep-pack with subliminal messages about her undying devotion to him. It's cruder than even that," Maissey insisted. "He gave her ceaseless input about her own unrequited cravings for him, gave instructions of the most sordid kind."

When he finally dehibered her after a month of these continuous subconscious messages, Maissey explained, they were the only ones on board stirring. "He did whatever he wanted to her. The most depraved acts imaginable," the *Piazzi's* iceman noted with too much relish. "And this defenseless woman cooperated with everything without any resistance. His sleep-packing had been *that* strong and *that* deeply imbedded into her receptive psyche." He paused, hoping to draw a disdainful response.

"So, what happened?" Chen finally asked, not upset but bored.

"Eventually, the AES dehibered the copilot without the iceman knowing. In his debauchery, he'd forgotten his most routine duties. The auto-emergency system roused a crewmember to investigate. A senior officer found the ensign chained to the iceman's bunk, bruised and bloody, yet offering no signs of protests."

Chen forced herself not to react, showing her iron will.

"Like all the *Plague Ship* tales," Maissey went on, "this story has various endings depending on the narrator. Some say she recovered fully. Others, that she skanked herself, since she never overcame those sleep-pack suggestions."

"That's just great," the captive listener responded with sarcasm that even the thick iceman didn't miss.

"Of the hiberman himself, a more exact history's known. After his court marshal, he was eventually stripped of his finger disks—a forced DRP—and exiled to a particularly harsh zone."

"What punishment is that?" Chen interjected. "Many UZs are the seat of such scabrous brutality anyway. Marsco can't clean up these cesspools overnight. That's merely sending this depraved rat bastard back to his own squalid element." Her response silenced the hiberman.

His disgusting story aside, the copilot had to admit that Maissey didn't seem as hopelessly inadequate as some icemen she had served with. He was fine before, though less crude. He was somewhat bumbling at times—poking a clumsy needle—but never totally incompetent. On their first outbound to Mars, all those he iced had suffered no hibersickness. No one dehibered dead. His HH GAS record was clean. No SWR listed. No trips to a UZ for anything degenerate; she had thoroughly checked. The only peculiar fact in his Security file was that he once visited Dr. Walter Miller at the dissident's Sac City grange. *Unusual furlough to be sure.*

To forestall any more of his coarse stories, Chen asked, "What did you think of our discussion last night?"

"Well," Maissey began, "it was striking for its outspokenness if nothing else."

"Yes, associates generally remain more circumspect."

"In a way, the commander seemed drunk," the iceman insisted.

"Not with booze obviously," she countered.

"No, but with knowledge. Power."

While the petty officer made final hiber adjustments, she asked him almost the way she would have asked Fuentes, "Why did the captain drill me like a plebe? He turned things pretty nasty."

At the end of their conversation on world history, over a chocolate bar for dessert, Wilkes inexplicably had pounced. "Tell me, Chen, the two major duties of a copilot before separation."

Unflustered, she answered with military smartness, the way the commander expected. "One, reconfiguration of ship's components. Two, loading, safety-checking, and securing of all bays and their cargo, sir."

He then spit out several barbed questions about the *Piazzi's* mods and whether she was confident that they were adequately secure and trim. Fuentes tried to move the officer off the topic but to no avail.

Maissey was expected to add nothing; he did as expected. *Doesn't apply to me. Icemen always stay out of a commander-to-subordinate berating.*

In answering her now, Maissey sounded like a trusted friend. "I don't know. Jealousy? After this sleep-pack cycle, you're taking your promotion exam. You'll pass, no prob, and move up the pecking order. Command of your own damn shuttle."

For the first time ever, Maissey sensed she accepted his confidence in her.

"You're gaining on his revered status, after all," he went on. "Some set-in-their-ways brass aren't so keen with women as equals or passing them in rank. Y'know our Wilkes."

"Yes, prewar."

Maissey adjusted an IV shunt in silence. He knew, looks aside, she had hidden steel within, honed to a fine edge. She had to, or else she wouldn't have graduated from Flight. Although no longer a male bastion, its training demanded cadets be physically and mentally fit. And Flight was only obtained after graduating from the Academy. No easy objective. "Whatever crap he dishes out," he stated firmly, "you can handle it."

Chen appreciated his support and smiled; it was the first genuine response she had ever given him.

Maissey was ecstatic.

At 0315 hours on the twelfth day of their flight, throughout the crew mod of the *Piazzi,* a harsh and undulating klaxon blasted.

The wailing woke Maissey from natural sleep as it registered to him that something was seriously wrong.

Moving as quickly as possible under the circumstances, the hiberman flew from his bunk and threw on some clothes.

He smelled nothing unusual—no noxious smoke, no acidic stench of smoldering microchips—a sure sign this was only a drill. *What's the skipper playing at?* The iceman muttered at the bulkhead, "Wilkes's really something to pull this chicken shit!"

Between 1630 and 2100 hours just past, he had been through each mod to check the entire network. He left all systems at optimum.

At 2230, he rechecked Chen, the only crewmember down. He ran a superfluous diagnostic on the monitors next to the clear hood covering the woman. The silky sleep suit gave her body a delicate, airy look. Her graceful breasts hardly moved in retarded breathing. Her lips were parted and ever so slightly pink although her skin was ashen.

These fastidious, lengthy visits, he rationalized, were part of his duty to guarantee the imperishability of the whole crew.

Only a few hours ago, he reasoned to the klaxon's pulse, *everything was within normal parameters, so if this is deep shit, it's not my fault.*

At his console, Maissey assessed the shuttle's ECS. All environmental systems were in their prescribed ranges. No loss of cabin pressure anywhere—that ruled out a collision. "Gravity's constant," he heard himself say. "Speed's as projected, still accelerating." He drummed his finger disks. "If an emergency exists, the computer doesn't know it!"

And still the klaxon pulsed.

Has to be a drill, Maissey thought as he raced toward Chen. With each stride in the .75-g, he was careful not to bounce off the bulkhead conduits above him. During such a crisis situation, procedures dictated that a hiberman rush to the iced crew. Flight deck assessment would indicate whether or not to cease auto-dehiber.

He had only a five-minute window to deactivate the automatic dehiber sequence. Five minutes to make a crucial decision, because coming out of hibernation, even during the best of circumstances, was a dangerous procedure. Plus, it was impossible to abort the sequence mid-course, because a human body couldn't stand the rigors of *beginning*, then *ceasing* deicing. Once commenced, the crewmember had to be brought back to complete and full consciousness. Should there prove to be no crisis, after a few days of awake-time, the whole laborious icing process would have to start over.

"Let the hibering lie," was the motto of icemen. A frozen crew may wake to find everything out-of-hand and lethal. If so, if they were dehibering into a shuttle absent of its life-sustaining environment, *well, better to die in your hiber,* concluded Maissey.

Spurred on by the emergency pulses, the running iceman reached the crew hiber-bay. He knew instantly: *a drill!*

There stood Fuentes and Wilkes, not at their stations in the command mod but waiting for the hiberman. The lieutenant turned off his wrist chronometer with an arrogant smile. He showed the readout to the CO, 8:52.89.

"Nearly nine bloody minutes, Petty Officer Maissey." The commander glared. "Four minutes late. Your work on Chen's gone to waste; she's on irreversible auto-de. You'll have to start all over when she awakes!"

"Sir!"

"Put this man on report," he barked. "And switch off that frigging alarm before it *does* wake the hibering." The flight officers strode past the iceman back to the command mod.

Even lingering over the diaphanous Chen didn't calm the hiberman.

Later that morning Wilkes asked, "Well, which is he? Washout or sex fiend?"

Fuentes confirmed, "Washout." Years before, Maissey had matriculated at the rigorous Academy but hadn't made it through the first year.

"Icemen!" the commander breathed out in frustration. "All of them bludge off the real working crew!"

"And did you see this?" The junior officer held up a small plastic bag containing a kilo of orange powder. "Want to try some?"

The commander looked askance at the suggestion.

"Seriously, it's sweet. It's a dehydrated citrus drink commonly associated with last-century's astronauts."

Wilkes stated bluntly, "You know, I think a shuttle *can* get through deep space *without* a hiberman. Computers auto-scan most protocols. An awake crewmember, *any* awake crewmember's capable of changing a few IVs now and again."

Precedents existed, the lieutenant reminded him, in which accidents in space eliminated a shuttle's hiberman. Those already in hiber-status survived because others competently supervised the remaining duration of sleep. "And this one," Fuentes stated flatly, "he seems mostly to stand over Chen's bunk."

"Or worse. Have you seen his virt rave?"

Fuentes, protective of his real Mei-Ling and angered by the degrading cyber one, tried not to show any feelings. "What else does he do?"

"He skulks about."

The lieutenant secretly regretted embarrassing the petty officer. The flier knew that he was near icing and would be putting himself totally in those disks. "'*Never* piss off an iceman,' Fuentes commented abruptly, "'they'll get back at you one way or another.' Nightmares and migraines induced by an altered sleep-pack. Intestinal infections—they'll stop up your elimination tubes."

Wilkes expected his subordinate to finish, but Fuentes continued. "Polyps. Peritonitis. Sphacelation. A bungled hiber's a retarded hell. Or death—sorry, sir."

Before Fuentes had interrupted him, Wilkes had been intently pouring over an obsolete NB, using a finger mouse thimble to control the unit. Notebooks of this type were for sensitive, highly confidential files. They used a finger mouse, even in the age of ubiquitous finger disks, and—for total security—each thimble was wedded to its unit, just like an old-fashioned, wire-attached mouse. Wilkes removed the rubber cone that fit over his right index finger.

"You know, that iced wallah in Pass Two has a unit something like yours," Fuentes noted. "But from the looks of it, his is newer." He wondered where the CO ever found such an antiquated machine, especially one that seemed in perfect working order; it was like a museum piece. He also wondered, *what did he want to keep so secret? Marsco doesn't condone much personal space and privacy.*

"I noticed," said the commander about the other NB. "Doesn't fit with mining consulting, does it? Makes him too secretive."

"Yes," Fuentes responded. Scuttlebutt around Vesta had it that this mysterious associate was not really a mining engineer but a surveillance operative. A lefter with an exclusive finger mouse notebook only fueled the speculations. He was keeping dozens of concealed files, that much was certain.

"Did I tell you what's in his sleep-pack?" Fuentes asked. "So says Maissey. Daily *Marsco Bulletin* converted to dream sequences and Lao-Tse's *The Art of War.*"

"No mining manuals? Tech updates? Shipping reports? Nothing that a mining consultant would be expected to be sleep-reading?"

"Nothing of the sort."

The colonel abruptly reminded his subordinate, "Don't forget to log an entry about vibrations in Pass Two and Cargo One after separation."

"Yes, sir."

Klaxon blaring, 2335 hours, sixteenth day out.

This time, when Maissey checked his console—*no drill!* A serious threat was imminent. An explosion had detonated in Cargo One, and its forward bulkhead was secured to Pass Two. Any damage to the container module might result in a cascading loss of cabin pressure throughout the remaining enviro-sealed pass mods.

Holy hell, he muttered as he bolted to where Chen and Fuentes lay iced. Unlike four days before, the day of the infamous drill, the cabin atmosphere was hazy with wisps of smoke. Maissey smelled smoldering circuitry.

The commander was waiting. *This is no exercise!* The klaxon wailed on.

Standing beside the iced-down crew, Wilkes ordered, "Let the auto-sequence rouse them! They might be needed!" The pressing crisis was a series of blasts in Cargo One, just beyond Pass Two where five passengers lie iced.

While the two rushed through the first module, another explosion rocked the shuttle. Something in a hold detonated violently. EDRs ignited, separating Cargo One and sending it perpendicular to the ship. The emergency detachment rockets pushed the damaged mod clear before it exploded.

"Holy hell!" Maissey picked himself up from the deck where the concussion hurled him. *What if,* he instantly thought, *what if that powerful blast happed with the mod still attached?* The near-ship explosion sent a shock wave great enough to slam the shuttle out of autopilot and computer-controlled trajectory.

"Shouldn't we send out a Code Black distress?" The hiberman suggested hastily.

"Negative! No conclusive evidence of that!"

How much more conclusive do you want? Maissey thought then started, "But sir—"

The pilot shouted over the iceman, "We may gimbal-lock! We're spiraling so much we might not re-control our tumbling!"

Even though Cargo One had exploded without destroying anything else, it was not well enough away from the shuttle to prevent collateral damage. Shards had punctured the hull of Pass Two, starting several potentially dangerous air leaks.

"Artificial-g is malfunctioning!" shouted Wilkes. "Down to less than half natural grav and falling!"

"Holy hell! Well below green lines!"

Besides pressurization loss, the fear of a burning shard hitting the gigantic fuel tanks in the propulsion units crossed his mind. Enough volatile vapors remained in those tanks to make a massive fireball of the *Piazzi*.

"You save Poindexter! I'll save the children!" Wilkes shouted.

Maissey obeyed without hesitation, even at great personal peril. There were other ways to save them, but this seemed the most expedient.

In this unplanned low-g, the commander and the iceman just might pull the hiber bunks out of Pass Two, safely manhandling them into the next compartment before anything else happened. Pass One's AG could be reactivated quickly and the hibernation process continued in a stable environment without any serious interruptions. To those on ice, these lifesaving movements would seem like a momentary power fluctuation and a fleeting dream.

The two rescuers had no time to spare. Only seconds remained before Pass Two was lost.

"The damaged mod," the commander shouted, "we'll have to jettison it once all human cargo's safe!"

As the iceman stepped toward Poindexter, he had no time to react before another explosion rocked the shuttle.

Anxious to save everyone, Maissey ignored the severity of the blast. Sparks crackled along the vital-signs monitor on the bulkhead.

Still time, the rescuer believed. *Still time! I've still got time!*

In the smoke and haste, he singed his finger disks trying to transfer commands. In the chaos, he failed to notice Wilkes retreating from Pass Two back to Pass One. The commander sealed the airlock behind him.

Another more powerful jolt rocked the shuttle. Pressurization was instantly compromised as a gaping hole, five meters wide, ripped open an exterior bulkhead. The rescue-focused hiberman was sucked into space. In weightless conditions, without a protective EVA suit, the remaining moist air in his lungs instantly exploded into the surrounding vacuum. His blood boiled off in seconds, leaving a barely discernable red-tinged vapor trail.

It took a moment longer for the still-iced Poindexter. Until his Plexiglas hood shattered, it protected him momentarily. But then like the hiberman, his lungs exploded away their last breath as his vital fluids vaporized, dissipating into the murderous void that had invaded the safety of the ship.

Through the viewport, Wilkes verified that the wallah's secretive notebook vanished and with it the cryptic records he had been amassing throughout his mission to the Belt. The commander visually verified that the unit's finger mouse thimble drifted amid debris carried out of the rupture. In the vast eternal blackness, the NB and finger mouse would never be reunited.

On the safe side of the bulkhead, Wilkes waited for his fifth planned explosion. He knew he had time to deactivate his sabotage. It was possible (with disk commands on his wrist remote) to disarm the last device. The next blast would activate the jettison boosters that would propel the module clear of the shuttle.

At least save the children? he thought momentarily, seeing that their pressurized hoods were still precariously holding. All he needed to do was override a few commands, stand in a virtual bay, and electronically control the robotic rescue inside the sabotaged Pass Two. Something Maissey might have safely done had the commander not urged the iceman directly into harm's way.

But why? he reasoned. *A few less wogs the better. If I kill two more, twenty more, what do I care? The Wars killed millions at a stroke.*

He felt the anticipated fifth explosion followed immediately by the expected ignition of EDRs. Pass Two separated from the main configuration of the shuttle. For a second time, reacting to the force of the emergency detachment rockets, the shuttle reeled out of trajectory and close to gimbal-lock. Then the autopilot fired its own correcting bursts of nitrogen from the dozens of nozzles placed around the remaining modules. The vaporous discharges brought the gyrating craft back to its correct flight path. Systems restarted artificial gravity as preprogrammed.

Before the very first explosion, using Maissey's computer, the commander had disengaged the preprogrammed dehiber protocols. No matter what had happened, even had his blasts done more damage than planned, the crew would never have been automatically deiced.

The rest—the wallah, the collateral wogs, that iceman: *the fortunes of war,* he thought as icily as surrounding space.

After the sabotage ran its course, and after the warning klaxon had stopped, the shuttle grew quiet. The *Piazzi* returned to her computer-controlled routine, as normal as any totally hibered-down shuttle.

In Pass One, Wilkes found everyone snug and trim. Stepping into the crew hiber-bay, he exchanged Fuentes's and Chen's sleep-packs for the secret ones he had already burned. As he engaged the last bytes of exec commands, his plans had reached fruition. He had everyone and everything exactly in place to start reshaping the world to his liking.

In the name of Wilkes, Colonel Hawkins sounded a mayday. It took twenty minutes for it to cross the void of space. He calculated the remaining time of Mars rendezvous to be three-and-one-half months. Several days prior, he would jettison the new sleep-packs, destroying the last shred of evidence.

Marsco had had it too easy, too cushy, these past twenty-five years. It put down periods of PRIM unrest. It dealt with cantankerous sids. It tangled with Luddites of various stripes. All mere child's play.

But Marsco would soon discover that Colonel Jarrod Hawkins, leader of three C-Powers attack carriers waiting at their hidden asteroid base, played for keeps.

Marsco had faced nothing like Hawkins and the forces at his command since the first round of the Continental Wars. Today, forty-eight Lightnings armed with thermonuclear weapons were poised for their surprise sortie. Nothing would stop the colonel when, in a single stroke, he decapitated the insidious cancer that dominated the Earth, nuked Marsco back to the vacuum-tube age.

The mythical Lost Fleet had waited long enough.

Colonel Hawkins had reached his point of no return.

NINE

PLAGUE SHIP

(On the asteroid Adams-Leverrier, 2095)

"It's solely an accident that brings this ship to your colony," Carlton Caruthers, the visiting Marsco liaison, assured the Independent colony's administration. Caruthers was an imposingly tall, muscular man. But that and his lefter status didn't hold sway over the six unwavering administrators seated around the conference table.

"This shuttle," Misha Paton, the colony superintendent, slipped on a finger mouse thimble to check his mobile screen, "this VBC *Gagarin*—we have denied, and we will continue to deny her permission to dock—especially if an accident's involved." Not versed in Marsco lore, Paton had no way of knowing how significant this port-of-call visit actually was.

The associate didn't blink. "She has every right to dock here," he fired at first. Then with a conciliatory gulp, he added, "But perhaps I spoke inaccurately. It's merely *coincidence* that brings this ship in to your spaceport."

Eleni Romanidu, the only woman in the conference room, broke in, "And *coincidence* that your ship's coming from the wrong side of the belt?" She tapped her fingernail—she was without disks—on a nicked-up and scored polymer table to emphasize her point. As the colony's legal expert, she kept Adams-Leverrier totally and truly independent from Marsco.

Caruthers glanced about at the half dozen faces with set jaws and determined looks. While his hair and moustache were trimmed and neat, the six Indies had that *Indie*-look. Paton sported a ponytail and a gold earring. Romanidu wore not just glasses but ones with dark lenses. The others looked peculiar as well.

Not one of them sported a single finger disk.

The viewpanel behind the colonists looked in toward the sun; its glare, even at this distance, still made the unnumbered stars and the close-at-hand asteroids impossible to see. But, somewhere out there, an expedition ship steadily approached. And the *Gagarin* was heading in at max, setting a Herriff-Miller speed record.

"Look," the liaison now continued with the expected tone of confrontation, "we don't have to ask permission to dock."

"Yes, yes," Superintendent Paton nodded, "Twelve Thrusters gives Marsco all the authority it needs."

The associate simply smirked. "And I don't need to give you a lecture on the movement of asteroids. Colonies line up differently relative to incoming and outgoing shuttles all the time. It's the nature of planetary orbits. Besides, as you've acknowledged, under Thrusters, ordinary traffic—"

"But," the legal counsel countered, her dark glasses giving away nothing, "the shuttle in question can't in any way be conceived as ordinary traffic. What's it doing out *that* way?" She motioned behind, through the Plexiglas. During the asteroid's rapid rotation, the view right then was outbound, toward endless space beyond the belt.

"Her mission's black." Caruthers dismissed her, hiding the fact that he thought her a shrill harpy standing in Marsco's way.

"I'll say," the legal wonk came back at him, her cynicism toward Marsco not disguised.

The superintendent thought it best to reenter this exchange before too much was said by the head of legal that should be left unsaid. Thimble-twitching his palm screen nervously, he brought up his chief concern. "The Von Braun Center has furnished us with a manifest of the crew but little else about this shuttle."

"As is standard for any docking craft, even Marsco-to-Marsco."

"But, the manifest lists six hibering crewmembers; lists them as—and I quote: 'Under quarantine.'"

"Matter of semantics, Mr. Paton, merely semantics," the associate stated. "You've known me for five years, as long as I've been this colony's liaison. I've helped in every matter possible during this time. We know each other; I hope we trust each other. You know that to Marsco, safety in space is its paramount goal."

The superintendent gave an obligatory nod, but the five other Indies saw that the associate was stalling, looking for a way out. The liaison himself knew this as well. And yet he stammered on, reassuring his hosts that Marsco expected cooperation even though it always respected legal Independents. Finally, mid-paragraph, he remembered the second associate present and immediately shifted his ramble onto him. "And Mr. Steerforth here, he's just in from the VBC on Mars which is home port of this craft. He's come out specifically to meet the *Gagarin.* He'll be most obliging with his answers—all of them forthcoming." The liaison responded with an unconvincing smile.

The visiting hibernation specialist, David Steerforth, looked from inflexible non-associate face to face in no hurry to respond. Much shorter and thinner than the lanky liaison, his looks betrayed no age because he had hibered a great deal. As typical with ice-tech drudges, he looked uneasy with live specimens, preferring to work with those already sleeping deeply. In a crowd of other men, he would easily be overlooked. Nonetheless, he came on with an all-too-familiar associate demeanor. "It's black, as previously stated. Marsco doesn't need your permission to dock, and it refuses your permission to inspect!"

"Is that a threat?" the regulatory specialist, Romanidu, retorted.

"Does it need to threaten?"

"It often does."

Both the superintendent and liaison were a flurry of arms and gestures trying to keep their respective subordinates and this visiting associate from escalating the discussion into open hostilities.

"Please, please," the chief colonist insisted, "you have to understand my point of view. I'm responsible for over 35K residents. And we know of plague ships—historical ones, perhaps mostly mythical, but others real nonetheless." He drew a measured breath, "And we know of the *Piazzi* some six months back."

"Eight to be exact," the recently arrived hiber specialist fired, growing impatient and feeling this was a sniper shot. "But that was the Asteroid Fleet—not Von Braun. In Marsco, two distinct entities."

"I realize that, but—" the legal specialist tried to retort.

"There *is* a vast difference."

"Realize that, too, but—"

"The *Gagarin's* on a scientific mission, the nature of which I cannot disclose. Obviously, every sensor on this asteroid tells you that she's coming in from outside the belt. Can't deny it. But what else's going on within her hull—that's classified."

"But it's within regs that my health team meet every crewmember," the legal expert insisted, "whether they leave the shuttle or not."

"Letting you on board's totally out of the question," Steerforth insisted. "The *Gagarin's* to dock, take on fuel, some supplies. It's been beyond the belt for over three years—"

Sounding more like *a* VBC rep than *the* VBC rep, the Marsco liaison interjected, "You've gotta admire the scientific marvel of *that feat!*"

"—but not all its crew will de-shuttle or deice, so *no,* you may *not* meet them. *Dot!*"

As both an Indie and a colonist, Eleni Romanidu, the head of the Adams-Leverrier's legal staff, was scrupulously cautious.

The confrontation three days earlier hadn't decreased her apprehension. Colonists needed ceaseless watchfulness lest space suck the life from their isolated pocket of frail existence amid this hostile, vacuous environment. On Earth or in space, Indies needed measured restraint rather than complacency when dealing with Marsco or else they would be crushed by its sheer size and might.

Her ancestors were Euros from the center of that continent, a location that always needed to balance the colliding extremes of East and West. Somewhat defeated, Eleni had felt like she was performing that same balancing act twenty-four hours ago when she watched the *Gagarin* glide up to a docking tether extended to greet her.

To read all the data the colony's sensors had amassed on this suspicious ship—Marsco had provided none beyond the troubling and vague manifest—she needed to sit at her work table and twitch her way through screens of data.

To do so, she wore a set of finger mouse thimbles. The system was ancient, but the adamant administration wouldn't let their tech specialists order anything Marsco. "We're Indies, and must act it," the superintendent argued convincingly. "As much as is feasible, we must support those few subsidiaries that have the moxie to stay out of Marsco's sway." A sign of his own stubbornness was the abject lack of finger disks throughout the colony and anything remotely approaching Marsco-standard finger mouse paraphernalia.

Eleni shrugged as she twitched her chip-embedded thimbles. Avoiding Marsco was an honorable but problematic sentiment to live by, especially considering that no one else made computers like it did. She looked at the trio of thimbles she had slipped onto her right hand. It was a wonder she was allowed to use even them.

The choice by these Independents to live free of Marsco rather than knuckle under had more repercussions than computer usage. The black hair framing her face was without luster or style. Bags hung under her eyes, but these were hard to notice because she wore dark glasses—another non-Marsco element—to protect her weakened sight and hide some of her strain. *Our life here is ceaselessly precarious,* she complained bitterly to no one in particular. Marsco on the threat horizon, arduous colony life, all this isolation to create their freedom—she was always just that close to jettisoning her independence for a modicum of an easier existence in some Earth-side Indie subsidiary.

For an hour, she reviewed all the Colony's reports on the mysterious shuttle. Partway through her examination, she needed to level the table she used as a desk, one as scratched as the colony's conference table where the Indies first met the two arrogant associates. She wadded up a piece of paper to slip it under a leg then tested her work station's stability. "Better," she whispered, "better than the bullshit cover story Marsco's manufactured."

Their first intel was spotty. The Adams-Leverrier's deep-space sensors had picked up an unusual bogie more than four months ago. After that, as the phantom came closer, the colony's tracking volume went up, out of self-interest if nothing else. It hit fever pitch three weeks earlier when the craft sent her initial and routine request to dock. Every colony took a plague threat seriously. And this shuttle's fatuous cover story, that she was coming in from Jupiter, only added to their tensions or suspicions. It ameliorated no one's qualms on the colony's admin staff. Not after the hushed-up *Piazzi.*

"Hell, why not claim that she's returning from Mercury!" she snickered.

Thimble-twitching through several reports, knowing she had already lost the first pawn in her opening chess match with Marsco, she mentally fumed, *Something isn't right! And that damn ship's tied to us right now!* Nonetheless, she swore she would gain a better grasp of the facts about the imposing shuttle.

Rising from her desk, Eleni stood at a viewport bubble where she watched the tethered brute.

Adams-Leverrier spun so quickly that dim sunlight hit the ship, passed it into shadow, and then once more into light four times an hour. The sunlight cycle created a creeping shadow along the entire ship's massive superstructure.

The craft was all wrong; even someone whose eyes were weakened by screens of regulatory minutia recognized that. The VBC ship had four propulsion units, all standard Herriff-Millers, but *four* thrusters, not the typical pair. And to supply the quartet of engine bells, she boasted extra fuel tanks plus extended crew mods. An extraordinary mule! A shuttle on steroids, dreamed up in the murky depths of the *Valles Marineris.* And anything anomalous, anything out of the norm, anything unexpected—and anything coming from Marsco—that was too much for any Indie.

"She's almost frightening," the colonist mumbled, knowing full well it was the mystery within the shuttle that was most frightening.

"I didn't know anything frightened you," someone whispered behind her.

She knew the voice before catching a man's reflection in the viewport. She didn't turn but slipped off her dark glasses.

"Zale, what if *plague* is?" She shrugged at the menace presently shrouded in shadow for the next several minutes. "This colony's been free of Neo-Con for its entirety, since before the Wars."

"You're getting panicky over the *Piazzi* cock-up." The man looked mixed-African. An adoption during the AIDS-ravaging times had brought one of his ancestors north from near the equator to a Central Continental Power earlier in the century. His looks might betray a mixed ancestry, but his speech and comportment were exclusively Euro. He spoke without a discernable accent. He stood behind her, gently resting his hands on her shoulders, and felt her relax into him without looking him in the face. After a dozen years together, his gesture was still cherished.

"Marsco gives me plenty of reasons—cover-ups, shifting regs, wallahs showing up, throwing their weight around."

"Twelve Thrusters?"

"That goes without saying!"

"And the *Piazzi.*"

"Yes, especially her, dammit!"

"But today, you got permission—"

"Finally!"

"—for the main thing we need. You'll go aboard with Anora, you'll see all's A-OK. That'll be the end of it."

"I'm not so sure it will be," Eleni replied, leaning back into the strength of her husband. "Will you come too?"

He laughed gently at one of her seemingly absurd suggestions he knew so well. "Bringing the colony's health officer, I'm sure Marsco'll buy. But why should an asteroid geologist come aboard?"

"Show of force, bringing our head of mining ops. Besides, I want your muscle."

"Don't go paranoid on me, Eleni. And more to the point, how do we justify a miner boarding them?"

"We want to verify they aren't illegally harvesting in this quadrant. We have a license from Marsco, a monopoly around here."

"Elli," Zale laughed at her predictable logic, "Elli, Elli, your legalistic mind."

"It's hiding something." She drew an irritated breath. "All their bullshit about Jupiter! *Jupiter!* Like it's just fuckin' next door." She pointed into the never-never just outside the Plexiglas for emphasis.

With the present colony orientation, Jupiter was bright enough to be the only object visible against the blackness, an orange ball not obliterated in the reflected station lights.

"The *Gagarin* ventured beyond and back into the belt—but for a reason. Hardly to go to damn Jupiter—no matter what the MAS or the VBC says. Why go there? Everything *there* is *here.* No, Marsco must be hiding something on that shuttle."

"No shit!" He feigned amazement at her bald-faced assertion. "It's always hiding something."

"I know, but I don't like it hiding that something while tethered to us."

"But what it has hidden isn't important so long as it isn't contagious. And Anora will know that by 1430 hours today." Turning her, he looked directly into her dark, bloodshot eyes. "We'll know. And I'm sure we're safe. But, yes, I'll go with, if that'll help."

"So, we've worked out this sort of compromise," David Steerforth explained to the hibernation specialist who had been on the expedition ship.

At this point in his career, Lieutenant Anthony "Zot" Grizotti of the *Gagarin* knew official bumf when confronted with it. Paton, the chief administrator from the Adams colony, Steerforth from the VBC. It made no difference. Both admins were generating self-importance, the iceman suspected. Although, he secretly admitted, he would believe Paton more than Steerforth any day.

Side by side the two made an odd pair. The VBC researcher stood shorter than the *Gagarin* iceman by more than a dozen centimeters. His frame was thin, lacking any muscle tone. Besides being taller, Zot seemed alert, engaged with his surroundings, attentive. His brown eyes were quick to focus and show immediate comprehension of any situation. His trimmed beard had a few gray strands as natural aging ran its course. He had grown it to full regulation size, which Steerforth, even at his age, couldn't manage.

Standing there silently, the visitor secretly glanced at his fellow iceman. He had dark southern Euro features and a sense of confidence that the visitor lacked. Steerforth envied Zot for his easygoing manner, unless working. Then, he was intense. It wasn't just his looks but his openness that the other man envied. People always liked Grizotti, even when he seemed to stand apart from the rest.

Although much older, Steerforth eagerly stretched his middle age out by hibering at every chance, his latest being the four-month crossing from Mars to the belt. Zot, on the other hand, had hibered reluctantly for short snatches during the years he had been on board the *Gagarin*. Although the flight crew and all members of the science team had iced in relays across the void, Zot stayed awake as long as necessary to keep his experiment stable and safe. As a science team member, Zot nevertheless helped out all he could. When the two flight crew icemen went under for six months at a stretch (at Zot's hands after the outward-bound ship left the belt nearly three and a half years ago) he made sure the hibering shuttle crew and his own cryo-frozen volunteers were all well tended.

"Do we know anything of their assessment team?" Zot asked at last.

As dangerous as trekking to Jupiter was, the hiberman was more concerned about this inspection. He wanted to know his foe—or friend—well before either approached. In the end, he never fully trusted Steerforth, but whatever info he shared on the colonists might prove helpful.

"Not much." Steerforth had gleaned from the Marsco liaison that the whole colony was mostly Euro with a stubborn streak of autonomy although nothing approaching Ludd beliefs. "Unusual sort of place, however. Some religious connection or another, or so Caruthers says. They're all thick-necked plus damned resilient."

"Have to be out here."

"Records acknowledge only a dozen or so residents have gone missing in the past five years—good retention, all things considered—living out next to nowhere."

"Where do they go when they leave?"

"How do you mean?"

"Do these fleeing Indies end up in Security? Does it seem like they can't wait to leave this place behind at any cost, thus they whore themselves in Security as legionnaires?"

"No, seems that most former colonists leave to join Earth-side sids." The specialist from Von Braun paused then asked pointedly, "By the way—why are you here?"

"Ask our fearless commander; she'll tell you." The hiberman, like most in his guild, had little love for shuttle pilots. "Has something to do with the science team not having gathered all Marsco HQ wanted at the Trojans." These asteroids, trailing the gigantic planet on an identical orbital plane, were the last locale explored by the *Gagarin.*

"*Marsco* HQ? Not Herriff and the VBC?" Like this colony, Herriff and his Von Braun Center on Mars enjoyed a large measure of autonomy from Marsco's Seattle-based general headquarters.

"Affirmative. Seattle stuck its head into our program."

"So, Seattle's pulling the Center's tail? Herriff's not liking that. But that delayed your Jovan egression?"

"Some balls-up like that. Plus crew incompetence."

"Incompetence? You are all hand-picked!"

"Well, all that and then Sparks sends the same sci-file twice. Put Seattle into a tizzy. We spent a week just asking ourselves what the hell was going on. By the time the flyboys and girls sorted it all out enough to satisfy the Seattle wallahs, we egressed ten days later than we should. Thus, we didn't align well with any belt colony—any Marsco colony."

He paused to look down at the asteroid, scores of its domes lit against the ashen, pocked surface. It was a large settlement in a relatively colony-free sector of the belt. "Adams had been a friendly place for years, I understand," the *Gagarin* iceman added at last.

"Yeah, the liaison reported that after each of his semiannual visits here." Steerforth joined his subordinate at the viewport.

"What's he like?"

"The usual ineffective drone: knows nothing but seems to know even less than that! Itinerant. He liaises with six or eight colonies but lives on Ceres—that's the largest Marsco colony near here although it is really at quite a distance at present. His wife and kids are there, and he has three or four babes on other colonies. None here."

Only Steerforth, Zot thought, *would concern himself with counting another man's women.*

After watching a slice of dim sunlight reflect off the surface domes, Steerforth confided, "Yes, friendly here once, well, until the *Piazzi.* From what I can gather—rumors at the VBC and grumblings here—that incident changed everything on several colonies."

Zot stated as dryly as possible, "What? Are sids and Indies beginning to doubt Big Red?"

"Cynicism doesn't help the situation, Anthony." Not knowing Zot well at all, Steerforth often used Grizotti's first name; to those who knew him, he was always Zot, just Zot.

"What did happen? Any idea?"

"Nothing official. Accident of some sort. There's to be an inquest. Or yet a second, or a third, or a continuing one, or God knows what else."

"Some butt's in it now. But, what did happen?" Zot asked insistently.

"Ask me about Von Braun and icing; no one will tell me squat even if they knew."

"C'mon, explosions on board shuttles just don't happen."

"Are you suggesting Ludds?"

"Or incredibly, poorly trained crews." Zot paused then ventured, "I knew someone on board."

"Know her well?"

"Him. No, just a friend. Classmate from my hiber-tech days. He was the iceman sucked into space—so far as we know."

"Yeah, we really don't know." Had Steerforth been a closer coworker, he would have offered his sympathy but didn't. "Look, it's 1100. Give me your prelim report. They'll be here at 1430."

As much as he dreaded this exchange, the hands-on *Gagarin* researcher had everything ready. At a small conference table, he had two screens booted with identical material, a précis of his work. It was an unflattering account of the methodology that initially placed six volunteers in cryogenic stasis, a system wholly unlike routine hibernation. And the person who had so thoroughly botched that primary workup was waiting to hear Zot's report.

When Grizotti initially came aboard the *Gagarin*, then in Mars orbit, the deep-iced guinea pigs had been in experimental cryo for half a year. Steerforth was quick to shift their responsibility over to Zot, to readily commit the subjects to his subordinate's finger disks, and to hastily de-shuttle on the last lander back to the planet's surface. At the start of the outward four-month crossing to the belt, the iceman needed to redo every aspect of the computer-assisted controls and monitors while still keeping everyone alive Steerforth had already frozen.

For his part, the VBC researcher had essentially copied Continental specs to freeze them but had dreamed up his own system for keeping them safe. Zot had to revise that system—in process—without endangering the frozen volunteers any more than they were and without ending the experiment prematurely by bringing them out of deep ice.

Grizotti was too kind to say outright, *I saved your ass, David,* so he spoke in generalities about the salvaged system, stressing more *his* alterations, *his* adjustments, *his* tweaks, as though he had added onto a working system, not redesigned an altogether failed one.

"All six were in yellow when I got them. I had them stable and safe within ten days."

"Not an easy task," Steerforth stated without emotion, even though his FD prints were all over those dysfunctional and bollixed fundamental protocols.

"They were all A-OK after eight weeks and are continuing so indefinitely."

The concept originator readily saw that Zot had implemented a wholly new system under the most difficult of conditions, life and death conditions. But after the report's conclusions, Steerforth played his part well and thanked the real designer for his forty-three months of ceaseless monitoring. "Excellent reconditioning of existing systems," he stated more than once.

Zot modestly thanked him for the acknowledgement. "Everyone's green-lining at present. They've been that way for the past forty-two months, one week."

"Outstanding! Plus their six months before—so well beyond four years total. Y'know, all six have agreed to stay under even after returning to the Center."

"We can then expect at least five years without problems—ten times hiber's current max."

"I've always maintained that twenty years is possible."

"If twenty, then fifty, one hundred. They're in stasis, after all, not hibernation. Just compare their body temps and vitals to green-lined hiber stats. And once safely in this stasis, eternity's the limit." Zot bit his tongue. *If a hundred, why not two or three? Post-solar is possible. Certainly not in this end-of-her-limits research ship but in some other spaceship that can be automated to go beyond Pluto and then safely away.*

But where?

After talking with the ten members of the flight crew complement and the twenty of the science research team, the Indie inspectors, accompanied by Caruthers, made their way aft to the hiber-station where they found both Steerforth and Grizotti in full uniform waiting for them.

The first thought that ran through Zot's mind was that the physician had an air about her like Tessa's. It was only in her deliberate and energetic manners, not her looks. Her blond hair was longer, fixed into a practical, non-ornamental braid that was curled up at the back of her head. Plus she looked strained from the rigors of life on an asteroid. Nonetheless, Tessa crossed Zot's mind until he mentally shook his head to clear himself of her memory.

Next to this no-nonsense inspector was an older woman with black bags under her anxious eyes, eyes partially hidden by dark glasses.

With them were two men, the superintendent and one other man obviously attached to the legal side of the inspection pair. He stood silently by, observing and noting everything without responding. Their names betrayed little: Zale and Eleni Romanidu, Misha Paton, and Anora Hauser.

The *Gagarin* cryo researcher made no attempt to garner meaning from names, races, and backgrounds. This was a postwar world, a Marsco world; all had been mixed, rearranged, sorted by techno-prowess. Or by choice to get as far away from Marsco as possible.

This sifting began with Divestiture and continued to this day. Only *associate, sid,* and *PRIM* remained as viable and discrete categories.

Unless you count these few Indies and the likes of Walter Miller as a fourth column. Once more, Zot mentally shook his head; he wasn't going anywhere near Tessa by thinking about her father.

Introductions over, the Indies gravitated to Zot's workstation in the midsection of the third personnel mod.

Usually, when a pair like these women entered to check up on logs and reports, one played soft, the other hard. This time, however, both came in as polished and resolute as asteroid nickel. The doctor asked pointed questions about the six crewmembers in medical isolation, while the other scrutinized the fragmentary records given to her. Believing their home colony in peril, they wanted to make sure every conceivable risk was avoided.

Through a bulkhead behind consoles and banks of monitors, the cryo-bay was closed off, its hatch sealed. Steerforth was determined to keep anyone from even so much as seeing the tech layout of his experimental system. Even so, it took only a moment and the doctor's sharp eye to raise concerns.

"You've given med charts for those six in hiber," Hauser stated with an accusatory voice. She motioned toward the locked-down bulkhead, "but they go back only four months." She addressed her question to Zot because he appeared to be the most honest of the three associates.

"And the problem is?" Steerforth interjected. He had been fussing around, keeping the inspectors from probing too deeply about his protocols.

"Your info doesn't match your hiber-logs," replied the legalistic Romanidu.

"And," the doctor interjected still to Zot, "just look at these readings—heart rate, body temp, whatever you select—your 'iced' crew are all *dead!*"

Defensively, the *Gagarin* iceman pulled up another screen. "Here's their respiration. They're very much alive, as you can see." He briskly pointed to a sine wave graphic that demonstrated their breathing rates as retarded but with verifiable patterns. A second screen showed the oxygen content of their slowly pulsing blood. "I'm not housing cadavers in there."

The doctor had never seen such hiber signs before. "You call *hibernation* 'icing,' but this really seems to be freezing someone," she commented in an unguarded outburst.

Neither Grizotti nor Steerforth felt obligated to respond.

"More to the point, Superintendent Paton," the liaison moved this confrontation back to its original purpose, "after examining for signs of Neo-Con, your med investigator here finds no evidence of plague, am I not correct?"

The accompanying physician nodded, still with an eye on Zot, an eye clearly pleased with his frank demeanor and kindness.

The inspection team murmured assent and prepared to leave when Zale, who had been a brooding presence thus far, brought out his own data file with a self-important flourish. "I haven't seen the records of your asteroid harvest. Where are those records?"

The two hibernation researchers were stunned by the question. "Why ask *us* that," Steerforth stammered. "Do I look like a sid astro-miner?"

Ignoring the slam, Zale stayed revved up, gunning for them. "The ship must have records." This charade covered his being on the inspection team, and it gave the two women more time to survey the hiber terminals.

Another aspect of this ship to distrust, Eleni noted, *this mega-bay. It's five, six times larger than it needs to be. Nothing makes sense here!* She didn't need to be a hiber-techie to observe that this workstation was beyond anything approaching normal. For starters its instrumentation was at least one hundred times larger than any standard system needed.

"Those records?" Zale asked the icemen again.

Even though flustered, Caruthers managed to evade the real issue. He was a minor official caught in a major situation well over his head. The VBC hadn't expected this trouble, or Herriff would have sent someone besides this inept Steerforth. The liaison drew a forceful breath. "These two are mere icemen—one wasn't even a member of the crew—why ask them?"

"Why not?"

"They know nothing of asteroid harvesting—*alleged* harvesting." He held up a disk-full hand, but that gesture held little sway with such Indies. "Besides *none* has taken place, I can assure you!"

"I don't buy that for a nano," the colonist spit his answer. "Why else is a ship going *outside* the belt and then looping back in? What else but for secretly harvesting our allotment and covering your tracks while doing such an odd loop?"

"These allegations are baseless, without substance," the liaison retorted.

The three associates glanced around at their Indie visitors. They then shared a mental epiphany: *they don't believe the* Gagarin *has been to Jupiter!*

Distrustful bastards, Grizotti thought. "What have we to hide? We've been on a scientific expedition." So as not to compound his statement with a direct lie, he added vaguely, "beyond the belt!"

Caruthers finally put his finger disks down. "Inspection's over. You see there's nothing for you to worry about or bother with, health-wise. As you've noted, you find no evidence of any disease present. And so now I really must insist: you're interfering with Marsco shuttle traffic! You've had your look-about, so please go. *Now!*"

Something was going on here, Romanidu knew; its nature she could only just imagine. Reflecting further, the Indie felt stiffening Marsco resolve. Knowing there was more here than met her eye but also convinced that the shuttle was truly plague-free, she concluded it was time to back off.

A week later when clear of the asteroid belt, the *Gagarin* headed toward Mars. With the hypergolic fuel taken on at Adams-Leverrier flaming through the quad engine bells, the expedition ship gathered speed for her last homeward leg.

"That extra pair will kick us along nicely," Steerforth commented to Zot as the latter prepared him for hibernation.

"You sure you want this? We'll be in Mars orbit in a little over three months."

"Three months of total blackness? What in solar for?"

Zot scoffed at the suggestion rather than reply. He had used his years beyond the belt to explore as best he could. He had augmented the ship's dish antenna for an enhanced scope to look deeply into space—for the pure science of it, something Marsco wasn't fond of lately. Even with that small-scale instrument, he had been able to gather files of substantial new data and gophered much more in cobweb sites long neglected by other associates. The whole universe beyond-solar waited for disks to explore it, yet it remained as unexamined as the far side of the moon in the middle of the last century.

"Let me ask you something else," Steerforth began, breaking the silence.

The hiberman nodded without speaking.

"Any good ass on board?"

The busy iceman ignored his colleague.

"C'mon, either it was sensational or you got zilch."

"How Marsco—so binary."

"Look—why d'you take this mother-of-all-sorties anyway? To become a monk? Or for all those Marsco Units? Cha-ching!"

"Who said I was a monk?"

"Oh-ho!" Steerforth stressed by drawing out the comment, "mending a broken heart, then. Hey, best way for that—" he gestured rhythmically and crudely. "It's like I've always said, 'there's always someone else to poke just down the hall.'"

Looking at the balding, short, unremarkable—and incompetent—middle-aged man, Zot tried not to laugh. "Chicks must cream in their thongs at just the mere thought of you."

Missing the intent, Steerforth gave a knowing wink. "Bingo! Bingo-bingo!"

Zot worked on in silence then asked, "Tell me something. What's this all for? I mean, this cryo? It's well beyond anything needed at present. And from what I've seen of Jupiter—why return? More than ninety-five percent of the belt asteroids aren't mined or inhabited. Marsco has no need—indeed, no desire—to go beyond the belt."

"Yeah, this expedition was the closest it's come to pure science in years."

"I guess you could say that."

"That's loaded—what the hell do you mean?"

"Pure science? We orbited Jupiter. Examined several of its moons. We went to the trailing Trojan asteroids. But last century's astronomers watching the Shoemaker-Levy comet collide with the surface learned more of Jupiter than we did. We looked for potential colony locales, for mining-worthy asteroids and moons. We looked for water-ice and frozen methane."

"And that's not science?"

"Not when you're really only looking for future mining sites."

Steerforth snidely countered, "Idealist."

"And you're *the realist?*"

"Damn straight." The older man's bloodshot eyes bore into Zot's brown. "Listen," he insisted, "learn this! You're an associate. The world's ours for the taking. We *can* have it all! Do whatever the hell we want. 'Just do it!' Quit all this sniveling about the past and about the future—live it up today! What did they say once, 'Seize the day'?"

"They were Romans, and they said it *carpe diem.* And their empire fell with quite a large bang, as history reports it."

"Well, better grab yours before—" He gave a gentle laugh, partly to signal his willingness to switch topics and partly out of his reluctant fondness for Grizotti. "Look, we didn't create this world. All we did was inherit it."

Zot wasn't answerable to Steerforth. And he knew in an hour the irritating associate would be out of his hair for three months.

Without comment, he picked up where he left off and continued prepping the VBC researcher.

"Hey," Steerforth grinned, "no hard feelings." He held out his hand, the gesture of shaking hands one not often shared in the Marsco world. The senior iceman knew enough never to tick off someone about to put you under. He would risk the FD-to-FD shock to avoid a horrid hiber. "Look, you asked *sort of,* so I'll tell you *sort of,*" he finally confided. "Off the record, nothing official." He paused, shrugged, and went on. "I don't know what ol' Herriff's got planned. Martin and I aren't exactly buds, if you catch? But I hear lots of rumors: a space ship—"

"Well, duh!"

"I mean one designed specifically for *deep* space."

"So," Zot concluded, "unlike the *Gagarin.*"

"Exactly."

Zot gave a shrug and looked out a viewport. "She really is just standard pieces added on to make an old-fashioned shuttle into an enhanced platform. Nothing new or special at all. Extra fuel tanks, another pair of engines. But more to the point, all this cryo-crap isn't just to make us obsolete?" They both laughed.

"No, far from it. We'll still be needed. And Herriff's aiming for a new engine concept."

"New design? How?"

"Like I know the specs? I only heard things, y'see, only heard them. I never saw anything, not even a single peep at the schematics or concept models. Something propelled by ions, not chemicals. And then the boss, Doc Herriff, he just says one day out of the dusty red Martian sky, 'David, push on with those cryo plans, stat!' Like I can pull such designs out of the air."

"Or out of a memory bank, a Continental memory bank."

"Look, it's all legit research, right? I checked their results and tests against mine, their data against my trials."

"Got me there."

"So, anyway, all I can confirm is that I *heard* that something's going down. But Christ, it'll be years, I tell you. I can see what's under construction in the orbiting docks—and there's nothing that seems remotely like it can do the impossible."

"Like house a crew in deep hiber for fifty, one-hundred years."

"One-fifty, two—I tell you, I've designed a system close to that."

"Well, *we* have designed."

Steerforth winked. "Got me there."

Grizotti had the IV tubes ready to start bringing the necessary fluids to keep the man safely asleep for months, a system far simpler and far less complicated than the future-oriented cryogenic stasis in the farther bay.

Steerforth reached out and stopped him. "One last point, Anthony. Think about this one, for Christ's sake. You'll either go back to the MAS Fleet or you'll stay with us at the VBC—I'd love to have you! Either way—not to Security, right? Y'know how many Academy grads end up as officers in the S & H mucking around patrolling hot zones?"

Zot shook his head.

"Lots, over forty percent this last grad year—well over. All that space-based bumf about shuttles and egress-my-ass those cadets had to learn and then, a few weeks past receiving their commissions, they're in urban gray with an Enfield and squads of troopers in tow."

"Something change while we were post-belt?"

"Not that on Mars I'd hear any more than you'd hear on board. But, rumors again, Anthony, rumors that something just ain't right on Earth. Some zones, even some run-down subsidiaries, they're all becoming IED-City. Christ, everyone carries an Enfield."

"Everyone?"

"Every associate. But y'know what I mean. It's hot down there on Old Blue these days, way hot, way too hot."

"'Needs no ghost.'"

"I know, I know, 'rotten in Denmark.' But seriously, watch your mouth, Anthony, Marsco-wise. It knows how to shut up those that open their yapper too much." He chomped his three times for emphasis.

"Yeah," Zot answered, "but don't worry. I'll be too busy saluting to complain."

"Be careful it's not you returning a salute from all your new troopers. When on patrol, you're too busy to complain, so CYA, my friend, CYA." Steerforth grinned one last time at his little witticism. "Y'know, you are as good as a monk, hearing my confession."

"Shall I give you a penance?"

"Not on your life! But I'll give you some free advice. Deice that blond in the fifth bay, the titty-luscious babe. If she's not space-crazed, she'll be willing. Types like her are always hornier than rabbits after hiber."

"The words of a master."

The senior specialist, winking before he drifted into hibernation, thought Grizotti's last remark was serious.

Most of the flight and science crews on the *Gagarin* went under hiber soon after the solitary passenger, Steerforth. The ship's own specialists took over after belt egression, leaving Zot to tend his six in cryo and work on his own scientific projects as time permitted. As promised, he supervised Steerforth personally, the VBC specialist not trusting anyone else.

At the cryogenic workstation, Zot was always alone. As the days passed into the first month, he thought about leaving Marsco. Dozens of Independent shuttles moved between the Earth and the belt. But the hiberman knew many of these were smaller ships that relied little on hibernation.

Or perhaps, he thought, *I'll really go near-Luddite, resign my commission, join Father Cavanaugh's SoAm PRIM school.* Zot had met the priest through the Millers, been down to his run-on-a-shoestring campus in the worst zone of Rio. Perhaps that would be his next move.

In the following weeks, he looked over his files of data about the post-solar universe. "Even if there were a confirmed Earth-like planet out there somewhere," he finally concluded half aloud, "even with a new deep-space craft and my cryo, who'd ever go? Ever want to go? Besides, what's *really, really* out there?"

After the hiberman dimmed all the lights in his cabin, the viewport filled with countless stars: dots merging into clusters, individual ones brighter than the rest, the backdrop of the Milky Way, a few larger lights obviously the post-belt planets. "All those stars and solar systems still years and years away," he confided hopelessly to himself. "Only Dante or Milton could conceive of a more vacuous hell."

Standing at the Plexiglas as if to get a closer view, he pondered infinity. He was nearly overwhelmed by its immense nothingness and its entire totality.

The only other thought that crossed his mind was Tessa. The Tessa he loved so deeply once, the Tessa lost to him completely. *Only Dante or Milton could conceive of a more vacuous hell than life without her,* he thought before busying himself to drive her from his mind.

TEN

THE BUTTERFLY CATCHER

(The SoAm Continental Zone, 2095)

"At current speed," the longtime associate explained to her solitary VIP, "we'll chew up the distance from Rio to your new home in under an hour-thirty."

Commander Andrea Pisanos had just joined Father Stephen Cavanaugh in the ventral gondola of the Marsco Sublunar Lander *Chico Mendes* where they watched the rainforest flash by fifty meters below.

Feeling the onset of airsickness, the gray-haired priest merely nodded.

"Easy jaunt," the pilot added, her own silver-enhanced hair shimmering.

"It's so kind of you to fuss over me," the green-turning dignitary managed to say.

"Not a bother, really," the woman insisted earnestly. "Merely completing my philanthropic duty by providing you all-weather survival gear for your reclusive two-week expedition—"

"—I'm collecting butterflies."

"Right, so you explained at HQ. And *twitch,*" her fingers tapped an imaginary air-computer pad, "three weeks later, I'm landering you 2,200 clicks into the interior."

"Nothing seems impossible for Marsco," mused the uncomfortable priest.

His host was not sure how to take that comment. Regardless, she took secret delight in making him airsick. She felt it was within the purview of her orders, which were to deliver this butterfly catcher to his distant hillside all the while getting him ready for Marsco's plans.

"Cavanaugh's famous," Mr. Giannini, a high wallah in Security and Hygiene, had explained to Pisanos ten days before. The wiry man looked hardened from Security work.

"*Infamous* some would say," added the wallah's assistant, a clone of his wizened superior. The younger one, a warrant officer, already looked calloused by his close-to-the-knuckle service, the likes of which the lander commander had avoided throughout her entire career.

"Well, yes, that. But notorious for his work in the Rio zones," the lefter, Giannini, went on. "Over the years he's become an outspoken critic of Marsco, a gadfly it tolerates because swatting him's hardly worth the effort."

"And yet," the pilot remarked to the pair, looking up from a palm unit on which she had been reading his Security file, "he's undeniably savvy in the ways of Marsco. His dossier reveals that."

His e-history showed an extraordinary calling. Born in the NoAm grain belt, he had studied at several prestigious schools before ordination. One of the first legally married priests the Vatican allowed, he lost his wife and young son, Margaret and Sean, in a Luddite attack seven years before the C-Wars. After the Wars, barred from another marriage by a regime change in Rome, he lived discreetly, as many other clergy then did, with his second spouse. They had no children. Isabella had passed on; he was now alone.

Despite that hidden personal note, the file explained that he had thrown himself into working among PRIMS, especially children, in one of the worst Rio zones.

"He can," commented the Security lefter, "fire up both ends of the candle and yet still not singe his fingers. This wily priest, who's been so long in a zone he's considered an all-but-disked PRIM, knows how to wheedle by grabbing between the flames. Usually, just enough to keep his inconsequential school up and running."

Pisanos took another cursory glance through a dossier that filled hundreds of screens. Clearly, there were blanks in the file, months at a time not accounted for. *Sloppy Security?* the woman wondered, looking at the two men with disbelief.

"Regardless of his PRIM-like life, he's sinewy, toughened by the rigor," the chief Security officer remarked with a mix of envy and disparagement. "It's no wonder he's gotten the nickname, 'the Emaciated Saint.'"

"Sainthood," his aide added, trying to sound sagacious, "is a subjective quality not easily attained or defined."

The pilot smiled slyly. "I take it from his file he's known to be energetic and sharp-witted."

"When needed," the warrant officer stated dryly without letting on his observation was from personal knowledge, "he can dress you down like a gunnery sergeant, though never near children—and always in English."

"He's a native speaker, I presume," Pisanos said.

"Of course," the wallah continued, "but more important to us, he has the survival instincts of a PRIM."

"In a UZ, one has to be cunning to endure," the assistant indirectly defended before catching himself. He then noted, "But he's tempered that craftiness with enough acumen to rival any diplomat. Plus, he's as dedicated as any Luddite."

"Yes," the lefter came back harshly, angry for the first time, "but for all this playing every angle—associates flock to volunteer at his shabby piss-ass school. Their way of showing 'Marsco philanthropy.'"

Right, Pisanos mentally noted, *and a few of those volunteers certainly gathered intel for the drafting of this dossier.*

"My best summation," concluded the Security officer, "he's formidable."

And so it was that Pisanos, skimming over the verdant Amazon canopy, took delight in her tacit instructions to airsick her solitary passenger.

Cavanaugh unintentionally flinched every time the *Mendes* swept closer to the forest. The lander engaged in military-type ground-hugging maneuvers, quite unnecessary for transiting anyone upriver.

"Takes some getting used to, doesn't it?" the commander remarked, betraying none of her delight. *Nausea'll tone him down a pixel or two.*

Standing behind, the flier watched the VIP tighten his safety harness, a measure of his nervousness because the craft remained at a constant fifty meters above the deck, rising and settling gently with the undulating terrain.

The guest had been on landers before, both Marsco and Indies plying their trade between So- and NoAm. His last trip was to Sac City three years ago, a monthlong rest he desperately needed—if staying at a dissident's grange just outside a zone was indeed restful. Previous flights were stratospheric, nothing like this canopy-top skim.

"We'll be straight and level soon as we pass these coastal hills," the pilot explained. Cavanaugh smiled but knew enough of landers and Marsco to surmise that this extraordinary display was just for him. He tolerated its condescension because he knew who was taking whom for a ride.

"Avionics in this beaut're modeled after the SSB-12B fighter—even predates the Lightning," the pilot explained further. "Marsco improved on them, of course. Another example of 'beating swords into plowshares.'"

The contrast between the two was startling. Cavanaugh wore plain, khaki bush pants, hiking boots, and a lightweight, drab cotton shirt without a Roman collar—all recently laundered if stained and frayed. He might have been a demobbed PRIM.

Like her entire crew, Commander Pisanos wore a pumpkin-colored flight suit. A breast patch, identifying her present Earth-side status, showed a gleaming aluminum lander circling the globe. Superimposed on the Earth was the stylized red M monogram.

Since the commander had worked her entire career based on landers, no confusion existed about her hiber-free age. She moved purposefully when she walked, carrying herself straight-backed with a trace of military precision. Although younger than the flier, the priest's years in zones had given him a slight limp.

A swath of sparkling river streaked under the *Mendes.* They were well in from the coast and crossing Amazon tributaries at a lower than necessary altitude. To provide her passenger with a true sense of "going upriver," the pilot had chosen this circuitous route.

From the observation deck, their velocity blurred everything directly beneath. The priest made nothing out except muddy tributaries broken by fingers of green. To him the entire view was a distorted smear of speed and color. He sat transfixed by it all.

"So, Commander Pisanos, you're an answer to this priest's prayers," Cavanaugh eventually remarked.

"It's nothing, really, to transport a dedicated lepidopterist into the interior."

"And such a luxurious lander."

"It's nothing, really."

"And to outfit me with absolutely every piece of gear I might need."

"Your ground transport for excursions out of base camp—*that* was a coup, I must say. You'll have a Marsco-standard hummer in top condition with liters of blend-cohol fuel. All in our bays and at your disposal."

From the chrome galley behind the seats, the commander poured seltzer water with a slice of fresh lemon. As she settled into one of the seven empty leather seats in front of its wide viewport, the priest mustered enough strength to taste his drink without a gag in his throat.

"On our lunar runs, passengers ate here," the associate explained. "A full complement always included four attendants."

"Oh, what are they called? *Hibermen?*"

"No, not to the Moon. No need. Sorry I couldn't roust one up. A feast'd be a real treat for a dignitary fresh from a UZ."

The priest smiled, but food was not on his mind. Turning to look at the pilot, he caught a dizzying peripheral glimpse of the world whizzing by.

Seeing him uneasy, the associate chuckled. "In space, you don't have anything streaking by, even when going twenty or thirty times faster. Watch the stationary horizon; you'll feel better."

A distant emerald line seemed fixed, so the inexperienced traveler concentrated on it to prevent any exploding sickness. The ploy worked, although his stomach still felt the lander hug the rolling terrain.

"She's no longer space-worthy, but she has fine lines. A sophisticated marvel." The commander paused to admire her ship. "Marsco did a top-tier job restoring her!" she stated emphatically as she rubbed her palm along the wooden armrest of polished mahogany held in place by sparkling chrome fittings. "Posh and strictly first-class from a bygone era. There's just something venerable about a prewar lander. The smell of leather seats, the feel of rich woods in the stateroom, the mirror-quality chrome. Marsco even restored her interior passenger compartments exactly as they were in her opulent heyday."

They both looked around the gleaming observation gondola. "Did you see the flight deck? We've updated the avionics to latest Lander Service specs; she operates with the best fly-by-wire controls

Marsco has to offer. The retrofitted computers take disk commands, but you still actually need your hand on a joystick to fly her."

"Is that an invitation? I'll take a crack."

The pilot didn't know whether he was serious or joking. "No, that's okay," she chuckled, "I've set the auto-controls and left a competent, well-disked copilot sitting there in case anything goes wrong. But it won't."

They sipped seltzer until the pilot continued, "Oh, I almost forgot, a memento of your trip." She handed him a Marsco Sublunar shoulder patch, a representation of the Lander Service's role. A brazen red *M* covered its woven Earth. The Moon and Mars sat in opposite corners where landers moved from their surfaces to orbiting docking ports.

"This'll decorate St. Teresa's trophy case."

"Let's just see how we're doing." With a few right-hand finger twitches, the commander booted a program; its display filled the starboard half of the viewport in front of Cavanaugh. As the projection became dark, the priest no longer saw through the Plexiglas. It suddenly seemed as if he sat behind half a solid wall, a comforting illusion to the queasy cleric.

The officer showed their preflight course in red with an overlay of their completed flight in blue. The whole line stretched from the Rio Lander Station, hugged the coast to the mouth of the Amazon then turned westward into the continent's interior.

The *Mendes* hadn't made the slightest deviation from her original flight plan even after covering half its course. "Vaunted Marsco precision," the pilot remarked. "You can actually observe the blue slowly covering the red; her speed's that great."

The priest responded with a tolerant smile.

"Now watch this," Commander Pisanos remarked earnestly. "Let me show you something that amazes me, and I even had a hand in its creation." Using her left-hand finger disks, she called up another program.

So, she is a lefter, the priest thought, confirming an earlier suspicion. *That explains her arrogance, her brashness.*

Left-pulling a secure menu, the pilot swiftly accessed info with her right disks. Soon a SoAm map filled the second half of the viewport. Its multi-shaded areas designated the whole continent although nothing showed the boundaries of any late twentieth-century country or former Continental Power. The projection had a surreal look, as though a computer game in which players made civilizations by moving glyphs around the screen.

The asymmetric realness of Marsco in our rearranged world, the priest thought.

Pisanos explained that various subsidiaries, like the Rubber Sid or Food Consortium, supervised most of SoAm, although many parts were still under explicit Marsco auspices. Without comment, they studied the projection. It was well understood that directly or indirectly Marsco actually controlled the entire map. "Although, it never straightforwardly interferes with subsidiary businesses or their employment practices," she said sipping her seltzer. "It acts in an advisory capacity only."

The priest's real, and secret, purpose alone kept him from being overtly confrontational, a stance that had made him legendary over the years.

"Even on a local level, I'm sure you'll agree, conditions are noticeably better."

The passenger nodded, admitting to that vague point. If nothing else, Marsco had stopped the death squads that once routinely patrolled the *favelas,* killing off street kids who had ventured away from zone boundaries.

"And in all fairness," the flier drove home her point, "as you must acknowledge, Marsco merely inherited PRIMS and UZs from the C-Powers. It didn't create any of them in the first place."

The priest, held in a captivity of his own making, gave a slight nod of acquiescence to his benefactor.

"Additionally, unlike the Powers, Marsco openly timelines to eliminate every single unincorporated zone eventually," the commander proudly pointed out. "We have clearly stated benchmarks!"

She drew a proud breath. "No wonder they say, 'If you want peace, work for Marsco.'"

"Yes, no wonder," answered the priest in a hollow voice. This was neither the time nor place for a verbal skirmish; he knew from experience how to pick, and win, his battles.

The associate, nonetheless, caught his drift. "With all due respect, Father Cavanaugh," she responded in a calm but forceful tone, "isn't it time to acknowledge that Marsco has kept all *countries* (as they were once called) from making war with each other for over twenty-five years now? Every single one of them! Trade-offs exist in every situation. It's binary. But on balance 'a world without war' is a stronger *either* than an *or.*"

Without an introduction to her segue, the commander flicked to a blowup projection of the clearing that was to become the priest's base camp. "We'll furnish you with a hard copy of this soon," she told him. "Notice here, in this valley to the west of your hillside, there's a shutdown V/STOL strip, used by Marsco as recently as nine years ago for reforestation work. Also an abandoned Conservation Corps camp five clicks to the east-northeast. It's north over the summit from your base camp, but best go around its crest than over. Marston mat road connecting the two, strip and camp."

The priest nodded blankly at the commander, not wanting to betray that he had already been given this exact information.

"All probably gone to jungle by now, but it's a prime migration route."

The pilot twitched up several graphics of indigenous butterflies. Clearing her throat, she began lecturing from rote about each high-resolution image, "In this ideal locale, you might be fortunate to spot the *Caligo memnon,* the owl butterfly, with ominous eyes on its wings." A twitch brought the next image. "Or even the elusive *Colias cesonia,* the Dog-Face Butterfly. Although it migrates throughout both No- and SoAm, all the way to the southern-most tip of the continent, this yellow beauty's considered rare in these parts." Twitch. "The *Heliconius charitonia* would be worth your effort, too, the zebra longwing."

The priest sat in silence.

Finally, the pilot pounced, "What exactly *do* you hope to see?"

Cavanaugh spit out the only name he knew. "The Monarch. You know, orange and black wings, antennae." He cared little for all this subterfuge. "It flutters."

"You are an optimist," the woman replied, playing along. "Although a tremendous migrating species, the *Danaus plexippus* never travels farther south than the central isthmus connecting the two continents." A few twitches showed the average yearly migration patterns that ended in old Mexico, well above the lander's present location. "But as a man of the cloth, perhaps you're expecting a miracle—and a strong wind from the north."

The two showed their opposite allegiances; each dug in with stern resolve.

An uneasy truce began, made clear by the flier remarking, "You should know that Ludds've taken over that deserted camp. So do be careful."

"Good of you to inform me, commander," the priest responded.

"Yes, I wouldn't want you to walk into something unforeseen. Something violent."

"I'd hypothesize," Cavanaugh spoke gently, knowing he must challenge the associate's last assumption, "that if my own experience with PRIMS has proven Marsco's stereotypes inaccurate, my introduction to these Ludds will also dispel your insinuations."

The woman was stunned by his abrupt reply.

"Aren't there scores of rumors like, 'They cut off all fingers with implants'?"

"Certainly," she replied, taken aback.

"And other ridiculous hearsay," he continued, gaining strength as he spoke. "They plan to destroy Marsco's computer Net. Not the software with some cyber virus, but the actual hardware itself—fiber network, wi-fi platforms, its nodes, downlink dishes, and all."

"That's more than a recurring fable. Look at how many times systems're cracked." The pilot found herself preparing to sortie into classified territory.

"Certainly there are violent cells," admitted the passenger. "Just like their namesake, they wish to destroy all machines with their bare hands if necessary and return to a simpler time."

Thinking they really agreed, the commander nodded, her silver hair gracefully following her head's movements.

"But *all* Ludds like that?" insisted the priest. "Every group of them? It's surely too ludicrous to be true. I've met dozens of nonviolent sects in my own zone and way up in NoAm at Miller's grange."

"Miller!" Mere mention of his name became the focus. "Doctor Miller?"

"Yes, Walter Miller."

"You know *the* Doctor Miller?" The pilot was thunderstruck. Nothing in Cavanaugh's dossier suggested the sagacious priest maintained such an incredible connection. A stunning oversight on Security's part.

"And his wife," he continued. "That is, I knew her. Actually, I knew Bethany Palmer from childhood. We were like brother and sister."

This was the priest's most alarming statement all day. It was beyond belief—that and the fact that Security had missed such a noteworthy association in Cavanaugh's past. "I didn't know," Pisanos slowly divulged.

"Or," the cagy priest ventured his own hypothesis, "has Security merely kept that part of my history from you, commander? If so, *why?* At least, that's the question I'd ask myself." He gave a chuckle and added. "Of course, I can't imagine Security not knowing of our mutual friendship, Walter's and mine. We're both under enough constant surveillance."

The associate was so troubled by this revelation she nearly let her guard slip. She wanted to ask specific questions about Miller, out of curiosity mixed with envy (and possibly an element of hero worship in praise of his rarely found independence), but then she quickly regained self-control. It was best for all associates concerned *not* to speak of Walter Miller.

The pilot found the priest's mental chess pieces expertly aligned against her. He defended himself with aplomb. *Well, I'd been warned.*

The lander continued to skim just above the unbroken canopy. What seemed like clouds on the distant horizon were steadily becoming the Andes.

To avoid further discussion, the pilot sipped her drink. But after a pause, she moved the conversation along in a different direction, "You know, on board there's someone from your remarkable little school—Warrant Officer Rivers."

"*Rivers?* That name doesn't sound like one of our graduates," the priest replied. Nonetheless, he couldn't help but be proud just at the mere suggestion that a student of his was an associate.

For nearly twenty-five years, he had kept St. Teresa's (named for Mother Teresa of Calcutta, "Patron Saint of PRIMS"), afloat in the worst shantytown. Each year the school sent a handful from that harsh zone to do common non-disk labor under the auspices of sid overseers. In time, some students actually went on to manage components of the Food Consortium or the Transportation Subsidiary where they were often single-disked.

The arrangement, however, always created uneasiness in the priest, all this rendering to Caesar.

And yet he knew it might be worse. The surest way to exit a zone was to volunteer for the Auxiliary. Trained by Security, dressed in their ominous gray-mottled fatigues for urban monitoring, they patrolled zones worldwide, often controlling them with an iron fist.

"I believe," the commander confidentially informed her passenger, "that when Warrant Officer Peter Rivers was your student he was known as Pedro Del Rio."

"Oh, yes, then I do remember him. Pedro! He must be doing well indeed if he's part of *your* competent crew," he responded, ever mindful of Marsco's other side—its known munificence that was currently propelling him on his secret quest.

"No, he's merely another passenger, like yourself," she replied. "We do have additional duties to attend to besides our little act of philanthropy."

Having made her point, the pilot returned to the topic of the refurbished lander. The gondola fittings shone with the same sparkle as the day she was initially commissioned to haul personnel and material to the Moon. Her cavernous cargo bays, only partially filled with jungle equipment, gave an indication of her enormous capacity.

"Sure could make landers back then. Of course, no more post-atmospheric trips for this one." She tapped the armrest as if to reassure the *Mendes* that the hardest part of the craft's life was past. "She enjoys her well-deserved semi-retirement," the pilot remarked affectionately.

"So, she's no longer whisking anyone to the Moon?"

"No. Marsco's designated her exclusively for SoAm reforestation duty. Her sister ship, the *Ken Saro-Wiwa,* plies her trade over Africa, assisting with woodland and savanna restoration there. When you return, permit me to fly you over Angel Falls. We can hover in the mist. Now that's a view! You can hear the cascade's roar over our Herriff units. Thunderous."

"I look forward to it, commander, if it's no further bother to you. I'm a simple zone man; my needs are few, but I wouldn't pass up such an offer!"

The lander commander hid a smirk. *You're the most dexterous and astute "simple man" I've ever met.* "At our speed, it won't be a bother. We'd have done it today, but I saw how anxious you were to set up base camp."

The com-link buzzed, and the pilot spoke briefly with the flight deck. "Twenty-five minutes ETA." She rose to leave. "If Warrant Officer Rivers can be spared, I'll send him down," she remarked while climbing spiral steps into the main fuselage. "I'm sure you'll have much to discuss after all these years," the retreating pilot called back down through the hatch.

After a moment an associate dressed in olive drab and dark-green tiger fatigues, because he was over the jungle and not in an urban patrol area, climbed down the spiral steps.

At the bottom, WO Peter Rivers paused awkwardly.

He was of small stature—childhood deprivation wasn't easily overcome—with handsome Latin features and wavy hair. In his early thirties, he had lost his boyish looks long ago as his body became taut and sinewy. He had been toughened both by his youth and by the hardships of his career. The pleasant, smiling boy the priest remembered was now grave-faced. Traces of that past self still existed behind the quick, dark eyes, but he kept his history under tight wraps.

He's done well, no vestige of the UZ hangs about him, the priest thought, *Marsco to the max.* Rivers had moved swiftly from being a raw PRIM Auxxie to a Security trooper, an actual associate. A vast distance to leap, but he had bridged the immense chasm.

The pair greeted each other warmly although the former teacher was reluctant to rise for his onetime student. Since the pilot left, the viewport again showed the endless canopy whizzing by continuously.

In his duty fatigues he might have been just another trooper patrolling any Earth-side hot spot. When the warrant officer sat down, he began, "You don't look much changed, Father."

"You look well, Pedro."

"I'm *Peter* in Marsco, Father."

"Oh, yes, of course."

"I don't have the luxury of a personal history," he explained in lowered tones, "having once been a PRIM." He held up the scar at the back of his left hand. "I am Warrant Officer Peter Rivers, an associate. That's all anyone needs to know."

"Yes, I understand."

The intense officer looked at the priest as if to say *Do you?* but went on, "Pedro Del Rio ceased to exist the day Peter Rivers upped to the Auxiliary."

"I understand," the priest commented again, looking hard for the slightest semblance between the laughing youth he had known and the serious man who sat beside him. He saw little remaining of the callow student, although he did see a language disk behind his right ear.

"How's everything back home?" the warrant officer asked.

"Fine," the priest replied in an off-handed manner then bluntly added, "Well, we need a new roof before the rainy season."

The school took in as many orphans and abandoned children as it could, the fortunate few from the teeming masses surrounding it. A dozen or more came for the day, as Pedro had, often returning at evening to corrugated steel and plastic shanties where they lived with a mother and a host of sibs and half-sibs. The teachers did their best to educate them. They shared with Cavanaugh the hope of moving a fraction out of the zone. Math. Enough English to prepare them for a language disk implant. The basics of computers.

"But we still have only finger mouse-driven units," the priest explained.

Peter laughed a bit, the first time while reminiscing that a smile crossed his serious face. "I bet they're the same ancient machines I used. Obsolete even back then!"

The priest lowered his eyes in embarrassed agreement.

"Remember when Tomás lost a precious finger mouse so one console couldn't be booted?"

The priest nodded happily. Once a crisis, it had become a humorous story to tell and retell.

"And what was it? Didn't Sister Claire finally find it in a crack in the floor? What chaos! One misplaced thimble with a QCA chip, and the school's in an uproar for a week!"

"Yes, what we wouldn't give for a bank of Marsco's latest technology. We're at a great disadvantage competing against sids, especially in computer skills. Many of them have a second disk before sitting for prelims."

They had unintentionally touched on one of the priest's internal conflicts—a defining inconsistency. Was it really better to send a few to Marsco than let them languish in a UZ? He had never reconciled his self-contradiction. Yet he was a man capable of guile, someone adept at manipulating that system as needed. He took little comfort in knowing he was not alone in this lingering ambiguity toward Marsco.

The priest often confided to his flock, rather too openly, that its own incongruity was overwhelming at times. Marsco might not care for tens of thousands of PRIM children, but then it might inexplicably turn around and send one or two dozen with Neo-Con to a sanatorium in the African savanna where the drier air speeded their recovery.

He thought deeply for a moment in silence. *But—and there always seems to be that "but"—am I putting young men and women in a position of temptation? Would they become too much like Marsco rather than an agent of change within Marsco?*

The priest had no answer, attempted no answer, except to say, "Well, recently I might've found a solution for our finger disk problem."

"How so?"

"There's an iceman I know—slightly. He says he's likely to resign his commission when he returns from Mars and come work at our school. Among the many attributes he will bring us is his training in disk-tech."

"That'd be great for the school, having someone to help with implants."

The priest laughed, "Yes, if *he* supplies the disks!"

In the distance, ridges continued to rise out of the rainforest. In the closest set of foothills, a clearing waited for the priest. Over one jagged crest, the Luddite camp was nestled. Farther west, well behind his hillcrest, higher steep peaks rose, ice-covered and cloud-shrouded.

For a moment, the two grew silent as the *Mendes* pulled her nose upward to climb the first set of foothills. The lander angled and tilted as needed to pass over three valleys and crest lines in rapid succession. Piloting here took quick twitches and steely concentration.

Peter resumed his serious tone, "I've never gone back. Not since leaving." A note of dejection rang with his confession. "Not even for my mother's funeral."

Deep in his gut, the priest felt he should confront Rivers, but he let the former student talk on.

"As young as possible, I joined an Auxiliary unit—*sid-level* but under Marsco officers. The training was hard, relentless. But being an Auxxie or a trooper's a little like being a priest," he tried to smile, "there's always need for our services." The warrant officer grew silent only for a moment. "Was fifteen when I upped. Got my first disks at nineteen—two at once. Had much catching up to do. I was nearly twenty-seven when I officially entered Marsco."

"So," asked his former teacher gently, "you're what they call a *centurion?*"

"Technically, no, not at present. A *legionnaire* is more accurate because I'm not as yet a commissioned officer," he added perhaps with too much eagerness. "A fine distinction, but these distinctions are made."

"I think I understand," the listener commented although he didn't catch all the nuance.

"Either way, Father Stephen, I am in Marsco, but both the terms *legionnaire* and *centurion* are derogatory, my friend, as is the case with *iceman*." He admonished lightly and then tapped his language disk nervously, the source of his fluent English and linguistic knowledge. "But regardless, I saw quite a bit of service before I made the final move into Marsco proper."

"I'm sure you have a fine record," the priest remarked as an off-handed compliment.

The former PRIM froze momentarily then continued. "I guess I was lucky."

"What St. Teresa's didn't give you, you got elsewhere. Bless you," the priest added. "You always had a way of getting ahead. Nothing seems to stop you."

The remark hit like an unexpected slap, not a tribute to his dogged work and unswerving devotion. Rivers finally replied in a taut manner, "Well, you gave me a start, a passage out of the zone and into a sid."

"But Marsco always was your ultimate goal."

"Yes, I didn't make it directly from St. Teresa's, but I did make it."

The lander turned 90 degrees and began cutting speed. A flat clearing came into view half a click ahead. The massive craft now seemed to move at a crawl, its exhaust and vectoring jets making gigantic trees that suddenly surrounded it sway in the engine blast.

"We're sending two to the Marsco Buenos Aires air-tech facility next week. Training to join the ground crews of landers like this one. A first! A pair of ours actually moving directly *into* Marsco." He held up two fingers in a "V" for emphasis.

"But what's this?" The legionnaire took the priest's right hand and turned it over. His index finger had the minimum adult implant.

"A gift from my cardinal. Every one of His Eminence's clergy has the latest. We're all on the Net." As the lander decelerated on its final approach, the priest picked at the hypodermal disk wistfully with his thumbnail. "I wish he'd fixed the school's leaking roof," he added too honestly. "He lives in a lavish terra cotta palace overlooking Ipanema and rebuilds his marble cathedral. He's already refurbished Christ the Redeemer."

"And you still live amid shanties."

"Yes, 'fraid so."

The lander's engine wash singed the lush grass of the hilltop clearing. Anti-g pulses flattened the withered grass as the craft hovered five meters above the ground before it came to rest on six pairs of landing pancakes.

"Here already," the priest announced, suddenly energetic. He took the hands of his student. "My prayers will be with you. St. Teresa's blessing to you."

"I have a confession to make, Father." The trooper unexpectedly didn't release the priest's hands. "I get a promotion for playing along, by talking to you. Marsco gets something; I get something. It's their SOP on these things." An uncomfortable awkwardness followed as the warrant gazed at the priest to see if he had taken all this in.

"Yes," replied the teacher with a chuckle that betrayed the fact that he was totally prepared for these remarks. "So your point is? When Marsco gives, Marsco expects?"

With a note of sadness in his glance, the trooper insisted in an earnest voice, "Don't de-lander. Don't stay alone in this clearing. Say you're sick. Force yourself to vomit. Feign a migraine."

The priest was confused. "Now I *really* don't understand you."

"There're Ludds nearby. They're camped on the far side of this hill. They've restored a V/STOL strip. They've also set up some sort of ECM umbrella—" Rivers saw from the priest's expression he needed to explain. "A countermeasures system. These buggers are sophisticated enough to block all our electronic probes. Simple radar jamming I can understand. But how they can block an infrared imagery scan remains a mystery. A technical impossibility. Even Marsco boffins can't explain how it's done, much less replicate it, counteract it."

The priest seemed impressed with the Ludds's ability to impede Marsco.

Security was impressed as well. When routine satellite surveillance sweeps were thwarted several months ago, it raised a red flag. Investigations increased, but all had failed. Neither Rivers nor Pisanso knew the full extent of those failures, although from the degree of interest Security was showing, both associates could guess.

The warrant officer continued, "We can't even watch from a satellite or high-level lander flyby. We routinely send surveillance platforms but immediately lose contract with our drones. Even real-time video links don't come back. I'm not sure you appreciate the advanced level of your adversary out there."

"Adversary? You're setting this up as a confrontation. It doesn't have to be."

Rivers brushed off the comment. "Security wants you in that camp to help us, well, to observe them for yourself. When you return—*if* you return—we'll gain much from your debriefing."

Jungle air suddenly filled the gondola as the ground hatch opened. The cabin grew thick with humidity. An afternoon storm was brewing, but the clouds didn't yet block the sun, lowering toward the horizon. The muggy air and somber words of the warrant officer made the priest dizzy. He assured himself it was vertigo caused by the treetop flight.

"Father Stephen," the associate began once more in a gentle tone, "for all intents and purposes, you're a PRIM."

To object, the priest held up his left hand which was without either a green glowing PRIM-disk or a scar caused by its surgical removal.

Rivers went on without hesitation, "Didn't you ever wonder why Marsco granted you such an unusual travel permit? And procured all this gear, no questions asked?"

He motioned out the viewport at three large containers being lowered from the Number Two cargo bay. Twin anti-g hooks had set each long crate safely on the ground in minutes. A swarm of associates, dressed in olive drab like Rivers, raced around setting up camp.

"See there," the warrant pointed, "at that associate starting your hummer."

Once it purred, the ground tech gave a thumb's-up sign while another associate arranged an uplink dish that was capable of communicating with any Marsco station, even those in deep space.

"I remember how to drive, even though it's been years. But use the high-end com equipment? Probably not."

"It's technological overkill, isn't it?"

Regardless, a dozen associates scurried about; each in turn giving the priest a wave to show all that was well with his on-loan gear.

The legionnaire had the priest note that these associates were wearing protective gloves. "Doesn't it seem odd that your camp's being prepared by Marsco personnel, not PRIM day-laborers or at least sids?"

Cavanaugh agreed with a silent nod.

"You see all this? Associates whipping your billet into shape? Disked personnel don't hump like PRIMS, after all," he added sharply then snapped, "to catch butterflies."

Fearing he might be confronted with a proposition he wouldn't accept, the priest slumped back into a seat, his vigorous energy gone.

"For your own good," insisted Rivers, "stay right there. I'll announce a med emergency. I'll order an evac, stat."

The passenger's face turned ashen with the slow realization his plan had collapsed even though this close. His insider had warned him that his cover story was transparent. "Doomed to fail," his source had cautioned. "Security will see through you in a nano."

Finally accepting his bitter failure, Cavanaugh said, "But I have to find them."

"Find them? Butterflies? Find who?"

"Two of my boys. I'm sure they were kidnapped!" The priest tried to hide his shame at his lies.

"Kidnapped?"

"Or lured. By a Luddite searcher. He comes often to the favelas. He gathers many around him, mesmerizes them with his plans to save PRIMS."

"Yes. 'The Leader' he calls himself, but he goes by several other names. Head of a dangerous group, the Nexus. His worldwide followers skirt just outside Marsco jurisdiction. They continuously scour UZs for misguided PRIMS. We know his plans." The Security warrant officer drew up short, "But how'd you know where to look?"

“Rumors in the zone mostly. And I gleaned some information from the Marsco Net—” he held up his single blue-green implant. “Even at the most elemental level, this opens many links.”

The warrant officer looked incredulous. “That’s asking the impossible from one adult implant, Father Stephen. You don’t gather much classified intel twitching a solitary disk. You couldn’t hack your way into anything black either. That’s the reason for them in the first place—to keep snoopers like you out!”

“Well, I have my sources within Marsco, you know. Or near enough *to* Marsco.” He remained elusive, cautious. “He did some checking for me. He knows how to use these.” He held up his index finger disk. “While I have one, he’s a lefter.”

“Must be some source!” The associate was amazed that his former teacher had so much access to the mysterious workings of Marsco. And this mole of his was not to be taken lightly. *But another time for that,* concluded the quick mind of the Security warrant. “But what about these boys?” he went on, dealing with first things first.

“Like you, Pedro, I mean Peter, really. Two from the school, orphans. One might not truly be an orphan but abandoned. We call one Antonio Naples, because he said his folks were PRIMS from the Naples Zone. Came to us when he was nine, about four years ago. Said his papa worked on landers under the auspices of the Trans Consortium. Brought the mama and son to Rio. Then, the papa is gone, next mama. Gone.”

Rivers knew the story, a repeated scenario.

“The other boy, we know him as Thax. Not really a name, but that’s what he called himself when he came to us. Said he was from the Mexi-City Zone, but who really knows? Never heard him speak anything at first but Spanglish—and now the little proper English we’ve taught him. He was nine when he came, maybe a little older—about the same time as Antonio. We don’t know his age for certain, but he’s small and frail.”

The priest looked into the distance as if visualizing two faces from many that pressed against the gates of St. Teresa’s.

"He arrived outside one night during a storm, like so many of the rest. He's a survivor but will end up a thief or collaborator without guidance. Who knows, he might as easily join this Ludd faction as willingly as he might join the Secur—" Cavanaugh caught himself, coughed slightly, and continued. "Where Antonio is kind, Thax is clever. And a leader, but I'm afraid, not the best sort for our school or Antonio. But good at heart. And, he's in the advanced stages of Neo-Con. Still treatable but extremely sick. He'll die without help."

Rivers saw the priest's fiery energy returning. He was a steadfast, stubborn man who let nothing deter him. He wouldn't be sitting there right then if he abandoned wild dreams easily.

"And you think," the hardened legionnaire began, "that you can just walk into this base, which might—*just might*—have these boys and announce, 'I'm chasing butterflies and reclaiming my lost sheep'?"

The warrant had grown angry but kept it in check. He knew the priest needed protecting from himself. These weren't just any Luddites; the Nexus were extremely dangerous, with an automatic shoot-to-kill order against them. His anger was born of frustration, wanting to protect someone bent on blindly hurting himself.

"What does the parish think of your plans?"

"No one knows I'm here," the priest replied in a whisper. "Semester's ended. Anyway, I gave up the parish duties five years ago to work solely with the school."

"So, should anything happen to you, no one will know!"

"Well, you'll know. And God, of course. Marsco and God! Can you think of two more omniscient entities?" The priest gave a chuckle, but the trooper didn't laugh. "And my Marsco friend. He'll know if anything happens to me." Cavanaugh looked away to head off this conversation. He eventually proceeded tangentially, "Anyway, it looks like I can text him with all that gear. Wonderful looking equipment. New hummer even."

"Stephen, be serious. Can't you see? Marsco supplied all this so that you can infiltrate that Ludd camp for Security. Whoever informed you about this secret base should have warned you about the dangers in there—"

"But he did."

"Obviously, it's made no impression." Their exchanged glances reminded each of the priest's obstinacy. "Look, we've already attempted to plant operatives three times, each summarily frustrated. Sending 'converts' to join the Nexus hasn't worked either."

The associate thought for a moment about those who had eagerly volunteered, trying to gain quick promotions through dangerous covert actions. All had failed.

"Any low-level photo recce shows a lush forest. Thick. Impenetrable. Satellite reconnaissance shows us nothing; each pass comes back a gray plot, as though its equipment's flawed. Ludds rely on little if any e-tech, and so there might be nothing for our lander flyby to observe anyway—mud huts, that sort of thing. Nonetheless, the gray plot shows these hostiles are projecting a tremendous ECM block. Quite tech-savvy, especially coming from the likes of them. That's partly what worries Security. These skinnies are stopping all our sensors, all our communications within their umbrella."

The look from Cavanaugh said, *These are hardly problems to me. I just want my students back.*

"Once in, no word comes out. We need ground surveillance. We know where they are, but we don't know their exact plans. Are they a serious threat or a group of separatist cranks bent on reliving the nineteenth century?"

The priest had no answer, so Rivers continued, "An associate's pretty obvious. As long as I can't dissuade you, here's what you can do."

"I understand," said the priest bluntly. "I was expecting this tradeoff sooner or later. I know how much Marsco's helped me."

"You needed its help to get this far."

"I'm to help it in return. *But I won't.* I go freely—or take me straight back."

The former student subtly changed tactics, "I won't tell you what the bodies we recovered looked like." The warrant reached for the cleric's right hand. "I will tell you, any finger with a disk was amputated."

"I'm a man of God. The Leader claims he is, too. We have that in common; I'll reason with him."

"You sure you won't change your mind?"

"Positive."

"Then, Stephen, for my sake, at least let us initialize your FD. We can trace you better then."

The priest looked deeply at his onetime student. "That might jeopardize me more, working openly with Marsco."

"It's for your own good, nothing that co-ops you into helping us." The officer insisted brusquely, "Security doesn't need help finding a few renegade Luddites."

"Oh, but it sounds like it does," the priest replied candidly, fiercely. "It needs my tough old hide in there." He motioned to the hill separating his camp from the other.

"For your own safety. For your boys. Let me initialize your FD."

Reluctantly, and only for the sake of his students, Cavanaugh agreed— his single compromise. He rationalized this to be the only way to be allowed to move without hindrance.

The associate performed the inputting with remarkable dispatch.

"How will this disk work?"

Rivers explained a Morse SOS and how to pressure the disk, even with his right thumb, to emit the dots and dashes.

"And what if I no longer have a right thumb?" he asked with a levity that hid the seriousness of his question.

Ignoring him, Rivers went on, "Press your finger disk onto anything but metal. Wood or plastic. Even a rock. Press hard, until it hurts. *'Dot, dot, dot'*—like I explained. Press hard, harder than twitching it normally. There's a dozen Security craft nearby, others besides the *Mendes* can pick you up in an emergency, in a matter of minutes."

"Press this finger disk—" the priest mumbled to himself.

"Yes, on anything that isn't metal."

The well-trained warrant officer debated with himself whether he should offer the priest his Enfield sidearm. He knew, however, he would never accept it. Besides, the weapon was wedded to his own implants, at present inoperative in anyone else's hands or disks. Dangerous and complicated to rededicate such a weapon to Cavanaugh's implant by disengaging its disk-safety lockout.

The gondola's com-link buzzed. Base camp was secure and operational.

The associate guided the priest, not to the spiral steps, but to an open side hatchway that had a ladder extended to the ground.

As he turned to go down the dozen steps, Cavanaugh glanced for a moment back at Rivers, looking at the toughened man.

"Take care of yourself," the associate beseeched.

"Yes, you too." Then the priest smirked, "Remember, 'It's a jungle out there.'"

"Yes, sir," the Security legionnaire snapped a smart salute as though to a superior. "Don't worry. I got your back."

The former student watched the priest descend to the waiting jungle clearing. In the distance, thunder sounded as a storm rose.

Rivers was upset for having failed the priest. He vowed he would do all in his powers to protect him. *But, God, I'd hate being in that forest all alone. Give me an urban zone with known hostiles any day, any time.*

From the gondola, the lander commander and the warrant officer watched a crew chief explain the equipment to the priest: standard com-link, food storage and preparation units, a rain-gathering device, his hygiene facility with solar panels assuring plenty of hot water. The priest was well supplied for a two-month stay.

The commander called over a prompt yeoman, "See that our friend gets this." It was a new butterfly net on a sturdy polymer handle made to resemble bamboo. "If nothing else, he can scoop up chrysalises with it." She also handed over a laminated map, freshly printed off the SDC data banks, detailing the area. "Also see he gets this," she ordered. "We can't give him recent ERIC images because of their ECM blocks. These'll have to do. Terrain's accurate at least, even if the dangers aren't marked. What's in store for him, we won't know for a while."

Turning back to the warrant officer, she added, "The Ludd camp's clearly designated. A blind man could find it. In addition to his map, the hummer's guidance computer has the coordinates, although GPS probably won't uplink once he's under their blacked-out umbrella."

"You're not taking any chances."

"Marsco rarely does."

The pair watched the priest studying the map. He soon acknowledged the gifts with a nod toward the gondola, his long-handled butterfly net resting awkwardly against his shoulder. When the ground personnel were satisfied that the jungle explorer was snugly settled on his hillside, they climbed back into the *Mendes.*

The commander gave orders to her copilot.

The lander used repeated pulses from several anti-g emitters to rise from the clearing and hover momentarily over the lush rainforest canopy. The craft then slowly gained attitude. In only seconds the waving butterfly catcher seemed small and vulnerable in his isolated base camp. Rivers stared hard down at the priest as his solitary figure grew smaller and smaller.

As soon as the *Mendes* established a safety envelope above the treetops, the craft accelerated and was gone.

ELEVEN

JUNGLE SORTIE

(Amazon Rainforest, 2095)

"Everything set, Mr. Rivers?" asked his superior, Mr. Giannini.

"Yes, sir. He's initialized. As ready as he'll ever be." Wishing more than knowing, the warrant added, "We'll get much intel when returns from this sortie."

If he does, the *Mendes* commander kept herself from adding.

In the tracking center, a small workstation crammed with sensors, Pisanos and Rivers stood with the associate who had earlier so eagerly demonstrated the hummer to Father Cavanaugh. Although dressed in fatigues with no badge of rank, anyone with an ounce of Marsco sense instantly realized that this lefter was not to be crossed.

The senior officer stood taller than Rivers by only five centimeters. And even though as old as the pilot, hiber had aged him more slowly. Other than these observable facts, he remained an enigma. She knew him only as Mr. Giannini. And now, as before, she never hesitated about obeying his orders.

From tracking, the associates monitored the priest's campsite, their faces lit by green readouts.

"What did you tell him to gain his cooperation?" the wallah asked.

"Everything," Cavanaugh's former student replied dryly.

Giannini stiffened. "Telling him openly might jeopardize this entire mission," he fumed.

"But his direct cooperation's tangential. He'll be helping by *not* helping. His intense focus to save his boys remains our best asset."

"This was to be a covert ops with the priest acting without his knowledge or consent."

"I found I couldn't lie to him."

"Where do your loyalties lie, Mr. Rivers?" the lefter demanded. "Your decision might very well interrupt your Marsco career."

"You misunderstand me, sir. I found I *needn't* lie to him." Rivers tapped the language disk behind his right ear, a common gesture to suggest that this implant was at fault when he misspoke. "I know Cavanaugh. He's on his own insane mission he sees as God's work. As such, he can't believe that anyone or anything will interfere. So what if he knows of our plans? Ours won't stop his. Through his ineffectual attempts to find those two boys, he covers our own plans perfectly."

By remote cam, the three watched the priest studying the hummer's GPS receiver.

"I'm not sure I follow your logic," the wallah finally stated.

"Don't you see? He had already assumed my pitch was coming. He was prepared to refuse our tradeoff offer. If I'd insisted—I know him—he would've gone straight home rather than cooperate. We'd have nothing but a scrubbed recon. Even when I told him everything, he didn't let that interfere with his scheme."

The warrant paused as they watched the priest wandering through his camp. He might have been surveying property for a new chapel; he looked so unperturbed while so near obvious danger.

"No, sir, he'll help us more without his complete cooperation. So he knows! He'll not lose sleep trying to figure it out. He'll focus on his primary mission, as self-destructive as it seems to be. Believe me, sir, by *not* helping us, in the end he'll help us more convincingly than we ever planned, ever imagined."

Giannini marveled at the innate sagacity of this former PRIM. *But what else should I expect?* he thought, glancing at the WO's left-hand scar.

"Mr. Rivers," he stated, pleased with his selection of an assistant, "I'm sure *ensign* isn't beyond your reach."

Contrary to popular Marsco wisdom, which professed that the best and brightest should go into the MAS Fleet, Giannini realized that this soon-to-be-centurion would be of greatest service by not going into shuttles.

Utilizing his single disk, Father Cavanaugh switched on his comlink. Activating a keyboard, he tapped out a short read-only message to Miller. "Arrived safely. All's well." The granger had assured the priest that he would receive the message through a freenet without Security tracing it.

In a similar way, he quickly twitched a message to the iceman, Zot, "Position waiting anytime you wish. Welcome!"

An evening thunderstorm left the base camp cooler but undamaged. The drenching rain, typical of sudden tropical downpours, was a welcome break from the oppressive afternoon heat.

As the winds subsided, the jungle just beyond the clearing teemed with foreboding noises. Exotic birds squawked out in the encircling bush. Annoying gnats and mosquitoes emerged to attack, not kept at bay by the insect-deterrent apparatus hanging from his tent, as an associate had assured Cavanaugh. Their aggressive buzzing interspersed with the louder jarring noises of cicada. A jaguar roared in preparation for her nocturnal prowl.

The priest reluctantly conceded that he longed for the familiar noises surrounding his school.

In a sprawling unincorporated zone, hunger and privation were restless. Babies wailed ceaselessly. Adults and children dying from Neo-Con coughed up blood the entire night. Echoes of cynical laughter, emitted after beating someone for his few meager possessions, lingered. Shouts broke out into arguments over scant building materials or a woman. In the distance Auxiliary non-leth engagements crackled and whooshed, often followed by the reports of Enfields as troopers moved in to control an increasingly tense situation.

And always, in the predawn light, the anguished murmurs of PRIM women lined up at a Marsco philanthropic pavilion for their meager food ration. There, they had their hypodermal BC strip checked. If it showed bright yellow through the skin along the left palm, signifying it needn't be replaced yet, they were provided a daily food allotment. Those who refused these implants altogether went away empty handed unless an older daughter or son, a father, had upped to the Auxiliary or Security.

Much was for sale in an UZ, the priest knew. It was always a buyers' market.

For an hour, Cavanaugh sat under a hurricane lamp reading his breviary and praying his beads. When finished, he moved to the borrowed hummer. Sitting on the passenger side, he engaged the nav-computer with his single disk.

The glowing digital map detailed all the known jungle tracks in the locale. The hillside camp faced south. To the north a steep, rocky ridge ran east-west. Going north was the crow-flies route to the Ludd compound. Farther up, the precipice was impassable, with jutting outcrops blocking every possible path for the vehicle. Going over the summit, consequently, was not the easiest way to the Nexus camp.

That route was due west along the base of the hill, a rugged spur off a larger range to the east. In five kilometers, the ridge sloped into the valley floor where the V/STOL strip and the approaches of the Luddite camp met. If the trails marked on the map were passable by hummer, he had a short drive tomorrow, even going the two longer sides of a triangle.

The thunderheads cleared away completely, leaving his camp bathed in the extra light of an already risen full Moon, a Marsco Moon. Large, ashen clouds blocked a clear view of surface craters. The old lunar man wore a clump of fuzzy white whiskers and pimples made from orbiting mining asteroids casting giant shadows.

—•—

"He's settled down for the night," Rivers reported. The listening associates heard rhythmic snoring mixed with the nocturnal sounds of the forest. Sensors picked up the breeze in the trees and the slow drip of rain off the tent.

"You have everything set for tracking him tomorrow?" asked Giannini.

"Affirmative. Wherever he goes, we'll be able to watch and listen. Unless he's under several meters of rock—not likely in a primitive Ludd camp."

"And the hummer?"

"The RS/VP can secretly leave behind two dozen remote sensors from its vehicle platform wherever we select. With any luck, we'll link with them better than previous drones. Give him a day rambling about, and we'll have remotes throughout the compound."

"And you're sure they can't detect our e-plants?" asked the lander pilot, unaccustomed to such clandestine ops. "This might backfire, tip them off."

"Such pongos characteristically forsake most tech," Giannini retorted needlessly, irritated with a jockey questioning his plan. "I seriously doubt they'll have the necessary scanners to detect and block our plants."

Rivers thought the contrary but said nothing. Given what ECM they already utilized—their umbrella even impossibly blocking IR sweeps—he wasn't confident in this surveillance at all. Sooner or later, he felt that someone would have to recce this camp personally. That was often the case in an urban UZ; drone intel platforms gather only so much. The experienced legionnaire knew the next step for Security, and he itched to join that recon.

Nothing in the priest's camp moved as Rivers conducted a final sweep with a real-time cam. "I'll just shut down for the night," he told his superiors. "He'll sleep until morning. I'll boot up then."

Without comment, Giannini removed his left glove to access an encrypted com channel for his nightly report. Neither Rivers nor Pisanos had clearance to boot such a secure transmission line. Both knew the signal to leave the senior officer by himself.

An hour after first light, just as promised, Cavanaugh found everything his nav-computer displayed. Driving down the ridge from his clearing, he soon joined a wide jungle track cutting through the thicker foliage. The hummer had no difficulty handling long-neglected paths as the priest moved westward without incident along the foot of the rocky spur.

And yet, all morning the solitary driver never shook the eerie feeling of being watched. *Someone or something's there in the bush,* he thought more than once, never losing that sense of being shadowed just beyond his view in the encroaching forest.

He drove slowly for an hour. Then hungry, he stopped for his first meal. He had ample provisions, although life in a zone kept him hardened and lean, accustomed to physical depravation. His body, conditioned by the rigors of a PRIM-like life, accepted what he demanded of it.

Moving once more through the jungle shadows, he soon found places that had grown thick with tangled vines. In marshy parts, Spanish moss hung above festering pools. In others places, the widening track unexpectedly seemed recently traversed and matted from continuous foot traffic.

In a pocket of dense growth, the hummer startled something in the bush. *A parrot? A jaguar?* He didn't know, but on he moved.

Moments later the trail cut through a lush obstruction like a tunnel. Branches and fronds gave way to a clearing on his right. Eventually the priest came to the abandoned strip mine marked on his e-map. Here water cascaded down the mountainside that he had been driving beside but never glimpsed through the dense growth. Miners had worked this spot more than 100 years ago, stripped it clean and moved on.

"Where is he?"

"The mining site."

Rivers's hidden cam revealed the remains of a slash-and-burn claim.

Last century, miners had dammed the stream to create a large pond. After burning back the jungle, they engaged high-powered pumps to hydraulically placer mine the hillside. Sodden topsoil and loosened gravel cascaded down into sluices where the heavier precious metal settled while the dancing sand and turbid water flowed away. It didn't take long for those powerful hydraulic nozzles to water-carve a hillside down to bedrock. Tons of earth were saturated, forced aside, abandoned. The rocky sediment lying in heaps attested to the pillaging.

"Such cuttings were often left unfit for further human habitation," the pilot concluded since restoring such sites had become her philanthropic avocation.

"Did you actually work down there?"

The pilot nodded. "Nature would have taken a millennium," replied the pilot-turned-environmentalist. "Marsco took several years. Where there'd once been barren slag heaps, we removed them and replanted indigenous saplings." Pisanos noted that even the trees were set randomly as though a natural grove, not a uniform plantation of identical rows.

As the associates watched, the priest entered a lean-to that stood to the side of the squatter site.

“Is that a relic of the mining era?” Rivers asked.

“No, it shows signs of recent habitation,” the pilot assured him.

This caught the wallah’s attention; here was something he didn’t know.

“Look, to starboard,” the pilot ordered. Rivers shifted the swiveling cam view. A latrine dug behind a tree hadn’t been carefully covered. Aseptic food packaging left in a shallow garbage pit suggested recent use. “The saplings cut from the hillside,” Pisanos noted, “clearly prove that squatters came *after* enviro-engineers left.”

The three conjectured who had been there. An associate gone native? Some sid shut out from the Marsco world, looking for a place of his own? A restless demobbed vet wandering twenty-five years after the Wars? A PRIM girl preferring to face jungle terrors alone rather than life in a crowded zone? Perhaps her child was buried near by—one of a myriad possibilities.

Cavanaugh shuddered. *Who’s been living out here so far from another Christian soul?*

That feeling of surveillance came over him once more. The grove of trees seemed to be aware of him. He sensed he was watched even if he didn’t see his observer. *The occupant of this lean-to? No, been empty for months.*

Rivers placed a sensor near the shelter. *Did some former associate build that?* he wondered, disparaging anyone foolish enough to leave Marsco.

A slow click later, Cavanaugh’s hummer forded a swift stream. The vehicle easily handled the viscous mud on both banks. As expected just beyond, the priest found the abandoned V/STOL strip nestled in a flat valley. Surprisingly, it was holding its own against the relentless growth around its edges. Accelerating down the runway, he discovered it was smooth and unbroken instead of vine covered. The tarmac for the most part was clear, even if here and there great roots buckled the macadam.

"Reached the strip?"

"Yes, sir. That's why I called you."

"Seems the same as from our earlier drone recon, don't you think?"

"No, look there." Rivers adjusted his cam to the left. "Don't you think there's a few more scattered hangers and maintenance bays under the canopy than we thought?"

"Yes."

"The whole field showed evidence of recent activity."

"Heavy use, too."

Parked on the tarmac, the priest once more sensed he was being watched. At the corner of a hanger hidden under swaying vines, he saw sudden movement. Driving over for a closer examination, he found the buildings still serviceable but locked and free of anyone about.

"Do an IR scan just along the jungle. Picking up anything?"

"Some disturbance, nothing definite."

"Could it be human?"

"Hard to say. Possibly a mammal, sir." Rivers shrugged. "It's a jungle. Monkeys. A tree sloth. Perhaps two, one on each side of the trunk."

"Stay with him."

"Yes, sir." Rivers continued accompanying the priest remotely. Checking the perimeter line of ECM projection, the warrant knew the wanderer would soon disappear under the Ludd umbrella.

The priest found the metal road running off toward the isolated Corps camp. The Nexus encampment was not more than five kilometers beyond. Crossing the strip and following the matted trail, he made good time.

Less than two clicks along, the jungle grew dense; it became a tangle of roots and branches hiding the remains of the road. But once through the thicket, the hummer entered an unexpected wide clearing. Although surrounded by rainforest, the clearing was inexplicably large, ten times that of his base camp. Because the camp sat on a rocky hill, it made sense that vegetation was sparse there. But Cavanaugh knew that here this clearing shouldn't exist at all.

To his horror, the priest found an explanation why. Carved out from the dank foliage, the clearing was the site of a burial ground, a pocked field with a hundred pits visible at a quick glance. Fifty, perhaps as many as another hundred, had already been reclaimed by the encroaching growth.

The mat road, which had all but disappeared in the jungle behind, was plainly visible, a rusty ribbon marking the right edge of the ripped-back jungle. Scores of pits stretched 300 meters ahead and 100 to the left until disappearing into the undisturbed green thicket.

From the *Mendes,* the associates watched the priest. "Any indication of these pits from our recce of this locale?"

"None, sir."

“Rather a morbid first find on this mission,” concluded Giannini.

Tuffs of grass sprouted in the indentation of each pit, giant dimples in the red dirt where once teaming, undisturbed vegetation stretched.

The three viewed the priest unclip the hummer’s shovel.

“It’s almost like he’s acting on orders,” commented the pilot.

He set to digging into the first pit.

“He’s driven by a need to know,” River conjectured. “He’s trying to discover who might be there.”

The pit eagerly gave up its mystery as the shovel revealed skeletal remains.

Rivers cataloged what they saw. “No clothing or shoes. No flesh. Just bones.”

“The long dead,” the wallah concurred, “all human.”

The entombed had been placed side by side, heads facing the same way, hands crossed over the chest.

“Execution site?” asked the lander pilot.

“Yes, war-era,” stated Giannini without emotion.

Had he wanted, the priest could have exhumed whole skeletons, but he quickly found enough. *Surely these were massacre victims long interred.* From the road reaching into the far forest, at least 150 other pits waited examination. The jungle had already reclaimed many beyond those. In silent prayer for the dead, the priest walked around the edges of several pits, a cratered moonscape of silent death.

Who had originally hidden these graves in the jungle? he wondered. *To what purpose?*

Something moved in the green curtain beyond. The priest whipped around to look, but the veil revealed no one.

Cavanaugh moved his hummer to the clearing's distant end and walked amid other pits that seemed different in depth and organization. Some near at hand were round. Others looked like fortification slit trenches. Several were L-shaped. They were scattered randomly in the newly made clearing, not placed in any particular order. They showed clear evidence of a hasty burial, victims covered over where they had been executed.

These pits gave up their secrets without digging; fleshless bones appeared in several.

"Look, a pelvis."

"And there's a partial skull."

"All close-range Enfield executions," responded Giannini flatly.

One skeleton remained totally unburied next to a closed-up pit. Through its ribcage, clinging vines sent tendrils out from bone to exposed bone. The last victim, forgotten years before in the haste of the moment.

The stunned priest wandered amid the killing field until he found what he feared most: five shallow pits that had been recently reopened. On one side of each was a mound of dirt. On the other, lay a jumble of broken exhumed remains, a femoral, two skulls, other odd bits of skeletons.

Like the first pit he had shoveled, the bones originally had been, after a fashion, neatly arranged. Now the pile showed that the bones had been dug up hastily and carelessly tossed into a confused heap, a mosaic of death.

Clearly these pits had been recently dug into for a second purpose.

The priest realized they had also been hurriedly refilled with the newly dead; too little dirt had been spread over the latest corpses.

Out of the earth, a few stared skyward. Their horrid remains—disfigured, distrustful of the living—looked up hauntingly, unconcerned with the clouds of black flies.

An undersized child. An old woman's paper-thin eyelids seemed to stare back from her shrunken, accusing face. A father, in the gesture of protection for his son, held a lifeless body. Both faces glared upward, their sockets shrunken into their skulls.

Beside the entwined pair, two other boys lay, their skeletons not yet picked clean by time or scavengers. Recovering his composure, the priest tried imagining them as his own. They were discouragingly similar—frail, helpless. *Antonio and Thax?* In such an advanced decomposition, Cavanaugh was unable to tell.

The putrid flesh attracted swarms of flies and knots of wriggling maggots. Brazen rats stayed at their gnawing, not frightened by the approaching man.

The nauseating stench made the priest swoon. Staggering to his feet after holding himself back from retching, he wasn't careful where he stepped. Almost falling into a nearby pit, his foot collapsed a still-covered grave, crushing a decaying ribcage, more evidence of a recent burial.

The priest, who had witnessed every sort of heinous crime before, heaved violently, his vomit hardly tempting the teeming flies.

Sitting at his tracking station, Rivers was horrified. Secret scanners and cam nodes kept the priest under a constant real-time surveillance. Remote control gave the trooper the ability to focus and zoom over the inexplicable landscape.

Marsco's stopping such slaughter, Rivers insisted to himself. *Security has stopped it.*

He anguished that he had urged the defenseless priest into this rotting, rank hell. That he had put such a peace-loving man into such jeopardy.

To the same grotesque images, neither Giannini nor Pisanos reacted. Although distasteful, the pits of mangled corpses were nothing new to either.

It was only when the hummer's remote came to rest near a recently opened grave that Giannini reacted. "Focus on the hands!" he urged, his excited words conflicting with his calm exterior. "Look at their hands!"

Rivers zoomed into a fly-covered pit.

"Yes, I see it," replied Pisanos, herself not squeamish at such a sight.

It took Rivers a moment to notice. Every decomposing hand had missing fingers. All the right index fingers were gone: every one, right hand after right hand, index finger after index finger. Other right fingers were cut off as well. Even some left hands had a finger or two missing.

Assuming a connection between the pits and the Luddites beyond, Giannini concluded, "Puts them in a whole new light, doesn't it?"

"Conclusive."

"Forced DRP to the max," commented the wallah in a weak attempt at macabre humor.

Perceiving the imminent danger for the priest and his foolhardy sortie, Rivers blamed himself for Cavanaugh being there.

The priest's hummer wound down the narrow track beyond the killing field. In a thicket, the squat hummer barely squeezed through a tangle of tree trunks and their intertwined roots. Beyond the end of the metal road, he was no longer sure if he was even on the passable track that formerly wound through here. He might be off a road altogether, might need to hike into the jungle to find the Nexus.

"What's happening?" Rivers spit out. The signals from the hummer were breaking up. The Ludds' electronic jamming seemed to be growing, reaching out farther and farther to surround the explorer.

For the past fifteen minutes, the hummer's signals had been fluctuating, weakening, then increasing in intensity, then weakening again. In a nano, all airwaves were completely lost.

Several silent minutes passed before Rivers acknowledged every e-link was broken.

"Cavanaugh might be out of touch permanently," he reported.

Around the stalled hummer, the bush moved in unison. The growth rose up as though the harrowing spirits of the dead who Cavanaugh had left behind had trailed and then surrounded him. In the verdant gloom, frightening apparitions stood before him, beside him, behind him. Out of the shadows they loomed hellish and sinister.

Twelve camouflaged figures silently encircled the hummer, their faces smeared green and black. Branches and vines hung from them. They weren't armed with advanced weapons; instead they carried machetes and assegai spears and bamboo staffs. One held a short blowgun.

The priest felt an unexpected sting on this upper arm where a sapphire insect stung him. He hastily tried to swat off the cobalt pest, barbed like a fishhook, but it had dug in deeply under his skin.

From that stinging instant, confused dreams began. Comforting dreams blended into other dreams that became ever more horrid with each shifting image. In a hallucination, menacing green hands reached for him. He tried escaping these apparitions, but they seemed solid, not imaginary.

Delirious, he dreamed of being carried a great distance.

"Anything?" Giannini asked.

"Nothing," was Rivers' despondent reply fourteen hours after the priest's channels broke down.

The *Mendes* continued on a slow circuit just outside the ECM umbrella. Sensors reported that the lander itself was being electronically probed. Beams emitted from inside the valley came at them, but the lander's own sensors were blind.

It was a position Marsco rarely found itself in.

Cavanaugh experienced many excruciating dreams his second night in the forest. Disturbing phantoms entered his mind, forcing their way in.

Behind his right eye, an intense headache throbbed. When he tried rubbing his forehead, his arms didn't move.

Threatening images came and went. He tried to wake himself but was unable to. *Is this like hibering?* he wondered. He next thought, *Am I to die a martyr? If so, my soul's ready, but I don't want to die.* Then, *Who'd know if I did? Not my bishop. No one at St. Teresa's. Marsco would know, that's for sure.* He found that somehow comforting. *Marsco would know!*

And still the intense pain behind his right eye throbbed.

Someone moved outside his dreams. *The watcher in the jungle?* Other images came and went. Then he no longer dreamed but slept soundly for hours.

After his unbroken dreamless slumber, the nightmares returned. Fragmented images ebbed and flowed. Each vision appeared more sinister and threatening than its predecessor. They shifted into growing shapes of ominous fury. Then they became jangled hallucinations. He saw himself lifeless at the bottom of one of the pits, the near-at-hand dead moving to embrace him, welcome him.

Half awake with heavy eyes open and quick gulps for breath, he thought he was about to die. He wanted to rouse himself to full consciousness, to end this lingering dream-horror, but soon he fell back into a heavy vacant stupor.

Hours later, when he dreamed, it was as though he watched himself on that first morning still in his clearing. *Was that only yesterday? No, probably two days ago—been asleep that long.*

In his dream, he watched himself making his trip as though watching from the tree line just out of sight: the jungle track, the miner's lean-to, the V/STOL strip, the mass graves. *Antonio's grave? Thax's?*

He thought, *Was someone watching there all the time? Something? A jaguar? A harmless spider monkey? Just out of sight? Trailing me? Over there—behind that second rubber tree. See him? Hidden in the Spanish moss! Look!*

Confused images followed, one upon the next. His dream abruptly shifted into momentary impressions. His head throbbed with the onset of a migraine he was unable to prevent. His trance became a nightmare of death.

Exhausted, he drifted off into unconscious dreamlessness.

For Rivers, the tedious hours stretched into a third day. Nothing changed, although the impeding Luddite ECM umbrella grew wider and stronger.

"Currently," the warrant reported, "even his base camp is jammed. Every device left by the hummer's silent. Twenty-four hours ago was our last full contact with any of them." He gave a succinct summary, "Priest, hummer, hillside base—all electronically gone."

The *Mendes* had the camp on visual, but in the darkness of night, the craft's thermal imaging scopes returned a gray cloudy reading, not a green-tinted image. "It's as though no starlight shines and no residual daytime heat radiates," the confounded pilot complained, as though the Ludds had cheated at a game Marsco always won.

Giannini exploded in frustration. "It's scientifically impossible, blocking off infrared signatures! And from jungle-hidden Ludds! Inconceivable! I mean, I'd believe it, if this were happening in an advanced subsidiary, but here? By these skinnies?"

Mother Teresa appeared in the dark. She beckoned the priest, welcomed him. But in a dream-trick, her white sari with its dark blue trim turned to dirty gray. Its blue strip became black. Her kindly face distorted into a crone's. Reassuring dreams of her became mad jangles of repulsion.

Then unexpectedly, a new menacing face appeared, a second crone.

The first witch examined him thoroughly but brusquely. The second hovered in the distance, a brooding angel of death. The scrutinizing one held up his right hand and angrily picked at its index finger with her stubby claws.

After that visit, Mother Teresa periodically returned. She always came pleasantly at first but ended up a hateful, frightening hag.

Then, for hours the priest slept, his rest periodically broken by the apparition of one or both withered, ominous faces.

Still the *Mendes* circled. Eventually, it spaced six drones evenly around the perimeter of the electronic disruption and the hill-top camp. Making sure all the probes were working properly, the lander returned to its Rio base.

"The drones," Rivers reported to his superiors, "are presently probing the umbrella."

One methodical unit ventured beyond the invisible electronic boundary; contact with it was lost. The others waited patiently to receive any faint signal from the priest.

Rivers feared it would never come.

"*Za!*" the wizened witch sneered, her head a dimly lit outline in the darkness. She offered the half-awake priest something to drink, which he refused.

I'm imprisoned, Cavanaugh concluded as his mind became clearer. He was sweaty, and the dank air made him feel clammy. He was lying on a cot, still dressed in his bush pants and shirt, although his boots were off. He remained groggy from all his restless and dream-filled sleep. He thought perhaps he had slept a full day. His head throbbed, and his upper left arm hurt from a painful, swollen welt.

"*Za!*" the witch ordered a second time.

Cavanaugh sat up and began reluctantly swallowing an amber liquid from a wooden bowl. It tasted sweet at first yet grew bitter as he drank deeply. He coughed at its unexpected sharpness. Indescribably thirsty, he found himself unwilling to cease from drinking.

The bowl drained, the witch refilled it. "*Za!*" He drank for a second time, finishing the bowl without its dregs bothering him.

"The jungle provides many gifts for the sha-woman who knows her," the witch spit at him. "Some gifts cure."

"Some ease illness." Another voice in the dark spoke up.

"For some, it offers comfort." Yet a third, younger voice spoke, taking up the lines like a chant.

"For some, death," the first witch cackled.

"What do you three offer me?" whispered the priest, his voice hoarse from her brackish drink.

The voices fell silent at his question.

The priest rubbed his beating temple with one hand, while still favoring his arm with the welt. He had perspired greatly; his cotton shirt showed signs of profuse night sweating. *Neo-Con,* he wondered, *or the onset of malaria?*

He surveyed his surroundings in the dim light. The walls of the stone room were beaded from the humidity; the air was still but surprisingly cool. *Must be underground,* he noted, *in a buried cell.*

Three human figures took shape behind a small table at the opposite end of his chamber. Two flickering candles gave their faces a yellow cast. One craggy face he recognized as the dream-witch. Although this crone was standing, so little of her torso was visible above the crudely crafted table, the priest concluded she was hardly taller than a dwarf. Her two cohorts sat on a stone ledge protruding from the wall.

He stopped rubbing his head; its throbbing abruptly vanished. Even the welt on his arm ceased irritating him.

Three sets of steely eyes scrutinized him without comfort or welcome. One sitting figure was as old and withered as the dream-witch but nearly bald. Her little tuff of short, white hair lay flat on her head. Even in the dim light, the priest saw in the other sitting figure a daughter's resemblance to the first crone.

"Who are you?" he asked, the first of many questions he wanted to put to these apparitions.

"We ask here," the youngest answered.

"Has your head left off pounding?" asked the dwarf-witch. To the priest's nodding she added, "A gift from the jungle."

"Your first," the other old witch keened.

"Your last?" asked the girl.

"That is for you to decide." The witches' remarks sounded like a chant-round with the dwarf-witch making their final comment.

The three were wrapped in homespun saris, woven of gray cloth with black stripes. They resembled those of the sisters who taught with him in the zone. *I see why I dreamt of Mother Teresa,* he realized.

The youngest kept her left arm in her sleeve because her wrist oozed from a large ulcerating lesion she tried hiding. The wound stained her sleeve with blood and pus. The man noted the infection notwithstanding the faint light.

"Tell us what these amulets are." The older sitting figure demanded.

These three, or some henchman, had obviously searched him. On the table lay his rosary and breviary alongside the Marsco Lander Fleet patch Commander Pisanos had given him.

The young woman spoke, "What of these beads, what talisman?" She seemed to have never seen the likes before.

"And you read!" The second witch stated as though a crime, thumbing through the pages of his breviary.

"And what of this?" The dream-witch asked, coming forward and holding up the woven shoulder patch. Placing it in his left hand, she reached for his other with both of hers. She turned over his right palm; the single finger disk, even in the dark cell, was clearly visible—a blue-green subcutaneous circle. "And what of *that?*"

"We will know—"

"—what we want to know," added two voices from the stone ledge.

"*Za!*" the dream-witch glowered. Turning, she motioned to the table where food waited. Weakened from his imprisonment, Cavanaugh didn't know from where it had appeared. If the food been there in the shadowy cavern long, he had failed to notice.

By means of a small wooden door, the three left him. A bowl of clean water sat next to the food. Before washing, the priest made sure the pitcher had enough to quench his thirst. Finding ample, he washed his hands and face, almost playfully splashing himself, before saying his blessing.

At first, not wanting to sit on the ledge previously occupied by the two witches, Cavanaugh stood to eat. His feet were cold from the stone floor, so he slipped them into his boots.

Standing at the table, he surveyed his meal. It offered a bit of roasted dry meat highly seasoned with salt and cayenne. He also had one meager, spicy yam. A bowl held a wrinkled orange. The drinking water was cool and fresh tasting. Soon exhaustion overtook him and he sat to eat.

After finishing what he assumed was his first food in at least forty-eight hours, Cavanaugh grew restless. He paced for a considerable time, walking along the table in two strides, turning to make two steps along the wall, turning at the bed, lowering at the wall with the door, then back along the table. He stopped at the water pitcher until he had drained it. The cell remained dimly lit from two candle stubs. Eventually, he lay back down on the damp cot.

This time, he knew he had been drugged. Perhaps the strong pepper covered some narcotic. He tried praying by counting his Hail Marys on his fingers since he no longer had his beads. He fought sleep with all his mental powers but with little success. He strained to stay awake as if his life depended on it. *Will you not watch with me?* he heard himself say, then his eyelids closed.

The priest didn't dream at all during his next lengthy, drug-induced sleep. Nonetheless, he heard many voices talking softly among themselves.

The first belonged to the haggard witch. He never dreamed her face, which gave him some measure of comfort, but she seemed to come and go intermittently, talking with him each time. She was no longer a silent looming figure in his sleep but a recurring, potent voice.

He recognized the second voice as his own, weak and halting. His mind wished to give no answers, but his will was unable to resist. This voice—his own distant voice—spoke names over and over, that was all he remembered ever saying, names: Warrant Officer Peter Rivers. Bethany Palmer. Stephen Cavanaugh. Commander Pisanos. Walter Miller. The *Mendes.* Tessa and Zot. Bella. St. Teresa's principal, Sister Dorothy Day Alvarez. Margaret and Sean. Antonio and Thax.

Over and over he repeated these as though in prayer. He heard his voice commanded to speak; he dare not disobey. Miller, Margaret, Antonio, Thax, Rivers, Tessa, and Zot. He heard the crone whispering with other, distant voices he only partially understood. She talked to two young voices, but he picked up only pieces of their conversation.

After a long period of dreamless sleep—he guessed he had been out for five or six days this time—someone touched his arm. He eventually awoke still in the same cell, as though he had slept only a single night.

From the distant Rio Cantonment, Rivers monitored the surveillance drones that loitered in the jungle. A dozen days passed with nothing changing while the legionnaire waited for the priest to reemerge unexpectedly from the heart of the forest darkness.

The warrant officer hated himself for sending Cavanaugh in to that impenetrable hell. He should have made him take an Enfield to give the naive cleric some measure of protection. As a well-trained associate, Rivers instinctively tapped a 9 mm holstered at his side. The weapon assured every associate of effortless and unrestrained passage outside the direct auspices of Marsco. Cavanaugh ought to have carried one.

The prisoner remained confined, unwashed, with no light except for a dim candle. A covered pot smelled from the corner. *Perhaps three, four days have passed,* he thought at the end of his second week. Waking from his induced sleep, he heard the distinctive chest rattle of someone in the bloody throes of Neo-Con and then heard soft whispering between children.

After a fortnight of prolonged sleep, he opened his eyes, seeing clearly for the first time since his single meal.

On the ledge behind the table sat Antonio and Thax, waiting for the captive to awaken.

TWELVE

THE JUNGLE SAGE

(In the Nexus Camp, 2095)

"I've been drugged!" Father Cavanaugh let loose, blinded by diffused sunlight.

The Leader of the Nexus approached the priest as the morning's first mottled light cut through the thick vines above them. His zealous throng surrounded the hostage, eager to see him for themselves, to witness this initial meeting between such renowned holy men.

"Interrogated!" The cleric went on, "Imprisoned! Today marks the first time I've set foot above ground for weeks." He spoke deliberately without hysteria. "I've not seen anyone during my solitary confinement except for three witches, and only once, the two boys, Thax and Antonio. Is this any kind of welcome?" Having spoken his mind, he wavered unsteadily.

Without giving a direct response to the captive, the Leader brought his clenched fists up to his shoulders then slowly opened his hands to show the palm side of his fingers. His hands were without disks although not free from implant removal scars. "As you see, Righteous Guest," the jungle sage spoke in a deep voice, "we are chaste toward the Evil One, as you are not."

The jostling faithful gave room to their spiritual head, but they pressed in on the priest so that even if he wanted to, he wasn't able to step away. The crush of believers standing in rapt silence, the morning's rising humidity, the depletion of his stamina: all made the prisoner dizzy. Nonetheless, he stood his ground.

The Leader was taller than the priest by twelve centimeters and was at least fifteen years younger. The rigors of life outside Marsco had not slowed him. The prophet wore a neatly trimmed sandy beard. His eyes were sea blue, his face sunburnt. He was dressed in a traditional-looking white cassock, more appropriate for the Bishop of Rome than a forest mystic. The rough cloth resembled the material of the witches' saris, only theirs were gray and not immaculately bleached.

Behind the Leader stood the three women, proud of their captive. They gloated over garnering so much information after his mysterious appearance in their remote reaches of the Amazon.

"Come, Mother, Sister, Daughter," the Leader spoke gently, "let's continue your praiseworthy reception for this, our revered visitor."

The fervent followers, who had been holding their collective breath waiting for a possible public sign of disapproval, sighed in agreement.

"Make immediate preparations for lodging our honored traveler in the visitor hut," Leader announced. At the back of the crowd of 400 followers, several scurried off without another word.

Turning to Cavanaugh, he commented loudly, "Most welcome you are, for your reputation for strength, compassion, and saintliness precedes you."

Even in his exhaustion, the wily priest smirked, "It's only through death that sainthood's bestowed. I hope I've not come for *that.*"

The Leader took the prisoner's right hand tenderly into his own hands. "Welcome. Ours is yours, holy man," he whispered to the priest's ear, still holding the hostage's right hand. "Welcome," he spoke softly to the other ear, "but we shall have to talk soon of *this.*" He looked down at the blue-green disk clearly visible under the skin of the right index finger.

His remarks broke Cavanaugh's resolve to greet the Leader without any sign of fatigue. The prisoner abruptly staggered forward, leaning onto his host's shoulder. "Three weeks underground have cost me much strength," Cavanaugh persisted hoarsely, then slumped onto several of the followers who eagerly assisted him.

The priest was immediately led through the throng to new quarters by four men who acted more as an honor guard than as captors. Cavanaugh noticed that they readily assisted him, urging him along with affection befitting a venerated guest. The roughness of his capture, the brusqueness of the dwarf: all that surliness dissipated in Leader's sanctifying gaze.

"Anything, ensign?"

"Nothing."

Rivers waited impatiently. Giannini demanded periodic reports, and yet for mounting weeks, nothing about the Luddites or Cavanaugh came back from the drones. Even a slow lander flyby over the valley for a visual recce revealed only dense, unbroken rainforest.

"Father Stephen's disappeared completely," his former student reported. "So have all signs of the Ludds except for their constant countermeasures."

Aggitated, Rivers could only watch and wait, keeping his impatience in check as best he could; even his recently added badge of rank did little to assuage his guilt.

Monitoring blank screens and silent com-links, the ensign waited. His first weeks as a centurion were marked by that single event—waiting.

The guest hut sat diagonally across from the Leader's central bungalow thirty meters from where the two had just met. As the four guards marched Cavanaugh along, Sister, as ordered by Mother, followed behind.

When they arrived, he stated with undisguised sarcasm, "Well, it's commodious compared to my previous digs." None of the Ludds caught his mockery.

In such a primitive hut, the flagstone floor was immediately striking. Its squares were multicolored but mismatched, cannibalized from midcentury buildings. And although the hut's exterior was rough timber, its inner walls were hand-hewn bricks. *PRIM work to be sure,* the priest noted, *all with prewar materials.*

The interior was a hodgepodge taken from many different sites. No attempt was made to match color or size. The Ludd masonry was mortared together with a mud and straw mixture of poor quality. The walls were already crumbling apart in the constant humidity.

Turning on the witch, the priest asked, "Why's the hut constructed this way?" The comment received no reply.

Along one wall of the largest room, windows without glass or screens faced toward the Leader's central bungalow. The only light, a green glow from the indirect sun passing through trellis vines, came from these openings. The hut offered no electricity or oil lamps. Nowhere was there a sign of pens, paper, or monitor. Anything even early-century.

The opposite end led to a smaller, private room with a bath barrel and water in three large stone jars. "It's splendidly kind of you," the priest sneered at the solitary guard who remained statue-faced in the larger room, "but no one needs to wash my back."

Cavanaugh found warm water in a ceramic ewer, a mirror, and a courtesy travel kit from the *Mendes.* He hadn't opened it before, but it held personal-sized containers of shampoo, shaving cream, and a razor. Marsco perks provided by Pisanos for the lepidopterist. On the bed waited a pair of his own khaki shorts, a cotton shirt, and clean underwear retrieved from his base camp.

"So, you've searched my gear thoroughly," the priest groused to his silent guard.

After bathing, the prisoner found himself alone. On an alcove shelf a meal waited, the largest since his capture. As he finished devouring the food, Daughter, the youngest witch, entered. Her thick black hair hung down over her shoulder, down her back, making her seem fresh and innocent.

She was slender and clearly coming of age. He looked tenderly at her as he would his own daughter. She seemed highly intelligent and had those classic features he had loved in his second wife, Isabella: high cheekbones; striking, penetrating black eyes; flawless olive skin.

But she carries such sadness in her face, her eyes, he thought with pity.

Cavanaugh studied her closely. She was all of sixteen, perhaps a year or two older. Her painful reserve was unmistakable. The prisoner saw she was originally born PRIM; a left hand scar provided evidence of that. And survival for such a woman, especially such an attractive one, often came at a steep personal price. She had paid that price, he instinctively knew. Paid it dearly.

"You're as incongruous as this hut," he stated calmly without her answering. "Like so much I've encountered here—everything, everyone's a curious mixture of styles and origins."

Through the front window, the priest surveyed the compound. From the steps of the Leader's bungalow ran a paved road in much disrepair. The bungalow and the other huts opposite were all draped in jungle vines that dangled from an intricate trellis system. Their supports were made from hundreds of wooden poles, all of them over five meters tall. Each was in turn anchored by guys and crisscrossed with thick cables along which the leafy vines traversed.

"Hops!" the priest exclaimed. "Looks like you're growing hops," he commented pleasantly, unconcerned with the silent girl's lack of response. Everywhere he looked around this camp, everything was under an elaborate trellis holding up lush vines that stretched into the rainforest without a break.

He turned to the young woman. "Well, I assume that these vines, like the reused bricks and flagstones, keep the huts cool—at least that's their intent."

She remained taciturn even though he was sure she understood perfectly. He thought of speaking in Brazilian or Mexican; she looked as though she knew both. Nonetheless, seeing that she was taking every comment in, he continued in English.

"The disorderly nature of the bricks seems to mimic the Leader's followers themselves." Sitting across the room from the silent woman, he received no response or encouragement.

"Those circling us at first, your esteemed Leader and me, so many seemed out of place here. Even with Marsco consistently shifting PRIMS, in this rainforest, I'd have expected more natives, for example. Or more like you—am I not correct in assuming you're from this continent?"

She gave no answer.

"And yet I saw many Asians; clearly I didn't expect any here. Several were Sikhs. I saw so many from India that I wondered if I hadn't been drugged and mysteriously spirited away from the upper Amazon and secretly conveyed to the Ganges half a world away. I'm correct in making that assumption, mistaken as it might be?"

The young woman remained still.

"In our Marsco world, nothing should surprise me," he breathed out in frustration. "Clearly—and I'm totally at a loss to explain my next hypothesis—a notable few, a handful at most, seemed *formerly* Marsco. Definitely associate material out there." He stopped and looked directly at her. "Does my rambling make any sense, my dear?"

He added with a chuckle, "More sense than associates *here!*"

The young woman stayed as stationary as ever.

Gently, the man rose to stand before his reticent companion. "You know, my child, I can see your infection." She remained motionless as he pulled back her sari from her left wrist where a festering, open wound ate into her flesh. "I might be able to help you. I'm no doctor, but years of tending children, well, I know a few methods that may fix you up."

At his words, the young woman swiftly withdrew her arm from view and shot the priest a hateful look.

"So be it. But do you know," he went on softly, staying next to her, wanting to confirm one last hypothesis, "the most peculiar thing I've witnessed thus far?" He asked while moving aside her long, black hair. Behind her right ear, an ELD was implanted. "This! Your disk! I believe it's properly called an English Language Disk. Miller would know. Regardless, it makes no sense, none. *Nada!* Not here, at least!"

Walter Miller tried repeatedly to contact Cavanaugh. If the priest didn't respond, the logical engineer theorized that only two alternatives existed. Either he was unable to answer, or he was unwilling to answer. Neither theory presented any satisfaction. The granger had been trying for weeks but was now past hope, anxious for any reply.

After Father Cavanaugh's siesta—a routine for his first week above ground—two escorts arrived. They were tall, dressed in lightweight tiger-scheme fatigues. Like all the Nexus followers who dealt with the priest after he met with the Leader that one and only time, they were cordial and polite.

This afternoon, they walked the captive past the Leader's bungalow toward a large pavilion 200 meters away. In this part of the compound, another forty huts were staggered along a 300-meter stretch of abandoned roadway fringed with long grass. As with everything the priest had seen above ground, these huts sat under the inexplicable trellisworks.

Moving along the broken pavement, the priest realized that the overhead system was larger than he had at first believed. Thick vines extended in every direction until they blended into the jungle.

The number of hidden huts surprised him as well; the camp was more expansive than he had imagined. And from these dozens of huts, scores of followers came and went. Most of the disciples he saw seemed older than his boys, but like that first gathering he witnessed, they looked like a mixture of PRIMS. He recognized a few others from obvious sid background, even a sprinkling whose bearing suggested previous associate status. As with the huts, the number of workers the priest caught at a glance astonished him; easily, 200 moved in all directions under the shading vines.

As his escort ushered the prisoner along, he was the only one to speak. "Conundrum upon conundrum," he stated out loud, hoping for any sort of response. "Here's one enigma after another."

Cavanaugh was brought to the largest compound building. Along this pavilion's walls, several icons and memorials hung. Here and there, he saw statues of armed knights; St. Michael and St. Ignatius with swords drawn; Joan of Arc in armor. On a far wall, crossed Zulu assegais hung next to a set of Marsco-issued shoulder-fired Enfields from the Continental Wars.

The Nexus inner circle waited at two low tables with twenty cushions arranged around them. The single, gold-trimmed cushion was Leader's. At his right Mother had one nearly twice its size; she seemed to swim in it. The sage didn't sit at the head but in the middle, so his position gave no indication of his pivotal standing.

The priest's cushion was directly across from Leader's, where the captive sat under his constant, intense gaze and Mother's suspicious stares. On the guest's right sat Sister and Daughter, on his left, a young man who sometimes acted as his escort.

Before their meal commenced, the witches rose and chanted, "His Holiness, Leader of the Nexus, bless us!"

Together the table raised their hands toward Leader to show their disk-free palms and replied in cadence, "Our Leader, who balances black and white, good and evil, bless us."

Rising, Leader responded "Amen," while once more gesturing that his hands were totally free of any subcutaneous implants.

For this meal, a mixed group assembled. As before, Cavanaugh noted that these PRIMS seemed common in worldwide zones but uncommon in the Amazon. All were adult except for Thax and Antonio, who sat too far away from the priest to speak with them. At least he saw them; he was thankful for that.

Antonio seems healthy, happy to greet me, the prisoner acknowledged, *but Thax looks seriously ill indeed. It's a miracle—by the grace of Our Mother and the intervention of St. Teresa—that he's able to sit at table.* The feverish boy's repeated cough worried Cavanaugh.

Their meal began. A type of wild game had been roasted with the same sharp seasonings the priest tasted before. Because everyone took from two overflowing platters, the guest didn't fear being drugged. Bowls of fruit graced the table: bananas, oranges, mangoes, and grapes picked (the priest learned) from the trellis covering the south side of the compound.

Never intimidated by his surroundings, as soon as he could, the captive spoke up. "This rainforest's not the healthiest place for Thax. He needs rest, medication, and isolation to protect the others from his highly contagious state." The boy had picked at his food the whole time. "A PRIM offered such a meal," the priest drove home his point, "doesn't hesitate."

Ignoring his guest, Leader commented, "See what the jungle has to offer those who know where to look."

Mother caught the priest's eye; in a menacing whisper she hissed, "So too the jungle gives to the sha-woman."

The hostage realized that Mother was implying she might drug, or even poison, him in front of the whole table if she chose.

As they continued to eat, Cavanaugh noticed the late twentieth-century affectation of gathering up many religious backgrounds to give the Leader an air of spiritual reality. Artifacts from every continent, every religion, encircled them. Jesus as a warrior. Kali with her many arms and flaming tongue. Aires as a Roman centurion prepared for battle. These and other elements of forged pomp provided credence for his followers.

It's a world hungry for any beacon of faith, the priest knew. He bided his time before bringing Thax up again.

Two young women, both dark-haired and graceful like Daughter, waited on them. The Leader beckoned the oldest, who was about twenty, to his side. "My child, show our guest your freedom."

She presented her PRIM scar to him, her disk removed when she joined the Nexus. Other scars came from hard labor and BC strips.

"See here," Leader showed the edge of her left palm. "Before coming here, my child, where did you live?"

"In the zone of the great Mexi-City, Leader," the young woman answered plainly. "Then our Yucatan camp."

"Enough of where next, my child."

"Yes, Leader."

"And from Marsco? What did you receive?" the Leader asked tenderly.

"Food from it only by taking its poison, here," she answered without hesitation, pointing to the BC incision on her left palm.

"Did you get much for your poison?"

"No, never enough."

Turning to the priest, he reminded him, "Marsco calls its food distribution *philanthropy.* A PRIM girl-child's fitted with venom under her skin. As long as she carries it, she's fed. But only a paltry amount. Still she must work." Turning back to the woman, he asked, "What work did you perform?"

"I scavenged rags in a sid dumping ground, as you know, my Leader," she answered in an unassuming voice. "Each day, rags for them, bits of rotting food for me."

The Leader closed her palm gently then bid her return to her chores. "This is light work compared to digging offal from festering heaps. Rags. Dressed in rags, picking rags, until we gathered her to us." The Leader paused. "*Marsco philanthropy:* 'Come to the pavilion all you who hunger, and it will give you food.' *And* poison."

The priest calmly responded, "I've been a resident of an Unincorporated Zone longer than anyone else present. Was in zones before Marsco began supervising them. The Continental Powers organized zones at first during Divestiture, to be sure. But, I know well what you allude to." Cavanaugh searched for the right words. He was trying to fathom rather than defend or apologize for Marsco. "Food for PRIMS comes with many trade-offs," he readily conceded. Most PRIMS worked at manual, menial jobs, hired by the day through the auspices of Subsidiary Labor Unions. And for the older girls and young women, an additional price was coerced: barrenness.

"We're in agreement then, my guest," the Leader continued in his kindly way, sure he had won over another convert. "Kip, come, my son."

The guard sitting next to the priest rose. An Indian about twenty-five, his features were deeply tanned. He wore black and green jungle colors and a turban. He looked lean, honed under the mantel of his uniform, but like all the other escorts of the captive, he displayed a pleasant demeanor.

As Kip stood by the priest, the Leader declared, "Notice how healthy and straight his feet are, my hallowed guest."

The priest nodded at the sound and proud disciple.

"Kip has been here—"

"It is being eight years at full summer, Leader."

"And before that?"

"Near Calcutta."

"But a PRIM zone."

"Yes, my Leader, in a zone of shanties along the Bay's edge."

"Doing what?"

"Breaking up, cutting up, old freighter ships for their metal."

"With what?"

"Hammer and chisel. Some acetylene torches we were using, though not many."

"By hand?"

"Yes, my Leader, was all working by hand. Many PRIMS with only a few tools. Beaching rusty freighter ships, it was then taking them apart bit by bit."

"And lifting?"

"Much lifting by ropes and chains and pulleys. And it was all being the backs and muscles of hauling PRIMS."

"A PRIM gang, holy guest," explained the jungle savior needlessly. "PRIM labor is so cheap that sids have them work *by hand.* These, my children, are less expensive than replacing broken machines with costly new ones. Repairing, oh," the Ludd leader waved off knowing the exact tech term, "oh, you must know better than I."

The priest reluctantly nodded. At the end of this century, such primitive physical labor sufficed because nearly all non-Marsco computers were still infected. Useless. By midcentury, nothing had run without embedded chips and computer control. The C-Wars corrupted the entire infrastructure.

"For all its promises," Leader noted, "this is what Marsco gives the PRIM world!"

"You're right," Cavanaugh added sadly. "Human labor's become that cheap."

"Human labor? PRIM labor! PRIM flesh!"

"Yes, PRIM flesh."

"Treated worst than animals."

The priest accepted the conclusion. "I've no wish to defend or justify Marsco actions on this or any score."

"And thus it must die!" interjected Mother. "Death to all of Marsco!" Whispers around the table showed assent.

"Isn't it possible for it to change?" the cleric shot at her. "There *are* precedents, even relatively recent ones. It *is* malleable—its members are at least, its *human* members?"

"All who are Marsco, or once were, deserve to die," the witch retorted. Like the priest, she wasn't backing down. "If they wear its mark, they deserve death." She held up her right hand in a defiant gesture.

"Unfortunately," commented the prisoner, ignoring the crone and keeping his remarks addressed to the sage, "as you've noted, and as we both witness daily, there is a constant, ready supply of PRIMS for such work, any work."

"And, Leader, it is asking much more of us PRIMS," joined Kip.

"Yes, much more, my son." The Leader looked lovingly and forgivingly at Daughter.

The priest easily surmised why they spoke of her so. Lowering her eyes from this obvious shame, she withdrew her left arm from view. Nonetheless, the arm had been visible during the meal. The priest saw that her ulcerated lesion oozed through the wrappings intended to hide her wound.

The Leader turned back to Kip, "This metal, what of it?"

"The subsidiary was selling it mostly to Marsco."

"And your feet?"

"I was barefooted."

"You were broken-footed once then, weren't you, my son?"

"Yes, Leader. Until Mother."

"He was nearly hobbled," the sage addressed his guest, "until we gathered him. With your shoulders stooped besides, was it not so, our son?"

"Yes."

"And Mother cured your round back and your broken feet so you walk strong and straight this day."

"Indeed, Leader." Kip drew himself up to show his regained stature.

"Do you not labor here with bricks, our son?"

"Yes, Leader. But here our task's honest and worthy. We are laboring but singing at our burdens. We're fed. Healed. We are having a rest when we tire."

"This forest home," the Leader turned to Cavanaugh, "built without crushing those who labor. Your hut, all its bricks and flagstones, not some destroying labor we demand but a tribute from happy and free people."

Once more the priest noticed the inside of the pavilion's walls. Like his hut, these were lined with mud-cemented, reclaimed bricks. Poorly pieced together, but the oddity of it was more stunning than the terrible workmanship.

"Here's the second camp I am building," offered Kip. "I also helped construct our Himalayan camp."

"Enough of that, my son."

"Yes, Leader."

"I feed the hungry, holy guest," the mystic explained in an undertone. "Mother makes the lame walk."

For countless nights until dawn, Rivers monitored silent receivers and gray screens. Nothing came back from the jungle darkness.

Has Stephen gone native? The ensign feared the worst; there were precedents.

The weeks stretched on as the utter stillness from bush and valley continued.

For a fortnight Cavanaugh took his evening meal alone. After that stretch, Kip escorted the priest to the Leader's bungalow.

In the main room, the Revered One waited cross-legged on a cushion. "My sole indulgence," Leader gestured as he offered the priest some green tea, "one more famous on another continent.

Here in this spot renowned for coffee, a few delicate tea plants of mine flourish higher up in the hills."

A skeptic, Cavanaugh wondered, *Ever even been to India?*

Sipping their tea, incense smoking up from behind, the Leader spoke in his customary soft voice. "I know of your tireless work already, my holy guest. Your reputation precedes you into my jungle." In the dark, the priest nodded at the compliment. "I know also of your, shall we say, traveling companions." He showed him the Marsco patch, the memento from the *Mendes.*

The prisoner stated a matter-of-fact tone, "Mother is ever so thorough in her, well, her *inducements.*"

"She's my right hand."

The priest mused slyly, "Does the left know of the right's doings?" He didn't resist the pointed dig, "'If your right hand leads you into sin—'"

"I know all," continued the Leader with a coldness that betrayed no emotion. "You have no secrets. No one does. Nor does Marsco—I know its mind. All minds."

Taking the Leader's boast as exaggeration, Cavanaugh replied, "I may be just a simple zone priest, but many before you have made such claims of omnipotence. Always hollow claims." He had never been one to shrink away from holding his position; imprisonment did not change that tenacity.

"Come, come," chided the prophet. "You're not the only pious holy man."

"I make fewer claims to holiness than I do to *effectiveness.* In some circles, St. Teresa's an empty file or an annoying pest. A boil on some associate's rump. But to me, it's significant. It'll live beyond me. That's one sure sign of its modest success."

"So, you're more *efficient* than *sanctified?*"

"If that's what it takes," he answered with a hint of smugness. In the silence between them, the prisoner sensed he must say something, so he asked quietly, "And what do you gain, Leader, in the end?"

"At my death," he bowed meekly, "a humble burial, if I am deemed worthy."

In the evening darkness, the Leader's white cassock seemed to glow. Cavanaugh wondered how the Ludds pulled off that trick. A black light seemed out of the question, but something made the Leader's homespun iridescent.

Sips of tea shifted the conversation. "You've come for two boys," the visionary pointed out knowingly, his accustomed gentleness slipping from his voice. "Have you not? A sick child and his friend; you've told Mother this yourself."

"No secret of that. Yes, two students."

"Why these two when there are so many? Perhaps they are your especial favorites, these delicate little ones?"

The priest held in his anger at the insidious insinuation. "Isn't that a bit crude, even coming from you?"

Leader made no reply to the rebuke.

"But, yes," the priest went on, "I've no wish to hide my reasons. Or defend them. I'm here honestly enough. The truth will out—always does, whether forced out or no—I came to reclaim these lost boys."

Leader remained silent.

"And so," Cavanaugh took the initiative, "your questions get us to the point rather precisely." Speaking as though he was talking about a computer upgrade, the energetic captive laid out his course of action. "I am better after, well let's say, after Mother's initial, gracious hospitality. Two, three weeks above ground does wonders. But, I'd like to leave here as soon as possible." Pushing for a conclusion whether the Leader agreed or not, he stated bluntly, "Tomorrow morning suits us fine. I've nothing else planned, actually. And, I'm sure you can arrange it—back all the way to the hummer or even my base camp."

"You're at liberty to leave us at any time," Leader answered without haste or feeling, "but take only what is your own."

"Why?"

"Perhaps it's not such an easy task, giving them away like this."

Mentally, Cavanaugh asked, *Why not? You stole them—give them back!* Wisely, he withheld his remarks.

"They come to me, because I feed the hungry. Mother heals the sick. I've seen the broken seals of the celestial scrolls," the spiritual master spoke in an unembellished style, letting the allusion catch the priest's attention. "If you join me, so you shall be saved. *I am* your true salvation; you shall be saved."

The mystic began speaking as though entranced. He looked up in to the corner of the ceiling and spoke to the vacant air, his distorted face and eyes hardening.

The sole witness of these grotesque changes, Cavanaugh found them chilling. At some point the Leader's voice was no longer meant to be soothing. His manners and words were without connection to reality. Cavanaugh felt they were spoken for him but not to him.

"'Fear not, for *I am* salvation. I've played with lions as though with kid goats. And with bears as though with lambs.' After the storm, *I am.* The peace-giver, *I am.*"

His words froze Cavanaugh.

Still in a trance, with his eyes gazing off to the transcendent realm, the sage continued, "'Marsco's pride shall be humbled; the haughtiness of associates will be brought low. I alone will be exalted, on that day, and all of its arrogance will be thrown down utterly.'"

The priest whispered faintly, "'Cease to do evil, do good, search for justice, help the oppressed, for a bruised reed he will not break.' Isaiah spoke of more than deadly retribution."

The entranced mystic whispered, "No! 'Start slaughtering the sons for the guilt of their fathers!'"

"'The sins of the father?' And what of peace?" the priest demanded. "And justice?"

"We'll find none while Marsco's with us, until its utter destruction."

"You ask much of yourself."

"No less than I ask of my devoted disciples. No more."

"That's considerable for one man."

"Perhaps in this darkness, you see poorly," the jungle savior cautioned. "For my part, 'I issue orders to my sacred warriors to serve my anger, my proud champions.' Soon, all will know—as my disciplines have proclaimed me to be—I will become Death, the Destroyer of Marsco."

"You will?"

"As my followers know and believe of me, I shall!"

Confronted with such revenge lust, the priest spoke pointedly. "Marsco is in error on many scores." He made out the prophet's head barely nodding to signal agreement. "But vengeance isn't ours to mete out willy-nilly. We must beat our swords to plowshares...as you well know."

"Only after we've finished with our righteous retribution."

At his uplink console, Miller repeatedly tried to connect with Cavanaugh but failed. For all intents and purposes, the Marsco system first used by the priest was dead.

As he had for more than a month, the granger went to sleep worrying about his friend. *What's happening?* Then he thought, *I should have convinced him not to go at all, except . . . he'd have gone anyway. I could have gone with him! Should have at least gone down to SoAm, talked some sense into the old fool!*

For the first time since coming to his Sac City grange, Miller felt alone.

Five days passed before Cavanaugh met with the Leader and his coterie once more. As soon as the inner circle finished the evening meal, the jungle mystic, taking the prisoner by the right hand, asked, "Why this?" In the torchlight of the pavilion, the single finger disk glowed blue-green. All twenty members of the Nexus saw it clearly.

"A gift from my cardinal," answered the priest. "He thought his clergy needed them."

"A gift?" Mother ruffled, angered at the slightest suggestion that anyone needed Marsco. "Would you accept a sharp-toothed piranha if offered? Or a writhing pit viper?"

"There, Mother," Leader broke in with a subtle smile. "Perhaps our guest *is* Daniel entering a lion's den or an apostle holding an adder by its tail?" He smiled in self-satisfaction.

"It's harmless, really," Cavanaugh explained, idly picking at the skin covering the implant with his thumb. "Use it to keep in touch with friends all over the world." Confronted with obvious allusions to his imminent death, the priest chattered on nervously: reckless he might be; suicidal he was not. "In space, too, but I know only one person there. Grizotti. Zot—fine man. Met him through Miller. He has come down to St. Teresa's even—two, three times. Students loved him. May come for an extended stay." Catching his rambling, the priest smiled at himself then added, "But, I do wish his eminence's gift had been a new roof."

Looking at the subcutaneous disk, the priest was reminded of Rivers's rescue code. *Has Mother drugged that out of me?*

The Leader grew solemn. "We do not see the harmlessness of this enslaver of humanity."

The prisoner began to answer with a reasoned argument, one that he had presented many times. "I've always believed that *technology,* in and of itself, is a marvelous extension of the God-given human mind. And as such, tech's neither harmful nor beneficial. It is the application of technology, the intention behind its use, that's where the goodness or evil enters."

The priest sensed the chill hatred of the room, the inner circle of the Leader disgusted; that anyone would defend Marsco or praise the use of its venomous tech, as they believed it to be, astounded them. This blasphemy was made all the worse for the presence of Leader and Mother enduring such heinous slander.

Sensing the tension, the priest nonetheless looked pointedly at Mother. "Anyone can *be* evil, *do* evil—it's a matter of choice." Cavanaugh had a streak of arrogance that often got himself into deeper difficulty when he didn't control it. Tonight, he didn't control it.

As though the hostage was still drugged, the decrepit hag grabbed his right hand roughly. Scrutinizing his finger, her craggy face seemed to grow even more malicious. "This *is* Marsco, and it inevitably brings death!" She scratched at the single disk as a dog might scratch at something it fears yet is intrigued by.

"Death comes for us all, Mother," the cleric retorted fearlessly. "That's still the realm of God, not Marsco. It may confuse itself with the Almighty, but most sane people don't make that mistake." He shot an accusatory glance back at the seated mystic. The priest suspected delusional mass psychosis here; it should be handled with dexterity and treated with compassion. He knew his barbed remarks were approaching sin, and he shouldn't sin. These murderous fanatics weren't worthy of his failings.

In silence, the Leader had been gathering his thoughts. When he finally spoke up, his retinue listened in hushed obeisance. The sage took the priest's hand, gently—unlike Mother—and held up its disk for all to see. "I weep at the thought that so devoted a venerable man's been willingly infected with Marsco."

He spoke deliberately, ethereally. "We believe Marsco is death. Marsco brought contagion death from its ventures into the unknown, into the sacred unknowable."

"And they tilt the heavens," Mother snarled, spitting through broken teeth. "The Blessed Moon! She crosses slower in the sky. Her blest face's polluted and her power clouded over."

For the past few nights, Cavanaugh had watched a new Moon rising through the trellisworks. It was not growing into a crescent shape but into a distorted slice with lumps and tuffs of clouds emanating from it. Shadowy blotches crossed the visible white of the lunar face. It illuminated the sky with an eerie blue-gray radiance brighter than a full Moon of last century.

"Hush, Mother, enough of that," her seer ordered quietly. He gathered himself once more before speaking. "Marsco *is* death. The Prince of Lies. It aims to infect us all. We must choose *this*—," he held up his own diskless right hand, "—or *that*." He next raised Father Cavanaugh's hand high.

The image was unmistakable: *death* by being a part of Marsco, *life* by being cut off from Marsco.

"The hated one promised us much for our blood, our tears, our sacrifice in that debacle of old. When we were first enslaved, Marsco promised us freedom. Willingly we gave it our bodies to be maimed and more, willingly our lives to be taken, to crush our shared foes. We stood shoulder-to-shoulder with it, sacrificed ourselves in our millions! Died in our millions! But for what? 'What a harlot it has become. Once integrity lived there, but now assassins.'"

The prophet paused to shift slightly. "We little knew then that the old Powers and new Marsco were so similar. We little knew—and suspected less then—that each in their own way was out to destroy us, destroy all PRIMS. Each in their own way! We knew little then that the Powers and Marsco were bound together in the destruction of PRIMS, each at its own turning. Shame, shame on us for first trusting either."

"Never again," Mother added. "For this day we trust only the sword that draws black blood."

The dwarf-witch's interruption brought another silence to the pavilion. A wind stirred, but nothing else made a sound in the nearby jungle.

As those around him gave their enthralled attention, the much-loved mystic continued, "The foe we defeated *for* Marsco, *in* Marsco's name—Marsco grew to become again. Gog and Magog becoming the same fiend. It assumed that malignant shape even as Hydra before it. Or a creature from Frankenstein's hands, rebuilding itself from the putrid flesh of others. Or of the Red Dragon in my scared scrolls, their seals now broken open."

Jungle noises increased. Outside, bats fluttered, undisturbed by any other movements in the night. Those followers in the bungalow room stayed in hushed reverence. The Leader spoke humbly, filled with a sanctified vision that the priest must share.

Although one of twenty listeners, the captive knew that he alone was the intended audience. All the rest were saved, all except him. Even in the dankness of his buried cell, he never felt such gnawing danger encircling tighter around him.

The Leader spoke anew, "This day, does Marsco ever see our children at work? Does it embrace them?"

"*No!*" came murmurs from those at table.

"Only its hirelings do that. Only sids ever touch wretched PRIMS. Marsco's conscience remains clear."

As the retinue listened intently to the Leader, even Cavanaugh seemed spellbound. As fearful as the message was, it conveyed much intriguing truth.

The holiest one went on. "And who helped bring about Marsco's utter domination?" He paused to catch the prisoner's eyes. "Who?"

"*PRIMS!*" those at table assented.

"And yet our children don't share in the victory spoils! Marsco wantonly used the fathers and grandfathers, the mothers and grandmothers of these, my children. Battle after battle! Slaughter after slaughter!"

The elders of the Nexus nodded in rapt agreement and memory. The young nodded in rote belief. Even the priest's head moved with involuntarily affirmation. *He tells them the horror they want to hear, want to savor.*

"Who pitted the helpless against the armies of the accursed Powers?"

"*Marsco!*" The twenty listeners answered in unison, in a resolute voice they were accustomed to using.

"Who made the PRIMS despised by their rulers?"

"*Marsco!*" the twenty answered as though in one voice.

"And in its war with the Powers, who suffered the most? *My PRIMS!*"

The table roared their assent, strongly echoing in their savior's whispered *PRIMS.*

"We thought them distinct from each other, Gog and Magog, but each was out only to destroy us."

Pausing, the Leader abruptly addressed this remark directly to the priest, "I'm sure you know, our holy guest, the Kikuyu proverb, 'When elephants fight, it is the grass that suffers.' Who suffered the greatest but PRIMS? Were PRIMS not the fodder for those far greater than us?"

With a slow nod, the spellbound priest assented to the righteous depiction of those times.

The mystic continued with deliberateness. "And what of our blood payment, bought at the cost of countless millions? When the dust and din of carnage came to rest at last, what did the victorious Marsco's PRIM armies earn? More death and more contagion brought down from the stars by Marsco itself. Plague after plague visited us, wiping out our remnant all the more! Death visited us by the uncounted millions! Our dead as uncounted as the stars!"

Reluctantly, the priest agreed with this depiction of those unremitting pandemics that dogged the world for years after the Wars.

"Those fell struggles between Marsco and the Powers—those malignant rulers who had first cast off their very own—crashed hardest on *us,* the weakest. Those two great battling elephants locked in a death grip. And with the ascent of glorious Marsco after the Wars, who spoke for the abject PRIMS in their wretchedness?"

"You, our Leader," whispered several voices unevenly within the pavilion.

"Sounds like Marsco itself in the early Divestiture times," shot the priest. Unwise, he knew, to so bait the seer just then. "Many originally became associates because Marsco promised to change the world, enhance the world. Things fell apart differently." It was no time for reasoned discourse, but no one was listening to him anyway.

The sage countered sharply, "May we remind you, holy guest, that our name is not *Luddite* by our own choice. Others christened us with that name, and we don't deign to argue their wise epithet. Yes, Luddites did smash enslaving machines with their own hands in their own time; we know who enslaves our brothers and sisters and children this day. Those who enslave them today betrayed them once before."

Leader paused to keep his audience mesmerized; even Cavanaugh was once more riveted to his every word.

"Those who now enslave the PRIMS betrayed them before. But we are not Luddites as of old. We are 'The Few.' 'The Chosen.' 'The Nexus.' A resurrected, a renewed clan. 'The least among you will become a clan and the smallest a mighty nation.'"

"Yes, Yahweh's promise to Abraham."

Ignoring his captive, Leader whispered, "We become renewed and newborn again. We bring the truths of light and dark as the Magi of old, of ethereal good and majestic evil as the Manicheans of old. We bring harmonic convergence. We bring the shine of crystal and the power of pyramids. We bring all the ancient truths into the renewal through our blood thirst. We are the warriors of Kali. Brothers of Michael, the fire-sworded archangel. Sisters of Joan, martyr for war. We descend from the incendiary Sherman whose burning brought freedom to PRIMS of old. We will grow to be as Pol Pot and bring purging beauty back to our people, purifying the masses with selective death! We are all those who love blood-purging and fire-storming. Our will is to earn freedom by slaughter and justice-blinding retribution."

"Yes, our Leader," whispered the retinue.

For self-preservation alone, the prisoner instinctively knew to hold back his caustic derision of this farcical melodrama.

"For it has sown the wind, and it shall reap the whirlwind! Sown fire and will reap the firestorm!"

"Yes," whispered the retinue.

"We shall become Death, the Destroyer of Marsco!"

"Yes, our Leader," whispered all those inside the pavilion.

Outside at the jungle's verge, other followers, gathering to hear the wisdom of their master, eagerly added approval.

In the softest voice yet, the Leader went on. "Marsco's visited upon this Earth three horsemen—war, pestilence, famine. We shall become the fourth!" He whispered more mildly than ever, "Death."

"Death," his followers repeated, first in a low whisper.

"Death!" he whispered so softly.

"*Death!*" they repeated loudly.

"Death to Marsco."

"*DEATH TO MARSCO!*" The Leader and his followers began an echo-chant: his barely audible whispers first, their shouts following. The ardent inner circle grew frantic, hysterical with a thirst for vengeance, even as their Leader's words stayed faint.

"Death," he spoke softly.

"*Death to Marsco!*" came back a louder reply.

"Death," ever so imperceptibly.

"*DEATH TO MARSCO!*" louder, stronger shouts in unison.

The sage and the captive remained a still center in the widening circle of revenge-chanting frenzy. The disciples demanded a symbol; Leader was theirs.

Death to Marsco! Bloody death to Marsco! Countless dead of Marsco!

As the curdling cries echoed back and forth, the priest realized the regularity of this holy man's homilies. This ritualized culmination, he concluded, took place often.

In the dimly lit pavilion, the noise increased so that soon the walls reverberated with the chanting. Leader remained the motionless eye around which a churning storm swirled.

Father Cavanaugh, in shocked disbelief at this display, noticed that only Thax, in his pale weakness, remained silent. And yet, on went the shrill mantra—pounding, threatening.

"Death," in a whisper.

"*Death to Marsco!*"

"Death," again in a hushed voice.

"*DEATH TO MARSCO!*" the Nexus disciples replied in a blasting, single voice.

As the spell-casting recital reached its crescendo, the priest knew he beheld utter madness in the followers, delusional depths he hadn't seen since the days of mass hysteria during the Wars. He understood instantly that Rivers was right: his solitary forest trip upstream was suicidal absurdity.

With a wide sweep of the Leader's arms, his devoted supporters fell into complete, rapt silence. Even a concert master rarely commanded that kind of practiced precision.

The message was strikingly clear: Fanaticism, yes! Yet under strictest control! Zealous unquestioning adoration: many rulers had sought this, but few ever achieved it. *Leader plays his cohort perfectly,* the prisoner realized, *and his cohort wants to be played perfectly.*

"You see how we wait," the Leader spoke as though the priest was a newly converted disciple, "anxious for the fitting omen. We wait for augury of the propitious moment to strike."

"Yes," added Mother with assured confidence, her face puffy from chanting. "We wait, as say the ancient scrolls of wisdom, for this foretoken, 'When the Moon is in the seventh house and Jupiter aligned with Mars—'"

Giddy, the captive jumped in, "'—then peace will rule the planet and,'" *and something, something, something*—. He snapped his fingers trying to remember an old song learned in his distant childhood, "'*The stars!*' Yes, I know," he answered sharply to the thunderstruck apostles.

Irate, Mother pointed an accusatory claw. "You've committed heinous sacrilege before us, desecrating our Holiest of Holy Writ."

Even seeing their vengeful glare didn't make the cleric refrain from his final contempt. "I know, I know, it may well cost of me my neck. You await 'the Dawning of the Age of Aquarius.' Yes, prophets of your ilk have come before with blaring trumpets and pounding cymbals and thundering drums, a few with all the eloquence of angels, but without—well, you catch."

That definitely signs my death warrant, the priest knew in a flash, his brazen effrontery not helping his cause.

Part of the crowd demanded his immediate execution as punishment while the other part wished the Leader to silence this utterance of sacrilege.

The simmering tension was broken by an uncontrollable outburst of Thax's coughing. A convulsing spasm from the afflicted boy shattered the spell and kept the spiritual master from commenting further on the priest's question.

"Excuse me, my Leader," the boy squeaked between fits. He rose unsteadily to leave, but Mother touched his arm to stay. He collapsed into the nearest cushion. Both the priest and Mother went to comfort the ashen lad as he lay back down.

Seizing the witch's weakness, Cavanaugh pounced. "I gather, Mother, this must be humiliating for you since I'm quite sure that you've openly tried to cure him. Am I conjecturing correctly? That your promised cure originally led the boy to flee our school? Harder than it looks, isn't it? Curing someone." He shifted his piercing glance, "As difficult as spiritually leading a congregation."

"Even though," the jungle leader answered, deigning to speak of this with such a heretic, straining to keep his voice kindly although hatred grew behind his words, fire flashed in his eyes, "you see how we help so many from the ravages of your zone, from the clutches of Marsco."

"The world is full of evil. Marsco doesn't have that sole distinction," returned the priest in a compassionate voice, his own arrogance subsiding. "And, indeed, I've seen it do wonders when it has a mind to, wonders even for PRIM children." His voice changed to an insistent tone. "Thax's deathly sick. He needs immediate medical attention. I *know* I can get him to the Marsco-supported dispensary near our school."

Cavanaugh hardly knew how to share his state of perpetual Marsco ambivalence with his host. He spoke rationally to the irrational believers all around him. It was an odd feeling, all this defending Marsco.

"Today, no medicine can cure Thax. Ours is a world where antibiotics generally no longer work. The boy's sickness is bacterium-spread, no question, and such diseases overwhelmed meds long before Marsco. And yet, I pray some DNA therapy may still work on the boy. Such transplants often create remission, but these aren't Thax's only hope. A sanatorium near the Serengeti might also help: its dry weather, its sanitary conditions."

Cavanaugh's looks were not of imploring so much as demanding. "Time's running out. Genome-therapy isn't a last-minute method of treatment; some healthy tissue needs to be in the boy's lungs to begin regrowing pulmonary sacs."

The jungle prophet leveled his skepticism. "Why should Marsco care of a single PRIM-child?"

"Yes, it's illogical, isn't it? It'll work like crazy to save an individual PRIM, especially if they seem a possible candidate for associate status. And yet, as a whole, no, it doesn't look after most zones as it has promised." The priest looked steadily at the prophet. "I pray constantly that it changes. In the meantime, if it offers to help Thax—"

The dwarf rose, "Marsco's medicine will slay him! My jungle shall cure him!"

"Mother," answered the captive, his ire toward his torturer not concealed, "then why does he suffer so? You've had him long enough, dammit! Cure him already!"

Thax broke into another unmanageable fit although he nearly choked trying to stop his involuntary spasms.

"The plague's eating out his lungs at an ever-increasing rate," Cavanaugh insisted. "His face betrays this; he's wasting away. Soon, his lungs'll be nothing but infected membrane and bloody pus. Too late for any therapy."

Mother murmured confidently, "The Moon. We wait for her full face."

"*The Moon?*" The priest was incredulous. "*The Marsco Moon?*"

Please, please, the cynical cleric prayed, *please join us in the damn twenty-first century!*

The dwarf-witch gazed around the faces visible in the half light, ensuring each disciple knew her intentions. "When enough nightly visits have passed and she is again at her full glory, with our holy one's permission, that brightest night we shall restore to soundness this little one."

"We give it gladly to save him," the Leader responded with a humble bow.

Unable to withhold his disdain, the hostage counterattacked. "And Daughter? What of her arm? If you can cure Thax, why not her lesions?"

The singled-out disciple withdrew her ulcerated arm deeper into her sari, frightened that she had unintentionally betrayed Mother. Even in the flickering light, visible panic crossed the young woman's face.

"Shall I not cure her then, Mother?" The PRIM-cunning captive astonished even himself with this heady boast. But his confidence was strong; he knew several remedies Mother only dreamed of. Cures that would impress even the thick-necked crowd pressing in on him. "A fair enough challenge, right Mother? A medicinal joust! You cure Thax; and I, Daughter." He found himself talking with the egotism expected from a well-disked and well-armed associate.

Mother ruffled herself up, a frightened, cornered clutch-hen doubling her size against a relentless, lethal predator.

It was the first time Cavanaugh saw her in any way flustered. He savored the sight, felt triumphant about it. Attacking her shawoman mastery had done the trick. With only a modicum of still-effective medicine, he had nursed hundreds of sick PRIMS in his charge. An infected rash would be easy, a cake walk, easier than curing tertiary Neo-Consumption.

"This jungle does hold many medicines," he admitted, on the offensive and unwilling to let his antagonist go undefeated. "From before the Continental Wars, and even after, the jungle gave up its secrets to true shamans and dedicated researchers alike. Many remedies, folk and refined, commenced from here. But the Kampaó natives are all gone. Their shamans are all dead. The C-Powers and the Rubber Subsidiary saw to that."

He bit his tongue but thought, *Plus you Nexus have had your murderous hands in their end, as well, I shouldn't wonder.* He remembered the putrid flesh of the newly buried he had discovered. *This crone is sure to eliminate any competition.* Chuckling at a joke he alone understood, he added, "You would make an excellent centurion for Security!"

In the silence that followed, the priest relished the thought that Mother was to be exposed as a charlatan, not a gifted healer. *Oh, she has found a scrap of jungle drugs, that's true—I know that from bitter first-hand experience—but her reliance of the Moon, talismans, and amulets cast serious doubts on her real medical ability.*

And the boy Thax was dying, and since Cavanaugh had come to rescue him, he must win this gamble. *Or...?* The prisoner forced himself not to complete that train of thought.

Taking up the challenge fiercely, the sha-woman added her own taunt, "We *command* you to cure Daughter-Child, since you boast of your skills so." The listening apostles showed their warped pleasure at Mother's defiance.

The priest assented readily. "Upon my victory," he agreed, "freedom for my two boys and me."

"Or pain of death," Mother added with finality. From her crevice-lined face above its diminutive frame, two dark eyes sparkled. Revenge was to be hers.

THIRTEEN

FIRE AND HOPE

(In the Nexus Camp, 2095)

"No! Dammit! I won't go back underground, you damn bitch!" Father Cavanaugh shouted, shaken awake by an unseen hand.

His hut remained black. Nocturnal noises filled the compound.

"A nightmare?" he asked out loud to the shadowy emptiness.

As the prisoner grew more conscious, he heard indistinguishable, distant sounds coming from the other side of the Leader's now-vacant bungalow. Muffled voices were abruptly followed by a tremor then an unexpected *yumph.* The ground shook violently, stronger than the initial jolt that woke him.

Earthquake? he wondered, hearing distinctly frantic voices. *Those shouts are panic!* He didn't understand any articulate commands, but the terror in their tone was unmistakable.

Dressing quickly, Cavanaugh stood on the verge of the sward. Over the thatched roof of the nearby bungalow, he made out bright flickering.

Surely lightning, he thought.

Through the trellisworks above him, the sky was clear. Beyond the thick, clinging vines, he saw stars and the smallest slice of a dying Moon before it disappeared completely. But the flashing was well below the trellis, not originating from above. It flared up yellow-red, growing into a bright white, like a bellows stoking a smoldering fire.

Another tremor caused him to stagger forward. Walking swiftly, the priest realized that this shaking emanated from underground explosions. *Pisanos? Rivers?* As he rounded the corner of the central bungalow he knew clearly disaster had struck—or Marsco.

When he reached the larger sward, he discovered that a hut, one placed twenty-five meters back from the abandoned road, was showering electrical sparks outward in a high arc. Its thatch roof and wooden walls blazed. Two other huts, each fifteen meters away from the fiery source, glowed from embers blown at them. In front of the bright orange flames, running figures crisscrossed the sward before darkness engulfed them. The unmistakable stench of an electrical fire hung in the air.

A bucket line had the two secondary hut fires under control. The single flaming hut gave yet another rumble from deep underground. The prisoner felt its jolt then saw a new sparkling arc explode outward.

From the darkness, Kip stood by the prisoner. In his polite way, the disciple whispered, "Holy one, you should be returning to your own dwelling." His gentleness did not hide his insistence.

"Is everything all right?" the priest asked. "Everyone okay?"

"As you are seeing, we are having all well under control."

Scores of uniformed followers—disciples the likes of which the hostage had never seen—swarmed out of the jungle and took over the bucket brigade. Those Nexus who had hauled water from the first silently formed a line of onlookers, partially blocking the priest's view.

"Anyone hurt? Does anyone need assistance?"

"Mother's here, holy one," the guard stated politely but increasingly insistent. Reluctantly, the captive turned away from the predawn excitement.

With Kip only a few paces behind, Cavanaugh remained quiet until he neared his hut. As he climbed its wooden steps, he remarked, "To me, of course, but then what does an *old* priest know living all these years in a UZ? But yet to me, those flaring arcs looked like electrical sparks." Commotion still filled the distant side of the compound. "And from *underground!* As though some gigantic electrical machine, a generator, something like that was exploding, catching fire and exploding. There *is* a definite electrical stench." He dramatically sniffed the night air. "I thought nothing mechanical was utilized in the camp."

"Oh, no!" responded Kip spiritedly, the emergency leaving him less guarded. In a nano, his voice seemed to hitch. "I am wishing you a good night," he added without enthusiasm.

"How long has it lasted?"

"So far, fifteen minutes and counting." Ensign Rivers alerted Mr. Giannini as soon as the Luddite's electronic countermeasures ceased.

The unexpected lapse in the jungle e-defenses gave only enough time to double-check the location of the missing hummer. "It's still at its last estimated location," the ensign reported. "In the exact spot where we assume Cavanaugh disappeared. All indications are that it hasn't moved in several weeks."

"Any other surveillance?"

"The in-place drones responded, relaying information about their surroundings. Mostly, they're in jungle. One's in a deserted rubber plantation."

By the time Pisanos was alerted to ready the *Mendes* for an immediate sortie, the EMC umbrella had returned as strong and large as ever.

The abrupt break lasted only two hours, then an electronic veil covered over the forest, valley, and hillside camp.

To his utter surprise, Miller was inexplicably in. From his grange he cracked into Cavanaugh's filing system. The engineer examined the encrypted records of the priest's com unit. The jungle visitor had received all of Miller's repeated messages. They came with increasing concern but sat unopened in an e-file.

In fact, Miller realized, Cavanaugh hadn't booted up since his first night on the hillside. Nor sent any messages except one to him and, oddly, another to Anthony Grizotti.

Is he even alive?

Miller tried gleaning other information, but in an instant, the system's pathways were blocked just as before. As unexpectedly as the granger had found them open, they slammed shut.

While the Leader was away over the next ten days, Cavanaugh's meals were brought to his hut. He always ate alone, although he asked repeatedly to see his two students. The second night of the Leader's absence was that of the fire. After that evening of blazing commotion, as soon as the captive finished eating, he was invited by Kip to walk away from the trellis-covered compound into the nearby jungle.

These evening strolls became a nightly ritual.

Kip always escorted him. This guard spoke little and rarely answered any questions fully. The Ludd never had another frank outburst as on the predawn morning of the fire. During each successive stroll, the Moon rose earlier and grew in size as it approached full. It climbed above the ridges of the surrounding hills, bringing with it bright trailing clouds.

On each ensuing night, the priest was allowed to go farther into the jungle. Even as the walking became more strenuous, his escort urged the hostage to step deeper into the unknown. Kip always took him on the same path that cut through the nearby tangles of jungle. At first, they kept under the overhanging trellis.

Later, their extended walks took them beyond the suspended vines and under the thick natural canopy.

After several nights, the priest commented, "I just realized that before reaching this location, the trellis ceases." Looking straight up, he saw stars through the massive branches above him.

In a week, he had his bearings from these repeated, lengthening excursions. From behind his hut, the closest one to the jungle, it was hardly half a click along the narrow trail to an abandoned rubber plantation. Here, captive and guard walked amid rows of trees that stood free of encumbering vines and tripping underbrush. Walking in that grove was quite easy. The hostage soon realized that someone attempting escape might traverse the plantation quickly, silently.

With each stroll, as Cavanaugh and Kip came to the plantation by the same path, they trekked deeper into the evenly spaced trees. Their direction always remained the same, always toward the far hills at the other side of the grove.

They regularly made it to the heart of the plantation. On these successive nights in the growing moonlight, the hostage made out a ridgeline in the distance through the overhanging branches.

If he was not mistaken, he had been below that very ridge when captured. Beyond it stood the higher, impassable ridge. On the other side of that jagged summit was his camp. His plan took shape in an instant.

It isn't possible to drive completely over that second crest but possible to climb over. We certainly can get over it in a single night. Indeed, a matter of hours. Perhaps all told it's three or four clicks from my hut to the hummer. When in the vehicle they could drive as close to the summit as possible. Then they would have only a steep climb through the remaining rocky outcrops to be at the top of the second ridgeline. His base camp should be visible from there, an easy descent for an old man with two young boys.

On the tenth night since the explosions, Cavanaugh and Kip walked farther out than any previous stroll. The jungle was alive with noise. The animals kept their night watch regardless of the illumination. A last squawk came from a toucan. A green parrot made its final evening flutter. Tree frogs began their nocturnal chorus. An occasional jaguar roared. Enormous bats woke and took wing.

The evening Moon had risen; its double brightness streamed through the forest like an auxiliary sun. It was nearly full and surrounded with thick debris thrown skyward from asteroid placements. Cavanaugh knew that with its coming to full, he was to face his adversary, Mother.

"Have you ever driven a hummer, Kip?" the priest asked on their way back to his hut.

"A hummer? As those the S & H Forces are patrolling in? No."

"Rather like driving a rover, really," the captive explained.

"I am having done that. But out here, there is being only one hummer—yours!" The Ludd cocked his head backward, indicating a direction behind the pair.

So, still there!

"It is being an odd thing, examining it thus," commented Kip, who kept his distance.

The priest knelt on one knee looking at the carcass of a forest kill. The prey had fallen about a week before, but bits of flesh had escaped being devoured. Flies and the stifling heat had bloated the putrid remains. Maggots wriggled when the priest kicked the rotting meat aside.

He picked up what he needed.

Marsco seems to be taking no chances although searching blind, Ensign Rivers concluded.

Aloud, the Security officer continued his briefing. "We know nothing more of the camp than we did three months ago." With backlit projections and dim lighting, Rivers saw no one distinctly in the audience. Anonymous noises, a whisper, a cough were the only responses to his bleak assessment.

"Not a single report has come out about the Nexus camp since the first day," the ensign reported. "Nothing comes through the sensors left behind by the hummer. Its cam's fully operational, but it broadcasts back only a gray screen. Two hours of clear channel came out only once—during a power fluctuation probably at its source. Nothing else gets picked up now but flickers of static."

"Have there been other attempts at a recce?" an unseen woman asked.

"Although not my area, I can report that satellite and low-level drone over-flights produce nothing as well." A yeoman fed a projection unit some data. "This's a look-down image of the locale in question. As you can see, it shows only a smudge where details of the Luddite camp should be."

A graphic that should have shown a green unbroken canopy instead showed a gray and distorted blotch in the center of the frame. The indistinct, fuzzy patch looked like a computer graphics error.

"Whatever these Ludds are utilizing," Rivers remarked, "it's totally effective against our surveillance measures."

Giannini added his single comment. "That fact alone makes this cell all the more dangerous. They're utilizing programs that even our own boffins can't replicate."

The room buzzed with excitement.

"Leader has returned. The Moon is growing full."

"Yes, I see."

"Prepare yourself," Kip urged with hollow sincerity.

"It's all in God's hands," replied the priest earnestly.

Ensign Rivers organized a second placement of six drones. Operational plans had been drawn for deploying two companies of Rangers on site. *These aren't Troopers sweeping a zone for skinnies without disks, not Auxxies with nonleths passing out burger vouchers to stray PRIM kidlets. Rangers play hard and for keeps.*

The ensign watched officers work with their heavily armed unit. Now assigned directly to Giannini, he knew he would not be on the ground with this crack team. The eager officer ached to command such an elite force just once.

On the night of their challenge, the full Moon and its clouds shimmered through the trellis. The pattern of lunar dust made the face's perfect circle seem bruised and swollen with a hank of hair streaming beyond its skull.

"The evil one has ruined her powers, polluted her saving graces," Mother lamented loudly so that those Nexus followers surrounding her to witness her upcoming miracle would know what Marsco mischief she was fighting against.

The priest replied cynically, "Hedging your bets, are you?" Not wise, he knew, but so satisfying to ridicule the poisonous dwarf.

The clearing chosen by the Mother for the healing ceremony was fifty meters beyond the main compound just beyond the trellisworks. All along the trail from the compound to the clearing stood a cadre of fervent followers who bowed as the sha-mother, Sister, and several young acolytes clad in gray passed. The clearing itself rose from the thickest jungle and was this night lit by flaming torches and fire pots. Daughter and Thax arrived, accompanied by Antonio. The healthy boy smiled but dared not speak. The jungle savior was there, aloof yet creating a commanding presence. At least 100 more came to witness the triumphant scene.

Full of confidence, Mother approached the priest to explain the finer points he might have misunderstood. "There are only three *chakras*," she noted with candor, sharing her wisdom. "*Power, love, hate.* You must hold *power,* love *power,* and hate losing *power.*"

Her black eyes burned in the torchlight, her pallid face wizen and sickly. She snarled her words at the unbeliever. "Hate those who have power over you. Hate yourself when your power weakens. Love power. Love to use power."

The priest touched Mother kindly on her slumped shoulder. "Mother, what about forgiveness? Patience? Loving your enemies?"

"Forgiveness?" she snickered, "show no sign of infirmity. Rip it from your breast. Patience? Use it only to destroy your enemies at a time of your own choosing. 'Waiting to avenge sharpens the blade that brings forth thick blood.' Keep hate in your heart; it manifests much power."

The priest was ordered to begin first. After silent prayers, he whispered to the frightened young woman who sat waiting in a low chair, "Don't worry, my child, I'm not half the rat Mother says I am." Just beyond the torches, which gave him adequate light, the crowd watched silently.

The diseased disciple herself let no expression cross her face. She was doing only what she was commanded; whatever happened, she feared the worst.

Over the previous few days, Cavanaugh had prepared by boiling, then drying, a dozen white cotton towels to cleanse Daughter's skin infection and to use as bandages. "They're as sterile as the primitive conditions allow," he remarked tenderly setting her arm on a small table. "My only reliable soap's the remaining shaving cream from the *Mendes's* courtesy kit. It has to substitute for any truly antiseptic solution," he explained while treating her.

While he worked, a few brave followers crept closer to see more clearly.

He began by gently washing her arm in warm water using his aerosol lather. "Just hold steady," Cavanaugh implored, "I don't mean to hurt you."

The zone resident had a trick or two up his sleeve that he delivered with theatrical gestures to rival any shaman. "You don't live as I have without learning scores of useful PRIM skills," the priest reassured his reluctant patient, confident his initial surprise would aid in the lesion's healing.

To clean the infection on the ulcerated wrist, the priest dropped wriggling maggots on the worst infected pockets, larva he found with Kip a few nights ago. They began eating at the wound relentlessly. "These puppies'll devour putrid flesh, my child, so no gangrene will plague you." As the crowd watched in as attentive silence as they gave Leader, the festering inflammation was reduced dramatically, seemingly right before their eyes. Several Nexus followers jockeyed for position to witness the voracious maggots perform their healing magic.

Mother snorted as though this was a technique she knew, although no one in the Nexus had ever seen it before.

"You're doing well, child," the priest whispered, asking the crowd to step back before removing the satiated worms. "I know you're on display here, as I am, so hang tough," he explained kindly. "Trust me, even though you're positive I'm one damned son of a bitch."

Aftershave lotion was the only alcohol at the priest's disposal. "Smells a bit girlie-man, but some women like it on their guys. Or they did in the last century." His exaggerated sniff of the small bottle brought a smile to the patient's face and a collective "ah!" from the spectators. "Never really intended to be medicinal, yet it's an adequate replacement for isopropyl alcohol or hydrogen peroxide."

Not one to pass up a dramatic moment playing to his advantage, Cavanaugh first flung a few drops of the lotion at the crowd as though using as asperges to shower his congregation with holy water. The Nexus's devoted ones were pleased with this inclusion of them. A few even blessed themselves until they saw Mother glower.

Next, he splashed this lotion directly onto the now-cleaned wound. When Daughter jerked her arm, Mother took special notice.

"I know it stings," the priest reassured the young woman, "but only initially."

Aside from the Leader's temperate words, the convert had found little compassion among the Nexus. Had she ever known her own father, she wished him to have this priest's gentleness. She wished any of the men who had so violently taken her before had shown her this much care. The stinging brought tears to her brown eyes, as did the memory of all her losses.

Before totally covering the wound, the priest had one last astonishing presentation to make.

With a flourish he explained to all witnessing his overly dramatic medical procedures, "Along with these clean bandages, I'm wrapping a poultice over the scrubbed lesions. Something from native lore of my own homeland, made from lichen with yellow-green mold." He continued tenderly, trying not to hurt the already frightened woman. "In bygone times, I'd have used antibiotic ointment, synthesized from this very bacterium."

His dramatic showmanship throughout the cleansing and bandaging only increased the amazement of the crowd. "Not as flamboyant as Mother's sleight of hand will undoubtedly be later this evening, ladies and gentlemen, but glitzy nonetheless," he stated with finality.

Behind Daughter's tears, Cavanaugh saw something he had yet to see amid these Ludds: the sparkle of sincere thanks.

Mother started her ritual by having Thax carried in to a measured drum beat. Four men carried his litter through the crowd with Kip pacing at the front to the pounding of a drum to clear a way. The movement was slow, purposeful, dramatic. At last, the sick child was set low to the ground to suit the crone's stature.

Placed evenly around the boy were four burning pots, each exactly positioned in the four compass directions. Knowing their portent, the crowd moved back from these flames. A larger pot flickered as Mother and an acolyte burned the entrails of a spider monkey. The hostage surmised that the flaming creature was to take the contagion essence away from the boy, thus freeing him from affliction. The stench of smoldering offal soon reeked about the sick child and Mother as she performed her smudging.

Sniffing the rising smoke of the consumed animal, the sha-mother discerned a powerful portent and, mumbling a chant that her acolytes echoed, she approached the prostrate boy.

She threw six tiny bones along his skeletal back. Taking up only five, she cupped them with her rough hands, circled through the choking, smoldering benediction, and at last threw them along his back a second time. After each throw she retrieved one fewer bone and repeated her blessings. Finally, with only one remaining, she tossed it along his back.

She divined its resting place on his spine was the strongest omen yet. Her crooked sneer assured her believers that her augury was working even in the perverted moonlight.

Although the crowd gave a pleased "ah!" after each of the sha-woman conjurer's gestures, the priest prayed fervently all the while, especially after realizing that each bone was a human finger.

After reading the signs, Mother removed the bones, all the while chanting with her acolytes. One attendant placed balled-up, wet cotton rags on the boy's back in four neat rows, three to each. Next, a second opened a polished wooden box and bowed before Mother. The offered box was lined with dark blue velvet, and from it the sha-woman withdrew a large drinking glass. It was not of any particularly striking design, but it was definitely crystal as its pure note attested after Mother pinged it with her claw. Holding the glass aloft, the witch circled the boy so all might see her talisman.

Finally, ceremoniously the witch squinted at the heavenly face through the cut crystal, entreating the Moon for healing strength. While thus praying, her acolyte lit one of the rag balls with an ember from the benediction fire.

The dwarf let the first rolled scrap on the boy's back burn until only half remained, then placed the glass over it before it was only embers. The crystal held in the smoke, which put out the flame but not until a large blister welted up. After the first rag, a second was lit. The hag officiously popped the glass off the child's back and placed it over this next rag. Mumbled incantations—chanted by Mother, answered by the acolytes—accompanied each ritualistic exercise. Soon a dozen red blisters lined Thax's weakened back.

My Lord and Savior, thought the shocked priest, *she's cupping the lad, 'drawing the poisons out.' This isn't even twentieth-century superstition; it's downright medieval.*

A week later, Daughter brought Father Cavanaugh his evening meal. Placing a tray down, she smiled. Instructed not to speak, she remained unresponsive but reluctantly showed him that her arm was healing steadily. Where before it had been oozing pus, tonight it was all dried scabs and patches of healthy skin.

"Yes," the prisoner remarked, "but my success's come with a severe price." He looked with pity into her deep brown eyes. "I pray they don't take this out on you."

As ordered, she said nothing but looked as though she understood.

The Leader came the next night with another young girl who carried the meal. "To what do I owe this extraordinary honor?" the captive asked. "Or, should I assume this means I'm not to fraternize with the servants?"

The Leader acted as though he didn't understand the sarcasm.

Both members of the Nexus stayed as the priest slowly ate. "You know," Cavanaugh finally remarked, "I believed that so long as you find me useful, I'm safe."

"Yours is a question I know not how to answer."

"Let me have a shot, then, if just for the hell of it. Perhaps I'm useful to you, as spiritual prophet, only as a fall guy playing opposite, and in contrast to, Mother."

The savior's visage betrayed a close-to-the-mark hit.

"Perhaps the façade of success has ceased for your *sha-woman*. Perhaps it dissipated completely—*poof!*—at my hands. I've seen the girl's wrist. Simple hygiene's done the trick for her."

Feeling this was his last chance to save the boys, the priest bore down. "Besides that, Thax's dying. You've not brought him to me *cured*. If he were in any remote way better, your old crone would be in here—*snap!*—in my face to gloat. *I* know that. *You* know that. He's wasting away by visible degrees each day, I'm sure. Anyone who sees him must recognize this."

The prophet remained seated without answering, stroking his beard but showing no other signs of listening to this bitter truth.

"Her bogus antics are a complete failure! Smoke and offal to impress your minions but an utter and complete medicinal failure! Rather humiliating, isn't it?" Knowing his own life was forfeit, Cavanaugh let loose his last insult. "Try as Mother might to blame her fiasco on Marsco and its polluted Moon, the boy's death rests in her claws even though I might have saved him. Or sent him somewhere he might have been saved. Your dwarf's missed her twitch!"

Hearing enough, Leader rose but Cavanaugh's next remark halted him. "Why of course, I see now! *You* know they are antics! But they're of great use to you, aren't they? Mother provides the ceremonial gimmickry; you provide the occult wisdom. Quite a duo! And all you need do is act engaged. But, damn, you see through it all, don't you?"

Leader behaved as though he was not listening. When the jungle holy man turned away, Cavanaugh—his second epiphany making what had once been murky instantly, blindingly clear—unleashed a surprise attack, "You asked me of the *boys* once! Insinuated the most disgusting things about them and me, remember? Well, fair enough, but let me ask you of all *these girls* surrounding *you!*"

With that, the mystic stormed out, his disciple following behind like a cold shadow.

An hour later, the scared girl came back. "To clean meal up," she whispered with terror in her voice.

"I can understand your fear, child."

As the girl began to leave, she set the tray aside. "You, holy one, truly heal. I seen her arm." With that she revealed her own infection, not as serious as Daughter's but open and festering all the same.

"Please, please," she begged, "heal me arm, fur Mother c'aint."

Over the following week, as he waited for the clan's next action, the priest remained alone, isolated. Except for a different follower bringing each meal and Kip walking with him each evening all the way into the deserted plantation, he saw no one. He wasn't drugged and tortured—for that he was thankful—but neither was he given much real freedom except for his regular nightly escorted excursions.

He had the sense, thinking in last century's terms, that his trial was over but that the jury was still out.

Finally Antonio and Father Cavanaugh met. As the prisoner walked the narrow trail back from the plantation, Kip was abruptly called away. The priest knew the path to his hut so continued on all alone.

Out of nowhere, Antonio and the unguarded hostage saw each other. "This chance meeting's indeed fortunate," the priest told his student.

The boy explained in halting English and broken Brazilian that he had just left a large hut on an errand.

"And insignificant errand, I'm sure, dammit," the priest swore in English, not caring if the boy understood or not. "I fear this *coincidence* has been orchestrated to give us three minutes together." The man looked around; they were truly on their own. He could see in the moonlight that every path nearby was empty. No one stirred from any close-by huts. As far as he was able to see down the trellisworks, nothing moved.

"Seems bogus, but nonetheless, we must make the most of this time."

The former student quickly informed him of Thax's worsening condition, his imminent death. When the boy pointed out that his friend hardly had strength enough to walk, the priest's mind was fixed. He had to act; they might not get another chance.

He implored Antonio, "We must escape. Tonight!"

"Where can we go?"

"Into the jungle! Then into the clouds! You must trust me!"

"*Sí*," whispered the boy, not sure if he understood the priest's English. "*Sí*, I away with you!"

The priest commanded in a low, imploring voice, "Bring Thax to my hut at midnight."

Two hours of moonlight remained when Antonio quietly opened the door of the guest hut and softly called to the priest.

Cavanaugh silently motioned Antonio and Thax toward the far back wall that faced the jungle. Behind the bed he had already loosened the poorly cemented bricks and punched an opening through. With little more than unspoken gestures for a explanation, the priest had the boys moving on their knees with him out through the hole.

"Rather like Alice," he whispered, sure the boys missed his allusion.

After crawling a few meters, they reached the narrow path Cavanaugh and Kip had taken every evening for nearly three weeks. Thick jungle totally hid the escaping three from view unless a pursuer was close at hand. Before walking long, they were well beyond the trellisworks.

In the half-click to the plantation, they had to stop for the first time. The priest planned—as hastily as he *had* planned—to get farther away before Thax needed rest. But after only a short walk, both the student and the teacher were totally exhausted. The child from the exertion, the man from the dread of discovery. They were drenched in sweat. He wished he had brought some water.

They sat leaning against the same thick tree trunk. Thax gasped for breath, sucking air into his bloody and weakened lungs. His eyes had grown so large their whites seemed like beacons in the dark. *It's all too much,* the prisoner reasoned. *I should take them back. It's death to me, but maybe they'll survive.*

After a series of quick gulping breaths, and after Thax's chest heaved less than at first, the tortured captive decided that all three must press on.

He soon mustered the strength to talk with Antonio, who stood slightly apart listening to the reassuring jungle noises.

"If jungle speak, no follows," the stronger boy explained; his short time here long enough for this clever PRIM to understand the forest darkness.

The sick youth rose to his feet unsteadily, using the tree for balance. He seemed disoriented and took a few halting steps back toward the compound.

"We should be going," the priest urged, turning Thax around and guiding him into the rows of trees. The boy resisted feebly, trying to move back in the opposite direction. With Antonio in front and the priest behind, the healthy pair steadily moved the sick boy along.

After fifty meters through the plantation, the priest asked Antonio, "Do you know if they moved my hummer?"

"Hummer? Not know what!"

"Something like a rover—I was driving when captured."

From the broken answer, the man gathered it remained outside the Nexus camp. Leader and Mother feared it might still be used by Marsco. The priest had to admit the sinister duo showed great sophistication in their reasoning about Security.

"If I can lead us there," the priest explained, "to the place where they've left my hummer, we can easily escape."

Antonio nodded and stood a moment while the priest took his bearings. Even in the semi-dark, the captive had a keen sense of direction. In due course, Cavanaugh pointed to the southeast through rows of evenly spaced trees. It seemed as though he had been practicing this escape for weeks.

The plantation dated from the '20s, yet its trunks hadn't been tapped for decades. The spaces between the trees were trampled down by more than his evening walks. The priest didn't stop to consider these signs of crumpled underbrush. The three moved among the trees with relative ease; that's all he noticed. They had to be swift; time grew short.

"Silence is important. You take the lead, Antonio, down this way." He pointed ahead. "Then Thax. I'll keep up the rear." They moved haltingly along. "We have about three more hard clicks," he explained to encourage them, "some of it uphill before my hummer. From there, we will drive as high as possible then walk over the taller ridge to my hillside camp. Marsco will keep us safe from there."

To the man's surprise, Thax balked. He started to scream, a cry cut short by a sharp onset of coughing.

"Perhaps he must rest," the priest rationalized. He too was winded by their swift trek. Walking with Kip, he had ambled leisurely to the far end of the grove. This time, he wanted to hurry along, yet both he and Thax were too exhausted. Sweat matted their hair; they breathed heavily. The dying boy coughed bloody phlegm in uneven fits.

Fear weakened the priest as well. He hadn't felt like this even in his cell. He knew what might lie ahead. "Even Our Lord feared in the garden," he tried reassuring himself and the students.

Antonio and Cavanaugh sat Thax down. The priest felt the boy's ribcage gasping for air, felt his pounding, straining heart. *So thin! So weak! Death's coming! He needs immediate treatment.* "Perhaps—and this'd truly be miraculous—the officers of the *Mendes* will extend their generosity even more," the priest spoke hastily, promising more than he might be able to deliver. "I might wrangle his way into a subsidiary hospital in Rio. Or perhaps a lander flight directly to a Serengeti sanatorium. When Marsco makes up its mind to do something—anything—little stands in its way."

After a moment, Thax regained his breath.

"How are you?" whispered the priest. "Can you continue?"

"Mo'their s-save me," the boy sobbed.

"There, there, I'm here—and Antonio," the priest spoke in his kindly way. "But, yes, Our Lady will save you."

"No, not *hers. Mo'their.* Tak'me Mo'their."

The priest looked shocked even in the last rays of moonlight. Antonio whispered, "Her's mucho magic." From his excited explanation, Cavanaugh gathered Thax had been talking like this ever since leaving the sick hut.

In that moment, the feverish child tenuously got to his trembling feet. In near-delirium, he started to retrace their way back. His companions caught him by his listless arms before he took half a dozen steps.

"We can't go single file; we must hold him," the priest realized. As winded as he was, he knew they must make straight for the hummer, still one and a half clicks away, without another stop.

At that point, a new fear darkened the mind of the priest. Once Thax grew quiet, the priest heard nothing. "What do you hear?" he demanded to Antonio.

"*Nada.*"

Nothing. A rainforest at night is never silent.

The darkness was stone quiet. No cicada chirped; no monkey chattered. It was ominous, foreboding. Deathly silent. Something, or someone, was moving unobtrusively without giving off a sound but making the whole jungle stop its own noises to allow the haunting gloom to pass. The priest felt the deepening silence behind them. The sense of impending doom was palpable. It waited to strike at just the right moment.

"We must move quickly now," the priest commanded Antonio. "Must push him along if that's what it takes."

Antonio guided them through the last rows of rubber trees. Even though Cavanaugh didn't want to stop, the sick child needed three gasping breaks. They had taken so long; hurrying had actually cost them time.

The predatory silence continued gaining on them; the priest felt it nearing even as they struggled to outrun it. If Antonio felt the imminent doom as well, he kept his fears in check by urging his two slower companions on.

Their backs to the plantation, at last the three faced the rising hill, the final barrier to the hummer and safety.

They started on a trail that wound its way gently up a slope of broken jungle surrounded by outcrops and grassy tuffs. This was farther than the hostage had ever come with Kip. But he remembered driving up something like this rocky incline the instant before his capture.

The Moon still gave out its glimmering light, but it was setting fast. Where the hillside rose above the jungle, the path seemed to shimmer at their feet. It was a glowing ribbon zigzagging up a green-black hill, between rock outcrops that kept the jungle thin here. Above them, the hill ended where the swath of stars began.

"Lord, give us strength," Cavanaugh prayed.

Thax moaned in his sweaty fever, turning his head back, still trying to break the grasp of the priest. Because they were on an exposed path, concealment was impossible. And the silence told him they were still being followed.

Each step seemed heavier than the last. The depletion of stamina by Mother's torture weighed the priest down. Yet still he pressed on. He felt himself pushing Thax more than guiding him; the boy's weight seemed to increase. So too, his reluctance to cooperate.

As they made a bend on the first low ridge, the priest gasped to Antonio, "Go ahead! See if this's the right place!" The path ran through some bare, jutting rocks then plunged into a thicket. If he was correct, through that patch of jungle, maybe 200 meters beyond, the hummer waited. "Run ahead! Go!"

As ordered, Antonio trotted out of sight.

The tired priest, relieved to be moving downhill at last, guided his reluctant charge with gentle urgency. On, on he pushed the breathless boy, meter after meter, not stopping even when the child's ribs began an uncontrolled spasm. *Jesus, he'll die here on this trail,* thought the priest. He then prayed, *Not here, Lord. Not on this trail, not here.*

His own ribs ached from the exertion of pushing the child uphill and then guiding him downhill. He doubted he would have the strength to drive the hummer once they reached it.

In that instant, the priest was again aware of *nothing.* The surrounding thickets and patches of bush, which should have been abuzz with noise, were silent. An ominous stillness stalked them.

Something unexpectedly moved ahead, coming out of the caatinga grove. From the shadows, a detached arm waved. The priest squinted a myopic eye, shaking with renewed terror. From the thicket, the arm waved once more. It soon grew a body—it was Antonio.

Five minutes later, the priest's prayers were answered. They sat in the hummer, all three taking a moment to regain their breath from their escape. The taller ridge waited. And beyond it, safety and escape. How far they would be able to drive, Cavanaugh didn't know, but it would be quite a distance.

Antonio tried lying his sick friend down in the back, but once Thax reclined, his coughing returned. The priest and Antonio agreed that the gasping child should sit upright in the passenger seat.

Only then did the escaping prisoner realize something was wrong. "It's," he choked out the words, "it's sat under vines for months, yet not a tendril clings to it." Breathlessly he went on, avoiding Brazilian so the boys wouldn't understand totally. "The key's in the ignition. It's even pointed toward safety, away from trouble—in the exact *opposite* direction I was driving that day." Without pause, the priest chattered on, "Something's wrong! Many things're all wrong! Like the placement of my hut *jungle side*, not set deep *within* the camp. Like my nightly walks with Kip that allowed me to reconnoiter this escape route."

Antonio, his PRIM senses strong, urged the priest to start the hummer.

But transfixed, Cavanaugh continued. "Like you meeting up with me—and both of us alone! Like the ease with which *you* were able to remove Thax from the sick hut at a moment's notice!"

With quick gestures, the PRIM boy urged the priest to flee.

"There's too much going that's all too pat—too coincidental for luck or even planning. A miracle *has* some plausible explanation. *But not all this!*"

He suddenly remembered his finger disk initialized to send a distress message. He reached his right hand forward to the metal dashboard and pressed his index finger in a rhythmic pattern. He felt a tinge of electric pain with each press. He continued forcing his solitary finger disk against the dash, sending out the SOS four distinct times before turning over the hummer's ignition.

"And when did the distress call commence?" asked Rivers, waking from an infrequent sleep break.

"O435, sir," a warrant officer reported. "Although it wasn't really 'a distress call.' We monitored a repeated and very faint *O-S-O,* then another *O-S-O.* Two batches hastily sent. Started picking them up about ten minutes ago."

"Undoubtedly our priest must've been flustered."

The warrant officer added, "The signal had metal interference. The sender must of not been thinking clearly enough to send a distraction-free message."

"You sure it's Cavanaugh?"

"Roger, it's his disk; we've verified that," commented the WO. "That's about all we're sure of."

Forty-five minutes later, plowing a path through the hillside thickets, the hummer found itself surrounded in the last grove before the safety of the high ridge.

There, the vehicle came to a stop. Around it, the bush moved in unison, in a direction not indicated by the early morning breeze. The tangled undergrowth rose up; the ominous silence that had followed them now engulfed them. Terrifying apparitions rose up in front, to each side, behind the hummer. Thax continued to moan for Mother, but the driver and other passenger were deathly still. Green and black faces stared from the forest. A hand reached in to turn off the ignition.

The prisoner recognized Kip standing at the front of the hummer, recognized his intense eyes even with his face smeared black and green.

"Were your feet healed so you could stalk the helpless?" the priest shot.

The hunter carried an assegai. Others, who had been Cavanaugh's guards or disciples around the table with the prophet, carried machetes and thrusting spears and bamboo laths—a poor man's truncheons. Their eyes were steeled for action.

Thax, in his fretful fever, moaned a last time, "Mo-their! Mo-their!"

The priest called out, "Father, forgive them, for they know not—"

A dozen Rangers repelled from the hull of the *Mendes.* Forty-eight of them formed a defensive posture around the priest's encampment. An additional dozen, inserted at first light, guarded the ridge along the hillcrest. Another twelve-man chalk dropped right into the camp and quickly searched it.

Commander Pisanos maneuvered the lander so that Rangers were placed below the camp and on the trail leading back down toward the abandoned V/STOL strip.

Each carried a shoulder-fired Enfield suited to the jungle. In camouflaged smocks and body armor, they were prepared, eager for any action.

Imagine leading them, Rivers thought with envy from the gondola of the lander where he coordinated the jungle sweep. *Imagine having a real enemy, not helpless PRIMS, to crush.*

The lieutenant on the ground called up to the *Mendes.* "Doesn't seem to be anyone around," he reported. "I'd say it's been at least eight, ten weeks, prob longer, since anyone's been here at all." The tech showed obvious signs of neglect. Tendrils clung to some of the hardware. Monkeys made free with provisions. But someone had thoroughly rifled through everything long before the monkeys took over.

"Keep alert, lieutenant," Giannini ordered. "Might still be trouble."

That's what we're itching for, the officer thought for his team. "Yes, sir. We'll handle any firefight," the ground commander reported with professional calmness while being keen to show this Security wallah how ass-kicking pumped his Rangers really were.

"Let's check out the hummer location," Giannini ordered. Pisanos disk-guided the *Mendes* beyond the deserted hillside, then up and over the jagged crest above.

In less than a minute, the lander hovered over the spot where the vehicle rested, just visible under a kapok tree. A detached Ranger squad had already secured the area, which seemed as calm as any jungle after a peaceful night.

A gruff veteran on the ground com-linked up to the officers on the flight deck. "Bedder cum-on down here see this."

Rivers soon found himself rappelling to the ground.

A young life in an UZ followed by several years of diligent urban duty had prepared the ensign for most nauseating sights, but nothing prepared him for this discovery.

Father Cavanaugh, his face beaten nearly beyond recognition, was spread out over the hood of his hummer. His eyes were open. No anger or resentment marred his look. Underneath each outstretched arm was a boy. The pair had been tortured as well.

On the priest's left was a sickly one, who was sure to die of NeoCon had his throat not been slit wide open. A healthy-looking one at the cleric's right bled from similar deep wounds.

The old man had an assegai driven into the left side of his ribcage, a heart-thrust delivered only after his death. A redundant symbol of execution.

Clouds of flies nestled in the stream of blood that ran down the hood and pooled near the front tire of the hummer.

"They haven't been dead all that long," Rivers reported emotionlessly, detached at this point from the carnage he unintentionally set up.

When the newly promoted centurion zipped Cavanaugh's remains into a body bag, he moved the man's arms. It was then that the Security officer got a closer look at the priest's consecrated hands: the right index finger was missing, clumsily hacked off at the knuckle.

FOURTEEN

A DIGNITARY COMES TO EARTH

(The Vandenberg Sector up to the Sac City Sid, 2096)

"Excuse me, sir," a husky voice stated to the back of a passenger hesitantly stepping toward a MAG LEV. Eight gleaming carriages waited as dozens of associates rushed forward to board.

"First-class's for associates only. Sids must prior arrange." A sid himself, the conductor gently ushered the wayward man away from the posh coach, steering him toward other top-quality cars farther down the platform.

"But I've reservations," explained the befuddled traveler. "All this bustling—this frenetic activity! And at one-g! Not used to it!"

Although the passenger was actually in his late eighties, no one would have questioned his age if he claimed to be twenty-five years younger. The sharp distinction between his chrono and physical age was that marked. Although slender, he wasn't frail. His straight hair was naturally gray, left long and pulled into a ponytail, a style forty years out of fashion. And he wore glasses, another sign that he was some well-to-do sid: associates had cornea surgery.

Most strikingly, he sported no finger disks.

The conductor, in an immaculate navy blue uniform, smiled courteously but firmly, "I don't have a rez for anyone *non-* in this coach." In his left hand, the conductor held a glowing mobile unit where certainly this rumbled sid wouldn't be listed. His right hand gestured politely for compliance.

The perplexed passenger looked hard. The blue-green dot was unmistakable under the lighter palm-side skin of the man's ebony hand.

Of course! Finger disks. The traveler recognized the minimum adult implant on the index finger. "Take me only a sec," he explained, fumbling for something in one pocket then another. "Just arrived from Mars, hiber-lag, y'know, not accustomed to all this g." Reaching inside his blazer at last, the passenger produced a small leather case from which he withdrew a single finger mouse from the dozen stored inside the velvet-lined container which might have contained cigars and not rubber thimbles.

The conductor hadn't witnessed this in years. In this age, even mid-range sids all had implants; few relied on serviceable yet all-but obsolete finger mouse hardware.

A stream of associates moved quickly across the platform toward the chrome and glass coaches even though the confused man partially blocked their way. A porter appeared to keep the rush running smoothly. No one would miss this express, even if this one troublesome sid held them up.

Slipping on a well-worn rubber thimble, the lost passenger was finally ready. "Sorry for the commotion," he explained. "I don't have disks. Never did."

The conductor replied with forbearance, "I *had* noticed, sir."

The traveler accessed the conductor's hand unit with a single thimble-twitch. He then pointed at the glowing LCD. "There I am—see—Martin Herriff."

The conductor half stumbled, half danced with excited politeness. "I'm am so sorry, *Doctor* Herriff. I was told only to expect a VIP, but I wasn't informed of—and I never suspect that *you,* well, without disks." He shrugged, "You can understand, of course."

The conductor and an instantly appearing porter were both attentive to the legendary dignitary. The frenzied pace of the platform seemed to slacken as travelers, associates, and bullet personnel admired this venerable personage.

Ushered along regally, in a few steps he was brought to the front of the bullet. Seating Herriff on the right side of the executive coach, the conductor explained, "The absolute best ride here, more to see." The VIP was immediately offered a beverage from a service cart. "Myriad to choose from. Even more than a Moon lander. This *is* Earth, after all."

This solicitous attention continued as the magnetically levitated express left the spotless, shinning platform on time and accelerated to maximum.

Ten minutes into the trip, the conductor, justifiably anxious about his passenger's route, confronted the Martian. "Doctor Herriff, y'know, we can still requie an exec hov' for you—someone so famous—meet you at the next station."

The Mars-based engineer respectfully refused. For many reasons, all kept to himself, he wanted to see as much from the ground as practicable. He had originally booked his homecoming straight through to his final destination, an itinerary from the Vandenberg Lunar Port directly to the Sac City Cantonment by lander. But before disembarking Earth-side, he changed his mind and opted for this circuitous ground transport to the subsidiary part of Sac City.

The conductor looked perplexed. "Shunning an HFC seems odd; after all, you are its designer." He whistled at the enormity of Herriff's contribution to civilization. He knew enough to add this analogy, "Indeed, as the airplane was to the twentieth century, so your hovercraft is to the twenty-first."

Herriff thanked him for his kind words, hyperbolic as they were.

"It's not uncommon," he continued eloquently, "to hear *Herriff*—oh, and Miller, I guess—mentioned with the same respect as Wilber and Orville. In many ways, *you* made the modern world possible."

Herriff smiled until left alone then shook his head to stop his mind from restarting that visceral internal dialog it endlessly had. *Can't lay all that at my feet,* his mind raced. *I only invented the HFC. I didn't muck up the second half of this century!*

The inventor of the hovercraft was adamant not to accept responsibility for its unintended repercussions brought about by reliable runabouts. To its credit, the HFC made city air cleaner with its fuel-efficient oxygen/hydrogen engine. Motorways and roads became less congested as so many HFC owners skimmed over surface gridlock.

But how others used, or abused, my invention—he had mentally hashed this out countless times while sitting alone on the Red Planet—*used and abused the HFC as they abused so many other tech-advances, it's not the fault of the designer.* He drew a sharp breath, failing to stop this torrent of thoughts. *Were the Wright brothers responsible for fire bombings of civilians? Einstein for Hiroshima or the Indi-Paki nuclear exchanges in the '20s? Might as well blame Priestley for fire as blame me for this century's economic and political shambles.*

Herriff took a sip of his drink to derail this mental anguish. Even during his prolonged hiber, induced sleep-pack dreams didn't totally remove these haunting dialogs. He had suffered though a horrible icing. Nearly three months of continuous dreams transformed into nightmares. He hadn't crossed while the Earth and Mars were in opposition, so the trip was a third longer than the most efficient trip. He was that anxious to get to Earth. All the while his restless mind kept returning to so many acrimonious arguments, several with Walter Miller.

Hence his choice, if this logic made any sense to anyone but himself, of the MAG LEV to Silicon, then on to Sac City by whatever train network means he could find.

He was returning Earth-side to gather data, to engage in primary research. By choice, he wasn't skimming over the surface to a Marsco cantonment; rather, he was purposely ground-transporting to analyze all he might witness firsthand. Eventually, he did need to make his way to the Seattle HQ, but in due time. Primarily, he wanted to explore a planet he hadn't visited in a quarter of a century. And look up a former friend and longtime collaborator he hadn't seen in more than fifteen years.

"Will there be anything else, sir?" the conductor asked, bringing his VIP a pillow and blanket. "This's pretty comfortable leather," he commented patting the back of the seat, "a guy fresh from space might curl up for a nice nap." The designer's haggard looks and puffy eyes behind the black titanium frames of his glasses betrayed his recent horrendous hibernation.

The coach was only half full, so Herriff had a four-seat pod around a small table to himself. Other associates sat quietly, some with their children. A few communicated with their workstations as the gleaming bullet cruised at top speed. Three associates twitched on notebooks. It was an efficient mode of transport for a relaxing half a day. He was glad the HFC hadn't rendered all this luxury from a byegone era totally obsolete.

The conductor soon returned. "Not like a shuttle, is it?"

"You don't get a sense of speed on a shuttle," the engineer replied absently as the sights closest to his window blurred by. Farther away, everything moved slowly, yet the passenger knew the MAG LEV was close to its maximum rate. "The perception of speed's always relative to distance; there's nothing to create that perspective in space."

"I know," the conductor replied, "one kid's in the Asteroid Service—not an Indie. Iceman, sort'a following his old man's footsteps. Flies with *Herriff*-Millers all the time."

The co-designer of the MAS's main thruster system smiled graciously.

"Earth-side long?"

"Only a few months."

"Not here to retire," the conductor stated emphatically.

"No, too young." Both laughed since they appeared to be around the same age.

"Have you ever ridden on our service before?"

"Not in a long, long time. Actually, this's my first trip off Mars to home in well over twenty-five years." The conductor gave a whistle. "The Von Braun Center keeps me extremely busy. But, more to the point, I haven't ridden a bullet in close to forty."

"Well, if this's your first ride in some time, much's changed," the railman explained. "All this predates the C-Wars, although extensively modified since. Computer retrofit. New chrome and stainless inside and out. Sid restoration work, of course. Complete re-glazing. Gold from asteroids—not SoAm strip mines as before—added to tint the Plexi just slightly."

Herriff noticed the honey-tinged panels that reduced even the harshest glare of sunlight.

"We run mostly along the coast through a series of sectors and some linked cantonments within a few sids." He ran on in a matter-of-fact tone. "We'll make several stops—Marsco Health Research Center, Marine Bio-Center in the Monterey Sector. Those kinds of places."

The conductor left his VIP. Through the expansive window, Herriff watched the ocean stretch away to the horizon. The sun painted the waves yellow, but any reflection off the sea was thoroughly tempered.

"May I join you?" a young associate asked the lone dignitary. While watching the changed Marsco world speed by, Herriff hadn't noticed an Academy cadet standing in the aisle. "The conductor told me you were on board, sir, and allowed me up from second-class." The twenty-year-old man held out his two-disked hand in greeting. They tentatively shook hands although the plebe was unable to conceal his surprise that the elderly associate didn't have any disks.

The cadet had a stern face with olive features, thick eyebrows, and brown eyes. He was attempting to soften his hard edge with

Marsco manners. Had Herriff been accustomed to trips to Earth, he would have seen the PRIM background of the cadet without any effort.

"Your reputation precedes you, of course," the young man remarked awkwardly.

"Thank you, ensign—"

"*Cadet,* sir. Cadet Maxwell Carter."

Herriff thought, *The name doesn't fit his face, but many associates rename themselves.*

The plebe traveled in a light blue uniform with gray piping and a shoulder patch signifying his Academy status. This uniform was a ticket to venture beyond many stoplines, but in this coach surrounded by so many lefters, his blues carried little weight.

"Traveling alone?" the designer asked without hesitation. "Do your friends wish to join us as well?" The doting conductor, overhearing, realized the cadet would be staying. A perk of rank.

"No I'm alone. On leave. Easier to catch a lander to Vandenberg and then take a bullet north. Better connects," Carter explained with only a trace of nervousness. What he didn't say was that, because his family still lived in an East Bay UZ under a decidedly different name, he had elected to approach home anonymously. This was better than going directly from Seattle to the Silicon lander field with fellow classmates and then possibly having to explain a great deal of his hidden personal history.

The bullet sped past several desalination plants in full operation that kept the nearby cantonments lush, even though the West was suffering through a serious ongoing drought. Accustomed to red, desolate dust, Herriff appreciated the fleeting view of thriving vegetation and stands of tall trees.

"These compounds are for associates," Carter noted. The housing units and high-rise offices overlooked magnificent vistas. All construction blended into the hillside to prevent any degradation of the frail ecosystem. All indigenous flora coexisted perfectly with Marsco.

"They're beautifully maintained." Herriff admired the thriving coastal oak and manzanita shaped by the constant ocean breeze. "Pleasant to see natural living things. Mars is barren, you know. The planet's bleak and inhospitable outside the colony's confines."

Carter nodded then added, "And no sign of drought here."

"Those desal-plants must be running 24/37/7," concluded the observant engineer. He caught himself then laughed. "Sorry, wrong planet. It's 24/7 here."

The cadet looked puzzled a moment until the Martian gave a hint. "Remember to apply your Intro to Planetary Science!"

The engineer had guessed at the course's name, but the clue jogged the student's mind just the same. "Oh, yeah, Mars's rotation is 37 minutes longer each day than Earth's. Doctor Miller has told that countless times. She gets off lecture at times in Propulsion Engineering and lets slip anecdotes about her younger life on Mars."

From the streaking bullet, the designer saw what he expected to see. During his years on Mars, he had heard repeated and ever-so optimistic reports about the numerous expanding sectors that were sprouting up as Marsco rebuilt the Earth after the C-Wars conflagration. Each locale the train sped through, each station where the train glided to a stop, the engineer found everything shining, exemplary, modern.

Over the years, quarterly statements from Seattle HQ had been filled with glowing stats of increased productivity, higher standards of living, increases in life expectancy. Those reports showed that everyone on this Blue Planet was moving ahead by leaps and bounds, even those huddled in revitalized sids and zones.

From his vantage point on the speeding MAG LEV, he witnessed in the passing cantonments the fulfillment of promises

Marsco had given when he was a young man. The longtime associate swelled with pride in its accomplishments.

"My I ask a personal question?" the cadet, comfortably settled in a leather seat across from the VIP, ventured to say.

Not accustomed to the decorum among associates that these days kept such inquiries to a minimum, the designer nodded.

"Are you planning to redesign the bullet?" Herriff didn't catch his drift. "Why *you?* On ground transport? You virtually invented everything that's flying these days."

"A good researcher never exaggerates!" Herriff gently admonished.

"But it's true—you did!"

"Not just me! I always worked with fine colleagues. Always a team effort—and there is no *I* in *T-E-A-M.* But, I've been away for years and years." He paused wistfully. "And I want to see as much as possible."

He stopped speaking as the bullet slowly approached a station. On both sides of the track stood ramshackle Housing Authorities—sights he hadn't expected to witness—the first sign of anything contrary to official proclamations. The blocks of low brick apartments were in poor repair. It reminded him of his childhood when the first signs of Divestiture were beginning to show. Poorly repaired roofs and boarded-up windows told their obvious tale. Hoards of PRIM kids played in littered streets rather than attended school.

In contrast a hilltop at a distance housed an expansive deep-space antenna array. The living quarters for its personnel were gated and guarded. The stopline clearly delineated the non-world from the associate world.

"It doesn't seem misplaced where it rests," Herriff noted about the sophisticated system. The impressed engineer focused on achievement rather than stagnation.

"Eagles and condors nest among the dishes," the cadet stated. Along the nearby river, he pointed out an osprey perched atop a reforested oak tree. "The whole area's been eco-salvaged after years of neglect. These're among the best postings," he pointed up the hill, "once you're on the other side of that stopline."

Another example, thought the designer, *of Marsco's evident concern for the Earth. Who wouldn't want to work and live in such a majestic locality?*

At a station platform, they waited silently as associates shuffled on and off first-class. Soon, the bullet effortlessly whisked away, leaving both an example of the polished Marsco world and the decrepit PRIM world behind.

"I've another question."

"Sure." Unaware of the self-contained and closed nature of Earth life, Herriff didn't know that few associates confided anything that mattered.

"Well, it's more about your co-designer, Doctor Miller. When we study propulsion dynamics in first year, the Herriff-Miller ignition concepts and combustion chamber schematics are thoroughly discussed. Plus, we get an extensive bio about you. Your life's work. Your legendary Hover/Flight Craft. Your Herriff-Grid—"

"What? *Mine?*" the designer shot, "Me? That's attributed to me?"

"Well, yes, of course."

"Historic oversimplification, to be sure. But no matter."

"So, you didn't invent the *Herriff*-Grid?"

"No! That system, even though it bears *my* name, is a software application. Has nothing to do with me—all I did was design the hovercraft—nothing whatsoever. Techno-nerds designed and booted the grid, not I. Marsco wonks integrated its super-computers; that's what makes it possible for thousands of HFCs to move in complete safety over vast crowded city skies."

"But they are your HFCs."

"Well, yes, my design, at first."

"But the grid invented an invisible superhighway. And with it, all airborne craft shared movement zones without fear of collision."

"Exactly. And the grid was necessary," Herriff defended. "Still is, I gather, but in those early years, in a matter of ten, twelve years, HFCs were skimming over congested ground traffic. But above, they shared airspace with fixed-wing and rotor craft that were quickly becoming obsolete."

"Museum pieces at present."

"Certainly," concluded the engineer, hiding his glee at his success.

"And skyscraper rooftops became natural landing pads."

"Exactly." Herriff slapped the leather arm. "'*And the rest is history!*'" he mimicked a voice the cadet had never before heard.

"Yes, well, here's my point," Carter went back to his question, "little, if anything's ever mentioned about Miller himself. Me and my friends—that's to say, my friends and *I*—well, we're max-curious about him, that's all. Is he dead?"

"Dead? Oh, no, very much alive."

"Is he like you? Permanently on Mars?"

"No, left years ago." That vague answer suggested that Miller might be hiber-exploring the solar system, so the older associate clarified, "He currently lives Earth-side."

"One plebe from Buenos Aries, she claims he's gone native, upped with some Amazon cult. You know, a Luddite."

"Oh, heavens, no!"

"Well, there are other rumors. Postings on blogs and webpages here and there, making all sorts of outrageous claims. Even bulletins pasted to Marsco documents, claiming he really never had that much to do with *your* engines. You know, disparaging sorts of e-Post-Its hacked onto one of our humungo assign-docs."

"Profs still work your butts off at the Academy?"

"I'll say."

"Props to them! But more to your point, we—Walter and I—worked with a large team, of course, but he was there in the thick of it. He has too much integrity to take credit for work he didn't substantially do," the chief engineer insisted. "The Herriff-*Miller* propulsion system very much deserves its name. Dot!"

Carter pondered a moment as another set of run-down housing units caught Herriff's eye. The designer seemed to watch then lose interest quickly.

Finally, the cadet asked rhetorically, "Isn't it odd that so famous, so influential an associate would eventually become a *persona non grata?* I mean, you can't find his e-address; he's only a slim factoid blurb in the Marsco-Wiki. Famous person like that can't just drop off the face of the Earth, can he?"

"Sometimes 'dropping off the face of the Earth' only takes leaving Marsco."

The young man found it hard to imagine anyone leaving what had initially been so difficult an organization for him to join.

Herriff thought better of his answer and purposely confused the issue. "He's on sort of an extended sabbatical, that's all."

The Martian witnessed an expansive subsidiary that seemed to be flourishing. "Of necessity," the cadet explained as though Herriff was unindoctrinated, "every sector needs a concomitant sid area for non-Marsco personnel who operate necessary mundane ancillary services. Transportation. Food distribution. Power grid utilization."

"Long list."

The plebe nodded but continued automatically, "Water services. Component assembly. PRIM labor unions."

What Herriff saw, to Marsco's credit, seemed held up to a standard of comfort unheard of for so many before the C-Wars. "It's sharing profits with largess," insisted the engineer.

The scene changed rapidly with the bullet's movement. Some shabbier sid areas, the visitor concluded wrongly, must be unincorporated zones.

"No, this train avoids most zones along the way," the cadet corrected and pointed. "What you're seeing is an HA. It's way too small for to be considered a real zone anyway. It's a Housing Authority site: units for selected PRIMS, something like trustees, within a sid or near Marsco sector."

Herriff hadn't known of these. *A few thousand PRIMS amid a sea of comfort.*

"Still, they're better off here than a hopeless zone," explained the associate defensively.

These views were further indications to Herriff that some of what he had been hearing was not squaring with what he was seeing.

Then he thought, chiding himself for his own naïveté, *Should I expect every word from Marsco, or any other bureaucracy for that matter, to be totally accurate?* After all, hadn't he once—over the objections of Miller—initially sent glowing test results to HQ after several preliminary trails for their new thrusters ended in dismal failure? Not really lies or fabrications, so much as "indications of the assumed potentialities of future positive test results," promises of what "would" be once certain shortcomings, glitches, incorrect calculations, and kinks were worked out. Dealing with a bureaucracy often meant dealing with reciprocal mendacity.

Nonetheless, as the MAG LEV soon sped through a score of opulent associate complexes and next streaked through tidy but modest subsidiary areas, the engineer began to feel depressed. Before his trip, he had hoped this visit would allay his worst fears, but so far, what he witnessed they only confirmed them. Life for an associate, to be sure, was gilded. For sids, especially the ones tied tightly and directly to Marsco, comfort and security. *For PRIMS? Well,* Herriff thought, *what's that old description of their life? "Nasty, brutish, and short."*

"May I ask another question?"

The older associate kindly acquiesced. "You've an insatiable appetite for knowledge. That's good in a researcher."

The cadet smiled. "I plan to jockey shuttles."

"Even so, ask away."

"There's an Academy prof, Lieutenant Tessa *Miller*. Doctor Miller."

"The Miller you mentioned who is from Mars?"

"Yes. Young. Bright. Been a prof about six years. Came straight from the Institute across the quad. No nonsense about her. Tough as nails. We call her 'Gunnery Sergeant—'" The student caught himself about to insult an officer and his advisor in front of one of Marsco's highest wallahs!

He softly and more politely continued, "There have always been countless rumors about her—that she's Doctor Miller's daughter. We've checked on her—girlhood on Mars overlaps with most of Miller's work there." He stopped, awaiting confirmation.

"You know, Cadet Carter, there're over 600 functioning Marsco colonies on the planet. Plus, about ninety more Indie ones. And Miller's a common enough name."

"Yes, coincidence probability at max threshold, I know."

"What else about her—aside from she's an excellent prof if she works you hard—brings you from this premise to your conclusion?"

"She graduated from the Academy then completed a doctorate at MIT with no other service break. Shows what Marsco expected of her."

"And from this fragmentary evidence you conclude that Marsco may have been protecting her?"

The plebe didn't catch the engineer's drift but went on. "She was a brilliant student, so everyone says. Other profs, her current colleagues, talk about her cadet years, one of those legends-in-her-own-time plebes. And she never confirms nor denies her lineage to Walter Miller, either."

Herriff had to chuckle. "If she keeps her past hidden and to herself," he knew this hadn't changed about Marsco, "is that *so* unusual for *any* associate?"

The cadet reluctantly admitted, that no, that wasn't at all.

"Well, I think I'll have to rely on that old dodge; it's best that I don't 'confirm or deny' anything."

"I understand perfectly."

They fell into a comfortable silence. The streamlined coach quietly sped inland, moving through an area cultivated by the Food Consortium. Under sid auspices, PRIMS toiled in the heat where once gigantic farm equipment worked.

As mealtime approached, the observant conductor gave Herriff a knowing look, *dining alone?* Enjoying the young man's company, the engineer asked the cadet to join him. The conductor obediently seated the VIP and the mere two-disker privately in the dining car. Attendants covered the table with a starched white cloth and placed a flawless rose in a vase between the two.

"Bethany Palmer always made sure we had flowers at the Center," Herriff stated, catching himself before he gave away Tessa's mother.

Sparkling crystal chargers graced each place at the table. The Marsco emblem was engraved on the bright handle of the cutlery, its sterling made from asteroid silver and lunar copper.

They ate their elegant meal silently. Crisp spinach salad with bay shrimp, fresh trout, veal in a white wine sauce. After this last course, the older passenger remarked, "I've seen much restoration already on my trip. Vandenberg—you wouldn't know it—had sustained much V-damage in the Wars."

"Been fully operational for over twenty years now. And the Cape, also back to full utilization."

"When I last left Earth, had to egress from Kuala Lumpur."

The two ate chocolate mousse and savored freshly ground coffee. "Something you don't get in space, Mr. Carter, so be prepared to bring your own supply when you board a shuttle."

"I'll remember that, sir."

"Beans don't seem to travel well through our supply system. Even freeze-dried. And so far, no one's developed hydroponic Arabica shrubs that yield any flavor. Bethany tried; never successful. More's the pity."

The conductor announced their imminent arrival at the SoBay terminal, the last stop before Silicon itself, the most important sector on this coast aside from the Seattle HQ.

Cadet Carter was certain that he and Herriff would part there. The plebe was relieved; their separation would help keep his own past a secret. He didn't know when they would meet professionally; his personal history best remain shrouded.

The attentive conductor was anxiously standing next to the two. "Doctor Herriff, d'I read your itinerary correctly? Still seems impossible. You *want* to transfer here, next stop? Head for the interior then toward Sac City?"

"Yes, that's right."

"*And* on ground transport?"

"Seems like a good idea at this moment."

"There're a few cantonments out that way, but why not liasie with a trav-assist agent? Can hand you over to Lander Service. Plus it's still not too late to requie a VIP HFC."

"A perfectly natural suggestion," Herriff smiled then added, "but no thanks, don't bother."

The cadet confided in a hushed tone, "There're several large zones between here and there. You ought to avoid them."

"I'll be safe, won't I?"

Both the conductor and student hurriedly assured the visitor of his safety. "Certainly, no one'll bother an associate, even one traveling alone," the conductor stated emphatically. "But the transport—bogus. Spotty at best. Connects terrible. Won't get luxury like this."

The cadet looked at the polished holster he wore, the handle of its Enfield sticking out from under a leather flap. *Makes movement easier,* he concluded, concerned for the unarmed wallah.

"But that's how I'm going," insisted the Martian traveler. From behind a befuddled veneer, his tenacity grew visible and resolute.

The cadet eased the tension. "I can escort Dr. Herriff up to the East Bay and get him to the correct train." To answer the conductor's inquisitive eyes and unasked question, he added, "Courier run. I have to enter the sid anyway."

The conductor noted that the young associate didn't have an attaché case handcuffed to his wrist—standard Marsco SOP—but said nothing.

Although face-to-face in the crush of haggard commuters, Herriff and Carter found it hard to talk over the confused noise of hundreds of common sids and PRIMS. "Not what you're used to!" declared the cadet over the commotion.

Herriff motioned with his head at the carriage. "I hadn't expected this kludge-level!"

"I'm sure in space, Marsco keeps everything in top condition."

"It never launched a *Mir,* if that's what you mean."

The filthy light rail needed basic repair—cracked windows, worn floor covering, torn up seats. Here and there, graffiti pathetically declared independence from Marsco. Herriff didn't want to imagine the jury-rigged ops side of the train.

"Pressed into continuous service without routine maintenance," the cadet shouted knowingly, "acute transport shortage."

Herriff's suitcases always seemed to be blocking the aisle. Carter was good-natured about having to repeatedly move them. Finally, both stood straddling a bag. The Martian noticed that when the surrounding passengers saw the Academy uniform—and realized he and the cadet were together—they gave the two a wide circle in reluctant acquiescence to their importance.

The LR crept northward along the east side of the Bay, stopping at several elevated platforms. It took more than two hours to traverse a fraction of the Martian's earlier bullet ride. Before they reached the second transfer point, the suffocating car began to empty. As the crowding subsided, cooler evening air entered whenever the doors opened. The two manhandled the suitcases a final time to slide them under a worn-out bench seat.

Once sitting, Herriff, who had been standing the whole time, realized he might have fainted had the carriage not emptied.

He's not used to this, the cadet realized. *Can't imagine what he's thinking, transporting like this. This isn't the Marsco world, his prewar world.*

"Can't thank you enough, Mr. Carter," the fatigued engineer huffed out. Beads of sweat formed on his forehead. Part of his ponytail stuck to his wet neck.

"You'll be all right heading up to Sac City? Still sure you want to go *this* way? There's ample time to get some proper transport."

"No, I prefer this," declared the displaced passenger. "I *must* go this way."

The nearly empty train came to gradual stop at the last elevated platform before Herriff's transfer point.

Pushing his face to the dirty window like a child, Herriff was able to see across to Marsco's side of the Bay, the tip of the peninsula, The City, and stretching down to Silicon. In deepening darkness, graceful skyscrapers glowed with all the radiance of a prosperous prewar city. Above that elegant skyline, thousands of HFCs glided effortlessly in unbroken rhythm, a Herriff-Grid in full operation. Quickly after the C-Wars, Marsco and a gaggle of cooperating sids returned that cross-bay area to its prewar elegance, status, and wealth.

The engineer's side of the Bay was almost totally black. Here the streets were only sporadically illuminated. The road system and light rail were in disrepair, hardly functional. Even on the Bay Bridge, only light traffic moved. Where once a toll plaza crossed the lanes of traffic, Security checkpoints searched the few ground transports attempting to cross over to the PRIM-free Marsco sector.

Herriff was not able to see much directly below the elevated tracks, but above the darkened skyline, he made out a score of Security HFCs on patrol. Two in the distance were at a silent hover with their searchlights probing the ground. They had spotted something in the menacing shadows worth a closer inspection. Other Security HFCs maintained their conspicuous vigilance with passive IR scopes.

Those shimmering lights across the Bay are moving steadily toward the twenty-second century, while this side is receding back to the twentieth, the associate concluded.

Waiting for the LR to move, the other remaining passengers coughed, whispered, shuffled. The air began to grow warm and thick in the delay. The engineer didn't know what to say to his guide. He commented amiably, "I'm sure I'm only delaying your leave. You've been more than kind to assist me."

"Don't mention it."

"Just get me to the correct train—I'll be fine."

"Marsco philanthropy. Not a bother."

His face at the window again, his diskless hands blocking any light, Herriff once more examined the street. As his eyes grew accustomed to the dark, he watched the moped and bike traffic swarming below the elevated tracks. Obsolete buses plied their routes through the throng. Passengers jammed inside while an intrepid few hung onto the sides by hooking arms through the missing windows and finding a tenuous foothold. Pedestrians crowded along the broken pavement. Food venders, clothing merchants, hawkers pushing this and that, all shouted in dozens of languages, none English.

The crowd parted as a slow-moving S & H hummer came patrolling down the street. Behind it, a larger, black Brad—armed with nonlethal ooze nozzle and stunner—followed the lead Security vehicle. Grim reminders of Marsco's supervisory presence in this deteriorating sid.

The LR tracks converged at the terminal buried several stories that linked with the city-connecting lines. An announcement screen stated a train heading east into the Central Valley was leaving in an hour, Platform #7.

Like the elevated platforms, the central terminal lacked basic repair and cleaning. Where there had once been rows of newsstands and food distribution points, about fifty PRIMS were living in cardboard boxes. Hordes of children sat among the squatters. An S & H officer and her Auxxie squad in gray and black uniforms mingled in the crush. Herriff noticed that some of the squatters and Auxxies were the same age; it was an easy transition from burlap sacks to uniforms.

"Security and Hygiene does a sanitize sweep through here once a week or so. Then these PRIMS are back like vermin. It's never like this across the Bay," Carter declared in an embarrassed way, "You'd never see this in a sector." He was glad the engineer didn't know that he grew up hard by here, a world he was leaving behind.

"It's unfortunate there isn't a food point," the Martian remarked. "I haven't eaten since the bullet."

"Another world ago," the cadet let slip.

"Nor have I had any water."

He thought back to Mars during the final weeks prior to his journey. A recent arrival on Mars, a fuel systems expert, having heard of Herriff's plan to visit an Earth-side subsidiary, offered this insistent advice, "Carry MREs along with a water bottle. And pack an Enfield." Herriff gently declined this caution. "It's been a long, long time," the young wonk concluded, "since you've visited Earth."

Herriff and Carter soon located the eastbound train. The finest car was at the front, a solitary second-class carriage whose best days were long past. The trailing coaches, for common sids and PRIMS, were in even worse condition.

The Martian found the second-class interior similar to the light rail with broken seats and windows repaired with duct tape.

"Hey'ya, whadda ya'doing?" a harried conductor shouted from down the poorly lit aisle. He had been on his feet all day and was in no mood for someone busting into the miniscule domain he ruled with an iron fist. He rushed forward but slowed when Cadet Carter stepped up to better show off his uniform.

"Yeah, yeah," the conductor muttered with a gruff tone that, if not conciliatory, was at least partially accommodating. The uniform might be that of a mere cadet, but it *was* a Marsco uniform. That was enough.

Herriff was totally spent. The Mars colonist didn't often have an adventure like this at full-g. He looked up at the conductor, who was negotiating with the plebe. His uniform was exactly the same as the bullet's personnel, but his was stained and smudged. Brass buttons were missing.

"How long's the trip?"

"About four how'ers, if d'Power Consort don't kill no juice. We're at dere mercy," the conductor explained in a disgruntled voice. Then in earnest frankness he added, "Ya duze know this ain't no lux'yuary bullet?" He stared hard to make sure Herriff understood.

Doing so, the designer got a good long look at the conductor. His fleshy face was broad with permanent anxiety lines and a fixed, unsympathetic glance. His eyes were bloodshot and quick to look away from anyone else's gaze, someone else's problems. This was his life, his strength, this routine of ordering around PRIMS and sids.

After Cadet Carter settled Herriff near the front of the car, he said his good-bye. "He knows you're Marsco," the young man motioned at the conductor. "That'll mean something, all things considered." With that he left the VIP all alone.

He was so helpful, the traveler thought, fighting off sleep. *He'll do Marsco proud.* Only after the train jerked out of the terminal did an ominous, foreboding thought cross the engineer's mind. *Had he been sent to watch me?* Herriff was unable to rid himself of that menacing notion.

Above ground for the first hour, the train traversed an urban area, acting like a commuter line, making several closely spaced, lengthy stops. The surly conductor stood at the door to screen riders. To a dozen sid overseers he recognized, he grudgingly slid aside, deigning to let them enter the forward coach, his best.

The cars trailing behind were jammed with day-workers, both sids and PRIMS who came in from neighboring zones. Theirs was a torturous, slow ride back out after twelve hours of hard labor.

The carriage's lights threw a shadowy glow, casting a yellow pall over the threadbare seats and frayed passengers. The conductor carried on a curt conversation with two particular riders, both junior managers in their early thirties. They were personnel contractors making the trip to Sac City with its juxtaposed ancillary UZs to arrange more workers for a factory complex.

"This ain't no commuter line all the way dare," the conductor burst out in a hostile voice. He had enough trouble moving through this solitary stretch of urban area.

"Hell, no. We ain't fools. Th'new PRIMS from the Valley'll be resettled t'a Housing Authority close to th'work sites." That seemed to settle the issue.

After thirty minutes without a stop, the train crossed a wide estuary on a dual-track bridge. Running parallel to the one span stood a second destroyed in the Wars. Beyond the crossing, the train came to a transfer point. The conductor informed Herriff there would be an hour stopover.

While the train stood on the siding, an old PRIM came aboard to take food orders, a nightly routine the conductor allowed.

"Y'never know what'ta dem wogs're cookin'," the conductor whispered to his passenger. Herriff noted, however, that he placed an order, shouting at the weathered PRIM as if he were deaf. The traveler politely asked for the same.

In ten minutes, a tiffin of steaming curry rice with a kabob of spiced meat and green peppers arrived. The traveler was especially grateful for the bottled water.

"Here, wallah," the PRIM gestured with a polite bow. "Y'will be enjoying this, is being good."

"How'd you come to be here?" Herriff reluctantly asked when the PRIM returned to gather the empty tiffins. "So far from home." He spoke as if the terms *far* and *home* still made sense in a Marsco world.

"Manys is living here, after the Great Wars," he stated, reluctant to look the wallah in the eye.

Herriff purposely overpaid the PRIM.

Part of the population rectification program, the Martian remembered a HQ bulletin. At subsidiaries request, ran the information, Marsco brought fresh labor to many population-depleted areas. Transfer of excess personnel, all initiated by sid needs.

After its hour-long stop, the train picked up speed. The carriage tipped and swayed, unlike the smooth bullet. While digging his teeth with a kabob skewer, the conductor declared to Herriff, "Dem wogs'll git outta of dat zone fuckin' quick. Work like dawgs. Clean, too. Dey'll bribe sumbuddy yet 'n git outta dare." The conductor concluded with a sigh of resignation, "Dat's whatta'u get fer losin' a fuckin' war—PRIMS everywhere."

With pitch-black night surrounding them, they moved around a low hill. As they traversed this bend at the hill's base, the conductor remarked with familiar expectation to the two men he had been grousing with earlier, "Let's see whatta s'does dis time, boys."

As if on cue, the carriage lights blinked several times, then stayed out. The electrical connections below the cars threw out a final shower of sparks in protest. The train immediately slowed to a complete stop. The conductor's voice declared in the dark, "Sure dis won't b'long." An announcement he was accustomed to saying but one that carried no assurance of its validity. The train stopped cold.

Shinning a small flashlight, the conductor came down the aisle toward Herriff. "We'll be movin' soon, I'm shure," he remarked in a way that reassured his unusual passenger that all was perfectly safe. The beleaguered railman knew that his misplaced, high wallah had never suffered through a journey like tonight's.

Herriff pointed toward the windows and asked what was flickering on the black mounds beyond the tracks. Hundreds of red dots glowed there. From close to the edge of the right of way as far as the designer could see, these lights flickered. A ridge crest 300 meters in the distance showed where things ended and the night stars began behind.

"Cook fires," the conductor answered. "Dat's a UZ. From here all d'way over hill. Bigges' in dis part of th' A & P League—" he caught himself. He went on, "Can't sees it too good in t'dark."

The train jerked forward and stopped. The lights didn't come back on. The cars jerked and stopped a second time and then a third, moving only a few meters forward with each lurch.

Through an open window, the smell of charcoal wafted in accompanied by the stench of burning cooking oil. Of feces and hooch. The smell of decay. The sounds of commotion.

As his eyes adjusted to the low light, Herriff was just barely able to make out cardboard and corrugated tin hovels in the glowing fires. A few dwellings were large drainage pipes resting aboveground with plastic sheeting draped at each end. Before them old women stooped, cooking over their low embers. The din of the place was a polyglot of languages, crying babies, Neo-Con coughing, and angry shouts.

Clearly, the PRIMS in those run-down Housing Authorities, PRIMS employed directly by Marsco, would find those conditions preferable to living here, the Martian realized, thinking back to his morning bullet ride. *Was that today? Was that only 200 clicks from here?*

A Security & Hygiene HFC noted the immobile train and ran its floodlights up and down between the carriages and the high fence marking the edge of the UZ—a show of strength to keep PRIMS inside the stopline. And yet, a few did venture near to the open windows of the carriages.

Someone in the dark at the back of the train shouted to no one in particular, "Hope some disease don't go floating in here."

A second voice shouted, "Hey, Mac, git uz'a coupl'e skanks, will ya?"

And answering passenger called out, "Can ya'magine whad ya'd pick up from dem!"

"HH GAS fur sure," came a reply.

"Not if you gets 'em yung enough," countered a knowing voice.

"We ain't goin' far soon," a last voice complained.

The conductor fumbled in a storage cabinet, eventually withdrawing two chemical emergency lights. He bent the plastic tubes nearly in two until they cracked loudly. Each soon emitted a soft green light. He hung one above Herriff and the other by his companions.

The dim hue hitting the windows reflected just enough to block out the orange cook fires. The bright bars of HFC searchlights crossed in the dark; Herriff still saw them. And nothing blocked the continued low noise of the PRIMS, an unmistakable dispirited din. Nor their stench. Several PRIMS outside called to the passengers about business of one sort or another.

"How long're we gonna be?" One of the younger men called out. "Bet the price's right," he muttered to himself.

"Ain't worth it," cautioned the conductor. "Dis is 'HH GAS Alley.'"

In the carriage window Herriff saw himself, a vague reflection. A haggard old man with a ponytail in disarray asked his likeness, *What did you expect to find?* When his image didn't reply, he accused. *You knew, you knew!* He berated himself, *Walter told you, but you didn't listen. Weren't listening.* Turning away, he closed his eyes.

The Martian traveler slept curled up on an entire bench seat because the carriage was empty enough for everyone to spread out. He didn't sleep deeply—at times he was almost awake; at times his mind seemed fully alert.

Around him floated random pieces of different worlds, worlds that didn't fit together, didn't belong together. Pieces of an old prewar world, the A & P Leagues, the Continental Powers. Pieces of Marsco. Rising Marsco in its early days of promise. The current Marsco he had only witnessed in snatches over the past twenty-four hours. Pieces of history set down in an anachronistic jumble. Hand-drawn carts. Bicycles and mopeds filling the congested twenty-first century streets. HFCs skimming overhead oblivious to the world of drudgery beneath. Labor gangs doing farm tasks by hand. Children everywhere, mostly in rags. Their older sisters for sale. Finger disks. Food in tiffins. A fresh rose decorating a splendid white tablecloth. Aseptic food packs and water bottles. Warnings about HH GAS. Hiber and icemen. Neo-Con. Herriff-Miller units pushing a research ship and her crew beyond the asteroid belt outbound toward Jupiter.

He wished he had packed an Enfield.

An abrupt jolt finally awoke Herriff. It was past dawn. The engineer didn't know what to expect on that hillside. He wasn't at all sure that he wanted to see that adjacent sprawling zone in clear morning light. Instead, he found the train at its final destination.

Pandemonium erupted at the Sac City station. Herriff's four-hour trip had taken all night. He arrived just as several light rails were disgorging their loads of PRIMS and sids.

"Welcom' t'Sacamenna, as oncet was," the conductor announced, his chin thick with growth, his uniform all the more wrinkled. "End uv'ta line, every buddy off. We're in Sac City."

Stiff from sleeping, Herriff found the daylight blinding. In his usual, kind voice he asked the conductor how he might get his bags off the train.

The conductor motioned with his head to the exit where several PRIMS waited with outstretched arms. The other passengers bushed past them. "Wallah, take bags! Wallah, me take," the eager PRIMS shouted, waving desperately to catch anyone's attention.

With gruff barks, the conductor chased away one who tried to rush in for the engineer's luggage. In the end, he stuck a thick finger into the chest of the largest and healthiest looking of the lot.

"What'll I do?" Herriff asked in confiding tones.

"Give 'um part of a token," came the curt answer, "he's yur prob now."

The deft PRIM balanced between Herriff's two cases and set off into the moiling chaos beside the train. He nimbly negotiated the swarm, pushing one bag ahead like a battering ram, dragging the other behind. Wide-eyed Herriff followed in his teeming wake.

Moving along, the Martian was nearly overwhelmed by the sights and sounds. Six commuter lines converged outside of the old brick terminal. During his boyhood, this had been capital of one of the thriving Atlantic and Pacific Leagues. While he was safely ensconced in the *Valles Marineris,* it had become the last governing seat of the faltering Continental Powers.

What was once a historically significant city had been PRIM-ified with this clashing juxtaposition of peoples and eras that didn't fix any logical pattern. PRIMS from all over the world pushed and shoved toward exits.

Another pair of decrepit and jam-packed commuter trains disgorged more PRIMS. The fortunate ones with consistent employment made their way to dilapidated buses waiting to transport them to their workstations. Large patches of rust ate through the paint. Windows were broken. *No gold tinting there,* Herriff found himself thinking.

To the Martian, the crush made no sense: obsolete transports and trains needing repair and PRIM children being led to work gangs.

Shouts in English filled the station as sid drivers collected who was theirs. A polyglot of languages answered, but supervisors kept everything in English. In the subsidiaries, as with Marsco, that was expected.

Herriff threaded his way through the surging mob by following his PRIM and his two rolling suitcases when a single voice cried above the horde.

A young PRIM hadn't connected with her overseer; her transport had gone on without her. She stood pleading, blocking an exit. The crowd pushed her aside, yet she continued howling and arguing with the sid gate-guard, another woman, who wouldn't let the PRIM through. A stream of heads interfered with their argument that went on unabated. Both the guard and worker looked identical to Herriff; only a uniform separated the two.

The platform supervisor, a seasoned hand with a single disk, wouldn't let the PRIM out when she appealed to him. Like the surly conductor, he ruled his tiny realm with petty fierceness. "Ya ain't goin' in'ta area withou' a valid permit!" he shouted at her. She didn't seem to know what he meant. "Unless ya' travel with yer overseer—," he motioned to the absent buses, "no enter here!"

She sobbed unrestrained tears. Just a few minutes ago, she had pushed to one side of the rush to chat with a friend who made his way to the station on a different train. When she looked up, her overseer was gone.

"No work today, no eat, sir," she mumbled tearfully.

"I can't help dat."

"Work not far. Can walk, sir."

"You ain't got no *access* permit," the supervisor yelled, pushing her way from the gate and back onto the platform. "You've got a *work* permit. *They* pick you up here—in them gone-away buses, you *no* walk."

"*No walk?* No can get to work—*loze job!*"

"Do day labor. There-there." He pointed to a holding pen off to one side where the wimpering girl might be picked for menial, one-shot jobs. She tried to stop crying. If she didn't look strong and willing to work, even a day's employment was out of the question.

In the middle of this, the supervisor had no hesitation letting Herriff, an out-of-place wallah and his PRIM, through the gate.

By this time, the traveler had had enough. He didn't need to see firsthand the expansive Sac City Subsidiary that surrounded the central Marsco Cantonment. Stopping his PRIM with a tap on the shoulder, he eagerly looked for assistance. Where once a gleaming marble floor greeted travelers, today Herriff found before him only a wide atrium marred by dirt and covered with trash. Finally, his search fixed on a Security warrant standing by herself. The hustling morning flow of sids and PRIMS created a wide, empty circle around the solitary associate.

The WO was the same age as Cadet Carter, but her skin was as dark as the bullet conductor's. Like the plebe, her uniform was immaculate and smart even amid the crush of humanity. The thought crossed Herriff's mind, *Did the conductor have a daughter?* Besides her neat uniform—the cleanest in the scurrying terminal—she wore an Enfield sidearm hanging from a shinning black belt. She was on routine duty, making sure her Auxxies kept everything in order.

While his PRIM stayed on the circumference not daring to approach, the Martian broke into the sacrosanct circle around the associate. Before the exhausted traveler made a comment or even huffed out his name, she stiffened into attentive posture.

"Good morning, Dr Herriff," she spoke in the affected tone of a valued subordinate, any vestige of monotonous duty gone. Her accent wasn't discernable, but the associate assumed she had African ancestry.

After sizing up the rumbled traveler, both his eyeglasses and ponytail askew, the warrant stated with unruffled self-assurance, "It's an honor for such a dignitary such as yourself to visit our subsidiary. I am to assist you in every way possible."

Herriff rarely pulled rank, but that morning he pressed his considerable advantage to its fullest. Skimming out to Miller's grange would be most satisfactory. "I want an HFC with a jockey," he ordered, his customary amiability replaced with associate haughtiness. "*Now!*"

FIFTEEN

AMONG FRIENDS

(Miller's Grange, 2096)

"Get in, get out!" the Security warrant barked through her com-link, as the whine of an HFC died down.

The eight-seater settled gently on its struts in front of the hedge break of a grange, one of a dozen that the craft had skimmed over since crossing a stopline several clicks back. Each enclosed settlement was a green oasis amid the dry and cracked tawny landscape, a signal that someone was living beyond Marsco with a degree of success. From the air, signs of the original inhabitants were clearly visible: evidence of old street grids, outlines of parks and school yards, the foundations of abandoned homes. The old, however, gave no indication of renewed life.

The WO at the lander controls looked around after her set-down. Inexplicably, a single stanchion holding a cam housing rose above the hedge and roofline. The Security apparatus focused into the grange beyond the open gate.

A trooper jumped out before the dust settled, his shoulder-fired weapon sweeping the calm scene.

A black, stocky dog eagerly trotted through the gate to greet the hovercraft. At the hiss of a charging Enfield, the inquisitive Io scooted away, her tail between her legs, her friendly bark turning to a distraught yelp.

A second trooper helped Herriff from the runabout, then gathered his luggage as though he were a porter. Setting the bags down, he covered his mate, who utilized his Enfield sight to scan beyond Miller's hedge.

No one seemed to be about, an uneasy omen in a hot zone where hostiles were not seen but expected.

The second trooper silently slipped past the first. Curiosity motivated both. A mystique surrounded this fringe-figure Miller. The pair might actually meet this legendary stopped-out associate for themselves.

Their commander still at the controls of the HFC kept the engines idling. "Get on with this," she shouted via a link, her voice tense, firm. "Drop the wallah, stat!"

Nothing excited her about seeing Miller's grange; she had been here before. She fidgeted with nervous excitement; other patrol areas needed her team.

When Deimos defiantly appeared, putting his whiffing nose in the open hatch, the commander shooed him away. Undaunted, the dog marked a strut and sniffed the luggage left in the middle of the abandoned road, then followed Herriff into the grange.

The two troopers picked up a stationary body signature ahead on their scopes. Exchanging hand signals, they leapfrogged deeper into the unknown, scanning the premises right and left, moving in protective unison through a side garden and down a shaded path toward the back of the rambling house.

The solitary heat signature spoke before the engineer knew anyone was standing around the corner. "I've been waiting for you, Dr. Herriff," a woman's voice announced.

Confronting the two legionnaires, the voice stood her ground, protective gloves off to show her lefter status. "Tell your warrant," she ordered, "you found an officer waiting for Elvis—*now get out!*"

Reluctantly, the troopers cast a final glance at their target, protective visors up for an undistorted look.

The woman's face was smudged with grime. Her work overalls, their legs cut short, were ripped where she had snagged herself. Her associate status and those slender legs suggested that every bit of what stood before the pair was totally HH GAS-free. Herriff was too old and exhausted to notice how shapely the legs were, a point not lost on the callow men as they shoved off.

What the traveler did notice was that he *was* expected. *Does everyone know I was heading here?*

Once the owner of the legs got a good look at her visitor, she embraced him. "Uncle Martin!" He returned an avuncular hug.

"What brings you to Earth?" Tessa asked, her voice now almost as chatty as a teenager's. "Father told me you were coming—a surprise announcement, your visit. Coming to *this* subsidiary—of sorts!" Her last remark hung awkwardly in the air until she noticed her hug had left dirt on the visitor. "Sorry, been under that unit," she motioned with her head as she dusted him off.

"Condenser problems? Water must be a scare around here to have a beast that size." It was twenty-five centimeters taller than the visitor and three meters square.

"Yes, actually Father has two other units with similar capacity down the way." Using her subcutaneous disks, Tessa double-checked its output readings. "At this humidity and temperature, should be pulling in close to 750 liters an hour more. Even with regulated and consistent drip irrigation, the cistern should be filling faster than it's draining."

"Power disruption?"

"Solar panels are at full—especially in this heat. Even with disruption, he's got a backup windmill system."

"Like life in space, contingency plans made for every contingency."

"He's a triple-redundancy guy!" Miller's daughter admitted.

The visiting engineer surveyed the extensive gardens. In this sweltering heat, any water loss could ruin a summer's harvest. It didn't surprise Herriff that Miller invested so much in his gardens. It also didn't surprise him that the granger seemed to have truly gone a little native.

After surveying everything, he asked, "Walter maintains this whole complex by himself?"

Ordinarily Tessa would have been reluctant to discuss anything about her father. This was a relatively safe area as quite-near-to-PRIM-locales go, but one had to be careful, nonetheless. Just a few weeks ago, as Tessa knew, a grange hard by the zone demarcation line had been ransacked. Someone killed. Someone raped. Roving PRIM youths, more than likely.

Tessa was more guarded than Walter, plus she was an associate alone in a threat-rich arena not a dozen clicks from a stopline separating off a sprawling and impoverished UZ. But she knew Herriff. *Frankly,* she thought, *I'm relieved to have company.*

"He does the best he can," she eventually replied. "I always spend my leave here, too, so we can catch up on tech maintenance. Throughout the growing season, a labor contractor comes around with his PRIM gang to help out. They do most of the planting and then the harvesting of the larger fields. Walter screened this contractor carefully. Mr. Fuji treats his PRIMS very well, else father wouldn't have him."

Climbing down to crawl under the condenser unit a second time that morning, she groused, "Found a leak in the hose orientations."

The unit rested on stacked slabs of broken concrete—the new placed on the crumbling old: an emblem of the Marsco world the Martian had discovered.

"Didn't find a glitch in the exec command protocols—*no!*" Her frustration was muffled as her boot heels pushed into the soft ground to shove her deeper beneath the retrieval equipment. Two tails disappeared completely with the woman's legs. "No, it *had* to be a hardware fault!" Her voice sounded distant and metallic. "Murphy-ed way down under here."

"Yes, software keeps you in a dry office, at a console, and out of puddles."

"Don't lick, Deimos, dammit!" her voice commanded, but not too sternly. "Some help you are! Look for ratters or black widows!"

"Condenser problems!" Standing there, Herriff announced loudly to no one in particular. "Sorry I can't help—wrong specialty." He squatted down to hear her answers clearly.

"Well, if you were in deep space and your water system sprang a leak, you'd specialize in hydro-systems stat." This wasn't a confiding tone of Marsco camaraderie; rather, the tone of a grilling prof flaming a plebe. Gone was that that precocious, intelligent girl at the Von Braun Center when Walter and Bethany were prominent researchers there.

Herriff replied, "Guess you're right."

"Although at the moment, I feel about as bright as a hiberman."

"So," he tried making small talk, "how's life as a propulsion engineer—something like your father?"

"A-OK I guess. Well, maybe you should ask my second years. Although at the moment I also wish I had taken more classes in hydro-retrieval systems."

"Like your mother."

"Affirmative." Several clanks emanated from under the raised unit. "Can you kick that wrench to me?"

When Herriff's foot hardly made the tool move, Tessa laughed. "You're too used to low-g life. Give it a good whack." After it slid to her, she worked on steadily.

Two cotton gloves stretched out from under the repaired condenser and pulled the woman out. She was dirtier than before, her face wet with rusty water and smudged with grease. "Done!"

"Small leaks *are* a pain. Always seems to be our problem. Of course, on-planet, low gravity and lack of air pressure complicate every aspect of the water recovery process."

"Well, I epoxyed everything in sight. That should be it."

"I'm surprised," he tapped the unit's housing, "this locality never needed condensers. It looks as though it's a Martian colony."

A puzzled expression crossed Tessa's face, who had stayed on the ground gazing up at him. "You haven't been back on Earth for a long time," she concluded with no emotion. Since the C-Wars, sids living this far from any green zone fended for themselves—water condensers and solar panels, defensive fences and thorny hedges surrounding Indie granges.

Back to the issue at hand, she continued, "This locale's several years behind in rainfall. Seriously behind." She pointed to what had been midcentury swimming pools now used as cisterns, one kidney-shaped close at hand, the other rectangular-shaped down the way. Covered to reduce evaporation and to prevent contamination, both were clearly outlined in bright blue plastic. "We resealed each last winter before the rainy season, such as it was."

The woman finally stood up and yoga-stretched her back. "Should have 98.0107% of capacity by 1300 hours today." The daughter spoke precisely like her mother.

As Tessa rechecked the water unit's monitor, Herriff had a long look at her for the first time. She wore her mother's ring, a Martian turquoise stone set in asteroid gold, on a chain around her neck. He saw in the associate the young girl he once knew. And he also saw her mother's face. "You know, you look the way Bethany looked when she first came to Mars."

"That's what many of his friends say, those I've met who knew her," she remarked with a tone that acknowledged her family devotion. Tessa was slender although muscular. She wore her auburn hair short, almost in a cadet cut, today covered with a bandana. She had her father's green eyes, but her mother's brush of freckles over her nose made her look a bit girlish, although she was a hiber-retarded thirty-something.

Dressed in Marsco-issued work overalls, which she'd cut off well above the knees, she had an unintentional tomboy-look. This side of herself, the visitor was certain, she never showed her students. Her girlhood and teenage hiber trips to and from Mars hadn't created a great discrepancy in her ages. In a rare thought about women in general, Herriff noted that slender women like her always look young in every pose anyway. Childless himself, he still let a parental thought crossed his mind, *The man she loves will be fortunate and blessed.*

In an hour, the two sat having iced tea on the shaded patio. Looking around the garden, the Martian commented, "Is it always so easy to walk in here? I mean, I just came in through an open gate."

"Yes, unfortunately!" Tessa retorted. "Pillaging's a nuance. Walter finally had to encircle the whole place to offer at least token resistance to marauding gangs." The grange was completely surrounded by a combination of thick hedges, stone walls, and high fences. But these had several wide gaps; his security was porous.

"From what I've seen, his house is a better structure than most out here," remarked Herriff casually.

"True." When Miller arrived a dozen years before, Tessa explained, all the houses along this road had fallen into disrepair. By cannibalizing several nearby structures, he had saved the best one. The main house was situated on a slight rise. Although extensively repaired so it was once more habitable, she found its outer layer of mismatched bricks hardly decorative.

Herriff nodded his understanding.

"The materials he didn't use," the daughter went on with pride, "he sold off, much as a pioneer sold off lumber from a farm he'd cleared."

"A sound practice."

"Yes."

"And Walter did all that?"

"He gets a lot of local PRIM help—and pays well for it." She paused a moment then added, "This locality predates the G-Wars.

Some granges were initially carved out by tractors and earthmovers; by the time Father arrived, such excavation had become PRIM hand-work."

Herriff gave a puzzled look. Too much had dominated his attention on Mars to remember every detail of the postwar years on Earth.

"Virus attacks on all OS systems—ruined almost every hard drive Earth-side."

The Martian gave slow acknowledgement to what should have immediately registered to him.

"A sid contractor came with his PRIM gang over his first summer here. They broke up the remaining concrete foundations." The visitor tried to imagine the laborious toil of sledgehammers, picks, and shovels. "Then they contoured the ground to plant his gardens and orchards."

Even in the afternoon heat, the two walked amid the cultivation, dogs at their heels. One garage remained next to the house, another one down beyond several raised plots. Like the house, the bricks and roofing shingles of the outbuildings didn't match. The weathered structures had half their windows boarded up rather than replaced.

Herriff examined the farther garage, which had several modern solar panels attached to it, incongruous additions to such a building. A dozen pipes ran from the structure. He noted that it was yet another example of the non-Marsco world. "Must be where he houses that other condenser," Herriff concluded incorrectly.

"No, that's his lab and workshop. He's come up with, oh, this and that in there," the daughter coyly deferred divulging anything further. "He wants to show you himself."

Boffin to the end, thought Herriff as their walk continued.

In the shade of the orchard, the heat wasn't so intense. Herriff recognized various apple trees, their blossoms long since gone, their fruit not yet ripe. "An abundant harvest on the horizon," he mused at the whole layout. The apricot and nectarine trees were heavy with fruit; any within arm's reach had already been picked. Close to the hedge stood almond and walnut trees.

"This Bing's possibly 100 years old," Tessa explained. "Look how he grafted a limb of a hybrid variety of the late-ripening Donovan reds."

Herriff paused, holding Tessa's arm to make sure he had her full attention. "You sound so like your mother. She was quite the gardener."

"It's all his work, or at least his supervision."

Beyond the tall fence in the desiccated, vacant plot adjacent to Miller's grange, a dust devil swirled twenty meters high, pulling dry sand upward to make the circling wind tawny. On this side, the wind swayed lush bounty.

"Everything's expertly laid out," Herriff commented, "like a motherboard."

"A handful of neighboring granges are even larger—their increase in size made possible by Walter helping them develop integrated systems."

"So, these neighbors haven't forsaken tech?"

"No, they're not Luddites," Tessa smiled, "just stubborn hardscrabblers."

"Let me just ask: does someone just grab the land?"

"Yes," Tessa acknowledged with a shrug, "in many ways, yes, that's it exactly." She explained that one Independent had walled in a portion of a former city park as an enclosed lot for his steers. Another included the playing fields of a schoolyard; he's sown it with drought-resistant wheat. "In this no-man's-land, it's mainly 'stake your own claim.'"

"Almost like Mars in the '50s." Herriff knew all about that planet rush firsthand.

To the south of the orchard, Tessa showed Herriff a piece of city park that Miller kept. “He exchanges grazing rights as barter,” the daughter explained. They climbed a stile into the field enclosed by a low stone wall. Two young men were tending their dairy herd, making sure they had water in the scorching sun. Tucked under what shade a solitary oak provided, a dozen cows ignored Io and Deimos, who ran at them. The pair spritely veered off when confronted by lowered horns.

“I want you to meet these brothers,” Tessa stated proudly.

The introductions were informal. Aaron and Jeremy Truman greeted the associates warmly. “Tessa,” Aaron stated first, outpacing his blushing younger brother, “that ’quipment’s boss!”

“We’re makin’ lots’a ice cream,” Jeremy stated, not yet looking up from the dogs he greeted playfully.

“It’s nothing,” Tessa assured them. To Herriff she stated, “I rounded up some kludgy gear for them.”

“Gear!” corrected Aaron. “Icemaker an’ two whole freezers fur a shuttle.”

“It all cum last fall.”

“Months ago and they’re still blogging on about it.”

“Here this hauler just cums through the fog, shakin’ the ground and scatterin’ cows. We thought, Pop ’n me, we wuz bein’ busted up outta here by Security—” He caught himself.

Jeremy thrust into the description. “Out of the fog it cums with massive bays filled—”

“Only 14.25% capacity,” Tessa stated, trying to keep accuracy for Herriff at 100 percent and praise for herself at a minimum. “Took me a while to find a partially filled cargo hauler coming this way.”

“You shudda see all th’stuff!” the persistent younger brother added.

“Obsolete hardware used to ground-train shuttle crews,” Tessa insisted to the other associate, “from a crew-mod mockup.”

“All hooked t’solars!” Jeremy went on, regaining his part of their thanks for Tessa’s generosity. “Then makin’ shore we cun use them.”

The woman deflected their accolades once more, assuring Herriff that she had not brought him out to this field just to hear all this rapture.

"You reconfigured fridge tech for photovoltaic power and non-disk utilization!" It was Herriff's turn to be adamant. "Painstaking work, a task not done quickly."

"Simple really," she countered with a knowing smile. "A few pieces of cooling schematics—"

"—and that 'lectric stove," Jeremy added.

The knowledgeable visiting colonist answered, "But solars *can't* power anything directly."

"*No,*" Jeremy shouted out, confusing even himself. "*Yes,* Tessa sent a transformer, too."

"Just castoff equipment?" Herriff looked at Tessa with a knowing smile.

She deflected the question. "Installers spend enough time with you?" she asked the young men.

"We're giggy, Aaron and me understan' everythin'."

"Well, the one spot where we wuz stuck at, Walter figgered out."

"Doc says that transformer's props."

"*New!*" Herriff filled in the gaps of the incomplete story.

"Why send solars that'll generate only 79.9876% when the latest maxs out at 96.0784?"

"Cum have ice cream later," Jeremy blushed out to Tessa.

"I'd like that," the older visitor replied to the young men.

Suspicious eyes darted from Herriff to Tessa. "Our closest friend," she explained hastily, "Father's best."

Trust was instantly reestablished.

As they left the brothers, Tessa explained, "Indies don't take easily to anything or anyone Marsco. But when they put it together just who you are, especially Aaron, who's aiming for the Academy, he'll be postal with excitement."

"Yes, Elvis *is* here!" Tessa explained to Walter as Herriff waited patiently for her to finish their call. "I'll tell him that. And yes, I won't mention *that.*"

Closing off her mobile unit, she laughed. "Was he always this directive? Or just to his daughter?"

These two, who knew Miller so well, had to chuckle at his prominent foible.

"Yes, and he was always late!"

"Yes, he often—almost always—spends way too much time at his projects. Most of what he's doing there, that's what I can't tell you."

"Can you tell me anything?"

"Just that he's started the research to develop an engine, all still experimental. An engine for a newly designed lander."

"Rather a retro step, isn't it?" They laughed since Herriff had solved that problem years before the Wars. "So, that's why he wasn't here to greet me?"

"He's been at this test for weeks. I was there overnight. Took an owl shift to give him a break. He's been working himself zonkers trying to meet a crucial deadline. Before I came down from Seattle, he was working nearly 'round the chronometer. I've pulled a few of the all-nighters for him so he might rest."

Herriff interjected, "Did he? 'Round the clock nonstop?" Knowing his former collaborator, he answered his own question, "Going 24/37/7, yes, that's him." He caught himself. "Guess I'm back to a 24-hour cycle, not 24/37."

With the tranquil afternoon edging by, they sat under an intertwined shading lattice. A mister cooled the air around them. Enjoying Miller's roses that climbed the west side of the patio trellis, the pair might have been sitting at a private Marsco vacation resort, space crew on leave after a long hiber-journey. It was another surprise to the visiting engineer, how quickly he could ignore the surrounding locale.

Their conversation changed after a moment. "Do many of Walter's friends visit him? Here?"

"As far as I know, you're the first—I mean of longtime friends—in the last three or four years. More came, and came regularly, right when he originally moved down here. When he lived in the Seattle Sid after Mars, of course, he had a constant stream of visitors, especially just after mom's death. They still had many friends, and then the HQ Sector is right by that subsidiary."

Herriff nodded in agreement.

Tessa added in painful acknowledgement. "I assume some friends who might wish to come here simply aren't allowed."

Herriff didn't pick up on the tenor of the remark; instead, he asked a tangential question. "And it's been eight years ago already, since Bethany's death?"

"No, just about thirteen. They left Mars more than fourteen years ago. She died a year and a half after their return."

"I remember when you *all* left."

"Memory does get confused in some people," Tessa replied with a gentle laugh, teasing the older associate in the way a only charming younger one can. "I left Mars to start the Academy two years *before* my parents permanently did."

"That's right! You were at the Marsco Institute of Technology in Seattle when she died."

"I was only at the Academy, a plebe." *Well,* thought Tessa, *the years go by quickly if you keep your nose to the monitor and your disks twitching. Friends' lives slip by as swiftly as your own.*

These were comforting, distracting thoughts. They kept her from associating any part of her own empty life with shuttle trips beyond the asteroid belt and hibernation advancements. She dare not ask about on-planet personnel engaged in cryogenic stasis experiments.

"Well, I *do* confuse things," Herriff stated, "what with so many colleagues coming and going over the years. Jonathan said I did so even on Earth. But you know I've directed the VBC for over forty years." His pause signaled a complexity of reflections. "After a time, I ceased ever leaving Mars. I've been on planet, well had *been* until I started this trip, over twenty-five continuous years. I did go on several test flights for our asteroid shuttles, even iced a bit on them, but that's hardly 'leaving the planet,' if you catch. Eventually, I stopped that—always on ground crew now—can't be hands-on forever. And, well, the time certainly got away from me."

"As director of the Von Braun Research Center, I can understand that."

"Never had a reason to return—no family left here. No one to show the Blue Planet to. And other considerations, of course," he remarked vaguely.

She knew what he implied: if an associate lived in space, why would he return to the plague-ridden, nearly totally destroyed Earth? For three years immediately after the Wars, the Earth remained frigid. Dust particles reflected away all the Sun's heat. Disease ridden. Politically temperamental. A period euphemistically called 'The Troubled Times' or more accurately, 'The Marsco Winter.' Staying comparatively safe in space, even with all its problematic hardships, was a decision many colony-based associates still made. It was the choice of her parents, after all. Even today, colonists returning to Earth by and large stayed exclusively in Marsco sectors to keep well away from sid areas and zones. Well away from PRIMS.

"You always worked too hard, Martin. Or at least that's what Walter says."

"He should talk."

Their reminiscing continued through a simple meal Tessa prepared, a salad with just-picked greens, homemade bread, and their neighbor's butter.

The visitor, surveying the gardens, made his point again. "All this reminds me of the Von Braun's extensive hydroponics gardens, the ones originally laid out by Bethany. I can see your mother's hands at work here. You know, of course, she came to the VBC station originally to be its chief hydrologist, but she was so much more. A real water generalist. Oh, how small we were in those days—such a collection of erratics."

Sounding like a lecturing professor, he explained, "You know *erratics,* those solitary misfit boulders picked up and pushed along by a glacier then left where they don't geologically belong." He turned away once more, looking off toward the hedges. "Everyone had to wear several helmets. But always one family! Her addition to the staff was an immediate morale boost. Her ideas and plans humanized *Valles Marineris.* Fresh fruit and vegetables from our own greenhouses, blooming flowers and green shrubs decorating hallways, climbing roses going up interior supports. Earth-like life and vitality. She wanted verdant life everywhere. She insisted we have it. Even today, all her hydroponics gardens still flourish."

"Everyone notices how similar this looks to her work," Tessa commented glancing around, then added, "I mean those few that knew her on Mars and who have actually visited here."

"Her gardens," Herriff recollected, "took my staff's minds off home and off prolonged duty rotations on planet with only periodic furloughs. I had wanted the VBC on Mars—and not on the Moon—for its isolation."

"Well, you got that, that's for sure!"

"With such extreme conditions, I also got what else I wanted: my entire staff working feverishly on projects with little break in their routine."

"Wasn't anything there to break the routine!"

Herriff nodded then confided, "But there's a steep price to be paid for working under such harsh, isolated conditions. I know everyone paid it, for all our achievements." He looked directly at the woman, almost as though apologizing. "Bethany's gardens were an acknowledgement that humankind cannot be totally cut off from life-sustaining Earth. We are—she made me realize—we are too wedded to our homes to be callously trans-located onto a barren, coldhearted planet."

Tessa had politely let Herriff recollect but did clarify, "Bethany was gone when Walter moved here." The visitor nodded in acknowledgement. "He did get help that first spring from their old friend, Father Cavanaugh."

"Oh, yes. Never met him, but I know he was a great friend of Walter."

"Best friends with mom originally. They grew up like brother and sister. Dad met him through her."

"Wasn't he just lost?"

"Yes, murdered last year, ten months ago next week, to be exact."

"How's he taking it?"

"Better than when he first heard."

"Must have been quite a shock."

"Yes. You know, I've only seen him so depressed one other time, at mom's passing. This winter, he threw himself into work like never before."

"Probably to handle the despair," the engineer concluded under his breath, knowing firsthand how to overcome such a great loss. He didn't think Tessa heard his mumbling.

She had, however. "You're right. I had a three-day leave before a lunar teaching-lab mission. I came down here, yet he worked all but eight hours of that whole time. And just like then, today he's throwing himself full throttle-up into this project."

"I can understand Walter pushing himself to keep his mind off things."

She paused, gathering up enough courage to make the next remark, "You know, in a certain way, I think he blames himself for Father Stephen."

An unbroken silence remained until Herriff asked, "Did you know him?"

"Yes, of course, another uncle." She reached over and tapped his arm, her finger disks tingling his skin. "When I was a plebe, I did a short stint at the Rio lander station. I went into the zone to visit him there several times—twice with Zot." She let that drop. "My first visit, I just arrived out of the blue."

She waited briefly before clarifying distinctly, "that first trip I was alone."

Herriff nodded that he understood.

The Academy officer went on, “I’d never been inside a zone before, not one *that* wretched and notorious. I was both fascinated and nauseated.” Remembering those distant events, her eyes focused above the hedge. “I mean, up until that time, I had only lived in your colony and in sectors or cantonments. I never imagined PRIMS, *people,* living like that. Horrifying! But I’m still thankful for the opportunity to make those visits.” Tessa took a sip of her iced tea.

Herriff’s inviting silence allowed her to continue.

“That first visit, Father Stephen wouldn’t let me walk out of the zone alone. I thought I was perfectly safe, being in uniform, and told him I could manage myself, take care of myself. I was too naive then to know how dangerous a place it really was. And too young to know that one associate in a sea of PRIMS might be at high-risk, a target of opportunity, regardless of my defensive training.”

The priest knew what the plebe didn’t: her death equaled her Enfield as a prize.

“And so he escorted me out. Everyone knew him, loved him in that UZ.”

Slipping her foot out of its sandal, she nudged Io’s thick black coat. The awakened dog stretched without getting up. The engineer’s interest in this story urged Tessa to continue.

“After other visits, he had two of his school’s nuns walk me to a secure checkpoint, even when I came with Zot. I mean, I saw PRIMS literally dead on the streets. Begging children clutching at my uniform, unsettling encounters I’ve never forgotten. It brought into focus much of what Bethany and Walter had been teaching me; it all made sense in a nano. Quite an epiphany!” She drew a breath, trying to keep a delicate balance of caring and accuracy. “A world without Marsco would be disastrous, because it invites in only more anarchy and chaos. But, can we humanize Marsco? I know we *must,* but *can* we?”

Herriff skipped her pointed question but wondered aloud how she had gotten into the zone to begin with, through the curtain of checkpoints and stoplines implemented to keep PRIMS separate from subsidiaries and Marsco complexes.

Tessa answered his probing question. She raised her right hand to show her implanted array. "Wasn't as full of course, but noticeable nonetheless. Clearly not a lefter then, but to an inexperienced Auxiliary grunt at some desolate stopline checkpoint, I might as well have been one." She shook her head in disbelief at her own immature bravado. "Auxxies are really often teens, as old as the Truman sons you just met. But, before that time, I never knew what portals and airlocks—cyber and actual—these opened."

She wiggled her fingers for emphasis, blue-green circles visible under the skin. "I just flashed them. In only one case did I have to shove my fingers in the nose of an old sid; she immediately became less intractable. *It's a Marsco world.* Showing these scream, 'Open sesame.'"

It was then that she noticed the incongruity of Herrill not having any FDs. Over the years, she had forgotten that obvious fact. Her own life crowded with Academy matriculation and then the complications of Zot, her graduate status, and then skyrocketing career, her habitual ambiguity toward Marsco. Most of her adult day-to-day life and tensions forced girlhood memories from her mind. Her eyes steadfastly fixed on the man's smooth fingertips. *Both hands should be laden with disks.*

"Oh, so you've observed my little secret," the Martian remarked with a shy grin and a trace of smug self-satisfaction. "I guess this comes," he examined both sets of natural fingertips, "from having already established myself as an expert, *the* propulsion and thruster *expert,* by the time disks had become ubiquitous. I'm probably the only associate without implants."

His eyes smiled at the sheer delight of being such a legendary Marsco outlier.

SIXTEEN

ENCOUNTERS

(Sac City Sid, 2096)

"Doctor Miller, aren't you coming home earlier than usual?" The Security officer who spoke eased into the vacant seat right next to the granger.

Having not given real eye contact to the other passenger before, Miller wondered how to reply to such an open-ended question. The engineer sat alone, although the nearly empty light rail gave ample opportunity for conversation, even if such familiarity was uncommon. The pair sat silently as the LR accelerated beyond a station.

"You *are* Doctor Walter Miller, right?" The questioner moved purposely close to the granger.

"Affirmative." The engineer looked down at his questioner's steady gaze because he was short compared to Miller. The officer appeared to be SoAm with an LD on his neck and gloves covering what looked to be a small disk array. In all, to the longstanding associate, the centurion didn't look that out of place in the Marsco world. "Now, may I ask you a question?" the granger finally responded.

"Certainly," the inquisitor replied stiffly.

"What's a Security officer doing taking a train?"

"Our destinies seem crossed," the centurion casually replied.

"An ominously vague response, my good man," Miller mused, avoiding any deeper conversation.

The lieutenant, however, kept speaking, "But, it seems odd seeing you here."

A wry smile crossed Miller's face. "Odder," he grinned, "than seeing a Security officer commuting?"

"Well, I do have an HFC at my disposal; allow me to offer you a skim."

"Thanks." Paying closer attention to the officer, Miller bent lower to read his nametag. "'*Lieutenant Rivers.*' Don't think we've met before."

"No, perhaps not."

"The Center needs our HFC this evening, else I'd have been brought home."

"Trudging along on antiquated ground transport from your Sac City Aerospace Associates Center—mostly east and a bit northward from here—doesn't seem practical." The SO nervously tapped his language disk.

"You seem to know a great deal about me."

"Your stop's only a half-click from the final checkpoint to your grange," the Security officer explained, showing that indeed he knew much of Miller. "You come home this way periodically."

"I can use the exercise."

"And tending your grange doesn't give you enough?"

Miller ignored that point by deflecting the conversation, "Fortunately for me, this past year, the light rail's reopened a platform closer to the stopline—and it's been dry."

"Nonetheless, it's still a hot walk. Please allow me to assist you."

The light rail itself, originally constructed during the midcentury, had given exemplary service prior to the Continental Wars. It was at present restored to minimal working conditions. Commuters were often forced to stand because so many seats were broken. No new coaches had been added even as clicks of derelict track were repaired and abandoned stations reopened. The carriages were layered with years of grime and abuse.

"Don't you find it ironic, Lieutenant Rivers," Miller pointed out, "that close to thiry years after the conflagration, restoration moves at a PRIM's pace. And that coaches are once more manufactured in this very sid, in the north—the thriving locale. Yet all those new, gleaming carriages are shipped worldwide to Sectors where efficient trains run on time, moving associates here and there." He paused making sure he was understood. "It's a foregone conclusion that *none* are put into service around here."

As Miller walked with the officer toward a Security HFC, a few mopeds buzzed past, propelled by home-distilled alcohol. A stream of sids and PRIMS walked along or scooted by on bicycles. Several jitneys wormed through the crowds, poking along with important sids heading to their compounds just north of the LR line.

Still an odd sight, Miller mentally conceded, seeing bikes and this size of a crowd walking along the wide expanse of this once-thriving suburban boulevard.

The hovercraft stood alongside an abandoned building. Swiftly, vectoring jets pushed the runabout above the din and crush of local residents.

"Generally," Rivers confided in a matter-of-fact tone, "the only HFCs seen around here are for Security and Hygiene personnel, except a few (like yours at the Center) that are still operational but in private hands. Lacking dense HFC traffic, this sid doesn't boast of a cyber efficient Herriff-Grid. No need." He tapped his neck nervously, his brown eyes alert but flicking side to side as though concerned about cross traffic.

"Was a fine system here when I was a boy, but it hasn't been reactivated."

"All in good time," Rivers responded.

Sitting silently in the second seat, Miller noticed something uneasy in the officer's eyes, as if the centurion, and not the granger, were the one marked for intense scrutiny.

The craft quickly gained considerable altitude for a skim, close to 2,500 meters. The whole area spread out beneath. Miller saw the LR line with its string of stations. He had left the train at the last open platform although an unserviceable right of way continued south into the hinterland of granges. Near the open line, streets were packed. Farther away, everything was devoid of activity.

The HFC skimmed above a former supermarket. "Twice weekly, on Wednesdays and Saturdays," Miller pointed out idly, sounding too much like a tour guide, "there's a farmers' market down there."

"And a black market," the officer added without emotion.

"I wouldn't know about that. I only barter for eggs and other fresh food grown in the surrounding granges. Periodically I secure soap or toothpaste or razor blades."

"Certainly, an associate of your status might still acquire anything online."

"Oh, I don't know. I prefer this method. A few kilos of my potatoes are nearly worth their weight in asteroid metal."

The irony wasn't lost on the engineer that in the years before the Continental Wars, residents bought produce and goods from around the world. Or they e-ordered whatever they wished. A FD twitch for asteroid gold and Martian turquoise jewelry. Or they spent the day trying on rings and bracelets at an outlet. Or landered to SoAm or Asia for such trinkets. Whatever the previous denizens of this once-prosperous area wanted, it was all there for them.

The constant scarcity now present reminded Miller that being non-Marsco was an arduous and continuous struggle. *Better than a PRIM's life,* he consoled himself. *But today down in this sid, life didn't seem all that different from that of a common PRIM.*

Miller gave instructions to be set down half a click from his protective hedge in the remains of a city park not yet claimed by any granger. It would be a hot walk to his back gate.

"But," Lieutenant Rivers protested, "*that's* your grange ahead!" The HFC still had enough altitude to see one lush grange end and to see Miller's begin in the distance. A stretch of parched landscape existed between the two verdant islands.

Miller explained, "I don't want to disturb my dogs when your runabout sets down."

As the three landing struts settled onto the broken pavement, before Miller moved, the granger asked bluntly, "Am I often to be thus treated? So officially? Or are your comments of an unofficial nature?" None of the questions came out as a compliment.

"I didn't explain," the officer stated as the hatch swung open and the engineer stepped out and stood next to the HFC, "that I knew Father Stephen—Father Cavanaugh—quite well."

The words had an instant effect on the granger who turned to stare at the officer. As this unexpected pronouncement sunk in, the granger seemed to deflate; he leaned forward to balance against the open hatch frame.

"I hope I didn't startle you with that intel," the centurion stated.

"No, I'm fine," Miller lied insistently, standing up tall and strong once more.

Seeing the effect his words had, the officer didn't believe him. "I'll come again," the centurion stated, "a courtesy visit, and we'll speak of our mutual friend."

The granger nodded ascent. Effortlessly, the centurion pushed the joystick forward and the runabout momentarily hovered before skimming away.

Miller stood alone with conflicted emotions and memories of Cavanaugh, wishing he had been more guarded, wondering at the whole incident, especially the final moment most of all. Any thought of the dead priest churned up Miller as though the murder of that innocent man was his own fault.

He drew a deep breath to gather strength.

With the HFC's disappearance, Miller finally turned toward home. He passed through the park, walking under the bare branches of the dead trees. The heat eased somewhat by the shadows of their stretching, barren limbs, deciduous sycamores, ash, maples, and deep-green conifers. Ornamental flowering trees from around the world. But all were dry. Even the indigenous valley oaks were dying. Many other species (such as towering coastal redwoods, once a common sight here), were already dead. On his left, what had been the park's rose garden was a winding track of lifeless bushes and PRIM encampments set back from the neglected gravel walkways. The artificial streams and ornamental waterfalls had become weed-choked. It had been so dry for so long that even the stagnant pools had turned to cracked patches of hard terra-cotta clay.

And last century, this was one of the most tree-populated cities in the world, the granger thought, remembering his halcyon boyhood fondly. "Everything's different at present," he remarked softly, "little of this city resembles its pre-Marsco prominence."

Miller moved along the broken sidewalk next to a brick wall and sentinel hedge that marked the border of a grange like his own but four times its size. At the side of the walkway was a wider dirt track used occasionally by lorries hauling heavy supplies.

A dark cloud hung over the granger. His mind was filled with memories of a thriving, lush city now a patchwork, with some parts dead and others thriving. And the ominous Security officer intruding on his space. What *that* meant, he didn't yet know.

After walking to his grange, his somber mood immediately subsided when he saw Martin Herriff sitting with Tessa in the flower garden. Several rose bushes were in bloom, red and pink, his wife's favorites. Sallosia shot up their colorful leaves along the deeply shaded edge of the garden. Pinched-back mums would bloom later in the autumn.

The two longtime friends broke into laughter and embraced as though a long-separated father and son.

Two days later their large afternoon meal ran late, with little concern for anything outside the hedges disturbing them. Herriff accepted Tessa's offer of a third piece of her specially prepared quiche.

"Fresh eggs are impossible to secure on a colony," the visitor rationalized his appetite. "I've not had real from-the-shell ones in over twenty-five years." Tessa's dish contained fresh spinach and zucchini. The eggs, butter, and cheese the granger had obtained through barter; two kilos of potatoes and one kilo of his ripe Bing cherries for two dozen eggs, the second to be delivered over the next week. Tessa had also made crusty bread in an early century machine, the summer sun providing ample power to the photovoltaic panels.

"How did you get butter?" Herriff asked his host, layering another slice thickly.

"I tutor Mr. Truman's son, Aaron. He owns—as much as anyone really owns anything around here—that big grange a few clicks east. And a large dairy herd. Well, relatively speaking, a dozen and a half cows. It's an exchange. And such a bright boy, Aaron."

Tessa nodded her approval. "We met them Martin's first afternoon here."

"Yes, we're to have ice cream with them," remembered the Martian. "Another luxury lacking at the VBC."

Miller was all business. "Possible Marsco scholarship for him—Tessa's working on that—but his computer usage is weak."

The guest continued to enjoy his meal as Tessa prepared him fresh coffee, another luxury often missing in space. "I can't understand it," he lamented after his first sip, "why can't coffee reach the colonies? I mean real coffee, not that ersatz crap we get."

Neither father nor daughter had an answer, but Tessa did say, "This is from Seattle. I stock up on those things Walter can't get here."

"You know," Miller went back to explaining about the boy, "you might be able to assist young Truman. He hasn't any disks." He wriggled his right fingers needlessly. "Certainly isn't getting any implants (although they're available legally *and* illegally around here) until after he sits for—and passes, of course—his Marsco exam. Being diskless puts him at a severe disadvantage. He's sharp, but so many others are much farther along in their schooling. Many parents do have their kids well-disked early. You ought to be able to give Aaron some valuable and unsurpassed pointers on finger mouse utilization. You must be the solar system's leading authority on accessing Marsco's latest computers with its oldest technology."

The visitor agreed that before his visit ended, he would make time for the young man, with or without ice cream thrown into the mix.

Tessa gave a shudder. "I wonder what a cow feels being milked by a disked hand. Must be irritating."

"They don't seem to mind me milking them," her father casually answered.

The Martian gave a laugh of admiration. "I appreciate the work and determination that you put forth to survive in a sid, especially this one, which seems to be falling backwards, not moving ahead."

"Yes, at times, this so-called subsidiary does resemble a zone—and one in steep disrepair. It's nothing like an area devoted to manufacturing important and necessary components for Marsco. But all that's farther north, and that locale is kept in much better shape."

"Anyway," the visitor continued, "you make quite a life for yourself here, albeit a lower-end life."

"Even so," conceded the granger, "look around beyond my hedges. It's what I've been sending you in my communication files, Martin; there's no incentive for Marsco to improve this subsidiary." He spoke in rapid bursts. "That old school behind us," he breathed out quickly, including Tessa in his hasty explanation, "there must've been thirty-five PRIMS in a gang there. Dismantling the vacant buildings. Now, if Marsco thought this subsidiary was potentially viable, it would be offering to rebuild schools, educating its teachers, paying them well, not tearing them up for stone and bricks. That's 'Marsco philanthropy'? You know the routine."

As their dinner grew longer, Miller asked his daughter, "aren't you running late? The light rail's sporadic. Too many power disruptions. Often sit for fifteen, thirty minutes until power's rebooted."

Tessa obediently rose to leave for her father's research center. She had the dog watch tonight during some fuel consumption tests. Yesterday all three engineers had witnessed the first series of these. Earlier in the day, they had studied the results of Miller's work. With only routine trials left, it fell to Tessa to watch them tonight without the pair of old friends there.

"I knew I'd be late getting out there with Martin still here," she explained imprecisely, "so I arranged alternate transportation."

A quizzical look crossed her father's face.

"Well, you approved the authorization," she informed her still-confounded father. "Bennie's picking me up in the Center's four-seater."

"Our Bennie? You mean Bennie Carton?"

"Yes. You remember: 'Approval of H/V HFC utilization for retrieval of essential personnel at 1745 hours for 1900 hours test sequence.' You twitched off on the authorization yourself." Tessa glowed with self-satisfaction.

"My dear, you've become Marsco *ad unguem.*" Miller shrugged with visible irritation. "So like a typical associate, 'to the fingertips,' using the system to your best advantage when needed. Showing off those disks. You didn't get that from Bethany or from me."

"Are you sure of that hypothesis?" his daughter countered, a deprecating grin crossing her face. Her green eyes danced. "I think I'm a damn sight too much like you, though I look like mom." Still chiding, she turned to Herriff. "I have them both covered, don't you think?"

"Oh, she's got you there, Walter. I'm sure you two are exactly alike," added the entertained witness to this domestic scene. Turning to the daughter, he expanded his theory, "Sounds like a trick *he* once pulled to secure *my* authorization to utilize our research dirigible to take your mother off alone. Not once, but *twice* he got away with that one."

Goaded by these two and growing slightly annoyed, Miller was truly shocked. “Those utilizations were always instrumentation test flights. Needed to calibrate sensors under actual high-altitude conditions. The upper reaches of Mars’s atmosphere approximate deep space itself. The dirigible acted as test platform.”

“With my hydrology specialist in tow? Who happened to be the most stunning *and* intelligent young woman on planet at the time?” Turning to Tessa, he added an aside, “You’ve grown up so much like her, as you say my dear.” Turning back, “After all, you weren’t sending water condensers into space. You were designing pyrotechnic thrusters.”

The daughter appreciated the ally on this pincer movement.

Miller roused himself from his reminiscences of those distant times. He snapped to all business, trying to cover his initial jolt with an explanation of the value of the single hovercraft to his research center. “When I came here ten years ago, the Center had three unserviceable and obsolete HFCs just sitting there. I thought I could cannibalize one to get the other two running. Turns out, it took two to get one running.” When he held up his fingers to count off these HFCs, his disks were clearly visible under his fingers’ epidermis. “That one’s irreplaceable. And so are *you*,” he retorted with finality, the concern in his voice palpable.

Tessa answered in a lower, confident voice, “It’s nothing like that with Bennie. I wanted to spend the extra time with Martin.” She turned to Herriff. “It’s been delightful. I’ll see you both in the morning.”

Her father next spoke as though his daughter were an inexperienced assistant, “Got the protocol data stick? Alpha file contains my preliminary results and a synopsis of first phase. Double-check those interpretations with tonight’s test. Complete at least three comprehensive runs. Everything should come in the same on the Kaiser scale.”

“Yes, of course,” Herriff mused, “you would be using the Kaiser scale.”

"And run a complete diagnostics, level four, between each test. And for goodness sake, make sure you reset all instrumentation beforehand."

Tessa arched her eyebrows in that *I've-conducted-these-tests-before* look.

Miller didn't flinch but went on, "We've a short time frame for optimum viability and little hypergolics left for a botched job. I leave it in your disks."

"Yes, sir," a Marsco's voice snapped with compliance. Father and daughter morphed into project manager and subordinate with a crucial deadline looming.

"And keep Bennie from always flying *my* HFC on fuel reserves." He turned to Herriff, "I don't think he actually understands your retrieval system." To Tessa he went on, "Make sure he brings *my* HFC back in one piece." His voice added an unsaid remark, "And, Lieutenant, don't you ever, ever pull this fast one again. I don't care who your father is!"

The tension was broken by the distinctive whine of vectoring jets as they throttled down from approach glide to hover mode. Three landing skids came to rest independently with triple thumps on the broken roadbed outside the grange's hedge. Even without seeing the set-down, the three engineers knew it was not graceful.

"He'll prang my kite yet," mumbled Miller.

Soon Bennie came into the grange ambling in a sideways walk like a crab, his awkward gait causing the yelping dogs to keep their distance. His young face was already scarred from carbuncles, the welts completely red and swollen. He wore common work overalls with one shoulder strap off either out of laziness or a warped sense of style. The bib and knees were ripped, a situation Miller had rectified by giving him a new set of overalls, although Bennie preferred these dirty, tattered ones.

"Ye-ah, nice place here, Doc, ain't it!" He grinned yellow-toothed, brushing his dirty brown hair out off his scarred forehead. "Wished I had me a place like this." Awkwardly, Tessa moved the intruder back out of the grange in quick fashion.

An odd feeling crossed Herriff's mind. The short scene was one of the few times he had ever seen Miller less than cordial with anyone.

After Tessa left, Herriff observed, "You're truly not pleased."

"Affirm that," he nearly snapped over his coffee. "I've seen this Bennie with some PRIMS we periodically hire. He's gruff, short-tempered, mean-spirited."

"And probably PRIM-stock himself, by the looks of him."

"Close enough, although that's not the issue."

"Certainly, she only wanted a quick skim out to the Center." Herriff tired to easy things, "Can't fault her for that! We even used that HFC yesterday. And my single experience with the local transport was enough for me. Living here must be nothing like life in a fully operational Sector."

"I know, the rail's sporadic. But, I don't like that behind-my-back method. Didn't it have that smack of an officer, any officer—Marsco or Continental Forces? You know the type."

"Yes. Deal with them all too often."

"And this Bennie, well—" his voice trailed off. "I'm sure he knows she's only charming him for the skim, but I know too much about him to trust him. Ever. Why I keep him at the Center's anybody's guess."

The father let slip more than he had intended, and he hoped his guest wouldn't pursue it. But his former colleague, who thought of Tessa as a niece, quickly noted this annoyance and did probe. "This sounds more serious than it looks."

"Bennie works mostly jockeying with that HFC. In one sense, he's a natural with it. But as I said, he doesn't take the time to really learn its operation. Never runs the fuel system properly, for instance."

The HFC's designer was taken aback, "But that's the beauty of the craft, self-refueling in flight!"

"I know—who doesn't? But *he* won't pay attention to anyone explaining the retrieval system long enough to learn about it. He *knows* already, such as he *knows,* if you catch."

"Yes, I know that type all too well. 'God's gift' pilots mostly."

"Anyway, we have plenty of equipment and sensors to haul. He can be a hard worker when he wants to be, but he is terrible—disastrous—near PRIMS. I refuse to assign him a detail that involves any. I've learned that much."

Miller drew in a breath and let out a plus-that's-my-daughter-with-him-at-this-moment sigh.

After a pause, the granger began, "He's been rejected *twice* for Marsco service, both Security and Hygiene *and* the Auxiliary Services. He asked me to check on why for him. This was, oh six, eight months ago, to see if there was something he could fix—or I could fix for him, I'm sure he was thinking."

"He wasn't really thinking *you* would use your pull with Marsco?" They were both thinking, *There's no longer any pull anyway; that fuel's spent!*

"Maybe he thought he'd wrangle some extra computer instruction, if that was keeping him out. You know, or maybe arrange to implant a disk or two. Easy enough in this or any sid. He's crazy to get into Marsco. Well, I did look into his entrance exams. He's bright enough, all right. But—" The engineer took a slow sip of coffee.

"There's always a 'But,' isn't there?"

Miller nodded and continued, "But, he's failed the psych profile. I've never met anyone who's somewhat bright—on the old IQ scale, close to 115—who's not gotten into Marsco in some status or another. But he's psychologically unfit."

"You have met really, really stellar people before; they're all a little off."

"Yes, eccentricity among geniuses is one thing, I grant you, but being crazed like Bennie is another." He then added spitefully, "and he's not *really* all that bright in an exceptional way! But still not even legionnaire quality, psych-wise!" Miller suddenly broke off.

"Now, that's low a threshold of emotional stability," concluded the visitor.

"Image Marsco thinking you're too damned whacked out to be an Auxxie goon to be unleashed on PRIMS. That ought to tell you something."

The guest understood his friend's concern.

"Marsco thinks his profile fits someone who's more than likely to join a resurgent Continental Powers faction or a Ludd cadre bent on something violent; take your pick. All for the sake of the violence, too, not out of commitment or devotion to some esoteric cause." Miller brooded silently for a moment. "Unfortunately, an all too typical young man or woman in an all too typical sid or zone at this epoch of history."

"There are that many?"

"Not all sids and PRIMS are clamoring to get into Marsco. And many clandestine cells do recruit around here."

Herriff nodded slowly. "I can see your apprehension. But I'm sure Tessa will be fine on one short skim."

"Oh, yes. I know she's packing."

"You know," the Martian colonist finally spoke after gathering the loose threads of their conversation and shifting it completely, "I'm rather shocked at the condition of this locale."

"Yes, I know," the granger replied. "But in all fairness, this sid's worse than most I've seen. Even so, it seems to be degenerating into zone status. I mean, Marsco shows off the Seattle Subsidiary and those coastal sids you passed through as the ideal models, but for all intents and purposes, they're just extensions of Marsco Sectors. No, I believe, from what I can gather—"

Is this an admission of some covert operation? Herriff wondered.

"—this subsidiary is by far well below the norm."

"But what we've been told on Mars—of course, I stay out of politics as much as possible—is 'that all subsidiaries are self-sustaining and flourishing. The UZs are to remain only temporary while they're being rebuilt.' What I see here doesn't square with what I've been hearing over the years."

Dr. Miller's eyes narrowed. "You doubted my reports?"

"No, not doubted. Just thought they were, well, part of your propensity to exaggerate. Not a good function of an engineer, I know, but a recurring phenomenon in you nonetheless."

"But I *didn't* exaggerate, did I?"

"No," the older associate reluctantly admitted, "no, I can see that you didn't. If anything, you understated by a magnitude of ten."

"Well, I'm glad you're here, so I can explain myself fully. I know many eyebrows went up when I announced we were suddenly leaving Von Braun. Bethany and I wanted to do something about Marsco. We'd come to feel, to believe, that Marsco hadn't actually thrown out the Continental Powers, it had simply replicated them, replaced one oligarchy for another. Nothing changed after the Continental Wars, really, nothing at all but the powerbrokers."

Herriff offered a half-hearted apologist's counterclaim, "But the Powers started the UZs—"

Miller cut him off. "Yes, but unfortunately the zones continue under Marsco. 'Oh, yes,' it rationalizes, 'things do take time to rebuild after the cataclysmic Continental Wars.' But the lion's share goes first to Marsco and little's left over for anyone else."

"And so this something you and Bethany wanted to do? What is it? Nothing violent, I suspect. You two were the least violent people I know."

"It was something I never thought I would be doing. I thought, 'What *if* a subsidiary produced something as good as Marsco did? And,' I reasoned further, 'what *if* this subsidiary remained independent while doing so?' And additionally, I thought, 'What *if* a subsidiary or two began flourishing again, on their own? Wouldn't that bring hope to the other ones?'"

Miller launched into an explanation of a plan he had been putting into practice for the past fifteen years. The Seattle Subsidiary still had lander manufacturing capacity and a history of making an excellent, reliable flight craft. Additionally, long before the Powers began to dominate, Sac City had been the home of thruster manufacturing. "Even some of the first engines that sent astronauts into space were assembled here, more than a century before."

He drew an excited breath.

"What if these two sids began assembling a new and better lander? With a new, highly efficient engine? Lighter airframe? That was my plan—fifty-five percent more power on a thirty-five percent lighter superstructure. I've sent you the exact specs already."

Herriff brushed aside the information he hadn't studied carefully but responded confidently, "Within the perimeters of possibility."

"The main byproduct, don't you see, would bring back viable work within two separate subsidiaries. These conceivably could prosper independently of Marsco. The tech-wonks from here wouldn't have to join Marsco. And then, maybe the electricity would stay on consistently. Instead of scratching out a bare existence, maybe there'd be a degree of prosperity here."

"Where would you go with this lander? You're not thinking of mining the belt? You're manufacturing a lander, not a shuttle."

"A shuttle? No, but not out of the question, either. Eventually, who knows? Maybe we just might move onto a new shuttle design. But first things first. There're plenty of Wanderer Asteroids still orbiting near to Earth—never been touched. Plus scores of erratic mining asteroids lost in wobbling orbits that missed their gravitational attraction from the Moon."

"Yes, capturing such asteroids would be a distinct possibility," conceded the senior engineer. "Perhaps there're more pitfalls than you realize, but if you risk nothing, you gain nothing."

"Besides," the granger continued with growing excitement, "we might sell our landers directly to Marsco or to other Indies. Independent sids do make up about ten percent of all space travel." His mind raced with myriad possibilities. "Even reclaiming satellites for their scrap would be lucrative. We have to start small, that's for sure."

"And so you think this inconsequential consortium might conceivably bring down Marsco?"

"No, never 'bring down' Marsco—I don't want to create another power vacuum. Such a vacuum brought Marsco to prominence in the first place."

Both remembered the worst of the times before and after the Continental Wars, even if witnessed from far away Mars.

"Besides, can you imagine what darker powers would rise up to replace Marsco stability? Imagine a world run by a squabbling collection of the most violent Luddite factions. Or worse, picture a return of the Continental Powers themselves, only in a more powerful, sinister configuration. The C-Powers themselves were for the most part the last vestiges of countries that wanted racial purity and nationalistic distinction as their guiding principal—after centuries of international exchanges and movements. At least Marsco got rid of the racial purification crap. That part of Marsco I respect and want to keep. But its lust for power, is that any different than C-Powers' lust for power? That thirst for dominance is what we have to overcome now, regardless of who is the driving force behind that absolute control. And so, I'm hoping our minuscule success will become a beacon that others might follow. I don't want to bring Marsco down in a nano. The chaos would make too many suffer, especially the PRIMS who suffer enough now as it is."

"I see, change the system from the inside."

"Something like that. Don't you know one of Gandhi's guiding principles: 'You must be the change you wish to see in the world'? We, Bethany and I, we thought we'd be able to move people, with gentle insistence, toward a better world. Not by toppling Marsco so much as changing its axis, its direction a tad. Make it evolve into something we can be proud of once more, like it was in its infancy. Make it live up to the humane language it spews."

Herriff interjected, playing the devil's advocate, "And yet, I detect your lingering contradiction about Marsco itself. After all, you didn't hesitate about sending your daughter to the Academy and then the Marsco Institute of Technology."

"'Marsco ambivalence,' that's what Cavanaugh called it. And no, neither Bethany nor I had any hesitation about Tessa's career.

Maybe she'll be the one to start all this change we desire. Even so, you're not a parent, so maybe you don't know what a parent feels. Would you hold your own child back? Keep her trapped in a world of sids and PRIMS and Neo-Con and bartering for eggs and butter? Constant surveillance and retina scans if you're on the outside, because of so many subversive Ludds? Hold her back? Especially if she can enter that safer world? Live in a world of comparative well-being? No, 'The time is now, and we are here.' She must make the best out of this world she inherited."

Two thoughts crossed the senior engineer's mind simultaneously. First, he wondered about his own HFC and lander designs. What if, forty or fifty years ago, he, Martin Herriff, had thought as Walter Miller was thinking today? Would the world be a different place had he been a forward-thinking Edison or Gates or Buffet? What if he had created his own transportation industry as a rival to, and not an offshoot of, Marsco?

Second, Herriff wondered, wouldn't Marsco put a stop to Miller? Self-preservation was one of its strongest tenets. The enthusiastic protégé was too influential within Marsco for Internal Security to stand in his way upon his return from Mars. (Hadn't he then been offered an immediate position at the Marsco Institute of Technology before it was widely known he was keeping his distance from Marsco?) After his wife's death, he seemed to fade and dwindle without direction or purpose, so over the past several years, Marsco seemed to ignore him.

At least that's what Herriff concluded on scant evidence. *He's just a crank,* Internal seemed to reason. A has-been associate imbued with eccentricity, a common-enough flaw among brainiac wonks. That is why it lets him live out some dissident charade. He can't be viewed as that dangerous, Marsco seemed to reason; his daughter was top in her class at the Academy and then at MIT where she earned a doctorate, following in his own footsteps. And currently, she is an Academy professor, an officer, a fellow associate. A lefter!

But, from what Herriff had gathered, Miller was too powerful outside Marsco for Seattle to ignore him any longer. Sometimes, in a world of shouting, silence makes the strongest impression. And Miller's whispering seemed to be reverberating throughout the whole Solar System. It brought Herriff here, after all.

The Martian shook his head. It was all too much for him to imagine. Miller had become the most famous *persona non grata* in the Marsco world. *How was he referred to at the VBC recently? He's become a "Sakharov"?*

When Herriff eventually looked up that vague reference on the Marsco Net, he found only a library cobweb site with no information beyond a few biographical remarks.

To his utmost surprise, Herriff immediately received a sharply worded email response from IS asking *him* why he had tried accessing such intel. He shouldn't have been shocked. Internal Security sending an e-message was part and parcel of the Marsco world.

But he was Doctor Martin Herriff and unaccustomed to being challenged like that.

Their discussions together grew longer. Even though not yet late, the Martian was tired. Because he was still confirming what he had journeyed to Earth to prove, he pushed on even though physically his endurance was accustomed to much less gravity.

After Miller and Herriff had been silent for several moments, each in separate deep thoughts, the granger said, "But my hopes are close to being crushed this time."

"How so?"

"I'm not sure Sac City will remain a discrete subsidiary for long."

"It would be better off being absorbed into a Sector."

"You misunderstand. Rumors, well-founded rumors—"

His undercover connections again? wondered Herriff.

"—persistent rumors circulate that this sid's to be reconfigured to UZ status soon. The change seems imminent. Look at its boundaries anyway, with its conjunctive UZs. The PRIM zones and sid areas are like fingers intertwined." He knitted his fingers for emphasis. "You don't need such a large subsidiary if it's a drain, not an asset, or at least that's how I imagine Marsco thinks about such things."

"Aren't all subsidiaries like this one?"

"I don't know. I guess so." Dr. Miller paused then added, "*No,* not all." Changing his mind, he went on, "The subsidiaries near Seattle are in great shape, of course. I know that some sids in northern Europe are doing quite well." He paused and thought a moment. "But the fact remains that this one was once the provisional capital and last capital of the Continental Powers. That may mean something to Marsco; it may not."

"Think it's because of you?"

Miller laughed cynically. "'Reports of my importance have been greatly exaggerated.'" He stressed his point by tapping his finger disks on the table. "But what makes you ask that?"

The guest from Mars made no answer.

The granger continued with his original point, "No, this doesn't look like a subsidiary that's flourishing. Even the limited services one usually expects are totally wanting although in theory easy to restore. Electricity runs only off and on. Water isn't running south of the cannery area. Nor has the Herriff-Grid been rebooted. And recently, even our C-phone capacity's out or it's spotty and totally unreliable. Unless it's a Marsco-provided unit on a secure link, a unit rarely works here at all, blocked somehow. Sometimes all uplinks to the Net are disrupted for days on end. No," he circled his hand to signify beyond his hedges, "it all looks like an incipient unincorporated zone to me."

"Yes," concurred Herriff, "as I've said several times, I was initially shocked at the deteriorating conditions here."

"I'm afraid we're only good for chipping bricks at this point, unless we can create viable reasons to exist and a way to stay independent."

A late afternoon wind picked up. Miller lowered PRIM-made bamboo blinds on the west side of the patio to block the intense setting sun.

"That's why the damnable rush to finish these experiments," Miller added tying down the last bamboo shade. "And why I let Tessa in on the project. She brought the latest Marsco protocols with her. Maybe this lander will become just something viable to sell to Marsco. And if we can develop one that's a success, and if we can get the manufacturing going top-notch, and if it wants our engines and landers, we have to have them up to speed."

The Martian replied, "An engineer's, a reformer's nightmare: 'If!'"

On their skim from the grange to the Center, Tessa sat quietly watching the ground beneath the HFC pass by. *Well,* she thought, *"skim" isn't quite the right description.* They moved along at full speed close to 1,500 meters above ground, higher than a skim, within what should have been a controlled zone had a Herriff-Grid been in full operation.

Although she was reluctant to speak first, Tessa eventually remarked almost wistfully, "It's nice, isn't it, not worrying about staying inside grid lines."

"Ye-ah." Bennie replied, managing to make the grunted *yeah* into two syllables. His hair hung in his eyes even though he constantly pushed it back.

"Open sky utilization's infrequent, unless you're manning an S & H craft on patrol," Tessa went on pedantically. "Above this sid, open's the norm."

"Ye-ah." In the small four-seater, she sat separated from him by only a swinging armrest. She was beginning to wish she had trusted the faulty light rail.

So far, though, Bennie had neither said nor done anything alarming.

In the clear afternoon sky as they moved along, she saw a dozen clicks in each direction. They were heading due east on what should be a short jaunt. Tessa was thankful for that. To the north, she saw the skyline of the city center. As the setting sun cast long shadows, she saw where power had been restored; illuminated windows began to glow. Somewhere in that skyline, although she was unable to make them out, were two signs of the world she had inherited: the cantonment with Marsco's HQ for this locale and the rotunda of the final provisional capital of the Continental Powers, long abandoned.

A few hundred meters below their HFC, Tessa made out islands of greenery, the hedged homesteads of Independent grangers dotting a sea of dry, tan earth and broken black macadam. She had skimmed over this subsidiary before. Memory plays funny tricks, but she seemed to remember the flourishing compounds as more numerous. Were Indies giving up their meager portion of autonomy and self-reliance? Her father seemed to think so, although confirmation of that hypothesis was impossible. *And Marsco isn't exactly conducting a census, either,* she concluded.

Farther south, the stopline was visible, dividing this fringe area of the subsidiary from the farther out but contiguous, spreading UZ. It was a snaking line just beginning to glow from its strong lights at staggered watchtowers and regularly spaced guard posts. Beyond the string of Auxiliary positions, it was easy to tell which side of the stopline was which. HFC over-flights on patrol at the same altitude as theirs were visible, probing, watching, waiting to pounce.

This HFC, she could hardly help but notice, ran without fully functional instrumentation. Odd her father considered it skimworthy. Understandable, she concluded, because he uses it only around the Center. In routine use, it probably never gained a quarter of the altitude Bennie had.

"This craft isn't in the best shape, is it?" she acknowledged, with an officer's edge in her voice that implied, 'You should glide to a surface-hugging skim and not be larking about at 1,500 meters.'

"Ye-ah," was the only reply.

Tessa noticed the fuel gauge and water vapor conversion status. The first was low, the second nil. He didn't have his water vapor intakes operational. Bennie wasn't making fuel for the craft; he was running off his water tank reserve.

In her severest listen-carefully-to-me voice, the professor stated, "The beauty of an HFC is its revolutionary and innovative fuel system." Bennie simply ignored her. "Utilizing a miniaturized nuclear reactor for power," she droned on academically, "this unit takes in atmospheric humidity, simple water vapor, separates the oxygen from the hydrogen, and then stores each volatile element in pressurized onboard fuel tanks. When catalytically reunited in the engines' combustion chambers behind the vectoring nozzles, the two gases ignite instantaneously for thrust."

"Ye-ah," Bennie uttered.

"You essentially gather fuel as you fly. SOP calls for only 10 percent onboard water at departure to save flight initiation weight. It's not uncommon, on a flight during atmospheric high humidity, to arrive with more fuel than you had at takeoff. The separator system's that effective. The engine's that efficient. In theory, you might have to dump water, stored before separation into hydrogen and oxygen, to attain the correct takeoff weight."

Her lecture was interrupted by Bennie repeating his "ye-ah," while not giving her any attention.

Abruptly, he angled the craft and banked into a turn that headed them north, away from Miller's SCAA Center and away from Tessa's engine tests.

SEVENTEEN

SCHEMERS AND DREAMERS

(Miller's Grange and the Sac City Sid, 2096)

"Truly impressive," Martin Herriff stated, "all this you've laid out." Walter Miller and his visitor walked through the grange's orchard at dusk. It was pleasant for the Martian to be among all the surrounding bounty.

Returning to the rose garden, Herriff recognized the fragrance of Bethany's flowers. He drew a deep breath. "That's the red Olympiad-Martian, a colony hybrid she originally grew for us. And that's the pink Elizabeth-Marsco, an Earth-side hybrid she'd also cultivated so successfully at the VBC."

"You know them well."

"I see them every day." On a trellis above them, a creamy Colony-Climber flourished, bred to climb up the interior girding of a dome support. On countless colonies, planters with earthen soil sat below open honeycomb frames graced with Bethany's work.

"She had been right," Herriff acknowledged, "about the need for something of home in our totally sterile and mechanical surroundings. But only a limited selection of blossoms, few and far between. Not lush abundance like here." He didn't add how much he had longed for Earth these past years. More than anyone knew, he had missed human connection.

"It's a spectacular sight," Tessa admitted. The red hues of an evening sunset caused by wind-driven dust gave the horizon spread before them its deepening tones. *At least it's not industrial pollution or smog.* Tessa took comfort in that. Crimson and burgundy passed into gray and black. The passenger grew more restless; they were still heading in the opposite direction of the Center.

As the evening grew darker, Bennie's route corkscrewed totally out of the way. Tessa lost all sense of landmarks. As a trained officer, not a comfortable position to be in. With surprising dexterity, the inept flier maneuvered the craft so it faced east and settled into hover at 2,000 meters, clicks away from Tessa's destination. As they hung there, the Moon rose.

The associate relaxed enough to observe that even with the clouds of Marsco's mining dust billowing out from its surface, it was a sight to behold.

In their silence, Tessa thought the scene almost romantic. *If the Moon hadn't become a cloud-encircled body. If its light reflected softly off the waves of some secluded lake. And if she were with Zot, and not with Bennie... If, if, if.*

No, don't go Boolean, she mentally demanded in her self-contained, self-controlling way. *He's out there amid the planets, and I'm down here virtually alone bathed in unnatural brightness, redlining a threat.*

"You know," the associate began, trying to start an inane conversation rather than let silence imply something else, "when I was a plebe back at the Academy, we had to calculate the increase in reflected light off the Moon—if the clouds' size were a constant. Of course, they're always changing. And some are in Earth's shadow anyway, just as part of the lunar surface is. Depends on how many and when and where asteroid-shard placements have occurred and what blasting's going on up there."

Bennie, although able, was unwilling to follow her remarks. He once more glided the craft in whatever direction he wished.

"My closest classmate then at the Academy, Anthony Grizotti, he won the McAuliffe prize for the best equation to predict the amount of consistent lunar dust albedo. *Albedo,* as you know, is reflected light off an object in space. Any moon, an asteroid, a body without its own luminance emanating from it, as a star or sun has."

In the green instrument glow of the cockpit, Bennie looked more and more sinister. As soon as he had shuffled sideways into the garden that afternoon, Tessa knew her mistake. Health for many was frightful in this post-antibiotic world, but basic hygiene was expected. A minor cut or skin abrasion might become fatally infected. Associates had a legit reason, she knew, for not mixing with PRIMS. Nonetheless, some of Bennie's problems he brought onto himself by refusing to wash his face.

Sitting there, Tessa witnessed a side of him she hadn't seen before. At her father's research center, he had been just another sid in the background, although one more like a PRIM. Tonight, Tessa knew she should have never put herself in this position. *Watchfulness* and *caution* were two keys of self-protection; every associate knew that.

Foolishly, dangerously, she had let her guard down earlier this evening. She was paying the price for such associate bravado.

It had grown quite dark as the two old friends lingered in Miller's garden. Candles Tessa had lit earlier in the evening burned but threw out little light. Only when the Marsco Moon cleared a row of trees growing just inside the grange's eastern hedge, did the garden brighten. In the radiance of that auxiliary sun, the two engineers remained in thoughtful tranquility.

Finally, the visitor stated, "I'm surprised Marsco still blasts clouds of lunar dust."

"You mean, although it promised long before the Continental Wars to cease such operations? Well, they're still in full swing."

"I see. I guess I've just grown long past being surprised by Marsco."

—

Seemingly out of nowhere, three green flares streaked by SCAA craft. Bennie's aimless meandering had caught the attention of Security. And now, the patrolling troopers were catching Bennie's attention, firing live ammunition across his bow.

"Ye-ah-ye-ah-ye-ah," was Bennie's only response, but he knew enough to lower his skids straight away and commence a landing glide. After the green flares would come bursts of red tracers that meant business. In the Marsco world, Bennie knew, questions were often asked later.

—

On the ground next to an abandoned grange, two troopers approached the barely skim-worthy HFC. "Kinda off the beaten track, aren't you?" one asked. The other stood aside, Enfield shoulder weapon at the ready.

Tessa removed her right and left gloves. Her gesture softened the posture of the trooper, as she knew it would. The second silent guard, assessing the situation, immediately slipped back to his own Security craft.

"Well," the remaining legionnaire explained, "you're missing some running lights." In the intense beam of his flashlight, he checked out the associate and her PRIM friend. Their eyes narrowed from the brightness like caught animals. An odd sight, an odd combination. If she were in trouble, she gave no sign, but it sickened the trooper to see such HH GAS-free prime with a common PRIM. "And I don't think your CAR is optimal, either. I buzzed your six, close enough to engage your collision avoidance radar, but you didn't change bearing, altitude, or direction. Negatory auto-evasion's a sure sign of malfunction."

"Ye-ah?" was Bennie's only response.

Throughout the evening, the two engineers spoke of old times, then sat in periods of pleasant silence. The visitor finally commented, "You know, the other morning after being on that train all night, I didn't come here directly." Because Miller was away when Herriff arrived, he hadn't heard this part of the story. "At the station I asked for, no, I *demanded,* an HFC to skim down here. But then I changed my mind."

The speaker poured himself another cup of coffee from a carafe thoughtfully left for them by Tessa. "I requested to be taken to the central HQ. I was given the use of their VIP suite to shower and rest."

"Of course," Miller said. "You must be the most important *lefter*—after a fashion—to visit here since the Armistice."

"You're undoubtedly correct," the Martian answered after a glance at his diskless fingertips. "Well, after a while, I tried to explain who you were and where I wanted to go, but I got the distinct impression that was unnecessary—that every single associate in the cantonment knew of you. Any mention of your name brought their beehive frenzy to a screeching halt."

"Doesn't surprise me. I'm under constant surveillance," the granger replied with a nonchalant air. Turning his chair forty-five degrees to face his guest fully, the Indie whispered, "Look over my left shoulder, up above the roof ridge. See an onion-shaped ball? That's a surveillance cam housing."

Herriff just made out a metallic shape against the backdrop of a dead tree beyond the grange. A wide, dark Plexiglas strip ran around the housing; through it, a cam was remotely aimed.

Miller explained that just to the northwest, a lamppost once stood at the corner of two residential streets. "Probably stood there in one form or another for over a century. After the Continental Wars, the metal of those poles became valuable, and few survived upright. Of all the light stanchions in this district, that's the only one Marsco reinstalled—two weeks after I arrived here from Seattle—but it never shines a light."

"Nothing's changed much," the guest added, "it was the case for many years prior to the C-Wars—indeed, prior to the creation of the C-Powers themselves—throughout any city were banks of cams."

"Yes, throughout our twenty-first century," Miller noted dryly, "whoever was in charge enjoyed the luxury of watching, watching, watching." He gave a light laugh before adding, "If nothing else, Security's constant, although there's not much to see most days."

"Can they hear us?"

"No, I've installed triple-redundant fuzzers with a fluctuating modulation system to disrupt any eavesdropping."

"I see. Random waves frustrate any overrides."

"Roger that. Fogs everything. I wish that I was able to do the same for those pesky IR sweeps, but I haven't access to that technology."

"Of course not. Very sophisticated, and in all probability, scientifically impossible to disrupt infrared light."

"Nonetheless, I wish I could," the granger stated in a tone of resignation. "Periodically, S & H sends a surveillance drone to hover above my garden. It has its snoop then goes away back over the hedge. I suspect it leaves a handful of bugs, but I don't think Security's broken my fuzzers yet."

"Incredible."

"Or, HQ arranges for people to just meet me. That happens often enough."

"Incredible," Herriff replied once more, thinking back to Cadet Carter on the train.

"It's a Marsco world." A wry smile crossed Miller's face. "I'm surprised it doesn't send in a bot some day—just to scare my dogs if nothing else."

"A robotic warrior? Aren't they obsolete?"

"Rendered useless by hacking and bot-tipping almost as soon as they were put into service but obsolete in every other sense as well."

"I don't follow your intuitive jump."

"There's too many PRIMS and poor sids who still man Auxiliary units and Security forces to stoop to malfunctioning faulty bots."

Herriff pondered his host's remarks. "And these drones, do they come because you've spoken out so forcefully against Marsco?"

"You say 'do they come,' but don't you actually mean 'are they sent'?

"Yes, but sent by whom?"

"Security."

"Security?"

"Yes, it certainly doesn't want me to have a following. Or at least, it wants to know who's in that following, if one exists."

"Does one?"

"Hell, no. I'm not that stupid. So, I tell people not to visit." This remark brought raised eyebrows from his guest. "I have an elaborate system to communicate with them. I think my messages get out undetected. I know my writings get posted, sometimes for weeks, before they're deleted by IOSS. Marsco's always had trouble protecting its own open Net. Basic ironic flaw in the system: let everyone on; some are bound to hack."

"And, that's not a following?"

"Blog readers are hardly 'a following' in that sense."

In the darkness, a sudden change came over Miller's voice. He went on with warm pride, "I've gotten quite good at e-posting an essay or two that reaches, potentially, millions. My links can be, if I modestly say so, quite ingenious. Someone in the London Sector may click to check the Martian weather and suddenly they find themselves tempted with a link to my writings."

Herriff was quite impressed. "How easy is it?"

"Too easy really. You should surf what's out there, posted by who knows who. Some violent cells, that's for sure. I'm sure some

Luddites aren't as anti-tech as they appear. Then, of course, there's always the disgruntled but still active Marsco associate, a mole, putting up this or that internally. Haven't you ever wondered how so many docs get pasted onto the Net, crashed by Marsco, then hacked on again?"

"Such as?"

"Historical documents, mainly, of the midcentury. I gather they're trying to give a truer analytical background of the past 100 years. And then there are stories of Marsco atrocities. Mainly revisionist history with a Continental Powers bent." Dr. Herriff didn't fully understand. "Widely known Powers atrocities, for example, are retold as though they were originally committed by Marsco. The Shanghai massacres of '57 come to mind as a perfect example. You have to be careful what you read. Even my cyber sources might be wrong, but I doubt it."

"But I've seen none of this."

"You *are* a model associate! Haven't you ever surfed looking for dissident writings?"

"Well, no, no I haven't."

"Then you're about the only associate who hasn't. No matter. I routinely sent you copies of everything I've written."

"Is that what you sent me over the years?"

Even in the dark, Herriff felt Miller's penetrating eyes. The granger spoke deliberately, "Yes, I used an old finger mouse NB to make those. I had Tessa take a few of them to Seattle and slip them to my old friends in the fleet. I've many other means at my disposal as well. Always hand-delivered."

The Martian wished he had read those smuggled dispatches more carefully. He had skimmed only a few. It might have saved him this recon trip. His Earth-side journey verified everything that Miller was suggesting in those essays that Herriff hadn't at first read thoroughly or totally believed when he did.

"And never delivered by the same courier."

"I noticed that! But isn't Tessa in jeopardy?"

"If I thought so, do you think I'd let her, for a moment, risk her life—"

"Life! Life? Is it that serious?"

"Potentially, it's that serious. Look, Marsco's playing for keeps. But no, Tessa isn't in jeopardy. It's only her career she's risking. Nonetheless, recently she's agreed. Besides, she's still important to Marsco—and I really haven't done anything wrong. I've committed no breech of internal regulations, although I've bent a few, that's for sure. I've only written a fair amount that question some statistics Marsco puts out. I call into question some of its philanthropic techniques. And the ulterior motives behind much of its so-called philanthropy. I don't call into question its authority. I certainly don't call for any violent acts against it. I'm not an Alaric, after all."

"Alaric," the visitor said under his breath, trying to place the prewar name. "Alaric," the visitor whispered a second time.

"Most vocal opponent of the Disenfranchise Movement, spoke up for PRIMS, he alleged, but by calling for a violent uprising." Using an antiquated system of mass media—a tattered obsolete system but the only one open to PRIMS—he was relentless and vitriolic in his condemnation, first, of the Continental Powers, then of Marsco. Many violent Luddites flocked to his airwave calls; many acts of insurrection were made at his behest."

When Herriff finally placed the notorious man, Miller continued, "In fact, I purposely reject direct contact with any group I suspect is violent. And my work gets quite a few hits a day, sometimes in the thousands."

"That many?"

"Yes, easily."

"I see," marveled the visitor, understanding his former colleague all the more.

"I ask questions, that's all. Hard questions—as any reputable scientist or philosopher or historian should do."

"But here you are and your own daughter works for Marsco."

"I know. Her choice. And I won't stop her. She's the one who has to juggle her feelings for me and her commitment to it. Besides, I worked for Marsco for many years; technically, I'm only on sabbatical. I still draw a portion of my full pay. And a portion of Bethany's, a bereavement benefit. But I think it is guilt money. Nonetheless, I deplore violence and am not advocating any use of it. What's more, I'm proud of my service at your VBC. I never deny that to anyone."

"That part of your story I don't understand," commented the visitor.

"Call it postwar ambiguity. Marsco is the world we know and inhabit. What else can we do?"

Their talk in Miller's garden continued. As everyone did in the Marsco world, Herriff eventually acted naturally, as though he wasn't being digitally recorded. Soon he stated, "Another thing surprised me on my trip. PRIMS? Why so many here?" It was a comment made without rancor, one made from the observation of an unexpected phenomenon rather than from bias.

"Yes, many more than you'd expect," the grange resident explained. "I love Marsco's euphemism: 'Labor shortages' to describe an area first devastated by the Continental Wars then ravaged by plagues. Another euphemism: 'the Troubled Times.'"

"It goes back to that?"

"No, it more than that." Miller looked into the heavens searching for the right explanation. "It's difficult explaining the system. In sum, Marsco moves PRIMS about. I estimate, about a hundred-K a day—in landers, just rounding them up and shipping them around."

"Why, that's over 35 mil yearly."

"Exactly, but as you can imagine, records are foggy."

"Yes."

"I estimate about 15 million are sent each year to Africa—"

"AIDS depletion?"

"As good a reason as any," Miller answered. "Others go to Asia, if you can believe that. But it's a swap, you see. Some move there, others move back here. A fourth-generation citizen might suddenly find herself whisked off to old Mexico or Uruguay or Natal. I use the former names for these locations, but they all house recent *diasporas.*"

"Impossible to imagine."

"Imagine it! Marsco SOP."

"But why?"

"Marsco doesn't want any groups forming around location, religion, culture. The Powers moved people for just the opposite reason, ethnic cleansing to make themselves, if not racially pure, certainly politically and ideologically rarified. Marsco moves anyone suspected of trouble. But it doesn't care what sort of mish-mash it creates or breaks up. When Security busts up PRIMS, many are sure to be shunted around, God knows where eventually. And, it collects the children, of course, for its schools."

"That I don't understand."

"Give them the basics, test them physically and mentally. Train the strongest, educate the smartest. Marsco needs associates; it's ever-expanding and needs more and more all the time."

"So, if I grasp your point, if you're a PRIM, you might just be snatched away from your family, your home?"

"Yes."

"And trained as Marsco sees fit."

"Yes. If you're strong and healthy and willing. And without any family or cultural ties, how would they know differently? PRIMS don't have much of either, but yes, if a PRIM isn't location-bound for employment, doesn't have some sid backing, then this PRIM might be snatched. Caught without a functioning PRIM-disk or when trouble breaks out—bread riots, protests against BC strips—large numbers of PRIMS are simply relocated."

"This's beyond sinister. The end of the twenty-first century, yet it sounds so like, like Rome."

The granger added softly, "Yes, Rome. Napoleon. The Third Reich. The Eastern Block. Rome." Miller paused thoughtfully and continued, "Father Cavanaugh's school was a conduit for training PRIMS who didn't have to go into Marsco. And oddly, almost perversely, Marsco supported his school although it rarely provided them with recruits. Here and there, a few got into Marsco. Cavanaugh was quite proud of that."

"That makes the least sense of anything you've said tonight."

"Well, Cavanaugh, ever the optimist, used to say, 'If Marsco is like Rome, we must pray that it'll have its Constantine.'"

"Before it's visited by Goths and Huns!"

"If my e-hits are any indication, it's an all too real and imminent possibility, Marsco being gothed in the near or distant future."

The Martian thought for a moment, "But how do you move millions upon millions of people, often against their wishes?"

"Two ways, mainly," Miller explained. "I've done a great deal of research on the subject, parallel historical events, because Marsco keeps almost everyone from writing or posting about 'These Recent Unpleasantries,' as I've seen them described. At any rate, the first way is to garner lots of help from the people you don't want to move."

"Buy their cooperation?"

"Exactly!" Even in the dark, the older visitor saw his host looking directly at him. "Do you know Cahill's writings on Rome? 'The Britons, the Gauls, the Africans, the Slavs who long ago had flocked to the Roman standard, forsaking their petty tribal loyalties and becoming Roman citizens, gained greatly. By exchanging tribal identity for the penumbra of citizenship, they won the protection of the *Pax Romana.*' Don't you see that the same thing has happened with Marsco? It is a sort of cyber Rome."

The guest had never heard that term.

"Join Roman-Marsco, cooperate, your life is one hellova lot easier."

"I see."

"We all fell under its spell, at first. We had such a poor *either/or* choice. Either we support the Continental Powers or join Marsco. But Marsco's nothing real. Or at least, once it wasn't. People formerly connected to it in a tenuous cyber way—*netizens,* we were called. But over time, like so many reformers, it grew into the problem." Miller drew an anxious breath; his task looming before him, portentous. "Marsco was once a noble ideal; it's presently been transformed into a hopelessly ominous entity. Well, not hopelessly. I'm banking on it not being in irreparable condition."

"Okay, yes, that's established, but how does it move millions upon millions of people over the year? At 100K a day?"

"As I said, you get the cooperation of many willing to serve Marsco rather than a discredited nationalistic system. So what if some other people aren't location bound anymore—if you cooperate, you skate, get a pass. Not all are connected to others in the same way as before anyway, but some are connected to an ideal, a cyber nation becoming a real, tangible fact."

"Yes, yes," Herriff stated bluntly not in agreement but in frustration. *Get on with it and skip the professorial analysis.*

"Well, the second reason is simple. Sublunar orbiter landers."

"How's that?" A defensive answer, their designer not wanting any additional blame for this world dumped on him by anyone, even Walter Miller.

"A lander has a tremendous cargo-carry capacity, Martin—you ought to know that; you initially designed it." Herriff nodded in reluctant agreement. Then Miller added thinking his logic was crystal clear, "Well, Marsco garners immediate cooperation when its minions shove an Enfield in some PRIMS' ribs."

Bennie nearly pranged the HFC as he landed hard on its skids at the bottom of a dry reservoir, facing a destroyed concrete dam in jagged ruins ahead of them down the valley. Several clicks back behind them, up a long sandy shore visible in the moonlight, were the remains of a bathing beach. The glow of low fires suggested PRIMS amid the trees higher up the slopes. Tessa oriented herself. Beyond the rubble of the dam and over the farthest valley ridge, an engine test might be initiated without her.

This was their second set-down of the night, and still Tessa was not any closer to the Center. The pair was clicks from anyone or anything.

In the C-Wars, the dam had taken a direct Vanovara hit (Type V-2, solid metal, she assumed) and had never been rebuilt. "It is sound military logic to take out a reservoir and not a nearby aerospace center, something Marsco might want to utilize later," she lectured in her disciplined way. Then, she allowed the seditious ideas running through her mind to cross her lips. "Inhumane, however," she confided, breaking ranks, "to destroy a civilian target, and worse yet, not to repair it in the following years."

These were all feelings she shouldn't be telling Bennie, but her father had had renewed influence on her thinking about Marsco. His beliefs brought a change in her, and these had altered their relationship, making the pair more like equals.

Not thinking at all of Bennie, her mind raced to other linked ideas about Marsco and its current role in the world. These thoughts weren't appealing. It was a world dominated by Marsco, but perception is reality and she perceived it differently now.

She examined the surrounding prewar reservoir. Dark blotches of scrub covered the hills. A few valley oaks grew above a still-discernable high-water mark. Below that line, new growth had reluctantly sprouted. In the continuing drought, neither the old growth above the waterline, nor the newer one below, was thriving.

Over the black hill outlined in the distance, her father's research center sat nestled out of sight. *Of course,* Tessa concluded, *"research" and "center" were loftier and grander terms than the reality.* For all its potential, it was more of a relic from the last century than anything approaching Herriff's genuine article on Mars.

Tessa shook her head. She had tolerated, almost humored, this near-PRIM long enough. Often, her initial response to conflict was to weigh all sides, hear all evidence. Works in research; in perilous situations her methology was potentially dangerous, even fatal. She must act as an associate and an officer. She resolved to take matters into her own finger disks.

"Relax," Bennie cajoled. He offered her some black market hooch. The officer had already smelled the oily drink on his breath. "When the team found out you'd be late 'cause of light rail disruption—power's sporadic after all—they goes on that they'd fire the first engine test without you."

"Without *me?*"

"Ye-ah."

"Didn't you tell them you were coming to get me?"

Bennie pushed the console arm between them out of his way. "Why should I tell 'em that?" he asked with a self-satisfied grin on his swollen face. He looked all the more blotched and puffed. He put his arm around her shoulder, his sour breath as menacing as his actions. His eyes held her in a determined stare.

"You know," the associate responded firmly, "I don't think this will get you very far. You *must* take me to the Center *now,*" she ordered in a determined voice without panic. She thought her officer's insistence carried all the force needed.

With his other hand on her thigh, he responded, "Come on. I seen that way you sucked up to me so nice to come and git you tonight."

"That was for my convenience."

"Do tell," the brazen man hissed, beginning to reach forward to kiss her. Although thin, he was powerful enough to overtake her if it came to that.

She pushed him away with her left hand. "You know, even though I'm on leave right now, I'm a Marsco associate. A lieutenant, in fact."

"Well, I'm man; you're girl!" he snipped, not retreating but regrouping to launch a second attack in the tight compartment of the four-seater. "And your little puss-oscity ought to be nice." He meant business, crude business. He wasn't some smart-ass cadet acting inappropriately. He was a serious hostile. "Come on, you'll love it, my big hard one comin' in you. And what's you bein' Marsco got t'do with?"

"Well *this*—" a sharp, metallic jab sent pain through Bennie's ribcage—"for starters."

He pulled back swiftly, but the pressure kept pushing against his ribs. Strong pressure that wasn't backing down, wasn't bluffing. Too strong to risk snatching at its source.

"Recognize this hard one?" Tessa coolly moved the metal object up and down his ribcage, painfully, over one bone at a time. "This's a fairly small-caliber unit, only 7.6 mm, Marsco-issued, Enfield. Thirty-shot clip. They're exploding shells; even though small, they'll make a mess. Laser designator, in case I'm not such a good aim. But can't miss from this range, right? Aerosol propellant that can three-burst before recharging. It blasts with a *pow-pow-pow.*" She shoved the barrel into his chest with each *pow.* "There's a few nanos delay, but then with little effort, *pow-pow-pow* a second time."

She ran the weapon against his bony frame with increased force. It surprised Bennie actually how strong she was. Panic crossed his face; his large eyes looking down, following every move of the insistent weapon. He refrained from resisting, fearing an accidental discharge with him as the sole target.

"But," Tessa continued her pressure, "my initial three-burst ought to be enough, don't you think?" Pressure. "Those first three blasts will blow one hell of a bloody hole through your scrawny-ass ribcage, don't you think?" More pressure. "Can't miss—point-blank? Bennie, does *eviscerate* mean anything to you?"

He shook his head, "Never heard of-of that!" Perspiration pasted his dirty hair onto his scarred forehead. He let his bangs alone; a movement to bush them aside might be misunderstood. His eyes stung; his greasy head glistened with sweat.

"Well, Bennie, there'll be enough blast power left over from those shells to lodge bone fragments in that hatch behind you. *Your* bone fragments from your ratty ribs and spineless back-bone." Running the tip of the muzzle over his torso was agonizing, threatening; she knew it. "Should I test our hypothesis?" By applying more pressure to the man's chest as she spoke, Tessa pushed him farther off his seat. He readily conceded his space yet was rapidly running out of room.

At her insistence, he fumbled with his left hand behind his back to open the hatch. As the gull-door sprung open smartly, he spilled out onto the ground.

"Crawl off over there!" Tessa motioned him away from any engine blast with a flicking motion of the hand-held's barrel. But its laser designator always returned to a position aimed at his chest. That red dot assured him of her accuracy and his death should she let loose a volley.

He thought about rushing her, but she wasn't leaning out of the craft that far and she was still armed. He edged away over the sandy ground, simpering like an injured animal, although only his pride was wounded.

"Before I go, take a look at this." She pointed the weapon skyward and pulled the trigger.

"Empty!" he shouted. He stood up to rush at her, but the dust from the vectoring nozzles temporary blinded him. "Bitch! I knew'd it all alon'! Not loaded, I knew'd it!" He stood in the gritty cloud, screaming at aft thrusters and the vastness of the barren reservoir. He took a few feeble strides to chase her, but the HFC was soon over the lip of the adjacent steep hill. She might be anywhere by the time he struggled up the stretching sandy embankment.

At the grange, the conversation of the old friends took a natural and relaxed pause. Miller offered to make fresh coffee, but his guest declined.

"So, what's your next step?" Herriff eventually asked.

"I suspect that we can put together a consortium to build and operate a small fleet. Ideally six landers, but I hope eventually twelve to twenty-four. Compete with Marsco in its own backyard."

"Who can give you financial backing? Who but Marsco?"

"There're two Hohenzollern concerns in a Euro sid; they've expressed interest. One's a metal fabricator, the other a chemical consortium. They manage to stay fairly autonomous of Marsco. They're both in the same strongly sovereign (and I underscore the term *sovereign*) subsidiary—one that's even begun issuing its own currency."

"And so?"

"And so we build our own fleet, one more advanced and economical than a Marsco lander." No snub echoed in Miller's voice.

"The Twelve Thruster Policy? Won't that ground you?" The Martian probed the details like in the old days, knowing clarity came from defending any idea from an onslaught of scrutiny. "Marsco used it in the past to create their monopoly in space. That single policy kept the Japanese, the Chinese, the Russians out of the game long before the Powers emerged."

"That's the beauty of my design: fifty-five percent higher fuel efficienty, thirty-five percent less weight, remember? Greater efficiency means we can leave from and return to Earth without refueling. Twelve Thrusters technically won't apply to an orbiter that doesn't need Marsco's refueling services in space."

"But what'll you do with this fleet?"

"For starters we'll mine close-approach asteroids. That'll make Marsco stand up and take notice! All those nearby Wanderers gliding by in and out of our nominal range. And we'll remain totally within Marsco regulations and restrictions: its mining ordinances apply solely to operations 'inside the asteroid belt.' Additionally, decades ago Marsco created the precedence of claiming unmanned equipment and random asteroids; we'll stand by the same rulings. Beat it at its old game."

"Yes, I see. That's why it hates lost asteroids; anyone can claim them."

"Anyone with the right tech support. There are hundreds drifting in close orbit right now. We'll legally glean from what's been captured by Earth."

"An impressive plan with an ultimate object, forcing Marsco to change."

"If I, well, my team—"

"—and Tessa—"

"Yes, *and Tessa,* if she's willing and if we all can get that engine running. We're so close. Time's running out. And all these delays caused by power grid letdowns and equipment failure. And copper. Do you know how hard it is to secure reliable tubing? Not to mention fiber optics materials. Polymer ingots. QVA chips without *something* Marsco embedded in them. And what I wouldn't give for a second fully functional hovercraft!"

Tessa maneuvered the runabout over a hillcrest and then brought it to a glide, landing on a flat ledge down from the summit. She was high enough on the third hill from Bennie to observe the Center from a great distance in complete safety. If he were foolhardy enough to chase her, he was hours behind.

She hadn't taken pilot training at the Academy; however, she was taught by Herriff himself how to handle an agile four-seater. Tonight, however, her own strong will to escape Bennie drove her forward. Even if she didn't know how to maneuver the craft, she would have tried desperately to operate it to elude her attacker.

After she set the craft on its skids—she hadn't bothered to retract them during her flight—her whole body began to shake. She broke into uncontrollable sobs. "I've never done anything like this. Never." Rightly or wrongly, she felt some responsibility for Bennie's actions, reprehensible as they were.

Her first mistake was putting him in such a power position. She should have kept her distance. Even without a patina of associate's arrogance, she had a sixth sense, especially about sids and PRIMS. She should have trusted herself more. Not like an associate viewing Bennie as a PRIM but as a woman simply knowing that clear dangers exist out there. It was a basic element of survival.

She had no right to ask a man like that to take her to the Center. On that score, her father had been absolutely correct. She was putting herself in harm's way. That part of this evening she should have avoided. Her inner sense and officer training warned her against such an untenable position.

Bennie's advances—as distasteful, as threatening as they were—bothered her less than her own lack of caution. She picked up her service weapon, which she usually carried unloaded. Taking no chances, in a few well-trained moves, she loaded a clip of exploding shells. Discharge propellant primed with its distinctive hiss.

"I'm growing so Marsco," she admitted with a frustrated sigh.

She double-checked the laser target designator that signaled the shells when to explode for maximum effect. She knew that earlier with Bennie at pointblank range, the shells (if she had had a loaded sidearm) would have passed through him before exploding, contrary to her threats. They would have been devastating to his ribcage but only as tumbling, solid bullets. A three-burst would have created enough havoc to make his torso nothing but red, mushy garbage.

This time, if she fired the weapon at any ribcage with the appropriate range, the torso would explode, blown apart in a detonating impact. Even a "winging" shot blew off someone's arm or leg or head.

That was the whole reason Marsco developed this weapon and its big-brother shoulder-fired version. During the C-Wars, Marsco was interested in a weapon that would kill efficiently in the hands of someone marginally trained. An Enfield made up for the poor quality of its operator. Its PRIM armies had been devastating, cutting a bloody swath through all they faced.

"It wuz easier," her gunnery sergeant had initially explained at a firing range many years prior, "to have a proximity shell with bodaciously complete lethality than train hairless-chimp PRIMS to shoot straight." It was an insidious, inhumane weapon. In a seasoned associate's disks, it was absolutely precise and relentlessly accurate. In lesser-trained hands, it still was greatly feared.

She stopped crying long enough to raise the Center, holding her thumb over the cam so she reported in on audio only.

"We expected you for the second test anyway," a faded, distorted image replied. "First candle's set to light up in five minutes; you're good until 2330."

"His engine has to burn! It has to!" she kept repeating to the engineer at the Center in an unguarded manner, uncharacteristic for the ever-inflexible, often emotionally rigid, associate.

"Oh, don't worry, Dr. Miller. Walter's candle will burn A-OK tonight." Tessa felt some reassurance that this evening's actions hadn't disrupted months of her father's work.

This update over, she stepped out of the hatch and effortlessly raised her Enfield at a tall oak tree fifteen meters to port where it stood at the edge of a steep drop-off. In the darkness, it was just an outline against the starlit sky. A red laser dot illuminated the exact spot where her shell would explode.

Gently squeezing, she sent a single 7.6 mm projectile just to the left of the two limbs diverging above the main trunk. The first branch shattered apart at that precise spot. She next aimed at the right branch, ruthlessly blowing it away from the truck. Two targets. Two shots. Two precise hits.

The branches burned; they were that dry and the weapon that effective. In their glow, the trunk now looked like an enormous standing man with his hands raised in the posture of surrender.

She imagined the defenseless tree was Bennie. One shot would blow his torso apart; a three-burst would blow him totally away. She heard her Academy weapon's instructor, a C-Wars vet with fingers missing from a near-blast of a shell, shouting at her, *Fry his fuckin' Continental-ass! Kill that son of a PRIM-bitch! Eviscerate the bastard! Disembowel him! Blow off his limp prick!*

But, before the wooden Bennie, she hesitated. She wasn't able to let go with those final rounds, even though her Enfield was three-burst primed. "Take down the bastard!" she screamed loudly, mimicking her gunny. "It's that asshole or you!" she let her voice rip. "Blast his fucking pimply PRIM face!"

She knew the language. She knew the drill.

Then, she heard her mother's voice, her father's, Zot's, voices distinct from Marsco. She holstered her weapon.

Behind the smoldering branches, down the hillside, an intense light flared up. Flames backlit billowing clouds of steam and smoke. In the shadowy distance beyond Tessa's perch, the first test ignited successfully with its blazing plume.

At the controls, she guided her HFC toward that solitary brightness. She wasn't as much Marsco as she believed.

The designer and his dreamer protégé continued their discussion long into the night. They had been interrupted only once, when well after midnight, Tessa called in a progress report of the second firing.

After that disrupting call, the visiting engineer took the opportunity to tell his tale. "And so, I had three reasons for returning. One, I wanted to see for myself—what was Marsco really up to? And I might add—I've seen enough. My mind is made up."

"About what?"

"It will become clear in a moment." He continued counting, "Two, I want to visit where I grew up one last time, see Baltimore."

"I'm afraid there probably isn't much remaining," explained Miller. "Most East Coast cities were prime targets for V-weapons. Vanovara strikes don't leave much behind, especially air burst fireballs, V-1 types."

"I suppose you're right. I think I knew that, but I still want to try to find my old neighborhood. Find my parents' graves—I buried them long before the C-Wars. It humors an old man."

"And three?"

"Three, I came to talk to you."

"I'm flattered to be sure, but you might have put yourself at risk."

"No, I don't think so. I'm too important for that. But 'number three' is better stated, 'I came to ask you personally, as a colleague and friend, to come back with me.'"

"I *am* touched, but why? The VBC's survived a good fifteen years without me."

"You've asked me to listen to your grand plans," the director of the Von Braun Center stated emphatically, "now you must listen to mine. Hear me out, before you say no. I came all this way to ask you to return, because I know you'll say yes once you hear my proposal."

The visitor took a sip of water. "Because of what Marsco has become, you have your plan. A good and noble plan: change it from the inside, if I catch your drift. Humanize it. Make it live up to all the potential it espouses."

Nodding agreement came from across the brightly lit garden.

"Well, at Von Braun, I've hatched a plan as well."

The silent listener bent forward in his chair to hear the whispered scheme. "Let me start with this point first. When you left *Valles Marineres,* you were on the verge of perfecting a new thruster, an ion engine. Something beyond chemical and hybergolic propulsion."

"That's right, using an unstable plutonium isotope, PU 239—volatile and dangerous material for fuel," Miller commented excitedly, yet with a degree of enthusiasm reminiscent of a VBC team meeting.

"You envisioned a deep-space exploration ship you believed could ultimately, *safely* leave our solar system."

"It's possible, using an ion plasma stream. Plutonium will give you plenty of go. Almost limitless. But a huge risk! So many variables!" Shifting about, Miller asked bluntly, "So you think my theoretical system will work?"

"Hypothetically, it's always worked. But now, *technically,* I believe we can travel anywhere in the galaxy."

Miller, his turn to cold-blanket an idea, added, "In the galaxy? That's plenty of real estate. And this ship's still well below light speed. Nearest stars are four, five light years away. Most are hundreds."

Herriff anticipated this from his former collaborator. "Of course, it won't be a fast ship, relatively speaking, but you never envisioned a fast ship. It'll be a tedious journey to any star system. Even at best speed, I estimate Alpha Centuri twenty or twenty-five years away. But why head there? No signs of a life-sustaining planet there. Besides, such a journey was always well beyond existing hiber tech."

"Wait a sec. What are you suggesting?" Miller was already leaping several steps ahead of the former co-designer.

The Martian took his time explaining. "The six-month boundary for hiber, it no longer exists. Marsco veils itself in secrecy. But, I'm its chief researcher for deep-space travel. And Von Braun was charged with developing a spacecraft that will take a crew beyond our own planetary system. And charged with developing the hibernation system, actually 'a cryogenic stasis system,' needed for such a journey. We're right now assembling such a spaceship. Indeed, assembling a real *star*ship."

Herriff let all that sink in, although it didn't look like Miller was at all surprised. Finally, he went on, "That's why your plans were rebooted. When you left, I had them set aside until an urgent directive seven years ago ordered me to activate every project dealing with post-solar system travel, however speculative. Yours of course, as you know, wasn't that theoretical."

"So all my materials and preliminary test results that had at first been ignored are being utilized? Your staff has successfully continued along the lines I suggested?"

"Exactly. And your lines were drawn precisely. You were further along than you remember. Besides, I've the best minds in the solar system working for me. At long last your theories have been put into an actual craft."

Miller couldn't help but swell with pride.

"I've a prototype only two or three years away from completion, I should hasten to add."

"You have a starship?" Miller asked eagerly even while still disbelieving what he was hearing. "A real starship?" This was unbelievable. While he was on Earth reinventing the wheel, Herriff's team back on Mars took his dream and made it reality. He stated as fact, "You have a real starship!"

"We'll have the first fully functional dog ship in two or three years," the Martian repeated. "She's actually a standard shuttle with the new propulsion system—*yours*—wedded to it for testing purposes. Since we believe all will run A-OK, we've started construction on another larger ship, muscled up from the schematics you left, a ship that will successfully achieve solar egression. Both the prototype engine system and the new ship are under construction as we speak. The project, I should add, is aptly named the *Sirius Odyssey.*"

"Don't bullshit me, Martin."

"Walter, I'm not. I'm building a real starship."

Miller held his forehead in his hands for a long time, his finger disks resting just below the hairline. At last, he stated, "There's so much to grasp at one go. Let me ask a few questions."

"Oh, your engine theories were sound," Herriff commented, anticipating the first of a barrage. "Design was the problem, always is, making that jump from informed intuition to a practical machine. Many fine engineers filled in your intuitive leaps with actual schematics, if that's a concern."

"No, I'm concerned about the, what's it called, the *cryo-status?*" Miller didn't let on that he knew about this process through contacts with Zot on the exploration to Jupiter.

"Steerforth, you remember, my chief hibernation specialist. He's developed that system. Like you, a theorist—"

"—and one with access to Continental databanks of test results," Miller finished the sentence without emphasis.

The director of the VBC looked askance at the granger. "I assure you he worked on his own theory."

"Are you sure, Martin? It's one of those known secrets," Miller insisted. "Practically everyone knows that the Powers were experimenting with some sort of long-duration hiber. If nothing else, it gives credence to all these persistent Lost Fleet rumors."

Both men held their own council even at this crucial juncture until Herriff insisted again, "I don't deal with myth, Walter, you know that. And it's not possible for Steerforth to delve into anything Continental. I'm sure it's his fresh research."

Accepting this, Miller asked about the team who helped with the icing prototype. Grizotti was never mentioned. Nor was the Jupiter run on which, Miller knew, Zot had actually tested these experimental cryogenic protocols. Tested and upgraded and improved them beyond measure.

The Martian visitor acted as though he knew nothing of Zot's role in these extensive tests. Perhaps he didn't, Miller conceded, if the Director concerned himself solely with test results and didn't bother with the methodology of the disks-on research that proved the preliminary schematics did indeed work. The VBC was vast. Herriff wasn't on top of every FD-twitch these days, like back at the beginning. Besides, once beyond Mars orbit, the *Gagarin* would have been an entity unto itself, even more remote than Von Braun from Seattle.

Miller spoke of the engineering terrain he was most familiar with, "So, why do you need me to return? I don't understand my role if your ions are up and cooking."

"A prototype's still not a successfully working spacecraft. There are design aspects I still can't—my staff still can't—work out. And we need some help with the latest Marsco protocols. The real hitch in your original ion recovery design was the need for an even faster computer than Marsco had yet developed when you conceived your theory. Gathering subatomic particles takes programming coordination undreamed of in your day. You should be proud of that: you were waiting for Marsco to catch up to you, not the other way around."

"But if you need an engineer with those computer skills, you need Tessa, not me. I'm the wrong *Doctor* Miller. I needed her help myself. She's up to speed on all the latest cyber tech interface and synergy." The father spoke with pride, wiggling his left disks as if to imply they were malfunctioning. "Even employing the kludge consols we have at the Center, she tripled our data output and thus increased fuel efficiency nearly 6.5%."

"Don't you see? I want you both."

"*Both?* How can that be arranged? I'm essentially a Marsco non-person."

"Maybe so, but I still have Jovan pull. HQ never denies me anything or anyone I ask for; it's only denied me the truth, as I've explained. Not a prob—if I ask, it'll assign you to me."

"I can't speak for myself yet; I need some time. However, if Tessa wants to go, God knows, I won't stand in her way." A gleam came to his eyes visible even at a distance. The father thought, *She can't stay tied in knots forever, I know that.* He also momentarily thought of Zot. He then concluded, *She has to decide about Marsco itself, sooner or later.* "Who knows," he went on wistfully, "maybe she'll go on a dirigible ride with a hydrologist?"

"You are so thick at times, Walter, my boy," his friend laughed, trying to get his colleague back to the drift of his conversation. "Don't you see? We have a starship under construction. In five, six years, we'll be ready for a shakedown."

A stunned silence extended between them. Finally Miller was able to ask, "And this affects me how?"

"I give up!" The visitor threw his disk-free hands heavenward, "Here it is in black and white. One," he counted off, "I need a jockey. I'm still working on that. He's got to know celestial navigation."

"Then someone with shuttle experience, clearly."

"Affirmative. And, two," he pointed to a second disk-free finger, "I need a computer wonk/engineer hybrid to keep our ion plasma units and propulsion systems—and all their damn ROM interfaces—up and running and online. Someone who understands the engineering concepts and the computer capacities."

"That's Tessa to be sure."

Herriff nodded agreement then went on. "And lastly," he touched a third finger, "I need someone who understands the whole bailiwick to get it up and keep it running. That's you. I've the cryo specialist already: Steerforth, its designer."

"For a test run?"

"Dammit man, you are as dense as asteroid iron," the Martian chuckled, as though talking to a recalcitrant plebe that didn't get elemental thermodynamics. "Not a test run, Walter! Not a run, but an escape!"

EIGHTEEN

ESCAPE

(Seattle and Vancouver Sectors, 2096)

"Escape?"

"It's my only viable option," Captain Mei-Ling Chen insisted. "Rather *that* than go through yet another sequence of hearings."

"Out of the question!" her counsel retorted too loudly for the quiet bistro. Decorated in a midcentury style, the restaurant had a bygone-era feel; hence it was Bryce's favorite. They had eaten lunch there several times during her ordeal; tonight was their first dinner. "You've lost the first round," he lowered his voice, "almost everyone does. We'll win on appeal."

Bryce O'Neill had been appointed by HQ HR to make sure Chen received proper due process. "Like my name," he explained at their first meeting, "I'm retro." She arched an eyebrow. "You must see my role as making sure you've the best advocate possible."

He had been true to his word, although they lost their initial confrontation.

"Look," she leaned in to him at their candlelit table and whispered, "I'm accustomed to action." She gazed around the room at the quiet diners, associates mostly, with a few high-end sids comfortable in such close proximity to the power center of Marsco.

Sitting back in their booth, Chen went on, "I'm not just waiting around for Fleet to come up with its next screw-me-over decision."

The pair sat alone, but she wished they had met privately rather than at this sid-owned establishment sequestered within the most important Marsco sector. The white linen, fresh fish on the grill, and Euro wines gave their meal a romantic feel. Even so, she activated a fuzzer, discreetly placing it under her starched napkin, and only then let him reach for her hands as a gesture of support.

Chen's counsel was natty in his somewhat formal attire. His blue blazer and soft-hued tie did give him an early century veneer. His trimmed hair, triangular face, firm jaw: all suggested vigor and determination. He wore half-lens glasses on occasion when reading. Chen hadn't seen an associate with glasses ever. This anachronism gave him charm and stability; even though only in his mid-thirties, he carried it off. He made himself appear to be trustworthy rather than affected; thus far, she'd not been disappointed.

Bryce sat straight-backed against the black leather of the booth. In any situation, he was a formidable force; handsome, fit, and replete with every ubiquitous associate attribute. He was brusque, to the point, sure of his stance with her career, her safety, and their personal interest, which for appearance's sake they kept submerged in so open a place.

Chen, her own attractiveness complementing his, was dressed in a simple black sheath with matching sequined bolero she at once slipped off to reveal her pumped arms and determined posture.

He enjoyed the sparkle in her almond eyes. Candlelight, catching her jet-black hair, gave it a glossy sheen. Over the months he counseled her, she had grown it longer. Instead of the reg-knot tied behind, tonight she let it down and softened it with graceful waves that brought her face into focus. Her delicate features betrayed nothing of her intensity beneath.

After a sip of Bordeaux, he went back to business. "Look, the first go-round took four months. We've been waiting nearly five for this appeal, the second go-round. Disappear at this juncture—it's admitting guilt!"

"You're right, of course," she smiled. "I won't quit. Won't just run out."

Her initial tribunal had convened in November 2095, a year and a half after "The *Piazzi* Incident" as it came to be referred to within the halls of Fleet HQ. But by this proceeding's first gavel, the chief witnesses against her were both gone.

"Vanished without a trace?" Bryce challenged that opening morning, his words falling on the deaf ears of the judges.

"Quite a coincidence!" He conjectured that the two missing officers had more to hide than the accused and innocent Captain Chen, who willingly stood before that august judicial body to face her charges. That day and every day, she attended in full dress MAS uniform.

The two men and one woman panel of arbiters were unimpressed. The chief judge reminded Chen's advocate on that bleak November day that these unprecedented proceedings, called at Fleet's behest, were to ferret out the truth of the unfortunate events on the *Piazzi;* they weren't a trial, per se, but "an internal tribunal."

"Nuance," defense claimed, "amounts to the same." He placed a gentle hand on her uniformed shoulder.

Trial, proceedings, internal tribunal—the words whirled through her mind. Standstill and then motion forward. More postponements. Recesses. Protracted searches for witnesses instigated and frustrated, the intermittent procedures finally resuming at a grinding pace.

Even alone at dinner with Bryce in his favorite bistro, snatches of these legal tangles were alive in Chen's mind.

Throughout all the tedium, her steadfast counsel hammered at every opportunity. "How can that be? That the principal witnesses against my client have simply 'gone missing?'" No longer reading, he pulled off his half-frames for emphasis. "That has to *mean* something! *Suggest* something!" His vociferous insistence was to no avail.

He repeatedly argued that the MAS Fleet had purposely shipped out the officers in question. He implied a conspiratorial connection.

The arbiters were absolutely dismayed at the mere possibility of this. Their candor was remarkable. “We shall investigate the *possible* collusion by Fleet HQ, but our disks are tied.”

Although necessitating more delays, the panel commissioned yet another thorough records search. A seven-week adjournment later, the only items this latest exhaustive hunt found were a fragmentary duty record for Wilkes and a complete duty record for Fuentes. What created so long a delay to retrieve this info, Chen never found out. Even so the officers in question were at present crewmembers on a shuttle heading for the belt; both were in hiber, unavailable for questioning or comments.

“A most unusual shuttle,” a court officer concluded with no inflection in her voice, “since it doesn’t exist in any vessel registry file. From all evidence this alleged shuttle’s never existed in the Fleet.”

A bright tribunal intern, even though a mere two-disker, unexpectedly discovered a craft by that name on a prewar registry. With more honesty than Marsco appreciated, she concluded. “The shuttle in question appears to have once been a Continental vessel commissioned in ’54.”

“In all likelihood,” the panel conjectured, “our chief witnesses are on a black mission.”

“Jupiter?”

“Not likely, but there’s no more information forthcoming. Absolutely none.”

Chen’s halting-paced proceedings were on once more but still with no possible way to cross-examine her accusers. The dragging twists and turns of bureaucracy, the abysmal serpentine mazes of regs, with only her advocate for consolation.

Even though the witnesses themselves made no appearance, the log entries of Lieutenant Colonel Arnold Wilkes and Lieutenant Julio Fuentes were admitted in January. Also introduced for the panel’s perusal was the log from the dead hibernation specialist, Warrant Officer Jamie Maissey. It was these chronicles versus Chen, who remembered nothing about the reconfiguration of the *Piazzi* mods prior to docking separation.

"Nothing?" asked the woman judge kindly, a kindred spirit.

"Affirmative, ma'am, absolutely nothing."

However prolonged each interminable delay, once the tribunal sat down to its business, justice was swift. In sum, those absent and dead recorded voices were enough to convict her of negligence.

"C'on, I'll walk you home," Bryce insisted after their uneventful dinner, the evening her first tribunal ended. Her flat was in a high-rise near city center, close to Fleet HQ and the proceedings site. The summer air stayed warm that evening. Neither was in a hurry for their time together to end.

The streets were packed with associates moving in and out of Marsco towers: beehives lit, occupied, humming 24/7. Permit-holding sids had coffee bars and shops along the busiest streets. A vetted PRIM sold flowers from a kiosk. "How retro," counsel whispered but knew enough to buy Mei-Ling a dozen yellow roses. His act was a gesture of kind friendship. Chen assumed that once upon a time, Julio would have bought her red ones.

At the entrance to her condo block, the rental of her suite made possible because she was still receiving her MAS pay, she turned to him. "Look, you know I'm under—"

He nodded to silence her. "An I-ON-U might be anywhere."

"*Are* everywhere."

They parted with a cordial, professional embrace and handshake.

Beginning the next week, her obligatory appeal was swift but the outcome the same. The accused and counsel hardly got a byte in.

Convicted, appeal run through the process a second time, appeal denied, conclusion the same.

In the end, the judges didn't know what to do with Chen except confine her to Earth. She retained her position in the Asteroid Fleet along with her rank, although shuttle duty, even lander duty on the lunar run, was strictly banned. She was stationed indefinitely on Earth with no specific duties.

"As for the rest," her defense advocate explained later while the two ate dinner alone, this time in her flat, "you're posted to HQ but given no specific assignment. Forthwith, you'll appear on no off-planet duty roster. Moreover, everything's treated as though *nothing* happened out there. And even if nothing *did* happen, nothing *will* happen, status-wise, for you."

"I don't copy."

"No pongo at HQ knows what to do with you exactly."

Chen's face went emotionless, Bryce noted.

"A conviction of negligence's serious enough to totally ruin your career. But in the suspicious ranks of IS, negligence in the belt's hardly tantamount to treason. Internal Security's always searching for major offenders like crippling OS hackers or seditious associates forming clandestine allegiances with some violent faction or other."

"I still don't copy."

"You're a little fish in a big pond."

"I am?"

"A harmless fish while gnarly sharks circle to attack."

"So, you're implying that these rumors every associate hears are true?"

"Can't speculate on rumors."

"HFCs exploding in crowded Herriff-Grids," her piercing almond eyes met his, "Earth-side R & R facilities having their water supply laced with bio-agents. An IED near a stopline. It doesn't take much more than hanging at an associate's watering hole to hear—"

"Can't comment on idle speculations but will say categorically, 'negligence' or 'omission of shuttle safety protocols,' as serious as Luddism? No. Career truncating? Yes." He paused as they looked deeply into each other's eyes, finding and giving solace. Finally, as softly as Fuentes might explain, he reiterated, "Summary dismissal from Marsco, no. You're still an associate."

"I didn't commit treason!"

"I'm convinced of that."

"Well, I'm equally convinced that someone else did."

For the only time after Julio, she let herself slip with Bryce that night.

After the verdict, Chen was required to stay within the Seattle Sector and the contiguous West Coast areas. That restriction gave her a wide berth while HQ further contemplated what else to do with its disgraced associate. It grew into a long contemplation made complicated by MAS having to surrender her case to Internal Security for obvious reasons. (As obvious as anything ever got in the hazy workings of Seattle.)

"Really, it's trying to forget about you altogether," Bryce remarked a few weeks later. He was growing colder, more distant. He had heard the grumbling about consorting with Chen, a *persona non grata.*

"I'm not paranoid, after all," she defended herself, catching the drift of his sudden chill. "Was *only* reprimanded. The panel never suspected me of being a threat, a hostile—you told me so yourself," she reassured him. "I'm just 'incompetent,' or so their evidence concluded. There're plenty of real threats around."

Her solitary defender and once-only lover soon asked to be transferred from her case.

Chen quickly discovered she was able to travel with relative ease on any light rail or bullet unhindered so long as she stayed within her confinement area. But that area was considerable, especially running north to south because so many Marsco Sectors were linked together along the West Coast. Starting one unseasonable gray and wet August morning, she began taking ground transport, sitting in a LR coach in a depressed stupor. That first time, she rode clear out to an end-of-the-sector station, a long platform between a set of parallel tracks. Every passenger (low-end sids and PRIMS with special permits) had to detrain and pass through a checkpoint at this stopline.

Beyond this last station was the beginning of an enormous unincorporated zone, *terra incognita,* and the beginning of the never-never for Chen. Only just recently disgraced, she didn't dare attempt to pass through the checkpoint. Instead, she crossed over the platform to the inbound side. She had essentially let her sleeve brush the edge of her confinement area, but she dared not cross its stopline. In a few moments she boarded a local coach heading back to her departure point, four hours going nowhere in particular. Her day was almost a truncated Mars-Belt-Mars circuit on a vastly reduced scale.

A week later, she trekked 200 clicks on a MAG LEV and several LRs out and back in the most zigzag course she could randomly set. She sat alone at the window, her eyes fixed on nothing in particular. No one bothered her.

She purposely disdained landers, preferring instead the luxurious restored bullet lines and rattling LR system. The grounded pilot walked along cam-observed platforms, passed retina scans. She twitched ticketing kiosks, her disks still opening every portal, real and cyber. Security knew where she was 24/7, yet she moved in open comfort on chrome and glass carriages throughout the western part of the continent or in cramped tub cars under Seattle.

The whole time, her only thoughts were that her life was in shambles, her career ruined. So she rode alone, a solitary brooding figure, surely observed. No chance remained of ever making shuttle commander or ever being a lefter.

She had lost everything, with Julio's betrayal cutting the deepest.

Because of the contiguous nature of Marsco Sectors, she made one trip south to Portland and then another all the way to Silicon. Without hindrance, she spent a week at Marsco's Monterey Rec Area, speeding there on a crowded bullet with scores of space crews on leave. She walked the beaches alone, hiked the windy bluffs alone, and ate alone. She passed up several eager liaison offers from other associates; every hookup invitation that presented itself, she declined.

In the warmth of that autumn's harvest, with special permission she traveled to Winnipeg, well beyond her confinement area, traveling through the great tracks of Marsco's breadbasket under Food Consortium cultivation. To secure her travel permit, she offered Security no explanation; none was asked. She traveled, was followed, did nothing unusual, and returned the exact nano, as authorized.

She still drew MAS on-planet pay. Yet, as one of her watchers noted, she spent next to nothing, racking up MMUs at a phenomenal rate like an iceman when a shuttle crew's hibered.

But during these four months of aimless and ceaseless travel, an escape plan began to coalesce.

The first comprehensive Security report concluded in part, "Captain Mei-Ling Chen spends her days wandering listlessly, a defeated, broken pilot tarnished by her own negligence. She knows she shall never again enter space; that seems punishment enough."

The third comprehensive report at year's end stated factually, "Captain Chen's quotidian actions are harmless. She does nothing out of the ordinary. In her off-duty uniform, she always looks straight ahead, sure of her direction and unconcerned about the crowd. She retains an officer's mien and demeanor."

Off the record, her watchers commented that such a prime HH GAS-free ass was going to waste. They gave her call signs. *Sister Chastity. Retro-Virgin. The Ice Bitch.*

That spring, Report Number Seven ran in part, "On the trains and in the stations, on the street outside her own small flat, Chen speaks with only a few associates and sids and an occasional PRIM. On the whole, she converses with no one out of the ordinary, certainly to no known or suspected Ludds."

Follow-up Report Number Eleven added, "She makes no new friends. She takes on no new lovers."

Report Number Sixteen concluded, "Too many hostiles to bother with this solitary grounded jockey."

Her watchers grew increasingly bored with the incessantly dull routine of her vacuous life. Careers stagnated watching her stagnated career. All that summer, suspected Ludd sympathizers siphoned off Security's attention and focus.

"Bryce?"

"My God, if this's traced!"

"Chill, it's a throw-away cell. Look, two things—*don't hang up!*"

He acted calm so his wife wouldn't grow suspicious at the late call.

"I need an Enfield. I need a doctor—"

"You're *not?*"

"Not that kind—*that* kind, if you catch."

"Oh, yes, *that* kind of finality."

"Roger that. Sure you'll know how to get me that intel without *it* being traced." She hung up.

Three weeks later, he sent a cryptic note: "Alves Leather Goods, Vancouver Sector. Doc Chamberlain, Sac City—somewhere. Contact at Pacific Suites."

Vancouver was rainy when Chen arrived late one November morning almost a year from the opening of her first hearing. From the bullet terminal, she rode a jitney throughout the subsidiary.

The harbor was to her right, the bay far over to her left, the park ahead in the distance. She seemed aimless, moving with no discernable goal in mind, passing through Yaletown, Gastown, and finally arriving back at Chinatown near the terminal.

Here, she set out on foot, milling around at stops, feeling a comfort she had not felt in years. Small businesses sold jade and silk to associates like she was and still is; business seemed brisk even in the cold afternoon. She stopped to eat, joining the thinning crowd of sids and employed PRIMS who savored bowls of noodles but kept their distance from the obvious associate.

When it was time to go, she let several trams proceed before she climbed on, seeming like she had no particular destination in mind. Somewhere off in the center of the Vancouver Sector was her target.

Stepping from a tram, she once more walked along crowded, wet streets toward the heart of the sector. Associates were everywhere, and thus the sids here prospered as the Seattle-Vancouver corridor expanded. Wherever she turned, Mei-Ling saw display windows brimming with quality goods, packed trams running on time, a functioning Herriff-Grid above. Hustling foot traffic lined the streets. No PRIMS begged—the only PRIMS she saw were diligently utilized by sids just as an associate would expect. It was almost pleasant, almost prewar.

Alves Leather Goods was easy enough to find, tucked into one of the ground floor showrooms off the hotel's atrium. The restored high-rise hotel was a museum piece of 19th century empire-building splendor, salvaged from the ravages of time by Marsco. The marble was as polished as every mirror. The chandeliers sparkled for associates as brilliantly as they had for diplomats and CEOs of the past millennium. The concierge stood as elegant as any of his forbearers, replete with a pet lobby dog to greet associates and high-end sid visitors alike.

Somewhere in this sid-owned splendor right under the nose of Security was a clandestine supplier of prohibited Enfield clones. The irony wasn't lost on Chen: a sid-run establishment that catered to associates as the cover for the black market.

Alves himself greeted the woman as she entered through the automatic glass doors. For his part, he was dressed with prewar dash: dark brown woolen slacks with a razor crease, burnt russet blazer, a muted orange and rich olive green ascot. He moved with all the ingratiating gestures of a well-placed sid. Soft lighting and music created an inviting aura for all who entered his posh showroom. His ways dictated their conversation as he glided her to a rack of fine-grain leather and wool skirts.

"Easy figure to grace," he oozed, pulling out one cut shorter than the next. "Try these three."

"I'm really not exactly looking for a skirt."

Moving aside, Alves motioned gracefully to racks of handmade supple jackets, several plain but a few tooled with frilled designs. "And this one—I call it 'a coat of many colors.'" He hummed a few bars of an old show tune.

The garment hung below her knees. Unlike the others, it was sown from several types and cures of leathers, creating a colorful flame design. From the hem, fire reached up her back, fanning to the shoulders and partly down the arms. "Rather apocalyptic," Mei-Ling smirked.

Alves produced a smile to seem amused.

The associate thought back to the inception of her Marsco world: the burning was too familiar to wear. Besides, she never wanted to stand out in any way.

Removing the coat, she stood at the rack of skirts again, as though musing about the shortest black one. "I'm really interested; you carry them I'm told—"

"Yes, Madam?"

Chen leaned in to him, their faces almost touching. Every sid was accustomed to an odd request now and again, even from an associate. Hers was the most startling in a while. “An Enfield,” she whispered. “A clone will do—with comp specs. Nothing traceable.”

Without any noticeable change in demeanor, he reached into a rack, pulling out a skirt so large she could step through it. “This’s a fine leather, cured on an island north of here. Handcrafted—totally PRIM-labor free.”

Holding so large a garment made them both grin at the absurdity of the whole situation.

“Clearly, I’ve no such merchandise, my dear,” the shop owner finally replied, putting the hanger back smoothly, betraying none of his internal agitation at her suggestion.

“My source was conclusive.”

He continued to slide hangers along the bar, listening but intent on finding what suited her perfectly.

“I’m not Security.”

“I never suspected—but such a request’ll bring those rat bastards—” He pulled up sharply, looked around his own exclusive showroom suspiciously, and moved on, ferreting out her exact skirt.

“Why I need one’s my own business,” she whispered, confiding too much. “But getting one will never involve you—if something goes—well, you can imagine. A woman can’t be too careful alone.”

“An associate?” It dawned on him he was dealing with one on the lam. Her vulnerability became *his* security. “So, we need to trust each other,” he finally concluded.

“I do like this one,” Chen smiled, picking up that black mini a third time.

“Excellent choice,” he concurred, “wonderfully supple leather.” He led the way to a changing room where she slipped into the garment.

“Fits stunningly,” he commented as she stood before a three-way mirror.

Would a man ever admire me again?

As that thought faded, she heard him say under his breath, "My son owns a small shop, leather goods as well. But he's less interested in, shall we say, *a Marsco connection.* Trying an Indie life even though still in this very subsidiary!"

"You know youth these days."

"Idealistic, I know."

"Where?"

"He's in Yaletown; it's not far. But too late to go there tonight. Try tomorrow if you don't like the selection here."

"But I like this one—I'll take it—but I'll look in on him tomorrow."

"Yes, you'll be quite safe walking there in the morning. Not now, not this late without, well, an associate after dark there, *without* what you're looking for—if you catch."

Chen twitched his register. He had a disk-record of her sale, thus more than enough info to ruin the officer should her visit turn sour.

Vulnerability and trust.

Mei-Ling spent the night alone in that very hotel tower. Her room was as fine as the luxurious polished atrium below suggested. It was as though she had stepped back a century to a long-gone world; even a chocolate mint graced her pillow.

Her windows, just below penthouse-level, afforded her a north view of the snow-capped hills beyond the sector's peninsula. Under those hills along the inlet, lights burned all night, sure signs of Marsco prosperity spilling over into the neighboring subsidiary.

Scores of HFCs moved through the towering buildings closest to hers. Crowds sought out evening entertainment along the streets. From her perch, the disgraced associate witnessed Marsco at its finest.

Before going to bed, Chen looked at today's purchases. Alves had even packed a cachet of jasmine within the box. The black skirt was indeed as finely made as the sid had assured her. It accentuated her perfectly but was totally useless. Wherever she was going, she wouldn't need this.

Earlier in Chinatown, she had bought two silk gowns with matching wraps, one bright red and the other midnight blue, lingerie as fine as any associate's. Standing before a mirror, her mind raced with memories of Julio. Up until hiber on the *Piazzi,* his was the best, the truest love she had ever experienced; she sensed she would never know such passion again.

In the end, she thought about wearing the red gown to bed but opted for a grey tee. Holding a pillow to her chest, she closed her eyes to the omnipresent Marsco luxury circling around and through her hotel tower and finally drifted off to sleep.

It was nearly ten when she left her hotel in a jitney heading toward the large park. From there she walked along a busy street. Half an hour later, she doubled back on herself to make sure she wasn't followed, then set off in earnest. It didn't take her long.

Down a cul-de-sac near another smaller park, dozens of stores bustled with sid customers. At the corner, an ice cream and sweets shop invited the locals in. Along the blind street, dozens of small establishments offered this and that hard to find, one of a kind. The sidewalk—patched but in good shape—met a set of brick steps going up the LR embankment that closed off the road. At that far end, in what had been a turning circle, a cargo-HFC (once Marsco, now sid-owned) hovered, set down, unloaded, and then rose skyward. All signs of normalcy. Her target was hidden in plain sight.

The door's lettering was neat and succinct: "Alves Leather Goods." As she entered, a buzzer alerted those in the back. No one was visible. Inside the small shop, half the size of the father's, Chen was met with rows of coats and handbags at the front with belts and heavy work aprons at the back. All the goods were designed for practicality and use, nothing like Alves Senior last night. All the displays were jammed in. No mannequins were graced with skirts or leather jackets. It was a practical, Indie establishment with no embellishments to induce associates to purchase merchandise.

Near the door, a simple printed sign read, "Everything handmade by sid labor."

"Yes?" a voice asked from a second room attached to the front showroom by an arch. The man still didn't show himself.

"Looking for a jacket," was all Chen gave away.

"Leather?"

"Of course—and handmade by sid labor." The voice didn't respond and obviously didn't have a sense of humor. Chen added, "I've ready tokens."

A lanky young man stepped forward. He wore his own handiwork, a visor not so much to protect his eyes than to hold back his long, tawny hair. Over a tie-dyed shirt, he had a tooled vest with rivets holding down strips of leather. He looked every inch an Indie with no time for anyone or anything Marsco.

Chen took a hard look at the lettering on his visor: "Live free or die." *What century do you inhabit?* the associate cynically asked herself.

Meanwhile, from the third room in back, a large man joined them by stepping through a beaded curtain. He looked like a humungous PRIM with Asian or Polynesian features, wearing a mullet. His hair in front was bleached platinum blond while at the back it hung black down beyond his shoulders, jet-black like Chen's. His girth was three times the size of his comrade's. He also had on tie-dye, but his gut was visible, his navel open like a second mouth demanding to be fed. He wore a pair of dark glasses as though he just stepped out of bright sunshine. From the storefront's third room, Chen heard sitar music and muffled voices, probably women and children.

As she came through the arch, the odor of leather gave way to the heavy scent of incense. The associate had never seen such a defiant pair, acting as though Divestiture and the Wars hadn't happened, as though Marsco wasn't somewhere just around the corner. But she was counting on that defiance if they would trust her.

Before she spoke, humongo stated, "She's clean. No weapons, nothing but disks."

So they're assuming I'm Marsco, she realized, *and using a pretty damn sophisticated scan system.*

Neither man moved or changed his blank expression.

"Look, you're either selling goods here or not."

"Either way, what if?"

"I've ready tokens." She motioned to a small purse at her side.

"It's still, 'What if?'"

"Look, guys, if I were Security, I'd be armed and you'd be splattered. Troopers don't ask questions of prats like you." She had never served with S & H, but she knew their routine.

"Tell us," the fat one said with his eyes hidden, both his mouths expressionless.

"The days of evidence, of trial—you're too young," she shrugged, "you don't remember all that."

"Shit," the little one spit out, "y'here to bullshit ur what?" He let his eyes dart to his companion. They shared a grin.

Not a chance, runt, Chen reassured herself. *It's tokens only with you two, not buying anything like that. Not from you.* "Since you're being blunt; I'll be blunt. I hear you sell leths—clones prob, but I'll take one. My pref's for a 9 mm."

Their grins switched back to blankness. The fat one started to move, but the runt held his arm. "Look, bitch, I ain't selling that shit. Marsco's got regs—"

"And mean-ass dawgs for troopers," Chen shot, playing their game, "that'll eat your guts just as soon as piss on you."

"As if you ain't."

"If I am, your boney and his fat ass would be fried in a nano. Those in the next room, too." The men leaned that way, protective of those hidden behind. "Now, we can play these

I'm-buffer-than-your-mother's-ass games, or you can sell me what I need." Neither moved. "Look, holes, if I walk without, Security'll be busting in so damn fast, you won't know what the fuck hit you."

Perhaps too truthfully, the boney one let down a bit, "Oh, I know. Seen shit happen." His head motioned over Chen's shoulder into the cul-de-sac. "Just out there."

"Sid life's fine," she argued, not pleading, just pointing out the obvious. "Imagine getting caught in a lander-sweep. PRIMification's never pretty."

The slender one inadvertently looked at the back of his scar-free left hand; nothing was guaranteed in his world, not even that. His status could be changed in a blink; he knew it.

The sids glanced at each other once more. "What's your assurance no troopers'll come after?"

"You'll have the goods on me—it's mutual trust or mutual destruction."

"How fuckin' retro," the skinny one unfortunately noted.

A teenager holding a baby came through the beaded curtain. She looked SoAm or possibly Med.

How like Marsco, Chen thought. *Lots of continental rep here.* The baby seemed to be the skinny one's. From under a red bandana, the girl's black hair fell down to her waist. Her skirt was panels of denim alternated with leather—a particular style several generations old. She hissed something the young man understood but Chen didn't.

"She says she wants you outta here."

"Fine, sell me that clone, and I'll be gone."

No one moved, distrust in the room palpable. Finally, Chen made up her mind. "Don't worry about Security," she softened. "They've given up watching me." She handed a ten-token to the reluctant young woman. "Here. It's A-OK. For the child," Mei-Ling explained.

Troopers threw stun grenades not tokens, the girl knew. She whispered at Alves Junior a second time.

"You sure?" he answered back softly in English this time. As the door buzzer sounded, he yelled at the disappearing associate, "Wait!"

In a boarded-up storefront next door, the two sids opened a plastic storage tub marked "Discards." Under some clean rags and tooled scraps, the leather maker showed the associate six clone sidearms. Four were smaller 7.6 mm models, easy to conceal. He urged her to try one of those. "It'll fit your hand nice," he noted.

Never one to accept limits, Chen took up one of the two 9 mms, the black matte model. She then took up the nickel piece, holding it in her right hand, then switching, weighing them both, feeling their grips as she aimed off into the distance at no particular target. "Disk locked?"

"Lever safety switch," Alves explained. "All the usual lasers for targeting but no disks necessary."

"Like a standard issue without twitching," Chen concluded under her breath.

"Plus," the humongo one added, "without disks, it's free from tracing."

"All the advantages of a Marsco weapon, none of the disadvantages," the young man stated in a voice and manner quiet similar to his respectable father.

"Clip?"

"Usual twenty for the 9 mm. Aerosol supply holds at least 100 shots."

Chen tripped the charger. A low hissing sound came from the grip as the firing chamber filled. The weapon pinged to acknowledge no projectiles were loaded in it. "Three bursts?"

"Or single shot, yes, like any M-co model," the larger man replied just like any sales rep eager to move his goods along.

"A four-burst model came out late last year," the other one stated knowledgeably, "but they still tend to jam." It was news to

Chen, although she took the info in without changing her expression. "My suppliers haven't worked the kinks out yet—as you can imagine, can't openly experiment with them."

The associate was pleased with the black clone—she would have picked it from among many—but to ask questions about its origin would only raise more suspicion that she was Security. Instead she asked where she could try it out.

"Can't near here—you'll have to trust *me* it works." The pair was locked in that vicious cycle once more because there was no way to test the weapon.

Finally, Chen asked a second question, "How much?"

"Two-twenty-five, but that'll give you two propellant cylinders—I'll put one in fresh—and 100 heads in clips." Not exactly an arsenal but more than enough for protection.

The fat man spoke once more, "Jacket?"

"Well, *that* was a dodge," Chen smiled, still coming to know the weapon as hers.

"No, he means we'll also sell you a holster."

The holster was a leather jacket with a hidden pocket under the left arm for the clone. "Slips into a pouch that's lined to deaden any surveillance scans. You'll walk as if—" His shrug let her know the scene.

He had three in her size, tan, black, or seal brown. "Leather's quite supple. Webbing's sown under the lining so it rides smooth, no tugging, bunching or sagging." It might hang on a rack alongside his father's goods and be right at home. He spoke with familial pride for his product. The young man may have bought that clone but made the garment himself, working out the details of hiding the concealing holster within it.

This attribute held true when he hand-stitched some lining at her left wrist that hung wrong. Slipping on a sewing thimble and bending to see the details in the shop's light, he looked more and more like his father at work. Chen noticed that his hands had brown stains from curing leather but had no PRIM-disk scar.

A toddler came and stood next to him, admiring his father's delicate work close up. He tapped the boy's head gently. Delighted, the child turned to Mei-Ling and grinned with happiness.

Chen went down on a knee with her arms open. "May I?" the associate asked the mother.

The child didn't know which way to turn, back toward his parents and sibling or into the open arms of the stranger. His mother urged him in whispers Chen didn't understand. Slowly the boy moved toward the waiting woman. "It's okay," she assured him, "I won't bite."

The reluctant boy finally changed his shy ways and jumped to the associate with open arms. "Pick 'im up," he said in a sing-song way.

His parents smiled as his father explained, "He thinks 'pick him up' is a command we have to obey."

Chen rose with the boy, humming and dancing a few steps while he giggled. In the end, he nestled his head into her neck, his arms around her. She stopped abruptly when the thought hit her, *Might've been ours had Julio and I lived in another world and another time.*

In the end, the tanner cut the label from the jacket; this final act made sure Alves Leather Goods remained invisible, impossible to trace.

NINETEEN

THE CAGE ROOM

(Sac City Sid, January 2097)

Make today as mundane as any other, Mei-Ling Chen willed herself.

Wrapped in seal-brown leather that clearly suggested importance—low-end sids shied away—Chen blended in with the higher-end ones around her. Although rare for anyone non-Marsco to be so well disked, it wasn't uncommon. Her status didn't create attention on a monitor screen.

After eight hours of second-class MAG LEV, she calmly exited the express at the North Bay Subsidiary well above Silicon. She left behind the chrome and marble Marsco side of the station and headed for the minimally repaired sid side.

Once a shuttle's out of the belt, she reminded herself, *the demarcation in space is PNR—Point of No Return.*

In the antiquated part of the station, she waited for a local. As she found a seat in a crowded car, she realized she was leaving Marsco behind, crossing a stopline as the train jerked out of the station. She ended up at a second transfer point and stepped onto a dilapidated inter-city line.

Every train she boarded was worse than the last and more and more jammed. Eventually, her last train deposited her at the Sac City Sid.

A thick blanket of fog made the January afternoon dark gray. Beads of moisture stood on any exposed metal. The fog dampened sounds. The detraining passengers up and down the platform blended into the single mass of sids and PRIMS as they herded toward the exit.

The fleeing officer moved amid the jostling throng. She planned on this chaos, counted on this bedlam. She walked, a palm unit to her face, as though talking to a colleague, a spouse, a child. The cam-operator who made her digital comparison found her an associate in good standing. Computers are reservoirs of junk. She was safe in the clutter of her files and Marsco's labyrinth of intel. Being non-hostile, Security hadn't reprogrammed anything about her.

At the gate separating the terminal building from the platforms, Chen made her way amid the teeming flow. A sid attendant kept the PRIMS moving along, but his actions were lax. As she approached his gate in the rusty metal fence, alarms sounded as the associate's FDs overloaded the e-spection scan.

"You're acting like I'm some diskless PRIM," Chen shouted with an edge.

When the gate attendant turned, he was confronted with a raised right hand, brimming with implants. As he hesitated, she began removing the left glove, upping the ante. The sid might snub a well-disked wallah; he'd dare not a lefter.

Her bluff worked. The flustered one-disker caved, erring on the side of the associate. He shouted orders for the pushing PRIMS to stop, and Chen stepped through the sensor system. A surveillance cam caught the whole action, unconcerned about a single associate in a sea of non-Marsco. Although scrutinized, she was free.

The attendant let the PRIM crowd restart its rush through his gate. He tried to watch the woman as she stepped away, but she was soon lost in the commotion. *I seen so many wallahs here lately, sumpthing must be up,* he thought, before returning to his duties. He then thought it best not to think at all. His eyes glazed as the monotonous routine was reestablished.

Carrying just a shoulder bag so she didn't look like someone prepared to stay long, Chen moved beyond the terminal. Where she expected to find a line of eager jitneys, the woman found none. *Nothing like Vancouver,* she acknowledged but quickly concluded, *so much the better.* She walked on into the ashen afternoon, needing only to go a dozen blocks through the old city center to reach the Pacific Suites.

For the first few blocks, most of the ground-floor windows were boarded up. Only foot and bike traffic went along the wide streets, moving aside for a battered trolley that sparked and rattled by. The crowd did the same as an Auxxie rover turned down the street.

"Check her, mate," a PRIM hissed to his companion when he saw Chen. Her stylish jacket, her determined pace, her bearing sent caution throughout those who passed by her.

"Recon for a lander sweep, y'think?" replied the second PRIM.

"Perfect place f'it," warned the first. The crowds moved along a cracked sidewalk across the street from a whole block that was being dismantled by PRIM gangs who still toiled even in the dying light. One corner was clear enough of rubble to support a lander whisking in with Auxxies and troopers to sweep the street clean.

Sensing this mounting tension as PRIMS and sids moved back to make a path for her, Chen kept on her course. *Sure signs of unrest,* she concluded. *Perhaps here's not so secure after all.*

Serving in space for years, she'd been led to believe that all subsidiaries were thriving, growing as Marsco grew, blooming as Marsco flourished. No HQ bulletin was farther from the truth. Several weeks back, Vancouver had seemed alive. Everything here suggested decay, further abandonment. Suspicion and wariness of Marsco.

The skeletal remains of burned-out vehicles convinced the associate that IEDs had recently exploded right here, as though this locale were an active hot zone. Strings of Enfield bursts dotted the adjacent buildings. The pilot wouldn't have been surprised to find herself caught up in a sudden Security sweep. She anguished as these thoughts brought up what Julio must have endured in the S & H for five torturous years.

She squeezed her left arm against the hidden Enfield; it was all that mattered now. She went on cautious, careful at every turn.

Just beyond the crumbling remains of several buildings, the associate spotted the faded and patched awning that proclaimed itself as the Pacific Suites. Although standing more than twenty stories, lights from its windows showed only the first five were in use.

A final few hurried steps brought Chen to the atrium of a once-posh hotel. Personal danger was worth the risk for anonymity, but the highly trained officer reached under her coat. It muffled the reassuring hiss of charging. Knowing that, she grew confident in her choice.

A handful of chairs were off to the side, but nothing invited the associate to sit a moment. What had been two-story-high windows to bring light into this once-elegant lobby were boarded up; they would have given little light in the clinging fog outside anyway. No businesses operated from the row of lobby shops. Whatever it had once been, the Suites had become little more than a flophouse. It didn't seem to have any wasted toke-heads, but its neighbors seemed to.

At the far end, steel bars enclosed what had previously been an open reception desk. There a greasy-faced old man in a cobbled-together cage watched her enter the otherwise empty, dim lobby. The old man put down his personal viewer although its screen continued to play, giving the cage a slight blue cast. It was explicit porn.

Like Chen, the man had obvious Asian features. But she focused on his PRIM-status more than anything else. Associate habits die hard; clearly his left hand should have been disked but wasn't.

"I need to stay for one night. Just me." She spoke with rigid pleasantry.

The oily face grinned with yellow teeth. "Room? No Marsco room here, missy."

In exasperation, she responded, "Why *Marsco?*"

They both looked at each other, seeing what was important in this world, not noting their distinct similarities. They reached the same conclusion, *Well, isn't it obvious?*

Chen continued, "Regardless of my alleged status, I want a single night."

"Sure? Sure, missy M'co, sure what y'wanna?" He grinned, his eyes darting between hers and the glowing screen at his left.

The lift had long since ceased operation, so Chen walked up three flights to her floor. On opposite sides of the landing were doors labeled *mens* and *womens.* Low murmurs emanated from the crowded room behind the men's sign. The other was quiet.

Carefully, the associate opened a door to find a chamber filled with thirty sleeping cages. They stood in five rows, each with two triple units standing back to back. Each cage was not much larger than a cadet bunk, separated from the one above by only a meter and a half. They all had locking doors through which the sleeper crawled.

One-night prison cells, the associate thought, *but that's all I need.*

"You wantin' anythin', hon?" a flat voice asked. "Du says you wuz cumin' up." A heavy woman sat in a small cluttered office to the left. "I'm Joanna," the room's matron offered without getting up, "and cun git you anythin' you need."

Chen nodded her acknowledgment, taking her bag off her shoulder.

"Don't need no locker, it looks." These lined one wall. "I cun sell y'a clean towel 'n soap for hot showers down ta'hall, all only a quarter unit."

The room was partially lit from a few bare bulbs. Paint peeled from the walls that once surrounded a conference room. Several cages were already filled. "Most clients're sids workin' 'n this area fur a week 'r so, then travel home to bedder lodgin's."

Chen hated to think of what *better* meant outside of Marsco auspices; from what she'd seen thus far, it wasn't promising.

A dozen bunks had a lived-in look rather than just the bare mattress, blanket, and clip lamp. Joanna whispered an apology, "A few privil'g'd PRIMS (workin' fur M'cos station'd here 'r a few best-off sids) they rents here, as long as they paid up 'n show no sign of Neo-Con. But give 'em no mind."

In several occupied cages around the room, the associate saw PRIM-disk glowing green. But to Chen, the distinction between sids and PRIMS had lost all contrast in this locale.

"Make sure y'pack up ev'thing tamarrah. Be out by eight—sharp!"

"0800, roger! No prob," the traveler assured the matron.

The other tenants in and out of their cages viewed the newcomer with suspicion. She was too Marsco, too polished for here. The PRIMS and sids checking her out assumed rightly she was disked, else why keep gloves over her hands?

For Chen, the night was her first time among so many PRIMS and low-end sids. She finally understood what Fuentes had to put up with, protecting these type of women from elements out to destroy the stability of their Marsco world. Everything here kept Julio in her mind.

For a moment, she paused, reluctant to pick a bunk, reluctant to enter farther into the ranks of cages. She hesitated about what to do with her gloves and with her leather jacket. *Act, I must act,* she ordered herself forward. *I'm still Marsco enough for my own protection here.*

At the far end, Chen found a relatively clean restroom. Its warm water gave an aura of sanitation, although only half the stalls worked. Fortunately, she was alone; the blue-green fingertips of her right hand were unmistakable.

After cleaning up, the associate locked her bag away in a bunk along the north wall. She was still restless and wanted night air before trying to sleep.

In the cage below hers, a child was curled up in a tattered blanket. The nine-year-old was ragged, dressed in soiled clothes. Her curly hair clung to her dirty face. Waking suddenly, she whispered, "Daddy?"

"No, honey," replied Chen softly.

The child's face was pale from exhaustion and hunger. She brushed aside her hair to reveal blue eyes and a bruised cheek. Her bare arms showed a bracelet of purple marks.

The associate questioned, "How'd your dad lock you in here?"

"He hadda dat woman do it." The girl pointed across the room.

"No, I mean, *why* did he?"

"He needdas be out alone. He sayz dat hers will brung me sum food."

The associate glanced over at Joanna, who shrugged; she'd nothing for someone else's kid. Chen withdrew a ration pack from her kit and offered it to the locked-in girl through the cage wire.

The child threw herself away from the package into the furthest corner. "Wuz's that?" She distrusted everyone Marsco, Chen realized. Although out of uniform, her status was not easily dispelled.

"Food for a shuttle crew. Ever hear of a Marsco shuttle?"

"M-co h'ar them basz'ards that done *all this,*" she hissed, obviously repeating an adult characterization. She shivered in fear.

That might be true, thought Chen, *but no associate'd lock up their own.* "It's good," she pleaded, smelling the aseptic wrap. "Try it, you'll like. Here, I'll start tearing it for you. You can rip open the rest. Rub the large pouch and it warms up." She read the MRE pack. "Chilli-mac! You like that?" She smiled encouragement. "Be good and eat your chocolate last." She pushed the pack through a wide hole in the mesh and let it fall onto the stained blanket.

Already, Chen had had plenty of the cage room.

In the stairwell, she overheard hushed voices talking one landing below. The officer was glad her clone was fully charged if needed.

A woman whispered in a husky tone, "Ya needsa yer freedom—lit her go."

"But, she'z m'daughter," a man insisted.

"Yer ain't sure of that. Y'*wuz* away a'lot! Lotz!"

"'Un thay'll takes gud car offa her, won't thay?"

"Course! An' give ya a doz'n units to boot."

As Chen descended past the pair, they looked at her with wariness but no remorse. In the dim light, the associate saw them embracing. They looked young, like the sids in Vancouver but unkempt and desperate. Their hands didn't glow.

Once Chen passed, the anxious woman resumed, "N' th'girls ge' treated real gud. Men ain't ne'er hurt them."

"I don't wanna nobudy to hurt her—I jus' cain't keeps her no moe," he stated defensively.

"I unnerstan'. I'm shore sh'll do real gud—men'll luv her."

Down at the first floor, Chen stopped before entering the lobby. It wasn't fear that shortened her breath; it was revulsion. She fully comprehended the veiled conversation. She thought of Marsco, how it worked feverishly to make that sort of despicable action impossible. Even so, the trade continued, flourished, festered in unsupervised locales like this one.

You'd never hear that among associates, she insisted, protecting her image of Marsco. *Even those leather-selling sids up in Vancouver would never do that.*

Her associate's commitment made her realize that she might be better off returning to Seattle. A grounded MAS pilot's life was preferable to anything offered here. And at least in *that* world, some semblance of decency remained. Her hesitation soon passed. No, she concluded, it was better to live as she wanted than in Marsco's gilded cage.

The officer found the clerk still watching the same porn. As earlier, she needed to compete with the glowing screen for his full attention.

"Tomorrow I need to meet a man called Chamberlain," she began in a low voice. "I believe he's hard to find, unless he wants to be found." Chen put four MMU tokens on the counter, twice what she given over for her bunk.

The Marsco monetary units caught his undivided attention. "Yes, missy, hem much diff'cult t'find. More diff'cult thun y'know," he stated with a deep philosophical look.

"But I've been told that folks here at the Suites *can* find him." She slid another token through the bars at the now-dutiful clerk.

"Ma'be find hem, missy-wallah, ma'be not." He was mesmerized by the tokens but knew how to pull the line just right when taut.

Chen lifted her palm slightly from the countertop to reveal six more shinning units. As tokens, and not debit strips, they were easily spent and impossible to trace. "Not until I know you'll help me find Chamberlain."

"Far—far frum here, missy. But I git yu'a hover. Quick skim. But missy, them six fir me, and a doz more—a'leas'—fur jockey and trip out."

"Arrange it," she ordered. "And leave the payment to me."

The associate left the lobby, heading away from the direction she had first come. Here a few shops and restaurants were still open. Their dirty look and greasy smell didn't tempt her enough to enter. Beyond the one lit strip, Chen found rows of other closed businesses. Only there did the woman find a milling crowd.

At first the officer joined them, relieved to find anything remotely resembling the life she knew. But soon she realized why this storefront attracted all the attention.

A nightclub operated there, selling home-distilled hooch and offering rave action in its dark, cavernous interior. Many common sids seemed to be enjoying themselves as they went in and out as couples or separate gangs of shiftless young men and women. The pilot even saw a few off-duty associates entering.

Next to the club's doorway, several skanks stood, girls the same age as the Vancouver mother. Even in the cold night, they showed legs, arms, shoulders. Their bling sparkled in the darkness.

This shit still, the associate thought, not from a puritanical stance but a hygienic one. *We're not post-AIDS in our HH GAS gone-wild world.*

The antics of the hookers attracted a dozen sids and a smattering of men who could only be associates. Chen knew from their close-cropped hair that some potential clients were off-duty Security personnel.

What bloody crap, she thought. *Bust them if they cross a stopline, yet frequent them here.*

The lone woman walked aimlessly for nearly an hour. Most places she passed looked totally deserted more than just closed down for the night.

From her cyber recce before escaping Seattle, Chen knew that just north of city center, a part of this subsidiary was emerging from its own rubble, beginning to flourish as scattered industries reopened. That prospering section had consistent electricity, running water, and more regular food distribution. Nothing on the Net had suggested that here, near city center, it wasn't doing likewise. But, the quarter she just walked through, although technically in the same subsidiary, resembled a longstanding unincorporated zone.

Moving on, Chen hoped that this Chamberlain was far from here.

"Shit!" someone shouted from a darkened doorway of an abandoned building.

The associate had her clone leveled in an instant; its laser designator pulsing a red dot on the chest of the first PRIM huddled at her feet.

"Troopers! Tol' ya dey're gitting reddy for undder fuckin' sweep!"

A dozen PRIMS were sprawled up the half flight of steps that led to the front door, their disks glowing faintly in the dark. How many were inside she didn't know. This group looked like two families that felt better protected here than amid the larger group inside.

At least some PRIMS take care of their own, the associate concluded. With that, she clicked off her laser and lowered the clone. "I'm not with Security," she announced and left.

As she walked on, Chen sensed this subsidiary was being PRIM-ified, reduced back to full-zone status. She shuddered. Associate born, Academy trained, she'd never ventured down such uncharted streets. Yet, her path was taking her out of Marsco safekeeping and into patrol districts like these.

Turning toward her lodging, she fortified herself with the thought, *One night. I need just one night, and then with Chamberlain's help, I'm free.*

“Wan somb-thing, wallah,” a gruff voice in shadowy doorway startled her. Instinctively she reached into her jacket but didn’t pull out her clone this time. The speaker stayed motionless. “Gots boyz. You wans some big-big tonight?” A sneer emanated from the shadows as the speaker gestured rhythmically at her.

“Yo! M’co!” Another guttural voice spoke up, “No one knows ya’re here, right? Cum ’un enjoy hot ass my place—no one tell.” Crude snickering followed.

“Maybe missy wanna girl?” the first voice continued snidely to his friendly competitor.

“We gotta girlz,” came the insistent reply. “Gotta girlz, gotta boyz. Licky yur pussy!”

After several quick blocks, Chen took the stairs two at a time and rushed into the cage room. Most cots were now filled with sleepers exhausted from their day’s labors. Some older women—mothers, aunts, sisters—crashed out with two or three small kids in one bunk, protecting them behind locked wire mesh.

Joanna sat in her small office, its yellow light the only one in the larger room. She was too tired even to feign interest.

When Chen reached her bunk, she found the one below empty. Discarded food wrappers remained behind on the grimy mattress.

Joanna never looked up.

TWENTY

SIGN OF THE TIMES

(Miller's Grange, January 2097)

"Tule fog, that's what it's called," Tessa Miller explained stiffly to Anthony Grizotti as they looked out onto the dark, mist-shrouded gardens of her father's grange. "Sac City's famous for it."

"I can name a few other things it's infamous for," the hiberman added, trying to keep their icy conversation going.

The pair stood at a window of the great room looking into the grey night. Fog had risen from the nearby river sloughs, blocking any signs of the stars. The closest neighbor's, whose house and outbuildings stood on a rise to the south, was also lost in the woolen mist.

Inside Miller's, Zot had found warmth and two glowing fires at opposite ends of the house, one behind him where Miller often spoke with his guests and the other down a long hallway in the dining room off the kitchen. But the warmth of fires didn't concern Zot; he was caught in Tessa's coldness.

After silently watching the night, they sat on opposite sides of the inviting hearth. How often Miller sat here discussing the Marsco world with other companions, the hiberman could only guess. Four large mismatched chairs circling the fire invited comradeship and amiable debate. Not so tonight.

Although they faced one another, an awkwardness separated them. The associates sat immobile in self-conscious stiffness. After not seeing each other for so long, they both had independently resolved to maintain a reserved distance until the other let any feelings be known first.

The fire cast a warm glow on Tessa's amber hair, giving it a sheen and luster Zot hadn't forgotten. Her green eyes seemed black in the light. If their color had changed, their intensity hadn't.

Without any introduction, the iceman volunteered, "I thought of you the whole way to Jupiter and back, four long years."

"It's been more than five since we've seen each other," Tessa replied tersely.

"Guess that's right," he answered sheepishly, unsure of what else to add.

"You've kept that beard." The professor ran her hand along her own chin, adding emphasis to her dislike of his breech of decorum.

"Iceman's prerogative." His was completely filled in, with only a few gray hairs emerging amid the dark brown.

"I hope you keep it neat," the Academy officer noted.

"I wear it trimmed and shaped to conform to regs." He added hastily as a last defense, "No one ever complained on board the *Gagarin*."

"Maybe so on a shuttle, but your hair's longer than regulations allow."

Is that all there's to say after all this time? the hiberman thought, looking into the fire's glow so as not to give away anything else.

"You've aged, matured," Tessa finally complimented. "You've lost that shy, boyish quality."

"*Boyish?* I was never *that*."

Tessa didn't hold herself back but pointed out that he had always seemed to stand reluctantly on the sidelines of Marsco, as though not quite fitting in. "Makes sense," she added to reassure that he caught her drift, "a sid resident entering Marsco the way you did. You often seemed silent, almost brooding. But after your little *Gagarin* expedition, you've returned—oh, I don't know—a seasoned officer and, more importantly, confident, controlled."

Grizotti felt the slam keenly and reminded her that he had been on a mission considered by many to be Marsco's greatest scientific feat. "A trip out to Jupiter, dammit! *Jupiter!* We went safely there and back!" His snit over, his next thought just slipped out. "I love you, Tessa," he whispered.

She ignored him. In the crackling firelight, her skin flushed with eagerness to greet her—*what?* She didn't have the right word for him; personal and professional confusion kept her at a loss. She knew she must maintain this gap between them. And she knew she must never close it or give him hope it would ever close. They must always remain apart. And so, needing to make a decision, Tessa sank into indecision.

"I love you, Tes," he whispered a second time.

"That was all so long ago, Anthony," Tessa eventually replied with no emotion.

But in a moment, Zot whispered, "Tes, I've never stopped."

All she dared reply was, "Don't even go there, dammit!" As much as she wanted to rush into his arms, much had to be settled first. She refused to drop her ridgid self-contained defense, a posture she skillfully employed over the years to keep most men at bay.

He watched the fire's quiet light, waiting for more of an answer.

For her part, she wanted to hold onto him tightly, to tell all she had to say, and yet was relieved to hear the whooshing of a landing HFC. That stopped her naturally as they listened, the craft's distinctive hover-whine distracting them momentarily.

A few moments after landing, the HFC increased its engines to climb back up into the foggy night.

"Whoever's piloting that better know how to skim," Zot concluded. "Was that your father's? From his Center? I visited once when he was cannibalizing old HFCs for pieces to make two others skim-worthy."

"He was able to salvage only one—but no, that's not it."

"How well does it skim?"

"Well enough," she evaded with an expression of veiled sadness. It wasn't the first time that evening Zot detected a resonance of melancholy, of loss.

Vaguely Tessa motioned with her head. "With all this fog, I'm surprised anyone's skimming about. Even a hovercraft's subject to weather conditions."

"You can't fly through soup like this, unless you're in one of Marsco's latest, especially since the Herriff-Grid's nonfunctioning here."

Looking at each other, they mouthed knowingly, *Security*.

But the flight of HFCs was far from Tessa's thoughts; her heart and mind muddled. "I think," she began then hesitated.

"Think what?"

"Nothing." Tessa wasn't playing coy; silence was her natural refuge.

"That wasn't it," Zot returned bluntly.

In the continuing stillness between them, Tessa's memory ran wild. She remembered her mother's funeral when she first saw Zot in a different light, a clearer light. As cadets, they had known each other for slightly over a year. He was just another cadet in the background. By virtue of her parents, she stood centerstage. At the service, several other classmates attended; Zot alone came for deeper reasons.

At that juncture in his fabled career, Walter Miller was still a distinguished star in the Marsco galaxy. Herriff and he had designed their innovative propulsion system that routinely sped to the asteroid belt. Being seen in the light of such a dignitary was a common act often made by some fledging associates on the move. Miller had learned to tolerate such ingratiating. During his wife's funeral, it was patently obvious who was there to be seen and who was there to comfort. And, as the grieving husband explained to his daughter later, Zot stood out because he clearly attended for those supportive reasons.

After the service, Zot held Tessa in a strong embrace. He whispered, "I know what it's like to lose a parent. I lost both of mine as a child." The words were intended to give reassurance to the stoic daughter. She had been standing composed and solitary (as she was still able to do) throughout the entire day. But hearing Zot, she softened in his arms, sobbing, letting herself go.

From then on, she viewed him as a kindred spirit, not as a sid in the background amid scores of Marsco-raised cadets. He had never been off Earth, for instance; many others had been raised on the Moon or on Mars as she was. They became close friends long before any passion roared.

Those ensuing months were hard for her. She retreated into herself. Cool reticence came easily to her, even to this day.

"You know," Tessa began hesitantly, trying to keep unsettling memories from forcing themselves into her mind, "there's something I don't understand about us—about *you*." She found it somehow a relief to enumerate to him their relational hotspots. "Years ago—it was in the spring—you told me you loved me," she stated without emotion, "right out there in Walter's garden. Yet that same night you asked my father—who wasn't by that time a glittering star in Marsco heavens any longer—to help *move along* your request for crew assignment to the *Gagarin*."

"For the Jupiter run."

"Your name was in the request file, but—"

"But no crew assignments had been made," he finished. "I thought Walter had some Jovan pull to get me on that crew assignment."

"Not Jovan, but *Martian* pull through *Herriff*, I think you mean." Tessa's remark caught Zot totally off guard.

"Let's just say, I asked him to use all avenues at his disposal."

"Okay, roger that, we'll just leave it vaguely 'for the Jupiter run.' And all the while I'm in Seattle and you're still on Earth prepping for this mission (because bulkhead hatches *did* open for your little sojourn across the solar system), you don't visit. Not even when I arrange for us to met here."

Zot studied the flickering fire.

"You're such a bastard sometimes, iceman." Tessa had always had a curious mixture of playfulness tempered by her severity.

Zot knew this wasn't one of those times. Tonight she was all revenge; she meant to torment him. "It sucks—you know that?—that after your first Mars cruise, when you were Earth-side and I was in grad school—"

"I didn't visit."

"That's right. Oh, I was busy enough, and I didn't need *you* to define *me*. But it did hurt. God, it hurt deeply." She wanted to go on, but doing so would confide too much, give away too much. She only asked, "Is that all I meant to you?"

"Course not, Tes, you know that—but you were hanging with that buff flyboy!"

"That was nothing. It went nowhere," she cut him off. "But more to the point, iceman, I'd like to know *from you* what *is* going on."

In the firelit room, they locked eyes. Both saw that love was still there if the Marsco world allowed them to share it. Vindictively Tessa held his gaze, then let it go. She had him where she wanted, and he was going to hear it from her outright, come what may.

"Well," Tessa went on, explaining Zot's part in their long history for him, "you're back from your first run to Mars. And then, bang, you're off again. And I mean *off*. Not on a safe, routine asteroid cruise to Vesta or Syracuse Six—"

"As if any run to the belt is 'typical' or 'out of harm's way.' Look at the *Piazzi*."

"Okay, let's. People died on that shuttle. But you're over the top on *yours!* Not a typical run at all; no, you're on an experimental ship to death-defying Jupiter. Marsco's farthest deep-space run ever." Her voice changed to a bitterly cynical tone, "I think you've a dramatic flair about you, 'death-defying Jupiter!'"

"Odd behavior, isn't it? Even for a hiberman." He failed to joke his way out of her uncomfortable explanation.

Yet, she was serious and not about to let him off the hook. "Odd? Yes. Acceptable? I'm not so sure, but I won't accept it again. Fully understood? Never again."

God help the cadet who crosses her, the iceman thought, then asked, "Forgivable?"

“That remains to be seen.” Her voice had an edge to it, the kind Tessa employed when she was all business. Even in the Marsco world, her emotions ran true but guarded. “Well?” she snapped, sure this time her voice conveyed the polar distance she wanted, “are you going to explain?”

“Will it change anything?”

“That remains to be seen,” she whispered, almost bending. In the next breath, she caught herself. “No! No, it won’t! I just want to hear it from you.”

Bitch! he thought, *damned when I do, damned when I don’t.*

His innate kindness was giving way to disappointment, then anger. Finally, reluctantly, he started in, knowing that this was probably the last he’d ever say to her. He began rambling quickly, bits and pieces of his personal history she knew. Before the C-Wars, as a boy he loved space. “Was crazy about it, read whatever I could find, both print and Net. In my parents’ extensive library, most public ones being closed or destroyed in the Wars.”

“Or gothed.”

“Yes, there was that, too, as you remember those days running up to the conflagration and after.”

“Vaguely. I was young and then taken to Mars, but yes, I remember some—or I’ve heard.”

“Well, it was tough to find stuff, but using a finger mouse, I surfed everything about space. Black holes. Red dwarfs.” He drew a breath. So far, he was covering old ground; she knew all this. “That’s when I came across Hubble, Edwin Powell Hubble. Such a mind! An astronomer so important that eventually the first orbiting telescope was named after him.”

“I remember this from first-year space exploration class with Klein.”

“Yes, the most significant platform of its day. It kicked ass for years. Enabled Earthbound astronomers to gather info about space and the universe and star systems millions of light years away.” He paused. “And so, don’t you see?”

"Wow, ice jockey! You've made quite a quantum leap here. Even *I* don't pull that on my students."

"I entered Marsco to be an explorer, not a pilot. I'd already read as much as possible about space. I read astrophysics as some read the sports Net."

"Not surprising considering your folks," she conceded without a trace of moderation. Both his parents were physicists killed in a Luddite attack on their research lab before the C-Wars.

"No, not at all."

"But at the Academy, you had the potential for being a shuttle pilot; that would've taken you into space."

"You're right, but I wanted *to study* it. I saw myself as primarily a scientist."

"Again, like your folks."

"Yes."

"But you had the prereqs for astrogeology and astrophysics. You might've doubled in both! You're intelligent and determined enough to handle either or both degrees at the Marsco Institute. An advanced degree in the theoretical sciences's certainly in your genes. You might've had all that, *and more,* all at the same time." *Like me,* Tessa implied.

The woman remembered those times almost in spite of herself. How everyone assumed they'd marry, a natural Marsco merger.

But then unexpectedly during the second half of the Academy, Flight wasn't for him. Because he was immersed in hard science, it was then assumed that he and Tessa would be at MIT together—she to study engineering, he the theoretical sciences. *We could've easily made a life on our small stipends. Love would've gotten us through,* Tessa had reasoned with herself for years. She felt certain of that and of him back then.

Zot broke in, "But, at MIT those are *applied* courses. They're instructed only to facilitate Marsco's mining and commerce. I'm sure you've noticed that in its engineering courses." His voice took on a sharp accusatory edge. "Did you ever design any exploration probes? Did Marsco ever launch an expedition that wasn't designed purely for the exploitation of space, not for its scientific exploration?"

"So, you're telling me I made a mistake in taking one of its degrees?" she snapped with sudden indignation.

"I'm a little like your father—I've gotten *out* of the business of telling people what to do. That's why I declined Flight."

"You're right! You're a *very* little like my father." She ground the words out without lightening up on her dig. "A dreamer of something that doesn't exist any longer. Can't bring it back, can you?"

Tessa didn't want to admit that Zot's idealism was what she fell in love with at first. A passionate dreamer who threw himself headlong into whatever he loved. The complete opposite, she sat tight and made her mistakes by inaction. He jumped in with both feet; that's why she loved him so. But tonight's explanation made her frustration with him rise all the more. "So why hiber-tech?" she spat, first trying to understand totally his erratic life and then to dismiss it. "The least-admired, least-respected collection of yahoos in space."

He tried to reach for her hand, thinking that as he explained, this would help, but she wouldn't keep hers in his.

"Well," he began, "out there on the *Gagarin,* when just about everyone was iced, I did whatever I wanted. There're always a few crewmembers awake, but I was chief iceman. I arranged my protocols so that I had plenty of free time each day to study what I hadn't yet pursued and do my own deep-space sensor readings. I rigged a backup communications dish as a radio telescope receiver."

"And they let you, the other officers? The *Gagarin's* commander?"

He shrugged her off. "At hiber-tech, we heard rumors about an iceman who once had kept up his daily hiber work while still managing to play every single FreeCell game combination when heading out to the belt. All 36,000 of them! He found the game on a cobweb site and downloaded it to a notebook. Don't you think my commander was more excited about me studying stars than playing 'Civ VIII: The Rise of Marsco?'"

"I guess TBS virts are better than what most icemen do!"

"Don't slander the guild, Tes; it's beneath you," Zot countered defensively.

"And so that's all?" she probed. "Not doing anything else?"

His mind raced. *Does she know?* "Were you expecting anything else?"

"I was expecting some clarity about your strange behavior." But her mind raced, *He's still hiding something!* She pushed the envelope. "Aren't you going to say something about your *other* experiments?"

He looked her full face, trying to hide what he could. "They're classified." His cryogen stasis work for the Von Braun Center was top secret and expected to stay black.

"Dammit, Grizotti, you're so Marsco."

"Actually, I think of myself along the lines of last century's academic scientists." She easily caught the vague reference. "Something like my parents—only without a research institute."

"And that's it?" She rejected his explanation. "I deserve more than this."

"More?"

"Frankly, yes. Like a reason why you threw away a career." She took slow, deliberate breaths so she wouldn't add, *and me.* "You had so much at your finger disks just for the asking."

Grizotti didn't know what to say. He thought of his trip through Sac City that afternoon. The old city center had recently been ravaged by Security; he was certain. Signs of Marsco's iron fist abounded around him as he moved from the cantonment southward for Miller's. The crackdown left the sids there shaken and disoriented.

He had even witnessed a lander sweep farther out, near an internal stopline. Scores of PRIMS were pushed into a massive lander bay even as dozens of others were tossed out: a mindless exchange of one group for another to keep PRIMS worldwide disoriented, unable to coalesce into any true opposition. What he witnessed that afternoon wasn't the Marsco of the Asteroid Fleet or, to Tessa's credit, of the Academy; it was the Marsco of unrelenting power, unopposed power, unrestrained power.

The iceman struggled with what to say next, not knowing how an engineering professor at Marsco's flagship Academy would receive his explanation. Marsco had slipped in his estimation. And that wasn't an easy to admit. "I joined up," he began, "because of what it offered. Its world vision. A third option between the Powers and mindless Goths trashing everything. Remember, my folks were killed in a blind act of terror by anti-science Luddites!"

He drew a painful breath. "Nonetheless, Tes, I now have my doubts about Marsco itself."

"Every associate struggles with *that.* We're damned if we do, damned if we don't. Everyone rationalizes about Marsco, *'That's not the Marsco I knew.'* Or, *'Marsco never did such 'n' such before I ever enlisted.'* Or, *'It's a different Marsco now.'*"

"But, you've become... *you* are so Marsco."

"Am I?" she asked, trying not to betray the answer.

Walter Miller interrupted his daughter and his guest by coming down the hallway from the kitchen and shouting as though he was calling in a group of plebes, "Hey, cadets, soup's on! Let's eat. I've visitors I want y'to meet." Miller was wearing an apron and was drying his hands in a towel, a symbol of midcentury cordial domesticity he tried to continue.

Embarrassed, Tessa rose with an apology, "Sorry, father, Anthony and I didn't help much with dinner. He was showing me some interesting, interesting stars—he'd observed on his flight—"

"Visible stars, Tessa, through those dirty windows and in this fog?" Father, daughter, and hiberman all looked at each other knowingly. "Do you know much about those dirigibles that Marsco boffins use on Mars?" the granger asked. The iceman missed the allusion, but Tessa reddened. "Anyway, I want Zot to meet these men."

The smell of what Miller was preparing met them in the hall as all three approached the kitchen. *Almost like old times,* Zot thought, *between the genial greeting from Walter and the smells of home.*

"Wonderful!" Tessa breathed in the steam from a bubbling pot of tomato sauce.

"It's Famous Grizotti," Miller boasted, "but with my tomatoes and herbs."

"'Fresh-grown taste in every bite, so treat *our* kitchen like it's *yours!*'" the iceman mimicked his grandmother whose trattoria he remembered fondly.

The three associates joined the sons of a local granger, Aaron and Jeremy Truman, at the farther end of Miller's stretching house.

"Undoubtedly, you heard that HFC hovering in," Miller noted wryly, suspecting Tessa and Zot's obliviousness to the rest of humanity a few moments before. "Lieutenant Rivers, of the local Security unit, skimmed Aaron down."

The former Indie explained with boyish excitement, "I'm temporarily attached to the sid's lander field over winter break. Disks-on duty."

The young man stood taller than Tessa remembered and certainly more fit. Unlike the hiberman, he wore his hair neat and had a shaved chin, although on his downy face no one would know. He was no longer as tanned as when Tessa last saw him, but that was in the summer when he was working outside tending his father's herd. He had been out of the elements these past few months of intensive classroom work.

The cadet wore a light gray uniform with cerulean trim showing he was attending a prep sanctioned by Marsco before entering the Academy. Shaking his hand, she noticed he had two recent implants.

"Let me see!" she demanded with a sisterly air, not an officer's. She held out the fledgling's hand for Zot's examination as though no tension existed between them.

"They're brilliant! So damn quick," Aaron explained eagerly. "Nano-fast! Quicker than any finger mouse I've ever used."

The young man stopped to admire them himself, as though he was only now just realizing he had blue-green dots under the epidermis of two fingers. "I'm still over twitching," he admitted.

"It just takes time and practice," Tessa reassured him. "I had my first adult disk, after all, when I was seven."

"Precocious child, indulging parents," Miller slipped in.

"But," the cadet complained, "they still irritate a great deal, especially when hot."

The well-disked associates all shared their particular soothing secrets.

"I ice mine down," Zot stated.

Tessa looked at him with a teasing smirk, "*Ice*man!" Her shifting attitude caught both the hiberman and herself off guard. She seemed like his significant once more, razzing him so. It passed as she remarked to Aaron, "I dip my fingertips in turpentine to toughen the outer skin. The more calloused, the less the heat bothers."

"Can't imagine you as calloused," the cadet blushed.

"Imagine it," Zot snorted.

Jeremy shot in his piece, "I jus' slip on a damn thimble." The youngest of the gathering, he still managed to sound like an old farmer. His tone suggested, *wuz good 'nuff in my day.*

"My third's coming soon," Aaron solemnly explained, waving an empty fingertip. Although both Millers were lefters, they expressed sincere admiration for that. "Say, is there any way I might email Herriff to thank him? That entrance exam: I'd have never done so well without his coaching and your tutoring, Dr. Miller."

"He's a standard address," Tessa suggested. "Marsco Net'll get you there."

"Oh, yeah," the neophyte realized belatedly. So many once-closed portals had suddenly opened to him with those recently acquired disks that it was easy to overlook the obvious.

"I've one," Zot confided, "that I know he's sure to receive *personally*. The standard one's definitely reviewed by some boffin or another."

The point was not lost of Tessa. *He knows more than he's telling about the Von Braun.*

At this point Aaron took a good look at Grizotti. His beard more than any shoulder patch had given him away instantly: Hibernation Service. But an iceman officer? It made no sense to the newest associate. Instinctively, the cadet grew standoffish.

Miller gave a laugh. "You've learned the pecking order quickly."

Like her father, Tessa felt the snub aimed at Zot. "You *are* clearly aiming for space service, aren't you?" She kidded him lightly in that familial way she had with her Truman brothers.

"Why aim for anything less?" the cadet asked, confident in his abilities, especially with his growing disk array.

"Well, before you look down on our hiber specialist here," Miller laughed at the absurdity of it all, "remember: he *was* a member of the *Gagarin* crew."

"*Am* a member," Zot corrected pointedly, looking from one associate's face to the next. His remark silenced everyone awkwardly for a moment.

But that fact cast Grizotti in a new glow. "Damn, sir!" the cadet let out an excited yelp. "The *Gagarin*? Jupiter?" Aaron's sudden enthusiasm didn't hide the young man's uneasiness, but Zot overlooked all that.

"Besides Jupiter, there was Europa, a Jovan moon. And the Trojans, the planet's trailing asteroids." Sensing continued discomfort in the young man, Zot then confided, "And I also started at prep like you. Got my first two implants then. Spent two full years there before Academy matriculation." He stated the fact as an olive branch, a point not lost on Tessa, who knew of his genuine compassionate nature underneath a hardened associate's exterior.

"Silicon Prep?"

"No, back in the Chi-Town Sector, a former college campus near the Lake shore. Wonderful place still resonating with Jesuitical logic and discipline."

Cadet Truman tapped his TLDT, a nervous action he picked up once implanted with the tutorial language disk, temporary. He knew his grammar had come a long way; his vocabulary was another matter.

Zot stressed, "Prep also helped with my agility and physical training and other necessary skills—disk utilization, HFC skimming, that sort of thing." He refrained from adding that it was there he first fired an Enfield.

Finding himself more comfortable with the affable Zot, the cadet remarked pointedly, "You can be on my icing crew anytime."

Guiding the conversation to include his other guest, Miller put a few questions to Jeremy about the dairy.

Having a farmer's reticence and an Indie's attitude toward associates, the young man remained silent in the corner of the kitchen, playing with the dogs. Above his head, three leather belts hung from coat pegs. On each belt an issued Enfield was holstered, one from the cadet and two from the officers, symbols of a world Jeremy didn't belong to or aspire to.

Miller then asked his neighbor, "And your plans? Being a vet still possible?"

Proudly, the younger brother acknowledged he was still on with the vet option. "Pa an' me got it worked out when I can 'prentice." His chosen world, the associates knew, was still stagnated in the past, while his brother's rocketed ahead.

He had none of the polish his brother had acquired at the Silicon prep. The younger man was weathered from his long hours with the family herd. And his smooth face was already becoming prematurely creased from his hard life. His hands were chapped, calloused from the daily tedium of hard labor. He was someone who worked like a PRIM at times but one who thought like a sid at all times. He remained fiercely proud of his Indie status.

Zot enjoyed Miller's dinner with unrestrained zeal. Hiring local PRIMS to help preserve his bounty, the granger had cooked his summer tomato harvest down to sauce according to Nona Grizotti's recipe. "Only diff's that it's frozen, not canned," the granger explained. His huge freezer, one designed for a belt shuttle, brimmed with more than a year's supply of food.

"Tastes like ours," the descendant of restaurateurs claimed, passing his plate for another helping. Only the dairyman outpaced him.

"Well, I made the bread," Tessa pouted, seemingly ignored in the heaped praise for Miller's crop and its transformation into spectacular sauce.

"Best machine-made I've had since the *Gagarin,*" Zot replied with a wink toward Aaron and an elbow to Jeremy, bringing the whole table to silence until Tessa smiled at her own folly and laughed aloud.

Inexplicably, she leaned into him and kissed his cheek. "Touché!"

Shit, woman, he thought, *consistency is all I ask.*

Tessa blushed at her own spontenaity. Zot's true nature toward both Aaron and Jeremy caught her attention. He was a good man; everyone knew him to be so. In only one breath, it seemed, she was glad she still loved him even if she didn't know what to do next.

As was his wont to include everyone at table, Miller turned to Jeremy to ask, "how's those new village homes working out?"

Zot didn't know what he meant but watched the young granger bristle at the very notion. "PRIMS so close—" Jeremy caught himself; it was Miller's idea to settle PRIMS nearby their granges. "They work hard, that's fur sure."

"But you're concerned about them still?" Miller looked at his other guests but without a sense of judgment or disappointment. Change takes time, especially among grangers who sought to keep their non-sid, non-PRIM status.

"I'm trying something," he explained to Zot. "A village, what, seven clicks from here?"

"Only five," Jeremy corrected, not liking PRIMS as close as that.

"Well, five clicks. I've fished out about two score PRIMS, I mean, engineers, electricians, trained men and women, their children. Some with DRP—"

"DRP?" Aaron asked, many of the Marsco acronyms still confusing to him.

"*Disk Removal Procedure,*" Tessa explained to the neophyte associate with tutorial thoroughness, "when someone with FDs—" she held up her own fingers, "—must surrender them."

"Well, *surrender*'s a bit euphemistic," her father countered. "But never mind that now. These villagers are conscientious, willing to help local grangers, even Allison's Ludds at the Enclave. I use a few of the engineers for my SCAA research. Others work here; I cultivate much more than one man can handle."

"Creating this village serves what purpose?" Zot asked.

"I'm trying to get them sid-status. Don't you all enjoy living without a RFID disk?"

No one needed to answer; even Jeremy looked at the back of his left hand: scar-free, never disked, never labeled a PRIM.

"And you pay them?"

"With crop-share and MMUs; like everyone should be, they're paid well for their honest labor."

Jeremy looked at his brother, at the iceman, at the two Millers, whom he trusted beyond anyone else, but he still couldn't grasp their misplaced belief in PRIMS. In the other room hung their Enfield holsters. Easy to trust PRIMS when strapped.

Seeing that look only sibs can interpret, Aaron tried swaying his brother. "I go to class with PRIMS."

"Easy 'nugh *there,*" the granger countered.

Zot joined in. "I also work with plenty of *former* PRIMS. Guys with tech savvy but not enough to master flight or engineering." He motioned at Aaron and Tessa. "I guess hiber attracts them. Deep space work for sure since no one hibers this side of the Moon. And the MAS's got some perks. As coworkers, they're fine fellows: hard-working, tireless, dedicated like no one's business."

Tessa smiled slyly. "*Guys?* How macho." For a second time, she leaned over and kissed Zot's cheek like old times. With witnesses, nothing else would happen.

He replied aloud, "Ice Service tends to be a guy thing, if that's what you mean." Mentally, the thought ran, *Don't bullshit me, woman! If I admitted a few ice-babes were hot, ready, and randy as hell, you'd be on me in a moment for that!*

The night grew long. After their leisurely meal, the Truman sons rose. "Promised Pa I'd help milk so Jeremy can take a morning off," Aaron explained.

The younger brother's sheepish grin showed his appreciation at the supportive gesture.

"I know this sounds high camp," Miller apologized, "but a digi-tal?" The engineer produced a small cam so quickly that no one dared decline. Tessa stood between the brothers with her arms around their strong shoulders.

Zot took over and Miller slid in behind, a tableau of three generations if allowances for hiber came into play.

"Now, all four," Miller directed, ushering in Zot next to Tessa.

In the nano it took, the thought crossed the iceman's mind that he was nearly old enough for the two young men to be their sons—Tessa's and his. With hiber-retarded age, it wasn't that far-fetched. Although smiling for Miller, Zot concluded sadly, *I'm imagining a world of happiness that exists only within the restricted confines of Marsco.*

"Dishes!" Tessa announced, sounding like a gunnery sergeant, setting the iceman to work. "Chefs don't do dishes!" she proclaimed, shooing her father out of this own kitchen.

He didn't argue as she embraced him to wish him good night. "Am I detecting a resolution?" he asked in a whisper.

"I think you are," the woman answered vaguely. Both her father and Zot noticed a different aspect to her, relaxed, natural, barriers down.

Miller left them alone, turning off lights in the dining room and hallway that led toward his suite.

"He looks great," Zot commented.

"Were you expecting something else?"

"His can't be an easy life—plus, trying to get that lander project literally off the ground."

"He's fine. Happiest I've seen him in years. Healthiest."

"Hibering trips from Mars helps, of course." A professional comment.

"Yes. He'd easily pass for mid-forties still although well into his sixties."

"I love this grange," the hiberman commented. "So comforting, welcoming."

"Where he found all this kitchenware, I don't know." Tessa looked around the gleaming stainless steel room. "Looks midcentury."

"And it all works."

"If it takes soldering or disks, he can fix it!"

Zot leaned into the sink where piles of pans remained. "Like a great cook—everything needs cleaning. Did enough of this as a kid!"

While drying, Tessa stood behind Zot but moved in closer each time she reached for a pot or lid. Her whole body came against his. He knew her well enough to know she wasn't a tease, but the man shook his head at her contradictory antics. He said nothing yet savored the pressure against him. For the first time all evening it seemed as though tension had dissipated between them.

She leaned in again, brushing him purposely. He felt sure her own mind was unclear, yet she wanted him to know she was there, to feel her presence. Tessa always had an element of mischievous repartee at odds with her seriousness. It puzzled Zot to feel that spunk resurfacing.

The kitchen finished, they drifted back down the long hallway and returned to the dying fire. For a few moments, Zot sat next to the hearth, stoking the embers with smaller branches and larger split pieces.

Unlike the tense uncomfortableness earlier that evening, watching the logs begin to glow, the pair shared a tone reminiscent of their old times. Zot stayed near the fire, and Tessa sat behind him but brushed his back now and again.

"What d'you think of his village idea?" she asked with concern in her voice.

"Had you heard of it before?"

Miller's idea made waves that lapped the shores of Academy in distant Seattle. "Only in bitter comments, 'Sir Miller, Lord of the Manor.' That sort of crap." She looked over at him. "Unlike *Grizotti,* Miller's a pretty common name—not every associate puts it together. So I hear quite a bit of unguarded complaints about him around campus."

"Or they pretend *not* to put it together, and want to dig into *him* and *you.*"

"Ah, yes, all your Med ancestry suspicion! But affirm that, you're so right there."

They agreed that Walter was always trying some scheme or another to get as many PRIMS out of that life and into some other status. His helping Allison at the Enclave was another example.

The fire blazed higher as the wood flamed, the heat welcome in the otherwise chilly room.

"You're very perceptive of others," Tessa stated as a solid compliment. "Know that?"

"You mean, 'for an iceman'? That sort of thing?"

"No, I'm serious. For instance, you were especially kind to Jeremy tonight," she noted, brushing her hair back and sitting down on the floor next to him. As they spoke, they soon sat leaning shoulder to shoulder.

"Kid has to learn a better way with PRIMS," Zot added without judgment.

"Whole damn world does."

"Well, Walter's off to a good start there. For all flak he'll get, that village is a fine idea."

"Talk of flak! Aaron was way out of line with his disdain for your hiber service."

"A guy gets used to it."

"Well, he changed soon as the *Gagarin* came up, but you were also considerate toward him."

"Maybe I lack that professorial way of squashing an impish plebe!" He laughed, putting on a stern grimace then dropped his flippancy. "He and I are a lot alike, actually. Maybe I just came from a better educated background—"

"Both your parents holding doctorates, gee, I'd say."

"But, sid-status, having to go to prep, wide-eyed and naive about Marsco. Never had any implanted disks of either variety: finger or PRIM. That sort of similar."

"I imagine a dairy farmer's son worked damn hard, but you must have, too. Helping with the family business."

They sat in renewed silence, Zot not knowing for all his perception where Tessa was going next.

"Do you remember our first real time together?" Tessa eventually asked.

"Certainly. We'd been apart for a few months over the summer."

"Yes, that break after the funeral but before you gave up your ambitions of Flight School."

"Does that really change anything?"

"Do I have to answer?"

"No," he responded. He didn't know what else to do or say; he was afraid of losing her totally. Hesitantly, he continued the reminiscing she had begun. "I'd been posted to some temp SoAm Security duty. Fortunately, a quiet sid. Amounted to nothing. Ended up mostly saluting centurions, yelling at Auxxies."

"Security transfers still hang over cadets today," Tessa interjected.

"Could that happen to Aaron?"

"Affirmative, happens all too often." She paused then admitted, "Forty percent of last year's class." Her voice rose in protest, "And he's only a boy."

"I'm sorry to hear of that. It shouldn't be that way, y'know." He drew himself up fearful this was the remark that would end it for them. "I think Marsco can change, *can be* changed, so it doesn't have to do that any longer." He was reluctant to add, *That was our dream once, Tes, remember? Changing Marsco for the better from the inside. Doing all that together.*

Tessa leaned to catch his eyes, seeing his real concern for the cadet, concern and love she had overlooked for much too long. "Anyway," she eventually confided, "that summer, our first real summer, I spent my free time here."

"How'd that feel?"

"I don't know. I guess I loved being even a small part of Walter's incipient life here. He'd been so depressed for months. I got him to laugh, cry, relax. We laid out the gardens, planted trees. I finally saw him happy again. This place renewed him."

"You care about him very much, don't you?"

"No one could have better parents, all things considered," she whispered. She held his hands, acknowledgement of his loss so many years ago. Finger disks on flesh sent a tingle, but Zot felt a different one for a different reason. "But, his coming here, starting all this," she went on, "it *was*—and to a certain degree still *is*—unfathomable, his non-Marsco life."

With that, she grew quiet, reflecting. She drew up her knees and leaned her chin on them, but at an angle so she watched Zot clearly. She stared into his brown eyes illuminated by the fire. The flickering light also brought out the reddish touches of her hair. It cast her skin in a glow that suggested anticipation. "The best part of that summer, I remember, was landering out to Chi-Town for a glorious week."

Zot had completed his SoAm duties and was spending his leave with the grandparents who had raised him. When Tessa came to visit, their friendship turned into love. One night, the cadets had a meal at Zot's grandparents' trattoria, an establishment that had defined the Grizotti family for generations going well back before Divestiture and the C-Wars.

By the time Tessa met them, the downsized business made do in a postwar, scaled-back subsidiary. Nonetheless, many associates from the Sector had discovered Grizotti's. Like his father, Zot had broken with family traditions. His father had moved into academics and research, Zot to Marsco, a natural progression.

After their meal (much like the one Walter had just prepared), they skimmed to a secluded (and PRIM-free) spot along the lake shore where a planetarium had once stood. As night fell, they watched their dichotomous world unfold in the background: the dark PRIM zone remains of the metropolis contrasted with the brightly lit Marsco Cantonment skyline. Over the zone, Security HFCs patrolled, searching for trouble. Over the Marsco side, a Herriff-Grid showed the renewed prosperity Marsco brought to its associates and those sids who cooperated with it. One suggested the end of an era, the other vitality and renewed progress. A tableau of their world: the contrasting still-black hulks and re-illuminated skyscrapers.

By then they had known each other for two years, but this night was totally different. Zot, who had lived entirely on Earth, was content to listen to her tell all about her childhood on Mars, how that for a long time, she was the only child at the Von Braun Center.

That indescribable night they ended up stargazing farther from the city along the restored dunes. He pointed out the Red

Planet and Venus, which any associate could spot, but he even found dim Saturn on the horizon and tiny Mercury lost in a cluster of stars. He then easily located dozens of constellations and ticked off several Messier objects.

And as they both later admitted, *she* first kissed *him.* Surprisingly, Tessa swept Zot in her arms and drew him to her, although he was initially hesitant.

He tried explaining his reluctance. "Tes, you're so Marsco through and through. I'm still virtually a sid!"

"But you've gained associate status *now!*"

He held up her hand, clearly visible in the light of a Marsco Moon. It had more disks than his. "There're some stoplines you just don't cross," he explained in the only images he knew.

She just kept whispering her love and assurance that this was what she wanted.

Leaning on his shoulder before her father's fireplace, she finally whispered, "That was all so long ago," as though he had been privy to her own conflicted memories.

"Yes, we share a long history, if that's what you mean."

"A deep history." Her words tested the bridge between that past and this present, but words failed her. She reverted to protective silence.

"Tes, look," Zot finally had the courage to begin, "I know, *I think* I know, what you're trying to tell me. It's all off between us. I may be going on a second mission—"

"Jupiter?"

"Possibly."

"You *really* want to go." She stated it as fact.

"Definitely."

"Not back into the MAS?"

"Shuttles? Always a possibly, I guess."

"Security?"

"Negatory! I'm technically assigned to the *Gagarin* through the Von Braun Center, but I'm still in the Fleet. Either way, a certain amount of 'hands-off' from that." He paused then reluctantly added, “More of a chance of that boy ending up in Security than me, at this point.”

“I’m glad you’ll be safe.”

“In that sense of safe, yes, I’ll be quite safe. No Security duty, no lander sweeps for me.” He drew a breath, “But how safe’s traveling in space?”

“Dammit,” Tessa finally let out, her deep passions held in check all evening finally erupting.

“Now, what’d I say?”

She leaned her head to kiss him full on, but he jerked away.

“Tes, can I get *one* direct statement from you *finally* tonight? I’ve gotten every conceivable message possible all day long, garbled, mixed, scornful, partial.”

She didn’t answer at first but embraced her long-absent iceman.

“Zot,” she whispered with ardent liveliness, “I don’t know if this is wise or not, considering all our loose ends, but I want you tonight as though we’ll never part again.”

TWENTY-ONE

THE CREATION OF LIEUTENANT SHANGHAI

(Sac City Sid and Zone, January 2097)

"Have way to yer new frien', missy M-co."

Mei-Ling Chen discovered the same greasy, low-end sid in the reception cage the next morning. His dirty hair pulled back into a ponytail, he had slept on a mat in a small office behind the bar-protected counter. He quickly gave her instructions to meet her skim in the city park beyond.

Hoping never to return, Chen was across the lobby in a dozen steps and outside.

As she left the lobby, the sid examined one of her tokens. She willingly gave over ample for the piddling he'd done. "M-co's rich, yes," he snorted. "Like rich missy an' her tokens."

The associate thought it best to approach her rendezvous cautiously, so she walked slowly, taking her time.

The morning was gray and cold with thinning fog. The fleeing pilot found the streets clogged with PRIMS, many only children, moving off to chip bricks from abandoned buildings. Scores of sids on bicycles thronged through the crowded streets. A few mopeds popped, adding blue smoke to the morning haze. Nothing skimmed above, not even Security.

The associate moved into the park without paying any attention at first. After a few moments, she did notice that the untended grounds offered hints of their long-lost elegance. The outline of sidewalks wound through weedy ornamental gardens. Ranks of trees grew wildly, their gnarled limbs no longer trimmed. The overgrown lawn suggested the former importance of this locale even as PRIMS huddled in shelters at every turn.

Ignoring the PRIMS and resisting the urge to pull out her clone, Chen didn't stop until she witnessed a dark shape break through the dense trees. There, looming before her, stood the menacing shell of a capital dome, its foggy outline unmistakable. Only then did she reassess the implication of escaping through Sac City: the last ruling seat of the Continental Powers. She shook but not from cold.

Perhaps, not the best place to come after all, she reflected, too late to change anything. *Chamberlain's here, but so's this!*

The capital's copper dome and white limestone walls were streaked with smoke damage. Even in ruins, the edifice's classical grandeur suggested its significance dating back a century before Divestiture. It had stood vacant since the Armistice.

Here, the last provisional wing of the C-Powers desperately held out, struggling in vain against Marsco's final onslaught. Capitulation was inevitable as Marsco forces circled for the final killing pounce. Even so, for a few desperate weeks, the failing Powers frantically tried to regroup.

Chen stared at the gutted structure. The historic impact of capitulation, signed in there nearly thirty years before, kept the shell from sledgehammers. Just beyond the park, neighboring buildings that once housed the A and P League bureaucracy, some ornately fashioned in granite and marble, were being systematically carved up by Marsco for reconstruction projects in Seattle or Silicon.

"Vanovaras and Enfields made victory by the Powers impossible. Marsco won handily," she mumbled, her words edged with associate pride. "That's the Marsco I knew, the one I willingly volunteered to serve."

Chen had thirty minutes before her skim arrived, so she walked through the park's arboretum lost in thought, her charged clone under her left arm.

She had only girlhood memories of the Powers, but they were not fond ones. The associate's mind was alive with contradictions. It was true that the Powers had brought the world Disenfranchisement and Divestiture, actions that originally cut up countries into the first unincorporated zones by casting off millions of their poorest and most diseased citizens. But at least the Powers were somewhat legitimate governments, the vestiges of the last elected legislative bodies.

Marsco then was more cyber than real, more an ideal than a ruling entity, a virtual nation that linked all right-thinking idealists who stood against C-Power oppression. Pondering it all, the escaping associate concluded that for all its excesses, Marsco was a damn site better than the Powers it had replaced—legality aside.

And, Marsco had promised that, after capitulation, all existing subsidiary areas and unincorporated zones would be temporary. It immediately declared that its own ascendancy as the sole world authority was accidental. Its current role as the exclusive sovereign state, the only guardian of peace, was only transitory. Marsco guaranteed that the world would soon regain normalcy as this new world ruler quickly returned to manufacturing computer chips and shunting asteroids across the solar system.

And yet, in all those years since those hostilities, Marsco's power hadn't diminished one byte.

Well, thought Mei-Ling, *I joined a different Marsco; today's is the altered one.*

She found herself at the northwest corner of the park. The terminal and its bullet back to Seattle were short walk away. She had palpable reasons for remaining a loyal associate, not the least of which was that stubborn attitude of standing up to the moribund, abusive Powers that had once so ravaged the world.

In the end, it was Julio and the *Piazzi* that made her turn as she did. Committed to her escape, the officer walked back toward the rotunda.

An hour and forty later, an obsolete four-seater thumped down hard on three extended skids twenty meters from where the impatient associate stood. It bore the insignia of the SCAA, but Chen didn't know what that meant.

After the gull-wing hatch opened, the craft's sole occupant, walking one-sided like a crab, came up to the woman. The approaching man wore dirty, torn overalls and had a 9 mm Enfield strapped cowboy-fashion to his thigh.

Chen concluded, *Security'd love seeing you strut like that, PRIMson.* She noted he was without a RFID disk. *Prob by mistake or he's ditched it.*

His face, a red and welted mass of carbuncles, gave a menacing grin. He leered, eyeing her up and down as though for sale or the taking. "Ye-ah! Y'mus' be the M-co wallah lookin' for a skim?"

"Does that piece of duct-taped crap accelerate?"

"Y'gots a' issue with it?" he barked at her, pushing his long brown hair out of his eyes. "'Cause, I ain't got none, an' I ain't got all day."

As soon as she fastened her safety harness, he turned on her, "I'm shore our contact mentioned m'price."

"Yes, twelve units."

"Ye-ah, that's your prob, ain't it? But it's two doz now." He held out his callused hand absent of any disks. "Prepay or walk."

Chen gave over the tokens. She needed his assistance and wanted the skim over this nano. In flight, he'd be too busy to continue leering at her. She took comfort in that and her hidden clone.

Gaining altitude, the HFC climbed through the upper reaches of the morning fog. Visual was all but impossible, and instrumentation was minimal. The craft might not have other traffic to contend with, but it needed a great deal of clearance amid the building hulks spiking up from the city center.

"A Herriff-Grid's sorely missed," Chen stated with an insistence in her voice that urged caution. She wondered how he flew, because half the flight consoles weren't activated, either from being inoperative or from this bottom-dwelling sid's inability to access their commands.

The skilled MAS pilot quickly realized that he was converting onboard stored water into hydrogen and oxygen and then straightaway recombining them for thrust. The system was designed to store the fuel as components in pressurized tanks by taking in water vapor; the liquid was a backup. He was operating the craft on the thinnest of safety margins.

Certainly hasn't had even the most elementary skim training, she noted. *Besides that, the onboard-nav's ancient.*

"How're you controlling this kludge?" she asked with a determined voice, one that said, *I know how the hell to fly massive shuttles, and all this just isn't right.* "This's worse than a blind belt egression."

"Ye-ah! Dead wreckin'. You don't need no fuckin' finger dickers to know where I'm goin'."

"No," she shot back at him, setting her boundaries and stoplines firmly, "you don't need a dick to fly."

The craft angled upward but then yawed suddenly to miss a skeletal tower looming in the fog.

"Are you sure you've adequate clearance?"

"Ye-ah, M-co, ain't nothin' here to wurry. Jus' hang." He punched the accelerator, and Chen sensed the least amount of increased propulsion she had ever before felt.

As the craft struggled for altitude, Chen was still able to see the ground through the mist. Rising to nearly 200 meters, the flier set a course following the straight path of light rail tracks heading due east. Where the tracks entered a stretching unincorporated zone, they abruptly ended, yet another indication of what stops at a stopline.

"Buggerin' up wha'ever's left of th'friggin' place," the flier snarled, his anger too close the surface to be missed.

"From down there?" she asked, tilting her head.

"Ye-ah!" His menacing tone ordered no further questions or sympathy.

The pair continued east, veered, then came to a southward heading. The landscape below changed from an obvious zone surrounded by ribbons of stoplines and towers, to one of hedges and signs of cultivation. Near the largest irrigation system, small villages dotted the surface: new places for PRIMS. This thriving system seemed superimposed on an older, tighter network that still showed here and there in old roadways, small bridges over culverts, and the derelict remains of former residences.

"So, what's down there now?" Chen pointed with her gloved hand. When he didn't reply, she asked again, not used to an officer's question going unanswered for so long.

"Asshole grangers tryin' to live Indie," he sneered. "Know of Miller? One's that's bastar's."

That Miller? Chen wondered. She had certainly heard of him for many reasons but lately not at all. It's as if he never existed. *Every associate's their own way of escaping,* she thought.

Ten clicks farther south, a stopline cut along the horizon. All grange tilling ended on this side of that demarcation. Beyond that boundary, a barren zone ran through the valley and foothills to the east.

In fifteen minutes, they were heading toward those hills a second time, passing over the same stretch of tracks, the same cluster of granges. Chen saw through his disorienting tactics and noted landmark peaks periodically outlined in the misty distance.

Eventually, the HFC broke through the top of the gray blanket and flew amid those rolling hills. “Ye-ah, that there fog sets in the valley fur weeks in winner. Up here, can be all brightish ’n sunny,” the flier remarked, as though amazed to find the sun during the day.

They’d climbed more than 1,500 meters. Higher mountains grew visible in the distance without any clouds blocking their view. By this time of year, the high peaks should’ve been snow-capped but weren’t.

After twenty minutes more of silent zigzagging, all the maneuvers following the contours of the rising hills and then higher mountains, the HFC began its landing glide, aiming for a large compound in a clearing surrounded by evergreen pine and oak.

Although the altimeter read five K, the craft was skimming barely twenty-five meters above a meadow a quarter click from the clearing. Three dozen sheep, tended by a solitary PRIM-boy and dog, grazed just down the hill from a set of landing markers.

“Oh, ye-ah!” the man shouted, jerking hard at the joystick to vector over the scattering flock. Jets of expanding steam knocked the boy off his feet and scared his fleeing dog.

“You could’ve avoided them!” Chen yelled, automatically pushing her feet as though on control pedals. “What a shitty thing to do, terrorize that boy.”

“Ye-ah!” The man’s eyes lit up with power.

By now, the gliding craft was hovering for its set-down between parallel lights on a flat, grassy outcrop.

The clearing ran about 100 meters to a side. A cracked black ribbon ran from the central buildings into the surrounding forest, a last remnant of a winding road that once ended here. Walking up the hill, the associate and the flier passed several unperturbed dairy cows with another PRIM-boy tending them. Herd and PRIM stared unconcerned; they had seen many visitors here before.

"I suppose if you'd seen this boy, you'd have knocked him on his ass, too."

"Ye-ah!"

"You'd have spoiled their milk, broken their legs, scaring them like that!"

"His loss!"

The main building, a large structure in excellent repair, stood on a bare knoll thirty meters up the hillside. Its roof was wooden shingles, its walls logs. Along the south and west sides ran a sweeping sundeck. Firewood was neatly stacked to the east. Inviting smoke curled from several stone chimneys.

Although it had lost most of its former luster, Chen understood from its size and location that in the prewar world it had been an upscale resort. Scattered around the main lodge was a typical assortment of cannibalized outbuildings. Some were from the Marsco era she knew, solar panels and three downlink dishes. Other devices predated them but seemed to be in working order: a freestanding sauna beside a hot tub.

Chen walked toward the lodge, outpacing the jockey. She enjoyed the difference in the air up here. It was fresh, bracing. She was easily above the snow line, had the dry winter provided any. The sun was bright but gave little heat. And yet, at long last she felt truly free.

She hurried across the sunporch and entered the airy, bright lodge. Stepping through one of several French doors, for the second time in as many days, the associate stood in an atrium of a bygone luxurious business. This one, she noted, was much better kept than the last. The lodge had rustic decorations—mounted trophies of deer and elk, crossed skis on the wall, faded Winter Olympics posters from the 2054 Oslo games. Wood Glen was carved above the unused reception desk; it boasted no protecting grille.

At the far end of the lobby, the woman found Dr. Chamberlain warming himself by a stone fireplace. Dressed in a flannel shirt and old-style jeans, he seemed ready to play the part of proprietor of Wood Glen, circa 2020. A tall man, his lean body was crowned with long dark hair streaked with gray. He showed signs of aging well for someone so obviously non-hibering.

His movements suggested a pleasant naturalness, although his first comment was, "You need to buzz that flock?"

"I wasn't skimming," Chen offered defensively.

"Oh," he nodded and told the woman to enter a smaller side room warmed by a Franklin stove.

"You can wait here," he ordered the jockey when he finally entered. "We'll be a while. Make yourself comfortable," he added coolly.

The young man crab-walked to a chair covered with a PRIM-woven blanket and threw himself down. Once settled, he withdrew his sidearm and began polishing the barrel.

"Unusual friend you have there," Chamberlain remarked when the two were alone. His first cordial sign was to motion her into a soft leather sofa. He stirred the fire in the potbelly before explaining, "I know my clients regularly need skims to reach me. As you can imagine, there's hardly a trace of any road network left up here. But I'd be reluctant, *very reluctant,* to recommend him. *Bennie,* I think's his name."

"I didn't ask."

"It may be; it may not be. It's hardly my business to know, and I'm not asking. PRIM-stock, I presume."

"Affirmative, but without a disk."

"Although he's only one of a few active freelancers around these days, I would have kept looking for another. I'm not *that* hard to find." He stopped long enough to check for a reaction from the woman.

Chen responded plaintively, "I had no choice. I only knew your name."

"I realize you had to make due with paltry pickings, but I wouldn't trust Bennie if I were you."

"I also had to trust that cage manager to find a way here."

"Oh, yes, him! Runs that flophouse, if he's the one I think—I can't say who exactly you mean—but he can't be trusted, either. There're also other places to stay down in Sac City, most without cages. Real rooms as though still midcentury. Sheets, towels. Best any subsidiary has to offer."

"I thought I might be watched there."

The doctor studied her for a moment. "You're watched just about everywhere, right?"

"Yes, prob."

"So, I guess you *aren't* worth watching, if you catch!"

"Oh, yes, I see. I guess you're right. But, I've come a long way." Anxiousness unexpectedly rose in her voice. For the first time, Chen worried she might be turned away. "My recce was totally indirect, gained through subterfuge. I'm in a bind where, if I must trust someone, it has to be blindly. You see, I—"

Chamberlain raised his hand to stop her. "Watch the TMI. It's better at this point that I know nothing of you except what I need to know."

He's still not ready to help me, Chen realized in that instant.

The doctor moved from the fire to his desk. "My real practice *is* totally legal; my side practice *isn't,* strictly speaking."

The associate nodded her understanding.

"But I have my scruples," he insisted. "I never have—and I never will—help any Continental war criminal, for instance. I won't help questionable personnel with a dubious history lose their old identity." He paused to make sure she was following his logic. "Additionally, I won't assist Ludd fanatics gain a new cover so they can infiltrate Marsco. I do get associates *out* occasionally; that is, in my side practice."

He stopped once more, and Chen nodded she was following.

"Openly, I help those who want in. Or at least I assist those who want a better chance at getting in through its rigorous entrance exam. Or they want, say, some low-level associate work. A one-disker type, possibly two. For me to implant that disk or two is legal. Piece of cake. Lots of regs but OK. And for them, beats the hell out of a life of continual servitude, really, in a dismal zone or in a shabby subsidiary like that one down in the valley, don't you think?"

Chen moved her head signaling affirmative.

"A well-respected associate, regardless of ancestry, can generally bring their family into a sector, or at least into its contiguous thriving subsidiary. Who can blame the parents for pushing children into Marsco under those conditions?"

The associate had to agree.

"I don't get into the politics of my clients, but I have my standards."

"Yes, but I'm in a situation where I must take care of myself," she bristled. "I've no one left I can trust—as you can see by my selection of that rat bastard." She motioned through the wall toward Bennie. "That mean-spirited piece a shit, scaring that kid. I'll take whatever help I can, even that pimply moke's, if that is what it takes."

"You'd have stopped him if you could?"

"Certainly."

Rising, Chamberlain tended the fire a second time, still deciding whether to continue his consultation or dismiss her.

As he shoved small pieces of wood into the grate, the associate noticed the room carefully. It was paneled with knotty pine and kept immaculately clean. One wall was lined with medical texts in identical binding. She also noted a new Marsco-issued finger mouse NB on a side table and, at a separate workstation, a finger disk console.

The room had a decidedly medical feel about it. A take-apart hand rested in a holder near the books. Its molded plastic pieces could be disassembled to reveal the next layer of anatomy. It was a right hand with subcutaneous finger disks inserted in three phalanges. On the wall behind the desk hung a framed écorché sketch, also of the right hand, also with finger disks.

Having finished with his contemplative fire, Chamberlain sat back at his desk. "Now, what can I do for you?"

Chen raised her right hand disks and explained, "I can't be Marsco anymore. You see, what happened was that—"

"I don't need to know why you are leaving, Marsco, just that you are." He reached for her hand to examine it more carefully. It was then that Chen noticed he was a lefter. "You've had this primary disk for many years, more than twenty-five, I'd venture to guess."

"I needed a child's oblong disk at first for two years—small hands. My primary adult disk was implanted when I was nine."

He gave a whistle. "You *are* Marsco. So, not a PRIM? I mean, originally of PRIM stock?"

She was reluctant to answer.

"Look, now I need to know how far back I must go."

"Both my parents," she explained purposely, "were Marsco. A merger of longtime associates. Even my grandparents, all of them, were of the old Marsco from long before the C-Wars. Both sides of my family were either in space or in transportation R and D." She pumped herself up proud. "They, *none of them,*" she stressed, "ever had anything to do with Security."

He still held her hand, not in the way a lover would, but as a physician. His examination had a paternal feel; indeed, Chamberlain was nearly the age of her father and just as kindly. She took comfort in that. The last man who held her hand had made love to her and then abandoned her. Chen gave a shudder as memories shifted to Julio. She also remembered the other man who'd held her hand medicinally like this, the hiberman who last put her on ice. He was now long dead; she was blamed for his death.

"You see," Chamberlain went on, "it isn't just removing the disks, DRP. I could do just that, but hell, you'd be condemned to a subsistence life in a zone or maybe a slightly better marginal life in a low-level sid like Sac City. Or living on the fringes like my hillside neighbors. But you've got a wonderful advantage with these; you might as well keep them."

"How? Don't they make me 'too Marsco?'"

"There are a few—enough not to raise suspicion—a few sids with this many disks." He raised his own left hand as evidence but with no further remark.

"So, you'll fix it so I blend in?" Chamberlain nodded *yes.* "How?"

"Well, in synopsis, I'll remove your prime disk and replace it with another. It'll be initialized to change your identity."

Chen looked the doctor straight on. "The system'll see through that! My primary has over twenty-five years of cyber record. And retina blinks here and there. Internal's quite thorough," she added as though explaining the obvious to the confused.

He held up his left hand to stop her and gently reassured her with a squeeze from his other. "You came to the right place. I've been at this business for, well, let's just say that you're not the first I've assisted. I've gotten sids in and gotten associates out. And I can—I won't bother you with the tech bumf—change your identity."

"Its files're vast," the escaping associate insisted, "Those ranks of wonks at Internal Security, pitiless." Chen's wrinkled brow told him she still didn't believe him.

Marsco's systems were immense and interconnected, virtually instantaneous. Every machine knew who was using a pad in a nano. Forging a Marsco file, cracking something into its systems, was serious business, a hack not to be attempted lightly.

"S & H computer scrutiny," she added with the first hint of fear in her voice, "is intense and unrelenting." Her intense eyes gave emphasis to her last point, “Armed Security wallahs’re intense and unrelenting. Can inflict much more pain than that jockey out there. You just don’t fuck with Marsco.”

Still holding her hand, Chamberlain countered, “But computers *are* really single-minded. If everything’s copasetic when you log on, they let you in. The standard anti-hacker check only goes so deep. All I need to do’s create a second-level file for you, one that reads consistently with your other disks and consistently within itself. In short, ‘if it looks real, it’ll be real.’ With no red flags, the computer lets you past the security barrier and onto the Net. It never double-checks after that. And the information in this—I’m afraid I have to use the term—*forged* file’ll look like any other associate’s. You know, DOB, Academy grad date, shuttle flight records.”

Chen began to follow his line of reasoning. “So, if the computer thinks I exist—this *new* me—it lets me in.”

“Yes, any retina scan input switches to the new you!”

“So, the rest of the system never verifies that the file is for a nonexistent person.”

“Essentially. Plausible duplication of Marsco files is not impossible. There are what? Two-hundred million associates on Earth and throughout the solar system, give or take? No one knows. Marsco counts but doesn’t disclose. Add dependents—nearly 3-, 4-, 500 more? At least. Then there’s certified sid users. What? Another 500 million? Six and a half? Seven hundred? Hard to say; Marsco never counts. Auxiliary units and their dependents? Does it count them? Hardly. And these three prime groups’re adding and subtracting files all the time—new sids coming in from PRIM status, children coming online. Disk upgrades. Someone going Ludd, deaths, an infrequent court martial.”

Chen’s hand twitched.

“And clearly, you aren’t PRIM; a PRIM never has access.”

Her hand relaxed. “And the system’ll be reading an active FD, not a PRIM-ID disk.”

"You got it! Besides, can a system ever totally verify embedded data in one file against millions of others in scattered files all over the place? Instantly? No! No user'd ever get on the Net. There's limits to Marsco's tech, after all."

"Guess so."

"Fortunately for you, instead the system creates 'safe files' and then only double-checks against these. If you are where you are supposed to be and who you are supposed to be, the system says, 'OK, you check out A+, so on you go.'"

Chen nodded that she was following his reasoning.

"And unless someone sits at a screen and double-checks your bogus record against an old crew manifest, for instance, or your supposed graduation date against the actual Academy records, my deception can't be discovered—but who'll do that? You'll look too legit. You'll look too Marsco-approved, since you'll be listed as a sid."

He paused to make this point perfectly clear. "And you won't be doing anything overtly stupid!"

He tapped his desktop with his left fingers, their disks adding a slight clicking sound. "And you also can't be traced back to me, so if you're caught being overtly stupid, your ass's history. And your own business. Marsco can't come after me."

"After the operation—after this changeover that creates a new me—then what'll I do?"

"Disappear! I presume that's what you want."

Chen nodded yes, but asked, "To do what?"

"Freelance. It's a big solar system. Still plenty of legal Indie shuttles operating outside of Marsco."

"But alongside."

"That's right." He looked again at her disk array. "You're probably a shuttle jockey judging from your number of disks and from how little you know about ground life." His head motioned through the door and toward where Bennie'd remained sitting, still cleaning his black market Enfield. "You haven't been around here, on Earth, a good deal."

Chen nodded affirmative.

"So, hypothetically, if you *are* a shuttle pilot, Indies are always looking for competent crews—mostly former associates, anyway. The Powers-trained crews Marsco absorbed into the MAS are all pretty much retired by this time."

He paused to prepare her for the next set of instructions. "I'd get off the Earth. The Security relay system on the Moon never re-verifies anyone with the Earth-Net. Once you're in space, you can pretty much travel, work, settle in a colony. Have kids, it won't matter. We'll hide you in plain sight of Marsco's backwaters. Roughly ten percent of space is Indie, anyway."

"10.3768%," Chen inserted with Marsco precision.

Chamberlain looked at her. "I rest my *wallah-case,* Marsco."

They both cordially laughed.

"But," he continued, "Marsco's so sure of its security that the space- and Earth-Nets rarely are rectified. In five years, seven, your new file'll have such a *legitimate* history, a virtual realness, that no one will bother to drill deeper into your record unless they've reasons to become suspicious. You can return to Earth then, seven years, ten tops."

"A few belt crossings—I might be hibering most of that time."

"Exactly. And who's to check on an iced crewmember? And if they do, what they find will check out as legit."

"Why's that, do you think?"

"Victory disease. Marsco won the C-Wars by its initial overwhelming cyber strikes. In a sense it won virtually in the first few hours, almost the first nanoseconds, although the C-Powers didn't realize it until much later. Fighting—real hostilities with casualties and collateral damage—raged for another three years." He spoke from cruel memories of those times. "And at present Marsco can't believe that anyone has the ability to outsmart it. It's the king of geeksters; therefore, no one *can* outsmart it—if you catch. Well, in a nutshell that's its convoluted logic."

"So what do I need?"

"Well, to start, 6,500 MMUs. I hate to sound so crass, but that has to be up front." Chen didn't blink. "Plus 3,750 for expenses." The associate showed him three debit cards, two worth 5,000 and the last 1,000. She carried six other five-K cards plus a dozen worth 500 each.

"We'll have to get them broken into hard pieces. Too easy to trace a card. Should we trust that jockey of yours as our gopher? In the northern section of Sac City there's a bank of sorts. It's honest—even if he isn't—and I still need my ten-K-two-fifty."

Chen agreed to hand over 12.5K in plastic. Chamberlain had a system in place for such a contingency. He disk-sealed her debits with a left twitch into a small box. "Bank knows what to do, and *he* won't know the contents." When he was finished, he called to the other room.

In a moment, the escaping woman watched Bennie head down the clearing toward the battered HFC in his sideways gait, not totally convinced she was ever going to see any of those units again.

"Now, another aspect of my business," Chamberlain returned to his task as hand, "y'know, this's a sideline for me. Marsco knows I'm here. I live in what it'd be consider an unincorporated zone, but the few PRIMS and everyone else who actually lives out here, *we don't make trouble.* I've a laid-back Ludd commune for neighbors, and unless they try to sell their stuff outside the area, then everything's square with the S & H."

The MAS officer wondered how often off-duty legionnaires came up to visit them but said nothing.

"My main business's implanting disks—legally. Slack time now, but I usually have five to eight patients lined up. More coming all the time. As soon as the Marsco entrance exam results are posted, sid parents will be here hammering down my door. 'My daughter failed; she needs another disk to do better...' 'My son wants to be a shuttle jockey...'"

Chen understood, so the doctor continued. "I've actually helped get many, many talented young sids into Marsco, legally;

they do better on their repeat exam. Pass and they're in. Marsco can't be faulted for that. It only takes talented volunteers; nothing else seems to matter. Race, gender, parents' nationality. Even PRIM background. Nothing holds you back."

"Health's all; you need excellent health. No trace of HH GAS." They both knew that this host of STIs still ravaged their world.

"Right!" he agreed but returned to his explanation. "And typically, when I do a good turn to these sids, they remember. I'm totally word of mouth. Except your word. I want no repeat business—*none!*—from your praise of my sideline work. Do you understand?"

Chen nodded.

The physician explained the procedure to substitute her primary for a new disk that would create a supplemental identity. "The operation and recovery will take a week, which you'll spend here."

"A week? Seems a long time."

Chamberlain smiled. "Part of that time you'll spend becoming your new you."

She nodded her understanding so he continued, "I've no other patients at present as I said, so you'll be safe from observation. Even if I had, I keep an isolated chalet in the woods, but as I think of it, if you prefer, you may have that."

"No," Chen answered and then demanded, "all I want is a local anesthetic, not a general." Her gaze assured him of her insistence. "The last time I was under anything—well, let's just say I wouldn't be here if my last hiber experience had been better." Chen thought she needed to continue. "You see, there was an inquest, a trial, then an appeal. You've probably heard about 'the *Piazzi* incident.'"

"Yes, I believe that I may have seen something about that." The doctor assumed she was being analogous, although nothing could compare to that hushed-over cock-up itself. "But I don't need to know much about your career, only enough to close out that old file."

"Fine, but I still want a local."

"Agreed." Chamberlain paused. "Well, if that's all settled, I'll need your full and *real* name, as it appears through your access disk." He slipped on a finger mouse thimble and started a confidential file on his secure, standalone NB.

"You're taking no chances. A lefter but using a separate notebook via a finger thimble."

"In my side business, you're right, I take no chances." He looked deeply into her almond eyes. "Name?"

"Chen. Captain, MAS. Mei-Ling Swanson Chen."

The focus of his eyes changed. He had heard *that* name before: the central figure in the *Piazzi* incident. Something he hadn't counted on. Chamberlain wondered if he should continue. Often in life, he realized, one stood on the verge of a wide gray area. Cross it, and you step from mediocre to champion. He always played safe on this side of stoplines with Marsco, never venturing too deeply into the gray swath now before him. No so today.

His thimble hung in the air. Should he twitch or close the screen? He drew that accepting breath and plunged ahead.

With each keystroke, he brushed aside all concern as he psyched himself up for this, his greatest challenge. He had that much confidence in his work; breaching Security protocols was his stock in trade. So what if this Chen might be so hot that Security was relentlessly searching for her? He knew he could outsmart those buggers and pull this off.

He soon finished with that preliminary aspect of his exam. Closing the NB he stated bluntly, "And another thing besides never returning here afterwards," he cautioned. "And you must never return to any place the good Captain Chen frequented. You know what you are giving up, then?"

She nodded.

There remained only the arduous task of creating the soon-to-be-sid a new identity. "Tell me about your family history. We need to create a shadow you, and it's best if it overlaps many aspects of your real life. Easier for you to remember the deceptions, keep up the pretense."

"Originally, my mother was Euro and an associate. My father's family's from Shanghai, but he grew up in NoAm. I was born back in Marsco's Shanghai Sector in '59."

"Excellent! Many PRIMS and sids from that locale passed their Marsco exams and entered during that timeframe. Makes your cover viable. Its personnel records are fragmentary from that era anyway, the Wars and all."

"I was only a child in the Shanghai Cantonment for part of the Wars then was taken to the Asian HQ, Kuala Lumpur Sector."

"*Perfect!* This'll all make it easier to fabricate your new history."

"How so?"

"Thirty years ago, many PRIMS changed their names and simply took their new ones from their region. You've just become *Lieutenant Ling Shanghai.*"

They continued through the afternoon with the finer points of Shanghai's personal history. When the HFC returned, the pimply faced jockey angled up to the pair holding the box. Its lid was bent out of shape, the lock broken.

"Ye-ah! Bank shorted you," he explained.

Shanghai counted out her 10.5K in large tokens, taking the strong-arm heist of 2K MMU in stride.

TWENTY-TWO

TRANSITIONS

(Miller's Grange, January 2097)

"If you're on the *Gagarin* for her second run," Tessa reminded Zot, "you'll be gone for another *four* years! Maybe *five!*"

The Jovan explorer had no answer. They were down the hall from the grange's kitchen in the great room with its warm fire as the winter afternoon passed slowly.

"Is that what you truly want?" Tessa asked, "being away that long? After what's just happened between us?" Even though it was here before the fire only two nights ago that she let their passion explode, she churned inside: all was still that unsettled.

"It's not like that, Tes. You know it isn't."

The weather hadn't changed over the past few days. The first week of January remained cold and foggy although warmer between the couple. Zot, who had arranged quarters in the cantonment just in case, found no need to leave. Miller was pleased to have him stay here, especially after seeing his only child so happy once more. The hiberman and Tessa were inseparable, until the issue of returning to space reared.

"Well," she reasoned, "how about taking a Mars run?"

"Shuttles?"

"Why not? That'd be almost a semester in length. Match my schedule. It gets pretty rough on me time-wise once a term begins, anyway."

"As if MAS HQ'd kindly arrange my schedule around yours—and its."

"At least give it a chance. Give *us* a chance."

"Inviting, I must say." He smiled and took her hand even though she didn't play along.

"Look," she came at him forcefully, "we have to make a decision here." She put her arms around him and pulled him close. Their eyes fixed. "I don't want to be left hanging. Haven't these past days meant anything?"

"Don't doubt that, love." He bent down and kissed her cheek. "But don't go retro on me either: career or relationship? Hmm?"

"I'm not that schematic," she shot more pointedly that she'd planned. "Be serious!"

"I am," he countered.

The hiber specialist tried enumerating all the ways things might work: being four or five years on the *Gagarin* was first on his list.

"That's a dangerous trip!" she responded without a second thought.

"Space's dangerous! Life is dangerous!" He tried another track: Tessa at Van Braun on Mars.

"Where will you be?"

"Can't say for sure," he replied honestly, "but the VBC can't be ruled out." He quickly ceased ruminating on that option because he didn't want to explain his integral connection with the Center's cryo-stasis research. It would involve many changes at *Valles Marinaris,* not the least of which was telling Herriff just how useless Steerforth really was as Chief of Hibernation Science.

Zot rubbed his forehead. Suggesting they might be together on Mars meant telling her too much of what really happened on his first Jupiter run.

"*If*," Tessa started her own proposal, "and I underscore *if, if* I did end up on Mars, would you reenter the MAS and be based from there?"

"You at the VBC?"

"Maybe! And there's precedent for couples there—happy couples!"

"I know, but I might be able to do better than shuttles."

"What does that mean?"

"Can't really say." He tried being loving while evasive.

"Don't play coy with my guts, iceman."

"Believe me, that's not my intention."

"Without sounding too much like 'the father of the young woman in question,'" Tessa began in a mock-serious tone, "'what *are* your intensions?'"

"Serious!"

They bundled up to face the cold afternoon, put up with the yelping Io and Deimos racing around their legs, and went for a long walk beyond the garden.

Winter brought most growth to an end. The remaining vegetable plants were raked into piles for mulching the beds. The orchard had been pruned in late autumn, leaving the once-bountiful branches stark and bare. Only the orange trees showed any signs of life, although most of the fruit had been gleaned. The ground was hard from freezing and from the lack of rain.

In the far field, where the Truman sons often brought their herd, the dogs scared up three frantic rabbits. When Tessa and Zot reached the re-created pasture's edge, they leaned against the low stone wall. Tessa pointed to the southeast where Miller's first village lie, invisible in the mist. "He has maintenance work for them at the Center until the spring," she explained.

They stood silently at the import of such a once-again normal life.

"It's almost like this fog has ghosts," Tessa finally remarked, her words coming out in white breath.

"How do you mean?"

"We're in a former school yard. Children once played here. Farther south was a park with an aerated, artificial lake surrounded by what Walter calls 'starter castles.' People lived here. Now look!" The area within the PRIM-built wall was clearly a restored grazing meadow. Beyond the stones, however, the once-fashionable lawns had become a thicket of thistles. The pond, a stagnant marsh. The remains of five mammoth houses, abandoned decades before, rose from wild bushes and bent trees.

"I still don't follow."

"Is it wrong that *couples* once lived here? They had kids, dogs. A life."

Zot resisted making a cute remark that trivialized what she was trying to explain. Instead he replied truthfully, "I think I understand. It's hard to imagine *us* having a life like that; is that it? White picket fences and all. Not without sinking totally into Marsco."

"I guess that's what I'm saying."

He stood up at long last, pulled her into his arms and whispered, "Tessa, I don't know how all this will work out for us, but I want you." As she started to pull away, he held her close. "I want *us* to marry."

"Zot, you know you don't have to—"

"I know I don't *have* to; I *want* to."

"I want to as well," she whispered between kisses, "more than anything else."

At first, the pair embraced in silence, overwhelmed by the seriousness of the moment. Juggling careers, past pain, current status: all that in the illusionary and transitory Marsco world they inhabited. Then they erupted in ecstatic laughter, their barriers down. Even the celebration of their long-simmering love the other night had been guarded. This afternoon, they were in the present and dared dream a future together.

Whirling her around in their excitement, Zot exclaimed, "It won't be a world like this old one, and it may be a world without Marsco, but we'll have a life, Tes, I promise you that."

"A happy life," she whispered out of breath.

"Yes, a life as one."

She kissed him, giddy with total love, happier than she had ever been. "Do I get to name the day?" she asked, returning to her earlier mock-serious tone.

"Do I get to name a condition?"

All lightheartedness ceased as she locked him in a dead-solemn stare before he spoke another word. "Condition?" She searched his eyes for his real meaning.

"Tes, I've got to know about the *Gagarin!*"

"Are you saying you'll walk from the altar to that shuttle?"

"It's more than a shuttle; it's an experimental ship, an expedition ship."

"It's still a *space* ship—and one taking you away!"

"Tessa, I'm saying I *have* to know what's up with our second expedition. Married or no, I have to know. I have to make up my mind based on whether there is to be a second Jupiter run."

"Pardon me, dearest one, but you're in jeopardy of moving rapidly from fiancé to fiasco."

Love is a leap of faith, so Tessa leapt.

She and Zot went to her father's library where they used the e-system to scan the iceman's messages.

It only took a moment before Zot thundered, "I just can't believe this Admin chicken shit!" There on a monitor glared his new orders. "Worse than I feared," he fumed. "Look, I'm transferred back to the MAS."

"They can do that?" Tessa hid her true feelings—her natural tactic—because this transfer might open several doors he perceived as still locked.

"Why the hell did Herriff cancel his most advanced ship? I mean, isn't the Center *more* than Martin Herriff? Damn! Isn't the VBC about *science?*"

"Can Herriff just shunt you off to the Asteroid Service?"

"I never really left. Besides, I answer directly to David Steerforth in hiber research. It was really all only temp, anyway. He's probably arranged to get me transferred off the *Gagarin,* not Herriff. Oh, damn, I see my confrere's greasy finger disks all over this more than the Old Man's. I've never even met Herriff—never been to the main Center, either. Icing research's conducted down the valley. Besides, I was on the *Gagarin,* mostly."

"Sounds all hush-hush, your work."

"That's Steerforth—before and after the Jupiter run."

Tessa grew silent and let Zot view her quiet demeanor as acquiescence and consolation.

She assumed she knew why Martin cut the *Gagarin* program. Steerforth's part she didn't know, but Herriff's part she could nail down. The Center had limited capacity; the director needed its engineers, its scientists, its whole gaggle of boffins running through his subterranean Martian colony, all of these wonks working toward his planned escape. In their frenzy, the workers wouldn't know this was the case, of course, but Tessa understood the system well. With no countering evidence, what was before her made the most deductive sense. It was a logical, syllogistic conclusion she didn't wish to share yet.

Herriff's plans to escape the solar system were taking shape. He even invited Miller and her to join his endeavor, but a loving partner finally sat next to her. *I'm not ready for that,* she concluded, *giving him up, losing him so soon. Walter may leave; I'm staying with Zot.*

"Don't you see?" she whispered to him, "we've other choices."

"Name a good one quick."

"You seem disappointed for a guy getting married," she shot him a harsh look, but soften, "*to me!*"

"You seem too happy about this."

"Look," she countered, her green eyes boring into his, "don't shove me into a corner, and don't push me away." He nodded. "You can go to MIT! I teach across a greensward, dammit!"

"In hiber-tech?"

"You're the one cobbling together a radio telescope on the *Gagarin.* You loved the exploration; that's what you'll miss, not icing folks."

"Oh, so all I do is just show up one morning, and the majestic Marsco Institute of Technology just takes me in with open arms? Stipend, lab coat, laptop. '*We're here to teach orphans and stray dogs!*' Is that their motto now?"

"Spare me the theatrics."

"Genetic flaw—all that Med peasantry in my blood."

"Look, I have some pull." She cut him off before he responded. "*I do,* not just my father. And besides, you don't need pull. You're a scientist who's been to bloody Jupiter! Get an astrophysics degree. Publish your results; do more research."

"What results? What research?" he sounded defensive, secretive.

His tone caught her unprepared. *Is he hiding something else?* "Look, I'll document my sources: *you!* You told me you set up a dish out there on that ship between nowhere particular and nowhere else. You're the one who told me that you became a junior-scout astronomer by night out there amid all that blackness—all of which now seems more inviting than me!"

"Oh, yeah, that," he whistled to cover his tracks. "The Academy? Look, aren't you the one who told me, 'the groves of the Academy are a thicket of egos'?"

Tessa laughed coyly. "Well, I probably did and that won't change, but what's that got to do with us?"

Each was hiding much, and both suspected the other of doing the same.

Even so, she stood so that her body leaned into his. The pressure of her breasts and thighs against him sent a thrill throughout his entire frame. She was that close finally—and nearly fully his. It was exhilarating, exciting, daunting all at once. A reminder of what he almost gave up, almost lost forever.

"Oh, screw it!" he let out his exasperation. "Let's just run off together!"

More so than his earlier ones, this remark caught her off guard. "Where?"

"Anywhere Marsco doesn't exist!"

"Dreamer." She pressed harder against him.

"Okay, okay," he finally gave in with soft laughter. "You've got me—totally. All of me. You're at the Academy; I'm doing whatever! How last-century. I've just become a 'house domestic-partner.'"

"We've choices, don't we?"

"The way Marsco views the world, I'm not so sure."

"Look, maybe we need to be in Marsco. It isn't changing from the outside."

Zot sounded like he wasn't listening. "Maybe Walter's right," the iceman signaled back toward the gardens, "stepping out like this."

"Or maybe Walter's wrong! Influence *can* come via my way, too, you know."

"From the inside?"

"From the inside."

Their eyes locked green to brown. Nothing else in the world mattered to him at that moment. Nothing else would. "Okay, okay, I said it. I mean it. I'm in."

"Good, now make me really, really happy." Zot tightened his grip on her muscular body, running his hands down her supple back. "I'm sorry to disappoint, but I'm a bit old-fashioned. Make me happy by going with me to tell Walter."

"I couldn't be more pleased—and surprised—for you both," Miller whispered into his daughter's ear. "I know the challenges you face! This isn't the way it was when Bethany and I—" He broke off.

"I know, or think I do," the daughter assured him.

He held her at arm's length. She was beaming. The only other time he witnessed such a glowing face was Bethany's while holding their newborn years ago. He prayed the pair would know such joy.

"Well, *son,*" the granger held out his hand to Zot, "welcome officially to our family, such as it is. I couldn't ask for Tessa to have anyone better." Their handshake became a full bear-hug.

"Thanks, Walter, I'll make her very happy, I promise."

"I can see that!" Tessa and Zot radiated their devotion. "Keep her safe—that's the most important thing, these days."

Miller caught himself looking vaguely off into the distance, not so much at space as at time. Sharing Tessa with Zot, but without Bethany, was a joyful sorrow but still a sorrow. After a few moments, he saddened even more. "Wish Father Stephen was here for the vows."

"Yes," Tessa agreed, sitting next to her father, putting her head on his shoulder. "I somehow always assumed he'd do them."

Love filled the grange. The fog stayed thick, the cold biting. But inside the rooms crackled with expectations.

The next evening, a Marsco Security and Hygiene officer stood warming himself by the blazing fireplace in the great room. Io and Deimos had settled down from their excited greeting to sleep at his feet.

"Lieutenant Rivers, I don't think you have yet met my daughter, the Lieutenant *and* Doctor *and* Professor Miller."

"Tessa's fine," she added with a cordial handshake.

"And Lieutenant Anthony Grizotti. Her fiancé and a hiber specialist late of the exploration ship the *Gagarin.*" Even though the Security officer'd never been in space, the mention of that shuttle impressed him.

"They've just become engaged," Miller added, obviously thrilled.

"My congratulations, then," the visitor stated formally, bowing and then shaking hands all around a second time.

The Security officer was in standard ashen uniform worn by off-duty urban personnel but had a prescribed air about him.

He stood straight and proud, the proudest there, even if the shortest. Tessa would certainly never be able to find fault with his hair, chin, or uniform. *If he's still only a lieutenant at his age,* the hiberman reasoned, *then he came up as a legionnaire through the ranks.* That bespoke of the centurion's devotion to Marsco more than anything else.

The officer was taut but almost too quick in his actions. With black hair, brown eyes, and darker skin, he seemed quite similar to Zot in many respects. Yet, he was never at ease with himself. He never produced a smile that seemed genuine.

Zot noticed—without being noticed—that Rivers had a language disk implanted behind his right ear.

"Peter's been to visit several times over the past few months," Miller explained, "since being posted as one of Marsco's advisors for the Sac City Sid."

"Yes," the officer explained further, "as Security does for most subsidiaries around the world, I'm here to provide trained officers for sid personnel."

His comment put a sudden damper on the cordial atmosphere of the grange.

"I hadn't been long in-sid before I heard stories of the famous recluse, Dr. Walter Miller, living south of the cantonment. Our mutual friend, Father Stephen, murdered almost two years ago already, would be pleased at such a fortuitous meeting." Rivers tapped his LD nervously.

The three Marsco officers and the former associate sat at table for a simple meal. The fireplace bathed them in golden light.

"I came to the conclusion in my first winter here," Miller explained, "that all these fireplaces were designed to be decorative and not practical." His sprawling home, reminiscent of a Roman villa, had eight bedroom suites and a dozen fireplaces. In true fashion for a hands-on engineer, he'd gutted the original hearth and installed a device of his own fabrication that made them fully functional.

Rivers gave a delighted nod. “It certainly throws out enough heat.”

“Last century’s firewood-tech, really, but it’s a practical setup, especially since even my best solars don’t convert much juice in this soup,” Miller commented. “I’m forced to keep the rest of the house rather cold this time of year, I’m afraid.”

“I should have brought you a survival power pack,” remarked Rivers. “Enough energy in it for days.”

“You know your bounty of coffee and sugar’s ample.”

“Well, it’s the least I can do, knowing I bring such other sad news. And on a propitious night. It’s just past the Epiphany: once, a night for gifts and celebrating.” His LD gave his voice a crisp, precise pronunciation.

“You brought fresh coffee?” the hiberman exclaimed, excited at the prospect.

“Zot brought us jam, too, father. Raspberry, your favorite.”

“And Spam, don’t forget,” Grizotti added.

“Wouldn’t want to forget *that!*” teased his host with a good-natured jab. The Spam was in its distinctive blue, although in aseptic wrapping, not a metal can.

“’Fraid they’re packed for deep space and post-code but still edible.”

Tessa darted an amused glace at him, “Shuttle cast-offs! For your future father-in-law? Such pleasantries, iceman?” She pinged his right ear with her finger disk.

Their light banter and high spirits continued.

The laughter was only broken when Rivers rose to his feet. Holding up his coffee mug, he began, “I want to toast this auspicious still-new year,” he began in formal disk-English. “To such a fine friend. A humanitarian. To his beautiful daughter and her espoused; they make a handsome duo, don’t they?” His eyes darted side to side as he continued, “May many blessings come to each of us this year.”

As though holding fine crystal stemware, the four rose to their feet and touched their mismatched polymer mugs one to another.

"Tonight's the night for wine," Tessa sighed, wishing for some vestige of engagement celebrations long past.

"You said something of sad news a while ago, Peter," Miller noted, returning to his seat. "On a night like this, surely you jest."

"I wish I did, sir. I don't know how to tell you, but I thought you'd like to hear from someone as soon as possible in case you feel it best to leave here."

"Leave?" Miller asked. "Me? Leave here?" Eyes shot across the table from Tessa to her father.

"The Seattle Subsidiary," the Security officer explained after some hesitation, "has been partially, but substantially, merged into the Marsco Sector. It's no longer independent."

"As though it ever was," Zot smirked.

"The non-merged remainder," Rivers continued, "won't be strong enough to be anything but an appendage to the Sector, with no hope of any autonomy. It's become (or, technically, more exactly, will become) a subsidiary supplier for the sector, nothing more."

Tessa exchanged glances with her father and whispered, "I'm so sorry." To Zot's surprise, under the table she reached and took his hand for strength, a tender, unexpected gesture of unity and need.

"Heard anything about this?" Miller asked her, a Seattle resident.

"Rumors only, but I've heard them for so long—over the past dozen years at least—since I started at Academy *as a student,*" she underscored. "I'm sure you'd heard this one before, too."

"Yes, I have. But even so, I hear so many Marsco rumors." To Rivers he asked, "When?"

"Officially, 1 July. Unofficially, the order was effective the first of this month."

"*Over a week ago!*" Miller thundered, in a rare outburst of emotion. "And no one from the Seattle lander plant bothered to inform me?"

A lugubrious silence descended on the table.

Rivers finally remarked, "They were probably instructed to say nothing." He added rhetorically, "Y'know how Marsco works, certainly."

"All too well," both Walter and Zot answered together.

The saddened engineer shook his head. In front of his guests, he uncharacteristically held his forehead in his hands, finger disks placed just below his short gray hair. Rousing himself after this lengthy pause, he surveyed his guests. His disks had left red marks on his skin from the exerted pressure. "D'you know where the stopline'll be?" he asked Rivers.

"Not exactly. I do know the lander plant's within the new boundary. It's grown too important for Marsco to ignore any longer. It'll be placed under its direct auspices."

"Marsco's wanted to do that for some time, I gather," Miller conjectured.

"You would know all that better than I," Rivers answered stiffly.

"How does this affect you?" the iceman asked. He had been given only a fragmentary overview of Miller's ultimate plan. *Hadn't Tessa trusted me with the whole story?* he wondered. Even so, he was able to deduce the ramifications of such a sweeping plan for himself. A lander fleet competing with Marsco, most of it constructed in Marsco's own backyard. *Now, that's something I could believe in!*

Miller began talking, seemingly to himself, "Yes, it all makes sense. We've had so many delays down here. Of course, up in Seattle they probably want to go with Marsco because my engines were too long in coming. That's it, I'm sure. Just good, old-fashioned business sense." His gaze begged his guests to believe this fatuous rationalization. "It's so hard for us to get components and material anyhow. And Bennie running off with our only reliable HFC last summer, just when we needed it."

He looked pointedly at Tessa but spoke without recrimination, "If you'd told me sooner about what he'd attempted, I'd have never let him back near the Center. You only told me after he'd swiped our one and only working runabout. Of course," he added hastily, so his daughter wouldn't think he was blaming her, "his actions weren't your fault."

Tessa and Zot exchanged glances. He thought, *There's another thing she's not telling me.*

All the while, Miller continued on with his monologue, "And composite material's so hard to come by. QCA-chips without embedded formats surreptitiously hidden in them. And metal, especially copper. And not enough damn electricity to run the assembly floor for a full day. I can't really understand why we always had such problems."

He looked face to face as though one of them was withholding this intel. "Other industries in this sid get everything they need. Adequate power—the electric grid's up and continuously serviced. It just seems to be us. I don't want to sound paranoid, but, I don't get it, why us? Always us! Jinxed, I guess."

He drew a deep breath. "But we'd completed six engines and already shipped them to Seattle. Enough for three landers."

Miller went on thinking everyone understood his situation and that these random remarks made perfect sense. "The Seattle crew thought they'd have two landers complete and running in a few months. Our first test flight—an orbital run—was tentatively scheduled for, for July 1. This summer!"

"How ironic!" added Tessa softly, "the day everything's to change."

"Officially change," Rivers replied.

After another pause, and for only the second time that evening, Miller burst out, "I can't believe Marsco's *that* threatened by a tiny damn fleet of Indie landers, for heaven's sake! Twelve, tops! *A dozen versus thousands!*"

The three guests waited for Miller to draw his final conclusion—what was to them an obvious conclusion—but he didn't.

Tessa rose, and standing behind her seated father, hugged him the way a little girl has to because her parent is so much taller. "I'm so sorry. All your work."

"Our work," he responded, tapping her embracing arms tenderly.

Slowly it dawned on him, "Well, silver lining. Being part of a Marsco Sector—especially the HQ complex—has to improve the lot of dozens of sid residents up there, that's for sure. Even PRIM lives will improve."

The four associates all thought, *This isn't the Marsco I believed in when I signed on.*

"Sorry I've ruined your meal!" Rivers began formally.

"Nonsense, Peter. I wanted to know. Needed to know. Eat now," he commanded. "Everyone eat. Tessa's made her famous quiche." He motioned to Zot, who never let anything stop him from a hearty meal. Miller dug into his slice as though nothing had happened. "Eggs too difficult to secure to let 'em go uneaten. There might not be a fresh dozen for a while."

After their nearly silent meal, the party broke up. Tessa and Zot walked off quietly together. As if they might overhear, Tessa shooed the dogs away.

She took his hands and raised them to her lips, kissing finger disks and all. "Zot, you know I love you. I don't think I can or will ever love anyone except you."

"You make me so happy—"

"But—"

"*But?*" He had a sense this was coming. He strained to slow down her words, to will them not to enter his consciousness. Or to enter so slowly they came without meaning, without the utter destruction of his life.

Even so, she began, "I don't think—it's just that—it's all off for us."

He was too shocked by her harsh directness to respond with anything other than a meager reply. "After the other night? After yesterday afternoon? I thought we'd settled—and I'm officially off the *Gagarin!* That's definite. I do something wrong? Say anything?"

"No, it isn't you. It's *Marsco.* I've been thinking this anyway for a long time, since I began reading Walter's *Ascendancy.*"

Zot knew that the work was Miller's attempt to chronicle how their out-of-kilter, muddled, bollixed-up world came into being.

Nonetheless, Tessa remained nebulous and elusive. "And tonight," she tried justifying, "after hearing about all those changes in Seattle, I made up my mind on another proposal I've had."

Grizotti looked puzzled.

"No, not like *that,* from Martin."

Zot still looked puzzled, "Herriff at the Von Braun Center on Mars." He stated the obvious in a dull, dry tone. Not bitter, not sharp, but flat.

"Yes, it's just, last summer Martin asked me once more to consider joining his research team—*insisted* I reconsider his long-standing offer to be the propulsion engineer for an experimental spacecraft. A Miller *Senior* design for an engine Herriff has ordered built at long last."

Everything clicked with the hiberman: new engines, new designs, new cryo-stasis system. He remembered Steerforth's veiled remarks on the *Gagarin* when the ship docked at the asteroid belt on her return from Jupiter. It explained perfectly why everything changed so suddenly at the Center; he realized all this in that nano. Even so, Tessa's connection to this black project blindsided him.

"Tonight," she began her guarded explanation, "as soon as I understood the full impact of what Rivers was saying, I just decided—" Her voice and emphasis changed swiftly, "It's doing *all this* to stop *him!* Don't you see?"

"Of course, I do, Tes. I understand fully." He reached to hold her gently, and she let him comfort her. "It's obvious. I'm only surprised Security took this long."

"Well, long or not, it's the last byte." She blended into his arms as though dancing, her action contrary to her declaration of their breakup.

This's where she belongs, he thought, then strained to say sympathetically, "So, Marsco ruins your father—pisses on him big time—and you want to stay with it, join it on Mars?"

"It's not as simple as that," she answered, finally pulling out of his embrace. "It's something I, I can't tell you—"

"Can't tell me! That's the crux of the issue, isn't it? You don't trust me."

"Nor you, me." The woman tried calming herself down. "We're both holding back something, many things, aren't we?" She almost mentioned his message about cryogenics to her father, the one she'd seen a few summers ago. He almost mentioned this Bennie moke stealing the HFC.

"We weren't holding back the other night," Zot whispered without an accusatory tone.

"Nor when you proposed," she admitted. "Our love's come to a stopline, that's it—and all of it." Her eyes shone with determination. If Zot thought there were tears, he was wrong. The resolute woman vowed never to cry over him again.

The hiberman replied softly as though to himself, "We've both become so Marsco, we've trashed any chance for our love."

Embracing him for her final time, Tessa whispered, "Know that my love isn't crushed, my darling. Now, go!"

She ran into the darkened cold rooms at the farthest end of the house.

Standing by the Security HFC, Rivers and Miller talked. The centurion offered Grizotti a skim to the bachelor quarters in the cantonment. The iceman accepted when it was clear from Tessa that she wanted him to go rather than stay. The two men waited while he packed up his kit.

Moisture from the muting fog hung thick on everything. The single I-ON-U stanchion was a dark shape in the gray distance. Water beaded on the composite flight surfaces of the HFC. Miller's dogs appeared from inside the house and joined their master. Sensing the cold, they soon returned to the warmth before the fire.

"I haven't told you the second half," Rivers began reluctantly, "the worst half of my unhappy news."

"Tonight's the night for it," the engineer answered, trying to stay resigned.

"I'm afraid that Marsco is going after *you!* We're to instigate a surveillance of your activities."

"Instigate? As if it hasn't already begun!"

"Well, *intensify.*" He tapped behind his right ear to suggest the language disk was the problem.

Doctor Miller stopped him by indirectly motioning to the onion-shaped surveillance housing visible even in the fog. Infrared cams were recording their every move although his in-place fuzzers frustrated them capturing any speech.

"Beyond that," Rivers explained.

"You mean more?"

"Yes, more than mere passive scans. I've delayed immediate implementation, of course, in deference to your daughter's situation. I didn't know about the iceman being here and his connection to her, but I think my delay helped both of them stay out of some Internal dossier. It's best for them not to meet here again. Even your daughter—she must leave and never return. I'll keep things as discreet as possible until she goes, but I can't delay my orders much longer."

"What more can they do?"

"Much more," the S & H officer shifted his explanation. "I owe a great deal to our friend, Stephen Cavanaugh—more than I can ever repay. It's in his name I help you, as I didn't help him when I should have, could have," he added vaguely.

Miller didn't understand fully; Rivers made no attempt to clarify.

"Security's thorough. This subsidiary: most of it will fall back into a zone."

"As if it wasn't already."

"But until now patrols kept roving PRIM gangs at bay. Soon, however, the shrunken sid is to keep the light industry and cannery sections in close proximity of the cantonment. But stoplines are to cut off the southern locale. Trains are to stop. Your grange will have even less security."

"There hasn't been much out here for years anyway. It's been falling toward UZ status, hasn't it?"

"It's been clear for a long time, starting from even before I was posted here, that this sid was slipping zone-towards."

"What was the lingo once?" Miller asked of no one in particular but his own memory of those horrid times long past, "during the prewar era of Abandonment? *PRIM-to?*"

Rivers shrugged. Even his ELD didn't pick up that slang.

"No matter," responded Miller. "When?"

"Same time frame as in Seattle, officially 1 July. But for all practical purposes, everything's already taken effect. The new main sto pline will be well beyond the light rail spur you often ride. Service to end soon at dozens of platforms."

"Thanks for telling me all this. I know how it must jeopardize your position."

Rivers didn't respond to that but added, "I'm sure part of its reasoning is that this sid was once so politically significant. You know, '*the last bastion of the C-Powers.*' But, it's also after *you,* I'm afraid."

"Is it that frightened? Of me? C'mon!"

"It is! You're a more powerful threat to it than you know. Be careful."

Disbelieving, Miller only nodded in disgust.

Rivers continued, "I'm sure Security thinks you came here because of the area's connection to the Powers."

"Oh, that's paranoid nonsense. I grew up near here!" He pointed vaguely northward. "Was on Mars—as an associate in good standing—when the Powers used this former *state* capital as their final *federal* capital. I came back here years later because of the vestiges of that research center, what I renamed Sac City Aerospace

Associates. When I came back, it was an economic decision. A research decision. A personal decision. Not a political one."

"Are there any distinctions between them in our world?" asked the Security lieutenant astutely.

The engineer didn't answer as they waited for Grizotti in silence.

After a time Rivers spoke up, "May I come again? Still a friendly visit of an unofficial nature."

"You're always welcome."

"So, you won't flee?"

"No, prob not. This's my home."

The centurion added in a confident low tone, "Watch out for *sudden* friends who might be Marsco. Be on your guard. I'll keep these upcoming changes at bay as long as possible, but my superiors are more determined than I am. They're bringing in a high wallah, a Mr. Giannini." He stopped to see if by chance the granger reacted to the man's name. "I've met him before. He'll pressure some misguided associate who's looking for a rapid get-ahead. Those callow youths who would sell out their best friends to gain any advantage as an associate. I know the type—I've been there."

"Well, maybe things might work differently this time."

"I've asked for a transfer so I don't have to—"

"I understand."

Grizotti joined the two outside. He'd been trying to talk to Tessa, but she wouldn't open her bedroom door.

As he came up, Miller asked the Security officer, "Still haven't found my missing HFC?"

"Your stolen runabout, don't you mean?"

"Well, yes, I guess Bennie did actually pinch it. I probably won't need it now, but I would like it back."

"We'll keep looking."

Cordial farewells went around as the two associates boarded the runabout. The craft rose thirty meters to clear the trees and the single surveillance stanchion and then disappeared, its discharge vapor hardly noticeable against the fog. After the engine noises died away, Miller remained, staring up at the thick blanket.

Tessa could not sleep.

Io found her. Although squat, the dog sprung effortlessly onto the bed and immediately nestled down next to the restless woman for warmth.

For her own part, Tessa thought of her father's work, his partially finished collection of materials about the history of Marsco. It wasn't a detailed chronicle so much as a pasted-up set of interviews and reminiscences made by associates, Luddites, troopers who fought on both sides during the Continental Wars. Statements from survivors. Fragmentary blogs and webcasts from those who didn't make it through the conflagration.

Her father's energy was incredible. Designing engines at his Center. Gathering all those interviews and historical documents. Tending his gardens.

It gave her pause and a headache.

The portion of *The Ascendancy* she saw over the past few years was instrumental in bringing her back to his grange. Her new understanding of Marsco's rise to prominence, her clearer perception of that era, helped ease the tensions between father and daughter. She comprehended her world so much better through him. She scoffed at the thought that Zot and she might find happiness while connected in any way to Marsco.

Although she knew she must not stay closely tied to Marsco, she knew it was wise to return to Mars and work for Herriff, to accept his ultimate proposal. She'd find a degree of autonomy on the Red Planet, and eventual escape seemed to be her only answer.

And Zot? She surprised herself by letting the question come to her mind. She shouldn't have let her guard down. She stonewalled him so long (and all other men); she knew she should have kept that stopline closed to him. She must tightly clamp down every feeling for him once more, as she had for nearly five years up to the other night. Her mind defended this unyielding stance. Her gut? That went unanswered.

Tessa rose quickly in the dark. Io danced around her feet as if they were going outside together in the dead of night. Deimos heard the commotion and joined them.

The three ended up standing outside of Miller's study. A light was on in the room, shining under the door, but Tessa heard only an occasional creak of a chair moving slightly. No papers rustled. No finger disks twitched a pad. Listening at the door, she was sure her father merely sat there gray-screening, thinking. Trying to understand it all. Praying.

Tessa wanted to burst in like a child and ask him what to do about Zot. She loved the man yet believed she must give him up completely.

Not sure what else to do, she sealed herself off from any decision. Steeling herself came naturally to her; a trait, she had been told, that was also strong in her mother. She ached for a crack in the mental casing of her own making, even as Zot tried to break through it, even as she let him break it down the other night.

Outside her father's study, she let herself be encased once more.

As she waited there, the room's light suddenly went off. The chair gave the clear sound of someone rising.

When Miller opened the door, he found the hallway empty.

Tessa appeared asleep in her room when he paternally looked in on her. In the dark, the shadowy dogs stirred without sharing their secrets.

Once settled into a room at the visiting officers' quarters at the cantonment, Zot killed time. Rather than think of Tessa and their now destroyed bond, he settled into his bunk. But his mind raced too much for sleep. Over the past few days he had been on the verge of watching her slip away, of having her totally, and then ultimately losing her forever.

The very notion of Tessa joining Herriff, worming herself even deeper into Marsco—the Marsco her own father rejected—became too much for him to bear.

Surrounded as he was at the cantonment by hundreds of eager associates, he felt bottled up. He wanted to scream, shout, smash a chair into the wall, but he had to remain in simmering silence. *I'm getting out,* he vowed with every fiber of his roiling mind. *I refuse to assist in the continuance of such an oppressive, destructive hegemony.*

"And Tessa be damned," he whispered hoarsely. "Tessa be damned!"

Two days later, the C-phone buzzed to life at Miller's grange. He couldn't get over the irony of it working suddenly, when every other service in the surrounding area was inexorably going downhill. In a matter of months, whatever was left of any infrastructure would be totally useless, except to malicious, revenging PRIM gangs who chafed at their chance to obliterate whatever they couldn't possess. The way of the world just beyond the fringe of Marsco.

The phone buzzed a second time. Someone was definitely trying to reach him.

A man's crackling voice, partially drowned out by static, stated calmly, "I really shouldn't say too much, because sometimes other people are listening in."

"Roger, I understand."

"And sometimes, my transmitter just rings a random number. Old system, pre-Marsco. Rings people haphazardly, hit or miss."

"Affirmative. We're all in that soup."

"Well, I'm trying to reach a Doctor Miller, Doctor *Walter* Miller. It doesn't matter who I am, although he knows me by reputation and has sent me an occasional client. I do lots of planting. And if this *is* or *isn't* Miller, you needn't confirm."

Silence acknowledged the situation.

"D'you know if Miller is allegedly still looking for a shepherd for his flock? I understood—y'know how these rumors fly around sids and zones—that he and a Martian colleague made inquiries last summer about that."

"I really shouldn't comment on that—"

"Well, let's assume that that's the case."

"I accept your hypothesis."

"In my line of work, I meet scores of people with many talents. I just met an extraordinarily talented woman this week—"

The line crackled so loudly the speaker had to repeat himself. He then continued, "She might even be affiliated with *his, Miller's,* former employer. Maybe she is; maybe she isn't. Maybe she *isn't any longer.* Can't really say. Not my place to say. Anyway, she was having trouble with an on-disk file and asked me to help open it."

"Did you?"

"No, lost the *whole* file. Had to reconstruct the information all over for her."

"Sounds complicated."

"No, it's surprisingly easy. Most extraordinary, I merely renamed her data on her disk and off she went."

"Why are you telling me of this?"

"Yes, well, see—she seems to be a high flier."

"Is that so?"

"Yes," said the crackling voice. "A talented high *high* flier."

"Tell me more."

"You and your friend *may* want to speak with her personally about that, if you're still looking for someone extraordinary."

"I shouldn't comment on my friend's interests."

"Oh, quite understand."

"But, she seems keen for *that* line of work?" Miller asked.

"Yes, and what I saw on her old data file shows much experience in that regard. She really *belted out* a long résumé. Three times, at least, I gather."

"Well maybe as a service for that longtime Martian friend of mine, I should meet with her, since she's on Earth and all."

"I have to say, in all fairness, you may not be overly fond of some of *her* friends."

"Oh?"

"Yes, well, one of them is using a, shall we say, a *borrowed* runabout."

"*Mine?*" The word burst from Miller; his only remark their whole conversation which wasn't delivered in a disinterested monotone.

"Well, I can't say *yours* because I can't exactly know for sure with whom I'm talking. But it did have the insignia of a former research center not 100 clicks from here. He seems to think that *you*—or someone at that alleged Center—loaned it to him."

"Permanently loaned it to him, I suspect he feels."

"I suspect you're right in your estimation of his rather low-threshold of honest feelings."

"Sounds like what Bennie Cart—"

"I say, don't give away anything, you understand."

"Oh yes, sorry." Miller caught his breath. Maybe here was the pilot for Herriff's escape flight out of the solar system, but was she trustworthy if she's associating with Bennie? He asked, "Does this friend seem particularly nasty? Not really a reliable sort? And does he walk sideways, crab-like? 'A youth carbuncular'?"

"That's an excellent characterization! He's brutally calloused and potentially dangerous, and personally I'd never have engaged his offered services—there's so many other choices. And, I'd have looked damn hard to find one. Y'know, she seemed to rely on him, regardless of how badly he treated her."

"Yes, some people, women mostly, do stay in relationships like that."

"'Fraid you might be right there."

"Oh, it's such a shame; that does make a difference about this extraordinarily talented woman."

"Well, I haven't said a word to her. Perhaps I shouldn't?"

"You know, I don't like the company she keeps. I have to be very careful about the kinds of tenants I have, women I'm seen with, that sort of thing. Sorry if that sounds old-fashioned. And possibly I'm misjudging her by her single friend, but no, perhaps it's best she and I don't meet after all."

Herriff needed a deep-space pilot, but Miller wouldn't recommend, wouldn't trust anyone associating herself with Bennie Carton. They weren't that desperate just yet.

"Shall I keep you in mind in case someone else just as extraordinary comes my way?"

"Yes, some other big-time jockey—male or female—please think of me."

With that, the C-phone abruptly went dead.

TWENTY-THREE

IN THE DARK

(Sac City, January 2097)

"Gloomy winter or bright summer," Colonel Jarrod Hawkins confided with uncharacteristic disclosure, "I pay little attention to such variable conditions after so many years in changeless space."

The colonel and Captain Julio Fuentes stood in the pitch-black command bunker seven stories underground, a single flashlight beam piercing the darkness.

Acting as the colonel's ADC, Fuentes mechanically switched on several battery lamps that radiated a soft yellow light. The bunker wasn't heated because the building above (formerly the capitol building itself) had fallen into disrepair. The air was damp; the ceiling dripped randomly here and there.

After a long pause, the aide-de-camp unthinkingly added, "The fact that topside it's winter means absolutely nothing to you."

"Affirm that. But slipping into this sid undetected *does.*" Hawkins kept speaking, trying to draw a telling remark from the former associate. "I think exclusively in strategic terms. Meteorology crosses my mind only when picking targets. 'What will my Lightnings face?' That's why weather mattered."

Fuentes made no response.

"A clear night with a late rising moon's ideal, much better than a foggy sortie. Although a Lightning could—and often did—attack through dirty soup."

No recognition of facts stirred in the subordinate.

Burning with impatience, the commander fumed, "Better a sudden, decisive attack than all this endless political waggling."

Fuentes listened, a blank expression on his face.

Hawkins walked around the bunker, the faint light illuminating several other rooms. In their present state, the concrete walls betrayed none of their former importance. "What decisions were once made here," the senior officer noted. "Now look." He bushed the nearest wall with his fingertips; white powder flaked off.

The com center had been stripped of situation maps and secure landlines. Nothing remained of the SDCs and telecom network that once ran through here. Nothing remained of the projectors that once displayed hot areas around the world and throughout the solar system twenty-eight years prior. Broken bits of tech were strewn about; useless wires hung from conduits.

"If anything did remain," Fuentes remarked at last but with no sense of Marsco pride, "they'd be kludge compared to today's ops."

Testing the waters, Hawkins ventured to add, "We're standing in the place of greatest dishonor for the Continental Forces."

"If that's so," Fuentes answered without emotion, "then the actions precipitating such a disgrace must have been heinous." His voice and eyes betrayed no connection between his words and their meaning. Behind his back, his fingers twitched the air, an odd habit that pleased Hawkins.

Late into the night, Lieutenant Peter Rivers sat in his HQ office twitching through a file he did not like seeing. Spartan, the office had curtains, but he hadn't bothered to lower them. The Sac City fog seemed to paste itself on the window glass; the office lights gave the panes an eerie glow. These effects meant nothing to the SO as he glanced through the detailed Internal report for the third time. *Too many*, he thought, *far too many high wallahs are coming here.* He looked up, saw the open curtains and adjusted them hours after dark, his way of avoiding an obvious conclusion. "Why come here? There is no here *here*," he smirked under his breath before sitting down.

On the opposite wall, a map of the redrawn stoplines illustrated that this sid was on the verge of shrinking drasticly. Miller's grange was outlined in red.

Are they here for Miller? He hoped not.

He hadn't spoken to Miller since Epiphany when he broke the devastating news to him about his failed lander plans, about Seattle gobbling up a relatively independent subsidiary in hopes of cutting the enterprising granger off from any allies in his quixotic ambition to challenge Marsco. And challenge it peacefully, legally, and technologically.

With a twitch using his most secure finger disk, Rivers opened his lastest dispatch from Security HQ in Seattle. Giannini was coming in just over a week to supervise Miller's treatment. If Rivers were to do anything, it must be done now.

But, the local SO knew he must first make sure Miller wasn't meeting with these influential sids who'd arrived singly and in pairs. Whatever was up with that, Miller had better not be involved or there was no helping him. Whatever was up, the centurion had to know stat.

Calling for a HFC, Rivers quickly amended his order. "Not a two-seater," he told the Ops duty officer, "get me the largest and a squad of troopers."

A dusty mahogany table stood in a conference room to the left of the com center. Each seat lacked a delegate's nameplate originally made from asteroid nickel and inlaid Martian lapis lazuli lettering outlined by lunar platinum. Fuentes found enough plastic seats for the soon-to-be-started meeting, not the leather chairs that the world's highest councilors once graced while deciding the destiny of the Powers.

"It was here that the legislative mandate to continue the struggle for freedom dissipated. Nearly twenty-eight years ago," Hawkins informed Fuentes in his precise, martial way.

The commander waited for any sign from his subordinate. None came, so he continued.

"Here civilian governments, against the express wishes of their military leaders, agreed to a cease-fire, agreed to end hostilities against Marsco. It was here, in this inauspicious spot, that Continental influence essentially ended. Here, that governments sold out their own fighting forces, sold out a military that had sworn to serve, uphold, and protect the bloody spineless bastards who let their proud warriors down. The buggers pushed our faces in the mud."

Fuentes drew Hawkins up short, "But twenty-eight years ago, Marsco had this bastion surrounded." Had the remark come with any degree of emotion, the colonel would have been worried. Instead, it came as a dry fact, nothing more.

Hawkins remembered those days. Belligerent hordes are a strong inducement to sign an Armistice. And with Marsco's forces poised outside the city, the final and harried Continental Powers's Delegate Council had to acknowledge that all was lost.

The ADC commented in a dead tone unaware of his words' import, "Those PRIMS were led brilliantly, but yes, it remains a humiliating defeat." After making his case, Fuentes remained silent, unmoved except for air-twitching behind his back.

"Beaten by rocks from space and the world's teaming rabble," the colonel acknowledged, his eyes fixed on his subordinate. "Undone by tech-geeks and whiz kids, and a few live moles sitting at *our* monitors, who with a few well-planned disk clicks, crashed our sophisticated command and control infrastructure. Marsco boffins who twitched nearly all our advanced weaponry systems into inoperability."

Hawkins now stood silently, all the while scrutinizing his aide for the slightest sign of independent thought.

Slowly the colonel continued, surprising only himself with the frank remark. "Of course, I was in space, already in cryo, when our final curtain fell." It was his way of defending his honor, by refusing to share in the disgrace of that ignominious capitulation.

Soon after the outbreak of hostilities all those years ago, the C-Powers forces were left without satellite links for communications and weapons control; their twenty-first century forces inexplicably found themselves fighting a conventional war as though it were 1916. On the ground, they faced the battle-arrayed throng of PRIMS who came on at them mercilessly, wave after wave, armed solely with three-burst Enfields.

Civilian control became nearly impossible when all non-military telecom and computer interaction ceased. Marsco trojans and cyber attacks were aimed at total annihilation of all military command structures and civilian government links. Populations soon found themselves without electricity and Herriff-Grids. Without Net information. Without broadcasts from reliable sources. Without adequate food distribution. Without the fabric of the sophisticated world they knew.

Hawkins deliberately focused on the junior officer. "I was not here for the slaughter," he admitted, almost embarrassed.

"I was on Earth as a child," Fuentes remarked dryly.

"Of course."

"Civilian panic spread," the aide added.

A stillness returned to the pair as memories overtook both. Marsco dominated the skies and anything orbiting the Earth. It destroyed or co-opted the use of all satellite weaponry and GPS technology, making strategic targeting by the C-Powers virtually impossible. Aiming artillery and ground-launched rocketry became unreliable, useless, even when PRIM encampments and fortifications were close at hand, within visual.

"In the times leading up to the C-Wars," Hawkins caustically admitted, "everything had become so computer-dominated that we joked, 'How pathetic, even a bow and arrow's impossible to aim without a command disk twitching over a pad!'" He held up his own red disk for emphasis, glaring at Fuentes, searching for any spark of a reaction. "Marsco's disruption of our civilian and military Net—which it essentially built—brought everything we had to a fatal, catastrophic termination. A cascade event, one crash bringing on the next."

"Yes, even though only a boy, I witnessed it all," was Fuentes's only whispered, emotionless reaction.

"But, what to target anyway?" Hawkins reluctantly let his mind slip back onto those horrid times as he ran down the questions that had plagued him for three decades: "How were we to retaliate against vital and essential parts of our own infrastructure and society? How were we to fight our own systemic, cyber network? A world that had become a virtually intertwined, Wi-Fi world: how do we attack the multinational geeks and wonks who controlled Marsco?"

Paying no attention to his aide, Hawkins ran on. "Marsco had become such an integral part of every developed nation. How could we fight *it* without tearing *ourselves* apart? Thriving pieces of the Pacific Rim, the Chinese coast, the Indian subcontinent. Japan, Korea, and Malaysia—the most tech-advanced parts. Almost all of No- and SoAm, Europe. Name the locale; it had grown thoroughly integrated with Marsco. What to do?"

"Waging war's simple," Fuentes conceded dryly, hardly responding to the diatribe. "Picking the correct enemy isn't." The former associate showed no discernable connection between his incisive words and their marked meaning.

These musings, Hawkins knew, were more than hypothetical scenarios to ponder over at war colleges on attack simulators. Defeating Marsco this time would take more than mock engagements and glyph maneuvers.

This wasn't a civil war against factions of a single country. It was war against the entire fabric of modern life. Until the C-Wars loomed, historically no armed forces had ever contemplated the fact that they might be called upon to fight essential parts of their very self. And the most vital parts—a point not lost on Hawkins, who tended to see the world clearly in starkly contrasting black and white.

"Nationalism," Hawkins lamented, "multinationalism, PRIMification, Divestiture, Abandonment: all produced such drastic changes in the political landscape by midcentury. Who was really prepared for this type of war?"

"No one except Marsco," Fuentes answered without embellishment except for hidden air twitches.

"Affirmative," the colonel replied, still eying his ADC for any signs of a crack, "the losers contemplate the lingering, unanswerable questions after a war, not the winners."

"And when hostilities began in January 2067," Fuentes added in a monotone, "Marsco did have obvious enemies to fight. And it fought them with remarkable, ruthless skill. Besides its crippling initial strokes, it rained down Vanovaras with pinpoint accuracy, hitting vital military and civilian targets at will."

"You know its history well," remarked Hawkins.

"I was very young then."

"Yes, of course."

"Needless to say, it was a short war, only thirty-four months. And the last such hostilities for nearly thirty years." Fuentes stopped, and looking around as though coming out of water after holding his breath for too long, he then added, "Yes, *Pax Marsco.*"

Hawkins stared, contemplating the blank speaker, making sure no spark of affection glimmered behind his dull eyes. But his aide had spoken all the while in a drab, continuous tone.

Spirited by these memories, the professional soldier had to grudgingly admit that, for a military amateur engaging in its first and only real conflict, Marsco fought superbly, brilliantly. He tried to tone down his admiration for his adversary's success. But next time, it'll be different; soon, if he'd anything to say about it.

"Marsco's the explicit, unequivocal target now," he noted, "the clear and present danger—the one suffering from Victory Disease."

His voice grew hot with excitement. "It's grown complacent after such an initial swift victory; foolishly, it believes it's impervious to rebellion or attack. While it's bloated with self-confidence, our time for a counterstroke approaches."

Marsco's grown to be so like the C-Powers themselves, forty odd years ago, Hawkins thought with emotions mixed with awe and envy. *Overripe, rotten at its core, ready for a band of Young Turks to knock it from the highest branch.* He savored the fact that history had set him here at this epoch. It was his destiny to reach for the highest limb and pluck all the waiting fruit he wanted.

The colonel's reverie was interrupted by the sounds of someone approaching. Three hawks from the bygone Continental Delegate Council, a trio who stubbornly resisted signing the mortifying December '69 Armistice, were making their way to the long-neglected bunker.

Turning to Fuentes, Hawkins ordered, "Make sure the remaining delegates arrive only after I've had a few moments with our first guests." He hadn't much time to earn these militants' support.

Showing that he wanted to obey his commander, the aide left with dispatch.

At first, the distinctive whine of the HFC's pinpoint landing glide went unnoticed. The thick fog and time of night deadened every sound. Rivers had his squad out and organized in a defensive perimeter around their target. If anything was happening inside, everyone was trapped.

"Don't let anyone out. Restrain first but don't hesitate to shoot."

"Yes, sir," a trooper answered tersely.

Charging his Enfield sidearm, the SO moved with caution toward the main entryway.

It was only then that two yelping dogs and the granger himself appeared in the gateway, stunned to see Rivers standing there armed with Marsco muscle in the shadows behind him. This was a change from previous visits when the officer came without brandishing the weapon he routinely carried.

"Is there something I can help you with, lieutenant?" the granger asked rather more formally than intended.

"Yes, Dr. Miller, you can answer a few simple questions."

The granger snorted a sharp laugh, "Is there such a thing coming from Security?"

"Are you alone?"

Miller called the dogs. Only after the auburn Deimos marked a landing skip of the HFC did he and the squat Io, the grange's protective pair, return silently to their master's side. "I'm with my dogs as you can see, here all alone. Tessa left three weeks ago; Zot about the same."

"No other visitors?"

"Do you want to rummage through each room? Look under every rug?" He gestured toward the inside of his house. "I guess asking to see your orders to do so is fruitless; plus, a search warrant's nonexistent in this world."

"Any other visitors of late?"

Miller laughed then pointed to the onion-shaped housing overlooking the grange. "Check your own surveillance records," he remarked in a restrained tone. Rivers was no longer the benign visitor—coincidentally sharing a mutual friend, the deceased priest Cavanaugh—but a fully engaged Security officer on a mission.

The centurion ushered Miller deeper into the grange away from the front gate where his Security squad stood on alert. A few meters inside the hedge, he softened. "This will be my last unofficial visit."

"Looks official to me."

"Forces are at play I can no longer control or influence. You must leave soon."

"Leave? Where to?"

"You must know of somewhere in the Marsco world where you can hide in plain sight."

"I thought I was doing just that right here."

Rivers spoke urgently, needing to return to his squad at once so as not to raise suspicion. "Everything here in Sac City changes toward you in a few days. It is best you are gone by then." At that point, Rivers finally released the discharge propellant pressure of the Enfield and holstered his sidearm. With no explanation, he added, "Please accept my apologies for interrupting your privacy, Dr. Miller."

The SO hadn't searched the premises, but he knew the granger wasn't lying. Miller was alone, in danger, and adamant about not fleeing.

The lieutenant felt his finger disks were clean. The granger had been warned under the optimum cover of hunting for high wallahs known to be moving about Sac City for no apparent reason.

For a few minutes, Miller watched the HFC rise six meters, hover, and then set a course due north back toward the center of Sac City. It flew without running lights, yet for a time the granger followed the faint glow of the vectoring jets even in the thick fog. "Off to roust someone else," he asserted to the alert dogs who seem to watch the lights with him. Marsco was that way, all three silently agreed.

The corridor outside the DC chambers brightened as the first delegate tentatively progressed toward Hawkins.

The officer turned on two additional camp lanterns. In the dim light his drab green and gold-trimmed uniform looked colorless. But to anyone old enough to have lived through the Wars, "the green and mustard" was immediately recognized. The uniform, once proudly worn, hadn't been seen since the Armistice.

As the delegates entered singly, the colonel was instantly struck by how much each had aged. He felt like a shuttle commander after an extended hiber-voyage viewing his elderly parents. In Hawkins' absence, the men had grown older, none gracefully.

The first into the room was Herr Neidlinger, who represented the old north-central European Hohenzollern State. With special permission, he also voted for the Baltic Tri-Power. Although not expected to attend because of age and illness, the Scandinavian delegate often took his cue from Neidlinger. Hawkins fervently courted the favor of this councilor, an important man who controlled two votes and swayed a third. The fate of most of old Northern Europe rested in Neidlinger's shaking hands.

Where once he sported thick sandy hair, today his head was covered with thinning gray strands combed from the back over his crown. The scar of his thunderous youth had faded but was still visible below his left eye. He had gained a pronounced limp during the intervening years that necessitated a cane, its handle decorated by an enormous black asteroid diamond. After fumbling with the cane, he shook Hawkins's hand in a cordial greeting. "Haven't met one-on-one since before those unfortunate times."

"During the Wars," Hawkins stated boldly coming to the point, "you favored many of my clandestine plans. I'm counting on your continued influence and support with the DC now."

"Yes, yes," the delegate murmured vaguely. "But since the Wars, our power bases—much smaller than the old prewar boundaries." He added as a concluding aside, "Everything's shrunk considerably. You've been away many years."

"Yes, of course, I know that. Away in space, but I know what's going on."

"Do you? Well, please allow me to fill you in on the *real* score," the old man chattered on with keen political emphasis, knowing their time together was limited. "Like the rest of the delegates, I currently represent subsidiaries initially drawn up at the dawn of Divestiture some seventy years ago but redrawn several times since then by both the Powers and lastly by Marsco. And you should know, many successful and independent sids are indeed flourishing, a point made by Marsco to show how its policies are working successfully." He shuffled toward a seat. "But before I go on, I must sit down."

The officer asked himself, *Have these old men lost their nerve?* Repeated realignments had changed the political realities, creating serious ramifications. *Can these delegates actually speak for their present constituents, many of them born after the C-Wars? Do they still command power? Wield power?*

Hawkins, for one, aimed to find out.

The delegate finally found a place to his liking. His walk in the dripping, damp corridors had tired him. Coming down flights of stairs—the lift wasn't functioning—and entering the chilly room agitated his knees. Seated, he bent his legs to sooth their aching, to massage away any lingering stiffness. These stretching antics, Hawkins had to admit, were like those of an old man, which of course he was.

"Odd you wanted to meet here, colonel." Neidlinger's pointed remark cautioned the officer about the way things might go.

Delegate Miklos Horthy, wearing a natty navy-blue suit in a mid-century cut, waited patiently in the corridor for Neidlinger to have his say before entering. He smoothed his styled hair, drew himself up perfectly straight, and walked into the chamber. Horthy was accustomed to entering only when the focus shifted solely to him. He did so that evening with the panache of a scripted politician. The debris-littered bunker complex was disappointingly empty, still his practiced entrance commanded attention.

"Delighted as always, *General* Hawkins," declared Horthy, unintentionally giving the colonel a promotion. His greeting, a gentlemanly embrace followed by a pro forma kiss on the officer's cheeks, was more cordial than Neidlinger's, if more embarrassing to the reluctant recipient.

Stepping back from the second delegate, the colonel noted that Horthy had aged as well. But yet, he wondered, *Does he still have fire enough to command?*

At one time, this delegate was the representative of the enormous East-Central Euro Power, now broken into a dozen or so subsidiaries. Once he was the most hawkish member of the old Delegate Council, outspoken to the last against any capitulation.

Would this thinning old man, who resembled more of a caricature rather than an energetic delegate, still command respect?

The third councilor entered and seated himself business-like after accepting Hawkins's greeting. Delegate Gobineau, who represented both the Gallic and Iberian Powers (although these constituted only one vote), was exactly like Hawkins in this one regard: he was a man of few words but decisive action. He had gray hair tied back in a ponytail of early-century style, and he sported a neatly trimmed gray beard. His round, puffy cheeks were bright red; his frame had thickened somewhat over the years.

Without rising, Councilor Neidlinger greeted Gobineau cordially, although the two had often been rivals.

Coming to the same conference table where capitulation had been discussed the last time any delegate sat there, Hawkins began his remarks. "Gentlemen, today, I'm expecting a total of eight delegates and the Council's military advisor. Instead of the fifteen members, I'll address the minimum needed for a quorum. But discussion of my plans will have to wait at the moment. I'm here to primarily seek unity."

"As in the old days?" Gobineau shot, as though personally smarting from Council disunity.

"Gentlemen," the colonel began once more, then stopped to make sure his fuzzer was set; its unheard static disrupted any possible clandestine recording of their conversation. If the room were bugged—or if a delegate were digitizing his words—playback would be nothing but crackling.

"Gentlemen," Hawkins began his third attempt at speaking, "the time has come to reassert ourselves. Your former and hacked up Powers have waited patiently under the thumb of Marsco. At this very moment, I'm prepared to strike—and strike such a decisive blow that Marsco will be sent reeling. With such an opening sortie, we'll so disrupt its ability to rule that each delegate can swiftly resume control and completely direct his own areas of interest. My opening stroke will create a vacuum which you'll more than adequately fill."

"In the same way that Marsco gained power in the first place," noted Gobineau, an off-handed remark offered with no intention to offend.

"Exactly," commented Horthy. "Marsco really didn't *win* the war; it merely disrupted our ability to maintain control long enough for its forces to move in." He thought a moment with a wise expression on his face. "Marsco merely made it impossible for us to win, that's all. Consider this, we resisted for only thirty-four months, less than three years!"

Tapping his black diamond on the side of the table, Neidlinger interjected with a noticeable degree of irritation. "Please, gentlemen, the purpose of this meeting isn't to rewrite history. We *lost;* let's not forget that! Thirty-four months or thirty-four years: we lost! And, the defeated lose even more by surrendering historical accuracy. Let's focus on the future."

"Yes, well," commented Hawkins, "the past *is* past, but back then the entire military command—except Staff General Igman, Military Advisor to the Delegate Council—was not eager to, nor prepared to capitulate. We *would,* and *could,* have continued the struggle indefinitely. Need I say, 'We were sold out'?"

"Perhaps the general knew something you didn't," responded Neidlinger sharply. "But that's another debate for future historians. Let someone disinterested solve these enigmas after we're long dead. Beside, it's rather a moot point. If we'd continued for even a few days longer thirty years ago—"

"—twenty-eight," corrected Horthy.

"—so be it, the truth remains the same: if we'd continued twenty-eight years ago, PRIM troopers would have sat where you're sitting now, handing us the capitulation pen. We were surrounded. We'd already lost. Back then we deluded ourselves into thinking we still controlled territory by merely repositioning our symbolic glyphs here and there on situation map projections." He threw his hand toward the empty com center to remind everyone of those bygone maps. "Territories that Marsco and its PRIM hordes already controlled—we were sending commands to as though—" He let history finish his comments.

Hawkins knew he had to win over this delegate. Neidinger was too powerful not to include in the forthcoming plans. Trying to ingratiate himself without too much coyness, the officer continued, "If victors write history, Herr Delegate, I intend to write the next one. But time's pressing, and I want to outline for you what I've planned before the rest arrive."

As the colonel spoke, it became clear to Neidlinger that Hawkins, along with the other two, had been working secretly on this scenario. All three delegates had already received an outline of the colonel's plan; each had a single hard copy delivered by courier. No other cyber or paper copy existed except the numbered printouts in delegate possession.

Plus, Neidlinger noted, Horthy often filled in the scenario gaps for Hawkins. Gathering of Enfield weapons to rearm the land forces, Horthy explained, was already well underway. *Is Delegate Balfour already in on this? Enfield assembly plants're in her subsidiary.* Neidlinger wasn't sure.

Hawkins outlined his plans quickly until the Hohenzollern delegate abruptly interrupted. "So the heart of the matter's this: you have a secret base in the belt—"

"I can't confirm or deny that statement, Herr Delegate," Hawkins retorted.

"Well, it can't be on Earth. You wouldn't surreptitiously cache space-launched weapons on this planet, because getting them into orbit gives them away. The Moon and Mars are so thoroughly Marsco you couldn't hide any substantial base there. Not one as large as you suggest here." He thumbed through the plan, "forty-eight Lightning fighters, their flight crews and launch personnel. *Three attack carriers!* The exact size of the rumored Lost Fleet."

"Originally provided by Dr. Genda's Asian Power, I believe," Gobineau added.

"Quite a force," Neidlinger concluded, "one never accounted for after Armistice. It has to be hidden somewhere. There's no space travel beyond the belt—"

"Until recently," corrected Gobineau.

"I'm clearly speaking of a time before the C-Wars," he shot at the interrupting delegate. Turning back to Hawkins, he concluded with pleased logic, "Ergo—the belt."

"Sound reasoning, Herr Delegate, as I'd expect. But I can't confirm or deny anything. I wouldn't want to compromise my base's security."

"Remember, colonel," the northern European delegate shot, his still-intense eyes glaring at the officer, "that 'my base' is really 'our base,' and that you *are to act,*" he stressed carefully, "*act* only with the Council's *direct* authorization, as in the past."

"I'll take that under advisement, Herr Delegate."

"Please do." Returning to the printed plans before him, the huffing councilor resumed his summary of the Hawkins plan. "So you move these secret squadrons from our belt base to—"

"Let's just talk about maneuvering the attack carriers undetected into launch position between the Moon and Earth. Once unleashed, most of my squadrons hit Marsco's essential targets on Earth, immobilizing and decapitating its HQ command structure in one massive strike. Shock and awe. A *coup de main.*"

Before continuing, the speaker looked at the delegates for confirmation of the daring plan's overwhelming intent. "A smaller attack hits high-priority lunar targets, (colonies, deep-space com arrays, docking ports) essentially isolating all its space-based personnel. We control or destroy the key parts of the Earth and Moon in a nano—it can't react."

Both Horthy and Gobineau were pleased with the simplicity and directness of the audacious plan—and the target selection well away from their people. The colonel's energetic explanation made a more favorable presentation than his text.

Pedantically, Gobineau added, "Hawkins meant *coup d'état,* not *coup de main.* Our actions'll be by those previously *in* power and rightly acting to regain what is ours *by law.*"

Hawkins bowed to the legal authority.

Delegate Neidlinger, as the other three suspected, brought up several concerns. The key one was simply, “E-viruses?”

“Not in these Lightnings. I’m not using corrupted prewar drones with their susceptible real-time remote control. I’ll have pilot butts in the seats this time.”

“Yes,” Neidlinger reminded them of the painful reality, “last time Marsco had no trouble wrenching control of our very own hardware from us.”

Horthy asked a question that showed his knowledge of the remarkably adaptive Lightning delivery system. “Won’t your changes—adding pilots—diminish the craft’s capabilities negatively?”

“No, sir, I don’t believe it will. As I’m sure you all recall, a drone Lightning can be retrofitted with a flight deck to accommodate a crew of four officers. The canopy and flight adaptation hardware reduces the mach-nine speed, but she’ll still be blindingly fast.”

“Weight?”

“Weapon carry characteristics change so that each ship will hump only eight thermals, not twelve. But eight’s enough for the job! That’s 360 weapons on target.”

“Isn’t your math wrong?” Gobineau quarried eruditely. “Isn’t that *384?*”

“Three ships are wild weasels flying as countersurveillance and weapon-suppression craft; these carry no offensive accessories.”

“And that’s it?” Neidlinger came back. “With 360 weapons you expect Marsco to roll over and play dead?”

“With all due respect, Herr Delegate, I don’t expect Marsco to *play* dead. I expect Marsco to *be* dead.”

The chamber erupted with several voices talking at once, as Fuentes dutifully escorted several other councilors to the long-empty conference room.

"This many delegates from the old DC shouldn't be together, at least not together *here,*" the youngest member of the Council stated emphatically. In his late fifties, Mr. Valmy still walked and talked with firmness and directness. Hawkins appreciated such characteristics in a man generally, even though personally he had no respect for this delegate.

"Did it have to be here?" someone whispered from the back. Hawkins recognized Doctor Genda, who spoke impeccable English with only a trace of an accent and no LD. Like Neidlinger and Horthy, he too had aged. His forceful, confident bearing was gone. Refusing to use a cane, he steadied himself against Valmy's arm.

His unsteady gait did not lessen his importance. Like Neidlinger, he carried two votes, the Pacific Co-Prosperity Sphere and Hong-Shang, one of the large and influential Powers carved out of the former nation of China. Years before, the burgeoning enclaves of Hong Kong and Shanghai had merged into a significant state by controlling or influencing other prosperous sections of the Asian mainland.

These regions had gathered themselves into the first Continental Power during the period of traumatic postrevolution anarchy in the late '30s. These economically viable sections survived by divesting themselves of their weakest parts and by seeking out other robust alliances. Such astute moves became the paradigm for other Continental Powers as the century unfolded: a template for divesting and abandoning ineffective parts of moribund countries and redrawing boundaries along fiscally thriving lines.

A major player, Genda needed deft handling. But as the colonel and his allies moved toward him, noises in the corridor caught everyone's attention.

Hawkins then heard the one voice that he assumed would give him the most trouble. The Commander of the Powers' combined forces, General Marshall Igman barked, "Who gave this man permission to be in *that* uniform?" Captain Fuentes was appropriately dressed in the green and gold of a staff officer. "No one's authorized to wear *that* uniform!"

"I gave permission, sir," Hawkins answered, cutting short Igman's angry remarks by stepping forward. It was the first time the recently arrived delegates saw his uniform clearly.

"I should've known Horthy wasn't behind this entirely by himself," Delegate Balfour groused. Another Euro councilor, she had entered with Igman. "Hawkins!" she burst out when she saw the colonel in the dim light. "In full uniform!" The sole woman delegate, she had aged gracefully, her spirit unbroken. Hawkins had always thought of her as a bint with no administrative aptitude or stomach for real governing. He endeavored to constrain his disrespect because he needed her vote and her Enfields.

Along with the military commander, Igman, and Delegate Balfour, Mr. Worthington entered. A NoAm Powers delegate, he was the last one elected president of the DC before Armistice. A savvy politician, he generally kept quiet during meetings, allowing those presenting to have their say—so long as it was short and to the point—before moving his agenda along with dispatch. As council president, however, he knew he had to exert more control over Hawkins.

Security hadn't really interrupted Miller earlier that evening. Rather their intrusion only confirmed to him that what stability he enjoyed at his grange was indeed crumbling. The reduction in the size of the Sac City sid for starters showed him he was living a dream. An illusion. His research center and the subsidiary lander assembly plant near Seattle—both soon to be absorbed into Marsco proper—were valuable assets Marsco would rather supervise directly than allow as rivals. Good fortune for those employed there but another visible sign that Marsco ultimately brooks no opposition. Closer at hand, amid all the local changes, even some Indies were abandoning their granges as rumors of the stopline pullback gained credibility. So far, the Trumans were staying put, but only because with Aaron in Marsco, the patina of associate status protected their grange somewhat.

If he really needed one, the final sign wasn't tonight's intrusion, Miller realized. It was Tessa's note sent a few days prior. He'd been brooding over it since first reading it. She had resigned her position at the Academy effective immediately and accepted an appointment with Herriff at the VBC. The director's longstanding invitation to join his staff became a stronger pull than remaining Earth-side, living in the Marsco sector with the highest comfort and security.

After reading her cryptic note, Miller sent his daughter one short question. When her response came back, "Yes," he knew he had to act. Tonight only confirmed it.

Before closing down his work for the night—work disrupted by more than Rivers and his Security squad—Miller tapped out a message to Herriff, for his eyes only: "Still room for me at VBC? Confirm ASAP."

For the first time since Bethany's death, Miller felt drained, as though he had just returned from Mars after a strenuous, prolonged spaceflight and needed to adjust to higher gravity. He shut down his computers, darkened his study, but walked more slowly toward his bedroom suite. His body ached from strain. The dogs were no fools; they were already asleep in a warm heap when he was finally ready for bed. He found his room ice cold. In addition to everything else, the damp chill of these last few months added to his misery.

Old bones and flesh shivered in the unheated room as the seven delegates, who nonetheless represented nine votes, found seats near old friends and away from old enemies. The buried room wasn't cold enough to show their breath but was cold enough for other reasons. Igman sat directly across from Hawkins so that his eyes never left the subordinate officer.

After all were seated, the colonel opened his remarks. "I'm sure you all have many questions of me."

"Yes," Doctor Genda grinned, "how'd you stay so young?" Genial laughter erupted among the delegates.

General Igman answered bluntly for the colonel, "Cryogenic stasis." His razor tone was intended to cut off any humor. He aimed to keep this a less-than-cordial meeting in which he still directed all military ops.

Unlike the other two officers, Igman was out of uniform, although his still fit his trim body. As chief military advisor of the DC, at Armistice he pledged never again to wear the green and mustard. The unnumbered dead of the C Wars and the darkened aftermath of that conflagration still haunted him. If he had been a better politician, the Wars could have been avoided. If he had been a better soldier, the Wars might have been won. Either way, he wanted no more war making.

Trying to take the initiative away from Hawkins, the general commented, "Twenty-eight years of peace have come at a steep price to be sure, but it's still worth the cost in the long run. Maybe this peace will hold up," the general pleaded, "for another thirty, fifty years. And maybe Marsco will soften. Seems to be a different attitude these days, better demeanor among the younger directors at its helm —"

"—especially since Cleary and Graves relinquished power," Worthington noted of two of the three iron-fisted founders of Marsco. This was the first remark made by the brooding DC president, who sat next to Igman.

"—yes," the general continued, "Marsco's Governing Board's more trustworthy, quite politically adroit, and they do listen to us."

"And many sids are flourishing at present," the president interjected with the general's permission, "we've ample evidence of that prosperity around this table."

Hawkins saw the nods from a few of Worthington's compatriots.

"This's certainly the case," the general continued, "in the north central Euro sids and many on the Pacific Rim." Neidlinger and Genda acknowledged the truth of his words.

"Who knows?" The general paused to state his point exactly. "Even with my doubts, I'm willing to let Marsco be and not risk starting another worldwide catastrophe. Certainly, nothing justifies renewing a conflict of that magnitude. The risk of such horrific fighting—" words failed him momentarily "—and of the countless dead again are certainly," he hit the table for emphasis "certainly too great to contemplate even in a tertiary manner."

Hawkins glared but proceeded with his agenda. "For those of you who spent extra time coming down to this command complex, my apologies," the officer stated in his usual directness.

"Hardly much left to command," General Igman retorted bluntly.

The colonel ignored his ostensible commander and continued, "I wanted you to see this old cherished, venerable building for yourselves. See how the marble and mahogany and oak are all gone. The gold stripped off by PRIM gangs. The place has been looted. See what's become of this proud—"

"Skip the vitriolic speech, colonel," injected the irritated president. "We all lived through the Wars and their aftermath—on Earth, in sids—or worse. We've witnessed the same organized Marsco vandalism worldwide often enough. 'To the victors....' as the saying goes. What's your point?"

Hawkins saw clearly that the old alignments within the governing council were re-forming. Except for Gobineau, the delegates seemed calcified into their former positions. *This's no way to govern, having to suck up to these impotent old men! No way to wage war, begging for their blessing!*

As the last delegate, Councilor Renzo, entered, he began a stinging pronouncement, his sarcasm hardly buried, "I must congratulate you, Delegate Gobineau. Or should I say *Associate* Gobineau?" Hawkins realized that Renzo must have been listening in the hallway. Finally seated, the last delegate bluntly continued, "After the Armistice, Gobineau, you so nimbly managed to seat yourself on the original Marsco ruling committee of your home Power. Your position allowed you to retain control, even though your old country's now chopped into a dozen subsidiaries."

Pretending to miss the snide intention, Gobineau bowed at his adversary.

Renzo, incensed all the more, continued, "You even assisted in advantageously realigning *all* borders and stoplines within your sphere of influence. Even helped organize, as none of us were able, several thriving sids."

"Yes, but all under the auspices of Marsco," the attacked councilor noted with feigned humility.

"Even so," Renzo pressed on, his disgust up to the surface, all political politeness dissipated, "you transitioned to Marsco very neatly, almost effortlessly."

"And in doing so, I saved my people much suffering," the councilor retorted. "Yet, regrettably our success's peaked. You know that."

Over the past decade, the prestige of his sid areas began to decline. All the while his natural and consistent rivals—Renzo's adjacent subsidiaries (ones that had been a single Euro power at one time)—rose. Witnessing this, Gobineau shifted his position gradually closer to Horthy's. Current tensions altered old alliances. Marsco wasn't doing enough for Gobineau's constituents. He knew there must be an immediate change, even if it meant throwing his lot in with the likes of Hawkins.

Watching this display of old mistrust and lingering unsettled scores, the colonel turned diplomat, realizing he must forge a new alliance from delegates who over the years had drifted back into their traditional rivalries.

During this jealous outburst, Hawkins was once again struck by the age of the diplomats. They seemed rheumy about the eyes, from the relentless hard years since the Wars and the icy chill of this bunker. Only Balfour's eyes shown bright; she'd recently had her corneas replaced. In some zone, there were two particular PRIMS, each minus a single cornea. A lucrative business, selling healthy body parts, mostly to Marsco. Her adolescent blue eyes (perfectly matched by an unethical ophthalmologist) gave her face a youthful radiance not seen in the others at the conference table.

"My point, Madame Delegate, distinguished delegates, and General Igman," Hawkins once more tried to bring the meeting toward his agenda, "comes out lucidly in my prepared remarks of which I have given you a synopsis. See page three, heading 'Planning and Implementation.' I haven't been idle in the past twenty-eight years."

"Cut to the quick," interrupted President Worthington, breaking his foreboding silence once more. "You sent us this synopsis over six months ago via Horthy, all cloak and dagger. We can gather from this," he crackled the pages, "what you're up to."

"If I might begin—"

General Igman took up his civilian commander's remarks, "Pretty clear what you're up to on page six, last item, 'Attack Scenario and Reacquisition of Continental Powers Control.' Marsco would love to read that."

Worthington jumped back in, "Treasonous material for us to receive. Do you have any idea of the potential harm you may have created for more than one subsidiary by merely distributing this seditious material?"

After slapping the table, Colonel Hawkins spoke deliberately and pointedly, "With all due respect, Mr. Worthington, you can only commit treason against your own country. Who committed the greatest treason by selling out when we—"

"Don't throw that crap at us," Delegate Renzo shouted after his own slap on the table. It was the anger of an old man, one whose younger days were filled with frequent, violent outbursts. Age, however, mellows everyone. He looked at Hawkins through thick old-style eyeglasses and still had difficulty focusing.

Clearly siding with Hawkins, Horthy inquired of his fellow delegates, "What choices are left to us?"

"Sometimes the choice of the *status quo,*" stated the council president, "is better than a choice of 'mutually assured destruction.'"

"My space fleet, Mr. Worthington," Hawkins replied confidently, "will make this 'Marsco assured destruction.'"

"Where was your space fleet to protect us from the V-weapons?" demanded Valmy hotly.

It was a question unrelated to anything said previously but one the Delegate had waited more than thirty years to ask the colonel face-to-face, since the first day of Marsco's space weaponry attacks. Old personal scores take a long time to settle. Valmy's festering one against Hawkins was as serious as the colonel's against Marsco itself.

Balfour added, "Marsco's June '66 incident, its so-called "Prewar Accident" over London, gave you plenty of time to reposition your forces appropriately."

London, the original capital of the Powers, had suffered the first Vanovara blast, a warning shot that Marsco pitifully described as "an unintentional orbital release of an asteroid fragment during routine shard operations." Many of these delegates here were fortunate to be alive after that initial V-hit. Much of the G-Powers bureaucracy was lost in the instantaneous incineration of the city center on that day several months before the real conflagration commenced.

"So this is it, then," Hawkins shouted above them, his disked hand giving another slap to the table with enough force to bring about immediate silence. "Bloody hell, you buggers have all gone soft and muzzy." With his steely gray eyes he looked around the room. "If you've read this proposal, you know we're in a position to regain our rightful rule of law. But we must act swiftly."

"Just how, exactly?" the military officer, Igman, asked. "You give a sketchy outline here in the synopsis." To compensate for hearing loss, the general kept staring at Hawkins to read his lips, a subtle method he'd picked up over the years.

"That's jumping ahead to page seven, *general.*"

"Well, then jump, *colonel,*" insisted the military advisor in a whisper that shouted his order. He made sure his gaze never left Hawkins.

The meeting's organizer flipped through his notes noisily until he came to the section of his prepared talk. "You see that 'Attack Scenario and Reacquisition of Continental Powers Control, Subpart D' means we decapitate Marsco with a coordinated series of sorties against Earth-side and lunar colony choke points that renders its command structure inoperative."

"Bold and decisive, isn't it?" commented Horthy, with Gobineau surprisingly nodding in agreement.

"Something like what it did to us with their initial cyber attack," President Worthington had to acknowledge.

"And their follow-up V-strikes," Igman conceded. London was not the only city to suffer from V-hits.

"Exactly, sirs. Only we do it from space with my Lightnings taking out all their essentials. Like what happened to us back then, Marsco will instantly find itself blind and unable to communicate. It'll offer no coordinated response. Again, similar to its offensive scenario with its dual cyber and Vanovara attacks. It'll all be over before Marsco can deploy any forces or mount any counterstrike."

"But their initial sorties were all cyber!" Igman shouted, his military logic impeccable. "You're hitting the Earth with megatons of raw power!"

"Your point is?"

Several delegates jumped on Hawkins before this personal dual escalated. Valmy attacked first. He insisted on knowing the status of the formerly virus-infected Lightning drones. "Marsco's brilliant e-strikes made these weapons, *our* weapons, inoperable. Or it totally turned those drones to weapons of its own use. What's been done to change that situation?"

Hawkins felt as though he were addressing a cadet class at the Academy. "You're correct, Councilor Valmy, about the Lightnings. During the last hostile period, drone utilization and remote control of said assets suffered severe setbacks."

Valmy and Igman rolled their eyes over such euphemisms, then the delegate retorted hotly. "Our Earth-based Lightning fleet was totally inoperable for most of the Wars, e-corrupted from the start of action. The corrupting viruses that ruined our cyber system still ravage some computer systems today."

Igman added, "Even some of Marsco systems weren't immune."

"Those were our counterstrikes," Hawkins retorted before he continued with his rudimentary lecture. "We can reconfigure a drone Lightning into a crew-based Lightning. It was designed with that dual purpose in mind, battlefield adjustment-wise. But, more to the point, we'll repeat Marsco's history lesson to us on them." He tapped the tabletop with his red C & C disk for emphasis.

"History teaches us," the usually reticent Genda replied with a philosophical air, "that these 'surprise attacks' don't always achieve their desired results. After their initial shock, the unexpected rebound can be devastating."

"If history teaches us anything, Doctor, it teaches us that 'Strength lies not in defense but in attack.'"

The comment pulled Igman up short, he thought he knew that military tag. As the discussion ranged around the table, he strove to remember its original source. Finally, it clicked. The general mumbled—louder than he expected because of his partial deafness, "Adolf Hitler, *Mein Kampf*."

The officer's sharp outburst caught everyone's attention. Stunned, they looked at him as he gathered his thoughts, "A series of sorties from space isn't enough." As military advisor, he wanted to punch holes in this idle shuttle jockey's ridiculous war scenario before it grew seriously out of hand. The colonel presented an easy target; his puerile tactics were absolute trash.

The general immediately unleashed his next salvo, "You'll need adequate ground personnel after this purported 'decapitation' to move in and seize the power centers. Calm the population. Keep order in the zones. Control the vast Security cantonment network—there's thousands of those—you can't possibly destroy all of them with a space-based attack. Plus control all those Marsco sectors, most extremely large. And don't forget, many Marsco Security cantonments within our sids can stand independently of central control and re-supply for weeks. Months, perhaps." He scowled at the colonel as if that gaze alone had won this strategic engagement. "What'll you deploy for ground troops?"

Hawkins seemed isolated, out on a limb. No delegate came to his aid. He replied slowly, "We'll be able to marshal our own troops, of course—"

"Not enough!" Igman was shooting accurately. "Marsco's using vast amounts of our own people at this very moment, both in sid Auxxie units and even sometimes in its Security battalions. Difficult, if not impossible, to sortie legions like that, ones more than likely to remain loyal to Marsco, or one that will be totally out of communications once you destroy its—and our—communications networks."

"Or," Worthington added, "caught in a thermal blast from our Lightning attacks, can you just order them to join us after we've just nuked them?" Along with Igman, the Council President was committed to stopping this madman right here, right now.

Hawkins forged ahead, ignoring every counterargument, "But for the rest, we will again take a page out of Marsco's book, general." The colonel tried to suppress his delight at the overall strength of his plan. "PRIMS. We'll do as Marsco did and *arm PRIMS!*"

Horthy added to the silent, appalled delegates, "None of you should be shocked. Marsco deployed hords of Enfield-armed PRIMS to tear us down the last war. In a short while, PRIMS will assist us in bringing down Marsco in the next war."

TWENTY-FOUR

SHORTENING THE LEASH

(Sac City Sid, 2097)

PRIMS!

The very thought hung in the icy air of the conference room until, with help from Horthy's assistant, Fuentes brought several trays of sandwiches and two pots of hot coffee. The food dispelled the frosty gloom that settled over the bunker at Hawkins' announcement that he was negotiating with remnants of their former foe.

"But Marsco keeps PRIMS disorganized." Igman launched his spoiler attack as soon as the Delegate Council reconvened.

"One man has been able to secretly organize a dedicated core of followers," the colonel explained. "Like me, their Leader's planning a decisive stoke against Marsco. If we combine forces, Marsco will be without options but defeat."

"And how did you make these contacts?" Igman demanded.

"I originally stumbled onto their plan several years ago while on one of my periodic trips to Earth."

"If you've 'stumbled on them,' hasn't Marsco?" the general dug. "Its Security's relentless. Pitiless."

Ignoring his superior, Hawkins plowed on, "I immediately seized upon the idea of linkage. These PRIMS need only a knockout punch to initiate their attack. I knew I needed grunts to weed out any remaining elements once its infrastructure is shattered. It's a natural blend of two complementary forces, theirs and mine."

"You mean, the 'Continental Forces,' correct?" Igman restated bluntly.

"Of course, I only represent the DC," came the crisp reply.

"Hardly seems like it," quipped President Worthington.

Over a cup of coffee that steamed in the cold bunker, Delegate Balfour questioned this proposed alliance. "Isn't it rather risky, trusting a PRIM army at this point? I needn't remind you; they essentially put Marsco into power in the first place."

"And then afterward they in turn were 'sold out,'" Hawkins shot.

"We seem to be using the phrase a great deal today," Horthy interjected, coming to Hawkins's aid. "Talk about sold out! PRIMS did most of the dying for Marsco and what'd they get in return? Unincorporated Zones. Disease. Marsco's further abandonment of them. The incipient Powers weren't the only ones to cut PRIMS loose."

"Yes, you're so right, to our shame," Valmy countered, arguing against Hawkins's plan. "The Powers originally started PRIMification. Of course, my country didn't have them back then because our population growth was under control. But we didn't condemn their original creation (on-continent and off-) sixty, seventy years ago. We never condemned the Divestiture Movement or the first Abandonment Policy, as it's more accurately labeled. Unincorporated Zones festered well before the Wars, most created by us."

Renzo concurred with Valmy, a position noted by Hawkins. *They'll vote as a block and vote against me.*

"None of those zones' originators are represented directly today, Bom-May and Hong-Shang," Genda reminded the table. "I vote for the Hong-Shang Power but only as they direct me. Nonetheless, let's not get into historical discussions about who's to blame for what."

"Moreover," Igman interjected, making his point succinctly as was his wont, "there's blame enough for the breakdown of democracy around the world. Elected, representative governance is always frail. Our forefathers let it die, wither, as they bickered and failed to compromise on anything." Not everyone was listening, but he felt these ideas must be expressed. "Doing away with education, with housing, with hospitals, to give a few rich a tax break." Those not remaining attentive sat in bored silence. His pro-citizenry argument had been offered before, rejected before.

Doctor Genda, who liked the status quo, further disregarded the general and moved the meeting along by announcing, "On that regard, I've instructions to vote for continued strong connections to Marsco."

He needed little encouragement to continue. "Granted, Marsco's broken up much of the Powers I represent into scores of smaller subsidiaries, but there's still much wealth to be made. A few resourceful and cooperative entrepreneurs in my areas know that to be the case. Regardless of who's totally and ultimately in control—the bygone Powers or the current Marsco—MMUs are being made by the fistful." To show emphasis for his ideas, he gestured slowly as an old man might. "And with the least difficulty as possible, I aim to keep in power those who are right now gaining the most. Disruption and changeovers are unfavorable for those to whom I answer."

Paying no heed to the Doctor, Renzo spoke up. "I'm not one to defend Marsco, but in point of fact, it only continued many policies the Powers actually began. With the unchecked overpopulation and continuing political chaos after the Indi-Paki nuclear exchange, we allowed Bombay and Malaysia to unite, following the Hong-Shang model. They carved out areas of interest that were economically viable and cast the rest adrift. And we Westerns and Euros granted them sovereignty." He looked around the table for acknowledgement. "For the second time in a decade, we let countries cast millions of citizens aside."

"Not us, exactly," Worthington pointed out for the sake of a historically accurate record. "Our 'grandfathers' in a sense."

Renzo nodded. "I accept your clarification. These initial, so-called 'Continental Powers' had sovereignty, but over what? The sweetest pickings of old China and the best fruit of the islands nearest it! Or, the most flourishing sections of the Bengal and Arabian waters! The best parts of the Asian subcontinent and the Malay Peninsula and some other islands. These incipient Powers picked and sorted; they took only the ripe fruit from the waiting trees. The rest, they left to fruitless anarchy, and *we acquiesced to it all.* Or at least, our forefathers did—and mothers too," he added in deference to Balfour.

Silent agreement circled the table accompanied by only a minute amount of shame. It had all happened before these delegates rose to power.

"And is Marsco," Renzo continued, "doing anything differently by creating its own sectors and fostering subsidiaries? No, it's only picking the best and leaving the rotten fruit on the ground. 'A page out of our book,' Colonel Hawkins."

"The zones," stated Valmy, "don't forget the history of the zones."

"Yes, quite so," continued Renzo. "We essentially blame Marsco for the UZs, but our grandparents started them when Marsco was still manufacturing chips and basking in the glow of its revolutionary Wi-Fi tech. Fostered zones? We required zones internally by law in most of our own countries. Putting migrants and refugees and the uneducated, other tattooed and pierced mokes, criminals and street people—our so-called 'undesirable citizens'—into ghettoized sections of our own cities. Then we 'divested' the rest of society from them. In some cases, we forced our own citizens onto other 'countries' we created out of our own larger countries as part of 'trade agreements.' These broke unions, lowered workers' costs."

"When you tax only enough to gild just that upper crust," Igman noted bitterly, "what do you expect to happen to the marginalized? It was a natural step, this abandonment."

"Natural, but politically unconscionable," added Worthington, planning to allow these hard-line hawks their say, and then letting rationality and reasoned political debate take over in the final analysis.

Once more, silent political embarrassment showed on a few of the faces at the table. The idealist Worthington seemed to be winning.

Had our forefathers really done such a heinous thing? A handful asked themselves speechlessly. Such a historical record couldn't be denied, only tweaked or spun. Democracy *had* abandoned many of its own citizens. And to keep the new borders secure, the Powers had drawn up internal and external stoplines and organized Auxiliary units to patrol them. Marsco's current system was only a macro-version of the same thing.

Renzo returned to his salient point, repeating himself as old men often do, "Soon after Hong-Shang grabbed Taiwan, that lush island of prosperity in a sea of despair, Bom-May was born."

"How poetic you are," hissed Horthy, trying to stem this ongoing outpouring of forgotten regret. "Those were other times. Talk of today."

Hawkins jumped in just as impatiently, "What's this schoolroom lesson got to do with anything, Renzo?" The colonel felt his control of the discussion was slipping.

The delegate took a moment to gather his thoughts. "*If* this Council's considering condemning Marsco, and *if* we're seriously contemplating a possible preemptive-*slash*-reprisal attack for its 'crimes against humanity,' I thought it only fair to remind the members of this esteemed body that some of these crimes are the exact ones our own august predecessors initiated." Looking at Hawkins through his thick eyeglasses, he asked hotly, "Does that make my point clearer?"

"Your Boolean logic's perfectly clear, sir, although irrelevant." The colonel's voice steamed with discontent.

General Igman, with uncharacteristic anger in his voice, reentered the fray. "Hawkins, you're running this meeting as though you already *have* our authorization to recommence hostilities. I don't believe," he ticked his finger to count, his red command disk clearly visible, "one, that we've given you such permission; two, that we still have any viable, palpable authority to do so; and three, that we are all rash and foolhearty and blatantly ignorant enough to authorize instantaneous mass murder."

"Perhaps that's another thing that's wrong with the world these days," Hawkins responded, throwing himself back into his chair with impatient disgust. "It's no wonder we lost the last war," he conjectured.

Amid the torrid debate and sharp recriminations around the table, Horthy alone kept his composure. Fists pounded. Voices rose higher, sharper. Clear lines were drawn between two camps with Genda and Balfour seeming to be the only holdouts, ones who hadn't stated any articulated position. And yet, amid it all, Horthy remained centered regardless of the excitement. His old eyes were never out of focus.

Inexplicably over the whirling din, he asked a seemingly irrelevant question. "Mr. Worthington, point of order! Point of order, please Mr. President! Will the parliamentarian clarify a point?" The delegate had to shout over the table's uproar. Once quiet, he asked in a manner that pulled everyone up short, "How long does the military advisor serve the Council?"

Like the others at the table, Worthington was caught off guard. Lacking an appointed parliamentarian, the president of the Council turned to Igman, the military advisor of the DC and his trusted friend. The two conferred silently. It had been almost three decades since the Council had met and nearly as long since it observed the nicety of electing its military advisor and having a debate along rules society enforced.

After a moment, the president of the DC stated, "As best we can recall, this advisory position, as with the economics and environmental advisors (both currently vacant), has a five-year term. A non-voting seat."

"Like the president's seat," Horthy's hand moved in a circle, "it rotates and does not vote."

Worthington nodded his agreement.

The Euro delegate went on with smug confidence. "It's been so long since this Council's met in earnest that the internal rules and bylaws need to be explained again to everyone's satisfaction."

Worthington slowly answered, "The only difference between the military advisor and council president is that no succeeding military advisor can come from the same Power. It differs from the chair in that respect. I—or any Council president—can be indefinitely re-elected, if the DC wishes. Also, anyone from my home Power, in this case, the NoAm A and P League Powers, may succeed me."

"With all due respect to you and General Igman, Mr. President," Horthy stated flatly, looking at no one, and lacking sincerity in his remarks, "I think we should, *we must,* continue today's consequential and momentous discussions only after the election of a new military advisor and Council president."

The whole table was thunderstruck.

Even Hawkins was caught off guard by this blindsiding suggestion at such a crucial point. As a buzz went around, Horthy alone remained controlled. The mid-continent politician was rising in stature among some of the group, especially most of the other Euros.

Moreover, the delegate had a plan afoot that Hawkins didn't fathom. Just like the rest, the colonel had been kept out of this loop.

"May I ask," Worthington inquired, "for what purpose do you make such a request?"

"Sir, with all due respect, we're here to discuss the methodology of reestablishing the legitimate rule of law on this planet and throughout the solar system. I think it best to begin with following our own bylaws first."

"But Mr. Horthy," Valmy stated with forced calm, "we don't have a quorum—"

Turning to the interloper, he cut him off, "Ah, but we do, Mr. Valmy."

Horthy was met with a skeptical look from his chief adversary, but it was Renzo who interjected, "We need ten members; we've only eight."

Horthy replied, "Let me enumerate. There were originally fifteen Powers represented by this Council." Nodded agreement all around. "Doctor Genda and Herr Neidlinger each vote for two by long-standing consent. The rest of us represent one each. Thus we have in a sense ten members represented, not eight."

Renzo countered, "That's only nine, because the chair doesn't vote."

A fellow Euro, Gobineau, threw his support to Horthy, "Just because the chair isn't a *voting member* doesn't mean his Power isn't represented. And so, ten. A quorum."

This's well planned, Hawkins observed the machinations prearranged behind his own back, a whirling cog inside his own whirling cog. *This's orchestrated with military precision.* He was being out maneuvered even as he tried to position himself. Fortunately, these plots played into his finger disks.

The Gallic and Iberian delegate continued, his backing of Horthy obvious, "Besides, Marsco totally sacked the resurgent SoAf government, Euros that resettled the Cape after that continent's AIDS depopulation. That makes only fourteen Powers remaining. Ten of fourteen is even a stronger quorum."

"What goddamned diff does it make if one particular Power was officially unseated by Marsco or not?" the outraged Worthington stated. "All Powers surrendered."

"I see your defeatist attitude, Mr. President," Horthy went on, ready to trounce any opposition. "At the conclusion of the Wars, yes, we were defeated. But according to the peace accords we signed with Marsco, the Continental Powers remained 'the legitimate and exclusive governing bodies of their existing constituents.' Marsco was to exert only temporary control of reconstruction-era events. 'A provisional and temporary governing power,' I believe the wording ran. We're technically still in power by law and fact."

"By fact?" General Igman blasted, raising his voice above the growing arguments around the table. "We haven't actually ruled anything since we signed the Armistice, here," he motioned to the ceiling, "seven stories above, right under the rotunda. Marsco's no more transitional than I am from Jupiter. In name, you may lead delegations, but of what? By whom? All the former boundaries have been repeatedly changed and shifted and redrawn seemingly at Seattle's whim. We're old men and one old woman. We no longer rule anything." Murmured consent came from Worthington's corner.

"Remarks out of order, Mr. President," Gobineau stated in high parliamentary style.

"Besides, General," Horthy interjected, "you never were part of the 'we' who ruled. You merely advised."

Hawkins had to marvel had the speed at which Horthy took absolute control. The delegate from the once-mammoth East-Central Euro Power obviously didn't want the president's position; he would cease voting then. But by quick succession he offered several points. First, General Igman was to be dispatched as military advisor. Hawkins wasn't sure what the final vote outcome would be, but Horthy needed only a simple majority of those present for that.

He and Gobineau were a sure alliance. Neidlinger joined them, bringing his two votes—a surprise to Hawkins because the rise of Neidlinger's people had pushed Gobineau into Horthy's camp in the first place. All that past bad blood seemed abruptly forgotten. Europe, at least a large section of it, wanted to control its own destiny once more. It didn't relish being dictated to by a powerful NoAm conglomerate aided by its Asian confederates.

Voting against were Valmy (from a Franco-Anglo NoAm Power), Renzo (the sole dissenting European), and Genda, who like Neidlinger, cast two votes. It stood four to four, especially since Hawkins, Igman, and Worthington had no votes.

Although he represented a large Atlantic and Pacific League Power, a significant world player once, as DC president Worthington couldn't cast a vote except to break a tie. Of more significance, no one present could cast it for him. The Council president wouldn't vote unless Balfour abstained. Only then would the chair be asked to cast his tiebreaker.

It's all up to Balfour, that bitch-gorgon, Hawkins thought. When the colonel realized her importance, he felt sure all was lost. She was not a significant player in his plans.

But yet, in further surprise, she voted squarely in the Horthy "Europe First" camp. Evidently she was more in than she let on. Five votes to oust Igman, four to keep. By a similar vote, Hawkins was straight away named military advisor.

Furious, Igman rose to stiffly leave the room. "Who the hell do you think you are? Casting votes along old boundary lines that ceased to exist years ago? It wasn't just the Cape Power that Marsco officially removed. By all intents and purposes, all of us were removed from power. It's been over seventy-five years since anything approaching a free and open election took place, parliaments and congresses being suspended during the early Divestiture periods and Abandonment Crisis."

"With all due respect, general," Horthy replied with no hesitation, "it's time for you to go."

The general took his leave in silence, followed by Renzo, who no longer had the stomach to watch the machinations of Horthy without making some gesture of protest. His exist prompted the leader of the new power block to ask Valmy, "Do you stay or go?"

As the most vocal remaining dissenter left, Hawkins motioned Fuentes to follow the dejected delegate. "This complex has many tunnels and rooms, and someone might easily get lost," the new MA reminded his ADC. "Or worse."

Old scores take a long time to settle, but with Hawkins they eventually were.

The clamorous exits caused a temporary break in the meeting. The colonel looked around the bunker before business resumed. The location he chose gave the proceedings a surreal quality. Broken pipes, dangling wires, the carnage of the looted complex substituted for the trappings of political influence and authority. Hawkins shook his head. And yet, the resonant voices echoing in the dampness reassured him that these decisions mattered. Legal governance must reassert itself on this planet, else all was doomed.

When the renegade delegates resumed their seats, Mr. Worthington, still acting as president and ostensibly still in charge of the agenda, immediately tried to close these proceedings before any further action on Hawkins's unthinkable, indefensible, proposal could be brought forward. But he had only Genda's two votes to count on. They weren't enough. Taking their cue from the other losing dissenters, the president left the buried chambers in disgust, the single vacillating delegate following behind.

With their exit, only Hawkins, Horthy, and his followers Gobineau, Neidlinger, and Balfour, remained in the room. Not enough to declare war but enough to authorize Hawkins to initiate the next level of preparedness and wait for explicit instructions.

Before the remaining group broke up, Horthy asked Hawkins a second time for a clarification about the reliability of the Lightnings. "Hadn't they been co-opted by Marsco's viruses before the previous hostilities?" he asked pointedly. "Hadn't Marsco left many trap doors in their programming?"

"As you know, the Earth-side squadrons were susceptible to virus infections, many of them embedded in the very Marsco chips we had utilized to construct onboards in the first place. Marsco long planned to make our weaponry inoperative, and so it created many Trojans it could later open at will. Its sinister longtime horizon plans were just another element in our claim to legitimacy. It was always against us. But to address your concerns, during the

Wars our drones ceased following their remote-pilot commands. Cruise and guided ordinance went off course, detonated over ocean or barren desert—coincidental? I think not. I see the FDs of Marsco in this."

"But your squadrons?" asked Gobineau. "How can you be sure of them?"

"In the slow orbit around the sun, asteroids change location. Three times in the past twenty-five years, my hidden base has migrated close to prime Marsco colonies. At those times, we've laid dormant, hunkered down. We sent out active and passive ECMs and waited for the natural, slow movement of the belt to take us away from trouble."

"Yes, we understand that from your synopsis," Horthy impatiently replied, fingering the colonel's report.

"When my base was on its own in a quiet sector, we scrubbed the viruses out of the command codes of all our hardware and software. I've had my tech staff read every line of exec language in every computer we deploy. We've successfully purged anything that's not to our purpose. My Lightnings are clean, totally virus-free, I assure you."

"Damn! That's tens of millions of lines of command code," responded Neidlinger, the member of the Euro faction least confident about Hawkins. "Impossible!"

"Herr Delegate, what else did those boffins have to do all those years? Some of remained in cryo-stasis, such as my pilots who are still iced. But even they're getting sleep-pack instructions on their targets. My attack crews are young and eager. Others, like myself, have been in intermittent cryo when the times weren't propitious. I had to dispatch one snooping S & H operative who had grown too hot. But at other times, we scanned input commands."

"And your weaponry? Pulse ordnance ready?" asked Gobineau.

"More than likely, we'll not be intercepted, so Lightnings won't need defensive armament."

"So what'll you hit with?"

"Smart, fire-and-forget weapons carrying a package or multiple packages in the ten- to twenty-megaton range."

Hawkins spoke without a connection to the words he uttered. A stunned silence settled round the conference table.

Eventually, Neidlinger responded. "Vanovaras, as you know, were kept in the low kiloton equivalency range. Even so, they produced so much smoke, dust, and airborne debris that the planet suffered a devastating cooling trend for years." Nodding acknowledgement went around the table. "Crops suffered in the global three-year cloud cover."

Horthy interjected, "Yes, the aptly named 'Marsco Winter.'"

"Name it what you will, we all suffered."

The colonel shot, "Unless you were some associate living in a space colony." Hawkins was trying to paint Marsco into even a darker corner and cover over his relatively easy off-planet life in the Asteroid Belt during this time.

Sure that the officer missed his own condemnation, Neidlinger continued. "The postwar famine killed an additional several hundred million. But," he emphasized with a tap on the table, "at least the winter-producing clouds were radiation-free. Your proposed use of these atomic weapons might be too much for the planet to withstand. Each warhead is a thousand times more powerful than any Vanovara; each is capable of producing tons of radioactive fallout with unpredictable and unprecedented consequences. Ones that will linger for a thousand years."

"The worst areas will be those closest to the initial hits: I concede that," Hawkins retorted. "But, in a sense, we'll be like the Romans with Carthage. The victorious legions plowed salt into the fields around the sacked city so no one could or would ever again live there. We'll be doing the same thing to Marsco."

"Can't we rely on something like a Vanovara?" Balfour asked, obviously taken aback. "They produced enormous destruction of their own accord."

"The beauty of a Lightning is its ability to leave its launch platform in space—"

"Its attack carrier?"

"Yes, leave their orbiting launch platforms then enter the atmosphere, deposit their accessories, and return safely to home. But package-separation height is too low for an effective V-strike. We have to be in visual range to engage our laser scopes; V-weapons are launched from orbit."

Horthy remarked, "So, in short, what you're saying is—"

"We'll incinerate the bloody bastards."

Balfour added under her breath, "Three hundred and sixty times."

Hawkins reiterated. "The collateral damage will send Marsco quite a message."

Horrified stillness gripped the room as the sheer magnitude of the audacious plan crystallized.

"Colonel Hawkins," Balfour finally asked, "I meant to put a follow-up question to you about the use of PRIMS. Are they trustworthy and dependable enough? Are they even healthy enough to fight a campaign? Life in most zones," she swallowed, searching for a euphemism, "is difficult and short." Showing a typical sid reaction to PRIMS, her concluding question was, "Can you adequately organize an army around such rabble we don't even trust?"

"I misspoke when I called them PRIMS," the colonel answered. "More accurately, we'll rely on Luddites. And Ludd battalions are being formed even as we speak."

Balfour was shocked by the answer, the most she had been the whole evening. "Luddites are even more unpredictable than PRIMS," she rebutted the officer forcefully. "If Ludds aim to destroy technology—can we trust them to follow us after we regain control—hypothetically regain control, of course?"

"We won't need to trust the Ludds then, ma'am. After I annihilate Marsco, we will exterminate them. 'Termination of program.'" He gave a slight chuckle. "Another page right out of Marsco's book."

Fuentes guided the HFC back to the secret quarters he and Hawkins maintained in the Sierras well away from the central valley and its former capital.

Their trip took close to an hour because the ADC didn't skim in any conspicuous way while in the heart of enemy territory. Theirs was one of the few non-Marsco HFCs in the sky. If detained, they'd be easily identified. Once high up into the mountain range, Fuentes discontinued his circuitous flight path and struck out directly for their secret base.

The colonel loosened the collar of his green tunic and stretched back in the unyielding seat beside his aide. Closing his eyes, he confided, "The first thing I need is a bigger staff. I'm sure I'll get a promotion of at least two stars now that I'm the military advisor to the DC. All those years of waiting paid off."

He grew quiet for a moment, then remarked. "Surprises me still," Hawkins stated with eyes closed and his hands behind his head, "how much control Horthy exercised over most of the other Euros."

Fuentes didn't react.

"That old geezer knew precisely what he was doing. I thought I'd called that group together to set the groundwork for exactly what Horthy ended up achieving. He and Gobineau planned the whole bloody thing out well beforehand."

He tried to get comfortable in the stiff seat. "I'm sure that cagy, old fox knew he could count on both Neidlinger and Balfour." The colonel's hesitance was a sign he was working it all out mentally. "If not, if he hadn't gotten those votes, he would have then let me take the fall." He paused, doing the political geometry, "Although he would have tried again later without me to organize this. He's a calculating and plotting old bugger."

"How's their reluctance to give you full attack authorization ultimately affect your plan?" Fuentes asked without emotion.

"Political wonks are always reluctant to use the weaponry at hand. But, no, not in the least. This doesn't delay us. We proceed as planned."

Guiding the HFC was second nature to Fuentes, but the former associate couldn't follow the tangles of Hawkins's line of reasoning. His mind wouldn't let him. Eventually the aide did ask, "Even to the point of initiating Lightning movement? Once we commit from the belt, there's no going back." Spoken like a Marsco-trained pilot who knew space travel and shuttle egression well.

"That was my first mistake today. I should *not* have asked permission."

"I don't copy."

"I should have told them outright this is my attack plan—live with it. It's in full swing. PNR: point of no return. Back it or suffer the disastrous consequences. Should have already had my carriers on their way. I should have told the Council only when they were sitting at launch point ready to destroy Marsco. I'll do things differently next time."

He rested philosophically for a moment, then resumed. "You know, over time, I've learned it's easier to ask for forgiveness than ask for permission. So, we'll just go ahead as arranged and force the DC to sustain our engagement scenario. What did they used to say last century? 'Lead, follow, or get out of the way.' I have that group of old men just where I want with just enough permission to act upon my plans in a way that looks like I'm following their orders. They think they've got me on a leash, but I'm the one holding theirs. They're tethered to me, not the other way around."

Hawkins wriggled in his rigid seat, his eyes still closed. He snorted with cynical laughter, "I like that the central block of this new continental delegation's solidly Euro. This way, no wogs or jigs to mix things up. That continues to be the central flaw of Marsco, after all," asserted the commander, "Marsco always mixes things that should remain separate, discrete," he explained. "But what'd you expect? Nearly 100 years ago, when Marsco formed initially—"

"—in 1999," came a distant, emotionless fact from Fuentes.

"—yes, back then, the three founding members were all mixed up. Only one was Euro. But the second Asian. The third African.

Well, by that time, the ancestry of all three had become inexplicably NoAm."

"Yes, Cleary, Fugiama, and Bridges."

Notwithstanding the exactness of Fuentes's input, this was Hawkins's diatribe on Marsco history. "It was always been mixed up for the start. It tolerated—even fostered—such mixing. Not good," he concluded, "all that combining." He gave a snide smirk. "Remember that copilot on the *Piazzi?*" he asked Fuentes directly.

The ADC tried to hide what he felt as Mei-Ling's memory forced itself into his mind.

"What was she? Some sort of Euro-Asian polyglot? Not right!"

Fuentes focused on the black night ahead.

"And those wogs in Pass Two—that much power going to brown wogs. Might as well have PRIMS mining the belt! And that black High Wallah was someone you knew right off you must never trust. And many of the hibering personnel, who survived the long crossing without an iceman, were a mish-mash, too. If it wouldn't have raised too much unwanted suspicion, I should have offed half of those bloody mongrels. May as well have started cleaning up Marsco's mess right there."

Hawkins drew a breath, contemplated a moment, and then continued, "No, it'll be better when the new Powers are all Euro ancestry. We can select some allies in NoAm but only the better partners. Y'know, the right kind, the decent kind. The Asians, as well, as long as they know what's what, I can tolerate them, especially if they help this time but keep their place."

The colonel stretched his back side to side and he gave a mocking snicker. "I think we'll turn Valmy's subsidiaries into frozen unincorporated zones for most of the Marsco POWs we take. It's frozen half the year anyway. Of course, there won't be that many after those Ludds cut loose. They clearly have a fire in their belly that I wish our troops had the last time." He snorted. "Affirm that: one big frozen UZ. Let them all freeze their arses off."

After a pause, he pondered out aloud with merciless clarity, "Is it correct to say 'the *former* Valmy's Power' or 'Valmy's *former* Power?'"

The message Walter Miller was waiting for finally arrived from Herriff. A VBC transport was leaving Vandenberg with a plutonium shipment in a week. It had room for him and a second passenger.

"Bring a discreet shuttle pilot," the message concluded.

Miller had already turned away one offer for a pilot when he was trying to help Herriff but not planning on going with him. Where would he find someone now, only days before leaving himself?

If he didn't have a pilot, he at least knew someone who might have the right man in mind. With few options and little time, Miller was forced to start there.

Horthy adjusted a second fuzzer and placed it opposite the first one he had already engaged. If anyone tried to electronically eavesdrop, they would get a double dose of crackling.

"You're extremely cautious," noted Dr. Genda.

It was three days since the Euro-only delegates met a second time with Hawkins in the abandoned bunker. And one night since they finalized their discussions that authorized Hawkins to make contact with the leadership of a Luddite faction.

At Horthy's request, Neidlinger, Gobineau, and Balfour met with this single Asian delegate in the finest restaurant in a thriving Sac City Sid district, an establishment even frequented by off-duty associates. What better place than a comfortable private room here, the Euro leader assured everyone; it shows Marsco they have nothing to hide.

Gobineau answered a polite knock on the door of their oak-paneled room. A waiter offered menus. "The food's fair by NoAm standards," the Euro pointed out.

Horthy added, "Moreover, the ambiance cloaks our real purpose. To anyone looking on, we're here to reestablish old trading ties with this part of the world."

During the past few intervening days, these delegates hadn't been idle. Genda, who initially stood against Horthy's and Hawkins's plans, had been pulled from his nonaligned position once the Euros explained the full benefits of a resurgent Continental presence.

"We know," Horthy convincingly argued, "that we'll never be able to totally replace or supplant Marsco, but we suspect we might rise up to be an equal counterbalance to it."

Such an argument was compelling; it swayed Genda just enough to listen to more logic.

"Many of the Euro and Asian sids are currently viable, to be sure." This had been Horthy's strongest point. "And powerful enough. It's lucidly clear to us in Europe, to stand up to Marsco once we're united. Seattle knows all this, and its HQ relies on us to keep everything and everyone in our locales peaceful."

Horthy paused a moment to set his trap. "Didn't you travel openly? I did!"

"Yes, moved about freely," Genda conceded.

"We all did. When we came to Sac City for these meetings, we landered without hesitation or need for disguise."

"So your point is?"

"All these are all signs of how important and how trusted we are."

"So this'll give us leverage?"

"Of course."

As Horthy adjusted his fuzzers once more, Genda explained to the conspirators, "The principal reason for my reluctance is Hawkins himself. Can he be trusted to stay completely under orders? Not act on his own?"

A confident smile crossed Horthy's face. "I understand totally, Doctor. But you should know and have faith in me; I do have Hawkins on a tight leash. He's a tethered dog brought out now and then to terrorize PRIMS with his bark and snarl. Never to actually bite. And his master has no intention of letting him go tearing into the crowds."

"Notwithstanding, it's Marsco you're trying to scare, and it doesn't flinch easily."

"Not to worry. He'll do the trick."

"So you say, but when he moves his battle fleet—that is to say, *our* attack carriers—into strike position, how can we control him then?" Genda's remark had the intended effect, reminding his listeners that these carriers were originally commissioned by his Power many years ago. Their names attested to their ancestry: *Akagi, Hiryu, Soryu.*

"That'll be at least two years from now. He has to return to his belt base—he's still on Earth—deice all his forces once he's there, and then move them surreptitiously to a sublunar launch site. He'll be out of the way for our real plans all that time."

"So then, you're using his carriers only as a threat you don't really intend to use?" posited the reluctant delegate.

"The key word here, Doctor, is *intimidation.* Marsco's nobody's fool. It'll know clearly that these weapons are fully armed and completely serviceable. None of its safety command overrides once surreptitiously embedded in our weaponry chips are functioning at this time. Everything's clear and clean! Totally reliable! Marsco HQ will be forced to concede to our demands once it perceives this is a real threat."

"Only if our threat's totally believable," added Balfour.

"Hawkins gives us that credence, believe me," Gobineau maintained confidently.

"But are you absolutely sure you can control him?" both Genda and Balfour asked at once.

"Hawkins's a military man, not a politician. Rather blunt, never subtle. In that regard, he's not at all like Igman, who is completely able to grasp finer policy affairs. But our doughty colonel will never act without authorization. He's an officer, after all. We only need to show him off, show his weaponry off. And Marsco will back down well before he's needed. He'll be like these lethality-armed troopers who disperse a bread riot. Have you ever seen an eager trooper place a laser designator on a PRIM? Right here?" He pointed to Gobineau's chest.

"Once that PRIM sees the laser spot and knows an Enfield blast is coming *right there,*" he tapped his comrade above the heart for emphasis, "then they back away PDQ."

"And Hawkins doesn't suspect your change in his plans?" Genda asked. "After all, his document's specific that he launches an all-out attack! Creating, what did he call his sortie, 'a decapitation'?"

"He won't even be blind-copied about our real plans and purposes. He's only a feint, although he doesn't know it. Doesn't suspect it. Makes him more credible, since he believes he's the Air Cavalry coming to the rescue."

Balfour commented, "That's the best place for Hawkins, kept out of it." The woman drew a breath and seemingly launched into a tangent. "He's a little like Shackleton. An esoteric historical anomaly, Ernest Henry Shackleton. An incredibly heroic explorer, but in the depths of the Antarctic, while he was saving his entire stranded band of intrepid adventurers from certain death, the world was blowing itself apart in the first Great War of the twentieth century. Like him, our colonel never really fought in the C-Wars; he only survived for years out in the desolate reaches of the asteroid belt. Has to prove himself, right?"

Genda, scientifically trained himself, added, "In another world, Hawkins's feat—getting to the belt, starting that colony—he would be hailed as a hero! But accomplish all that during the C-Wars?" He shrugged with contempt.

"Hawkins's never lived down that smear, that he bolted when times got hot. Sat idly by on the sidelines during the worst of Earth's hell."

"Yes, well," Horthy interjected, "enough of your psychoanalysis of the good colonel. What of my strategy?"

"The beauty of your plan," added Gobineau, "is the interjection of the Ludds into the mix but then to ultimately crush them. They're a menace to everyone." General agreement circled the table.

"I'll say," joined Neidlinger, who'd listened silently most of the evening. "A violent group (I hope not the one he's been negotiating with), recently sabotaged one of our newest chem plants, to quote, 'save the environment.' Also blew up several server complexes. Up- and down-link farms. New ones we'd only recently installed. Destroyed millions of MMUs worth of tech equipment. Left a section of our sid without Wi-Fi for three months. And our sid needs all the rebooting it can muster. It certainly doesn't need any Ludds tearing up the progress we're making so they can make some retro-statement."

"Anyone killed?"

"Not really. PRIMS mostly."

Horthy saw future events falling along the straight line he was so carefully drawing. He assured his followers, "And so, Marsco eases up on us since it needs us and can see we are more than equal to it. And next, it then increases pressure on these nuisance Ludds. It's win-win for us."

Genda still showed his reticence. "You're banking on three entirely and utterly discrete groups to do exactly as you wish: Marsco, these Ludds, and Hawkins."

"That's the beauty of my plan," countered Horthy. "Hawkins scares Marsco into giving us more independence. We disarm Hawkins—"

"Whom we never intended to use anyway," reassured Gobineau.

"That's right."

"And these violent Ludds? I fear them more."

"And so does Marsco. It'll have to annihilate them, weakening itself. In the long run we keep rising without doing anything more than sitting back and bearing our teeth in a snarl, then moving in when the situation arises. We risk little but gain much."

The plan was set in motion, but Balfour and Genda still had serious doubts, which they disclosed to no one, not even each other. By helping divert Enfields (to be delivered by Hawkins to his allied Luddite group), Balfour had anted up but not increased her wager. In the end, she was actually risking little. She'd laundered the weapons shipments so well they could never be traced directly back to her personally should anything go wrong. Everyone would know *where* the weapons were produced, since only her subsidiary manufactures them, but *her* disks were clean.

Likewise, at this point in the scheme, Genda needed to provide little to the plotters in exchange for great future rewards. He was banking on his Power's prewar investment of the trio of carriers, a debt still owned to his people. Genda's Power had provided the striking arm of the fleet before the C-Wars, but had never collected any payment—the Wars were lost that soon after delivery.

Separately, both of the more reluctant delegates feared Horthy's plans greatly. It was risky threatening Marsco, even vaguely. And this was overt. A plucky PRIM never was so brash. Why should a powerful subsidiary be this bold? But both delegates knew that if Horthy's plans began to unravel, they could quickly side with Marsco and put this trouble behind them.

Gobineau, too, knew he could lay all failures, should they come to pass, at Horthy's feet.

"Subsidiaries only improve if Marsco stays in power," Horthy insisted. "A Marsco we modify, of course, but one in power nonetheless. None of us in our growing sids want Luddites or PRIMS sharing in that power, our power. But why should Marsco continue to get the lion's share? It's time for our dogs to wag our own tails."

TWENTY-FIVE

WAITING

(Sac City Sid, 2097)

"Any associate from outside our cantonment's an honored guest," Lieutenant Peter Rivers stated, welcoming Anthony Grizotti to Security HQ.

"It's good of you to have me," the fellow lieutenant replied without much enthusiasm. "I fear I'm putting you out."

"Nonsense, nonsense," the centurion assured the iceman. "You break the monotony of duty and bring news from beyond this patrol area." As Zot messed with his newfound companions, Rivers further commented, "You entertain my staff with such hair-raising tales of the moon, Europa, and the—what's that exact name? Ah yes, the Trojan asteroids."

Although merely a lowly hiberman (certain reputations crossed all branches), deep space experience gave Zot a "wondrous, fascinating aura," as Rivers termed it, even though in the MAS Fleet itself he was of the lowest caste.

Grizotti let the appearance of enjoyment mask what he really felt. Tessa plagued him.

Every associate at HQ was soon calling Zot "The Explorer" and looking forward to joining him in the mess. He sat drinking coffee with them until assignments thinned his gathering of off-duty warrants and officers, Euros mostly, or of Euro-descent, with a healthy mixture of Asians and Africans.

Nearly a week after Rivers had been to Miller's grange the last time, Zot and Rivers talked quietly by themselves. "I'm between postings and have three more weeks Earth-side before I'm to proceed, via lander, to a lunar docking station."

"Such a destination, it sounds so—" Rivers searched for the correct word, a quick nervous tap to his language disk acting as an aid. "—so, romantic."

Grizotti dipped his head to hide his lying. "After transit to Mars, I'm expecting to begin prep for that follow-up mission to Jupiter."

"That far? You want to go *that far*?"

"You're right to question my quixotic choice. And, you're right that, by virtue of my prior *Gagarin* experience, I've earned a less demanding within-belt mission. Or perhaps even a posting at Hiber-Tech. But, yes, I plan on volunteering for a second four-year trip." It was easy to lie to the Earth-side Security officer.

"Although this's not a certainty, am I not right?"

Does he know something about Herriff and my MAS status? Zot wondered. The iceman nodded at the question, assuming it was a Security officer's duty to pose it. "Much depends on the next few days here."

"I see," Rivers probed, guessing, because he knew strikingly little about the Fleet and the VBC. "You are possibly shunning a somewhat routine belt run to make up for a personal loss?"

"I don't think a routine belt run is less hazardous than a second Jovan trek," the iceman smirked to his host. "Jamie Maissey, a fellow hiberman, ended up seriously dead in a mishap on a so-called routine run."

Truly out of his league, Rivers commented nothing further.

“I know, yours is a dangerous job, as well,” Zot added hastily, not wanting to seem arrogant about his off-Earth status. “You do more than meets the eye.”

“How do you mean?” the reticent Security officer shot back.

Suspicion grew on all sides.

“Scuttlebutt, that’s all,” concluded the hiberman. “Praise for your leadership.”

They let the subjects drop.

The security officer was busy with duties most of the next few days, but he made time for Grizotti at meals. Zot, meanwhile, busied himself with nothing in particular.

Tessa filled his mind, but the iceman found himself thinking of the capricious nature, the backwater eddies and the unhindered, flowing channels of a Marsco life. His career might easily have been like Rivers’s. The men looked roughly the same age but had followed separate tributaries of the Marsco system. Zot’s sid background wasn’t exactly easy, living through the C-Wars as a child, for instance. Yet, he passed exams, made grades, eventually entered the Academy proudly, with honors. Since then, he hibered often enough to shave off half a dozen years from his physical age. He still seemed in his early thirties.

Born after the C-Wars, Rivers never knew a world without Marsco domination. He traveled ways that were Earthbound, stagnant, but still filled with danger. It was clear from how he looked: several years older than he really was. PRIM youth and then the rigors of Security added lines to his face and gray to his once thick black hair. The SO and iceman might be taken for the same age but for different reasons. They even looked a bit alike with Zot’s Med features and Rivers’s SoAm coloring. Except the beard.

Yet, beneath it all, the two associates were linked. Each was devoted to Walter Miller. The idealism in Zot made this a natural choice, even with his severed ties to Tessa. Rivers never expressed his connection directly, but he had an inexplicable devotion to the granger that was unmistakable.

Also, beneath it all, both were searching for something. With Zot, the search went on. For Rivers, he found his home in Marsco, his surrogate family. Security work for him was the destination after a problematic PRIM life without consequence, direction, or hope. He was proud of his distinguished life, even though until recently, he'd skirted duties that put him in collision with Miller. Until the other night, he was steadfast in assisting the granger, if not openly, at least as much as he dared.

At this point in his career, Rivers was the senior officer at this cantonment, in control of one single outpost of four dozen in and around Sac City answering to a central headquarters.

"It is nice, comfortable," the S & H officer stated, looking skyward as though the dull gray mess ceiling held an answer. "Central HQ is clicks from here."

"So, you're in your own fiefdom with virtually complete control of this patrol area, answering to higher wallahs only when necessary."

At first, Rivers looked puzzled. He then smiled. "Oh, yes, I see."

The officer explained his manor's layout. The main complex within the sid took up several city blocks. The central building—his own HQ offices, officers' mess and living quarters—spanned an entire block. Rivers bragged that Marsco staffed more than 55,000 such urban complexes throughout the world in subsidiaries and unincorporated zones.

"Many started from before the Wars," Zot noted. Marsco prewar philanthropy brought it into locales where law had broken down, or more accurately, had been withdrawn. Marsco brought a sense of order, the basics of civilization, by supplying food and medicine and welcome protection from roving gangs of armed youths who were trying to assert their own control over these newly created, powerless PRIMS. It was a side to Marsco, this protective side, that attracted many associates of Miller's generation. Back then, if the new Continental Powers weren't going to take care of their own cast-off citizens, Marsco was.

"Yes, Marsco has been in many places for generations, but all these subsidiary locales now, today," the Security officer insisted, "have requested Marsco tech support in maintaining peace. Security's presence is always at a sid's invitation."

"*Always!*" Zot added nothing more to challenge the fervent officer's belief.

"As example of Marsco efficiency," Rivers continued, skirting the issue, "the layout of each large complex's standardized so that an associate entering one anywhere will know their way around."

His architectural blah-blah continued with a description of the main blockhouse that was a uniform seven stories, made of indigenous brick, festooned with antennas and dishes at one end of the roof and a lander pad at the other. Its basement was an arsenal. "The central keep contains all the com and deployment equipment Security needs should it be temporarily cut off from HQ."

"Can't imagine that scenario," Zot replied, burying his snide tone with an innocuous stroke of his hiber-service beard.

Next to the main building stood several modernized barracks for Security troopers and Auxiliary personnel. "Generally, Auxxies—sid and PRIM volunteers all—carry only nonlethal weapons, unless a situation presents the need for full arms."

"In that rare eventuality," Zot retorted wryly, "I'm sure the arsenal provides ample supplies of leths."

"Of course."

Over the past few weeks, under Rivers's supervision, the Auxillary units had already added leths to their nonleths; each boot now carried an Enfield sidearm. Some individual units were even issued Enfield shoulder weapons. "Speculation about your real purpose here," whispered Rivers, "is not the only rumor spreading through the ranks these days."

"Then these rumblings about possible trouble, expected trouble," Zot noted, "are true?" Always eager to head off any serious unrest, Marsco was quietly muscling up the local Security units and arming Auxiliary battalions accordingly.

"I'm sure all this upscaling of weaponry only adds to the speculations about you, my friend," Rivers concluded, "but regardless of what my troopers whisper about you, remember you're an officer on temporary assignment in this zone. So, as a matter of course, carry your Enfield at all times."

"Yes. Was issued one when I came Earth-side. But are things here that dangerous?"

"Don't consider my request in those terms," Rivers attempted to gloss over. "Let me only encourage you to be at the ready while here."

Without attempting to hide his cutting tone, Zot responded, "And, as with any official command structure, encouragement from a senior officer carries the weight of a direct order."

Almost as an afterthought, Rivers added stiffly, "Need I remind you, lieutenant, that although a MAS officer, you're under an obligation to join an S & H detachment should any emergency arise? To Marsco, at least in theory, an iceman (or any fleet member with warrant rank or higher) needs to merely exchange their Earth-side uniform for the urban gray of Security regulars and be fully functional and integrated." It was the closest Rivers had ever come to demanding Zot, the maggot, give him fifty.

The iceman laughed. "I've always believed that that was something that happened only to newly minted Academy officers. Security duties, in lieu of Fleet posting, have interrupted more than one career."

"Believe what you will, my friend."

The hiberman believed he would be back in space soon. The possibility of a Security tour never entered his mind.

The sun glared off the polished canards and upper surfaces of the gleaming HFC Miller had secured, along with a competent and tactful jockey named Karo. *Shame he's not a shuttle pilot,* Miller thought more than once. Even before the HFC broke into full sun, the pilot wore aviator glasses. The dark lenses and a soft cap kept his features hidden, yet his ebony skin was not out of place in the Marsco world.

"Good to see such bright light again," the granger commented to his taciturn pilot. The flier's large frame was stuffed into the command seat, but his hand movements and finger twitches were agile, quick, responsive. *He shows no signs of hiber,* Miller concluded, *naturally ageless, probably in his late forties.*

The pair was twenty minutes from the dissident's grange, well up into the Sierras. In a normal winter, snow would be deep here by January, but nothing approaching normal had fallen in years. The unbroken forest below showed signs of drought. At least the craft was above the blanket of low clouds that settled over Sac City behind them.

"That tule fog's really gripping the Valley," was Karo's only reply. He was a reticent man, not angry or suspicious. He always spoke to the point.

"Winter soup seems worse than when I was a boy down there," Miller answered.

"Everything's worse now than back then."

After hearing from Herriff, it took Miller less than an hour to find the coordinates for Chamberlain's and find this jockey for hire. The dissident's skills on the Marsco Net and his computer setup were nearly comparable to Marsco's. Secure windows opened to his left twitches as though he were in Internal. While he searched, a line learned in childhood ran through his mind: "Desperate times call for desperate measures." Miller had to act swiftly, possibly cutting some corners to pull all this off.

The pilot had a booked schedule, but Miller's MMUs freed him for a whole day. Karo was worth it because Miller wasn't sure how long any protracted negotiations might take. His steep price didn't bother the granger either. That was something Karo hadn't expected: Miller accepting his services with no attempt to barter or knock off a few MMUs.

Must need this trip badly, the pilot concluded. *And he can't be your ordinary granger.* But his tokens were too generous for any serious questions.

Miller scanned the craft's instruments. Their heading and ETA readings were spot-on with his handheld unit. Karo hadn't deviated one degree from the optimum course.

"Can I ask: were you in Marsco?" Miller began.

Karo held up his right hand, a red FD visible under the index finger's skin. "Twenty years."

"Security?"

"Hauler and lander transports, never in space. NoAm division mostly."

"That where you learned to skim so well?"

"Essentially." He adjusted the craft's flight attitude to take into account the hills below that grew steeper than expected. "When I left, I did so just at the time of an auction of a shitload of surplus equipment. Got this puppy and its larger brother, a hauler six times the size. Been at it four years now, hauling supplies for sids, moving folks like you around. Well," he added flatly, looking over his instruments, "not really like *you*, if you catch."

"Yes, but let's not make much of that."

"No prob."

After a pause, Miller shifted his focus. "Was this a Security unit?"

"For VIP personnel. Never armed but did have more anti-tracking devices. All that got stripped when I bought it." Polymer covers over what had been instrument panels attested to that fact.

Chamberlain's spread came into view on the next hilltop, a pinpoint approach as accurate as any Marsco skim.

"Where do you want me to set down?" Karo asked between adjustments to the vectoring jets and twitches to lower his skids.

"No one's expecting me, so in as visible a location as possible."

Karo pointed to a flat space in a large pasture that was in the line of sight from the main lodge. "This looks good. No one can suspect we're up to something nasty if we land where they can clearly watch us from up top."

The former hauler pilot set the HFC on its skids without so much as disturbing the grass. "You'd think I was still Marsco," he commented softly. Once he shut down his vectors and conversion units, he asked, "You want me to go up there with you?" He pointed to the lodge about thirty meters up a gentle slope. Two figures stood on the terrace watching, a man and woman.

"It's up to you."

"Can use a stretch," Karo answered, reaching over to a compartment and removing an Enfield and leather holster. To Miller's glance, he answered, "Former associate. Never walk into the unfamiliar without this." In one fluid motion, he unfolded himself from the command seat and had the holster fastened.

By the time the arriving pair reached the lodge, only the man was waiting. He motioned them to a set of deck chairs in the sun.

"You've been here before," Chamberlain remarked bluntly to Karo, sizing him up, showing no welcome, unconcerned about the Enfield.

"Year or so back. And you *did* ask me to forget the trip."

To Miller, Chamberlain stood back, hesitant. "You certainly don't need any more disks," the physician said at last.

"If you'll recall," the granger explained to the stern listener, "we *accidently* spoke on c-phone a while back about the possibility of you having connections to a shuttle pilot."

"May have."

"I'm not sure if you are still in communication with the individual we spoke about."

Chamberlain gave no indication either way.

Sliding a memory stick from his hand-unit, Miller went on, "If your shuttle-experienced friend wants to leave Earth, I'm going in a matter of days. Not more than four. If your friend needs to find my place, look here, these are the coordinates to my grange."

He waved the stick. "If interested, we can discuss the matter further right now." He looked around but saw no one. "Or down the Valley at my place. Any time, day or night. But in less than four days."

When Chamberlain didn't take the stick from him, Miller set it down on his chair's arm.

"I won't bother you any longer," Miller concluded, turning to leave.

"I might be back, who knows?" Karo explained. "Business is real good, and it's booming just now."

In a few strides, the pilot caught up to the granger. Since they were heading down hill to the waiting HFC, their pace was quicker than their climb up to the lodge.

After the Indie HFC had turning clearance, it swung around, gained height to miss the closest trees, and was gone. Both Chamberlain and Shanghai watched it glide away, picking up speed as it did.

The physician left the sunny deck without a word or an indication of what sat on the chair's arm.

Alone, the pilot looked at the stick. Snatching it, she placed it safely in a zippered pocket next to her hidden Enfield.

As Zot languished, he was amazed at what he learned. He gained firsthand validation of his long-held suspicions about Marsco and the conditions of Earth. Very early on, the iceman asked repeated questions to reluctant junior officers. His age and obvious status loosened many tongues.

One WO, fresh-faced and eager for more action, told much to the iceman. From this warrant (a Euro but one raised in Africa where his parents were sids), Zot learned that Marsco gathered volunteers for zone work who weren't connected ethnically or culturally with the majority of the indigenous PRIMS.

"Is it always done this way?"

In an exact factual manner that hid the legionnaire's true feelings and kept a veneer of loyalty in the forefront, he explained, that in this sid, Security utilized the services of six battalions of troopers for patrol duties. They came with ample Auxiliary units, as well: nine additional battalions, mostly from the South West Equatorial Pacific Islands.

"How ready are they?" Zot asked with a bland tone.

To the warrant, the iceman clearly seemed to be loyalty-probing. That being the case, he replied candidly, "Three Auxxie units aren't fully trained yet but are receiving complete training on site. Primarily those three assist with inconsequential patrol duties."

After a few go-rounds of Zot's intense questioning at the mess table, Rivers had to pull him aside. "My new friend, you're terrifying my junior officers and warrants more and more."

"How so?"

"Your questions. Iceman or no, to them it's like you're checking their allegiance. They're concerned, justly so."

"Is it wrong to ask such questions?"

"Wrong? No. Wise? Also, no. But the answer to almost everything you ask is always the same: 'It's a Marsco world.'"

Yet, Zot kept asking.

The mess hall talk circulated about Zot, an officer who seemed to have nothing particular to do. The stigma of Internal Security clung to him the way a scar on the back of his left hand would have if he'd ever had a PRIM-disk removed.

Another officer, convinced she knew why the alleged iceman was actually there, tried staying on his good side. She proved to be extremely open, explaining after several pointed questions that in Sac City, the arrangement of service personnel coming from around the world worked so well that the Auxxies began settling their families here permanently. They'd established a thriving compound to the east of the city center, a place called "the Colony."

The iceman already knew of it from Dr. Miller. In fact, Zot had an open invitation from the Colony's leader, Xiao P'hing, to visit at any time.

Nonetheless, the visitor questioned, "So they've forsaken their traditional homelands for here?"

Of such a question, the listening officers collectively thought, *What do you expect from an iceman?* But one, hedging her bet in case Grizotti was with Internal, stated in a matter-of-fact manner, "Are there such things as 'traditional homelands' anymore?" Her proper answer put the other uncomfortable warrants clustered around the probing Zot at ease.

Another time, one of the hiberman's new acquaintances was proud to tell him about her battalion structure. "Besides imported troopers, many indigenous PRIMS (teenage boys and girls) are trained to assist with security duties here," she explained with Marsco pride. "They're especially adept at monitoring food distribution and water rationing. Should they pass muster, these locals will soon be on their way to more intense training and eventual deployment to a different UZ, ideally half a continent away."

"I see," noted Grizotti. "And am I right that, mostly, their duties, these trusted locals, are to promote total cooperation between indigenous peoples and their out-located overseers?"

"Affirm that."

"And all these legionnaires-in-waiting are Neo-Con free, am I not right?"

"Roger, sir. The single-most important volunteer threshold."

"And quite young. Thirteen? Fourteen?"

"All within regs, sir."

Nothing the iceman heard surprised him. He was gaining valuable intel about the underside of Marsco, but it was what he suspected all along. Running an empire takes a shadowy, furtive side that rarely sees the light of day.

"Don't you feel up for a furlough at a more luxurious location?" Rivers asked the next morning at table. "And temperate? Foggy Sac City seems an unlikely a place to remain for a few weeks. You have the choice of scores of Marsco rec areas with their many perks." He gave a wry smile. "An associate counts on every hookup there being free of HH GAS and Neo-Con."

The hiberman managed his own smile. "Since you extended an invitation to this less-than-glamorous locale, I plan to spend my entire time here."

Rivers lowered his voice. "But some of my junior officers secretly suspect that you are actually on an Internal mission, as often happens. Well, so I'm told." He gave a knowing look, then another, side to side. "See how they stay aloof these meals, except when your hiberman tales about Jupiter grow too exhilarating?"

The centurion motioned for Zot to look around the mess. The iceman had begun noticing that when he spoke of space, these reluctant associates joined in. Many, he surmised, believed it better to play along with a covert wallah and his thin cover story than stand back only to have him cast a long glance their way.

Grizotti gloated at this fact, since the hidden, real reason he stayed was the close proximity to Tessa. He was hoping that she would eventually contact him here. He had already waited one bleak, winter week without a word. Although surrounded by other eager companions, he longed for Tessa. After passionately reigniting their love and then in a nano having it all come crashing down around him, Zot was unwilling to surrender her to Marsco.

Later in the meal, the Security lieutenant felt the need to justify Marsco's actions. "By selecting personnel from different political and ethnic backgrounds," Rivers stated flatly, without betraying any personal connections with this policy, "Marsco completed two tasks at once. First, it removes many youths, especially boys, although many young women also serve. Removing them keeps them from—" Rivers let a shrug be his word.

Zot motioned he understood. "And getting them so young breaks down any ties to region, religion, culture, language."

"Goes without saying. And teens, who once might cause trouble in their own zones, now receive discipline, training, and motivation to be responsible citizens of the world."

Or so Marsco's spin would have it, Zot thought while looking blankly. He added a pro forma remark, "Marsco's been doing this for decades."

"Yes, yes, since even before the Wars," Rivers remarked then returned to his salient point. "And second, there's a compelling reason for each sid or PRIM in service to cooperate. A percentage of the successful Security unit's earnings go back to its home sid or UZ."

"A welcome addition to any family's income, I'm sure," responded Zot scornfully. "So, if a unit doesn't perform its job well, everyone has their fam's extras cut off." He made the remark as a statement of fact, not as a question.

"All is determined by the individual performance rating at the squad level."

"I guess that the old expression 'One bad apple…' aptly applies here," concluded the iceman. "One goldbrick or reluctant legionnaire, and bingo: all perks withheld from the whole unit."

Rivers added without a trace of irony, "Marsco's method ensures high morale and sustained motivation."

"So," Zot went on needling, "what if the PRIMS don't cooperate? I mean the *patrolled* PRIMS, not the *patrolling* PRIMS."

In the calm, reasoned way training had taught him, Rivers explained. "If resident PRIMS in a particular zone didn't cooperate with Security or Auxiliary personnel, then it would be that food and water distributions are impossible to conduct peacefully. Sometimes this means weeklong disruptions (possibly longer) to the whole supply pipeline for that zone or portion of zone, for that matter. It means shutdowns in the chain of resupply for safety concerns."

"Safety concerns? Not punitive measures?"

"Safety concerns! The same might happen with electricity and heating reserves."

"In those locations fortunate to have them, in high-end zones, for example."

"Exactly. And for factories, rudimentary as they might be in this zone. They're forced to cease operations. Even slight trouble in a patrol area brings near-total cessation of services."

"This never happens in the subsidiaries proper?"

"Or, your questions! Sids generally run themselves. But, certainly, any sid that ceases to cooperate with Marsco, surely—"

"Yes, I know, PRIM-to. Reduced to zone status before the sid knows what the hell happened and why."

"You know the kit, my friend, so why all these questions?"

"Just curious, I guess."

"You sound like our mutual friend, Miller."

"Well, all this is one way to ensure cooperation," the iceman eventually concluded, layering his synopsis in a skeptical tone.

Rivers ignored the jab. "Consequently," he went on with assured confidence in the policies as though Zot were in total agreement, "all PRIMS work toward smooth operations of support services. That's *all* Marsco wants."

"So what you're saying is that without total and complete local cooperation, then Security safety measures prevent any distribution of essential supplies for fear of further disruptions."

Pleased the iceman finally got it, Rivers added with emphasis, "Marsco expects and generally receives full compliance."

"I'm sure it finds that the two groups—supervisor and supervised—soon cooperate fully and that the patrolled zones, along with their overseers, are quiet and contented."

“That’s the plan. But generally, even in the worst zones, something as flashpoint-controversial as BC strip checks before food distribution, go smoothly because Marsco wants it that way.”

And Marsco wants its own way 24/7, Zot noted. After thinking a bit, the iceman commented, “I can’t imagine what happens if no cooperation’s forthcoming.”

“Regrettably,” Rivers explained slowly, “if all doesn’t go well, Marsco has stronger means.”

“Via other troopers at its disposal, ones trained to make sure peace’s maintained at any cost. Rather a piss-poor system,” Zot concluded bluntly.

The iceman’s explanation collided violently with the centurion’s deepest feelings. “It doesn’t hesitate to utilize crack specialists, if that’s what you’re implying.” The Security officer’s internal conflict made the tone of this rationalization sound hollow.

Zot easily understood the vagueness of the fellow’s remarks. And he came to see the dichotomous nature of Rivers. He would soldier on without a gram of reluctance; he continued to bleed Marsco red without a nano of hesitation. And yet he was of PRIM stock.

The only exception seemed to be with Walter Miller. Zot realized almost from the first time they met that Rivers had a leniency toward the granger and his daughter for reasons the hiberman didn’t know and possibly never would. The centurion’s benevolence toward the pair was palpable.

“It always surprises me,” Zot commented the next evening to Rivers, “that Marsco continues to play one group against another to keep control of its zones.”

“Its? All unincorporated zones are run by subsidiaries; Marsco only assists in their governmental control.”

“So be it,” Grizotti replied, acquiescing to the obvious party line.

They had driven north of the old city center near Rivers's locale to an area that was once again flourishing. The unlikely pair walked along an expansive strip where restaurants and shops conducted their modest businesses peacefully, remaining safely open until an extended curfew. In a coffee bar, the associates sat at a small table enjoying the bustle of the orderly crowd just beyond the window. Bundled-up sids scurried by. The weeks of valley fog didn't seem to dampen their spirits. Their breath showed white as they headed for warm homes.

So last century, thought Zot.

Under the glow of newly installed street lamps—each one with an additional onion-shaped cam housing—sids briskly conducted their affairs, buying and selling. Something approaching a Marsco-standard Herriff-Grid operated above. HFCs whooshed by or hovered with skids down for a glide landing. *Someone's making plenty of MMUs here,* Zot realized. Even if constantly under invisible, vigilant eyes, these sids were content. It seemed a small trade-off.

The iceman noticed it first and then pointed it out to the Security officer. "See how many walking by have bandages on their right hands, specifically the tips of their index fingers." These were sids starting from scratch, ones who had never been disked.

"Yes, new implants."

"For sids?"

"A sure sign things're improving here."

"I gather they were thoroughly checked out before disking."

"Not my department, but assuredly. It's the old dilemma," commented the Security officer, trying to stay noncommittal. "How do we have absolute safety in the most efficient way?"

"Well, I'm glad I don't have deal with that."

"Yes, of course, but you must remember that any officer in the locality can expect to be utilized if an emergency arises. 'Familiarization of the immediate area via ground recce.' That's how I've justified letting you engage a Security HFC and hummer. And why I expect you to carry your Enfield."

"So, you *are* expecting trouble."

The Security officer sipped his coffee but didn't respond. He watched the contented crowd flow by reasonably. His silence confirmed to Grizotti that all was not quite right very near here.

"Have you seen both Millers lately?" the iceman finally asked.

"I've only seen the one," the local officer answered. It was clear which one he meant even though his answer remained evasive. "Let me once more give you some advice. Move on to a real R & R area for the remainder of your leave. May I suggest Ipanema, near Rio? Summertime there now. Excellent facilities. Beautiful beaches. *And other scenery*. And frankly, the sids are friendly, female wise." In a lowered voice Rivers added, "It grows unsafe here, I'm afraid, even for Marsco S & H forces."

"Unsafe? Here? For an associate in a subsidiary as peaceful as Sac City?" Zot milked it, motioning to the tranquil street outside the coffee bar. "You're expecting trouble *here,* in such a serene setting?"

"You know, my friend," retorted the S & H officer as he tapped the subcutaneous disk behind his right ear, "my LD is quite thorough. It's mostly eliminated my Brazilian PRIM accent, linguistically, no small accomplishment. And yet, I still have trouble understanding your tone, your hidden meanings. *Innuendos,* I believe they're called. Are you speaking seriously?"

"Of course!" Zot's tone changed immediately. "What sort of trouble can happen here? I mean, you have quite a grip on the situation, don't you?"

Rivers didn't answer.

"Oh, so you're referring to the redrawn stoplines?"

"You know what I mean. Some places will be safe; others, maybe not."

"And Walter? His grange?"

"It officially reverts back to a UZ at the end of June, as you know. All these years, he's lived in a tenuously defined gray area. All those Indie farmers as neighbors. That attempt at a PRIM village." He tapped his language disk needlessly as though to increase its efficiency, "All those self-reliant grangers are so close to the former

UZ demarcation anyway. In a few months, after the drawback—" A shrug completed his comment.

Rivers took a sip of coffee then continued, "Those granges will all be in part of the expanding zone, in a true random patrol locale, not a 'gray area,' at all." He gave another shrug. "The stopline will cordon this prospering district and the other such locations in the northern or eastern environs of the subsidiary plus around the old city center, where there's the most important industry, the canneries, and better housing blocks. And around the Colony, of course. That will be well-protected even if we don't protect it."

"Naturally," Zot concluded, "the Colony has to be included in any new patrol area."

The S & H officer once more answered by shrugging, "You expected otherwise?" He clarified, "I doubt we'll make any runs very far down south toward Miller's, unless there's trouble we wish to control. Of course, some trouble we have to let burn out by itself."

"Like wildfires left unattended, even in forests Marsco's worked so hard to preserve."

"Nature must take its course. And then there's that new Hygiene Center."

"Neo-Con, here? A serious threat?"

Rivers looked around the dimly lit coffee bar to make sure no one was listening. He wished he had had the foresight to bring a fuzzer to break up any electronic eavesdropping. His voice fell to a whisper. "The fog and damp winter. A serious outbreak in a southern UZ spread widely over the past months. We're to set up a hygiene area, not more than five clicks south of Miller's. He's in no immediate danger from this facility, but it will make many things more difficult if he wishes to remain. And, if we don't get adequate winter rains, I also fear for cholera in the blazing summer." The officer paused and gave a sardonic chuckle, "And if the rains come hard, I fear malaria, West Nile, and encephalitis."

"A shitload of everything, I suppose."

The senior officer tapped his LD. "Very poetic. But near to any PRIM area there's always a threat of many spreading diseases."

Neither spoke again until Rivers abruptly changed the direction of the conversation. "Where's your family from? Originally from, say your grand-, or great-grandparents?"

"Most from what was the Midwest, generally around Chi-Town. And well before that, as the name implies, Italy. But on my paternal side, the Euro ancestry is a long stretch back. We have a smattering of other Euro-stock mixed in there as well. Common enough for someone on this continent for two centuries. My maternal side is closer to the Med. My mother's actually from Italy itself, Basilicata, but raised on this continent." His brown eyes gave Rivers a penetrating glance. "But such ideas of ancestry belong to last century."

"You know much of your own family, a Marsco oddity."

"I also know, unlike here, that my home sid's prospering. But much of the old city's carved into zones and housing authorities."

"Yes, so little really changes, doesn't it?"

"Well to the south of those locales, the prime farmland's leased from Marsco by several Food Consortiums. But even the zones back in Chi-Town, they've had running water for dozens of years, winter heat."

"I've lived without both—" Rivers caught himself. He wasn't from sid background. He wasn't able to speak of a paternal and maternal ancestry with any of the authority Zot had. "Never mind," he half whispered.

Grizotti looked across the table at Rivers. The centurion's name told much, that he had distanced himself from ancestry to become an associate. Zot knew he was Brazilian, hence linked to Europe centuries before, not at all unlike himself. But, there was much SoAm mixed in, possibly both indigenous and African—typical, but completely unknown, absolutely unknowable. Genealogy and DNA searches were dead social sciences. In the Security officer's Marsco, Zot realized, self-knowledge and ancestral history were luxuries not afforded every associate. Marsco associate or sid or

PRIM were the only identities allowed. The iceman doubted that a category for the Truman sons, for instance, even existed.

A long silence followed, both men absorbed in their personal thoughts. Finally, Zot spoke apropos of nothing, “I think I understand; they should get out.”

“Who they?”

“The Millers.”

“He’s down there alone at present.”

“And the other Doctor Miller?”

“Assuredly, she left early the next morning following our Epiphany dinner.”

The iceman lowered his saddened eyes and stared into his milky coffee.

TWENTY-SIX

MORNING AND AFTERNOON

(Sac City Sid and Zone, 2097)

"Excuse me, sir," a WO supervising an Auxxie squad shouted at Grizotti from across the vehicle park. "You shouldn't ought take that one, sir."

In the gray morning light, Zot had climbed behind the wheel of a hummer in the motor pool where a dozen rovers and hummers sat ready for use. Rivers had given him access to a fuel-cell vehicle, and the iceman was exercising his freedom. With much on his mind, so much so it gave him a headache, he still wanted to see several sections of the zone and sid. In an invisible and insignificant sign of protest, he wanted to personally verify or disprove Marsco proclamations.

In the cold blanket of fog, the insistent warrant officer wore only a gray T-shirt. It had the motto "Service and Protection" in dark letters across the front. His carrot hair was chopped close; his face was clean-shaven, except for a neat, reg-trimmed moustache. He looked every inch an Earth-side trooper: sinewy and accepting no nonsense, especially from a mere hiberman, officer or not.

"We've already substituted her nonleths, sir." The warrant motioned to the long-barreled weapon behind the driver's seat. A 12.7 mm stood on a swivel mount rising through the open hatch.

"That much muscle? Expecting trouble?" Zot asked pointedly.

Ignoring the question, the WO explained, "We only let them out on armed patrol. They're too prized for their kick to just go out alone."

As the surrounding zone fell back into its isolated savagery, even Zot's 7.6 mm sidearm was coveted in a territory of resurgent violence.

"Take that one, if y'don't mind." The warrant pointed to a rover with a pair of nonlethals that hadn't yet been substituted.

The vehicle's main weapon was a McGrath stunner that sent out an electrical charge like a lightning bolt into a milling crowd of PRIMS. With optimum weather and ground conditions (air not too humid, ground not too wet), it was stun-capable up to 100 PRIMS in a mob. It gave an incapacitating jolt that periodically blinded its targets permanently.

The secondary unit looked something like a mounted fire hose. Its oozy liquid turned viscous on contact, making natural and easy movements impossible. PRIMS were immobilized in the heavy, glutinous jelly. Although considered nonlethal, on many occasions it suffocated its doused recipient: PRIM noses and throats sealed by the hardening ooze. If scuttlebutt were true, its discharge created a deterrent for latent anti-Marsco activities: choking to death.

As with the stunner's battery housings, the jelly tanks were empty in anticipation of weapon substitution. The rover appeared formidable but wasn't.

"I know you've permission, sir, to wander at will—from Rivers himself, sir—but be careful with this here gear. We've reason to believe that V/STOL flights took place in the extreme south zone. Ain't a good sign for safety, personnel-wise, sir. You're a significant asset to any violent pongos, as a hostage. Both you and your sidearm, sir, and them equipping on the rov."

Zot realized this WO meant business even as he feigned courtesy.

"Pardon me, sir. I know you're in the Fleet, and all." His voice carried an edge that approached insubordination in anyone's army. "And you're prob really a high wallah who can bust my butt at a drop, if you catch, but don't take no stupid-ass chances. Copy? Don't get your fuckin' hole bunged up with any skinnies! Not on my watch!" He blinked then gave a compliant toothy grin. "Sir!"

The officer had to suppress his outrage at such defiance.

"Worse yet, sir, if you really are jus' a mother icer, don't get your fuckin' meddling ass in a bind, dumb-shit-wise, that I gots to get it out of."

Iceman, Zot thought, *always the butt of it.* Assuring the warrant that his first destination was the Colony had a soothing effect.

"Safest places in the whole damn sid, sir!" The retort came unctuously polite. "To be officially placed within the newly redistricted green zone soon. Always a secure destination even these days."

Closest to the cantonment, Zot found the Sac City sid run-down but with signs of better things to come. Here the old city grid still held true, although the streets were dotted with foot, bicycle, and moped traffic. An occasional jitney came past. A Security vehicle.

He maneuvered through several areas once devoted to housing. An elevated freeway stood useless above him, unrepaired for several decades, made obsolete by a Herriff-Grid. The iceman was glad that the rover had good traction; surface streets hadn't been repaved since before the Wars. Traffic alone pounded them into a beaten track.

Because this area would be well within any new stopline, an old school, brimming with children, had reopened, clearly under direct auspices of Marsco. *One hand of Marsco and its largesse, but what's the other doing?* the iceman wondered.

After an hour of wandering, the sights changed rapidly. Farther out, away from anything Marsco deemed productive, the hiberman found signs he expected in a zone, not a sid. PRIMS lived on the streets. He passed several well-guarded food distribution points with long queues. All the PRIMS seemed old or children. Teens and young adults were either away in work gangs or scooped up in lander sweeps.

Turning a corner five clicks deeper into the sid, Zot approached a narrow street where two dozen adventuresome skinnies had thrown up a roadblock using empty oil drums and bricks. It was the last thing the iceman expected, being rousted for a protection toll in the middle of a sid. Eight young PRIMS, eating off to the side, grabbed crudely-fashioned clubs to greet their unforeseen prize.

Thought you've all gone to the Auxiliary, Zot mused until he saw the look in their eyes. He was one lone associate, a soft target. A dozen rocks fell around him. Taunts followed. Rivers's plan wasn't as thorough as the Security officer had boasted.

The iceman tapped his holster but backed away from the flashpoint instead. He knew what these street punks didn't. Once a recce drone spotted them, Marsco was bound to hit here hard. If lucky, these daring PRIMS would find themselves in Patagonia or Basra by nightfall. If unlucky, their folks might find their bodies.

Entering the Colony, Zot was stopped twice. Once at the thick concertina wire of the compound perimeter and a second time three-quarters of a click within it at a second defended gate beside the original residential area. The iceman marveled at these guards: boys and girls too young to be Auxxie volunteers themselves but obviously trained by their fathers or siblings in thorough search procedures. And Enfield-armed.

What a leg up in life, he thought sarcastically, *by eleven or twelve years they can use Enfields. And they're not at a roadblock shaking down random traffic.*

Zot sipped the oolong tea offered to him, surprised at the Colonists' hospitality. And yet, it was no wonder. To them, the iceman was Marsco *"ad unguem," to the fingertips,* and their entire livelihood came from working diligently, selflessly, to serve Marsco.

During a previous visit to Miller's, Zot had met Xiao P'hing, a longstanding Auxiliary leader and one of the first to bring his family here. It was Xiao who initially envisioned the Colony, and he was justly proud of it. Hardened by the rigors of duty, the Auxxie had also become softened by its rewards.

"So glad you've come to my home. An officer here! We're so pleased." Xiao nodded to his wife, who sat behind.

The Auxxie himself was a squat, square-shouldered man with close-cut hair. It was clear that as a member of the Auxiliary, he knew his business. As a host of an associate, he knew hospitality. *Maybe he'll teach that WO back at the cantonment a few lessons,* Zot thought. As a venerable leader of this sid's ancillary Security units, he wielded much more power than mere rank.

"I hope you admire what you see," he stated, pouring the iceman another cup of tea. His twisting head pointed to the four corners of the Colony. His gesticulating gave Zot a glance at his language disk.

Explains the proper English, the iceman mentally commented. "It's an out-of-sid experience," the hiberman finally replied aloud, smiling back at Xiao's contented family. The esteemed visitor and residents all sat in a darkened room, lit by candles, scented by smoking sticks. The older boys all had FDs, but they didn't need any language disks. Marsco's only an exam away, the hiberman realized. No shakedown roadblocks for them, no recce drones overhead, no lander sweeps.

The Colony housed roughly 1,000 Auxxies along the winding streets of a former subdivision. The restored houses and salvaged gardens were in excellent shape. Some residents here had been on station for more than twenty-five years, almost since the cessation of the C-Wars. Over time, they brought their families from the privations of their original zones to this considerably more stable locale half a world away.

"By now, of course," Xaio was quick to explain, "we're comfortably resettled here."

"You'd say, this's home?"

"Yes, it's our home. Marsco made it so."

After their noon meal, Xaio took Zot to the Colony's central water tower. They scaled up a spiraling catwalk to an OP on top that afforded a 360-degree vista, although today everything was seen through an ashen mist. The tower spouted Marsco's most sophisticated surveillance gear. From this vantage point, the panorama of the Colony spread out before them. What was beyond was under constant visual and CCTV observation.

Fences and watchtowers surrounded the former parklands that once graced this suburban area. Relentless vigilance kept PRIMS out of the extensive gardens and fields that stretched out along the riverbank. Two footbridges connected the Colony proper to the far side of the river where a former wildlife preserve afforded more retro-cropland and grazing space for their cattle.

Here, armed guards stood watch 24/7. At a typical outpost in a calm sid, an Auxiliary member would most likely carry only nonleths or at the most a sidearm. Here, off-duty Auxxies and their families were heavily armed with shoulder-fired Enfields. To the Colonists, just beyond their field of vision, the adjoining mogged territory teemed with hordes of restless hostiles. With Marsco's blessing they intended to protect their own.

His language disk working perfectly, Xaio proudly explained to Zot, "Our cultivation is a lush island amid a sea of roaming unknowns, sids, thousands of renegade PRIMS, Luddites of all stripes. The very elements we patrol stoplines to control. All these make their homes just beyond our wire." The Colony was an oasis of bounty within a teeming sea of continuing postwar chaos.

A barbed-wire fence surrounded the central area, an incongruous line of curling rusty tendrils running next to restored, early-century homes. A jarring juxtaposition to the iceman, never totally resigned to such sights.

Beyond the central living area, residents carefully tended their PRIM-made gardens. These were surrounded by another distant fence sprouting several evenly spaced towers. a formidable barrier prohibiting entrance without permission.

Most stoplines, Zot noted, don't have that thickness and stalwartness. Many were in fact only an imaginary line, a patrol designation. A line of I-ON-Us and PRIM-monitors linked to a cantonment command center.

"We're protecting our own, not just Marsco's. Here, the line in the sand is kept perfectly clearer."

"Yes, I see," the visitor commented dryly.

Xaio added, "'Good stoplines make good neighbors.'"

Zot nodded in mute agreement.

From their watchtower vantage point, Xaio eventually pointed out the Enclave, barely visible on the southern horizon along the river. "Ludds continue to salvage a university campus there." Like the Colony, the Enclave was a thriving oasis of order and safety within the greater poverty of the destitute subsidiary.

"Yes, in much the same ways as you have developed this parkland."

"No, much different, much," the iceman's host insisted.

Through a scope, Zot made out several distant buildings, once the library, dorms, and classrooms.

"Those Ludds are a threat to my very own."

"How so? From all that I've heard, they're passive, hard-working. They cause no one any trouble."

"No matter, they're Ludds and don't belong there." Xaio held his breath so he didn't fog up the scope's eyepiece and focused for a deeper look into enemy territory.

Zot sensed that Allison's Enclave was marked for particular attention as stoplines pulled back.

On her last morning with him, Ling Shanghai sat relaxing with Doctor Chamberlain on his sundeck, bathed in bracing winter light. They wore PRIM-knitted sweaters, but their faces and hands warmed in the brightness. The compound was nestled far enough up into the mountains to have brilliant sunshine pouring down while the Sac valley, invisible out beyond the down slope, languished in fog. On the wind-sheltered deck, they watched morning shadows disappear in the dense, dry forest on the opposite hillside. As the sun climbed higher, Shanghai felt safe and contented.

"Everything checked out," the physician remarked about his patient's final medical exam earlier that day. "Your finger's healed completely."

She inspected her fingertip to be sure, gingerly picking at the new disk with her thumbnail.

"It'll take close scrutiny," he noted with professional satisfaction, "to find scar tissue from the first hypodermic implant and its subsequent replacement. There might be some slight evidence of surgery around your primary disk, but no one can tell at a glance we've switched."

He took her hand, but not with the touch of a doctor.

"I can't thank you enough." Shanghai still talked as a patient even with her hand in his.

"Remember," he cautioned, "Marsco doesn't consider you a threat, so you're safe on that score, *if you're smart.*"

"Don't worry; I won't bring Security down on you."

"That's not my concern. I meant that you're so extreme, you're apt to do something rash, that's all. Although, I admire your grit."

"Have to be. I've only myself for protection."

The winter sun streamed down on them, still hand in hand. Shanghai asked without breaking the aura created by the radiance, "What's been substituted in the Marsco files?"

"Nothing really *substituted.* And you've memorized the synopsis of your new past life. That associate who skimmed up here sometime last week is still fully functional in the cyber files. Shanghai's newly initiated, but her records go back twenty-five years or more. Anyone looking for that earlier associate will find her quietly residing, as required, in Seattle near the Marsco HQ."

Shanghai nodded that she understood, as he explained further, "If someone keeps accessing her factoid and keeps getting the same answer, suspicion might grow. But I've found that generally Internal Security isn't that thorough on minor matters."

"And negligence is minor?"

"To IS? Yes. Think of Marsco's real threats. Compare that disgraced associate to some other associates covertly joining violent factions and then acting as moles. Compare that disgraced associate to some crazed cracker gone native and disrupting any number of exec ops."

As Chamberlain looked out over the wooded valley, Shanghai watched him intently. Older but without any hiber-retarded aging, he remained vigorous. His isolated life gave him an air of ruggedness, of individuality so often lacking in her uniformed world. His graying hair gave him a mature attraction.

He eventually continued. "Five months ago, hackers—from Earth, mind you—took control of the guidance commands of a mining asteroid coming in from the belt. These hackers actually altered its trajectory so that instead of being captured in lunar orbit, it used the Moon to fling onto a new course, a collision course with a lander."

He drew a breath, still staring into the distance, still showing a striking profile to Shanghai. "A catastrophic impact was averted by quick-disked evasive action by the lander copilot."

"Can always count on those live ones at the flight deck," the flier noted.

"Nonetheless, that gives you an idea of what Marsco faces. And that's not the half of what some committed Ludds can and will do. Rover bombs at newly reopened malls in prosperous subsidiaries. Bio-attacks! Euro-sids and Sectors have had outbreaks of disease: weaponized influenza, anthrax. Some faction or another's planted virulent microbes where occurrences hadn't been a problem for years, since the Wars."

"Even in space, I've heard such rumors."

"Something Marsco doesn't brag about."

"I can't imagine that number of incidents."

"Imagine it; it happens! Several Marsco research institutes recently had their data storage vandalized, their physical experiments destroyed—recombinant DNA fields, that sort of thing. Net postings about 'Franken-food!'"

"Sounds like the first few decades of this century, all this sci-tech gothing."

"Much like!" He looked at her directly, "So, you still think negligence's a major prob for Internal? It has its disks full of real dangers, real hostiles. Chen was convicted as a bungler of MAS SOP, that's all." He paused to make sure that she didn't take these harsh remarks personally then tapped her shoulder gently. "On scant evidence with terrible council."

Shanghai forced her mind not to return to her multiple betrayers.

"Yes, that associate's alleged ineptitude seems mild compared to many, many others who have stopped out of Marsco and now want revenge against her. Sometimes it's quite easy for a former associate 'to be turned,' as the spook slang goes. So, I'm convinced that Internal will be leaving her alone if she behaves herself. At most, an IS boffin might randomly check on her, but my program will keep stating she's in the Seattle Sector, minding her own business."

Shanghai seemed relieved. Between their deck loungers, their hands remained entwined.

"Yes," he added to completely reassure Ling, "that disgraced associate's existing cyber file will seem complete to a cursory glance, and she will seem to be totally complying with the tribunal's decision."

"Well, actually, *indecision,*" Shanghai stated. "The panel didn't know what the hell to do with me." She caught Chamberlain's cautionary glance. "With her. Technically, I'm, she's, still on Earth-side pay."

"Which reminds me," the physician redirected her remarks. "I can transfer over everything in that woman's bank account."

"Really?"

"It'll take some time, and Shanghai needs an account of her own, one that's been around for a while. Six months from now, MMUs can move over electronically without a trace. It'll take a small fee to launder, of course, so there's a 25% service charge."

"Fine," Shanghai smiled but thought that Bennie filched much less than one quarter of her units. "But more to the point, what about Chen? Actually?"

"Just hanging, doing what someone does on Earth."

"So, you're saying, she's no different from any other MAS jockey between missions. You know, deep down, I think Internal's really ferreting out Wilkes and Fuentes; there's something unresolved about *them* more than *her.*"

"Precisely. And if you—*and she*—don't cause any hassles, no one'll notice. So long as you stay out of trouble." He squeezed her hand for emphasis.

"Well, if there are any complications, I'm ready," she replied. Instinctively she pulled out her clone from under the leather jacket she had placed on a chair next to her. During her week here, she was never far from it.

"An Enfield?"

Feeling so shielded by him, she refrained from showing or discussing the weapon until that moment.

"Issued model?" he asked a second time.

"Black market," she explained, "took a chance up in the Vancouver Sid to get one. It's a clone; made sure of that."

"Wise precaution. Harder to trace."

"Nearly impossible."

"You've taken some incredible risks," he observed. "Stay that course."

"I'm not planning on offing anyone, if that's what you mean."

"Something like that. Don't employ your new identity to seek revenge."

"I'm still a little concerned about it." Shanghai motioned to her clone. "Should I leave it here? What conclusions will S & H draw from me having this?"

"Can you carry it concealed? I never knew, although, of course, I assumed, but never got anything." He stopped short of admitting he scanned her before their first meeting.

After an awkward pause, she continued. "It's easily hidden. The jacket has sort of a weapon-fogger sown in, which is also its holster."

"Well-hidden, easy to conceal, no one knows you have it. That being the case, so long as you're careful, I don't see a prob. Quite against regs, but then again, some sids move about armed and aren't detained so long as they *don't cause trouble.*" He hitched his voice as he spoke those words so they came out with a lilt of humor.

She gave a flirty-finger wiggle at him. "You keep saying that, 'Don't cause trouble.'"

"Because I mean it."

"I only plan on making the kind of trouble that's expected," the flight officer whispered vaguely. She gave him a glance with her deep brown eyes that showed her desire to comply.

He took her hand once more as they held that gaze. After a moment, she asked slowly, "Meanwhile, I'm free to do as I please?"

"Within reason, yes. But get off-planet as quickly as possible." The pair ignored the elephant in the room; neither mentioned Miller's unexpected visit. "And," the physician continued, "stay off for a good many years. Marsco leases egress launching pads to Indie landers at both Vandenberg and the Cape. And does the same with its lunar docking ports. Look around for a legit shuttle crew that's heading for deep space. There're only two or three every month or so, but you ought to find something PDQ."

"Far fewer launches than Fleet."

"Yes, so get on the Net and see what's out there. Many free-lance ops are constantly looking for qualified, experienced pilots. Most are above boards."

"They're almost all Marsco-trained, anyway," Shanghai added with pride.

"And most have mixed crews, so you won't have to become a fuck-buddy to get along."

"I can take care of myself."

"No doubt." He reverted to an earlier point. "Indies don't ask questions; it's their hallmark."

The woman had so many questions she longed to ask, not the least of which was about Miller's offer.

He cautioned further, "And make smooth lander-to-shuttle transit; don't hang around the lunar colonies."

Shanghai understood. Marsco was really a small world. She might run into an old classmate, a former lover anywhere.

In a moment, she blurted out, "Couldn't we just kill Ch-, I mean that *other* associate? Destroy her cyber files or put in a terminal date of her life?"

"Raises too many questions. At present, Security thinks she would never go to such an extreme as *this.*" He gently held up her compliant hand. "When it finds out she's actually gone, Internal may rely on catching her once she initiates some pad with her disk, to click some blog or chatroom, anything."

"But that's totally impossible, right? You've removed that disk."

“Affirmative! So, for six months, a year (if Internal Security is indeed looking for her) let their ops think she’s somewhere near Seattle. Let it think that, for whatever reason, that other associate is electing not to initiate any e-messages or Net links—”

“They take a disk log-on.”

He nodded and resumed, “Let Internal think she’s upped with some indigenous passive Ludds in a contiguous Seattle zone. Some commune of retros up in the Cascades somewhere. Or on Vancouver Island. Let it think anything.”

“I wouldn’t be the first associate to do so, just stop out for a time or drop out altogether.”

“Exactly. Meanwhile, you’re that much farther away in deep space and have established that much more of a plausible deniability as a freelance pilot.”

“I understand.”

It was only then that Chamberlain let go of her hand.

“I’ve already given you, as Lieutenant Ling Shanghai, an honorable discharge after ten years’ service. Medical discharge. You have developed a slight heart murmur. Occurs naturally and disappears sometimes as we age. Funny, that’s what’s happened to you. You’ll pass any pre-flight physical and Neo-Con blotch test with ease.”

“But my age?”

“Chrono and physical get distorted in the shuttle service. Especially after all that hiber I gave you. Besides, you’re blessed with those changeless looks most women envy and many men desire. It’s impossible to guess your age by just looking at you. And I’m sure many people, especially men, look at you.” His comment included a long gaze into her eyes. “You’re maybe twenty-seven, maybe thirty-eight.”

Finally, Shanghai forced herself to ask, “And this Miller?”

“Bit of a crank, mostly,” Chamberlain replied. “He runs hot and cold towards Marsco. In, out, not in, not in. Tried to start up a lander corporation but it seems to have been crushed by Marsco.”

“But, he’s heading to space stat.”

"True, true. But I'm not sure exactly what he wants a flight crew for. And he's always under surveillance. Surprised he risked coming up here. It actually pissed me off, him just showing up like that. I don't need extra Security monitoring, that's for sure."

"But why did he suspect some pilot like me was here?"

"I'd heard once he was on the lookout for a flier. At first, I thought he might be able to assist you, so I did contact him once. Thought you would be able to trust him. But not now. Especially, not after his display the other day." The physician paused then added, "He seems desperate."

"Desperate people take reckless chances," the newly created sid concluded. As a viable avenue for her safety, Miller was out entirely.

Shanghai put out her hand to thank Chamberlain.

Taking it, he cautioned once more, "Remember, never, never return here." Their handshake became a cordial hug.

Instinctively, she almost recoiled violently. After Julio last enfolded her in his arms, he betrayed her. While in this unfaltering embrace, she was agitated by her contradictory feelings. She wanted his sheltering but knew she had to safeguard herself at whatever the cost. She wanted to trust; she did not trust. Not at present. Even so, she lingered in his arms. *Would there ever be another?* she wondered in a fleeting moment of hesitation. She wished she had no need to run away.

The woman also knew that as much as she projected an air of total control, she was coiled, prepared to strike to ensure self-preservation. The slightest provocation might set her off. She knew this but hid it from him.

After he moved back, Chamberlain asked with concern, "Another thing—you sure you want that jockey taking you back to sid central? Look who Miller used. I can find you another trustworthy—"

Shanghai shook her head. "No. I've already arranged for him to meet me here this afternoon. Better for *you* if he knows I'm gone," she reasoned. "I wouldn't want him to sic Security on you if he gets an idea I might be worth something—you know, a reward."

"Oh, he makes too much ferrying folks and material up here as it is. You saw how he *earned* extra from you. If he narks, my neighbors will refuse his services, as unreliable as he is. Fear of losing his borderline-sid status keeps him somewhat honest. Nonetheless, I'll give him a stern warning when he comes. That should keep him in line."

Chamberlain looked out over the forested mountain. Curls of chimney smoke rose from a distant compound, his closest neighbor, another outlander making do in this rugged remoteness. "Besides," he continued, "Marsco doesn't want to shut down my *legal* practice. I provide it with an invaluable service. As far as my side concern—since I never work on anyone truly harmful to it—I think it knows yet tolerates me."

Shanghai looked alarmed.

"I told you, I don't take chances on that, and I don't keep records."

"I hope that continues."

"It will! And anyway, I've got the goods on too many wallahs who have previously engaged my services. Disked more than one bed-down partner, for instance, so they can move in Marsco circles."

To Shanghai, Chamberlain's stories smacked of what was all too typical of Marsco. On the surface, the institution was discreet, Victorian, even puritanical. Underneath, it smoldered with the same driving energies and plaguing obsessions as other opulent empires preceding it. She had to keep reminding herself that Marsco was as human as the rest of mankind.

Once outside of the Colony, Zot checked his nav-computer. This area beyond the fences had never been a part the subsidiary proper but rather part of its adjoining unincorporated zone. Most houses were made habitable by utilizing other structures for stone, brick, wood, anything serviceable in the current harsh realities. Here and there, window frames were glass lined, but mostly canvas or plastic sheeting served to block any broken panes. Originally quite modest, these habs were a pathetic sight considering the former importance of this city.

It depressed Zot, these sites that seemed to be from times past or from other continents. Once all this happened at a great distance; at present in this locale, it was now just across a stopline.

During the entire *Gagarin* mission, the crew received reassuring bulletins describing the marvelous improvements to the subsidiaries worldwide and the great strides taken in most zones. The iceman found no evidence of any of that here. As is the case in the worst of UZs, this one had no running water or electricity. Little sanitation. Prosperous sids and the Colonists lived under the umbrella of the restored power grid. Or like Miller, they generated their own electricity from solar panels. Not so here.

Farther into the zone, Zot found crowds of idle PRIMS. Signs of malnutrition were rampant, even though the strongest residents of this UZ—men, women, and children—were frequently employed as day laborers on work gangs.

Moving along these broken streets, the rover passed scattered bundles off to the side near crumbling building foundations. Only when the cover of one blew back in the wind did Zot realize he was passing PRIMS who died in the night.

So, it's come to this! the iceman thought. *Citizens of what was once the most affluent nation ever, dying on the streets. The way of all empires!*

Chamberlain provided Shanghai with clothing appropriate for a freelance crew. It lacked an identification patch, but the style was reminiscent of the breed of self-reliant jockeys. She donned the gray turtleneck but stopped dressing to examine the navy blue V-neck top.

Shanghai was reluctant to put on the second sweater. The last time she wore one (in blue silk, not cotton) her lover had taken it off before his betrayal.

Did Julio really betray me? Yes, dammit! Yes! Why else would he disappear before my tribunal? Would Chamberlain help the likes of him? Probably not. No, definitely not! But certainly other less scrupulous implant specialists exist!

When they stood together again in the sun, the doctor kissed her hard. Then silently, he removed that blue top. Shanghai didn't resist.

Lovers, she thought, *lovers never turn against lovers.* She was prepared to do anything to remain free, even believing in what was contrary to her own experience.

Two hours later than expected, Bennie skid-bounced his HFC inside the remote compound, nearly pranging it. He had been drinking hooch all afternoon.

Several PRIMS looked up from around smoky fires as Zot slowly drove the Security rover in to their small encampment.

Not the threatening group Marsco makes them out to be. Near one of the shanties, Zot brought the rover to rest. The iceman had reached what he assumed was the absolute bottom the PRIM heap in this zone. PRIMS who had just given up totally.

"Can I leave this here?" he asked them.

"Yes, wallah." The nearest one spoke avoiding his gaze. "As y'pleeze."

The woman lived in a lean-to, a shanty made from plastic sheeting and pieces of boards. Nothing like the reasonably strong habs he had just passed north of here. She sat next to a glowing fire, her rationed potatoes buried underneath low embers. The orange light etched her face with lines.

In the fog and red glow of the fire, the woman seemed aged. *But she's probably younger than she looks,* the hiberman thought.

It's difficult to judge the age of someone in the Fleet who hibers a great deal, but try guessing her age, someone ravaged by harshness unimagined in this country just fifty years before.

A sickly young girl rested her head on the woman's knee, laying as close as she dared to the coals for warmth. She coughed that distinctive death grip of Neo-Con.

"Is she not well, mother?" he asked. "How long's she been so sick?"

"Too long, she's suff'd too long, too much."

As they spoke, the child recoiled from the associate, digging her face deeper into her mother's crocked arm.

Wouldn't laugh at a Spam-pack here, he thought.

Leaving them, Zot walked among the other shanties scattered under the trees just beyond a high-water mark of the river. Sandy clearings were dotted with fires as PRIMS made do here in the damp and clinging fog. In a flat wooded area near the remains of a levee, other lean-tos stood in an area often deluged in the spring. The PRIMS were unaware of Zot's presence or were unconcerned about him generally. A single Fleet associate in their midst hardly roused curiosity anymore. Even an armed trooper in urban gray camouflage would go unnoticed.

As he walked on, the hiberman heard several more children coughing. *Can you imagine,* he thought, *running blotch tests here? No "Marsco pink" in this group. There'll be many deaths here by spring.*

PRIMS. Zot thought of the term as he walked aimlessly. As an associate, he was conditioned to think of PRIMS collectively, if at all. As with these close at hand, they didn't seem any particular race; they were just PRIMS.

Only in that instance did the hiberman realize the first woman was probably of Med-ancestry like himself. Or SoAm like Rivers, if those distinctions made sense in this world of shifting and shifted populations. Some even seemed Asian, others African.

"But only as I think back on them," Zot confided softly under his white breath. "My first trained response is to see them only as PRIMS." He looked around the clearings as if to be sure that disks glowed as they should. "Indeed, gender or age doesn't matter with PRIMS since they're all merely PRIMS and as such worth no notice."

Since the C-Wars, most of the world's surviving population had been reduced to this single word: *PRIMS*. No other term need describe them. PRIMS did exist, it was true, from before the Wars. But they, like the ones Zot saw today, essentially, had no history. They were merely PRIMS, and PRIMS were just PRIMS. Nothing else. File empty. Dot.

Even the term's etymology, the iceman didn't know for sure. Was it shortened from *prim*itive? Or more than likely: *P*ersonnel, *R*efugee/*I*ndigenous, *M*arsco-*S*upervised. This idea stemmed from the old Marsco, the Marsco concerned with philanthropy when the midcentury was gripped by a series of pandemics and by millions of refugees, the first teeming dispossessed exiles of the Abandonment Era. Back then Marsco did what the Powers wouldn't; it was moved by pity and self-interest into to help alleviate human suffering. Thus PRIMS and Marsco were inexorably linked.

Zot shook his head. This was an unknowable history.

In any event, all the shanties around the iceman were a far cry from the restored homes and thriving gardens of the Colony. *Of course, Auxxies cooperate fully with Marsco,* he concluded cynically. Marsco is obliged to pay them off. Here, people only managed to survive. Or die. He remembered the girl beside the low fire. Born into the Marsco world but totally shut out from it, as he hadn't been, as Tessa hadn't been.

"Nasty, brutish, and short," he whispered hoarsely.

On a rutted dirt road running atop the levee, the iceman drove southward toward the Enclave, which sprung up on what had been a university campus.

Where the levee ran along the east side of the former campus, Zot left his rover. Heading into the campus proper, the iceman followed once-paved walkways that had long since become foot-beaten trails. Here, where in years past swarms of students strolled, large parts of the campus quads had been converted into vast communal gardens, dormant in the winter. During the growing season, the furrowed fields drew water from the neighboring river through a sophisticated network of pipes and ditches. Although much larger, the computer-activated irrigation system rivaled Miller's. Zot saw the granger's disks at work helping to organize these productive fields.

Unexpectedly from behind the associate, a deep voice called out, "Yur M-Co, ain't ya?" The voice seemed to materialize from the lowering fog. The speaker betrayed boiling rage rarely openly aimed at an associate.

Startled, Zot wheeled to face his hostile, his hand instinctively leveling his Enfield. A quick twitch and the laser designator put a red dot at the voice's sternum. A single-burst, even from its small caliber, would decapitate its target.

"Typical ov'ya yung wallahs," the ominous voice intensified its spleen. "Ya don't knowd a'ole alley when ya sees one." The old PRIM tried standing parade-ground straight. He had one useless eye and bore the facial scars of shrapnel wounds. He had once been dangerously close to exploding shells. Too close to remain unharmed but far enough away to survive. His face was now steeled and darkened by the elements.

As Zot stood face-to-face with the PRIM, the target unexpectedly barked out guttural sounds with no logic or pattern to them. Zot froze but kept his Enfield at the ready, its laser remaining on the PRIM's abdomen.

A small crowd gathered, twenty more specters out of the mist. "He ain't right in ta'head," a bent old PRIM explained to the associate. Turning on her cane toward the disfigured man, she laughed, "Ain't tha' righ', Ol' Joe?"

Words returned to the confused vet, "I fought fur it, I did. 'N I git this." He pointed to his craggy face. Fingers were missing from his right hand. "N'this." He pulled at his ragged sleeve to eagerly display other deep scars.

Another woman stepped forward and stopped the old PRIM with a calming touch to his arm. "There now, Joe," whispered this new PRIM, "this wallah here, he understands."

"With M-co, I wuz. Believe' it, I did. Had m'own Enfield. Th'shoulder 9 mm. Chromed-breach. Non-disk."

"Shh, there now, Joe." A comforting, calming voice. "Don't go back. You needn't go back." The soothing woman looked at the small crowd, then at the intruder over her shoulder as if to say, *For whatever reason you're here, Marsco, go away from him at least. He's suffered enough.*

Her stance between the associate and the vet placed the red targeting dot on her chest. Seeing this laser placement, Zot finally holstered his Enfield.

At that moment, the iceman recognized her as Allison, the leader of the Enclave, who often visited Miller's. For her part she didn't recognize him.

"Only taking a look around," he hastily explained. "At this old campus. Was a college once, a fine university—"

A man's voice from the back of the knot of onlookers remarked, "We know that, wallah. Some of us hold degrees from here."

"Or taught here," a woman commented firmly from the side of the PRIMS.

Not knowing what to say further, Zot said, "Well, I won't disturb you further. Sorry I upset him."

The leader of the group reassured her Ludds that this particular Marsco wasn't to be feared. Silently, she ushered Old Joe into the care of waiting hands. Moving toward the iceman, she asked, "Why are you here?"

Zot fumbled for the answers; he wasn't sure himself. "Looking around, mostly," he blurted, knowing that his explanation suggested a Security recce and not his real intention. "I know Doctor Miller—"

"Which one?"

"Well, both, actually." Zot continued. "But we've met before, too." He saw this didn't register. "At Miller's grange." He motioned over his shoulder in a vague direction.

Allison let a slight smile cross her lips. "I'm sorry, Marsco. I've met many there. And all this—" she pinched at his sleeve "—uniform, leveled Enfield. I'm sorry; you all *look* the same. *Act* the same."

The others who overheard this snippet gave a slight laugh, not belittling but amused by the sight of this armed associate, especially now that he was no longer threatening anyone.

Allison was like no one the hiberman ever knew. Her gray hair was pulled back into a knot, not stylish but practical. Her homespun the same: clean, neat, practical. Leading the Luddite Enclave left little time for anything frivolous. Her blue eyes, however gently they gazed, were intense. Her calm belied her fierceness at preserving this haven from Marsco encroachment.

Zot wasn't sure, but something distantly "Marsco" struck him about the Ludd leader, a former associate, perhaps? If he had her story correct, in the prewar era—she was in her sixties—she was known for her beauty, charisma, and sharp-witted mind. Their vestiges were still present.

As if mesmerized by Allison's penetrating eyes, Zot blurted out, "I'm thinking of joining you."

"If so, perhaps you should know us a bit better," Allison replied.

The Luddite took the associate farther into the central quad. Here, the grass hadn't been tilled but remained a greensward between many buildings.

"These dorms are again housing residents," she explained. Window panels were retrofitted with whatever the Ludds could manage to block out the elements. "These were all designed for central heat and air. We've made them serviceable even without being on the electric grid." Solar collectors lined the roof and the south face of the building, running everything at minimum in the fog.

The visitor responded, "You seem to have created a more cohesive community than is generally found among PRIMS."

Allison let the condescending remark pass.

In the middle of a second quad, scavenged from Marsco only knows where, stood a water tower. "A solar-driven system designed by Walter fills the storage tank," Allison explained proudly. "It's purified first, of course."

"Your tower doesn't also act as an OP—an observation post," he commented dryly. "It's not armed like the Colony's."

The Ludd looked at him without comment.

The two approached the library, the size and height of a Security blockhouse. Here Allison noted that it was coming back online soon. Salvaged solar panels would provide the power.

"From Miller again?"

"No, actually, we found our own and restored them." She pointed toward the roofline. "The dish link we're in the process of refurbishing. The whole system should be operational in June."

"Here?" Zot asked.

"You shouldn't seem surprised. There are many engineers among us. Walter employs several who are developing his lander fleet. We're not against *technology.*" She took Zot's right hand gently, palm up. "We're against *these.*" Zot's finger disks, blue-green under his epidermis, were covered by a glove, but he caught her meaning.

Inside the building, the associate found a bank of computers, finger mouse units waiting for an eager set of thimble commands to twitch them. "They're outmoded, to be sure, slow and kludgy, and seemingly useless relics from a bygone era," Allison admitted. "But they'll soon be integrated into a central network."

The iceman remarked, "If any roving bands of PRIM looters knew of this library, it would be vandalized. To them, computers are for gothing."

"You think like an associate, wallah," Allison admonished softly. "Some PRIMS do tear apart and destroy, but usually only that which they're unable to use or to understand. If nothing else, it's their only sign of power in their own powerless world."

"And how do you protect yourself. At the Colony—"

She waved him off. "We're on guard, always, but we're unarmed. We wish to survive, not threaten anyone."

The associate was not sure he understood her totally.

"To the casual observer," Allison explained, "the Enclave doesn't appear to be prospering, but it's thriving. Our gardens provide food. The university's once-famous arboretum: we've transformed it, restored it, so that we've much for bartering. We provide many grangers with saplings for windbreaks and grafts for their orchards. Even Marsco enviro-engineers eagerly come to us; much of Sac City's restored foliage started here."

In the distance, tucked under what had been a stadium, acetylene sparks flew and a blue light glowed then disappeared. "That's our workshop's welding torches. We're known for our adaptive equipment work."

The Enclave's engineers collected solar cells for reutilization. They cobbled together civilian rovers and hummers. Even cannibalized heavy equipment, welding two or three abandoned construction cranes into one serviceable unit, having e-scrubbed its onboard computer of any latent viruses.

"As sections of the sid reemerge from postwar decay, our work's had a hand in its re-tech development." She paused then added, "It's all *Marsco-free* development."

"And all the while, your own hands remain without finger disks?"

"Yes, we live and work outside direct Marsco supervision. We value our autonomy."

Nearby, in a three-story dorm, once a grad residence, these Ludds created an austere hospital. "Not a zone confinement area where the dying are cordoned off and left to fend for themselves," Allison explained, coming close to a bitter tone for the first time. "In other places, the sick left to die alone."

To no one in particular, Zot muttered. "Marsco philanthropy."

"Not particularly," Allison replied then added, "Although it has medicines, here we tend the dying with some final dignity."

"Even as your caregivers risk further transmission of the highly contagious disease?"

"We're as careful as any hospital. But here, mothers watch children. Children watch parents. Strangers tend orphans. Street PRIMS, with a vestige of altruism supposedly absent, watch the elderly."

"You're not as devoid of human spirit as Marsco makes you out to be," replied Zot as though making an insightful statement.

Allison's compassion kept her from a sharp, belittling reply.

At the far edge of the campus, two buildings were being taken apart at the hands of a PRIM work gang. One coming down brick by brick was the empty admin building. "Marsco wants the stadium, which you saw we're using." The woman drew a near-defeated breath. "I fear that eventually, the heart of our community will be vacated—perhaps at the barrel of an Enfield—and dismantled for its serviceable pieces."

"Seems reasonable to assume," the iceman replied sullenly, hiding what he suspected about the Colonists.

"Marsco has its ways of reducing communities such as ours, making sure they don't really flourish unless directly connected to it."

"Actually," Zot retorted, "I'm surprised you've lasted this long. When they come—"

"*When?*"

"*If* they come, gangs will dismantle more than bricks," Grizotti stated, covering over what he suspected.

"Yes," Allison added flatly, "Marsco sees us as a greater threat than any cadre of armed Ludds. Whether at the hands of Marsco or at the hands of others with its complicity, those similar to us are rarely allowed to prosper. At best, we're only delaying the inevitable. And all too often, for the younger, healthier ones, escape means joining an Auxiliary battalion and patrolling some other UZ a continent away."

"Or worse!"

"Yes, or worse."

After looking thoughtfully into the hazy indistinguishable horizon, the iceman finally pleaded, “Is it possible for me to join you?”

“Anyone may join us,” Allison candidly answered, “on three strict conditions that you fail to meet: no uniform, no finger disks, no Enfield.”

TWENTY-SEVEN

DEAD RECKONING

(Sac City, 2097)

"These PRIMS live close to us because we help them," Allison stated in a matter-of-fact voice while she and Grizotti proceeded along a levee near the Enclave.

"So unlike Marsco," the associate noted, "who feels they belonged at arm's length or expects something in return."

"You know it well, wallah."

"Well, the one I want you to see, this girl, is dying."

"We'll do what we can."

As the late afternoon closed in on them, Zot found himself in a dark wood, guided by Allison. Had the iceman been alone, he might have staggered in the dense tangle of wild undergrowth, but the Luddite leader knew the labrynth of trails well.

They walked hurriedly atop the levee, stopping only once at the eastern edge of the former campus. Here years ago, a footbridge spanned the river; only two pilings near each bank remained. Orange fires glowed on both sides of the slow water and stretched around a bend ahead of them. The smoldering embers beside the shanties scarcely cut the dense shroud of rising mist.

As the pair approached Zot's parked Security rover, Allison asked flatly, "Where did you get this?"

"It's a Marsco world," Zot smirked, fully aware that he and Tessa, and even her father in some convoluted way, benefited tremendously from that world, a world that the iceman was on the verge of rejecting forever. "The girl's only a few minutes down the levee."

Bennie held the joystick lazily, blowing off all safety protocols.

Shanghai wasn't impressed with his bravado. *Typical arrogant pilot. I've seen such antics before.* Finally, she demanded, "Is your nav-computer functioning?"

He shrugged but didn't answer. For the third time, he pulled the craft above the layer of thickset fog to get his visual bearings, then sank back down toward the floor of the blanketed valley.

"Some obstructions are only apparent when you're nearly on top of them," she barked with an officer's edge.

Bennie didn't reply but kept on with his dead reckoning.

He isn't as stupid or inept as he looks or pretends to be, Shanghai thought, knowing he was calculating every move in advance. She saw his keen, dangerous edge and smelled his hooch.

In the old city center many unmarked hazards lurked. Bennie was no longer on a skim over the countryside looking for points of recognition in the distance. He had taken them amid the skeletal high rises of the downtown, each relic capable of crippling the HFC. This wasn't a prewar metropolis ablaze with its affluence and completely covered with an integrated, fully functional Herriff-Grid. Below—and sometimes surrounding the HFC—was an ominous, post-apocalyptic wasteland.

To the north a glow illuminated the horizon where a stopline wound. The better sid areas displayed their recent reconnection to the power network. Shanghai saw sporadic HFC traffic above that distant glow. Not enough to merit a grid but enough to show signs of economic recovery. Here, on Bennie's side of that stopline, nothing.

They continued aimlessly another twenty minutes through the early evening darkness. When their HFC passed over a well-lit checkpoint along an internal stopline, Shanghai realized they were heading north once more. She grew tense. They were re-crossing the city center; they had been here earlier heading west.

"We're flying in circles!"

"Ye-ah?"

"Why've you doubled back on yourself?" Shanghai thundered. "We've made this loop already!" Her voice was insistent, not panicked.

"Ye-ah? Well, I like to caddiwonk m'way around," Bennie replied slowly, without giving her eye contact. "Keeps anyone from followin' t'cloze, if y'catch."

"You've plenty of instruments to do that," she barked, "like your CAR: *C*ollision *A*voidance *R*adar. Use *that* to check your six." Clearly she was in danger but held herself firm. "Get me as close to the light rail station as possible," she ordered as though still in control.

He guided the HFC without any adherence to her instructions.

"Ye-ah," he responded eventually. "Gots t'git y'back to m'friend's place," he hissed with a sideways leer.

A chill ran through Shanghai; she sat up ridge. "You know how Chamberlain warned you!" She repeated his remarks verbatim, "'If anything happens to Shanghai, you'll never work up here again. Dot.'"

"Ye-ah, oh, I ain't worried' 'bout things happenin' to 'Shanghai,'" he replied with a threatening glance. His carbuncles appeared greasy in the instrument glow of the flight deck. His eyes took on a terrifying look. "No, it ain't Shanghai's gots to worry; it'z some puss named 'Chen.'"

"You have to trust me," Zot whispered to the terrified child. Although his uniform struck fear into the PRIMS, Allison's presence helped. "We've a better place for your daughter," the iceman explained softly.

With the Ludd's assistance, Zot shepherded the sick child and her mother out of their lean-to.

"Our hospital will provide some comfort for your little one," Allison reassured the terrified woman as they headed back to the Enclave. "Warmth, a decent meal, a bed."

If she's to die, Zot knew, *it'd be better amid those surroundings than out here alone.*

As Allison moved the mother along, Zot carried the child. It wasn't far, less than two clicks, nothing once in his rover. The girl was easy for the associate to handle. She caused no trouble, and in the end, was compliant to his wishes. She held him tightly around the neck with her thin arms.

As Zot settled the child and her mother into the rover, the Ludd leader repeated several times, "All will be well, all will be well, you'll see."

The near-PRIM sid and Indie pilot rode above Sac City and the surrounding zones for another hour in tense silence. Until he set the craft down, there wasn't much she could do but wait. Threatening him (an Enfield blast would take them both in such close quarters) or grabbing the controls was out of the question at this altitude. The craft zigzagged the whole time. Clearly, this caddiwonking was intended to confuse her, disrupt her bearings, put her at his mercy, break down her resistance.

Bennie's maneuvers actually had the opposite effect. Shanghai filled with resolve for her safety, for her eventual escape. Relying on her flight training, she had her bearings well enough to know roughly where they were.

Reaching under her jacket, she felt the grip of her clone. The right moment would come.

Zot waited an hour for news. A nurse informed him that the child was resting comfortably with her mother at her side. “Time will tell; she’s quite sick.”

The hiberman found himself with nothing else to do but return to the cantonment. As he walked through the night back toward his parked rover, an extraordinary thought, one quite unforeseen, crossed his mind. *Had our love held us together, this child might have been ours, Tessa’s and mine.*

For several paces he wondered, *Where’s that world? Where had it gone? Our world where I carry our child to her safe, warm room? What happened that made such an ordinary act all but impossible? Why was that world never born to us?*

What should have taken thirty minutes, forty tops, took nearly two hours. By the time the HFC lowered its skids, late-afternoon gloom had given way to blackest night.

Below Bennie’s hovering runabout, five orange panels appeared on top of a run-down building. The two-meter-long chemical strips, glowing amid the grayness of the sid, sent a clear signal. The building, once a bustling hotel, was almost entirely black from lack of power. Next to the run-down high-rise, three green strips illuminated a set-down spot at street level.

“Someone knows we’re coming,” whispered Shanghai, not frightened nor shocked, just aware. As the craft went from flight to glide to hover, the former associate saw that only the first five stories of the adjacent building was dimly lit.

With an unexpected fearful shudder, she realized they were back at the cages where she spent her one solitary night in the Sac City Sid.

"I'm not going in there," Shanghai declared adamantly.

She relented only when Bennie countered, "Ye-ah. *You* won't, but *Chen* will."

The escaping pilot felt she had no choice. She didn't know what kind of trouble Bennie would make or had made. *Has he contracted Security? Are troopers already inside?* She had to find out then make a clean break.

Reluctantly entering the darkened lobby, Shanghai heard an obnoxious voice calling to her. "G'evenin', missy wallah. Back s'soon, yes? Back t'see me." The voice spoke from behind its protective cage where nothing had changed in the past several days, not even the digital porn.

The brown eyes of the two met and glared. As they stared, Bennie sidled his way around behind her, ready to stop her if she bolted.

"I've only one thing to say, missy. '*Chen.*' Mean anythin'?"

"Roger that," Shanghai retorted, "where can we talk?" She wanted this discussion to be absolutely private and over quickly.

"We talk here, missy Chen."

"Stop calling me that."

"Okay, better 'missy M-co'?"

"I'm *not* Marsco, either! I'm part of a crew from an Independent shuttle." She pulled at her sweater, which came close to being a uniform, as if it were evidence.

The cage man's grinning ceased as he snapped, "Then name it, missy! Can you? Can you, say, name y'comman'er?"

Bennie eased further around behind.

"How much do you want?"

"How much y'got?" The cage man's grin reappeared as she grew more reasonable. Considering the volatile situation, he was suddenly all smiles and agreeableness.

A gruff voice behind her hissed, "She's gots lots. I seen her pay plenty already fur nothin', and not missin' nothin' neither. Ain't that right, hon?"

"Of course, my debit cards. You rat bastard! You got more than just those extra units." He smirked in self-satisfaction. "You're a brighter moke than you look, an easy task, considering."

It all made sense what each man wanted. The one, her *units.* The other, *her.*

As she felt danger approaching from behind, the former associate instinctively bolted a few meters into the atrium, away from both Bennie and the exit. As trained, she backed herself against a wall to keep the pair of hostiles in full view.

"Ye-ah. Y'understand uz," Bennie glowered. He moved slightly toward her.

"Don't think I don't catch, didn't figure you out."

"Let's uz be friendly like," Bennie declared, trying to edge toward her a little at a time. He wasn't a large or powerful man, but he was scrappy. Physically, he felt sure he could take her as brutally as he wanted.

"No here for'at," the cage man snapped harshly at Bennie. His appeasing grin then reappeared. "When I'm done, negotiatin', take her—" The cage manager stopped speaking abruptly and turned ashen. His eyes froze.

For a moment, Bennie had turned away from Shanghai to look at the manager. When he turned back toward her, he was facing the business end of her hissing 9 mm.

"Let's just call it a day, shall we, gentleman," Shanghai remarked in a stage whisper, drawing a bead on Bennie's head. The red laser designator glowed squarely on his carbuncled forehead. "At this range, a few meters, I can't miss. You'll be bloody meat and pus in an instant." His hand moved slowly. "Touch your weapon and you're a dead piece of shit."

She lowered the laser dot to his crotch. "You think you're such a big man," she smirked. The dot moved left to right between his pants and holster. "Drop that weapon slowly with your left hand."

After complying, Bennie stepped away from his gun belt on the floor. Initially terrified, he then feigned exaggerated laughter. He turned to his partner and caricatured fear, motioning over his shoulder as though the armed associate was the funniest woman in the world.

The whole time, Shanghai kept designating his head and temple with the red dot. Turning around and shouldering up so he became an even clearer target, he growled, "Bitch, I knowed that ain't loaded." His laughter ceased. Hate burned in his eyes illuminated by the laser's red glow.

He eased himself closer to the cage in his sideways walk, one small sliding step at a time. He was so positioned that he was able to slip toward Shanghai as he moved closer to the cage. "Bitches never load them things!" he declared.

"Keep back! Keep your hands where I can see them!" Shanghai glided sideways toward the exit, keeping herself pressed to the wall of the dimly lit lobby in case of an unseen third confederate. The designator never left Bennie's forehead. "One squeeze and you're trash, pus-face." A few more meters across the cluttered lobby and both men would be on the same side of the trapped woman, on her right.

To her left, the door and escape.

She motioned him toward the cage, and for his part, he obeyed. But he kept coming toward her incrementally, inching closer to her as they passed: he in the middle of the lobby; she along its wall. He moved slowly toward the cage; she away from it, toward her freedom. Each move by him slid him away from the weapon on the floor, but he knew he could take her down and then take her without *that* weapon. He had weapons enough for that.

As the escaping woman moved, so Bennie moved. He was actually getting closer to her, facing her full front, and glaring at her. His blustering gave her an even better target. But as she went in one direction along the wall, and he in the other toward the counter, he continued closing the gap between them.

He slowly gained on her in their opposite movements. He was now less than three meters away and edging nearer while appearing to be moving closer toward the reception desk. The cage man was stationary, fixed in one spot, with only his torso visible above the counter.

"I'm goin' to love takin' us upstairs, ain't I," Bennie glowered, his eyes burning with power.

"Shut up, dammit!" Shanghai shouted. She was too well trained to become flustered, but he was getting to her. The tribunal, her derailed Marsco career, all her betrayals by love. They all forced themselves up into her consciousness where she had buried all the boiling rage of rejection and disappointment.

Contradictory thoughts flooded in so abruptly that she nearly lost concentration. On the *Piazzi* Fuentes and her shadow lover, Maissey: one gone, one dead. Wilkes. Bryce and the tribunal. Making love that very afternoon to ensure silence. Bennie's HFC, his smelly hooch, his leering glare.

Her mind snapped back to the threatening moment. Her hand tightened around the clone. No one was going to force her to do anything again. Bennie and his comrade were tops on her list of catching the first dramatic statement of her new course in life. She was letting no one ever stand in her way.

"Do as s'she s'says," the cage man urged in a loud whisper, as if Shanghai wouldn't hear. His game was up. He was willing to let the armed woman escape. His life for her departure, a fair exchange.

Although moving toward the cage, Bennie was getting noticeably closer to the woman.

"Bitch ain't loaded that thing! I knowed it," he insisted, creeping along. His position relative to the associate almost hid the cage man in the shadowy end of the deserted lobby.

The would-be attacker kept his arms extended to grab her when he lunged. With his red and swollen face, with his dirty outstretched hands, he looked a caricature of a villainous monster from one of last century's horror films. Only, he was truly threatening, breathing heavily with contempt and wrath.

As Shanghai and Bennie both moved, he was gaining on her, a dozen centimeters at a time. His voice and menacing movements began to unhinge her intense fearlessness.

Shanghai knew if he came much closer, the clone's shells might wound her when they exploded. But at least at this range, one shot would stop him cold.

The armed woman reached a break in the wall. By now Bennie was out of her way. Behind her waited the empty hallway leading to the street. Stepping tentatively backward, she stumbled over something. Not a good plan of action; she was trained to know her escape options clearly.

As she stumbled, Bennie took a sudden step toward her. "Come on, bitch, gimme that thing!" He jumped but she avoided him, agilely rolling and tumbling away from his heavy thud. She put another two meters between herself and her attacker.

"Move back toward the cage! Get back! Don't follow!" she commanded. With the two men out of her way, she was only a dozen meters from safety

Bennie, in a ball on the floor, remained still. "You ain't leavin'!" he barked. "I'm takin' you down! You'll love it!"

In the dark, Shanghai didn't noticed Bennie setting his legs for another spring. This time, his lunge came closer.

Swinging downward with her weapon, she gashed his temple with its hardened plastic grip. His head smarted from instant pain, infuriating him all the more. She was stronger and more nimble than he'd imagined. So much the better when he had her; she was lively, and he wanted to crush that liveliness.

When he rose, gaze fixed on her, blood ran down his left cheek from the slash beside his eye. Her blow cut open a swollen carbuncle, but she hoped he got the message and would finally stand back.

"I don't want to last-resort you, but I will if you come at me again. *There'll be no warning shot!*" Shanghai declared.

As he stood up, his hand bloody from feeling his wound, he seemed to come apart with fury. "See, bitch ain't loaded it!" He yelled to his caged confederate, trying to convince himself. "She's not shootin' it!"

Bennie wanted her and then wanted her dead. Shanghai saw the loathing in his enflamed eyes. "I'm goin' to have you, bitch," he humped to demonstrate what he meant, "you fuckin' bitch."

Shanghai made another movement backward but tripped over the three steps that went up from the lobby into a long hallway leading to the street exit itself.

As the woman sprawled with her legs open, Bennie advanced.

Trying to act vicious, the would-be attacker attempted to yell, "Bitch, I knowed it ain't loaded!" but an exploding shell hit his sternum first. The detonation inside his torso blasted his pulpy heart and lungs out of his erupting back and through the wire cage. Splattered by Bennie's internal organs, the cage man hit the floor.

Flung awkwardly over some broken furniture, the lifeless body had been an easy target. Shanghai fired a second time. That shell exploded inside his left shoulder, blowing off his arm.

Strewn with Bennie's entrails but unharmed, the cage man cringed behind a solid reception counter, unlikely to rise up and shout demands. Her escape route was wide open.

Shanghai had little time to think. With a quick flip, she set the fire rate from single shot to three-burst. The weapon fired without the slightest recoil to misalign its aim. The noise of discharge and explosion blocked its hissing recharge. One after another, exploding shell after exploding shell tore into the caged reception desk before erupting. She blasted away three shells at a time although her training would have had her first assess the danger level of the situation.

The room filled with the pungent odor of the discharge propellant and the detonating rounds. Flames burst out on both sides of the counter: dry wood, igniting shells, Marsco efficiency.

Without visual of her second target, she was sure he was sprawled dead, probably in pieces like Bennie. No one survived the carnage of fifteen explosions pumped rapidly into so confined and unprotected space.

Shanghai knew her twenty-bullet clip was almost depleted. It surprised her how quickly she expended seventeen shots, certainly in less than eight seconds. Standing exhilarated in the smoke, she straddled Bennie's body. Even at the risk of collaterally blasting her own feet, she prepared to squeeze her final shot into the lifeless head with its acne-swollen face. His body was as threatening as a PRIM crushed by a Security Brad.

You make such a fucking good primary target, she mused, savoring her victory. It came to her in a rush. *Damn them all! Damn you, Bennie, and damn that grinning trash behind the desk, and damn Wilkes and damn Bryce. I'd off those bastards, if they were here.*

It surprised Shanghai that she didn't cry. Chen might have, but Chen was now dead.

She gripped the clone in both hands, pointing its barrel downward, dangerously close to the once-menacing skull of her slaughtered attacker.

"What's going on?" a man shouted from behind her.

She whirled around and would have fired except he was obviously Marsco; from the looks of his uniform, a MAS hiberman.

In the deserted lobby lit by crackling fire at one end, the pair of MAS associates stared at each other. Although his Enfield was drawn, the iceman facing her wouldn't have fired. Shanghai was convinced of that—even in the fleeting glance she got of his face and eyes in the flickering light, she was convinced he wouldn't harm her.

"There's been some sort of shooting," she reported in a direct, detached tone, holstering her weapon and stepping over the bloody corpse at her feet as though the offal wasn't there.

"What are you doing? I think you should stay," the iceman semi-ordered, although without any real threat. Only then did he finally holster his Enfield.

As soon as her hand was free of her weapon, she held up her gloved right palm to imply she was disked. Her left hand was still covered, but she let it suggest another array.

For that single instance, the iceman saw the woman full-face. Those alert eyes, abruptly purged of anger and resolve, mesmerized him momentarily. It made no sense. Although he hadn't actually seen her firing, at the very least, she was standing all alone in the incendiary smoke and was threatening to blow apart the skull of what must have once been a PRIM.

"I'll get Security," she declared with an assured Marsco tone of authority.

"Where you going?" The iceman shouted to the retreating back of the fleeing associate. "Aren't you Marsco?" She was gone. "Of course she is! Idiot!" he shouted at himself as she disappeared.

Shanghai lifted the HFC off the ground before the dazed hiberman attempted to stop her. In hover-mode at 400 meters, she reclipped her sidearm, which for a clone, had performed flawlessly. She sensed she might need it again before the night was out.

The obsolete nav-computer had never been retro-functionalized, she realized. Before her, the flight console's GPS reader was not serviceable. CAR was not operational, nor was the radar detection scanner.

She climbed into the clear night above the layer of fog, circling the run-down subsidiary without direction. A partial Marsco moon had risen, illuminating the top of the mist but making visual recognition through the ground-clinging cover even more difficult. With no working nav-equipment, she skimmed aimlessly for fifteen minutes. She slowly moved above the fog bank debating if she should set a course for Chamberlain. But how?

As she made up her mind, time passed. She paid attention to nothing. She knew she must not return to the mountain compound; her actions might bring the S & H. But she didn't know where else to turn.

Finally, with resolve, she yawed to starboard then set a heading for what she hoped was a receptive man. She was going back up those hills in the misty distance.

Three bright flares shot out in front of Shanghai. Shots across the bow, the green streaks sliced through the night gloom. The associate was being rather insistently hailed by Security: land or be fired at with 25-mm exploding shells.

After what she had just witnessed (she didn't allow herself to think, *After the havoc I've just wrought*), she wanted no part of the business end of any shell, especially one of a higher caliber than her own 9 mm. Twin 25 mm would cut through her hovercraft and flesh with keen, merciless Marsco efficiency.

The fleeing woman lowered her skids and twitched her landing lights to full, both actions signs of compliance. She throttled back and brought the craft into a landing glide and then to a hover. Easing her craft through the darkness beneath her—her craft lacked proper controls for such a safe nighttime set-down—she hoped she had ample clearance for her blind landing.

The Security HFC blazed the area below with spotlights so that both craft landed side by side in a field of what had once been a municipal park. A dozen fires glowed under the still-standing trees that lined the long, narrow, empty spaces. One of Shanghai's skids landed in a soft, grassless spot, a kidney-shape of sand she hadn't expected to find in the tree-surrounded lane.

Taking a deep breath, she opened the gull-wing hatch to watch the pair of S & H personnel, an officer approaching her and a trooper armed with a shoulder-fired weapon remaining next to the Security HFC.

"Good evening," the officer stated politely.

Shanghai was at first taken aback by his polished manners. He had Latin features similar to Fuentes, about the same build but without a MAS badge of rank because he wore urban gray camouflage fatigues. He was probably a dozen years younger than Julio but physically worn from his S & H life. Like Fuentes, he had no PRIM-disk scar, his left hand clearly visible in the moonlight.

"May I ask your destination?" the officer asked, his armed trooper standing twenty paces off.

Shanghai's eyes fell on the SCAA lettering on the runabout's fuselage. "Back to home base," she answered vaguely but confidently. She pointed at the logo.

"Oh, Miller's Center," the young officer commented, then realized he should be more circumspect.

The thought crossed her mind, *If I come out blazing, I can cut both of them down!* But lying her way out might prove a better way. "Yes, Miller." She knew roughly that his grange was somewhere in the opposite direction she'd been heading. It was worth a bluff. "Just ran him home to his grange." (*Are we talking of the same Miller?*)

To the officer, the craft's orientation was enough to support her story. Yet, before he could dig deeper into her explanation, the second trooper, who had remained with the Security HFC, approached. "Command call coming in for you, sir."

The stoic trooper now stood next to the woman while the officer while went back to his HFC. The legionnaire soon sniffed the air. After a third good whiff, he left her to talk with his commander.

When the pair returned, the officer asked if she was armed. "I'm a retired MAS associate, a pilot, now a sid in good standing. I ought to have a right to a weapon."

The officer held out his hand, and she surrendered up her clone. He held what looked like a service weapon to his nose. "You ought to keep better care of your weapon; it might save your life."

She replied solidly Marsco, "Yes, sir, I had intended to."

"Intentions are not enough! Smells like it's two, three days old." The officer didn't bother to use a forensic computer to analyze the weapon's firing history.

"Yes, sir." Shanghai was now without a weapon. More lying was her only course. "Target practice and busy schedule. No time to clean up properly."

"That's not the way things are done in Marsco! Isn't that right, Lieutenant?"

"*Former* officer. But quite right, a gunny would rip me a new one for this."

Confident of Marsco camaraderie, he handed back the weapon.

She slipped her clone into its concealed holster.

"This HFC's no longer equipped for night utilization or navigation, tech-functionality-wise," the officer stated with concern.

"Dr. Miller's aware of that. We take the risk," Shanghai spoke with Marsco poise.

"Look, there's been some sort of trouble, serious touble in Sac City, the downtown. Hazy what it is." Marsco collegiality dies hard. The callow officer was trained to scrutinize PRIMS and low-life sids, not Marsco-trained pilots with plausible cover stories. "Get somewhere PDQ because you'll be stopped again if you skim this piece of crap."

The Security HFC lifted off leaving Shanghai shaken. The interlude was more stressful than having to defend herself from Bennie who was such a clear threat. In that situation, she had control; not so this one. This time she had to be more guarded yet cagey. Almost cloak and dagger.

She pulled out her clone. She either had to keep blasting, keep lying, or hunker down in this locale and live under the cloud of a constant threat of discovery.

"No," she whispered. "Chamberlain's right." Getting off planet ASAP was her best course.

Only hours before, she had sealed what she hoped was the physician's absolute silence. Returning to him now, after he said never to do so, was complicated, too risky. His reaction to her an unknown. And with Security on high alert because of her own actions, getting up to his lodge had become even more dangerous, if not totally impossible.

Here? Stay here somewhere? she pondered.

"Out of the question," the fleeing pilot grumbled.

Counting and discarding these dead-end choices left her with only two: skimming in any direction in this battered, broken-down HFC until she or it could go no further (hardly a choice, since it only delayed making a real decision) or chancing it with Miller.

Before she had time to counter-argue, she found the granger's memory stick and inserted it into her reader. He was less than five minutes of low-altitude skimming away.

Io and Deimos barked wildly before Walter Miller was aware that an HFC was gliding down toward his grange.

Standing at his gate, the granger was surprised to see his stolen hovercraft, which he hadn't seen in months, with a woman at the controls. As she walked into his grange, he noticed she was about his daughter's age and carried herself with that marked Marsco mien Tessa often displayed.

The vistor was all business as she stepped toward the puzzled granger.

"I haven't time for a lengthy explanation," Shanghai stated emphatically. "And I don't think I *can* explain my reasons thoroughly." Her voice implied, *Don't argue with me; we can sort this out later.*

"I'm afraid I don't fully understand," the granger protested.

Shanghai cut him off. "If you're looking for a pilot, a shuttle pilot, you found her. We must leave here tonight!"

TWENTY-EIGHT

THE DESERTED GRANGE

(Sac City, 2097)

"Readout confirms the iceman's after-action report," the red-haired warrant officer declared to his superiors. Zot didn't fire his Enfield last night; the weapon hadn't been discharged in six weeks and never by him.

Rivers's nose had told him so, and now the forensic history from an embedded chip in the grip confirmed this.

The Security lieutenant, the iceman, and a third officer, a high wallah from Internal, met in the conference room. The local centurion was convinced that Zot had nothing to do with last night's shooting. And because the iceman wasn't hiding anything, Rivers arranged for this morning's obligatory interrogation to take place in the comfortable room adjacent to the officers' mess.

A decorative wall heater resembling an old-fashioned fireplace radiated ample warmth through artfully contrived logs and tasteful scarlet embers. It gave the room a homey feel, although on the wall hung three foreboding maps of the subsidiary and the newly designated zones outlined in red. Miller's grange was also circled, the only Indie grange so noted. In the redrawn subsidiary and contiguous unincorporated zones, Miller's grange stood well beyond any stopline. It sat in what was quickly becoming a new wasteland created in a few twitches by Marsco.

The wallah slipped a mouse thimble over his right index finger, covering a red disk, and then input the weapon's firing history info into a confidential notebook.

He's keeping awfully private records, realized Zot. *Time to play Marsco to the hilt.* "Excuse me," he said politely, with a tone in his voice that conveyed the impression, *I know there's a mistake here on your part, but I'm not going to make any trouble about it.* "Might I have your name?"

"Certainly, I'm Giannini."

"Hey, *pisano*—" Zot's Med eyes met the brown eyes of mysterious official whose aura of inscrutability was enhanced by his lack of uniform. He wore an out-of-style blue blazer over an old-fashioned button-down collar and woven tie, knotted tightly.

"*Pisan?* Yes, something like that," the IS wallah responded dryly. With a swift return to Marsco formality, he explained, "I happened to be in this area. I'm supervising safety protocols of sid subcontractor plants."

Zot feigned amazement.

The visiting officer continued, "Those industries with high security clearance."

"Yes," replied the iceman with a boyish grin, "that explains the situation quite satisfactorily."

"Since I was in the vicinity, Lieutenant Rivers asked me to oversee this investigation." He got down to business. "Now, we know definitely it wasn't your sidearm that was fired. Couldn't have been you last night at all, unless you have hidden a different weapon."

Zot shook his head *no* to Giannini and shrugged a *What's up?* to Rivers.

"We suspect the 9 mm weapon was an S & H Enfield," the local Security officer added, "or a close cousin."

"Mine was issued to me when I came to Earth, not by Security. Technically, I guess really it's a MAS issue."

"No," Giannini corrected, "it's Security issue. They all are. Always. But yours is a smaller caliber than the one was fired last night. That mother was humongous. Not to mention, fired ostensibly by an associate." The iceman sensed the seriousness lay in the fact that the shooter might've been an associate, not that two near-PRIM sids were offed. "You saw her disks?"

"Yes!" The iceman thought a moment. "Well, no, not actually."

"Well, which is it? *Yes* or *no?*"

"She had on protective gloves, but clearly she was the one firing away. When I entered, she shoved her gloves in my face to imply she *was* disked."

"That's a common enough dodge," Rivers commented.

"A lefter?" asked Giannini.

"Wasn't able to ascertain that for sure. I suspected she was, but now that I think about it, she probably had a complete set, or nearly so, on the right. Not so fancy as your array, but a handful to be sure."

"But you're guessing, right? You really saw no disks."

"*Conjecturing*, more than *guessing*, but affirmative, I didn't see any disks, only gloves."

"And this woman—she was clearly a woman, right?"

"Right on that! No doubt!"

"Asian, you say, or perhaps Euro-Asian?"

The hiberman shook his head. "Indistinguishable features, really," he remarked dully. "She might have been Med. You know, like us, Tuscan or Iberian." He had her faced completely fixed in his mind but tried to disclose as little about her as possible. He didn't know why.

Zot repeated almost verbatim what he had previously stated for his report. He was driving through the old city center, stopped the rover to walk around. He saw the HFC in a hover glide and recognized its SCAA emblem.

Ten, fifteen minutes later when he drove up to the landed runabout, heard Enfield shots, two singly at first, then a rapid succession of three bursts. "I couldn't tell you how many, they came so quickly together." Rushing into the atrium, he shouted his presence, not thinking he might become the next target.

In the lobby, a woman, possibly—*probably*—an associate, looked as if she was about to blow away a corpse she was straddling. "That's what struck me the most," the hiberman stated. "Those exploding shells might have, *would have,* taken her own legs off below the knees. She seemed that intent on further mutilating the corpse."

"He was dead already, you're certain?"

"Yes, without one arm, his left I think, his chest a bloody shambles." Zot was still shocked by the sight; the whole scene was difficult to comprehend and more difficult to explain.

"Look, I'm an iceman, after all," he went on, "not a trooper. Never had that pleasure. I've never seen anything like that room before—ever. And I'm old enough to vividly remember the C-Wars and the Troubles." He added, parenthetically thinking of the mysterious wallah's red C & C disk, "Must have been a common sight for those who were actually there. Fully functional, I mean, and fully adult."

He returned to his action summary, "As I came to a stop near her, her right hand disks are in my face as a sign of full authorization. She then cuts past me and scoots out the door. The next second, before I can react—that room! It brought me up short. Fire at one end, a dead, bloody carcass, the smell of burning flesh. Well, then in a nano, I hear acceleration lift from that same HFC I had just seen. She's gone before I had time to react."

"When you say, 'right-hand *disks,*' we've established you mean her right-hand *glove,* right?" The high wallah put forward the questions; Rivers only listened.

"Affirmative, but dammit, it was dark; I was spooked! I thought, then and now, that her glove *had* to be covering plenty of disks."

"But you got a good look at her?" Giannini asked.

"No—yes—I guess I did."

"But you're sure she had enough disks to be an associate?"

"I'm guessing yes, but not an array like yours, as I explained once already."

"For a while, it was *conjecturing*. Now it's *guessing*." The SI officer grilled the hiberman.

"Look, I wasn't able to tell whether she was a lefter, like you. But she *was* right-loaded—I feel I'm right to assume that. Rank of captain, I'd say. Certainly a lieutenant nearing promotion, but I can't be sure. But look, it was threatening in that lobby, chaotic, smoky, and—frankly—I was scared! If someone else in there was ready to squeeze off a few rounds at anybody Marsco, we made two excellent targets. I didn't fully comprehend what was happening until she was gone. It all happened that nano fast."

"And why were you there?"

"I told you. Lieutenant Rivers has been allowing me use of a rover. I was on sort of 'a personal recce.'"

"That's right," confirmed the cantonment officer, "full use of our vehicles."

"And full run of the district?" Giannini shot a questioning look at Rivers but added nothing more.

"I'd driven throughout the UZ yesterday—"

"—that's pretty far to drive—"

"Well, the parts being PRIM-to from the sid—"

"Rather odd for an iceman to be poking around the retrenching pieces of a far-flung zone, isn't it?" The question was addressed to both officers.

Is another branch of Internal doing a separate investigation of this locale? wondered Giannini. *"Iceman" may be his cover. Wouldn't surprised me if it were—that stopped-out associate Miller's worth that much scrutiny.*

Grizotti had Rivers's back. "It certainly wasn't the lieutenant's fault if I overstepped my bounds. He said I should stay close to the cantonment but never stated it directly." He gave a look to the Security officer to ask, "Was I under direct orders to stay close?" Receiving no answer, he continued, "I'd been invited by Xiao to the Colony. Well, one thing led to another. He—Lieutenant Rivers—did say to carry my Enfield, which I did, as you know. So, nothing I did should reflect badly on him."

Both of the listening officers were satisfied with the iceman's explanation for different reasons.

"Later that afternoon, you drove to the old university." The wallah didn't call it "the pacifist Luddite Enclave." He was quick to note, "Singularly an odd place to visit, isn't it?"

"It wasn't off limits."

"The nav-logs confirm his destination, sir," Rivers added. He summarized the record. "Next, the lieutenant made his way to the city center. Stopped for thirty-five minutes near the old C-Powers capitol. It's quite near the locale of the blasting when—"

"You stopped there? Why?"

"Most famous victory accord *ever* was signed right there under that rotunda," replied Zot with a chest bursting with fulsome Marsco pride, the most pseudo-enthusiastic remark he ever mustered. "Marsco ought to build a memorial there. A commemorative plaque of some kind. A distinctive cenotaph with an inscription for those who paid the ultimate price. History was made there, although there's a stench of death about the place."

"You went inside?"

Before the iceman got too deep, Rivers interjected, "He was preparing to make his way back to HQ when—"

"Yes, Lieutenant Grizotti, please, if you will, explain that part again."

"I first saw an HFC coming in for hover," Zot began, hiding his exasperation at this whole repetitive ordeal. "Well, heard more than saw—dark and foggy night. But a few minutes later, I saw it resting on its skids. An obsolete model."

This time Zot didn't explain that he recognized the insignia from Miller's research center on the runabout. *Too late to leave that part out,* he concluded, *but I don't need to dwell on it.* "Engine heat was still rising from its nacelles. I thought, 'I'm in an S & H rover. Here's an HFC that clearly doesn't belong in a zone or a sid or wherever I was exactly stopline designation-wise.' I thought I ought to at least take a look. When I stopped the rover, the street was quiet. Past curfew, about 2015 hours."

"Nav-log records confirm all this, as well. It was 2017," Rivers added.

"That's why," the iceman went on, "when all hell broke loose *inside,* I was able to hear the explosions from *outside.* An Enfield's uniquely distinctive! I drew my weapon for self-defense and entered. You know the rest," he concluded.

To break the silence that followed, the iceman emphasized, "I'm sure she was Marsco, which's why I didn't shoot her myself. I saw there already was enough bloodshed—well, *blood splatter,* it was a shambles in there—without adding her blood to the carnage."

The wallah seemed satisfied with the consistency in the retelling of the chain of events. He dismissed the hiberman.

"Any reports of a missing HFC?" he asked Rivers.

"Nothing official."

"Unofficial?"

"The old experimental propulsion and production center—"

"—that's Miller place. With that pompous name, 'Sac City Aerospace Associates.' How rank. They will no more get into space on their redesigned sublunar orbiter than I would by farting."

"Yes, sir, something like that. Odd that there was theft from this assembly plant. It will become part of the protected restructured area of the redrawn sid. Marsco likes its testbed foundations."

"So, looting?"

"More of an inside job." Rivers wasn't prepared to disclose how he knew, disclose his former friendship with the granger. "But no official report of any theft. That's what makes it hard to trace; we have no record of it in our system."

"Very well," Giannini said. He bent over the radiating heat from the ersatz fire to warm his hands. He then added tangentially, "Worse than the HFC business is the unauthorized use of an issued Enfield."

"Or an unlicensed clone."

"Yes, that's another possibility. Equally as troubling."

"More so from my local point of view," Rivers noted. "Do you think some of the Ludds are now armed?"

"Not with Enfields. They eschew even finger disks. No, most Ludds are out of the question. Besides, why would a Ludd from around here kill a pair of low-end sids?"

"Then who?"

Giannini shrugged an answer. He simply didn't know and didn't want to speculate. "Any reports of weapons loss?"

"None." Rivers's tone was unmistakably defensive. *I run a tight Security unit,* it said, *by the book.* Even the rogue iceman was technically well within the district Security officer's purview and auspices.

"Anything suspicious down below the old stopline?"

"Beyond isolated, and expected, trouble with the locals, nothing. A shakedown roadblock here and there, nothing we didn't handle with dispatch. A few sightings, nothing confirmed however, of a V/STOL stealth craft. That's all farther south, though, 2-, 300 clicks beyond the original demarcation lines."

"Anti-radar and IR-evading hardware on board that craft, I'm sure. Even though it's using obsolete technology, it's still viable. I think we can suspect which Ludd group that is. This far north?"

"Only speculation at this point," the local SO explained. "Sid HQ will provide more details; they coordinate down-zone surveillance."

The Nexus! Both associates imagined the possibilities if this were true. The enigmatic Internal Security officer knew how malignant and virulent that particular enemy was. The local Security officer eagerly—desperately—wanted a second chance to meet with that clandestine cell. That cadre had killed Cavanaugh. Rivers didn't show it on the surface, but internally, he churned with desire to settle that old score. And when they next met, he'd have a clear kill-on-sight target.

Giannini prepared to leave the room. "Well," he commented in an off-the-record manner. "At least both victims were diskless scum of questionable worth. I think, technically, they were actually sids but of PRIM-value, essentially. As if PRIMS have any intrinsic value. Internal should have PRIM-disked those two years ago. However, I abhor the thought of an associate gone native. One of our own. Or gone over to some emergent, violent faction. She sure blasted the bloody hell out of that place."

"A full 9 mm clip would do it."

"Affirm that!"

Giannini felt fortunate for the incident. It gave credence to his presence in the subsidiary at this particular time. It provided him with an excellent, conceivable cover. Plus, it supplied him ample freedom to scrutinize his current project: the granger, Doctor Walter Miller.

A Security squad found Miller's grange deserted and quiet. Troopers fanned out and searched the abandoned premises in silence. The house was open, still fully functional but empty and forsaken, confirming a hasty departure within the past twenty-four hours.

Outside the gate, a four-seat HFC sat. The broken-down craft showed signs it had once been meticulously restored for Miller's SCAA, but now it suffered from months of poor handling and neglect. It lacked basic maintenance that undoubtedly the SCAA would have provided their valuable runabout. On the empty front passenger seat sat a loaded 9 mm clone.

Forensic readouts proved the weapon was involved in the recent slaughter in Sac City. It provided no clues as to how the weapon related to Miller, only suspicions which Giannini and Internal was eager to exploit.

The wind came up that night blowing hard over the delta and into the Sac Valley. It brought no rain, but it thinned the heavy ground fog. Clear winter skies were coming with the increasing wind, a sign that additional changes were speeding on their way as well.

Other ominous changes were obvious throughout the entire Sac City Sid.

The valley weather became unusually cold and clear the third day after the shooting spree. In the subsidiary, more residents noticed the lack of winter rains than the violent deaths of two local mooks.

Of more concern was finding out the exact demarcation of the rumored stopline. Where was it to snake along? Who were to be the winners, who the losers? Would it be a porous line of PRIM monitors or a real solid barrier? Was it better to move out before the upcoming line was known, or move out immediately based on rumors? They all suspected that when the new line was clearer, it might then be too late.

Obviously, anyone just inside the old stopline was in trouble, and many sids living near the current lines were taking no chances. An exodus, only a trickle at first, had started. Although settling in permanently would come later, many sids were on the move toward the city center and environs of the Marsco cantonments, their best guess of safety.

Almost immediately, some of the less successful grangers deserted their claims. The larger and stronger ones decided to wait out the newly drawn demarcation and hoped that a thorny hedge and an Enfield were protection enough.

That sunny morning, Zot requisitioned an HFC and skimmed to Doctor Miller's.

The associate carried two message disks for Walter and Tessa. He hoped that these adequately explained his current status and his upcoming disappearance. For disappear was what he planned to do. Instead of rejoining the Asteroid Fleet as ordered, he planned to join Allison at the Enclave. He would hand in his commission more to protect his new comrades than out of any feeling of loyalty to them. His actions were more anti-Marsco than pro-Enclave. Anything against Marsco right then seemed his best course of action.

On the disk addressed to Miller, Zot explained his anger and frustration at the failure of the engineer's lander scheme. "I'd hoped," the iceman's message ran, "that a sid-constructed fleet (*your lander fleet*) would send Marsco a strong message. I share your disappointment deeply."

He ended his message with a short announcement and a request. "I'm going to leave Marsco within a few days, legally or not, although I don't suspect MAS HQ will stop me. Icemen are easy enough to replace, even one with a history of working in the black as I have. I can no longer serve it, as I did, in good conscience even on a shuttle in the Asteroid Fleet. Additionally, one last favor," he ended, "would you see that Tessa gets the disk addressed to her? It's of consequential significance."

To Tessa he was more critical, savaging her for her continued work within Marsco through the Von Braun Center. "You ought to have ascertained by this time that in just conscience we (or anyone) can no longer participate in Marsco's continued domination of the solar system. We must strenuously work against this all-pervasive entity that rules with such draconian means. I can no longer proudly wear any Marsco uniform."

As passionate men often declare, Zot ended his remarks to Tessa with a castigating statement, "I'm shocked, shocked, at your cavalier attitude toward the magnitude of Marsco's heinous crimes. You can't distance yourself from them by simultaneously living on Mars (thus ignoring the situation) while continuing to do research for it (thus perpetuating the situation). You have to choose, Tessa," he concluded bluntly, "my insights into the situation and my love, or Marsco."

It often happens that men blinded by spurned love don't realize that the absent erstwhile beloved has already made her choice perfectly clear.

As Zot opened the gull-wing hatch of the HFC at the dissident's grange, he immediately noticed that everything was wrong. The whole area was eerily silent; no yelping dogs greeted him. The signs before him were unmistakable. Clearly the grange had been gothed.

The front door and north-facing windows of Miller's rambling house were smashed, wood and glass shards scattered everywhere.

Confronted by this unknown threat, Zot slipped unseen through the garden gate. His 7.6 mm in hand, he moved along noiselessly. He was still Marsco enough to sense imminent danger for a lone associate without backup.

Inside the hedge, all the greenhouses and potting beds had been vandalized. Zot found the drip irrigation's piping ripped up, twisted in knots, useless. The orchard trees were broken and snapped, their trunks brought down by brute force alone, not by an axe blade. Solar panels were trashed beyond recognition. Only one power generator remained loyally operational, its low humming the only background noise.

In the house, furniture was upended, broken apart. Miller's library was particularly savaged, his books in tatters on the floor. The non-readers of the Marsco world had had their way with them. The extensive computer array was smashed. Enough power still surged from the single solar-gen outside to send sparks flashing and jumping randomly from the broken-up hardware that smoldered. An acrid smell hung about the place.

It wasn't Marsco, Zot realized; no exploding shells had been fired. *At least not Marsco directly.* In fact, the pillaging showed no signs of any weaponry besides brute force and clubs. Nothing greater than sledgehammers had been wielded by enraged brawn and terrorizing diskless hands.

In that way, the atrium shooting and this sight were different. In another way, they were the same. Some group had had enough, had reached their limit, had gone postal-max, had taken it out on the secluded grange. And no blood—that was another difference. Zot was sure Miller's remains weren't strewn about. Sure, the granger hadn't witnessed the ransacking of his home, a home he so carefully restored and enhanced. Sure, he'd been saved that ordeal. But the iceman had no visual evidence of Miller's safety, or Tessa's.

Walking cautiously back through the gardens a second time, Zot noticed something submerged halfway to the bottom of the closest cistern. Whatever was suspended in the now-cloudy water was too small to be a whole body, but it was hairy and trailing blood. Instantly, the iceman imagined the worst. A horrific thought crossed his mind: a severed head. His mind raced. Its hair was the color of Tessa's.

He scrutinized the lifeless object. Deimos, severed in two, drifted in the water. Io floated in the other cistern, her entrails ripped open. Other objects drifted with her. An arm; its hand, diskless, clearly a sid's. Not too far away, a butchered boy, perhaps sixteen years old. Face up, the tormented remains revealed all the excruciating pain of the final horrific moments of Jeremy Truman's young granger life.

It was a wrenching, sickening sight. Trailed by the dogs, the innocent youth had come down from his father's spread to investigate only to be caught up in the maelstrom of furious destruction. Unintentionally, he had become the symbol for those ferocious, unstoppable fanatics who sought to destroy everything the grange stood for.

How often, the associate realized, are the blameless and harmless sucked up into a violent vortex and crushed amid blind, brutal carnage.

"What a way to die! What a world to die in!" Zot erupted.

Someone purposely poisoned the cisterns, trashed the gardens, tore apart the house. Whoever razed this grange wanted no one else ever living here.

The iceman had no idea where Miller was. Or Tessa. Or even if father and daughter were still alive. Either might be anywhere in Marsco's solar system or tossed aside in the ransacked gardens, as horribly mutilated as Jeremy.

Zot spent two silent hours burying the young granger in the patio garden closest to Miller's great room where the Marsco dissident had spent countless hours talking to his visitors about way to best avoid this kind of blind, savage bloodletting. A few steps down from the sliding door of Miller's inviting room, Zot found a patch of undisturbed garden. The loamy soil here was easy to dig. It was shaded by a tall valley oak near a thriving rose trellis, reminders of the grange's peaceful beauty in times past. The iceman laid the dogs to rest beside the future veterinarian, a gesture of guardianship and companionship in the loneliness of this isolated tomb.

Above the horizon a crescent day-moon hung in the winter-blue sky. Clouds streaked outward from the lunar surface, as pale as its partial reflection, a common enough sight from Earth. Other sinister and darker clouds crossed the winter blue sky, smoke and embers from neighboring granges now also gothed.

A walk to the upper pasture confirmed everything. The whole of what Walter had tried to create at his grange and the spreads of his neighbors were totally wrecked. The local dairy herd was mercilessly butchered. The iceman caught the stench of distant slaughtered livestock driven by the wind. The PRIM-sid village, a sign of hope amid hopelessness, was in flames.

The vandalizing was widespread and thorough. *Condoned by Marsco HQ?* the iceman wondered. *Initiated by Security? Sanctioned? Quelled only after it went too far or as far as the S & H wallahs wanted? Taking place in spite of the threat of Security coming in to restore order with an iron fist?*

The recently conceived Marsco dissident had no idea who had blood on their hands, on their finger disks.

And more crushing still, for this realization tightened his chest with fear, Zot didn't know where Miller and Tessa were.

All alone in the surrounding ruins, Zot spit in disgust, "It's a Marsco world."

(End of Book One of *The Marsco Saga*)

GLOSSARY FOR *THE MARSCO SAGA*

75-g. Also **.75-g.** Not seventy-five times the gravity of Earth, but seventy-five percent of that force. This shorthand/slang expression refers to the default setting of **artificial gravity** on a transiting shuttle in deep space. To keep hibernating crews safe, their environment must be at a constant 75 percent gravity of Earth's, thus .75-g. When speaking, it is more natural to say "75-g" than to say "point-75-g." No **associate** is confused by this shorthand.

Abandonment: Also known as **The Policy of Abandonment.** Cf: **Divestiture.** In the midcentury, industrialized nations began this policy of disenfranchising their own citizens, those citizens who would eventually become known as **PRIMS.** In the casting off of citizens, industrialized nations divested themselves of poorer, sickly, less educated members of their societies. *Abandonment* is the official policy name although the euphemism **divestiture** is often used to disguise the intent of these laws that cut apart a larger, partent nation into many newer, smaller nations, several of them unable to care for their citizens because the parent nation kept all the wealth, industry, and infrastructure.

Artificial Gravity. Also **AG:** Midcentury scientific advancement that, along with **hibernation,** makes space-crossing journeys possible. On colonies with less than Earth's gravity, such as on Mars or an asteroid, artificial gravity keeps human life as close to Earth's as possible. In space and on colonies, the most efficient setting of AG is **75-g.**

Associate: Any member of **Marsco.**

Attack Carrier or Service Carrier. A spaceship that is the mother ship to attack fighters, such as the **Lightning**. An attack carrier travels in space and orbits a planet or moon while launching and retrieving its fighter squadrons. Fighters are stored outside the hull of the carrier. These large vessels travel into deep space with the same capabilities as a **shuttle**. See also: **Lightning** and **Lost Fleet, Myth of**.

Auxiliary: Auxiliary Unit. A lightly armed patrol unit that dates from the era of the **Continental Powers.** In the postwar world, members of the Auxiliary are not yet members of **Marsco.** Auxiliary units are often equipped with **nonlethal weapons** but are then protected by **Security** troopers. A member of an Auxiliary unit who shows extraordinary skill and devotion is moved to Security, thus into Marsco itself.

Auxxie. Slang term for an individual Auxiliary member. Also referes to anything related to the Auxilliary, e. g., an Auxxie patrol.

Bradley: Also **Brad.** The generic name for various types of armored personnel vehicles (APV) modeled after the famous late twentieth-century military vehicle. Depending on the model, Bradleys hold six to twenty armed troops and carry a variety of weapons. Each has a crew of two to four. Auxiliary-controlled Bradleys are armed with nonlethal weapons. Security Bradleys carry either lethal or nonlethal armaments. Both terms Bradley and Brad are generically applied to any armored personnel vehicle larger than a **Hummer.**

Buff: Two mutually exclusive definitions. 1) Acronym for *b*ig *u*gly *f*at *f*ellow. (A well-known expletive is often substituted for "fellow.") Commonly said in the twentieth century of large, unsightly aircraft, for instance, a cargo plane. 2) A twentieth-century term still used in Marsco world to describe an attractive, muscular man or woman.

Cantonment: See **Marsco Sector** and **Marsco Cantonment.**

Centurion: Slang name for someone who started as a **PRIM** or **sid** then moved to officer status in the **Security & Hygiene Forces.** See also **Legionnaire.**

Command and control disk: See **finger disk.**

Continental Forces: The combined military of the **Continental Powers,** roughly equal to 20th century NATO or Warsaw Pact commands.

Continental Powers: Also, the **C-Powers.** The most advanced and highly technical nations, dating roughly from 2030 to 2069. The C-Powers began the practice of creating **unincorporated zones** (**UZs**) within their own borders and the practice of divesting themselves of unproductive personnel and territories. (These UZs were created to control crime and disease.) The C-Powers began dictating internal policies to poorer nations for various reasons, such as, forcing the underdeveloped nations to form unincorporated zones of their own to control immigration to richer countries. The C-Powers' attempt to rein in Marsco was one of a series of events that started the Continental Wars. (See also **Abandonment.**)

Continental Wars: Also often referred to as "The C-Wars." War that tried to bring down Marsco, 2067 to 2069. These are the dates Marsco gives, even though some fighting raged on until 2072. Although a single war, it is always referred to as "wars" for no apparent reason. Like most wars, it was brutal and nasty, although not short. It introduced many high-tech weapons, for example, Marsco's so-called *third wave cyber weapons,* **Enfields,** and **Vanovara weapons.**

Cryogenic Stasis. Also **cryo-stasis:** Not to be confused with **hibernation**. Although those under cryogenic stasis are hibernating, it is a different scientific and technical process that keeps the person safe. This method is an advancement that allows for a safe suspended animation well beyond the usual six-month hibernation duration. Cryogenic stasis has been used to keep people safe for twenty-five years; in theory, 200 to 300 years of cryogenic stasis is possible. If these experiments hold true, leaving the solar system safely is not beyond possibility.

Divestiture: Euphemism for **Abandonment** or **the Policy of Abandonment.**

Dog Ship: See also **Mule** or **Mule Ship**. Not a derogatory term for a problematic or troublesome spaceship. Aviation slang term dating almost from the inception of aircraft in the early 20th century. The term refers to a prototype spacecraft or a spacecraft used as a testing platform that undergoes many alterations in the course of its test flights.

DRP or **Disk Removal Procedure.** The removal of finger disks. Although DRP may be voluntary, the term usually implies the forced removal of finger disks, which in effect removes someone from **associate** or higher **sid**-status.

Enfield: Marsco's weapon of choice for its Security forces. It is an advancement over the gunpowder-fired weapon. An ignitable aerosol explodes to propel the bullet at a target. The bullet itself is explosive and quite lethal. Most Enfields charge with a slight hiss of the aerosol and fire a three-burst before recharging in a fraction of a second. An Enfield may be handheld or shoulder-fired. Models also exist that replace the **SAW** (*s*quad *a*utomatic *w*eapon) and machine gun. See **SAW**.

EVA and **E-VMU:** Protective space suits needed to move outside a space ship. Both are old NASA acronyms still in use in the Marsco Asteroid Service. An *E*xtra-*V*ehicular *A*ctivity (EVA) suit may or may not be tethered to an outer space vehicle. *E*xtra-*V*ehicular *M*obility *U*nit (E-VMU) is not tethered but relies on jet packs for maneuverability. Both types of suits have the necessary life support. Although less bulky and more graceful than NASA-era spacesuits, they are cumbersome and physically challenging to use.

Finger disks: Also **FD**. Starting in 2030, **finger mouse** technology was superceded by these disks. The wearer of the disk has immediate access to any Marsco terminal and through it the

Marsco Net. By 2080 virtually every computer runs by utilizing finger disks, although some finger mouse units still exist. Each disk allows the wearer to access more and more important files and portals of the Marsco net. (See **finger mouse.**) Each round, flat disk is a subcutaneous implant along the palm side of fingers, starting with the right index finger. Ordinary finger disks show dark blue-green under the skin and glow slightly when in use. Marsco Security and Hygiene officers (and earlier fighter pilots and other military officers) have a single bright red command and control finger disk in their right trigger finger besides the blue disks in other fingers. For the first fifteen years of this computer advancement, until roughly 2045, a quick way to tell if someone was a Marsco associate was to check for finger disks. Although later it was common for some people working for subsidiaries to have a few finger disks, the disks are always associated with Marsco. Although in theory nothing prevents a PRIM from having a finger disk, in practice, none have them. For a Marsco associate, eventually all the right-hand fingers might have one or more disks. If more disks are needed after the right hand is fully arrayed, additional disks can be implanted on the left hand. Such associates are extremely important in Marsco and are often referred to as a ***lefters*** or ***wallahs*** or ***high wallahs.*** (These last two names, however, can be applied to anyone of real or imagined importance who does not have disks.) The disks themselves are made of durable, flexible polymer QCA chips so the wearer may use his or her hands normally. To protect and/or hide disks, gloves are often worn. Some gloves commonly worn over FDs allow full finger disk use without interference. Finger disks are embedded with the user's identification, so the computer instantly knows who is operating the unit. In addition, a user with many disks, generally a lefter, can override another user's commands. Marsco worked out the problem of finger disks coming through the skin; these implants are permanent.

Finger mouse: Can refer both to the finger-covering thimble-unit itself or to finger mouse-driven PC laptops, notebooks, and in some cases, desktops. These are old-style (but still in use) personal computers without the typical late-twentieth-century wire-attached mouse. The finger mouse itself is a rubber thimble device with a QCA microchip that slips over the finger (or fingers) of the user. A finger disk does all the command functions of an old-fashioned, wire-attached mouse. For security reasons, each finger disk is wedded to its unit; no other finger mouse may operate that unit. Marsco's 2021 revolutionary invention of the finger mouse pushed it into the forefront of computer technology. After the advent of finger disks, sids, (especially sid students), and rarely, a few trusted PRIMS, still used the old technology of finger mouse units. Additionally, some Luddite factions allow their members to use finger mouse units because they do not allow implanted finger disks. Even well into the finger disk era, Marsco still produced and distributed state-of-the-art finger mouse PC units that were used to store ultra-secret documents. Even lefter wallahs use finger mouse laptops and notebooks for personal or black and sheltered materials.

Fogger: See **fuzzer.**

Fuzzer: Interchangeable with **fogger,** although fuzzer is the more common expression. A fuzzer's size may range from a small, easily hidden device for individual use to a whole system surrounding a large complex of buildings. The fuzzer electronically breaks up any vocal signatures so that someone under surveillance may speak without having his or her voice understood or recorded by an eavesdropper using electronic equipment. On a digital recording system, voices protected by a fuzzer come through as fuzzy, hence the name. The visual recording will be accurate, so lip-reading is still possible. To avoid that, someone using a fuzzer may speak into a handkerchief or hand to hide his or her lips while speaking. In the Marsco world, because surveillance is ubiquitous, the use of fuzzers is common, even among associates on a Marsco assignment.

Herriff-Grid: See also **HFC.** Computer system that allows tens of thousands of HFCs to operate safely above any location (usually a vast city center) without fear of in-flight collisions. The

Herriff-Grid made it possible to utilize the HFC in much the same way as the twentieth century used the automobile. Metaphorically, the grid produces a superhighway system above a city of invisible trunk freeways and lanes. This device is misnamed, because Herriff had nothing to do with its invention. In a postwar world, a sure sign that a location is flourishing again is the reinstitution of its Herriff-Grid.

HFC: See also **Runabout.** Official name: *Horizontal/Vertical Hover Flight Craft* and so often called an H/V HFC. A small, reliable, and versatile aircraft that takes off and lands by hovering. The HFC is like a heliocopter in that sense except it does not rely on blades for lift; it relies on its engines alone for lift. It does not need a special airport, like a conventional airplane, but can land on any hard, flat surface. They are relatively easy to pilot and navigate, thanks to GPS. Some runabouts are small, two-person units. Others can carry several metric tons of freight or up to forty passengers. This type of craft was a technological advancement from the common helicopter and **V/STOL** aircraft were in use worldwide by the middle of the twenty-first century. This flight advancement couples the capabilities of helicopters and airplanes, rendering these two aircraft types obsolete. Originally designed by several inventors and engineers, it was Dr. Herriff, the century's greatest flight engineer and designer, who made the first models for mass production and general use. Consequently, Herriff is credited with the HFC's invention. Sometimes HFC is thought incorrectly to mean *Herriff Flight Craft.*

HH GAS: Pronounced "Ha-ha gas." *H*erpes, *H*epatitis, *G*onorrhea, *A*IDS, *S*yphilis. In the AIDS-devastated world of the late twenty-first century, special care is taken care to avoid partners with HH GAS. See **Security and Hygiene**.

Hiberman: Another name for a hibernation specialist who puts passengers into hibernation, monitors them, and brings them out of hibernation safely. Cf: **Iceman.**

Hibernation: Technical advance that made it possible to safely transit space crews to Mars and the asteroid belt. By keeping crews hibernated, shuttles need to carry less life support; thus, larger crews can transit. Hibernation makes it possible to colonize Mars and the Asteroid Belt. The maximum hibernation period is six months. Cf: **cryogenic stasis.** Hibernation is widely used, quite safe, and reliable but limited in duration. It is a common experience when traveling beyond the Moon to Mars or the Asteroid Belt.

Housing Authority: Whenever PRIMS are allowed to live in or near a **subsidiary area** or **Marsco Sector** because of their employment situation, they are housed in guarded complexes that make up a Housing Authority. Generally, such locations are placed out of sight and are kept to a maximum of a few thousand residents. Conditions are substantially better than life in a typical UZ, which makes them appealing to a PRIM, although not a place where a Marsco associate would reside. (One benefit of a housing authority, for example, is that ample food is provided.) Resident PRIM workers living in a housing authority are under the constant supervision of their sid overseers.

Hummer: Four-wheel drive vehicle used by civilian control personnel and Marsco security forces. Heavy and rugged, it takes its name from the late twentieth-century vehicle it resembles. Hummers are larger and heavier than a standard **rover.**

Iceman: Derogatory term for a *hiberman.* Suggests the hibernation specialist merely puts people on ice and does little else. Cf: **Hiberman** and **Hibernation**.

Internal Security: See **Security and Hygiene.**

I-ON-U: Slang spelling of "eye-on-you" which is how the term is pronounced. The word refers to surveillance equipment on stanchions and within buildings that make it possible for nearly everyone to be under closed-circuit TV (CCTV) observation.

IR: As in the twentieth century, infrared. Many scientific devices and Enfield scopes utilize IR technology.

Kirkwood Gap: Twentieth-century astrological term for the naturally occurring gaps in the flow of the asteroid belt.

Kludge: In the Marsco world, pronounced like "judge" or "fudge." This is the only variant spelling and pronunciation since the C-Wars. Carries the same meaning as in the early twenty-first century; that is, a poorly constructed computer system or a mismatched set of components. Hence, a system or solution that is clumsy or inelegant. Now also describes temperamental Marsco equipment that works only intermittently or not as successfully as designed. Thus it describes new and improved devices that fail to be as good as the original, simpler versions or equipment that works well on Earth but not in space.

Labor Unions: See **Unions.**

Lander: See also **Sublunar Orbiter.** A combined aircraft and spacecraft that can fly at great speeds on Earth (as a jumbo jet) and even make trips to the Moon (as a spacecraft). It hovers to land. This design of craft is always used for sublunar travel because it contains no hibernation bays and is not suited (for various other technical reasons) for deep-space travel, that is, travel beyond lunar obit. Original landers were posh compared to later Marsco versions. Because no passengers hibernated on them, every conceivable travel luxury was provided to keep passengers comfortable and entertained. Originally, a non-Marsco consortium developed landers, another reason for their luxurious nature, because Marsco spacecraft tend to take on a practical and economic hue. The term *lander* has stuck to any spacecraft used to service an orbiting docking port. Thus, there are landers on Mars that transport personnel and supplies to and from the surface colonies to the shuttle spaceports orbiting above. Now, rarely called **sublunar orbiters** or **subs.** Many Marsco landers utilized exclusively for air transport on Earth are older, restored sublunar orbiters or landers that are no longer space worthy.

Language Disk or **English Language Disk:** Also **LD** or **ELD.** As the second name implies, an implanted disk that allows the wearer to speak grammatical, accent-free English. The disk is placed behind the right ear and is often visible below the epidermis because it is blue-green like a finger disk. Sometimes, a native speaker of English whose grammar is nonstandard is given an LD temporarily until the user learns standard grammar and idiom. These are T-ELDs, *T*emporary *E*nglish *L*anguage *D*isks.

Late Twentieth Century: Also **LTC**. The era spanning the last few decades of the twentieth century until the first decade of the twenty-first century, roughly 1980 to 2010. LTC is not an exact date so much as a term to describe attitudes, geography, technology, and computer components that predate Marsco's rise to dominance starting about 2025. LTC often implies that the thing or idea in question is outdated, obsolete, or of questionable value because it is so old and, more importantly, pre-Marsco.

Lefter: A person with disks implanted in his or her left-hand fingers. Almost always an extremely important Marsco associate, although theoretically a sid (someone non-Marsco) could become a lefter. See **finger disk** and **wallah.**

Legionnaire: A common trooper in Security and Hygiene who started as a **PRIM** or **sid.** Cf: **Centurion**. In point of fact, most troopers in Security are Legionnaires.

Lethal weapon or **leth:** In the Marsco world, almost always some form of **Enfield**, its most ubiquituous and effective and lethal weapon.

Lightning: A Continental Powers weapon of immense destructive capability. Originally designed as a remote-controlled drone, individual craft were often retrofitted for on-board flight crews. They carry conventional or nuclear weaponry. Lightning attacks were known to break up PRIM formations during the C-Wars. Although capable of flight like an airplane within the Earth's atmosphere, it is a space-launched and space-retrieved craft. As such, each squadron is carried outside the hull of an attendant **attack carrier**, or **service carrier**, to transport it to its launch site close to the fighting. During the C-Wars, Lightnings launched several strikes against Earth and lunar targets. See **attack carrier** and **Lost Fleet, Myth of.**

Light Rail or **LR:** See also: **MAG LEV.** Any rail transit system that resembles twentieth-century trains and inner-city lines. Can be above ground or subway or a mixture of both. Some light rail systems carry passenger traffic between major MAG LEV hubs. Essentially, light rail is any rail system that is not MAG LEV. In most cases, unless specifically stated, light rail systems are run-down and patched together; their use is mainly for sid or PRIM commuters.

Lost Fleet, Myth of the. A large strike force of four Lightning squadrons on three attack carriers heading for Mars to attack Marsco targets there when the cessation of hostilities canceled this sortie. This massive and deadly fleet never returned to Earth because it apparently did not have enough supplies to return, theirs being presumably a one-way, suicide mission. That fleet's disappearance began the ***Lost Fleet*** myth. See **attack carrier** and **Lightning**.

Luddites: Also **Ludds.** Not to be confused with **PRIMS.** Anyone can be a Luddite, per se, if willing to give up most technology, especially the finger disk. Some Luddite factions are pacifist and live simply in communes as much as possible apart from Marsco. Other violent Ludd cells are committed to the destruction of advanced technology, especially Marsco's. (In both cases, it is conceivable that even a disgruntled Marsco associate might join the Luddite ranks.) Violent cells tend to be clandestine and loosely organized. A quasi-religious leader known as "the Leader" or "the One" and "His Holiness" (among other names) leads the largest and most dangerous Luddite cell, **the Nexus**, which Marsco fears the most. Not all Luddites are bent on Marsco's destruction; some have merely chosen an alternative lifestyle, i.e., utilizing little or no twenty-first century technology. Also, there is a tendency among various Luddite groups to pick and choose what technology they wish to keep; some will allow finger mouse technology, for instance, some not. Generally, all Luddites agree on the absolute rejection of any and all subcutaneous finger disk implants.

MAG LEV: Magnetically levitated trains. These are luxurious because they have been restored to their midcentury elegance. The vast, interconnected system was built by the countries that predated the Continental Powers. Cf: **Light Rail.**

Marsco: Company formed by merging Japanese microchip and American aerospace and computer software industries in the early twenty-first century. These companies and conglomerates had their roots in mergers, acquisitions, and buyouts from the 1990s. Rather presumptuous to call itself "Marsco" when one of the first parent companies formed, but to quote an original prospectus, "We're aiming high." First products were chips made from synthetic crystals manufactured in space. Their products increased chip speed 100 times at first, then 1,000 times. Three university grads working in Seattle began the computer research aspect of the parent company. Three founders: Sito Fugiama, Tyron Bridges, and Michael Cleary. For his Ph.D. thesis in 2017, Bridges wrote a universal application that linked all OS systems to a single language superceding BIOS. With it, he made millions before defending his dissertation. By the end of the twenty-first century, there are hundreds of millions of Marsco associates and their dependents. Approximately 350,000 of these live in space.

Marsco Net: In the postwar world, the only fully functional Internet system. Because of finger disks and **Internal Security's** scrutiny, use of the Marsco Net is tightly controlled.

Marsco Sector and **Marsco Cantonment:** Any one of several hundred locations on Earth that are exclusively designated for Marsco associates, although PRIMS and sids enter to work there. It is necessary that PRIMS and sids live nearby to service these areas. An individual **sector** may be extremely large, sometimes as large as a twentieth-century country or a state or province within a former twentieth-century country. The new sector boundaries frequently disregard any previous boundaries. A **cantonment** is generally city-sized or smaller, situated in or near an important subsidiary area. Depending on location and need, there may in fact be several small cantonments throughout an important subsidiary to help maintain essential services, to assist with hygiene control, and to offer technical support and material assistance with security. Generally, smaller cantonments are expanding, as it is the policy of Marsco to annex the better parts of contiguous subsidiary areas. After the Continental Wars, there was no need to designate a Marsco colony in space per se, because virtually everything in space was now Marsco's. (There are a few notably independent colonies on the Moon and in the Asteroid Belt.) It is most important to note that the terms *Marsco sectors* and *Marsco cantonments* apply solely to an Earth-side location.

Marsco Winter: See **Troubled Times**.

MAS: 1) *M*arsco *A*steroid *S*huttle. These shuttles travel between lunar docking ports and Mars or the asteroid belt. 2) *M*arsco *A*steroid *S*ervice. The branch of Marsco that operates its shuttles. See also **shuttle**. 3) *M*utually *A*greed *S*ex. Consensual sex. Cf: **SWR**. See also **UA**.

MMU: *M*arsco *M*onetary *U*nit. Marsco's currency. It is the only currency in use at this time. MMUs may used in token form, in a sort of prepaid debit card, and in electronic format. Tokens are smaller denominations and impossible to trace, just as bills and coins were in the twentieth century. Larger amounts of MMUs are transferred electronically, just like current banking systems. An associate or important sid would have disk capability (either finger disk or finger mouse) to twitch MMUs like current debit cards or credit cards; thus such cards are superfluous. MMU tokens are the ubiquitous monetary device, although prepaid token cards are in wide use but can be traced.

Mogged: Military slang term dating from the late twentieth century, shortened from the name of Somalia's capital, Mogadishu. As the Somali civil war destroyed its capital city, the term rose among UN occupying Peace Keepers to describe a once-modern city now in rubble. Marsco uses the term to apply to just that, any formerly advanced cities now in rubble with little likelihood of restoration. A mogged locale is an area in shambles and despair.

MR SoD: Pronounced “Mister Sod.” *M*arsco *R*ed *S*creen *o*f *D*eath. Marsco Internal Security has the power to disable another user’s computer. When IS does so, the remaining useless screen is entirely red, hence, MR SoD.

Mule or **Mule Ship:** See also **Dog Ship.** A long-standing aviation slang term for an aircraft that performs many assorted tasks and can carry a large quantity of cargo. These crafts are designed for heavy lifting, not beauty. Marsco has retrofitted many former landers that originally were outfitted for luxury in the pre C-Wars day. Marsco uses these for more practical uses. These are now clearly *mules.* A few old hacks still use the term *dog ship* and *mule* interchangeably, as would have been the case with some aircraft in the mid-twentieth century.

Neo-Consumption: Also **Neo-Con.** The most widespread and deadly of several diseases that were pandemic before and after the C-Wars. This disease takes its name from the original one for tuberculosis, “consumption,” because it resembles the symptoms of this deadly ailment. In its early, undetected stage, it is highly contagious. In tertiary stages, symptoms include deep coughing that brings up bloody mucus, severe fever, listlessness, delirium, and eventual death. Several of these diseases existed before the C-Wars but ran rampant during the **Troubled Times,** especially in **UZs.** Many plague outbreaks were incorrectly given the name Neo-Con for lack of any exact diagnosis. A constant rumor, spread by many Luddite groups, is that Neo-Con was caused by Marsco negligence, that the disease was transported to Earth accidentally by Marsco, a Martian microorganism brought by an early Marsco expedition. (See **Plague Ship.**) Independent scientists and researchers have never confirmed this hypothesis.

Nexus, the. The most violent Luddite faction plotting against Marsco.

Nonlethal weapons, or **nonleths:** Weapons stemming from twentieth-century attempts at crowd and riot control via nonlethal means. Generally in the Marsco world this means ooze nozzles that spray the recipient with a slurry coating that hardens to immobilize the recipient. Electric stunners are also used. Both types of weapons can be handheld or mounted on Brads and Hummers. Often, Auxxies carry nonleths until the situation dictates them being fully armed with Enfields. Most Auxxies have learned how to utilize a nonleth *lethally.*

***Plague Ship*, the Myth of:** During the midcentury, pandemic diseases swept the Earth in three devastating waves. Although these were natural occurrences, rumors circulated that Martian microbes were unintentionally brought to Earth on a Marsco shuttle. Variants of these rumors blame Bethany Palmer for unleashing these microbes. Luddites often fan the flames of these rumors to blame Marsco as much as possible for these disease pandemics.

PRIM and **PRIMS:** Not to be confused with **Luddites.** Continental Powers term that predates Marsco's ascendancy as a world power. It refers to the sickest, poorest, and least technically advanced peoples of the world, those originally "let go" by the Continental Powers. As such, it is applied to these people regardless of race or ethnic identity. Marsco armed and led **PRIM** armies against the C-Powers but did not disband their **unincorporated zones** after the C-Wars, as promised. At the end of the twenty-first century, most PRIMS continue to live in these zones. PRIMS still do most of the manual labor in subsidiary areas and Marsco sectors. A census of PRIMS on Earth is never undertaken; such a calculation would serve no purpose. Estimates vary, but the best guesstimate of their numbers is between 3.5 to 4 billion. Most live in UZs with perhaps a quarter of a billion living in better conditions because they work in subsidiary areas or Marsco sectors. There are no PRIMS in space. Most Luddites, especially the fanatically violent and rebellious ones, began as PRIMS; Luddites still recruit, albeit in a clandestine manner, among this discarded population. The term's etymology is unclear. Most likely, it is a capitalization of the letters *p-r-i-m* from the beginning of the word *primitive.* One unsubstantiated etymology is *P*ersonnel, *R*elocated and /or *I*ndigenous, *M*arsco-*S*upervised, thus the acronym PRIMS. NB: as a noun the word may refer to a single person and thus be shortened to *PRIM* to conform to standard English grammar, as in, "An old PRIM sleeping on the street." The word may be pluralized: "PRIMS do not live near here." The word can be an adjective as is the case with many English nouns: "a PRIM-made garment." Rarely, it may be a verb, as in: "He tried to PRIM down the merchant's price." The term is no longer always derogatory but rather can be thought of as a neutral term for those who are simply PRIMS.

PRIM disk: An ID disk placed under the skin at the back of a PRIM's left hand. This disk acts as a RFID (radio frequency ID) for location detection. It glows green when fully functioning, amber when not.

PRIM-ification: Originally, the official policy of making new nations into nations of PRIMS by removing any means for them to educate or employ their populations. By making many former citizens into PRIMS, the C-Powers prospered. Over time, the term came to mean any action or decision that lowers a person's status, even if that lower status is not PRIM status. For instance, an associate may become a sid, yet the action may be called a *PRIM-ification.*

PRIM-to: Slang for something turning into or being made into a PRIM zone or areas. Not necessarily an official policy. To say something has become "PRIM-to" suggests it is run-down, worthless, worthy only of PRIMS. Also a voluntary act of being like a PRIM, much like the old expression "gone native." "He's gone PRIM-to…" thus implies the person wants to be more PRIM-like for whatever reason.

P-W/O-D: *P*RIM *W*ith*o*ut *D*isk. A PRIM who has removed a PRIM disk without authorization. Not a former PRIM who has joined the Auxiliary or become a legal sid whose PRIM-disk is removed legally. P-W/O-D is a serious infraction of Marsco regulations. Pronounce *pwŏd* or *pwăd.*

Rangers: Most highly trained troopers of the S & H. Rangers are trained for combat, not just patrolling **UZs** and other hotspots. They are trained in multiple insertion and terrain survival techniques along the lines of commandos, special ops, and SEALS of the early 21st century.

RFID: Radio Frequency ID. An early twenty-first century inventory device made into a humanity movement control device in the later half of the century. An integral part of a PRIM disk.

Rover: Four-wheel drive vehicle resembling a jeep. A generic term for any soft-skinned, small, light transport or patrol vehicle of this type. Sometimes armed as needed with lethal and nonlethal weapons. Smaller than a **hummer.**

RSVP: Remote Surveillance Vehicle Platform. Surveillance equipment on a vehicle that can secretly leave hidden sensors wherever the vehicle travels. Although he does know not this, Father Cavanaugh's Hummer is secretly rigged by Marsco Security with an RSVP to infiltrate a Luddite camp.

Runabout: Another term for an **HFC.** This particular term tends to be used for small HFC, those under twelve-seat capacity.

SAW: *S*quad *A*utomatic *W*eapon. Twentieth-century military slang applied to an advanced Enfield that fires more than three bursts. Belt fed, like a conventional machine gun, it fires rapidly and accurately. Any reference to a SAW is to an Enfield SAW, not a twentieth-century military SAW.

Security and Hygiene: Also **Security** and **S & H.** The quasi-military units that enforce Marsco's dicta. The Security troopers patrol subsidiary areas and unincorporated zones, lead Auxiliary units, and keep order when as needed throughout the Marsco world. Although nonlethal weapons are available to them, most Security personnel carry **Enfields.** The Hygiene portion of the S & H ensures disease outbreaks are controlled. It additionally investigates associates whose behavior may be spreading **HH GAS. Internal Security** or **ISOS (Internal Security Operating Systems)** investigates uses of the Marsco Net that are not approved. If discovered to be on the Net illegally, IS can destroy an unapproved user's system so that the screen shows only Marsco red or **MR SoD.**

Shuttle: Space vehicles used exclusively for deep-space travel. The closest they approach Earth is orbiting docking ports circling the Moon. Shuttle are modular and are configured or "refabricated" differently each time they commence a deep-space voyage, as their flight mission dictates. Each shuttle is always made of two propulsion modules and a command and crew module. To these are attached cargo bays and/or passenger compartments with their hibernation bays and attendant hiberman personnel. A shuttle can be refabricated into any number of configurations utilizing this modular system. Shuttles first began traveling from orbiting lunar docking ports to Mars; thus, their original name was *Mars Shuttle.* The command mod of a newer Marsco Asteroid Shuttle, the type that routinely travels to the asteroid belt, is named for the astronomers who first studied the asteroid belt or for NASA astronauts. Regardless of configuration, the shuttle takes its name from its command mod. Shuttles never land; they dock at orbiting ports to be serviced by landers.

Sid: The name given to anyone living in a **subsidiary area.** Unlike **PRIMS**, a sid worker lives a better, albeit modest, life. Sids provide a great deal of technical labor for Marsco. They also supervise any PRIMS who are doing physical labor for Marsco or for any subsidiary industries. When used by a Marsco associate, the term *sid* may have a derogatory ring to it, depending on context. There are perhaps three-quarters of a billion sids worldwide. Around 175,000 live in space under the auspices of independent contractors. The ultimate goal of most sids is to become a Marsco associate by whatever means. NB: no confusion should exist when the term *sid* refers to an individual resident from a subsidiary area or a subsidiary area itself; context makes the distinction clear. Both meanings are constantly at play and consistently used.

Stopline: Boundary between a Marsco locale and a **subsidiary area** or an **unincorporated zone.** The boundary line may be real or virtual. Computer and observation methods make movement impossible without permission. Additionally, there are internal stoplines or checkpoints within a patrol area. Slang expression: "To cross a stopline" implies doing or saying something forbidden.

Sublunar orbiters: Also referred to as *subs.* See also **Lander.** In a technical sense, these craft are no different than a lander. The main difference is in application. A sublunar orbiter is used exclusively for space travel from Earth to the Moon. A lander may be of the same design but consigned to shifting personnel and supplies to orbiting shuttle docking ports and their Martian colonies. Even when on Mars, which is obviously not "sublunar," these craft may be called "subs" or "landers" interchangeably. Marsco-produced sublunar orbiters tend to be modern but spartan. Older subs or landers tend to be more luxurious if they predate the explosion of space travel to Mars by Marsco. Nonetheless, often the terms *sublunar, subs, orbiters,* and *landers* are used interchangeably for spacecraft that can land on a planet's or the Moon's surface and also enter space. They are never confused with a *shuttle,* which is used exclusively for deep-spaceflight.

Subsidiary Areas: See also **sid.** Highly developed areas that were the heartland of the industrial and technical Continental Powers. These are areas that Marsco needs for manufacturing non Marsco products and for the majority of its food production. Marsco makes most of its profit by trading with these areas. A resident of one of these areas is a **sid.** There are generally one or more subsidiary areas contiguous to every Marsco sector or cantonment to act in part as a buffer separating any **UZs** from Marsco. When PRIMS work in subsidiary areas or Marsco sectors, they always do so under the auspices of sid management.

SWR: Sex with resistance. Pronounced like "soar." May also be spelled SWR-D, for "sex with resistance—definitely." In that case, pronounced like "sword" or "soared." In the Marsco world, these are all a euphemisms for rape. Clearly a male (and often a female) associate has a great deal of power and authority over sids or PRIMS. SWR is that authority and power abused to its worst and fullest extent. Often the term is applied for acts when the associate buys someone in a **UZ** for carnal purposes. These acronyms may be used as a boast even if the act isn't completed or even contemplated, as is the case with Maissey bragging to Grizotti.

Trooper: A member of Security forces not of officer rank. Cf: **Legionnaire** and **Auxxie.**

Troubled Times, the: The five-to-seven year period after the C-Wars of the worst incidences of worldwide plagues, especially the pandemic Neo-Con. Because of war-induced debris in the atmosphere, the global temperature plummeted. Also known as the **Marsco Winter**.

Twelve Thruster Policy: In 2029, Marsco started its "Twelve Thruster Policy," which essentially limited what vehicles could travel in space. The first policy set at twelve the number of engine types Marsco would service in space. This forced every nation to comply with Marsco's maintenance and fueling requirements. Through this policy, Marsco de facto established a monopoly on space travel. Marsco claimed its policy was nothing more than "a standardization of space travel" in much the same way as nineteenth-century railroads standardized their track gauges or the twentieth-century computer community standardized its hardware and software. This policy began the Marsco Motto: "Everything off the Earth goes Marsco."

UA: Unauthorized ass. Long-standing term for consensual sex with inappropriate partner, for example, with a colleague's wife while the husband is posted away. In the Marsco world, it has taken on the added meaning of a liaison at work (as in a work cubicle) during work-related conditions or during a duty shift. Partners are always consensual; thus UA cannot be SWR.

Unincorporated Zones: Confinement camps originally begun by the Continental Powers themselves, a point not lost on Marsco. By the middle of the twenty-first century, the poorest and least "salvageable" populations were confined to these zones, "for their own good," mostly to control crime and disease. Some industrialized nations exerted extreme political pressure on underdeveloped nations to coerce them to set up their own permanent, internal refugee camps to diminish the demand for immigration from poorer nations to richer ones. Soon emerging nations divested of their poorer citizens in this manner as well to create a small portion of elite citizens. Before the C-Wars, Marsco began its policy of "philanthropy" to help these camps have a healthier and improved standard of living. Marsco's interest in **PRIMS** dates from this time. Although publicly stating it would eliminate the UZs after the C-Wars, Marsco kept this prewar confinement policy in force to reduce the risk of diseases being spread when it initially assumed control. By the Marsco era, many zones are the size of twentieth-century countries.

Unions: Also known as **Labor Unions.** When PRIMS are given employment permits for work in a Subsidiary Area or Marsco Sector, they are screened by Unions to make sure they are reliable and, more important, free of any traces of disease, especially Neo-Con. Like the term *housing authority,* which also goes back to the twentieth century, the term has changed its meaning in the Marsco world; the term *union* is an old word serving a new purpose.

Vanovara weapons: Either one of two types of meteorite weapons employed by Marsco. The V-1 was the frozen, depleted nucleus of a comet guided to its target from orbit. Accelerating speed of descent and gravity compression of the frozen gases, which make up the nucleus, cause a tremendous explosion when detonated as an air burst. These were used against soft targets such as troop concentrations and communications centers. The V-2 was a solid metallic asteroid guided to a ground strike, usually against hardened targets (such as military compounds) or major infrastructure targets (such as dams and vital industrial sites). Neither warhead was extremely large, the V-1 slightly being larger than the heavier V-2. Usually, they were under several tons and measured less than a few meters by detonation or impact. Marsco kept their impact value between ten to twenty-five kilotons each. Their small size, plus the fact that literally thousands of asteroids orbited the Earth as debris from the larger mining asteroids Marsco had brought there, made detection nearly impossible. By the time Marsco rained Vanovaras down, the C-Powers' military communication network was virus-infected beyond use; radar and satellite detection arrays ceased to be functional. On the other hand, years of plotting precise trajectories for mining asteroids across millions of kilometers of space gave Marsco the technical ability to send V-1s and V-2s to Earth with extraordinary precision. Marsco after-action reports claim an 89.9082% accuracy of hits, but as with nuclear weapons, a near miss was generally as effective as a direct hit. Quite possibly, microbes from the frozen nuclei of the V-1s brought virulent opportunistic diseases to Earth. Thus plague outbreaks after the C-Wars are also attributed to Marsco by some detractors. Blast debris contributed to the Marsco Winter. See **Troubled Times**.

VR: As in the twentieth century, virtual reality. Many Marsco projection devices are VR and allow for 3D reality viewing of another person (as in a recorded message) or an object being scrutinized for scientific investigation.

V/STOL: *V*ertical and *S*hort *T*ake*o*ff and *L*anding aircraft. Although designed in the twentieth century, by the middle of the twenty-first century V/STOL craft have large carrying capacity and near-total stealth capability. They are exceedingly sophisticated aircraft but of the last generation predating lander advances and HFC runabout technology. Unlike a fully functional lander, a V/STOL can never enter space or orbit. A favorite means of air travel among some Luddite factions.

Wall Unit: An associate in a dead-end job in Marsco. Such an associate is someone not likely to be demoted (or de-disked) yet is someone in all likelihood that will spend the rest of his or her career at one desk. These associates are like old-fashioned *wall unit* equipment, not used much but there is no use redecorating to get them off the wall. Can also describe a quaint, unfashionable idea. "It's a wall unit deal to think PRIMS should be educated."

Wallah or often **high wallah:** Slang name for a Marsco associate of great importance. Usually, this person is a lefter. Term can also be applied to anyone of real or imagined self-importance; all those thinking they are important when they are not, thus a pompous, pretentious sid might be called a wallah. In its first meaning, it is generally not condescending; in its second, it always is.

ABOUT THE AUTHOR

James A. Zarzana earned a BA in English from Saint Mary's College of California, an MA from Sacramento State University, and a PhD from the University of Notre Dame. In 1989, he joined the Southwest Minnesota State University English Department.

Zarzana's novel *The Marsco Dissident* is the first of four works of speculative fiction in *The Marsco Saga*. *Marsco Triumphant* is slated for release in March 2015, *The Marsco Sustainability Project* in December 2015, and *The Ascendancy of Marsco* in December 2016. Drawing parallels to the Roman and British empires, the novels explore human conflict and the abuse of power.

Zarzana is married to fellow Notre Dame graduate, SMSU professor, and poet Marianne Murphy Zarzana. Their daughter, Elaine, is also a Notre Dame graduate, educator, and writer. The author is an avid ND Irish football fan who enjoys cooking and loves dogs.

Website: www.TheMarscoSaga.com

Facebook: The Marsco Saga